Valhalla

The Valkyries Fire

An Epic Fantasy Novel
Book 1

A.J. TORRES

Valhalla
The Valkyries Fire

Cover Illustration and Interior Knot Art by Nicole Deal
Chapter Header Designs by Marcus Kennedy
Chapter Header Digital Inking by Adlin J. Kennedy Torres

Despite the obstacles placed before you, may your fire fuel you, and your light shine a path ahead.

Other Stories
By A.J. Torres

Content Warning/Trigger

Out of respect for my readers that want to be warned about triggering elements before reading, please be advised that this book contains the following:

Blood and Gore
Death
Fire/Death by Fire
Forced Sex/Kiss
Misogyny
Corpse/s
Depictions of PTSD
Fear of Darkness
Mentions of Abuse/Harassment from a Sibling
Mentions of Assault/Rape

CONTENTS

Realm of Midgard

Ellinika

Zarago

Mikadzuki

Dessert of
Khufu

Mahaanbrahman

Eemheide

Weida
Long

Veerence

Elviser Forest

Liftlatinn

Vandr

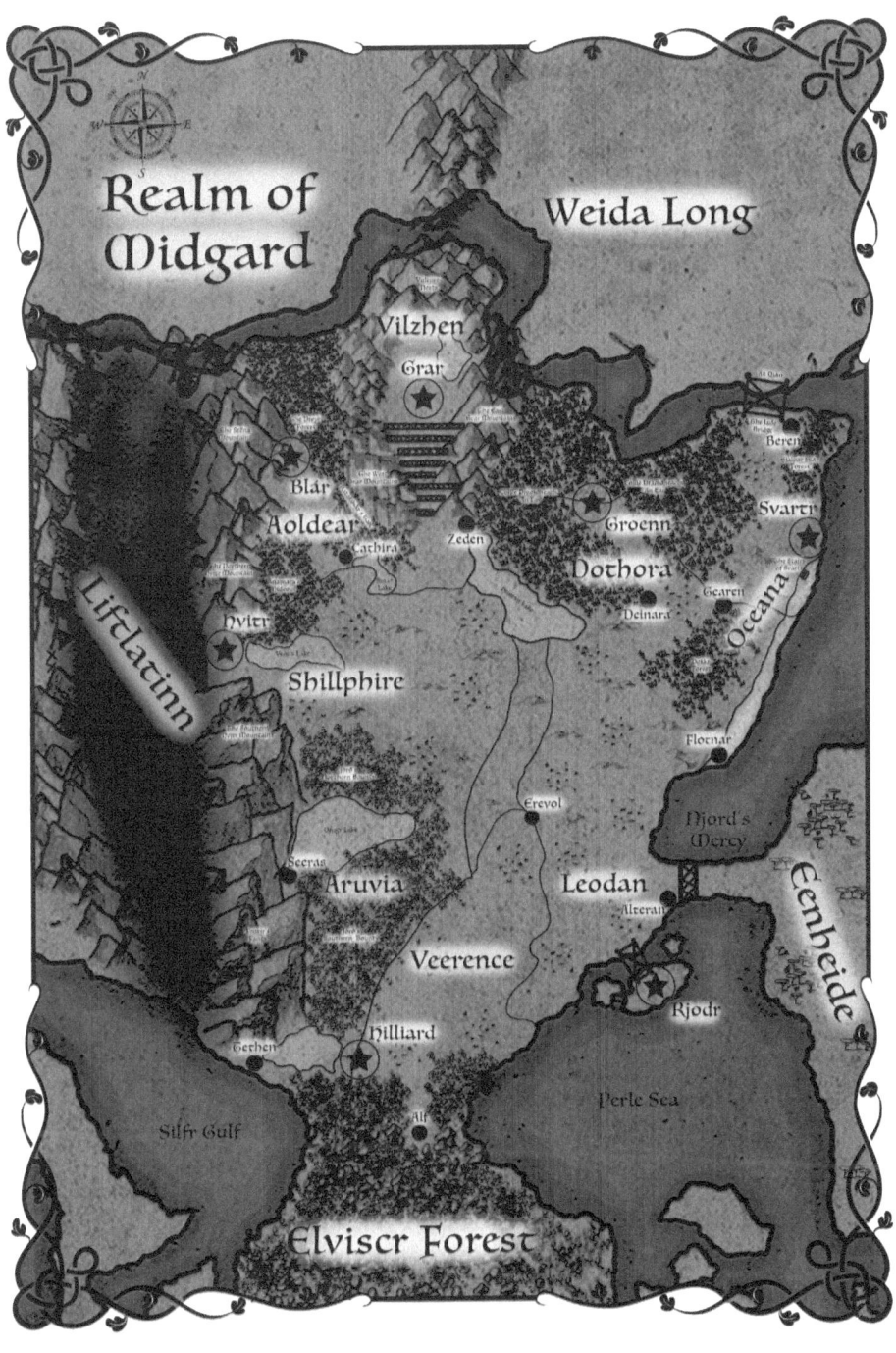

Pronunciation Guide

Here you can learn the names of important characters and places in this book. If you'd like to learn the various Norse/Nordic terms, you will find the glossary at the back of the book.

Part 1

Characters

Eilert Önnîka — *Aye-lort Oe-nee-ka*

Saya Önnîka — *Suh-yuh Oe-nee-ka*

Valhalla Önnîka — *Val-ha-luh Oe-nee-ka*

Edan — *A-duhn*

Tarik Grunr — *Tear-ee-k Gruh-n-r*

Kiara Vitaliadottir — *Kee-uh-ruh Vee-tuh-lee-uh-doh-teer*

Loki Ódinson — *Loh-kee Oo-dihn-sun*

Aura Vitaliadottir — *Uh-rah Vee-tuh-lee-uh-doh-teer*

Thora Andradadottir — *Thou-ruh Ahn-dru-duh-doh-teer*

Arianwen Andradadottir — *Uh-ree-uhn-wane Ahn-dru-duh-doh-teer*

Cascade — *Kas-kay-d*

Heimdall Ódinson — *Hi-m-duh-l Oo-dihn-sun*

Anita Petoradottir — *Uh-nee-tuh P-eh-toh-ruh-doh-teer*

Frigg Fiorgyndottir — *F-ree-guh Fee-ohr-geen-doh-teer*

Syn — *S-ee-n*

Fulla Fiorgyndottir — *F-oo-luh Fee-ohr-geen-doh-teer*

Thor Ódinson — *Thou-r Oo-dihn-sun*

Vitalia — *Vee-tuh-lee-uh*

Vardan Loyalen — *V-ah-r-den Loh-yah-lane*

Diamantina Athenan — *Dee-uh-muh-n-tee-nuh Uh-the-nuh-n*

Sigurdr Sirgonson — *See-guh-r-d-r See-r-goh-n-sun*

Places

Seeras — *See-ruh-s*

Veerence — *Vee-ruhn-c*

Asgard — *Ahs-gah-r-d*

Bifrost — *Bi-f-ruh-s-t*

Marglod — *Muh-r-g-luh-d*

Alf — *Ah-l-f*

Part 2
Characters
Alistair Hilliard — *Ah-lay-s-tear He-lee-uh-r-d*
Shu Yen Ling — *Shoo Yan Lee-n-g*
Madame — *Mah-duh-m*
Eilis Hilliard — *Aye-liss He-lee-uh-r-d*
Embla Hilliard — *M-b-lah He-lee-uh-r-d*
Lorna Hilliard — *Loh-r-nah He-lee-uh-r-d*
Druoga Drigarrson — *D-ruh-oh-gah D-ree-gah-r-sun*
Velondr Grár — *Vay-luh-n-duhr G-r-au-r*
Ing Favrine — *Ee-n-g Fah-v-ree-n*
Places
Hilliard — *He-lee-uh-r-d*
Grár — *G-r-au-r*

Part 3
Characters
Yggdrasil — *Ee-g-drah-seel*
Verdrfolnir — *Vear-dur-foh-l-near*
Ratatoskr — *Rah-tuh-toh-s-kur*
Nidhoggr — *Nee-d-huh-gur*
Hel — *Hale*
Hermódur Ódinson — *Hair-moo-duh-r Oo-dihn-sun*
Jörmungandr Lokison — *Joh-r-muh-n-gah-n-dur Loh-kee-sun*
Fenrir Lokison — *F-aye-n-reer Loh-kee-sun*
Angrboda — *Ahn-gur-boh-dah*
Narfi Lokison — *Nah-r-fee Loh-kee-sun*
Nari Lokison — *Nah-ree Loh-kee-sun*
Sigyn — *See-guh-n*
Huginn and Muninn — *Hue-gee-n and Mew-n-een*
Geri and Freki — *Geh-ree and F-reh-kee*
Garmr — *Gah-r-mur*
Kaledvrishoth — *Kah-lay-d-vree-shoh-th*
Ayunli Nealfire Svartr — *Ah-yuh-n-lee Nee-ahl-fih-ur S-vah-r-tur*
Aegir Svartr — *Aye-gee-r S-vah-r-tur*

Places
Fensalir — *F-aye-n-suh-leer*
Helheim — *Hale-hi-m*
River Gjöll — *G-jooh-l*
Helvegr Path — *Hale-vay-gur*
Svartr — *S-vah-r-tur*

Part 4
Characters
Daeymyn Svartr — *Day-m-ihn S-vah-r-tur*
Njörd — *Nee-jooh-r-d*
Albrecht Svartr — *Ahl-b-ray-k-t S-vah-r-tur*
Tamanna Gadhavi — *Tuh-mah-nuh Guh-dah-vee*
Emera — *Ah-mee-rah*
Logír — *Loh-gee-r*
Lilianna — *Lee-lee-ah-nah*
Scald Yorath — *Yoh-rah-th*
Thorin — *Thou-r-een*
Places
Mahaanbrahma — *Mah-ha-ahn-brah-mah*
Raseela — *Ray-see-lah*
Rjóðr — *Ree-oo-thur*
Eenheid — *Aye-n-ha-eet*

Part
I

PROLOGUE

"**Y**ou must grasp the hilt firmly. If you don't, the sword can easily be knocked from your hand."

"Like this?" A boy of about seven years of age, Uhtred, pink eyes and a black mop of hair atop his head, locked eyes on his instructor. Tightening his grip around the hilt of his wooden training sword, he shifted his stance for defense.

Eilert knelt before the boy, inspected him from top to bottom, and smiled approvingly. "That's good," He said, standing to address the group of Aruvian boys and girls of varying ages. "With a strong grip, you have full control of not only your weapon, but of the battle as well."

Taking a few steps and stopping before them, he crossed his hands behind his back. "Once you have control of your weapon, and by extension your opponent, the possibilities are endless. You can overtake them in various ways. Whether to protect yourself," Eilert paused, looking away from the group to a young girl at his right just outside of the arena, her grin beaming. She held healing herbs in one hand and waved happily to him with the other. Touching the tips of his fingers to his lips, he kissed them gently and waved his hand toward her. "Or to protect those you care about." Eilert returned his attention to the group. "Learn to fight, find your reason to succeed, and the battle will be yours. Do you all understand me?"

"Yes, Lord Eilert!" The kids grinned. They all stood tall, straightening their backs and holding their heads high. The show of confidence made him chuckle.

His hand flew to his silver and violet rapier, Lightpiercer, and drew it, holding the sword before him. The silver blade shone white against the bright sun. The kids all stared at its brilliance, eyes wide and several with mouths agape. One audibly gasped. "Whether your blade is great, striking slow and strong, or be it light, swift, and piercing, it's a part of you. Whatever weapon you choose, never turn it on those you love."

The kids stared at him, taken aback. Eilert closed his eyes. With a swipe and a flourish, Lightpiercer nestled into its sheath once more. "Why don't you all practice a few swings for now, then we'll be done for the morning."

"Yes, Lord Eilert!" The kids raised their wooden swords high in the air and swung them forward, repeating the pattern of strikes.

"Please, Mama." The little girl with the herbs leaned toward her mother, pink eyes large and pleading.

Saya Önníka, the Duchess of Seeras and Gydja[1] of the Temple of Kveykva, his wife, looked to their daughter with brows curved disapprovingly. Eilert then approached, garnering their attention.

Standing before them, he placed a hand to his hip. "All right, you two, what's wrong?"

The little girl, Valhalla Önníka, clasped her hands before her chest and greeted him with a joyous smile. "I want you to train me in the way of the sword, Papa."

Her feelings on the matter rested clearly on her face, his wife's expression stern and body rigid. She had always been too overprotective, but that's what he loved about her.

Attempting to defuse the situation, he met her look with a smirk. "I don't see why not."

"Eilert!" She exclaimed, her tone short and objecting.

"Saya, there's no harm in her learning to defend herself."

She stood to speak face-to-face with him. "No, that's what the High Prince is for. By the time they are wed, he will be well-versed in swordplay and should be able to protect her. Valhalla would be far better served focusing on herbs until she's ready to start training in light magic. She doesn't need training with a blade."

With a sigh, Eilert glanced down at his wife's hand resting over her stomach, her fingers trembling lightly. He walked up to her, cupping her small belly, and touched his forehead to hers. "My lovely Saya, it's only training. It's not as if we are sending Valla to battle."

She took a deep breath, her eyes staring at her daughter for a long moment.

---

1   Gydja is Celnor(Norse) for Priestess.

"I know," she sighed in defeat, "I know. I can't help myself, it's just . . . Are you sure?" She looked up at him with pursed lips and eyes shining with concern.

Releasing a soft breath and smiling serenely, he felt the light kicks of their next child in her womb. "I think you worry too much."

Smiling sweetly, she let out a soft giggle. "And I think you don't worry enough, but I suppose that's what makes us so great together." She flashed him a playful smile, her beautiful pink garnet eyes twinkling in the sunlight.

The sight sent his heart aflutter. He then pressed his lips to hers, kissing her deeply. As they parted, his heart longed to remain in the embrace. "I love you."

"And I you." Her smile softened and her cheeks flushed.

A tiny squeal of excitement startled them.

Valhalla's wide eyes darted back and forth between them, her hands clasped over her lips, cheeks bright pink. Eilert let out a loud laugh, surprised by his daughter's reaction. "Come on, you." Valhalla rushed beside her father and took his hand as they approached the Madr Bardagi Arena, where the other kids busied themselves with training.

"All right everyone, that's enough for today, but before you go . . ." Eilert scanned the kids in the front row and smirked. "Uhtred, was it?"

Uhtred beamed. "Yes, me Lord?"

"Would you lend Valhalla your training sword? Just temporarily until I can commission one for her."

"Of course, me Lord."

The other kids rushed over and stood on the left side of the arena. Valhalla ran to Uhtred, grasping the hilt of the wooden sword. The boy helped her adjust her stance. "Here, grab hold, and stand just like this."

Valhalla let out a shrill giggle and positioned her legs under her long white dress.

Eilert took a sudden short breath. Although this was simply a training session, the sight of her holding the sword caused a visceral reaction within him. His pulse spiked and heart thumped a bit quicker, making him feel dizzy. A day would come when his daughter would need to wield it. The thought startled him to his core. The sense of foreboding settled into his chest. He shook it away. With a prayer to the mighty Ódin in Asgard, he pleaded that such a day might never come.

Eilert cleared his throat, then noticed the sudden quiet fall over the area. "Do you know how to hold it, Valla?"

She nodded and stood as straight as she could. The tip of the long sword nestled into the ground. Her arms shook, struggling to hold the wooden sword.

"Good, can you raise it?"

"Umm," Valhalla's face scrunched and went bright red, her body tensing as she pulled on the fake sword. With a loud breath, she exhaled and her shoulders slumped, unable to raise the tip even a little. "No." She frowned.

Before Eilert could say a word, Uhtred wrapped his hands around hers and raised her arms high in the air. "There you go."

As he let go of the sword, its weight pulled Valhalla back. Uhtred gently nudged her forward, likely intending to help find her footing to swing the training sword downward. She only managed one step before becoming entangled in her white dress and falling, landing squarely on her face.

Eilert startled. Saya jumped with a heavy gasp. Uhtred stared at Valhalla with eyes wide, unsure if he should rush to her side for comfort or to treat her as he would any of the other trainees, to allow her this moment to show her strength of character.

His wife, on the other hand, didn't hesitate. She walked over to tend to their daughter, kneeling beside Valhalla and placing her hands on their child's waist, to help her up off the ground.

All the children stared at Valhalla, faces scrunching in anticipation of the tears which would soon follow. Saya smiled sweetly at Uhtred, catching him off guard. "It's all right, dear, it was only an accident."

Eilert watched his wife turn Valhalla to face her. His daughter's tiny hands covered her face. Valhalla sniffled lightly, dirt smudged across her porcelain white skin. Light tears flowed from the corners of her eyes.

Saya wiped away the dirt and tears from Valhalla's face. "Hush now my little one, stop your tears. Now tell me, are you well?"

Valhalla removed her hands from her still-teary face, her nose scrunched and red. "It-it hurts."

"Good." She stated, gently grasping Valhalla's chin with one hand, and guided her daughter's gaze up to meet her own. Valhalla's eyes widened with confusion.

"Let the pain remind you that you are mortal, that it will be waiting for you if you're not careful." Valhalla's eyes trembled lightly at her mother's words, but her calm smile remained. "We mortals are capable of extraordinary and, oftentimes, incredible things, but pain is our counsel. Listen to it when it voices itself to you." Her mother removed her hand from Valhalla's chin and softly tapped her nose, causing their daughter to giggle. "So, what is it telling you?"

"Umm," Valhalla looked away from her mother to her white dress, stretching past her knees all the way to the ground, and covering her small feet. She grabbed bundles of the fabric in both hands, lifting them lightly off the ground. Looking back at her mother with a grin, she answered, "Wrong clothes."

Saya and the other children giggled at her response. Her mother nodded and cupped his daughter's face, touching Valhalla's forehead to her own. "I know you will never intentionally worry me, Valhalla, but know that I'll always worry for you." She then wrapped her arms around her daughter and embraced her warmly. The girl's eyes shook, then closed as she embraced her mother in return.

A strong gust of wind raced all around the arena. Eilert braced, watching helplessly as Saya, Valhalla, and the children struggled to keep their footing. Hair and clothing fluttered about wildly in the torrent. The leaves and branches of nearby trees swayed violently, looking as though the winds would pluck them from the soil at any moment. He turned in the direction of the gale, staring at the Haed Valley just outside their city of Seeras.

The winds blew toward the center of the valley, swirling fast. A small, dark sphere began to form at the heart of the howling gale. His people looked shaken. He felt a sense of dread bloom in his gut at the thought of just what might be the cause of such a sudden change in the weather. Those caught in the streets struggled to get indoors, to take shelter within their turf homes and longhouses to protect themselves from the coming storm.

Picking up their daughter, Saya held her tightly against her chest as the winds pushed them forward. Many simply stared at the growing sphere outside their small city, eyes trembling and feet frozen in place out of fear.

"Children," Eilert called, pulling their attention from the storm, "I want you all to return home. Don't stop for any reason, unless it's for your parents!" The children all nodded, not a single one arguing with the Duke, and dispersed.

The gale picked up, roaring with each burst, crashing into them like waves on a sandy shore. Eilert and Saya struggled to stand firm. He raised his gaze back to the sphere. Valhalla wrapped her arms tightly around her mother's neck. Eilert's breath hitched in his throat as Saya startled with a gasp. The sphere quickly grew and grew, now the size of a horse and still expanding.

"Saya," Eilert said, his voice tight with urgency. She turned to meet her husband's furrowed gaze as he drew Lightpiercer. "You and Valhalla take refuge in the temple!"

She looked back at the sphere outside of the small city, only managing a few steps before it burst and out poured clouds of pure darkness. They expanded, racing high into the once clear blue sky, enveloping the city on all sides, and trapping the citizens against the Fenrir's Fangs Mountains at their backs. Shouts began ringing out across the city, the names of loved ones carried on the winds as families searched for one another. The blackened clouds choked the sun's rays, shrouding everything in grim gray shadows.

Eilert quaked at the sight, unsure of what ill tidings this would bring, but he had never been one to take chances. He spun around to his wife and took a deep breath. "Now, Saya!"

Jumping, his wife nodded. As she started to head back into their home of the temple, Eilert made a mad dash heading to the front entrance of their small city of Seeras. On his way, he found people still gawking at the ominous event transpiring around them.

His brows furrowed over his eyes and he skidded to a halt. "Everyone, please listen!" Eilert bellowed, catching the people's ears. "I need every able-bodied person to the wall, NOW! Everyone else, barricade yourselves indoors!" Eilert then continued his flight toward the half-man-sized wall that encircled the outskirts of the city. Before he knew it, many people followed close behind.

Reaching the entrance of Seeras, a few soldiers stood before the city gates, their bodies trembling. Eilert's breath grew heavy, but it was nothing compared to the hard pounding of his heart against his chest. The people of the city were scared; he knew it, understood it even. Fear clung to him just as it did them, but he knew they couldn't let it control them, lest they allow the Norns to write their fates.

"What do you think you're doing!?" Eilert bellowed, startling the soldiers. Their eyes all fell to him. "Get those gates closed immediately!"

"Yes, Lord Eilert!" His soldiers scrambled to follow his command.

Eilert glanced to his right at a longhouse where they stored armor and weapons. He walked up to it and swung the doors wide open. Braziers burned brightly, illuminating the various handed-down armors and weapons resting on the shelves, all originating from their neighboring castle cities of Hilliard and Hvítr. Seeras was still small, not yet capable of mass-producing their own, and so relied on their allies for support.

He turned to face his soldiers and those volunteers still arriving. "I want archers at the wall at once! Everyone else, grab a chest piece and a sword. Be prepared for anything!"

"Yes, Lord!"

The unarmed rushed in and grabbed armor and weapons. Eilert grabbed the closest chest piece. With the aid of one of his soldiers, he slipped it on and strapped it closed, then exited the longhouse.

"Lord Eilert, come look!"

Eilert turned his gaze to the wall by the gate, to one of his Captains pointing outward with a trembling hand. "There-There's something coming forth."

Eilert's heart froze and he hastened over to the Captain. He placed a hand flat on the wall and looked out. Breath caught in his throat, Eilert's eyes widened at the sight of the shifting black clouds still pouring from the sphere.

A shadowy figure appeared from within the twisted, black shroud. The figure emerged and stopped about a mile out from the city. Eilert stared at the mysterious person with trembling eyes. He didn't know this person's identity or how they could wield such powerful seidr able to rival that of a god, but he vowed to the mighty Ódin that if things came to a fight, he and his people would somehow prevail, and hoped that the powerful Týr and Thor were on their side.

Eilert glanced left and right, his brows heavy with worry. These lands had always been peaceful, and most of the citizens had never fought more than a passing bandit. Still, no amount of training could substitute for real combat. They had heart, at least. He hoped that would be enough.

He settled his nerves as best he could as the small number of soldiers and volunteers spread out around him. They readied themselves behind the small wall, swords and arrows in hand. His gaze swept the barrier, landing on the space where a group should have been. "Dammit, where are the völvxs? Has no one sent word yet?"

"I'm sorry, me Lord. All this is happenin' so fast."

Eilert's heart skipped a beat. He returned his attention to the figure in the distance and his eyes slowly began to tremble.

Creatures started emerging from the shroud and stood beside the mysterious stranger. They moved as one with the shadows, forms somehow both of tissue and wispy smoke.

A creature much larger than a horse, covered in thin spikes, slithered forward and hissed. Massive wolf-like beasts stood on their hind legs, bearing sharp fangs and howling in guttural tones.

The figure who led them raised what looked like a weapon and pointed it in the city's direction. The creatures charged the city from all sides, their numbers endlessly pouring from the clouded vale.

Eilert's body shuddered in terror. They couldn't falter, not now.

The monsters were on the move, Eilert ordered all archers to loose their arrows upon the horde. In an instant, arrow after arrow flew through the sky and rained down on the beasts, piercing fur, scale, and flesh.

The soldiers, let alone the volunteers, lacked the training to face such an attack, but their lives depended on their actions here and now.

He looked to his left, surveying the condition of his soldiers. The ones on the wall shook. The Captain beside Eilert watched with fear plastered on his face. Sweat slid down the side of his forehead. Terror had him.

The Captain retreated several more paces, ending up by a turf house. He flinched and froze in place as something fell on his cheek. The Captain wiped it away with a shaking hand, pinching the strange sticky substance between his fingers. Just then, a soft growl from above caused him to jolt. Eilert's stomach fell as he saw the creature before the Captain did, but he could do nothing to avert the man's fate.

The Captain slowly let his head fall back, his eyes widening as he too saw the wolf-like creature. The monster let out an ear-splitting roar. Opening his mouth to scream, the Captain grasped for his sword, but the beast moved far too fast and lunged at him.

Eilert stared with mouth agape, unable to move as the creature wrapped its lengthy, clawed fingers around the Captain's torso. It dug its nails deep into the man's back. Saliva slid down the corner of its mouth as it sank its sharp fangs into one of the man's shoulders.

He let out a loud yelp and called out for help. A few of the soldiers heard his plea and turned to answer his call, but as their eyes fell on the fiend, fear froze them as it had Eilert. The monstrous creature towered before them, a mixture of beast and man.

It sank its teeth deeper into the Captain, ripping into muscle and bone, and tugged its head back. Hot crimson liquid flooded out of the wound, staining his clothes. Bile rose in Eilert's throat while his knees trembled, ready to buckle beneath his weight.

The Captain's sword dropped to the floor and his head fell back, lifeless. The monster sank its teeth in once more and with a tug, ripped the arm from the man's body. The soldiers stumbled back and fell onto the archers behind them. Men screamed as arrows loosed, some flying aimlessly and a few slamming into fellow soldiers.

The creature bellowed menacingly as it dropped the Captain's dead body to the now muddied ground. It cocked its head to the side, tossing the severed arm at the soldiers feet, and flashed them a bloody grin. The grisly sight gave way to panic.

Everything fell into disarray. Some soldiers stayed in position while many abandoned their posts. The creature raised a clawed hand and swiped at the soldiers as they tried to run, tearing through armor as if it were nothing but soft linen.

Screams started echoing throughout the city. Eilert, regaining what little composure he could, spun around and scanned the area as cries called out in all directions.

"Oh no!" He whispered as dread filled his every being. Eilert's heart twisted in his chest. The archers were now mostly defenseless, save for the few guards who remained. The monsters swiftly overtook the wall.

"Shit! Fall back!" Eilert commanded. "RETREAT TO THE TEMPLE!"

~*~

Saya stood in the opening of her temple, holding Valhalla tightly to her chest. She looked back at her small city, at the carnage raging through Seeras, and choked back tears.

Blood stained the walls of homes. Corpses littered the streets in all directions. A handful of people clad in white robes poured through the chaos. She could see their mouths moving, but could not hear their words. Their hands burst alight with flame, startling her. A barrage of fiery blasts bombarded the monsters, charring their bodies, leaving little more than ash and a putrid odor that seemed to stick in the air.

A few of the völvxs summoned balls of light between their palms, growing in girth and radiance. Thrusting their arms forward, the light flew toward their attackers. The magical blasts raced through the air and made contact with a cacophonous boom, disintegrating anything they touched, leaving mutilated, pulsating remains in their wake.

Saya sighed with relief. Perhaps they had a chance after all.

The spark of hope left her almost as quickly as it had appeared. The screams of her people intensified nearby, causing her to jolt. Her eyes darted left and right, watching as a sea of people filled the streets, likely fleeing an overrun part of the city. With the influx of people, it became more difficult for the robed völvxs to hold the creatures at bay.

A couple with a small child got cornered by one of the tall snake-like creatures. A fire völva nearby readied a spell and extended her hands forward. Just as she let loose the spell, a person crashed hard into her from behind, causing the torrent of flame to miss the creature. Instead, the blaze crashed through the closing doors of the adjacent longhouse. The building erupted with fire and screams followed from those trapped inside. Smoke billowed from the entryway. Embers spread, carried by the winds.

Turning back to the light völvxs; panic rose in their eyes. The creatures seemed to increase in speed, dodging spells with sudden ease. Their movements became so fast that their forms appeared only as black blurs to her eyes.

Smoke from the burning homes obscured the already darkened area. Flashes of figures could be seen through the smoke as magic burst within. Some of the blasts sailed clear of the smoke, crashing into the mud and homes with booming clatter. Those citizens unlucky enough to be caught in the spell's path fared little better than the creatures.

Chaos struck fear into Saya's heart. She commanded her body to flee, but all she could manage was to inch her way back into the open foyer of the temple. Her stomach churned. Bile climbed her throat. She squeezed Valhalla tightly to her chest.

Eilert then slid into her view. His lips moved, but she couldn't hear his words. The screams of those dying and the victorious screeches of the bloodthirsty creatures drowned out his pleas. He grabbed one of her arms and pulled her deeper into the temple.

They flashed past stairs and rooms filled with offerings for their gods in Asgard. They continued until Eilert stopped and threw her through the entryway of a large room. She stumbled in, almost falling to her knees, but managed to keep herself upright.

Looking up, she found herself staring at a white stone statue of the Valkyrie of light. She spun around, alarmed at the loud scurry of footsteps of soldiers storming into the room, likely all that survived the initial onslaught. They rushed behind the double doors, readying to close and bar the entrance once every last living soul was through.

As the last of the soldiers rushed in, creatures hurtled toward them from close behind. Eilert stood in the doorway and raised his rapier vertically before him with both hands clasped around the hilt. He scrunched his brows, summoning a red magical circle before him, and aimed it down the hall.

A fire glyph appeared at the circle's center, surrounded by ancient Celnor runes. Sparks exploded out from the center of the incantation, followed by a burst of flame. It roared through the hall and consumed all within.

He held fast, allowing the flames to pour forth and cleanse the temple of the monstrous creatures. The fire burned with righteous fury, scorching everything in its path. He then broke the spell with a swipe of his arm, extinguishing the fire. The monsters had come mere feet from eviscerating him, all now turned to charred husks of ash.

Eilert retreated inside the room and his soldiers began sealing the doors. More monsters came rushing down the hall, barreling through the remains of their burnt brethren. As the doors drew closed, the soldiers grabbed anything and everything not nailed down and piled it all in a makeshift barricade against the doors.

A few of the soldiers looked to Eilert, their eyes pleading for guidance, for any semblance of hope he could offer them, but when he spun back to her, she knew in her heart they could do nothing more. His body visibly shivered in exhaustion, shaking as if snow filled the room. Eilert's eyes then fixed on the doors before him.

Saya's heart raced hard within her chest, worrying for her husband standing a short distance away. Only the gods knew what may have been going through his head at this moment. She wanted so badly to embrace him.

"Eilert?" She called softly, her voice causing him to flinch.

He turned to her, his trembling eyes confused and filled with terror. Sweat slid down his face. Her daughter's cry caught their attention.

Shushing Valhalla gently, she tried to comfort her, knowing it to be in vain. Saya then raised her eyes to her husband.

He dropped his silver rapier, rushed to them both, and wrapped his arms around them. "I'm sorry. I'm so sorry." His voice cracked.

Her breath hitched. The defeat in his voice hit her with the strength of an ox. There had to be a way out for them, there had to be. If not for them, then for their daughter at least.

She glanced around, hoping beyond hope to find some way out of this nightmare, but all she saw were the four familiar stone walls and the burning iron sconces she had known all her life. There was no other door, no openings to the outside, no matter how hard she wished it. Nothing could save them now.

Releasing a steady breath, she rested her chin on Eilert's shoulder. With one arm wrapped around his waist, she held him and Valhalla close. Her eyes trembled.

This truly was the end for them, she thought darkly.

Sliding her hand up to her husband's face, she placed it on his cheek. She brushed her lips against his opposite cheek and kissed him softly.

They parted for only a moment and stared into each other's eyes. A small resigned smile rested on her face. She gazed up at him, staring at his trembling but beautiful Hillian blue eyes, shimmering like sapphires against the firelight. The hopelessness extinguished his fire within.

The frown on his face spread deep, casting her smile away. He closed his eyes and buried his face in the crook of her neck. She could feel the light tears as they fell against her skin, her body shuddering as a result.

She raised a hand to his loosened black hair, rubbing the back of his head, and turned her glance to the white stone statue of their Valkyrie of Light, wondering why she had forsaken them so. Then Saya's eyes traveled to the statue's right shoulder and followed the outstretched arm pointed toward the floor. Releasing Eilert, she stepped toward the spot indicated by the statue.

There, she found four creases within the floorboard and jolted, remembering the space below. This offering room just happened to house a compartment used as a food store in case of emergencies.

She released a quick breath and called Eilert's attention, her eyes fixed on the trapdoor before them. He stared for a moment before the realization struck him as well.

As he rushed to the trapdoor, the doors of the offering room banged loudly once, startling everyone within. The room fell silent again, and she immediately knelt to the floor, squeezing her fingers through a small opening between the floorboards and the trapdoor, and pulled it open.

Many large, blue ceramic jars filled with grain and dried meat occupied the space. Only one person could fit.

Saya and Eilert looked at each other, silent, her eyes wide, but steady. He shook his head, rejecting what she knew they must do.

Answering with furrowed brows, conviction blossomed in her chest. "If only one of us is to survive this massacre, allow it to be our daughter, Eilert."

He stared back, a wall of tears rising in his eyes, and teeth gritted. His breath labored, unable to hold back the heartache as he looked away, and simply nodded in understanding.

A pang of guilt and anguish swelled in her chest. She understood why he hesitated, but it had to be done. No matter how much it pained them both.

Another bang sounded on the door, hardening Saya's resolve. Placing Valhalla at arm's length, she looked at her daughter with a small smile, pressing her lips against the girl's forehead, and sat her between the jars.

As she readied to pull back, Valhalla reached out, grabbing two of her mother's fingers, and clutched them tightly within her tiny hand. Saya paused, her eyes welling with tears as she stared at her daughter, hoping Valhalla could find comfort from her touch, the last they would ever share, and gently rubbed her thumb against her daughter's fingers.

Eyes filled with tears, she managed to force a smile. "Valhalla, no matter what happens, no matter what you hear . . . I want you to be as quiet as possible, all right?"

Valhalla squeezed her mother's fingers tightly, her little face a mixture of fear and confusion, but hesitantly nodded.

Eilert slid in next to Saya and placed a hand on Valhalla's head, a gentle smile of his own showing on his face. His eyes lingered, steady, a wall of tears locked behind his loving gaze.

"My little Valla, I know not who caused this, but no matter what happens next . . . revenge isn't the answer. It can transform the most true-hearted person into a monster. Do you understand me?"

Valhalla stared at her father, her eyes trembling. She knew Valhalla couldn't understand why her mother and father were saying such things, but as she stared at her daughter for the last time, her heart broke.

Her lips trembled. She wanted to tell her daughter all would be well, that they would fetch her once everything quieted, but she couldn't bring herself to speak. She didn't want her last words to be a lie.

Another bang sounded at the doors, causing Valhalla to flinch. The furniture scraped against the floor. It wouldn't be long now.

Saya held her eyes on her daughter, soaking her in as long as she could.

Valhalla looked to Eilert as his hand rose above her head for only a moment. His eyes closed, and he took a deep breath, his lips tightly pursed. He then opened his eyes and exhaled.

"Lord Eilert!"

The sudden loud call startled Valhalla. Panic flashed in her daughter's eyes, a terror Saya knew deep down would likely haunt her child long after this day.

Still, this was the only way. This had to be done. It must. She repeated the words to herself over and over again, trying to make them as true as possible. So long as Valhalla was safe, nothing else mattered.

Valhalla turned to her mother, then to her father, and nodded.

Tears flowed down Eilert's face, but his smile never wavered. "This is the only lesson left I can teach you. Be brave. I want you to know, your mother and I love you so very much. We will always be with you. Please, take care of yourself, my little Eldr[2]." He leaned down, pressed his lips against Valhalla's forehead, and kissed her softly. He tapped his forehead against hers, as some of his tears landed on his daughter's face, and let out a shaky breath.

Valhalla raised her other hand to Eilert, to touch his face, but he stood too fast and turned to face the banging doors. Didn't turn to see him. Instead, she kept her eyes on her daughter, only on Valhalla, as Eilert walked away.

Taking in her daughter as long as she could. A lump formed in her throat for how much of herself she could see in Valhalla, from her ebony black hair to her porcelain white skin and Aruvian pink eyes, except for her nose. Her daughter had her father's nose and round chin.

Saya giggled softly to herself. Tears continued to flow down her round cheeks. Both she and her daughter remained quiet, the noisy thuds against the door powerless to infringe on this moment.

Her lips quivered. There was so much more left to say, but they were out of time. The thought wrenched her stomach into knots. It would be so easy to give in to despair. However, she had hope, hope that her daughter would survive, that Valhalla would be the tiny part of her and Eilert left in this world.

She pleaded. Begged even. To Ódin, Frigg, Lady of Light, to anyone on high that would listen, to allow Valhalla to live. Live long enough to find a new family. True Love. Perhaps even marriage and a family of her own. To give Valhalla a chance to grow into an old woman and die peacefully in her sleep. To allow her daughter to live a full and happy life, whatever that could be, and to

---

2   Eldr is Celnor(Norse) for Fire.

keep Valhalla safe from harm.

Pulling her hand from her daughter's grasp, she slipped away from those tiny fingers.

Valhalla stumbled forward and reached out to her mother, eyes wide. "Mama?" She called softly.

Saya released a quick breath as she grabbed hold of the trapdoor. Her heart twisted tightly in her chest as she choked down the urge to scoop up her daughter one last time. She held her smile firm, forcing it to remain even though it pained her fiercely.

She stared at her daughter for a moment longer and stole this last fleeting moment to hold on to. The banging increased with every beat of her racing heart. As she heard the barricade scrape on the wooden floor, ready to give way, she pulled her arm back and slammed the trapdoor shut, leaving Valhalla alone in the darkness.

Lady Red

A Chase Through A Forrest

A MONSTROUS ROAR RANG OUT over the otherwise quiet forest, shaking the very trees to their roots. Valhalla broke through the brush of the dense forest, running in a mad attempt to escape her pursuer. She moved as quickly as her legs would carry her, fleeing the komod dragon den now a reasonable distance behind her.

The forest was just south of Elviscr, beyond the borders of Veerence, and was vastly more expansive than she could've imagined. Dodging each trunk and low-hanging bough blocking her path, she navigated her way over the sea of thick roots. Stray branches clipped at her clothes as she narrowly zigzagged and ducked beneath as she passed. Crashing through a dense shrub, she nearly crashed into a fallen tree mere feet in front of her. Its trunk was as thick as she was tall. With great effort, she lunged, putting all of her strength and momentum into the leap and just barely cleared the broken trunk.

Her chest tightened, and her lungs blazed with the fiery pain of exertion. Sweat slid down the side of her face. Her short, thick, ebony hair was drenched and caught on her skin. She held her red cape tightly in one hand, making sure it didn't catch on anything. Her hand-and-a-half longsword banged rhythmically against her left leg.

A light rumble beneath her feet threatened to send her tumbling over the shifting twigs, leaves, and rocks below. Leaves rustled closely behind her, sending her heart into her throat.

A short growl sent a shiver up her spine. Turning her head to the left, there she spotted a young komod dragonling the size of two stallions.

Its body slithered through the forest, its mass carried by four strong legs. Unlike their winged cousins, Komod dragons couldn't fly. They had a strong connection to the earth, and their breath was so powerful it could heal nearly any wound or ailment.

Valhalla! My födra[1] is not far behind! The young komod's voice rang clear, its sound not perceptible by earshot, but instead a whisper among her thoughts, causing a light tingling sensation as it washed over her.

To each bank of dragons belonged gems specific to their species. Komods had large sard gems embedded in the very center of their foreheads.

Valhalla? The komod called with a raised brow.

"All right, you ready, Barna?" Valhalla yelled back with heavy breath.

She glanced at him, awaiting his answer, his face grimacing heavily with doubt. *Art thou sure about this?*

Valhalla hesitated a moment, understanding his concern. Who in their right mind would use themselves as bait to distract an Elder Dragon?

"Yes!" She answered confidently, even though she thought it was probably a terrible idea.

You dost know I can hear your thoughts, right? Barna replied.

"Just aim for that crystal on his back, I'll be fine!" She hoped it really would be.

Barna's scaly eyelids narrowed in worry, but he nodded reluctantly. He slithered away to a safe distance, climbed up a slanted tree, and dove headfirst into the earth, disappearing underground.

Valhalla silently thanked her friend with a smile, ignoring her second thoughts.

Her eyes flashed wide, seeing a tree fall just before her. She vaulted over the bough with a heavy grunt. As her feet touched the ground, she rolled forward,

---

1   Födra is Dragon for Father.

stopping her momentum by slamming her hands against the dirt, and found herself in a large clearing.

She stood up to gain her bearings, getting a good feel for the surroundings. Scanning over and agreeing with herself that the spot would do. Her heart raced hard against her chest.

The ground beneath her feet quaked fiercely, almost toppling her, but she managed to stand firm. A massive komod dragon sprang from the ground for a short distance before her and landed hard on all fours, startling her back a couple of steps.

"Just-Just keep your eyes on me, Elder Bron." She whispered with a trembling breath, grounding herself as firmly as possible before the great komod.

Her eyes squinted at the creature, noticing his sickly form hidden from the sun within the shadows cast by the surrounding trees. Bron's scales were paler than the usually shimmering amber brown hue typical of the komods. His once reddish brown eyes were now as black as the night sky. Even the long tuft of dark brown hair under his chin had turned a dark gray.

He growled in a deep, menacing tone, the sound shaking the earth around them in a reverberating guttural threat. A shiver ran down her spine.

His large, jagged, dark brown horns protruded far from his head. At this distance, he was as grand as a small mountain. Bron's lengthy body far surpassed the young dragonling who separated from her moments ago. When held high, his head surpassed the cover of the very trees around them. His sharp claws dug deep into the dirt, as the pads of his feet crunched the grass flat underneath.

Bron's eyelids began to flutter to a close, almost like he was struggling to keep himself awake. He shook his head, looking irritated. His stance loosened, his head falling fast to the ground, but instead of crashing down, his massive nostrils tapped the dirt, and he let out another harsh growl. The dirt and leaves beneath his face flew in a cloud before him.

Her heart swelled for the Elder, but she was curious as to what could be wrong with him. Valhalla continued to inspect the great dragon, careful to keep her distance.

Bron shook his head again, this time with agitated vigor. His gaze went unfocused and now seemed to pay her no mind. She guessed he had turned his attention inward, focusing on something unseen, and by the scrunch of his brow, was battling within his mind.

Valhalla took a deep breath. This was her chance to strike, to incapacitate the Elder. Due to Bron's strong affinity to earth, air seidr would have been the most effective for the task at hand. Unfortunately, that form of magic wasn't one Valhalla possessed. Her seidr affinity was strongest with the element of fire.

Hopefully, her years of study and training with the valkyries would pay off.

Valhalla clenched her fingers into tight fists.

She closed her eyes and concentrated on summoning forth her Fjölkyngi Völva, or as the humans of Midgard called it, Völva Sage level seidr. Glowing red runes of fire and Celnor knots slowly appeared on her skin, glowing brighter and brighter. Her connection with the element smoldered at first and quickly rose to blistering heights.

A roar pierced through the quietness of the moment, startling Valhalla out of her concentration, causing the glowing red runes to fade from her skin.

Bron's eyes quickly opened, and he turned to look behind him. Just as he did, Barna hopped off a tall tree and landed on the Elder's back. The dragonling latched onto a long, dark crystal embedded in Bron's back between his shoulder blades, trying with all his might to pull it out.

Bron roared fiercely as Barna attempted to pull the crystal free. The Elder twirled and whirled in a frenzy, trying to throw Barna off, but the young dragonling latched onto the crystal, determined not to let go of his father.

Bron raised his front legs high into the air with a deafening roar, the sound so intense that Valhalla had to cover her ears to stop the pain ringing in her head. The Elder slammed his claws down and rushed toward her with such speed that her heart leapt into her throat.

She jumped to her right, just barely dodging Bron's massive, rectangular-shaped head. Valhalla somersaulted away and watched his body turn as his back bashed against a thick tree. The trunk just barely tilted from the impact, its roots hanging on for dear life beneath the ground.

Bron then rushed to another tree and bashed against it as well. He tried to remove Barna by sheer force.

Valhalla! What-What dost thou suggest now!? Barna exclaimed.

"Pull the crystal out fast, before it fully takes over your father!" She screamed with a tremble in her eyes.

That is easier for thou to say—Barna let out a heavy growl, his grip loosening from the crystal—*Get him to stop moving will thee!*

Valhalla's fingers twitched, and she raised her hands, right palm open wide and left firmly holding onto her wrist. She returned her concentration to summoning her Fjölkyngi Völva and closed her eyes to focus. The runes on her body burst with a red glow, so bright they illuminated her surroundings.

A swirl of heat formed on the palm of her hand, growing hotter and hotter, causing the strands of her hair to float and softly brush against her cheeks. A sizzling energy flowed from her fingertips to the very center of her hand, releasing an explosion of swirling heat so intense that her hand recoiled slightly under the pressure.

Valhalla, watch out! Barna screamed.

Her eyes snapped open, feeling the energy inside her rise and emanate a bright, fiery light from her eyes; her Fródleikr Völva powers had awakened. As Bron rushed toward her, she pulled her right arm back and thrusted forward, hurling a massive fireball at the Elder.

It hit him square between the eyes, causing him to falter. He tripped on his claws and crashed into the dirt in a spray of rock and earth, followed by a shower of leaves. His weight was so great, his momentum carried him toward her, leaving a line of sundered earth in his wake.

Valhalla retreated, attempting to dodge the great beast, but tripped in her hurried step and fell flat on her backside. Bron's flaring nostrils came to a stop mere inches from her feet.

It Wasn't a Crystal!?

Valhalla released a long sigh of relief. The Elder's eyes were closed. His breath came quick and harsh. She attempted to stand, her knees weak from the fear of having almost been trampled by the massive dragon.

As she walked around Bron's head, she spotted Barna. He had fallen off his father and was shaking his head, dazed from the hard landing. Quickly slithering to Bron's back, Barna grabbed hold of the crystal once more.

The young dragonling tugged at the smooth crystal, his nails scratching against the surface. Barna pulled with everything he had. The black crystal jerked and, with a soft hiss, finally slid out of his father. A waterfall of thick, golden brown blood seeped from the round wound.

Barna tossed the crystal away from his father. Both he and Valhalla rushed to Bron's wound, inspecting the severity. Valhalla, fearing the worst, let out a light gasp. The opening was about the size of a large, well-fed cat. She could see through the dragon's hide and muscle within, his organs bruised and bloodied. Golden brown blood poured in a spurting stream from the hole.

"We need to heal this wound," Valhalla said with trembling lips.

I-I know, but . . . but I dost not know how to use our kin's healing breath yet. Barna replied, his eyes quivering.

Joining Valhalla at his father's head, she watched as he peered at the unconscious Elder. His expression sent a pang of empathy through her chest. Bron's eyes remained closed, and in the back of her mind, she worried it was too late. Tears began to fall from Barna's large, round, reddish brown eyes, and he gently tapped the crystal on his father's forehead.

Valhalla's chest went tight. She was trying to figure out a way to save the Elder dragon. She thought about calling upon two of her valkyrie companions, Cascade or Anita, as they know healing seidr. However, before she could do anything, the ground beneath her feet started to quake again, startling her from her thoughts. The rumble grew stronger, causing her to stumble to the dirt.

Large holes opened up all around them, and many komod dragons sprang from the ground. They landed firmly, staring on in equal parts poise and stoicism.

A komod dragon with a masculine build slithered forward, leading the bank. He was much larger than his companions, almost as massive as Bron. Almost. His name was Bryn, a dragonling of Bron, and from what stories the Elder dragon had shared with her of his children, he was one of the oldest.

He slithered close to Valhalla with an intense glare in his reddish brown eyes. *Step aside, human!*

Valhalla hastily stumbled back from Bryn's snarling fangs, bowing as she stepped aside to show her respect, allowing Bryn a clear look at his father and the wound.

The dragon lowered his head to the flowing opening on Bron's back, inspecting it. Bryn took a deep breath. As he exhaled, a soft, shimmering green mist poured over the wound from his barely pursed lips.

The mist floated into Bron's body, coating the organs and blood in emeralds. Sparks of green firelight flickered within the opening, jumping from one organ to another like little shooting stars. A loud hissing sound emanated from the edge of the wound, glowing brightly green.

The Elder's skin began to move, the hole closing as his skin stretched inward. Bron gave out a fierce growl. His face tightly scrunched, and his claws dug into the dirt.

Valhalla sighed with relief as the wound steadily came to a close, happy

Bryn arrived in time to save his father. Thanks to their connection to the land, they could cast their senses a great distance, and as long as whatever they were seeking was touching the ground, they would find it. Turning away from the komods, she was unnerved by the dark crystal lying several feet from her.

How could something like this crystal pierce a dragon's scale? Nothing could pierce their bodies except the claws and fangs of other dragons. Could seidr alone really be enough to penetrate their iron-like scales?

Valhalla gazed down at her longsword hanging on the left side of her waist. She grasped the crimson hilt with a firm grip and pulled it slightly from the scabbard, the visible portion of the silverish-red blade gleaming in the sunlight.

The dwarves of Nidavellir had forged it. Thanks to their pact with the dragons, all of their gear was forged from components harvested from the great creatures upon their deaths. Claws, fangs, and bones all melted down, shaped, and sharpened to fit a warrior's need in combat, be it a small stiletto or a massive greatsword. Their scales, horns, and hair made for the finest of armor, be it a robe or heavy plate. Valhalla's crimson outfit and lightweight black armor had been forged in this way, giving her greater protection from cuts and scrapes than standard Midgardian armor, but did nothing for bruises.

Her brows lowered. How could the crystal have possibly pierced the Elder's iron-like scales? It didn't make any sense.

How dost thou plan to destroy that wretched thing!? Bryn growled, startling Valhalla from her thoughts.

Brödíga![1] Show some respect to our födra's savior! Barna retorted.

Bryn jerked his head to his younger brother, an unsettling rage in his large, round eyes. His nostrils flared, and his fangs peered through trembling lips. Valhalla watched with concern, but remained quiet. Barna cowered before his massive brother.

Silence! It is due to her reckless actions that our födra was almost killed! Bryn snarled.

The accusation took her aback. She knew she had taken every precaution possible with freeing the Elder, never once even drawing her sword, and although she cast her fire seidr, it hadn't caused him any real harm. She had to act fast when she arrived, finding the massive dragon harming his own kin. If she had done nothing, many of them would've surely died. What else was she supposed to do?

Another komod slithered forward, shielding Barna from Bryn's wrath, and glared at him in return. Her frame was much thinner than Bryn's, as was common for many female-born dragons, but she exuded an air of defiance and

---

1 Brödíga is Dragon for Brother.

confidence not many could claim to possess.

I think that is quite enough, brödíga. If perhaps thou showed some sort of competence in dealing with Födra, then mayhap Valhalla would not have, as thou would claim it, needed to use such reckless measures. Dinali retorted, a friend and dragonling of Bron, another of his eldest hatchlings.

Arsara,[2] thou would side with a human of all things!? Bryn exclaimed, slithering closer to Dinali. He snorted strongly, blowing a few strands of her dark brown hair behind her jagged horns. Her scaly eyelids narrowed.

Thou better watch thyself, neölate.[3] She responded coldly.

Bryn's maw curled back, light glinting off his silverish fangs. A deep rumble started in his chest and built into a growl that vibrated into Valhalla's bones. He was furious at the slight, and understandably so for one of his age. The term roughly translates to youngling in their tongue.

Valhalla shuddered at the tension rising between the two, feeling as though battle could break out at any moment. She looked to the other komods around them, all seemingly just as apprehensive as her. Her eyes moved quickly between the two eldest dragonlings, her feet frozen in place, and she wondered what she could do to diffuse the situation.

She took a step toward them. "Listen! I'm sorry—"

Dost not apologize, Crimson Dragon. Thou took it upon thyself to act as bait to lure our födra away from killing his kin. Thou at least had the sensible idea to do something. Dinali interrupted without breaking eye contact with Bryn.

Bryn's eyes widened in anger. *I did not see thee try to help!* He snapped at his sister.

I can at least admit—

That is enough, the lot of you!

Everyone startled and turned to the Elder komod, Bron, his reddish-brown eyes tired, but open. His breath was heavy. Sliding his front legs underneath his bulk, he tried hard to push himself up to stand. His thick legs wobbled beneath his weight.

Barna flinched and rushed to his father's aid. Although he was much smaller than Bron, the young dragonling did well in helping his father stand, and Valhalla found herself donning a smile as wide as the one spreading on his face. Once fully stood, the Elder thanked his young son with a nod, sweetly nuzzling his nose, and turned to his oldest dragonlings, his expression despondent.

He steadily raised his head high, his strength returning, and approached Bryn. *The ability to admit to thy fears can make thee a stronger Elder.*

---

2   Arsara is Dragon for Sister.

3   Neölate is Dragon for Youngling.

Bryn remained silent and simply turned away from his father, ashamed.

Bron then turned his gaze to his daughter, seeming equally disappointed. *Being able to understand another's fears can make thee a compassionate Elder.*

Dinali's eyes softened at her father's words.

Ye both came from the same nest, hatched together. I will be entrusting my bank to ye both. If ye cannot work together, then how can I entrust ye to care for thy kind?

Both Bryn and Dinali closed their eyes with defeat and apologetically lowered their heads to the Elder. Bron nodded with a stern but loving stare. *I will forgive ye for now, but I must see thee make an effort, together. Dost thou understand?*

Ay, Födra. Both Bryn and Dinali answered in unison.

Bron nodded once more, then slithered over to Valhalla. His amber brown scales had returned to their shimmering radiance. Even his beard and mustache returned to their former lush glory.

She flashed him a warm smile, causing him to do the same in return as he lowered his head to her. *My dear Crimson Dragon, I am glad to see thee unscathed from my chase.*

Taken aback, Valhalla inspected him with curiosity. "Wait, Elder, do you truly remember all you did?"

Bron glanced away momentarily, his chin lightly touching the ground. His eyes began to tremble, likely recalling the uncomfortable memories of his actions at the dragon's den.

For . . . the most part. Voices came to me, clouding my mind, filling me with-with . . . He closed his eyes. Taking a deep breath, he lowered his body to the ground to rest.

She stepped toward him, placing her hands on his snout, and was surprised by the softness of his large scales. The shine of the sun's light had returned to them.

Valhalla gazed up and watched as his eyes opened again. He stared at her for a long moment, a mixture of curiosity and concern clear in his face. *I must know, Valhalla, what dost thou plan for that vile thing?*

She swallowed, unsure. Glancing over her shoulder at the black crystal, she eyed it uneasily.

"As much as I would like to send it to Asgard for study," Valhalla released a sigh of defeat as she spun toward the crystal and approached it cautiously, "they have no place to store such an item, to safeguard it from those who would use it for ill intent. I know of a means to teleport it, but I haven't yet perfected the spell and still need direct contact. With that said, I do not dare touch it myself for fear of corruption. So, that leaves me only one course of action."

She stopped mere feet from the crystal, feeling something radiating from it. The strange feeling sent a cold shiver up her spine. She then heard a low humming, like a swarm of bees emanating from a deep cave, echoing and flowing in waves.

Valhalla's hands clenched at her sides, and her eyes slowly widened. She felt an odd sensation as if something were trying to worm its way into her mind. Strange whispers. So many of them, low enough that she couldn't discern what it was they were saying, but knew they were calling to her.

Crimson Dragon? Dinali called out, her tone filled with concern.

Valhalla flinched from the dragoness' voice and turned to her with a faint smile to calm her trouble. She gave Dinali a nod to show she was fine and focused on the dark crystal.

She raised both hands level with her chest, held wide in the air in front of her, and closed her eyes. Concentrating, she pictured an object left in her bedchamber back in Asgard.

Valhalla brought her hands closer together, the tips of her thumbs closing until they touched. A swirl of heat burst to life, causing her hair and cape to flow about her in gentle waves. Her eyes flashed open as a burst of fire erupted in mid-air and spread horizontally to her left and right in a long line.

As the fire dissipated outwards, it sent bursts of heat in all directions. Her ebony hair strands brushed against her cheeks. She closed her hands around the crimson and black hilt, this sword much longer than the one hanging about her waist, still nestled in its scabbard. Valhalla twirled the weapon about, reacclimating to its heft after having not needed it for some time, preferring instead to use her longsword due to its lighter weight, giving her more mobility in combat.

She stabbed the tip of her silverish red blade into the dirt. In the very center of the weapon's guard was a seidr glyph of fire. The symbol and sword once belonged to another, but were now her's to bear. Valhalla inspected the two-handed greatsword for a moment. It was an extravagant broadsword, yet much too heavy to wield for long periods, even with it being dragon forged.

She took a deep breath and exhaled steadily. "I have to destroy this thing."

Hearing no objections from the dragons, she gripped the hilt tightly with both hands and heaved it out of the ground, raising the blade high in the air. After a brief pause, Valhalla swung her sword downward with every ounce of strength she could muster.

Just as her longsword's blade came from dragon claws and fangs, so too was the blade of her greatsword. It was able to cut clean through even the strongest of materials, and this crystal was no exception. Her blade bellowed with a thunderous boom as it struck the black crystal, shattering it straight down the middle.

The corner of her lips twitched with a smirk, but quickly faded as something began to seep out of the crystal. A burst of dark clouds exploded from the opening, blasting past her and ascending high into the sky at an alarming speed, shrouding the area in a haze.

It dawned on her that the crystal was no mere crystal, but a container for dark seidr. Valhalla's heart dropped into her stomach.

Darkness spewed out. A thick, sludge-like mist poured out and spilled to the ground, spreading fast, and enveloped Valhalla's feet. It climbed up her legs and nearly made its way to her knees before she could react. Her muscles were tense with fear. She struggled to step back, trying to put some distance between herself and the crystal. Something squeezed tightly around her ankles.

She let out a horrified shriek as she spotted something resembling tentacles grabbing hold of her feet and wrapping around her shins. Valhalla shuffled as she tried to escape their hold and fell back onto the ground. Staring into darkness, it continued to spread and thicken, darkening the world around her, as though it would consume her whole.

Screaming, fire, then cold, silent darkness. All she could see was black. Her elbows hit something hard, and pain shot up her arm. She yearned to stretch out her stiff joints, but the space was so tight she could barely even move. All she could do was sit there, alone with her only companion, the hunger tearing at her stomach.

A strong gale slapped her face, pulling her back to the present. Her eyes were wide, and a lump formed in her throat, body trembling. She spun away as fast as she could, shielding her face with an arm.

Winds like a raging hurricane picked up around her. A wailing howl pierced her eardrums. The leaves swayed violently in the wind. Trees ripped from the ground and fell, causing the ground to shudder with each crashing trunk.

With her every sense pushed to its breaking point, her mind flashed back to the last moment she had seen her parents. An eerie sense of familiarity fell over her, bringing more than a small amount of discomfort, and just as it had happened back then, a lingering silence overtook the area.

The heat of the sun warmed her porcelain white skin. Valhalla slowly raised her head to the sky, vision obscured by the bright light. She rubbed her eyes, then opened them again, finding herself surrounded by shimmering brown scales.

Valhalla followed the scales to her left and was surprised to find Bryn's snout mere inches from her face. He had somehow pulled her from the darkness and shuttled her to safety. Her eyes were wide, unsure of what to say.

A soft smirk rested on his face. He exhaled a quick puff of air from his nostrils, jostling her from her shock. She slowly sat herself up, her gaze locked on him. "Thank you," She said, her voice soft and lips quivering.

Bryn nodded and unwrapped his body from around her. He gently shook his body to and fro, the motion similar to that of a dog ridding its fur of water, and slithered over to his father, Bron, whom Dinali had shielded.

Valhalla rested on the ground for a moment, gathering her thoughts. She felt the smooth leather wrap of her greatsword's hilt in her left hand. Valhalla glanced at the weapon, her eyes drifting across its surface as trepidation filled her thoughts.

Her hand shook, wondering how such a thing as the crystal came to be, and for what purpose. Was it simply to manipulate Bron into violence against his kin, or was there more to it? Valhalla's eyes narrowed as anger rose within her, sure of her suspicions. It was her, it had to be.

Her lips quaked as terror washed over her. If Valhalla were ever to face this former valkyrie again, she honestly doubted she could defeat her, let alone survive the encounter.

She shook the thought away and dismissed her greatsword in a whirl of fire, returning it to her bedchamber in Asgard. With one hand on her knee and the other on the ground, she pushed herself up with a labored breath. Her body felt oddly heavy. Her nerves were on edge.

Valhalla shook away the pins and needles in her hands and gazed up, intent on sending what was left of the shattered crystal to Asgard, but found no trace of it, not even a single shard.

"Wait . . . How? It was just here!" Valhalla's heart raced within her chest, and she filled with dread.

Valhalla? Bron's concerned tone echoed in her mind.

She jolted, forgetting for a moment that she wasn't alone, and turned to the komods. They were preparing to depart, to return home through a newly formed massive hole in the ground.

Will thou be all right? He asked with a small but worried frown.

She took a breath and forced a smile. "Yes, thank you for asking, Elder." Valhalla raised a hand to her chest and curtsied low to him and his kin. She then lifted her head back to Bron. "Don't worry about me, return to your den and get some rest. You deserve it."

Bron bowed his head low. With that, they dove one by one into the hole, disappearing into the earth. The last dragon to enter was Bron's eldest daughter, Dinali. *Please, stay safe, Crimson Dragon.*

"You as well, Dinali." The two bowed their heads in farewell, and Dinali dove into the opening, sealing it behind her.

After a few moments, Valhalla found herself alone and fell to her knees. She wrapped her arms around herself, trying to quell her rising fears as cold sweat slid down the side of her face.

The darkness, she despised it. From moonless nights to candleless rooms, she hated it in all of its forms, ever since that day, thirteen years ago, trapped under the floor in the temple's storage compartment.

She raised a hand to her lips, feeling them tremble. Valhalla slowly grew angry, with herself most of all. Rolling her bottom lip into her mouth and in between her teeth, she bit down, nearly breaking the skin.

"Dammit, I truly am terrified to face her and her seidr. Gods! This feeling is fucking terrible." She scolded herself.

Valhalla buried her face in the palm of her hands and chuckled uneasily, hoping to ease her troubled mind. It helped a little, even if only slightly.

Words from a memory long forgotten suddenly stirred in her mind: *Let the pain remind you that you are mortal, that it will be waiting for you if you aren't careful. We mortals are capable of extraordinary and, oftentimes, incredible things, but pain is our counsel. Listen to it when it voices itself to you.*

Valhalla flinched at the memory of her mother's words, still clear after thirteen years. A small, warm smile grew on her face as she recalled her mother's following question after her child self tripped and fell on her face: *So, what is it telling you?*

She released a steady sigh and answered. "Don't face the valkyrie. Not alone, at least."

Valhalla chuckled softly again, feeling uplifted, and raised a hand to her lips. Curling them over her teeth and inserting her index finger and thumb into her mouth, she whistled so loudly it echoed for miles.

After a brief moment, the ground before her began to glow with a bright orange light. The dirt and grass slowly charred. The orange glow spread like fire to kindling, bubbling and swirling as it expanded. Fire erupted, and out sprang forth a beautiful, black Clydesdale. His mane, tail, and hooves were alight with flame. Bright crimson eyes looked upon her with worry.

He trotted over to her, still kneeling on the ground, and tapped his nose against her forehead. Hot air blew from his nostrils. She gently cupped his chin, burying her face in his.

Valhalla, are you all right? Please, don't scare me like that again. I can't bear to lose another rider, especially one as wonderful as you. The clydesdale said into her mind.

Like dragons, the valkyries' clydesdales were able to speak telepathically, though the horses needed no gems in the center of their foreheads. As to how that worked, Valhalla didn't fully comprehend it, knowing only that it was a form of summoning only possible to the Asgardian völvxs.

She smiled happily at her friend, flattered. "Edan, I'm fine, I promise. I didn't expect this trip to turn out as it did. Then again, I don't think Keeya did either."

Honestly, if they had, they and the other valkyries would've been with us. Edan snorted out a hot gust of air, blowing Valhalla's ebony hair strands from her face. *Are you well enough to ride, or do you need to call Lord Heimdall?*

"No, please, I would like to ride for a bit. I want to clear my head before we return to Asgard to discuss this business about Bron."

Edan nodded in understanding as Valhalla pushed herself off the ground and stood. He turned to his side, allowing her to climb into the scarlet saddle on his back.

You are forever alone.

Valhalla paused, hearing the eerie whisper enter her mind. The voice was hoarse and foreboding, sending a light shiver down her spine. She turned and glanced around, but found only the vast green forest about them, not a soul in sight.

"That's . . . odd."

What is? Edan's question entered her mind.

"Hmm? It's nothing. I thought I heard something."

Valhalla placed her hands on the saddle and climbed up Edan's side, seating herself carefully atop him. She grabbed the leather reins around his face and suddenly froze.

Another old memory flashed through her mind, of when she was young, clinging to her mother and filled with fear. Her heart quickened, her body tensed, and her jaw clenched. Chest tightening, she suddenly found it hard to breathe. Valhalla's body trembled as her heart was now pounding against her chest.

Her eyes widened as the memory grew clearer. Fires roared through streets, burning bodies and homes. Blood drenched the dirt roads. Terrified screams, too many to count, echoed in all directions.

She desperately cursed at herself, taking a deep breath, she shook her head to rid herself of those terrible nightmares.

Valhalla pulled on the reins and turned Edan to the right. "Ride, Edan, please! Just ride. I need to feel the wind on my face."

Then you shall have it. Edan replied, picturing him with a confident smirk.

He kicked up, neighing proudly, and dashed forward in a gallop, carrying her swiftly through the forest. The wind blew her hair from her face and dried the tears as they fell from her eyes.

Valhalla

Escorting a Mysterious Noble

The sun hung heavy in the sky, its rays shining upon Valhalla. The heat bathed her skin with its warm caress, replenishing her depleted seidr stores used during the fight with the Elder komod, Bron. She closed her eyes, taking slow and steady breaths. Her mind hung heavy from the encounter with the black crystal.

Feeling better, Valla? Edan asked as he walked down the unkempt forest path.

Opening her eyes, her gaze fixed on her hands resting on the leather reins. "A little, but . . ." Valhalla's grip tightened as old memories attempted to resurface, the painful past she would rather not revisit.

Visions of monsters, blood, and death haunted her throughout childhood, often emerging in moments of silence, when alone in the darkness of night. Her home was gone, her parents dead. Everything she knew and loved was taken from her. She had waited for death to find her in that small storage space. Never in her wildest dreams did she expect to be saved, least of all by her patron saint Aura and the valkyries, but the moment that door opened and Aura appeared, Valhalla knew she could trust them. They brought her to safety, to a place shimmering in gold, with a bright yellow sky, and seidr the likes of which she thought only existed in legend and folktales.

Want to talk about it? Edan asked, trying to mask the worry in his voice.

Valhalla shook her head and sighed heavily. "No, at least, not here. I'd prefer we find a safer place than this vast open forest. I'm feeling odd, unsettled in this place."

You think it's safer to talk in Asgard? Edan chuckled.

Valhalla's lips stretched into a small smile. Asgard had been her home for a very long time, but to say it was a safe place for her would be misleading, regardless of her status given by the Asgardian royal family and her close ties to the valkyries.

There were those amongst the Æsir who glare down on the so-called lesser races of Midgard, humans especially. She had never shed the need to constantly look over her shoulder, feeling angered stares and distrustful eyes looming from the shadows.

Her smile faltered for a moment before responding. "No way. I *much* prefer A—"

She was interrupted by the rustling of bushes to her right. Startled, her hand darted to the sword hilt hanging from her waist. Just as she was about to draw her blade, out fell a well-dressed man in crimson and black. He hit the ground hard, causing Edan to jolt and hop a couple of steps away.

Valhalla stared at the man, baffled as to what purpose might've brought him so far into this forest, the nearest human settlement being roughly a ten-day journey by horse.

His clothing and leathers were in pristine condition, barely a scratch nor spot of dirt on him. The cloth shined in the light, likely silk. She assumed him to be a nobleman.

He squirmed on the ground for a moment. His jostled ebony hair, which glimmered in a dark emerald sheen, and hands obscured his face as he let out a groan of pain.

She slowly climbed down Edan, cautious of the man. "Who are you?"

Unanswering, he placed a hand on the dirt. The other remained on his face, still shielded by his long hair. He pushed himself up off the ground, attempting to stand. As the man moved his right leg forward, he fell to his side with a loud grunt and reached for his ankle.

Valhalla sprang forward, knelt down behind him, and gently rubbed his back with a hand for comfort. "What is it? Where's the pain?"

"M-My right ankle! Ngh, I think I twisted it."

She helped him turn onto his back to better inspect his ankle and, if lucky, get a good look at his face. His tawny skin was pale, not sickly, as though he hadn't been out of the sun's light for some time. She thought him to possibly be about her age, if not a bit older. The man's youthful face was contorted in pain, making it difficult to be certain. She was unable to see his eyes and a majority of his face due to his ebony hair, which covered just over half of it. What she was able to make out was a single thin scar that stretched across his lips. Valhalla assumed the man received the injury from sword training or the like.

Something about him was familiar to her, but she couldn't place a finger on what. Valhalla was taken aback for a moment, turning her attention to his right ankle covered by heavily laced, black leather boots.

"Oh my, you're a beautiful one."

Valhalla paused, unsure how to react to the compliment. Her hands flinched away from his ankle and hung still in the air. She glanced back at the nobleman's face, seeing a curious grin resting on his face. Her cheeks heated up, unsure if she should be flattered as unease set in. She never felt right when receiving compliments. She wouldn't, couldn't trust them. At all. To her, they were lies. A ploy to get something out of her. Ever since *him*, Valhalla hadn't had the chance to get over it.

The young man chuckled, bringing Valhalla out of her thoughts. "I didn't mean to distract you."

"It . . . It's nothing." Her gaze snapped back to his ankle. Valhalla's cheeks continued to warm, but not out of embarrassment,

His gaze, a look she had seen too many times before, was one typically worn by lecherous men. She hated that look ever since *then*. The thought sent a strong shiver down her spine.

Valhalla pushed the past out of mind and focused on the task at hand, checking the condition of his right ankle. The man gently grasped one of her hands and rubbed his thumb across her skin. "Such a beauty. Your hand, it's soft, yet it belies your strength."

He caressed the fair white skin of her exposed fingers, avoiding the crimson fabric of her gloves. She raised her shoulders, caring little for his rough touch. Valhalla firmly raised her gaze to meet his. She hated the look in his eyes, causing her skin to crawl. Valhalla quickly slid her hand out of his grip, glaring at him with distrust.

The nobleman snickered loudly. "I'm sorry, I have poor impulse control.

My name's Tarik Grunr, son of the Grand Duke of Castle Ormr."

Valhalla stared at him, dumbfounded, having never heard of such a title as Grand Duke or any castle having the name Ormr, for that matter. She thought over the titles she had learned and knew to still be in use in Veerence, the highest ranks of nobility aside from Kings and Queens, were that of Duke and Duchess. Valhalla supposed a Grand Duke could be higher than a Duke. Because of that, it would be a good idea to watch what she said; however, if he ever touched her again without her permission, she vowed he would be walking away with more than just a sprained ankle.

Tarik chuckled softly. "I guess you aren't from Kveldúlfr, are you?" He smirked curiously.

"Kveld—Oh, no. I'm from the northern realm of Veerence. My home lies beyond this vast forest."

"Ah, you know I've always wanted to travel north, and now I think I will, knowing there are such lovely gems as you to be found." Tarik leaned closer to Valhalla, cocking his head to the side as though trying to see her face.

She kept her eyes on him while inspecting his ankle. Skeptical as she was of his intentions, she would be ready if he tried anything. Valhalla wasn't going to fall victim to a scoundrel should he turn out to be one, but if this wasn't a ploy and he really needed help, she wasn't going to leave him out here alone to fend for himself. Lips thinned, it turned into a sour frown. "Um, right. Where's your family's castle?"

"It isn't far. If we continue down this path, you'll spot it shortly." He leaned back, propping himself up with arms planted on the ground behind him, and tilted his head, resting on his left shoulder. The strange smile remained on his face while watching her tend to the wound.

Was he trying to be charming? Tarik seemed friendly enough, if not a little too friendly. He might have been just a bit awkward and overcompensating, but it was equally possible that his intentions were less than honest. She just couldn't shake the uncomfortable feeling. Maybe it was just in her head. Even still, Valhalla's stomach churned with unease.

"I don't see any external signs of a major injury, no gashes or blood soaked into the leather, which is good." Valhalla removed her hands. "I hesitate to loosen the straps and remove the boot for further inspection, though, just in case there's an issue with the joint, that pressure could be all that's holding things together. We should get you back home so that someone more experienced, who has the proper tools, can see to it. So, I suppose we should get you up on my horse." Valhalla slung one of Tarik's arms around her shoulders and carefully helped him stand, surprised she hadn't noticed the scent of calluna and lingonberry about him until now.

She turned him around to face Edan, and as he spotted the fiery steed, his eyes widened. "Amazing! Your horse is on fire. How did I not notice that until now?" Tarik's excitement beamed from eye to eye.

Valhalla chuckled, looking at her companion. Edan rolled his crimson eyes in annoyance and shook his head, releasing a heavy snort. He was well past tired of people's same old reaction, especially from the humans of Midgard, though he had come to expect it at this point.

"He's a horse made from seidr, old magic. Edan was a gift from the almighty Ódin," She said with a playful smile.

As Valhalla glanced at Tarik, it quickly faded. His face was momentarily cold. "I can imagine . . ." He then cleared his throat and turned to her with an eerie smirk. "Makes sense, I've never seen seidr like this done by humans."

Valhalla grew more nervous as her pink garnet eyes darted back and forth from Tarik and Edan. "R-Right, why don't I help you up then?" She helped him over to Edan, supporting his side with the limp.

Reaching Edan, Valhalla released Tarik and knelt on the ground, locking her fingers together, and glanced at her steed for a moment. "Edan, do you mind bending a knee, please?"

He nickered and bent one of his front legs as though bowing. She looked up at Tari and nodded. With a thankful smile, he placed his left foot in her hands. Valhalla, taking a deep breath, hoisted him up as he swung his right leg over Edan, situating himself in the saddle, and made room for her to join him.

She placed a foot in the stirrup and pulled herself up, careful not to kick Tarik. As Valhalla placed herself on the saddle, she grabbed her crimson cape and wrapped it around an arm so it wouldn't flutter into the Lord as they traveled.

With the fabric secured, she took the leather reins and readied to leave for the castle. She then felt Tarik's hands slide around her waist and fought back the urge to vomit.

The sickly feeling fell over her fast, her stomach churning with discomfort. Valhalla quickly glanced down at her tightening hands, her brows furrowed over her eyes. She needed to calm down. Although the touch was a bit too forward, Tarik needed to hold on somehow.

"Is everything all right?"

"What? Yes. Sorry, everything's fine." With a deep breath, Valhalla leaned forward, ignoring Tarik's tightening grasp on her waist, and tried to push down her unsettled nerves.

"Listen, I'm sorry for how I've behaved. Honestly, I have trouble controlling myself around beautiful women, especially one such as yourself." He flashed her a sly grin.

Glancing back at him, she blushed in frustration and spun away. Speechless, she focused on breathing. Valhalla released a troubled sigh and answered softly, "Don't worry about it." She then leaned forward and patted Edan gently on his neck. "Let's go, Edan, and please be gentle."

Her companion nodded and started forward, down the unkempt path of the forest, their destination, Castle Ormr.

Valhalla

A God's Deception

Valhalla and Tarik journeyed along the road atop Edan, traveling at a relaxed but steady pace to avoid upsetting the man's injury any further. A strange unease lingered in the back of Valhalla's thoughts. It was as if the entire area felt wrong somehow.

Her stomach churned, trepidation growing with every step. It was as if all the trees, bushes, and even the air itself were watching her. Valhalla's hands fidgeted with Edan's reins.

What was going on with her? Was there something wrong with this place that she just couldn't see? Was she walking into a trap? No, she forced the thought away. She wanted to give him a chance, the same chance anyone deserved. Valhalla didn't wish for the past wrongs she'd suffered to govern her actions. She would give him the benefit of the doubt, and if he let her down, well, it wasn't like she was helpless, not anymore.

"Is everything all right?" Tarik asked.

Valhalla startled lightly at the sound of his voice. "What? Sorry, everything's fine. How much further is it now? To your castle, I mean."

"We're almost there. See the top of the tower just above the treetops?"

Valhalla turned her gaze ahead and looked upward. Just above the treeline was the top of a stone, cone-shaped tower. Atop it, a green flag flailed wildly in the breeze, so much so that she was unable to make out the castle's insignia.

Her jaw clenched as a trickle of sweat slid down the side of her face. "Tell me, how long have you lived in this forest?" She asked, a hint of anxiety in her tone.

"Oh, about three years, give or take." Tarik answered with a flourish of his wrist.

The hairs on the nape of Valhalla's neck bristled as his hands slowly ventured up her sides. It made her skin crawl. She quickly turned to Tarik with wide, glaring eyes. "What in Yggdrasil's shade are you doing!?"

He grabbed her shoulders and pressed his lips intimately against her ear. "Why don't we have some fun before getting to the castle. I'm dying to see every bit of your body, especially your—"

Valhalla raised an arm high and swung her elbow back with as much force as she could muster, slamming into Tarik's gut. An intense flame burned in the depths of her pink garnet eyes. "Now listen here, you! I'm not some traveling whore, here to help you feel like a man for what I can only imagine would be a few pathetic moments before reality returns and you have to face the truth of the sad little man you are. I'm a passerby who, beyond all good sense, ignored your unwanted advances and chose to show you kindness, to take you home instead of leaving you where you lay because it was the right thing to do. You'll keep your hands to yourself for the remainder of our time together unless you want to lose them," She said in a contemptuous tone.

Valhalla returned her attention to the path, her brows furrowed over her eyes, and her grip tightened on the reins. "Edan, please continue. The faster we get there, the faster we'll be rid of *Lord* Tarik."

As you wish, my friend. Edan replied in agreement and hastened to a gallop.

Soon they reached Castle Ormr, passing through a tall, open set of iron gates. Valhalla was surprised to find just how clean the state of the castle was, even more so by the lack of guards.

Colorful flowers wove through lush, leafy green garlands wrapped around stone railings on either side of a small bridge leading to the castle. The ungroomed greenery of the forest hadn't touched this place.

As they passed a large, though simple, circular fountain centered in the small courtyard, a servant maiden wearing a form-fitted black dress and white apron waited before the steps of the castle. The woman greeted them silently with a curtsy.

Valhalla signaled for Edan to stop and climbed down. She allowed her cape to fall from her arm and drape down her back, then walked to the servant maiden. "If the Grunr family has a healer, could you fetch them for Lord Tarik? He has . . . a sprained ankle . . ." Valhalla paused as she spoke, staring at the servant maiden with suspicion.

The woman's hair was so dark, it was as if looking into the night sky. A faint hint of azure glistened in the sun's light. She was tall with porcelain-white skin and felt strangely familiar. The woman raised her head to Valhalla, eyes closed. As the lengthy strands of hair slid away from her long face, Valhalla's heart skipped a beat.

Eyes widening as the realization set in, Valhalla's blood ran cold. It was Kiara.

Kiara's deep sapphire monolid eyes flashed open, and her lips stretched into a condescending smirk. She stood upright, placing one hand on her small, squared hips and cocked her head to the side, inspecting Valhalla with a snide expression of judgment.

"You've grown so much since the last time I saw you. Three years, was it? My dear Lady Red, you've become so strong, so sure of yourself, but you—still—fear—us, don't you?"

Valhalla jolted and quickly turned to find Tarik standing, no longer favoring one leg. A terrifying, hungry grin stretched across his face. His hand rested on Edan's back. A burst of darkness then exploded from beneath the man's feet and quickly formed into writhing, cloudy tendrils as long as he was tall.

Edan roared out a neigh of terror and leapt away to the edge of the courtyard. Valhalla rushed over and embraced him momentarily. Her body trembled. With a deep breath, she turned to face them with eyes wide, heart racing, and panic was reaching a boiling point.

"What's wrong, Ódin's dear Valhalla? You look like you've seen a draugr." Kiara sneered. She then made her way over to join Tarik, and as she stopped at his side, the cloud of darkness covered them both. The energy swirled faster and tighter, growing so thick Valhalla could no longer see them through the vortex.

After a moment, the black clouds fell to the ground and churned around their feet, spreading across the ground toward Valhalla. Her knees went weak and nearly buckled under her weight. Fear threatened to freeze her in place. The dark seidr hung low and hovered in a thick mist. Kiara, the Valkyrie of Shadows, stood tall and imposing.

She wore shining, raven-decorated black armor. Spikes jutted here and there about the plate, as though a bramble of a thousand thorns were her protection. Even her flowing garment underneath was black. She was as darkness incarnate. Her ebony hair twirled long over her left shoulder, hanging to her waist. Kiara's sapphire monolid eyes glared at Valhalla beneath her pointed raven visor hanging over her forehead.

Valhalla glanced to Kiara's right, to where Tarik had been. He was gone, and in his place now stood Prince Loki Ódinson, the God of Mischief and Chaos, with a look of contempt on his face. This man, no, Æsir, was the one who massacred her home city of Seeras when she was just five falls young.

Valhalla's emotions soared back and forth between terror and anger. She should feel hatred toward the god who took everything from her, her parents, her friends, and her home, but Valhalla was equally afraid. Loki was a god and was said to wield some of the most powerful seidr in all of Asgard. If he could single-handedly wipe out a city, what chance did she stand against such power?

Crimson-threaded depictions of encircled serpents and wolves shimmered against Loki's otherwise midnight black garments. A few short strands of his ebony, tied-back hair hung loose over his right eye. The single thin scar on his lips, as Tarik, was now three, accompanied by a few other faint marks between them. A gold bangle gripped his left bicep. On it was a repeated symbol, two snakes forming an S shape, one pointed north and the other south, each grasping the other's tail within its mouth.

Kiara began sauntering toward Valhalla. Every fiber of Valhalla's body told her to flee. She instinctively stepped back in a panicked retreat, but bumped into Edan, who seemed to be just as frightened as her. There was nowhere to go. What was she to do? There was no way she could face them on her own.

"Oh look, my Prince, she's petrified. My dear Loki, I think it's about time I end this wretched young parasite's life and finish what you started all those years ago." Kiara stretched out an arm, her palm open wide. A black cloud formed atop her hand in a swirl. The darkness stretched horizontally to either side of her hand in a line, the clouds pouring down like a misty waterfall, and revealed a shining, black two-handed greatsword she named Fridrgaeta.

Unlike Kiara's armor, the sword was quite elegant in design. Most of the weapon was as black as ink, but the handle stood out, a mixture of azure and violet. The ebony pommel was an ornate raven, its wings wrapped around the very end of the handle. The guard was also forged into the shape of a black raven, fierce as though it could come to life and attack at any moment. Its beak held tightly onto the blade, and its wings stretched far to either side. To describe the blade as being solid black would be insufficient. Even the light itself avoided its touch, a void that stretched two arm lengths from end to end.

"Not yet." Loki answered, his voice calm and stopping Kiara, causing the valkyrie to look at him with curiosity. "I first want her to suffer. I want her screams to be loud enough for that treacherous whore to hear all the way in Asgard."

He raised an arm to Valhalla, his hand opened wide. A black seidr sphere of energy formed and began to spin.

Valhalla was suddenly off balance. She looked down and found both she and Edan were now encircled by darkness. The void swallowed her feet and Edan's hooves completely. She'd already sunk to her ankles. Dark claw-like hands sprang from the blackness and grabbed hold of their legs, pulling them down, down, down.

Valhalla's breath quickened as she fought to escape their hold, dragged deeper and deeper into the black pool. She tried to pull her legs free, but the clawed hands' grip tightened in response.

Her heart raced wildly, feeling as if it were ready to burst. Beads of sweat formed on her brow, and her body shook uncontrollably with terror. She was about to be faced with darkness once again, about to be embraced by its choking hold.

She attempted to summon her fire seidr, but as the energies sparked and started to swell within her, the clawed hands grabbed hold of her arms and pulled them back toward the darkness. Now submerged to her waist, the lower half of her body went cold.

"NO!" Valhalla cried out.

She looked up at the blue sky above, about to call to Heimdall for help. However, as she opened her mouth and took a deep breath, the clawed hands reached up from behind and their sharp fingers wrapped tightly around her throat. They squeezed so hard she could barely get out a whimper. Vahalla gasped for air. Her sight soon faded, and the encroaching darkness slid over her vision.

The sky vanished in dark, stormy clouds. A torrent of wind danced all around. The once pristine castle crumbled and faded, falling into ruins.

As her chest disappeared beneath the darkness, her eyes fluttered closed. Valhalla was losing consciousness, and her breath was dangerously shallow. Her thoughts were fragmented, unable to focus, and she just barely noticed Loki's approach. He stood looming over her, atop the darkness as though the substance were as solid as stone.

Loki knelt before her, gently taking her chin, and lifted her tired gaze to meet his. He brought his face in close, the tips of their noses mere inches apart.

In her faded vision, she noticed something unusual about his eyes. The All Mother, Frigg, when willing to speak of her son Loki, always described his eyes as being a beautiful shade of blue-green, bright and more vibrant than any gemstone found in Nidavellir. His irises in that moment, however, were as black as ink, just as Bron's had been.

Valhalla's eyes flickered with life. Was he trying to tell her something?

"Lo—" Her voice cut short as her chin slid out of his fingers, a short breath escaping as the darkness brushed around her jaw and bottom lip.

She then heard screams, loud and piercing, fading in and out of earshot. Valhalla forced her eyes open and gasped for air. Her vision cleared through sheer force of will. Valhalla wanted to break free. She had to.

Looking up into the sky one last time and desperately trying to scream out Heimdall's name, she could barely let out a single audible syllable. Tears stung her eyes from the pain of the claws clenched about her throat, her fear of the darkness nearly dooming her to inaction. Valhalla didn't know what to do.

Her vision faltered. Spots of black and white danced in and out of sight. Valhalla's eyelids fluttered. Something appeared in the graying clouds far above. It seemed to be a white star. It blinked into existence, dispersing the clouds around it, surrounded by a circle of blue. The star grew brighter and brighter, as though it was hurtling toward her.

Valhalla attempted to raise an arm, hoping to grab hold of it, to bring it with her into the darkness. She struggled against the clawed hands, feeling her elbow begin to slip free. An explosion of white surrounded her, and though she fought with every ounce of strength and willpower she could muster, the strain was too much. Fatigue took its toll, and she lost consciousness.

5

Valhalla

A Friend's Aid

Valhalla's eyes flashed open, her sight a blur. She gasped, coughing and grasping her pained throat. Her breath came in rushed and shallow. The fast thumping of her heartbeat against her chest caused more than a bit of discomfort. Her thoughts felt cloudy and confused. What was that light? And how was she out of the darkness all of a sudden?

The hard stone was cold against her skin. Small blades of grass poked at her palm and between her fingers, a welcome sensation compared to the darkness that had threatened to surround her.

Valhalla attempted a deep breath, followed by a heavy string of choked coughs. She glanced back to check on Edan and found him in the same state as her. He stared at her with a glint of relief in his crimson eyes, then blinked and nodded his head lightly. Reassured, Valhalla was glad to see he was all right, bringing a small smile to her face.

It was then that she realized she and Edan were surrounded. She startled as the figures before her cleared, the murk leaving her vision. Her friends came; they actually came to her aid.

Seven of the nine Valkyries of Asgard stood around them. The woman leading the group, Aura Vitaliadottir, the Valkyrie of Light, and Valhalla's dearest friend, sent her heart soaring.

Aura was garbed in her white and golden armor. Her symbol, the eight-pointed star, gleamed on her shield, gauntlets, chest, and visor. The white fabric of her gown rippled beneath her armor like moonlight reflected on water, appearing as though it were composed of light itself. The sight had brought warmth to Valhalla ever since the woman found her under the floorboards thirteen years ago.

A sigh of relief escaped Valhalla's lips. She then noticed Aura hadn't turned to greet her, instead facing away and standing at the ready, her round buckle shield on her left arm and her one-handed, knightly styled shortsword, Stiarna, held firmly in her right hand.

Although Valhalla felt great power flowing through this place, especially with the additions of the valkyries, each one of them held their weapons in hand. Their powers put a great weight on her, making it hard to think, let alone breathe. Her heart pounded hard in her chest. She wasn't sure if Aura planned to fight, but she knew deep down that nothing good would come of it if the valkyries did.

Valhalla gazed past Aura and spotted Kiara and Loki a short distance away. She wanted to reach out to her friend to warn Aura from doing anything reckless, but her entire body trembled from exhaustion. She could barely move, let alone raise a hand.

"Prince Loki Ódinson. Lady Kiara Vitaliadottir. For your crimes against the nine realms, you are both hereby sentenced to death by order of Ódin Borrson, Hávi, All Father of the nine realms and King of the golden city of Asgard." Aura spoke in a reserved tone through gritted teeth, clearly trying to control her anger.

Loki's expression was stern and sullen. The winds blew wildly, tree limbs creaking and leaves rustling. "I see, my so-called father has run short of patience for me. So be it." Long, writhing tendrils burst from beneath his feet and swirled about, surrounding him and Kiara.

The valkyrie beside Aura stepped forward to answer. Intricate warbraids held her flaxen hair tightly back, and her armor of gold and white was decorated with lightning bolts. The Valkyrie of Lightning, Thora Andradadottir. "Of course your father no longer bears patience for you! You've rampaged across the nine realms for almost thirteen years; enough is enough. Now, come quietly or we will use force, your *Highness!*" Her words dripped with contempt. She twirled her long silver warhammer, Ljudmil, then let it land to rest on her shoulder with a thunderclap.

Loki's expression grew grim, and his dark eyes burned with rage. His tendrils swirling about hastened and swayed erratically.

The rest of the valkyries stood around Valhalla prepared for conflict, readying their various weapons in anticipation of the fight to come. Valhalla's muscles tensed as the air seemingly thickened. Her body felt heavier than it ever had before. Knowing her body wouldn't heed her command to stand and assist her friends, she was helpless.

Confusion whirled around in her head, making her a little dizzy. Ódin promised Frigg and Vitalia that no harm would come to their son and daughter, that Loki and Kiara were to be captured, questioned, and then imprisoned for their crimes. Valhalla's brows furrowed lightly. She had a feeling that Ódin's council was behind this change of verdict. Only they could pressure him into this course of action.

Valhalla closed her eyes and took a deep breath to calm herself. She had to do something, but what? What could she do in this situation?

"Wait!" Valhalla exclaimed. The heat of the Valkyries' stares sent static across her skin, but she dared not tear her gaze away from Loki. "Your Highness, Loki, Kiara is the one who killed Lady Ildri. It can't have been Aura. Please remember, she was away from Asgard for days, dealing with the rebellious band of Jotunns in Jotunheim. Aura couldn't possibly have been there to kill her sister, but someone else was there. You must know it in your heart. It was she who slew her!"

Her words screamed out, hoping they would be daggers of truth to Loki's heart. If she couldn't sway him in this moment, perhaps she could set the spark to cause a rift between him and Kiara.

The black tendrils swirling about Loki and Kiara slowly calmed, then receded back into his shadow. His expression turned to one of disinterest, but his eyes rested on Valhalla. "How dull. Kiara, do you mind? I've grown quite tired of this game."

He turned away and stepped into his frozen shadow on the floor. As he stopped, he faltered briefly, a slight trip in his step and hand brought to his face. Valhalla jolted at the unusual movement. However, before she could speak, Kiara clapped her hands high in the air, creating an explosion of darkness speeding toward them at an alarming rate.

"DAMMIT!" Aura raised her shortsword, Stiarna, vertically in the air before her, creating a barrier of light to shield herself and everyone behind her.

The force of the darkness threatened to push her back, her wedged sollerets ground against the stone ground. Her jaw clenched in exertion. Aura grunted harshly, arms trembled.

Valhalla desperately wanted to assist her in some way, to hold her in place, but could do nothing. Both Thora and her twin sister, Arianwen, the Valkyrie of Ice and Snow, stepped behind Aura and held her in place. Reaching around Aura, the two valkyries grabbed hold of the sword, placing their hands upon hers, and pushed with all their combined might to withstand the torrent of darkness battering the barrier of light.

Valhalla struggled up to a knee, watching as the darkness pressed against the barrier with such force it was unclear which would give first.

Minutes seemed to stretch, and fear shrouded Valhalla's thoughts. All of a sudden, the darkness relented, dispersing into nothing. Neither Loki nor Kiara were in sight.

Valhalla released a disappointed sigh, and once her panic subsided, she thought over the events from the moment Loki had revealed himself. She knew what she saw; she just hoped it was enough to prove his innocence.

Aura dismissed her light shield. She stood as still as a statue, frozen in that moment and lost to thought. Aura's left hand balled into a tight fist, the metal plates over her fingers softly creaking as they ground against each other.

Thora gently patted Aura on the back with a somber frown, then turned to Valhalla. Her expression quickly changed as their eyes met. The golden valkyrie smiled warmly, and her bright blue eyes, the shade as beautiful as Midgard's sky, twinkled. She leaned down with an outstretched, armored hand.

Valhalla smiled in return and accepted the valkyrie's hand. Thora then carefully aided her up. It felt like a massive weight was still upon her body. As though chains of iron were wrapped around her, pulling her back to the earth.

Once on her own two feet, Valhalla let out a heavy breath and struggled to keep her footing. She placed a hand on Thora's shoulder to brace herself on the valkyrie's strong posture.

"You all right?" Thora asked with concerned eyes.

"Yes." Valhalla lied, trying to keep her friend from worrying. "Thank you, Thora."

"I will make you a healing bath as soon as we return to Asgard." One of the other valkyries chimed in, her unmistakable Ellinikan accent still thick after so many years away from her home as an Æsir. "That should ease your aching muscles, Valla."

Valhalla turned her head to meet Cascade, the Valkyrie of Water, standing beside her. The woman's ocean blue eyes seemed troubled. She had tawny skin, and her bright blue hair shone in neatly tied back, elegant braids.

She was a beautiful woman. In her past life, she lived as a human of Midgard, born on the massive island country of Ellinika far to the northeast of Veerence. She sacrificed herself to rescue a beloved friend from a terrible fate, which proved her worthy of becoming a Valkyrie of Asgard.

Every one of them had a tragic past which led them to become the valkyries they were. Valhalla wondered if her life would also end as tragically as theirs. Would she have the strength of character to be worthy of joining their ranks?

Unlike Aura and the other valkyries, Cascade wore an azure and gold armor akin to Ellinikan soldiers, decorated to resemble seashells with carvings of ocean waves about the armor's surface. Even her bright blue garments underneath were of Ellinikan fashion. The fabric was lightweight, flowing, and quite revealing compared to that of Veerencian clothing. Her weapon was a golden and azure trident she named Medusa, decorated with pink pearls.

Valhalla heard Ellinika was like no place she had ever been, with unique architecture, clothing, and even flowers found nowhere else in all the nine realms. She would like to go to Ellinika with Cascade one day, when Cascade is ready to return.

She flashed Cascade an appreciative nod as Valhalla removed her hand from Thora's shoulder and did her best to stand on her own. "A healing bath sounds wonderful. Thank you, Casca—"

Arianwen sighed loudly with aggravation, causing everyone to turn to her, standing beside Aura. "So, what do you want to do now, Aura?"

"Now, we return to Asgard. I'll report to Ódin and Frigg, tell them of my failure to capture the two."

"This isn't a damn failure! We were just—"

Aura placed a hand on Arianwen's shoulder, interrupting her outburst with a kind smile. This inadvertently infuriated the ice valkyrie. She gently swiped away Aura's hand and turned away.

"For fucks sake, you're impossible to talk to. Fine, do whatever you want. See if I care."

Aura grinned. "Thank you, Arianwen. I know I'm hard to deal with sometimes, but thank you for understanding," She said with a gentle chuckle.

She then turned and dismissed Stiarna and her shield in a bright white flash. Cupping her hands together before the placard of her armor, she began summoning a different item forth.

A similar light appeared above her palms in the form of a sizable ball.

As it shattered into many twinkling starry lights, it revealed a white battlehorn decorated in intricate Celnor designs depicting stars and swirling knots, with amethyst gems about them.

Aura raised her gaze to Valhalla, her monolid amethyst eyes looking her up and down worriedly. "I know you've had an exhausting day, Valhalla, but my mother wishes to see you immediately. She said it's urgent. Can you meet with her before you rest?"

Valhalla understood and quickly nodded, ignoring her fatigue. She forced a smile. "Of course. If Lady Vitalia says it's urgent, then who am I to make her wait?"

Aura stared at her a moment, skeptical, but nodded as well. She pressed the tip of the horn to her lips and blew. A loud, booming sound echoed throughout the forest, signaling Heimdall that they were ready to leave.

A long, quiet moment followed. As a soft breeze rustled the leaves on the nearby trees, birds chirped in the distance.

An even louder boom from somewhere above broke the peace and answered. Valhalla gazed up and watched as a white star appeared in the clear sky. It grew brighter and brighter until it enveloped her, Edan, and the valkyries in a pillar of rainbow light, pulling them up into the sky and transporting them straight to the realm of the gods, Asgard.

Valhalla

The Golden Realm of Asgard

"**W**elcome back to Asgard." Heimdall Óðinson, Keeper of the Bifrost, Guardian of Asgard, and the God of Protection, greeted the valkyries and Valhalla.

He stood on a round golden dais at the center of the Bifrost, tall and broad-shouldered, as if one of the statues of the legendary Æsir of old had come to life. From her firsthand experience and the tales sung of the man, he was a stalwart guardian like no other. His golden, raven-decorated armor shone against the bright yellow sky. Beneath the armor, he wore a white garment draped over his light umber skin. His golden eyes shimmered, and a look of worry hung on his face. "Is everyone all right?"

"Yes, we're fine, but . . ." Aura glanced back to Valhalla with concern returning to her amethyst monolid eyes.

Valhalla forced a smile, though her posture told a different story. She stood hunched with an arm resting over her stomach. Both Cascade and Anita Petoradottir, the Valkyrie of Wind, stood at her sides. Of all the valkyries, they were the only two proficient in the arts of healing.

"I'm fine, I promise. Why don't we—"

"Lady Vitalia is aware of your condition." Heimdall respectfully interrupted. "She's willing to wait if you need time to recover. Vitalia is expecting your meeting with her to be long, so she prefers you to be well-rested."

"O-Oh, all right then. I guess I am pretty tired." Valhalla chuckled, glancing at Cascade and Anita with embarrassment.

Cascade giggled as she brushed a few thick strands of Valhalla's black hair behind her ear. "Come on, let's go to my bedchamber to get your bath ready. Everything I need is already there."

"I'll fetch your nightgown as you bathe too, so you can nap on Cascade's bed while we meet with Vitalia." Anita added with a warm grin.

Valhalla paused a moment before nodding, then followed as the valkyries escorted her toward the main entrance of the spherical golden hall of the Bifrost. Each time she returned to this place, she felt overcome with a sense of amazement. Following her friends, she gazed about the hall, taking in the craftsmanship.

At the edges of the hall were placed eight circular gates leading out to the other realms, four to the left and four to the right. Each one was emblazoned with decorative knots representing their respective realm. Between Midgard and Niflheim was a large circular opening, allowing Heimdall to peer into the open, pastel yellow skies and golden sea, stretching far past the horizon.

As the group reached the entrance of the Bifrost, Valhalla stopped and turned around to face Aura. "Wait! There's something I have to tell you about Loki."

"Oh, all right then, what is it?" Aura was visibly taken aback by Valhalla's burst of energy, given her current state, and walked to meet her.

"Back in Midgard, Elder Bron moved as though possessed due to a black crystal embedded in his back. When I was face to face with him, his eyes were different; they were as black as the darkest night's sky. It was only after the crystals' removal that he became himself again, and his eyes returned to normal. When I was facing Kiara and Loki, before I was swallowed by the darkness, I saw Loki's eyes. His irises were the same as Bron's."

Aura blinked with surprise.

"Then, just before Kiara concealed their retreat, I know I saw Loki falter. His hand flew to his face, and he flinched. If I'm right, he was battling to retake control of his mind. I think he's under her control."

Aura sighed. "Valhalla—"

"Please, Aura!" Valhalla yelled out, even surprising herself. She had blamed Loki for so long, hated him even when Frigg sought to better her understanding of the Æsir. She had told her much of his life, both the good and bad, painting a vivid picture of who he had been before the tragedy that changed the direction of her life. The realization that someone else might've been the cause of her suffering made her second-guess everything she had felt concerning Loki. She could never fully forgive him, but if she was right, he didn't deserve her complete condemnation.

"I have no love for Loki after what he did to my home, but if he is under her control now, he may have been back then as well. If he's a puppet in all of this, then he's a victim as much as I am. Besides," she took a deep breath, "Ódin promised Frigg and Vitalia that he wouldn't order their death. Frigg would be devastated if you brought Loki back dead."

Aura's lips tightened, and she released a soft breath. Valhalla held her gaze steadfast, certain of her theory.

From what Valhalla understood, Frigg had fallen into a deep depression after Loki's transgressions and became a recluse for a time. Valhalla hadn't met her until several months after being brought to Asgard and living with the valkyries. Eventually, she was introduced to Queen Frigg by Vitalia and Ódin. She didn't remember much of that day, save for the change in Frigg's eyes as the goddess stared down at her. It was as subtle as the changing of fall to spring, an ember of life returning, a refocusing of the iris. Frigg snapped out of her stupor. A deep sadness remained, but it no longer clung to her.

"Are you sure, Valhalla?" Aura's face grew serious. "We can't give Frigg false hope. I'm not sure she could withstand another blow like the one she took that day."

"I'm positive. I know what I witnessed. I'd stake my life on it. If you want, I can explain it to Ódin—"

"No, let me. You still need your rest, Valhalla. You've done enough for us today." Aura smiled, raising a hand to the back of Valhalla's neck and the other to her shoulder. She pulled Valhalla down to embrace her. The scent of magnolia and pine washed over Valhalla. Her pink garnet eyes closed, accepting Aura's warmth and comfort.

Aura stood shorter than Valhalla's six-foot stature, herself standing at about five foot five. Valhalla felt the valkyrie gently begin to stroke her hair, the feeling soothing her worry.

"Please, Valla, go rest. You gave us all such a fright when we heard you were face to face with Loki and my sister. Rest, for my sake." Aura whispered.

She placed her hands on Valhalla's shoulders and held her out at arm's length, her expression soft and sweet.

Valhalla stared at her for a moment in surprise, having not realized until now just how worried Aura had been. Growing up in Asgard, Aura had always been like an older sister to her. Tender and caring, teaching her right from wrong, and even the way of the sword. She had always been there for Valhalla.

She stared at Aura for a moment longer, then nodded. Aura turned Valhalla around and gently nudged her toward the entrance of the Bifrost, accompanied by both Cascade and Anita. Valhalla fiddled with her hands, having never felt comfortable when tended to by her friends, feeling as though she were a burden to them.

The light of the sun blinded her for a moment as she passed through the golden entrance. She rubbed her eyes to clear her vision and gazed up into the sky.

Standing upon the glittering rainbow bridge connecting the Bifrost to Asgard, she watched the ocean waves crash against the massive tree roots below. Beyond the bridge was the golden city itself, grand and vast. Many of the buildings stretched high toward the bright sky, reaching higher than the most splendid castles found throughout the nine realms.

Even after all these years of living in this magical place, it still took her breath away. Asgard was like nothing else in all the nine realms.

Most of the buildings here shared similarities to what could be found in Midgard, but on a much grander scale. Toward the edges of the city were ringed fortresses, each serving as a great hall to one of the gods like Tyr, Forseti, Freyja, and many others. They also housed various warriors and völvxs, or spellcasters, to hone their skills in battle and the use of seidr.

Beyond the ringed fortresses stood various longhouses stretching higher and higher, the deeper into Asgard you traveled. Vast stretches of countryside and turf houses peppered the city. Far to Valhalla's right, where the cliffside met the waters, she could scarcely see the boating houses and Lord Njord's hall towering above them. The gateway to Lord Aegir's hall, held beneath the sea, was just a bit further down the beach past Njord's hall. Knarrs and byrdings sailed in and out of view. Other small boats scattered about the golden waters.

Bright, colorful spring flowers and glittering fabrics decorated pillars and windows throughout the city. The Æsir were preparing for Ostara, a time when the realms rejuvenate, celebrating fertility and growth.

Although the ground was abuzz, with some traveling on horseback and others inside carriages, which admittedly wasn't terribly different from what was typical of any city in Midgard, there was another sort of transportation only found here in Asgard. Flying contraptions called vagn. They were similar to carriages, with rounded bottoms and benches inside that could seat several Æsir, but soared through the open air. A large mast and sail jutted from the center of the vessel. Ornate knotwork was etched all across the bottom and sides, surrounding a depiction of Verdrfolnir, Yggdrasil's great falcon, with wings outstretched.

The wind blew softly, brushing Valhalla's hair against her bare skin. She took a deep breath, soaking in the wondrous floral scent wafting from the city. Then the clip-clop of Edan's hooves called her from her daydreaming. As he stopped beside her, she brushed a hand against his soft black fur.

You are weak. They don't trust you. Use your Fire.

A sudden pain erupted in Valhalla's head, as though all her nerves were firing at once, causing an intense, constant barrage against her senses. She let out a short gasp, shallow as a whimper. Her hands flew to the sides of her head, and her body hunched over.

You are nothing. They despise you. Burn them all.

She stumbled forward, letting out a soft shriek. It was like her eyes ripped from their sockets. A scratching sensation burned the inside of her skull, almost as if something were desperately trying to escape.

The vision in her left eye blurred and darkened, casting a shroud over her surroundings. Black tendrils slowly crawled into view, slithering and making their way across her right eye. Her breath quickened. Valhalla's heart pounded hard within her chest, and her body shuddered.

You are useless. They wish you dead. Reduce them to ash.

"Wha-What's going on? This pain. These voices. WHAT'S HAPPENING TO ME!?" Valhalla's voice shook as she struggled with the searing pain in her head, feeling as though someone had dunked her in molten iron. She let out a raspy shriek and stumbled forward.

"Valhalla, what is it? What's——"

"STAY AWAY FROM ME!" Valhalla screamed out. She spun around and unleashed a wave of fire at the ground between herself, Cascade, and Anita, pushing them to a safe distance. She released another fierce wave of fire, crashing before the other valkyries who were slowly approaching.

Valhalla took several steps back. Her thoughts became scrambled, and she wailed out in pain. A raging inferno sparked to life at Valhalla's feet, engulfing her completely and swirling in a fiery tempest. She hunched within the wall of fire. A thought crossed her mind. She wondered if they would hurt her instead of coming to her aid.

No. They wouldn't. Why would she think that? What was she doing? What were these dark thoughts drowning her mind? Filling her like a constant wave washing over her, never giving her a moment to breathe. Her friends had always been there for her. Making her strong.

Right?

Before she knew it, she was silently pleading. Begging for someone, anyone, to help her.

Hot tears streamed from her tightly closed eyes, instantly drying in the heat of the blaze. She wanted so desperately for the pain to stop. The whispering voices were like shards of metal scraping against stone in her mind. Her body shivered, her mind was confused, and her heart was full of fear.

You are a burden. They are coming. Attack! Kill them. You will—

"VALHALLA!" A voice called out from behind.

Valhalla forced her eyes open, and the unknown voices momentarily quieted, giving her a brief reprieve. The fire around her slowed and faded to a faint flicker in a ring around her feet. She turned to see who had screamed out her name, to see who had quieted those dreadful, whispering voices as the sound of something lightly jingled against each other.

The tendrils receded from her right eye, but her left remained lost in darkness. Valhalla's eyes shot wide as she spotted the blonde-haired Queen of Asgard, the All Mother herself, Frigg Fiorgyndottir.

Frigg's indigo eyes trembled with worry. Her hand raised to Valhalla, as though trying to calm her. Frigg's guardian, Syn, stood at the ready beside her Queen. The woman's hands were tightly clenched around the hilt of her sword, drawn and held high.

It was her duty to protect the Queen at any cost. Syn didn't know Valhalla well, having only met when visiting Frigg, and never had a meaningful conversation, and right now, likely appeared as a threat. Valhalla was sure that from the guardian's point of view, all she could see was a young woman whose fire seidr had just blazed out of control.

Syn was a stern and strong woman. Her heterochromatic eyes were quite beautiful, one blue and one green. A cautious glare rested on her face. She wore light armor over her fitted garments. Her copper warbraids were as intricate as they were beautiful.

Frigg slowly and calmly raised her other hand before Valhalla, spreading her arms wide in an inviting embrace, and cautiously approached. "My dear Valhalla, everything will be all right. Please, tell me what's wrong? Talk to me. You know I'm always here for you."

The All Mother's voice was soothing, her words relaxing Valhalla's tensed muscles. The whispers quickly returned, louder than before, and continued their assault on her senses.

"The-The voices—They're . . . saying terrible things, such terrible things. They won't stop. Please, MAKE THEM STOP!"

More tears flowed down Valhalla's cheeks. She clutched at her head with both hands, hoping to somehow relieve the pain, though it remained and worsened. Tendrils shot across her right eye again and nearly overtook her sight completely. She tightly closed her eyes, hoping that would somehow slow the progression.

The All Mother hates you.

Valhalla's breath was heavy. She shook her head and screamed for the whispers to stop.

Burn her flesh!

Her knees quaked and weakened, threatening to buckle under her weight.

You're worthless!

Valhalla was nearing her limits. She could feel herself losing control. Opening her eyes, she could now only see the smallest glimpses of light through her right eye. The tendrils thrashed wildly. Her eyes shot wide with fear.

Let your fire blaze—

"Valhalla!"

She jolted and looked up to face Frigg, her kind, warm smile giving Valhalla a small measure of hope. The whispers slowly quieted, but lingered in the recesses of her thoughts.

"Valhalla, come to me. I can help you. Please, trust me as you always have. You know I would never bring you to harm." Frigg held her arms wide and continued toward Valhalla cautiously.

"Your Majesty, please—"

Frigg gestured to silence Syn's protest, shooting her a look to keep her distance, then returned her attention to Valhalla.

Valhalla desperately wanted to walk to Frigg, to accept whatever aid the Queen could give, but doubt crept its way into her thoughts. Her mind twisted, unsure if she could trust the All Mother.

There were those thoughts again. Why would Valhalla believe Frigg would harm her? She knew better. Frigg treated Valhalla like a daughter, and yet, here she was, hesitating.

Valhalla closed her eyes and took a deep breath, trying to force herself to calm through sheer willpower. She demanded her feet to move, even scolding herself to do so. Perhaps Frigg knew of a way to help her get rid of these terrible thoughts, trying to bombard her senses again.

She slowly reopened her eyes. Her body was shaking. Valhalla attempted a step, her foot sliding forward, then followed with her other. Stumbling, she commanded her body to move. Her eyes darted back and forth between the glittering rainbow bridge at her feet to the All Mother, whose warm smile and worried eyes didn't waver from Valhalla.

Valhalla reached out to Frigg as she drew closer. The All Mother brought her hands forward, awaiting Valhalla's touch. The Queen's hands were clean and soft, her nails shining with white and violet paint which matched her gown. Various keys hung from a golden girdle wrapped about her waist.

Valhalla always felt safe in Frigg's arms. It was as true now as it was when she was small. The All Mother's embrace was warm, and her braided blonde hair tickled Valhalla's nose. The scent of apples and flowers was all-consuming. When she closed her eyes, it was like being transported to one of Frigg's many beautiful gardens.

She stood before the All Mother. Friggs' gentle, loving smile beamed down upon her, but still, Valhalla hesitated to touch the Queen's hands. She gazed down at the All Mother's inviting palms as hers hovered in place.

Valhalla's breath was labored, and her hands trembled. Her eyes stung from the tears, and her round cheeks were red. Everything was going to be all right, she was sure of it. It had to be all right. Frigg had never done Valhalla wrong.

A sudden dark thought invaded her mind. What if Valhalla accidentally hurt the All Mother? What if Frigg was planning to harm her instead?

No.

She couldn't let those thoughts win. Thoughts that weren't her own.

Thoughts she was beginning to hate.

"It's all right, Valhalla, just take my hands and everything will be fine."

Her hands flinched, withdrawing at the sound of Frigg's voice.

She stared at the Queen's hands. Like Aura, Frigg had been there for Valhalla since she was a child. The Queen always tended to her. Frigg had provided her lessons in etiquette, reading, writing, music, and so much more over the years. She gave her a home and treated her as a daughter. She had found herself with loving parents, something she had thought forever lost to her since that fateful day.

The pain intensified. She placed her hands in Frigg's and watched as the Queen's fingers slowly wrapped around Valhalla's. Her porcelain-white skin was warm, save for the cold metal, white gold rings about Frigg's fingers. The Queen then leaned down and tapped her simple diamond and amethyst-encrusted, white gold circlet against Valhalla's forehead.

Her breath softened, slowing and eventually falling in unison with the Queen's. Something seeped into her hands; it was warm, but invasive.

"Lika, láta minn kveykva 'nvepuley hennar. Láta inn kveykva upp hennar hyggiandi. Láta inn 'idan hennar til myrkr aen illr at mein hennar hyggiandi. Láta minn kveykva vísa hennar."* Frigg whispered softly.

She was instantly aware of what the All Mother was doing; she was conjuring a spell.

Frigg suddenly pulled Valhalla's hands toward her, bringing her into a tight embrace. The Queen placed a hand on her back and the other behind her head. She began to glow brightly white, and Valhalla's being followed.

Her breath heaved, and her heart wavered. The words in her mind came fast and loud. The unknown's tone was harsh, but behind the words was a hint of trepidation. Something pulled within her. It felt as though it had bored its way into her soul and was now being ripped from her physical form. Whatever it was, it grabbed hold of her tightly, refusing to let go.

Squirming in Frigg's embrace, she writhed in agony. She wanted to scream out, to push the Queen away, but Frigg held her tight and buried Valhalla's face in her chest.

"Lika, láta minn kveykva 'nvepuley hennar. Láta inn kveykva upp hennar hyggiandi. Láta inn 'idan hennar til myrkr aen illr at mein hennar hyggiandi! Láta minn kveykva vísa hennar!"¹ Frigg repeated the spell loudly, and the light around them glowed ever brighter.

---

1   Frigg's spell is Celnor(Norse) for Please, let my light envelope her. Let it light up her mind. Let it rid her of darkness and evil that plagues her thoughts. Let my light guide her.

Valhalla's head spun, and her body weakened. Her knees finally gave out. Frigg allowed the two to lower to their knees. She held her like she was but a small child again.

"Mo-Mother?" Valhalla questioned, lying against Frigg's chest as she heard a light gasp escape from the Queen. A hand caressed her forehead and brushed the thick strands of hair away from her face.

"Hush now. As I said, everything will be all right." Frigg then kissed the top of her head.

Eyelids growing heavy, they then fluttered. Her vision blurred, and the realm about her faded into darkness.

Valhalla

There's Still Hope

Valhalla's world was dark, her body heavy, and cool to the touch. The scent of sweet flowers filled her nostrils. She tried to open her eyes, but they betrayed her as though mired in honey. Overcome by exhaustion, Valhalla struggled to move her limbs. Her hands twitched, fingers churning soil with the effort of moving mountains. She took a breath and held the content of her lungs until it started to burn, waiting for her muscles to relax before exhaling.

"Frigg, she wakes."

Valhalla knew that voice; it belonged to Fulla, Frigg's handmaiden. What could they be doing in her bed chamber?

Her eyes flickered open, her vision a blur.

Firelight danced on the walls of the bedchamber. A figure moved to her left, along with the sound of more jingling, and placed something at the very corner of the bed. Valhalla let out a moan and managed to raise a hand to her eyes, gently rubbing them to clear her vision.

"Are you all right, dear?"

"All Mother?" Valhalla asked with a dry throat. "Where am I?"

Frigg took Valhalla's left hand, still lying on the bed, and held it tightly. Valhalla reopened her eyes, able to see a little clearer now. Around the chamber were many lit candles, and the fireplace was fully ablaze, its warmth lightly caressing her skin. She recognized her bedchamber, at least one of them, and it was the one in the Hall of the Valkyr.

Revebjelle flowers sat at the very edge of her bedchamber. Blue wisterias hung from her ceiling, masking the golden stones of Marglod, the mountain home of the valkyries of Asgard.

She slowly glanced to her left toward a large window. The shudders were wide open. Valhalla could see the beautiful city outside and the sea in the distance. The sky was no longer brightly awash in vibrant yellow hues; now, it was the darkness of night. Many stars twinkled in the deep violet blanketing Asgard. A masculine figure stood in the nook, the azure silk curtains hiding the person.

A tall, broad man with bright, fiery red hair tied back in warbraids swayed gently behind him. He donned a comfortable-looking garb of crimson and gold over his deep brown skin. It shone lightly in the firelight, making it easier to see him the closer he got. Approaching, he stopped at the edge of Valhalla's bed, beside Frigg, placing his hands flat against the silk azure sheets. He leaned down over Valhalla with a relieved smile upon his fully bearded face. A slight redness surrounded his emerald eyes, as if he had been crying. The sight took Valhalla by surprise. Thor rarely cried.

"I see the Princess has finally awakened from her slumber." He said with a warm chuckle.

"Thor?" She questioned while rubbing her eyes. "I told you not to call me that. I'm no Princess." Valhalla replied, her words soft and her strength slowly returning. She struggled to hold back her smile.

"All Father adopted you, so therefore, you're my sister, which makes you a Princess." Thor grinned, causing her cheeks to burn.

Thor was massive. He was both a mighty and intimidating warrior with a temper, but despite all that, she had always found him to be a big softie. Kind. Playful. He drank more than any living being in existence. Over time, she found he had a bit of an overprotective streak concerning his siblings, at least those he liked. Most of all, his temper was not one to ever take lightly, let alone get on the wrong side of. Thor explained to her once that there were only two people in existence who could calm his rage: his wife, Sif, and his brother Loki, who more often than not, tried to rile him up for fun. Valhalla missed her big oaf of a brother.

He raised a hand to her forehead, gently swiping a few loose ebony strands of hair away from her face, and placed his warm palm on her forehead. Thor then turned to the All-Mother. "She's cool, the fever has finally left her."

Frigg sighed with relief, though her grip on Valhalla's hand remained firm. "That's good to hear."

"Fever? You know I don't get—" She paused, recalling what had happened to her on the rainbow bridge. Her eyes opened wide, and she quickly pushed herself up from her bed. "Wait! What—"

A sudden pain flashed in her head, as though she had been struck by a hammer. Her left hand was still in Frigg's grasp, and so she rushed her right hand to her face, covering her right eye. Her face scrunched tightly and contorted.

She felt two heavy hands gently grasp her shoulders and attempt to guide her back toward the bed. Anchoring herself with her right arm, she refused to lie back down.

"You have to lie still, you haven't yet fully recovered," Thor said.

She shook her head, not wanting to lie down, her stubbornness overruling the advice of those around her. Slowly opening her eyes, her vision swayed between clear and blurry as the pounding in her head persisted.

Frigg took her left hand and pulled it forward. Valhalla felt her squeeze lightly, the All Mother's palm warm and soft. Looking down to the Queen's hand cupping hers, her gaze then moved up her arms, and to Frigg's worried, welling indigo eyes.

"Please, lie down, and we'll talk. We won't force you to sleep, I promise."

Valhalla trembled, staring back apologetically, and acquiesced, allowing Thor to softly lay her back down. He sat beside her, adjusting her feathered pillows, and gently slid his fingers through her hair.

She stared up at the ceiling, at the wisterias hanging over her, upset and confused about what had happened to her. Valhalla tightened her grip on the All Mother's hands, took a deep breath through her nostrils, and exhaled through pursed lips. "What—"

"Hush for now, dear. Thor, do you still have it?"

"Yes, All Mother, just a moment."

Thor turned away from Valhalla and reached for something hanging from his black leather belt. He returned to her and unwrapped a white cloth, revealing thinly sliced wedges of Asgard's most precious treasure, a golden apple.

The golden apples were tended and guarded by the young goddess Idunn of Youth. The fruit gave the Æsir the gift of long life, lasting even longer than elves, dwarves, and dragons combined.

He plucked a piece from the cloth and handed it to Valhalla. "We'll answer any questions we can, but first, have some. You've been asleep here for some time. I don't want a repeat of what nearly happened before. So please, eat."

"You don't have to tell me twice." Valhalla smiled weakly and took the piece of apple from him, staring at it for a moment.

Although the golden apples are best known for their use by the Æsir, they could also help non Æsir, like Valhalla, to survive in Asgard. The energy flowing throughout the realm comes from Yggdrasil and sustains the Æsir, granting them powers beyond belief, including seidr not seen anywhere else throughout the nine realms. Unfortunately, those not born of this realm are unable to withstand the immense pressure it wreaks on their bodies. Without regular consumption of the golden apples, the effect is similar to a costrel overfilling with water; over time, it will eventually burst at the seams.

Valhalla once made that mistake and found the description to be quite accurate. It was as if she was being pushed open from the inside. She had been preoccupied with something and had not realized how much time had gone by. That excuse didn't stop Ódin from scolding her. Now, whenever she returned to Asgard, there was usually an apple waiting with Heimdall and the valkyries, just to be safe.

It had been theorized that these apples, paired with her time raised in Asgard, were why Valhalla had become so powerful with seidr, able to even achieve the power of both Fjölkyngi Völva and Fródleikr Völva, Sage and Eternal Sage, in such a short amount of time.

After eating the apple, she looked at Thor and then Frigg. "So, what happened to me?"

"It seems you fell under the dark chaos' influence when you were in Midgard. For how long, however, that's only something you can tell us." Frigg replied, her expression stern, but unable to mask her caring, worried gaze.

"Why me?"

"What exactly happened when you were there?" Thor asked, his face even more serious than the All Mother's.

"The valkyries didn't tell you?"

"I've heard their version of events, but I want to hear it from you, please, Valla?" His face quickly changed to one of concern.

Her throat tightened, hating it when he looked at her in that way, and felt guilty for making them both worry.

Valhalla gazed down at the sheets draped over her. She wasn't sure if she should tell them everything, especially after Aura had done that already. Valhalla then assumed that maybe Thor needed confirmation? But what kind?

She returned her gaze to Thor, his dark emerald eyes trembling, and hers reacted in kind. Valhalla decided to tell them what had happened since entering Midgard.

Thor and Frigg remained quiet as she recounted all that had happened from the moment she saw the Elder komod dragon attacking his kin, how he gave chase after her, and her battle with him. They were taken aback as she detailed the moment of the crystal's breaking and the power it unleashed, only to disappear right afterward. Then she told them of her accidental encounter with Loki and Kiara, and how she hated not heeding her feelings about the so-called noble she met in the forest. Valhalla got an extreme reaction from the All Mother when explaining the appearance of Loki's eyes before she had nearly been swallowed by darkness.

"So-So it's true . . ." Frigg turned away from Valhalla, staring at the deep azure marble floor. Her blonde hair blocked her face from Valhalla's view. She then spotted Fulla, Frigg's Handmaiden and little sister, who stepped toward her and placed a hand on Frigg's shoulder, consoling the Queen.

Valhalla's heart ached for her; no mother wanted to feel so helpless in aiding their child. She sat up again, carefully situating herself, and turned to Frigg. "All Mother, can't you help Loki? As you did me?"

"Not yet, we still need *definitive* proof," Thor interjected with a slight sarcastic tone.

Brows furrowed, she was confused by what he meant. "Definitive? I don't understand."

"My brother—" Thor started, his tone harsh, but stopped himself. He closed his eyes and took a deep breath, pinching the bridge of his nose. After a moment, he exhaled in a long sigh and continued. "My brother . . ." His voice now softened, "is either being controlled by another, OR the chaos within him has grown out of hand. Either way, we need to capture him to be sure."

"Capture? Are you saying—" She exclaimed before being interrupted.

"Now that's enough," Frigg stood from her bed and patted down the skirt of her white and violet gown.

She gracefully turned to Valhalla and interlocked her fingers over her stomach. A small smile was upon her face, as though she was trying to hide her annoyance, but she had the feeling it wasn't about her. "There will be plenty of time for that. Vitalia would like to speak to you, especially concerning today's events. Are you well enough to stand, my Valla?"

Smiling in return with a light blush, she nodded to her Queen. "Yes, I'm sure I am, All Mother."

Valhalla slid the silk sheets off her and pushed herself to the edge of the bed. She found herself wearing one of her white, fitted nightgowns, the softness of the cloth welcoming against her skin, and looked to the floor where a set of matching slippers awaited her. She slid her feet into the shoes one by one, and as she was about to stand, Thor held out a hand in front of her.

She gazed up, his broad stature towering over her. Valhalla took his hand, and he carefully helped her up, cautioning her to take it slow.

Fulla, a woman as tall as Frigg, approached with a cup in hand. She had fair skin, a golden circlet she oddly named Orsnood wrapped around her honey blonde hair, and blue eyes. "It's filled with water. I figured your throat may be a bit dry, if not a little sore."

"Thank you, Lady Fulla."

Valhalla grinned with relief and accepted the cup. She placed the rim to her lips, tilted it forward, and let the cold liquid soothe her throat.

She exhaled, refreshed, and placed the cup on the nightstand behind her. As Valhalla turned to follow Frigg, Thor stopped her and turned her to him. "Listen, I'm glad you still harbor hope for my brother. Honestly, it means a lot. Many of us need that." He wrapped his arms around her, the scent of rain and leather about him, and leaned down to whisper in her ear. "All Mother, especially, thank you."

Valhalla exhaled softly in return. "Of course, Brother."

He gave her a tight squeeze and released her. A large, thankful grin was beaming on his face. She giggled bashfully, then hugged one of his arms, and they followed after Frigg and Fulla, who now stood before Syn.

Valhalla startled as the muscular, olive-skinned woman leaned against the door and shot her a stern expression with arms crossed tightly over her stocky chest. One of Syn's brows raised high. "Are you ready to go, or not?"

Frigg rolled her eyes, looking a little flustered. "Syn, honestly, what am I going to do with you?"

"What? I was just askin'."

"Yes," All Mother sighed, "I figured."

Valhalla couldn't help but laugh. "I'm sorry, I'm ready to go. Honest."

Syn nodded approvingly. "All right then." She hopped off the door and opened it in one quick motion. Syn was the first out the door, looking left and right. "All right, Your Majesty, the hall is safe."

"It should be. I'd call anyone a fool who sought to break into a place belonging to the valkyries." Frigg walked out and pulled a white key from her golden girdle with a swan carved at the end, with Fulla shadowing behind her. Valhalla then took a deep breath, clutching onto Thor's arm, and followed to meet with Vitalia down below.

Valhalla

Danger in Hilliard

Walking the quiet halls of Marglod, Valhalla lost herself in the scent of flowers and greenery filling the air from the Ostara decorations adorning the Hall of the Valkyr. Blazing, elegant golden sconces lit her way.

Colorful spring flowers hung low from golden marble arches and beams, showering her with their sweet fragrance. Similar glittering fabrics hung from the walls in archways and encircled railings with bundles of flowers sewn about.

Frigg and Thor walked in front of her, looking back now and then to make sure she was all right.

Valhalla had always enjoyed this time of year. For her, the month of Einmánudur could not arrive soon enough. She was a child of fall, but had always felt drawn to the spring. The flowers, the birds, the spring rains, she loved it all, and wouldn't change it for anything in all the nine realms.

Lost in all her gazing, she hadn't noticed they had already reached the first floor of Marglod. To their left was the entrance of the Hall of the Valkyr, and to the right a hallway leading to Vitalia's chamber, the Hall of Souls.

Before Valhalla could make her turn toward Vitalia's chamber, Frigg called to her. "Valhalla, a moment, please."

She turned to the Asgardian Queen, standing tall, poised as she always was, and gazed at her with the happiest of smiles Valhalla had ever seen. "Yes, All Mother."

"I'll be parting ways with you here. Everything has already been discussed with Vitalia, so please listen carefully, all right?"

Valhalla nodded and approached Frigg, quickly embracing her in farewell. The hug caught the Queen by surprise. She flinched at first but quickly composed herself and embraced Valhalla in return.

"Oh my dear child. You just returned to me, and already I must say farewell."

"I can stay longer, if you'd like. All you have to do is ask."

Frigg laughed as she placed her hands on Valhalla's shoulders, holding her out at arm's length. "I would love nothing more than to do just that, but—" Her face grew serious as she briefly glanced away before returning to Valhalla. "This next task is crucial, Valhalla. I . . . We need you to do all you can for the one seeking aid."

Valhalla blinked with curiosity, causing a small smile to return to Frigg's face. "As I said, everything will be explained after you meet with Vitalia." Frigg leaned down and kissed Valhalla gently on her forehead and brushed a few misplaced ebony strands of hair behind Valhalla's ear. "Goodnight, my Valla. Please, stay safe, and may Yggdrasil shade you from your woes."

"I will, and goodnight to you, All Mother. May the Great Tree always shade you from evil." Valhalla curtsied to her Queen, her head low. Frigg turned to her Handmaiden Fulla and Syn, then nodded for their leave.

Thor stepped forward and sighed. "You ready?"

"Yes," Valhalla tilted her head at him, "are you all right?"

"Sort of. Come, I think we've kept them waiting long enough."

"Them?" Valhalla raised her brows high with curiosity, causing Thor to chuckle softly.

"Yes, all the valkyries have gathered for this meeting. As All Mother said, this task is important. Whatever it is." He replied with a shrug.

Thor walked forward and led Valhalla down the painted hall. She was surprised to find the way to the Hall of Souls was devoid of Ostara decorations and inspected the old mural lining the way. Valhalla assumed it was to make sure The Battle for Asgard wasn't obstructed from view.

Long ago, a battle took place between the current King of Asgard, Ódin, and his oldest brother, Ragnarök. The murals of the great battle on either side of the hall depicted not only Æsir fighting against Æsir, but also creatures of seidr, both dark and light, interspersed throughout. Ferocious monsters fought with claws and fangs dripping with blood. Angelic beings shone so brightly, their light blinded the opposition. Soldiers donning gold and violet armor stabbed at each other with swords, spears, and arrows. Valhalla shuddered at the vivid detail.

As they reached the end of the hall and the mural's ending, there, Ragnarök, Ódin's older brother, was surrounded by darkness and chains. Ódin stabbed him with his own sword. On the opposite wall, Vitalia stood tall, her grand white and black wings spread wide, and her one-and-a-half style longsword, Lifdagar, raised high in the air. Not only was the light described as being as bright as the sun, but it also disintegrated the creatures of darkness around her.

Valhalla, although unsettled by the knotted mural, was amazed at the detail throughout, which accurately depicted even the smallest of intricacies in each weapon and piece of armor.

She then noticed Thor had stopped, standing before a massive golden door decorated with depictions of those same angelic beings found on the mural. The angels on the left had ruby eyes, and those on the right had sapphire.

The ones before him at the door's center stood side by side, their hands touching. As he opened the doors leading into the Hall of Souls, a line appeared, splitting the image down the middle.

He pushed the door open wide enough to allow them both entrance into the chamber. Thor then stepped to the side and bowed playfully. Valhalla smirked at the gesture and curtsied with a hearty thank you and walked right in.

Valhalla stopped and took in the grandeur of the chamber. Lit, hanging lanterns dotted the walls, and eight round pillars stood far apart from each other. The ceiling was dome-shaped and stretched high above them with a circular hole at its center, allowing in the natural light.

In the very center of the chamber waited eight of the nine valkyries, seven of which were sitting on beautiful wooden benches marked with Celnor knots to represent the Asgardian tree, Yggdrasil.

At the center of the chamber was the eighth valkyrie, Vitalia. She stood before a beautiful waist-high stone well, held up by ten statues of angelic beings; it was named the Well of Foresight. Vitalia, the first and most powerful of them all, stared at Valhalla and Thor as they entered.

As was true of all Asgard-born Æsir, she towered over Valhalla, strong and poised. She wore a slim, fitted mahogany-colored gown with golden knots stitched at its very edges. Vitalia's ebony hair fell long, reaching down to her ankles, with a few braids here and there. She had porcelain white skin like Valhalla, and her monolid eyes were of two differing hues, the left crimson and the right azure.

Though her eyes were beautiful to behold in the firelight, they were unnatural. There was no distinction between iris or pupil; instead, in each eye was a singular disc of color in their respective shade, shrouded in a cloudy haze. The valkyrie was, for a time, blinded for reasons Valhalla had never been told, and she never dared to ask, assuming Vitalia preferred to keep it that way. All she knew was that with the aid of Yggdrasil Herself, Vitalia's vision was returned to her, in a way.

Living beings were composed of energy, life energy linked to the great Deity Herself. It was through Yggdrasil's blessing that Vitalia was able to see the energy within every living being, vividly sparkling in violet silhouettes. It was described to Valhalla that with each movement, the hue cascaded in waves, bathing her surroundings and making everything clear as day.

Something shimmered faintly against the firelight toward the far right of the chamber, catching Valhalla's attention. A feminine figure stood still as a statue before another set of massive golden doors, similar to the ones she had just entered. She squinted lightly and saw the mysterious ninth valkyrie, known as the Valkyrie of Sleep and Time, standing before the doors.

She knew next to nothing about the woman, except that she was given two special weapons, the Sword of Sleep and the Staff of Time, and that the woman stood guard before the gates of Valhalla when Vitalia was otherwise occupied. Valhalla herself didn't enter this chamber as much as the valkyries, but when she did, the woman never removed her armor, choosing to keep her identity hidden.

She had asked about the valkyrie in the past; however, none dared to answer. The valkyrie's appearance, past, and even her name were a mystery.

Valhalla returned to Vitalia, feeling somewhat intimidated in the tall woman's presence. Vitalia's demeanor was almost always stoic, and her strength was clear. In her presence, she felt as though she had to carry herself as obediently and well-mannered as possible, though Vitalia had never demanded it.

Vitalia stared at her, almost appearing disinterested. Just then, a small smile of relief grew on the woman's face as she curtsied to welcome the pair. Valhalla returned it and formally greeted her in kind, trying to appear as proper as possible.

"I'm glad to see you're doing well." Vitalia stood again, gesturing toward Valhalla. "Your life energy glows as brightly as any Æsir. Tell me, how're you feeling, little Valla?" Her voice carried a flicker of jest in the pronunciation of the nickname.

Laughing bashfully, now disarmed, her cheeks were blushing bright pink. "I'm doing well, thanks to the All Mother. Now you *tell* me," she crossed her arms over her chest, the facade now playful, "are you really still calling me *little* Valla?"

Vitalia chuckled softly. "I suppose you aren't a little girl anymore. You're a fully grown and quite capable young woman." She stretched out a hand toward her. "Come here, my dear, there are things we must discuss."

Valhalla nodded in understanding and approached the great valkyrie, placing a hand in the woman's. Vitalia unexpectedly placed her other hand on Valhalla's shoulder as the valkyrie's smile faded into a worried frown.

"Listen to me, Valhalla, after speaking with both Ódin and Frigg, we have all decided you should cease your investigation into Kiara and Loki."

"What!?" Her eyes widened with disbelief. "But I—"

"Please, understand," Vitalia's grip on her shoulder tightened, "this isn't a punishment. You've had one too many encounters with Kiara, this time even involving Loki, which ended with you being severely injured. They're getting bolder." Turning away from Valhalla, her eyes glossed. "This last encounter . . . gave us such a fright. We weren't sure if we would reach you in time. Please, *please* understand." Returning her gaze to Valhalla, Vitalia's expression was uncharacteristically full of distress.

She stared at the tall woman, pink garnet eyes trembling, and now realized the depths of her friend's concern for her. Turning slightly to look at Thor behind her, he nodded in agreement, the same unsettled stare on his face.

Valhalla didn't realize just how disturbed her friends had been since coming to her aid. Could this be due to the dark seidr magic that was expelled from her body? She never meant to scare them all, then again, she never expected to encounter both Loki and Kiara either. She promised to try to be more careful from now on, for everyone's sake.

Sighing, she nodded to Vitalia. "All right, I understand. But I can't guarantee they'll leave me be; they always end up finding *me*."

"I know, Heimdall and I will take extra precautions from now on when you are away from Asgard. We'll watch over you for as long as we are able. I promise, Valhalla." Vitalia bowed her head with assurance.

Smiling softly, she embraced her warmly, breathing in the wonderful scent of apples and strawberries about the valkyrie. Vitalia jolted lightly in surprise.

"I'm grateful for everything you've done for me. Truly." She released Vitalia. "How about I stay in Alf for a while. I'll be out of the way, and if you need me, you'll know exactly where to find me."

Vitalia blinked at Valhalla, then nodded, seemingly satisfied with the idea. "Very well, we'll visit you and pass on any messages when we can."

"Thank you, was there anything else you wished to speak to me about?"

"Yes, there's still one more thing." Vitalia turned around and stood beside Valhalla before the Well of Foresight.

She raised a hand and reached into the thick mist flowing in the well. Moving her hand in a circular motion, she caused the mist to follow. As she raised her hand, the mist swirled around, opening up at the center, and spilled over the rim of the well, flowing over the floor.

A thick, silver liquid rested within. Its surface rippled, an image slowly forming. After a moment, a city became visible. It was massive and shone with golden yellow stones. Lanterns covered in dragons and violet banners with a black raven at their centers hung from the walls. A grand, golden stone castle was just barely visible at the very heart of the city.

"What is this place?" Valhalla leaned in to better make out the image. She inspected the many roads and buildings, resembling the ones here in Asgard, longhouses, countrysides, and ritual houses. She also saw designs belonging to the Celnor race, who heavily worshiped the Gods of Asgard.

Knots of ravens, dragons, and other creatures decorated the many buildings. Soldiers donning dragon-decorated golden armor patrolled the streets. Children ran and played in the many gardens placed throughout the city. People walked from stall to stall, shopping, some with smiles on their faces, and others looking a bit more dour.

"This is the castle city of Hilliard. The capital of Veerence." Vitalia answered.

Valhalla gazed at her in surprise, having never seen a city of its size in Midgard. "Really?" She asked curiously.

Vitalia nodded and softly responded, "Your messenger, Sigurdr Sirgonson, has a letter for you from the High Queen of Veerence herself." Her smile became that of a slight frown. "Something . . . has happened to her heir."

"That can't be good news. Is this message waiting for me in Alf?"

"It is," Aura answered and stood up from a bench beside her mother, Vitalia.

Seeing the two next to each other, one wouldn't have guessed they were of the same blood. Aura didn't resemble her mother as Kiara did. Aura, instead, resembled her human father more than her Æsir mother.

"Sigurdr has the letter along with an oral message deemed too important to be trusted to paper. I believe Sigurdr is waiting inside the Red Dragon Tavern at the moment."

"All right, is there anything else I need to know?" Valhalla asked.

"No," Aura shook her head, "I think it's best if he tells you the rest. Her Grace, Queen Eilis Hilliard, is desperate to safeguard her family. Word of your deeds has reached her ears, which is why she sought you out. We'd like you to see her and aid her in any way you can. Do you feel up to traveling to Midgard tonight?"

Valhalla was taken aback. She hadn't expected they would send her on another errand so quickly. Though insisting to everyone that she was fine, she still felt weak from the ordeal with Loki. Her legs trembled under her nightgown.

She took a few folds of the fabric in hand and stared down at the floor, her lips curling into her mouth, not confident in her would be answer. She glanced up at Aura, seeing the wariness on her face.

Valhalla could always sleep in Alf and travel to Hilliard the next morning using her horn. Her strength would have undoubtedly returned by then. She sighed and raised her head, looking at everyone, and faked an assuring smile. "Yes, I should—"

"Wait a moment," Thor stepped forward with a stern, but suspicious look in his dark emerald eyes, "after Valhalla's encounter with my brother and sister earlier today, she should rest, at least for a few days."

"Thor, I understand your concern for Valhalla's wellbeing, but I wouldn't ask her to leave so soon if I didn't think this was important, and besides," Aura paused, turning her stare to Valhalla and her tone shifting to one of command, "once met with Sigurdr, she can rest the night there and start her travel the next day. I'm no fool and wouldn't ask more of her than I feel she is capable of. I just need her to receive the High Queen's message tonight. The rest will be up to Valhalla to decide." Aura gave a gentle nod to her.

"Besides, many of us believe the situation in Hilliard could grow dire if not handled swiftly. Rumors of what has become of the High Queen's heir have started to spread throughout the city. It won't be long until panic spreads by way of those of nobility who didn't favor the heir." Thora, one of the valkyries, added as she looked at Thor, and then to Valhalla, also nodding in confidence.

Thor's eyes narrowed at the valkyries, and small sparks of lightning danced around his fingers. Valhalla's heart dropped into her stomach. She knew Thor cared for her deeply and was generally quite sweet, though she had seen his temper get the best of him in the past. If he felt he was being talked down to or that his favorite siblings were in harm's way, his anger would reverberate across Asgard.

"What's your sudden interest in this mortal city?" Thor asked, his very words carrying a small electric current through the air. "As you all should know, it's forbidden for Æsir to interfere with their lives for any reason."

"We do have our reasons, Thor. Please, trust me. Valhalla's safety will always be our priority, and everything will be explained in due time." Vitalia eyed Thor, and even Valhalla could see something had made the valkyries anxious.

Thor stared back in silence with his lips pursed, not saying a word as he exhaled loudly through his nose, trying to calm himself. After a moment, he took a deep breath, and his posture relaxed. He hesitantly gestured for Vitalia to proceed.

Valhalla turned to him with a small smile and approached. Stopping before Thor, she gazed up at him and grasped his index and middle fingers. She once did this as a small child to help comfort him and to tell him all would be well. "Don't worry, Thor, I'll be careful. You'll see. Whatever the High Queen needs, I'm sure I can handle it." She stepped close to Thor, standing on her tiptoes now, and wrapped an arm around his neck, embracing him.

He leaned down a little to accept her embrace, but she still sensed his hesitation. After a moment, she felt his arm wrap around her waist, squeezing her tightly. "Please, *please* be safe, little sister. I couldn't bear losing you, too." Thor whispered to Valhalla.

"I will, dear brother." She whispered. Withdrawing her arm from around his neck, she slid her hand to his broad chest and gently put him at half an arm's length away.

He placed his hand over hers on his chest, holding on to it a little longer before letting go. His eyes glossed lightly, making her wince, but he forced a smile. Thor then allowed her to leave.

She returned to Vitalia and Aura. "I'll go change and head out immediately. If I don't see you tonight, sleep well, all of you. Please, don't be strangers." Valhalla smirked playfully.

The valkyries chuckled warmly with her and bowed their heads in farewell. Valhalla curtsied goodbye to both Vitalia and Aura. Turning back to Thor for a brief moment, she paused before making her exit and raised a hand to his shoulder.

She couldn't tell if he was blushing under his trimmed beard as he leaned down to her and gently closed his eyes. Tiptoeing again, she softly pressed her lips to his hairy cheek. "Until next we meet, dear brother. May Yggdrasil always bring you strength."

9

Valhalla

To My Second Home

Garbed in an ankle-length black dress with long sleeves and a crimson smokkr stretching to her knees, Valhalla fastened her cape to two brooches just below her collarbone. The two silver plates showcased the symbol of Ódin's house, the valknut, three interlocked triangles. Between them hung several rows of black, blue, and crimson beads which tapped gently against her chest. She laid the rest of her black leather armor out on her bed, making sure she had everything she would need.

Knots of fire decorated her light armor. She brushed a finger along one of the designs. The fact that someone sat down and was able to stitch in such beautiful, intricate details was amazing. The skills of dwarven smiths and leather workers were truly something to behold.

After one last look, she grabbed her belt and slid it around her waist, pulling the strap tight and buckling it closed. She placed her bracer over her left forearm and fiddled with the straps, readying it as best she could on her own. However, as she looked down to grab the right bracer, it was missing from the bed. Valhalla glanced left and right, sure she saw it before strapping the left bracer on.

It slid into view, held by a slender hand. She turned and, to her surprise, found Aura there. Valhalla chuckled with relief. "One of these days you'll have to teach me to move as silently as you."

"Sorry, your door was open. I hope you don't mind that I let myself in." Aura laughed apologetically, having not meant to come off as intrusive.

"Not at all, thank you." Valhalla took the bracer and began struggling with the straps.

"You know," Aura started, her tone jovial, "I find it easier to put on armor with the aid of a friend, and you just so happen to have one standing beside you."

Both Valhalla and Aura stared at each other for a moment, then laughed heartily. Valhalla held out her arm to Aura, a large grin on her face. "If you don't mind?"

"No, of course not. If you have to do this alone in the future, it helps to raise a leg and rest your forearm on your thigh. Then you hug the bracer against your stomach. It makes closing the straps much easier." Aura shrugged.

"Thank you again, Aura. Did you come to see me off?"

Aura nodded, "It's been a while since I last saw you. So, I thought we could talk on your way out." She closed the final strap of the bracer, allowing Valhalla to inspect it to be sure the fit was comfortable.

"Perfect." Valhalla flicked her wrist forward and leaned down to grab her longsword from the side of the bed, strapping it to her belt. "I suppose it has been three weeks since last we . . . Oh wait! Is it true, Ódin really did change his mind about Loki?" Valhalla asked with wide eyes.

Aura nodded in confirmation as she pointed toward the door. "Come, I'll tell you about the meeting."

The two walked out of the bedchamber. Valhalla waved a hand, snuffing out the fires within, and locked the door behind her. The night air was chilly, yet comfortable, but Aura seemed unusually tense. They walked toward the stairs leading down Marglod.

"After you passed out on the rainbow bridge, I asked Cascade and Anita to tend to you." Aura glanced at Valhalla as they made their way down the stairs. "Thank Yggdrasil's light, Queen Frigg glimpsed the near future and saw what would transpire on the bridge. I want you to know, it was difficult to pry her from your side, but she saw wisdom after I told her of your findings and convinced her to meet with Ódin and his council."

Valhalla took a nervous breath, unable to imagine what must've been going through everyone's minds when she passed out. All she could remember was casting fire at her friends, the whispering voices clawing at her mind, and Queen Frigg's calming voice.

She shook the memories away and exhaled steadily. "The meeting must've gone well if you were able to change their minds."

"It . . . went as well as you'd expect," Aura stated with a frustrated frown.

Valhalla's brows curved over her eyes with disappointment. "That bad?"

"Sort of, but the meeting would've been worse were it not for Thor, Tyr, Heimdall, Bragi, Balder, and Hodr. And you, of course." Aura smiled, confusing Valhalla.

"What do you mean by me? Wait, Tyr, Bragi, *and* Heimdall were there as well. He seldom leaves the Bifrost!"

Aura chuckled lightly. "Yes, *you.* Thanks to what Frigg purged from your body, it proved an undeniable case in favor of Loki, and—" Aura quickly shook her head, falling silent.

"What did she purge from my body?" Valhalla asked nervously.

"Darkness, a great deal of it." Aura suddenly whispered harshly to herself. "I was right beside you and missed it!"

Valhalla's eyes softened at her friend. "Aura?"

"Hm? Sorry, it's nothing. Also, I know, I too was surprised when Tyr and Bragi showed up, but after what they heard from Arianwen and Frigg, they came at the request of the All Mother." Aura shrugged. "You know how much Tyr respects his mother. Bragi just wanted to help you and Frigg however he could. Heimdall came because he believed his presence was necessary. He witnessed all that transpired on the bridge, possibly even saw more than the rest of us through his gifted sight. Balder was . . . *present,* as usual." Aura rolled her eyes.

A shiver ran down Valhalla's spine. His was a name that brought nothing but bad memories. It had been two years since that incident. If it weren't for Frigg wanting to check on Valhalla, he would've—Her blood went cold, and her posture retracted. At least she would be staying in Alf for a while.

"By Yggdrasil's shade! Valhalla, I'm sorry I—"

"No," Valhalla shook her head and smiled weakly, "it's all right. I promise." She paused, taking a breath and loosening her grip on the hilt of her sword. "Anyway, I noticed you didn't mention Vídar and Váli. Not allowed in council meetings yet?" She forced laughter, hoping to fool her friend into believing she was fine.

Vídar and Váli were the youngest sons of Ódin, but not Frigg's. Ódin had many partners throughout Asgard, all women, but most were not married to him.

Currently, there were seven, to be exact, but only six bore the King of Asgard's children. There was also Hermódur, who was adopted by the King and Queen shortly after Valhalla had been.

Tyr, Balder, Hodr, and Loki were the only ones Valhalla knew to be of Ódin and Frigg's union. The rest were of Ódin's other partners, or had been magically born like Heimdall. Frigg, being Ódins first wife, bore the title of Queen of Asgard and All Mother. She promised to love and care for all children without scorn or prejudice. She was the Goddess of Marriage and Motherhood after all.

Aura raised a skeptical brow to Valhalla, but nodded in understanding. "Pretty much. Thor and Tyr considered them to be far too young for the meeting, even if they're the same age as you. They simply can't match your maturity." Aura winked. "They, in fact, threw quite the fit during their seidr training today." She smirked playfully. "I heard their Master's hair had been completely burned off his head, even his eyebrows." Aura laughed.

Valhalla covered her mouth and snorted. "Oh no, the poor Æsir. That's too bad, though. I know how much those two want to be involved in their family's affairs." Her words quieted and trailed off as a thought entered her mind. She stopped and looked into Aura's eyes, her face serious. "What about—"

Aura's expression soured as she turned away, continuing toward the exit of Marglod. "If you're going to ask about Kiara, her fate is still undecided. Ódin has ordered her capture, by force should it come to that. Loki will require care when capturing him. I'm just—" She sighed, "I'm just not sure how long I . . . or, we can keep doing this." Aura looked back and up to Valhalla, her brows heavily curved over her monolid eyes. "It's been thirteen years, Valhalla. I don't—"

"Don't despair, Aura," Valhalla stated intently, causing Aura to blink with surprise. "I know you think you can't defeat them, but you can, especially with your friends by your side." Valhalla smiled with confidence.

Aura was speechless for a moment, then let out a burst of laughter, her eyes tearing lightly. "Thank you, Valla, I needed to hear that. Come on, we're almost to the stable."

Aura wiped the tears from her cheeks as the two continued to the stable. Valhalla was surprised to find how quiet the Asgardian night was. She was so used to hearing the cheers and celebrations of the city. She shrugged. Valhalla had no idea she was asleep for so long. Even the fireworks had ceased.

Valhalla, having been lost in thought, noticed how far ahead Aura had walked and so picked up her pace. They both soon arrived at the stable on the left side of Marglod. It was massive by Midgardian standards and quite cozy, decorated with a lot of greenery and a few flowers. Valhalla's friend, Anita, claimed the flowers gave the building some character. The space within was large enough to house each of the valkyries' clydesdales with plenty of room to rest.

They walked through the vine-covered entrance and spotted the mounts of the valkyries. The horses of various colored coats and manes slept peacefully in their pens, each space having been lightly decorated by the horse's respective rider.

Aura's Clydesdale, Bleikr, a gorgeous white steed whose coat and mane shimmered beautifully in the moonlight, slept in a pen coated in violet. A thick, clean sheet hung on the pen's wall with bright lavender Celnor knots stitched at its edges, depicting horses. The leather reins were fastened on a hook on the opposite side. At the center of the violet-painted wall before him was a white, sixteen-pointed star carved from stone. Even the bristles on the brushes lining the shelf were violet.

Valhalla chortled to herself. She wondered if he hated seeing that color every day. She noticed him groan on occasion when Aura brought him to the stables for rest. Snickering, she tried to hide it from Aura. The valkyrie simply eyed her with a raised brow in response.

Awkwardly clearing her throat, she turned her head away to the left. A fiery glow was coming from one of the pens. She took a couple of steps forward, passing several snoring clydesdales, and found Edan sleeping soundly within his pen, standing on all fours.

She smiled happily at finding he hadn't been injured. She walked to him, careful not to startle him awake. Standing beside him, she gently patted his neck. "Edan, can you wake up? I have to go to Alf." She whispered.

His eyelids fluttered lightly, stirring awake. He slowly opened his eyes, shining brightly in crimson, and gazed at her groggily. *Valla? Are you well? Should you even be up?* Edan's eyes squinted skeptically, as though unsure if she was really here or if she were a dream.

Valhalla nodded. "I am, thank you for asking, my friend, and yes. I'm well enough to stand and walk, and should be fine to ride, I promise." She brushed her fingers through his black fur, trying to ease his concerns. "The question is, are you well enough to travel? A message awaits me in Alf. It's urgent that I read it, or so I was told."

Is that so? One moment, then.

Stepping back, she allowed him room to shake himself awake. He twisted his head from side to side, then bobbed it up and down. She watched his fiery mane flap against his thick neck. Edan then tapped his hooves against the hay-filled ground, one by one, in an attempt to stretch.

Once finished, he looked at her again, then nodded. *I'm ready.*

She grinned in thanks and turned to his saddle, hanging on the pen's wall behind her. Grabbing it, she stopped for a moment, realizing how barren his pen was compared to the other horses.

When she was much younger, she wanted to decorate the pen with flowers; however, Edan was adamant that his pen remain the way it was. He was especially against a heavy coating of flora as the pollen caused him miserable sneezing fits. She sighed with disappointment, but respected his wishes, given he was the one who would spend most of his time here.

Valhalla smirked with a light shrug and turned around to slide the dark crimson saddle onto his back. She adjusted the blanket beneath the saddle, making sure it didn't bunch, and gently tightened the cinches over Edan's stomach.

After double-checking that everything had been set correctly, she climbed up Edan, slid her feet into each stirrup, pulled the reins, and made her way out of the stable where Aura waited. Valhalla asked Edan to stop as her eyes met the valkyrie's curiously. "Tell me, this situation in Hilliard, how . . . bad is it?"

Aura took a deep breath before answering. "It's dire. If anything happens to the High Queen's heir, her daughter, it opens the gates for something to happen to her son, or even her youngest sister."

"Because either would be next in line for the throne?"

"Sort of . . . The passing of the crown can be a complicated matter, almost as complicated as Hilliard's history. As you might know, Valla, for several centuries, only women have been allowed to rule that city. The other castle cities have either passed the crown down to whoever was the oldest child of royal blood at the time, or allowed the children to pass it on to their siblings if they wished, forsaking their claim and the responsibilities that came with it."

Aura glanced away to the white cobblestone ground beneath them and held her chin. "For years, there has been . . . *tension* between upper society and Hilliard's ruling family. There has been tension within the family since the High Prince and Princess were born. Some of the noble houses have attempted to pit the siblings against each other, to force a change to the city." She shrugged, "What kind of change do they seek? I'm not sure, to be honest, but I don't really care. What I do care about is the potential for another great war to arise, brought about by their foolishness. The entire realm of Veerence will be engulfed in fire and blood, should this matter not be resolved quickly. And besides, I think my mother sympathizes with the High Queen."

"Because they both fear for their children?" Valhalla asked with softened eyes.

"Yes," Aura nodded in affirmation, "and . . ." She sighed as she hugged her arms, rubbing her biceps as a small frown formed on her face. "I'm going to be honest, Valhalla. I know . . . I know we aren't allowed to interfere with the affairs of other realms, but . . . I don't—I won't allow another war like those of Midgard's past if there's something we can do to prevent it. So many people died. Men, women, AND children. War knows no discrimination. And trust me when I say Hilliard has seen enough of war." She looked up, her eyes shining with determination.

"I can imagine. All right, I'll be sure to receive the message from Sigurdr tonight and will take a portal to Hilliard in the morning."

"Already made a decision, have we?" Aura asked with a knowing smirk.

"What can I say? Who am I to deny a mother's need for aid when it concerns her children's safety?" Valhalla responded with a challenging smirk, causing her friend to chuckle.

"All right then, sounds like a plan." She raised a hand to Valhalla, and the two clasped each other's wrists. "Please, take care, Valla."

"I will. Please hear my call should I need aid."

"You know we will." Aura released Valhalla and waved goodbye.

Valhalla gently kicked Edan's sides, signaling she was ready for their leave. He reared up on his back legs and stomped down hard, galloping onward to the rainbow bridge and further to the slowly spinning spherical golden hall of the Bifrost.

Once at the entrance to the hall, they came to a stop. She and Edan entered and greeted Heimdall. Bowing his head in return, he watched as they entered the swirling rainbow portal to Midgard.

10

Valhalla

The Town of Alf

Valhalla and Edan emerged into the realm of Midgard. She glanced back to the rainbow portal and watched as it burst into various tiny shards of light, disappearing as Edan's hooves met the green, grassy soil.

A chill air blew, sending a shiver down her body. She didn't expect it to still be so cold this far south in Veerence. Rubbing her hands together, she blew into them. A fiery hot glow appeared in her palms, her body temperature rising. Perhaps Ēostre's spring air hadn't yet reached Alf.

Shrugging, she looked ahead. Even though the night was dark and the moon was high, the people of Alf danced and sang with the energy of midday. Vibrant and jubilant were the people of this large town.

They were mostly former refugees from across the realm. For many, this was the first place they could be happy and safe in their lives. As far back as Valhalla knew, this town was free of hardship and war, persecution and discrimination. The people were able to be whoever they wished and to celebrate however they liked. Valhalla couldn't help but grin at the ceaseless festivities whenever she visited this place.

All right, let's head to the tavern so that you may rest. Edan stated bluntly, shaking his head with disinterest.

"Me? What about you?" Valhalla chuckled playfully.

You went from facing a komod Elder to combating, if we can even call it that, two Æsirs. Edan answered, shaking his fiery mane. *I think you've had enough excitement for one day.*

She let out a giggle and patted the side of his neck. "All right, all right. You win, but first, I want to meet with Eldira. I really should thank them for the ointment they gave me. It's been several weeks since that Frost Jotunn sprained my wrist, and their medicine did wonders."

Very well, but then rest, young lady. Edan glanced back at her with a sternness in his crimson eyes.

"Of course, Lord Edan, I would *never* go against your wishes." She said with a smirk and bowed exaggeratedly in her saddle.

They both shared a laugh as he began to enter the town. Alf was decorated for Ostara. Flowers wrapped around green garlands decorating the edges of turf homes and longhouses. Wreaths hung at the top of doorways, and bright petals decorated the ground, many now buried in the cold mud.

Valhalla always found happiness here, regardless of the happenings in the rest of the nine realms. The people had always been warm and inviting. Their homes were cozy and brought her comfort. This place felt more like a home to her than Asgard ever could, regardless of how welcoming Frigg and Aura tried to make her feel.

As she and Edan walked through Alf, basking in the fiery glow of the town, someone called out to her from far to her right. "Oi! Lady Red 'as returned."

The people about the surrounding area turned and grinned, raising their fists and horns in greeting. She smiled back and waved at everyone. Soon, a few of them approached to offer greetings.

"So how long will ya be in town for?"

"Maybe we can grab a drink together."

"As if she would spend time with you. You smell, brother!"

Valhalla and the people around all laughed. "I'm sorry, all, but I'm afraid this visit will be a short one. I'm only here to receive a message and will be leaving in the morning, but when I return, I'll be sure to make my stay much longer. I'll be working with Diamantina when I return."

A young girl of ten pushed through the small crowd, her smile beaming as she stretched out a fisted hand to Valhalla. "I'll hold ya to that, Red Lady."

The people laughed. The girl's grin was infectious. Valhalla stretched out a fisted hand to the little girl in return and tapped the back of her hand. "I'll see you all again when I return, and I'll be sure to visit you first, little one."

The group around her nodded and waved goodbye, giving her many well wishes as she and Edan continued their way. While walking the muddy road to the tavern, many more people approached to greet her and see how she was doing. She hadn't been gone for long, but seeing the people's smiling faces always warmed her heart. Valhalla truly missed this place and was glad to be staying for a while, at least until after her Hilliard task was complete.

After many greetings and farewells, Valhalla and Edan arrived at the tavern. She was taken aback at seeing how fervently the owner had decorated for Ostara, as the woman had never really been fond of flowers. The pollen gave her headaches. However, Valhalla let out a small chuckle as she remembered how it once took enough ale to hobble a dwarf just to get the owner to admit to their beauty.

The entryway leading into the tall, extravagant longhouse was lit by a lantern on either side of the door, blazing brightly. An iron crimson sign hung at the top right corner. On it was a depiction of a drake, two open wings, and four bent legs. The creature was encircled by the name of the massive five-floor building, reading The Red Dragon Tavern and Inn.

Before heading for the doorway, she looked to her left past the tavern to a large lake called Vatn. Her eyes followed the bank down toward the surrounding forest. There, shrouded heavily by the darkness of the woods around the town, was a turf house covered in all manner of flora from all over Veerence, with no sign of life in nor around it.

It seemed Eldira wasn't home, a shame really, as Valhalla was hoping to catch them with a quick greeting before leaving tomorrow. Valhalla shrugged, assuming the völvx, a prophetess and sorceress, was busy traversing the woods in search of herbs.

She hopped off Edan, cupped his chin in her hands, and gazed at him with a soft smile. "Why not go around back to the stable and rest, my friend. I'll come and get you tomorrow morning, all right?"

He tapped his nose gently against her cheek with a soft nicker. *Sounds good. Hopefully, Diamantina has found someone to properly clean the stables. It was just atrocious spending the night the last time we were here.* He sighed with disgust.

Valhalla chuckled and gave him an apologetic look as she scratched under his chin. "I know, again, I'm sorry about that. Maybe it'll be better this time."

I can't imagine it being any worse. Edan shook his head and bowed, wishing her goodnight. She waved farewell and watched as he disappeared behind the tavern for the night.

Valhalla then headed to the inn's entrance. Now, before the door, she took a deep breath, and wondered who she would find inside other than Sigurdr and Diamantina. If *he* were here, she wasn't sure what she would do. Her heart began to race. The man was known to be quite overprotective when it came to her safety, not unlike Thor. She wondered if Aura had told her lover about what happened to Valhalla earlier.

Her brows furrowed as she fiddled with one of her middle fingers.

Whatever happened, she was sure it would be fine. It wasn't like the time when she faced muggers in Flotnar; she was even able to walk away without even a bruise from the altercation. She quickly sighed with a heavy groan.

Valhalla quickly slapped her palms against her cheeks to snap her out of her dilemma. Releasing a short breath, she pushed the doors open and announced, "Drinks are on me tonight!"

11

Valhalla

A Letter from the High Queen

All the patrons turned to the doors to greet the generous newcomer. Upon seeing Valhalla, their eyes widened with joy, and cheers rang throughout the tavern with mugs raised.

Valhalla chuckled, her cheeks heating with excitement. After only taking a couple of steps inside, she stopped dead in her tracks. A familiar figure turned to her.

A broad man sat at the head of the table before her, dressed in black with a beige tunic beneath his leather coat. His one beautiful golden eye stared at her from beneath his messy, wavy, charcoal black mop of hair falling just past his shoulders. The corner of his lips twitched into a smirk as he slightly raised his mug to her in greeting.

Valhalla's breath caught in her throat, but she swiftly cleared it and crossed her arms over her chest. She flashed him a playful smirk. "Vardan," she greeted with an accidental shrill in her voice.

Just as Thor and Ódin, Vardan Loyalen had always been there for her. He had watched over her every time she stayed in Midgard, training her in unique fighting styles unknown to any in Veerence except him, and was the first to introduce her to her love of the sea.

He was Aura's mortal lover from Midgard and was one of the founders of Alf. Vardan had been alive since even before the creation of the black castle city of Svartr. He was now over five hundred years old, thanks to the golden apples of the Æsir, given to him by Aura herself. Vardan consumed at least one every year to keep his immortality and good health.

"Does Aura know you're fondling the tavern owner tonight?" Valhalla jabbed with a laugh.

The question caught Vardan by surprise just as he was in the middle of drinking his ale, causing him to choke. He gave her a stern glare once he stopped coughing. "That's not funny." Although he spoke Enskr like she did, he had an accent that was clear and brisk with clipped tones like most Oceanans.

Valhalla let out a weak and embarrassed chuckle, her cheeks glowing red. "Right, sorry." She uncrossed her arms, her fingers fidgeting, and realized she had made an error in her poor choice of words.

Vardan proudly shared his heart with two vastly different women, Aura of Asgard and Diamantina of Midgard, and they proudly shared their hearts with him. Both women were immortal warriors, strong, compassionate, kind, and even cared for one another.

Valhalla found their love to be inspirational, sometimes finding herself questioning if she could ever find something as real and pure as theirs. Her smile wavered slightly at the thought. Perhaps one day she might.

She approached Vardan and patted his left shoulder, apologizing, and leaned down to kiss him on the top of his head. Before she could step away to find the tavern owner, Vardan grabbed her wrist and turned her to face him. Worry shone in his one good eye. His right eye was scarred, blinded, and hidden under a black leather eye patch.

"Wait." He slid his hand down to her hand and brushed his thumb over the leather, fingerless gloves covering her knuckles. His gaze softened.

Her heart skipped a beat, suspicious that he knew of what happened to her in Asgard, but she chose to play innocent. She took his hand and forced a grin. "Is everything all right?"

"That depends," he chuckled softly, "are *you* well?"

She swallowed nervously, her mouth slowly drying. "O–Of course, why wouldn't I be?" Her innocent smile lightly wavered, having never been very adept at lying.

Vardan studied her carefully, his rugged jaw clenched and his grip firm. Her warmth faded at seeing his concern. He knew. She was sure of it. Licking and biting her dry lips, she met his eyes and held her breath. "Did . . . Did Aura—"

Interrupting her, he stood from his seat and wrapped his arms around her in a warm embrace. She blushed and released a sigh, hugging him in return. Valhalla rested her head on his broad shoulder, happy and taking comfort in the scent of the sea about his clothes. There was also something else, something she had never smelled before, but found it quite pleasant.

He gave her a tight squeeze, then slid his hands to her shoulders, placing her at half an arm's length in front of him. "I'm turning in for the night, but if you *ever* need to talk, just knock. I'm always free to listen to my little dragon." He tapped his forehead against hers, then kissed it gently. Letting her go, Vardan grabbed his mug off the table and took a quick swig of what remained inside, then headed to a staircase to retire for the night.

Valhalla watched as he made his way up the stairs. He stopped for a moment and glanced back at her, flashing a confident smile. She gave him one in return and waved goodnight. Vardan bowed his head farewell and disappeared beyond the ceiling.

She lingered a moment longer then returned to searching for the tavern owner. Valhalla glanced toward the counter and saw crowds of people before it. If the owner were around, she couldn't see her at all. So it was probably best to get closer. Carefully.

Walking toward the counter, she avoided the many drunk patrons who haphazardly spilled their drinks and food, and even dodged the occasional swinging fist.

Just as she reached the counter, yelling broke out over the already joyous hum filling the tavern. She glanced to her right and were it not for her reflexes, she would've slammed between a beast of a man and the bar. As she stepped back, the man flew past her, crashing into the counter, and toppled to the floor. His nose was heavily crooked, clearly broken as blood flowed down his round, chubby face. An uproar of laughter sounded from where the man had likely been before his sudden flight.

Seeing the situation had been resolved, Valhalla continued her search and cautiously stepped over the man lying unconscious on the ground. Reaching the end of the counter with a clear pathway into the kitchen, Valhalla peered inside, but the tavern owner was nowhere in sight.

She turned around to inspect the rest of the tavern, but couldn't see through the people crowding the floor. The search was growing just a little harder now.

As she continued her search, she took in the craftsmanship of the longhouse. Dragon ornamentation decorated the long hall, the details illuminated by the large stone fireplace in the back, and the many iron chandeliers hanging from the ceiling. Tables dotted the floor, built to accommodate both humans and dwarves.

This tavern was a wonder to behold. There weren't many places in Veerence so accommodating to non-humans. An air of relaxation came over her as she took in each lovingly detailed carving of the dragons flying about the walls.

"Welcome back, Lady Red."

Valhalla startled lightly, surprised at the familiar, lightly accented voice, and turned to find the petite tavern owner herself, Diamantina Athenan, emerging from the bright violet curtain of the kitchen. Diamantina was a kind but guarded woman, keeping nearly all of her past to herself. All Valhalla knew of the woman was that she was from a small island country near Ellinika and was once a member of the immortal Amazons. Very few even knew that much about the woman. She, like Vardan, was also one of the founders of Alf.

"Dia, there you are, I've been looking for you. How've you been?" Valhalla greeted her warmly.

Diamantina sighed from exhaustion, shrugging her shoulders nonchalantly with a grin, and took a few steps past the kitchen's entryway. "So, I hear drinks are on you." She said flatly, her teeth lightly gritted.

Valhalla snorted in nervous laughter. "Don't worry, I have enough crowns to set you for a while."

"You better have the crowns to set me for life." Diamantina pounded her fists on her hips, straightening her back, and scowled.

A long silence followed between them as the two stared each other down, unblinking. Valhalla straightened as well, planting her feet firmly and slowly drawing her hand to the hilt of her sword. After a long moment of quiet, the two suddenly burst into laughter, unable to keep up the charade.

"Oh come on, that's impossible!" Valhalla exclaimed.

Diamantina raised a hand to her ebony, shoulder-length hair and swiped a few loose strands away from her face, revealing her copper skin and dark brown eyes. "Aye, the benefit of being immortal." She chortled lightly.

Valhalla took a seat on a stool at the end of the counter as Diamantina approached. The petite woman walked past the counter. She wore a simple violet dress and had a leather apron over the top. Valhalla, even when seated, had to look down to meet her. The Amazon's stature was much shorter than her own, standing only at about four foot nine.

Diamantina hopped up on the stool next to Valhalla and placed an elbow on the counter, raising a hand to the tall red warrior. "Well, hand them over."

Valhalla chuckled playfully, giving in without a fight. "All right, all right, a promise is a promise." She reached into her belt and pulled out a simple azure coin purse stuffed with Veerecian currency, both crowns and an older currency that was becoming rarer and rarer to come across, barvs. She pulled on the thin white string, keeping the pouch closed, and pushed it open with only two fingers. Diving in, she pulled out forty gold crowns with ravens adorning their faces and handed them to Diamantina. "Here, this should be more than enough to last you a while. I also have this—" Sinking her fingers into her coin purse again, she pulled out a shimmering violet gem in the shape of a square, handing it to Diamantina. "Not long ago, Aura gave me this to give to you," Valhalla said with a wink. "She figured Vardan's crew was likely causing problems for your tavern, not paying their fair share for meals and bedding, and likely being rowdier than your average lot." She laughed knowingly.

Diamantina burst out with laughter. "I see, well, the dwarven ale and mead are almost out. This will be a perfect payment for the drinks." She took the shimmering gemstone and inspected it against the hanging firelight.

"Oh, and Dia?"

"Hmm?" Diamantina turned to Valhalla with a pleased smile.

"Something happened recently, requiring me to stay in Alf for some time once my current task is complete. I was just wondering, is there any work for me here? Something to keep me busy until I'm called elsewhere?"

"Of course, I could always use some help cleaning up the tavern once everyone has gone for the night. Some of my servers half-ass their duties when they think I'm not looking." Diamantina answered as she shoved the gold crowns and jewels into the pocket of her apron.

Valhalla bowed her head lightly. "Thank you, Dia."

"No need to thank me." Diamantina tapped her fingers rhythmically against the bar. "You know I'll always help you out, little sister. Now, what can I do for you this *lovely* evening?"

Valhalla giggled, happy to have so many good friends like Diamantina, Vardan, and the valkyries by her side. "I'm looking for a certain someone and hoped you'd know where I could find him."

"Oh? And who is this *someone*?"

"Sigurdr, I was told he bears a message for me."

"Oh him, yes, actually." Diamantina pointed with her thumb toward the back of the tavern, to an alcove by the massive stone fireplace. "He's at his usual table."

There, through the crowd of patrons in the flickering light of the fire, a dwarf draped in violet and ebony garments sat alone at a table. His long, curly, orange-red hair, adorned with a few braids, fell over his stocky shoulders. His legs rested, crossed on the tabletop. He chugged back what looked to be his third mug of brew, judging by the two empty flagons lying on their sides.

"He ordered his meal a while ago, but didn't want me to bring it out until after you'd arrived."

Valhalla turned to Diamantina, pleased. "Thank you, Dia, can I have a bowl of your bear soup? I've been dying for that recently." Her expression shone with hunger. Diamantina's bear-made meals were a favorite of Valhalla's ever since she had first traveled to Alf. It was a creamy soup with chopped vegetables and golden potatoes that melted in your mouth.

"One plate of boar meat and one bowl of bear soup coming right up." Diamantina nodded, blushing, and hopped off the stool, disappearing into her kitchen behind the counter. She loved compliments, especially those aimed at her cooking, even though she would never admit it.

Valhalla's belly rumbled with excitement. Gazing back at Sigurdr, who made himself busy chugging the contents of his mug, she noticed the way to him was crowded, but manageable. She hurried over to the dwarf, squeezing through the drunken patrons who sang and danced without a care. Valhalla couldn't help but feel warmed by their revelry.

Once through, she was able to see the ornamentation on the dwarf's garments unobscured. Sigurdr was adorned with amethyst and black onyx gemstones, marking him proudly as a member of the Amethyst Sun Clan of Nidavellir. Even the leatherwork had chiseled dwarven runes throughout, surrounded by poised griffons guarding a stylized rune of the sun. His cloak, which protected him from turning to stone under the sun's light, was draped over his shoulders, the fabric's edges bedazzled with many gems and metals.

Although not one of the founders of Alf himself, Sigurdr's grandfather had been. His family was a part of the town even before its inception, traveling around Veerence trying to rescue dragons, elves, and dwarves from capture and enslavement. Valhalla wished Veerence's history had been as pleasant as the lands were beautiful, but it seemed no matter where you were from, bloodshed and death were a commonality shared in everyone's past.

Once Valhalla reached Sigurdr, she greeted him with a warm smile. But before she could even open her mouth, he grunted impatiently. "Ye're late." He spoke with an accent very similar to that of the Dothorian-born folk who lived far to the northeast of Alf.

Valhalla's spirits diminished as she sighed, having hoped for a warmer welcome, though she expected as much. "Well, hello to you, too." She said as she slumped down at the table, its size more suited to accommodate those of dwarven height instead of one as tall as her. She stretched her legs out while shifting and forcing herself into the ill-suited chair. "Excuse me, I was preoccupied with an ill-timed surprise engagement with a god . . . or two." Valhalla turned away, her nerves still raw from the encounter with Loki and Kiara.

Sigurdr immediately placed the mug on the table, concern filling his amethyst eyes as he inspected her up and down. "Loki and that Valkyrie again?"

She took a moment before meeting his gaze again and nodded, chest twisting still. Noticing the rolled-up piece of parchment near the edge of the table, she turned her chair toward him and pointed, ready to change the subject. "Is that for me?"

He nodded as he picked it up and held it out to her. "Aye, it's from the High Queen of Veerence, if ye can believe it."

"Veerence? So she rules the whole country, not just Hilliard?"

"How have ye lived here for so long and not know that?" Sigurdr snorted and eyed her with a raised brow.

Valhalla shrugged, having never paid any attention to the going-ons in Veerence politics and high society. "Honestly, when you find yourself running errands throughout the nine realms, it's hard to keep up with who rules what region. Besides, with King Ódin being the All Father, and having spoken with gods and Æsir, keeping up with Midgards ever changing royalty feels as necessary as knowing the names of every blacksmith's apprentice in Nidavellir."

She gazed down at the parchment and began inspecting it. The paper was unusually white and clean, bound by a silver ribbon, and sealed by a purple wax bearing a raven insignia. Its wings were spread wide with a sixteen-pointed star above its head and a pointed crown below its feet, and was surrounded by a laurel on each side of the creature.

Valhalla squinted with curiosity, then glanced back to Sigurdr. "I was told two silver guards came to deliver the message, but by any chance, did the High Queen—"

Sigurdr shook his head as he grabbed his mug, smelling its honey and berry contents. "No. Just two of the High Queen's royal guards. They found me while I was on the road here—"

Valhalla blinked at him with surprise. "Wait, you took the surface road instead of the tunnel?" The tunnel had been specifically built to safeguard those who had been, in the past, hunted by humans as they traveled from Nidavellir to the Midgard entrance near Alf. It was constructed shortly after the town's inception hundreds of years ago.

Sigurdr chuckled at her bemusement. "Aye, Berlena refused to enter the tunnel. I'm not sure why. I assume she just wanted to stretch her wings."

Valhalla's face lit up. "Awe, you brought your griffon?" She rested her chin on the palms of her hands, beaming.

He laughed softly. "Aye aye. She threw a fit the last time I came without her, so I brought her along. Good thing too, made the trip much faster than the iron carriage. She's a lovely creature, but the surest way to death is to piss off a griffon. Anyway, we landed on one of those crossroads. That's when the silver guards found me and gave me both messages."

"Both? What's the other message?"

"They said ye should read that first before I give ye the verbal one."

Valhalla nodded and pulled the wax from the parchment, slipping the ribbon off. She unrolled the letter and began to read.

Dear Lady Red, whoever you may be, I am the High Queen of Hilliard and Veerence, Eilis Hilliard. Something terrible has happened to my family, and I find myself in need of your aid. I've heard that you pride yourself on helping those in need, and I am in need. It's urgent that you come to Hilliard as soon as possible.

Please, I fear my son's life and the life of my sisters may be taken from me, or I from them.

Valhalla flipped the paper over, inspecting to see if there was more, surprised at how small the message was, and how little information was given. She raised a brow and placed a hand on the back of her neck, unsure of what to make of the situation.

"It doesn't say much, just to come to Hilliard as soon as possible. What's the second message?"

Sigurdr nodded, but before he could answer, Diamantina appeared with their meals and drinks. "Here you go, you two. One bear soup with a honey berry mead for Valla. And one plate of boar meat and a golden ale for Sigurdr."

Diamantina set both meals and drinks down on the table and snickered as Sigurdr's face lit up with excitement. His lips stretched from ear to ear under his neatly groomed beard and mustache, eyeing the two boar legs, large thigh, and a mountain of mashed potatoes drowning in gravy. "Now this is what I need. Ye know, I always say—"

"A happy dwarf is a dwarf with a belly filled with food." Both Valhalla and Diamantina interrupted.

The two women glanced at each other and burst into laughter. He narrowed his eyes in annoyance, and his cheeks flushed brightly pink.

Their laughter soon died down, wiping the tears from their cheeks. "Well, enjoy your meals, you two. If you need anything else, don't hesitate to ask." Diamantina winked and as she turned to return to the counter, Valhalla tapped a hand on the petite woman's muscular arm.

"Dia, have you seen Eldira recently? I wanted to thank them for the ointment they gave me the last time I was here."

Diamantina shook her head. "Sorry, the völvx is out traversing the forest for herbs. I told them it was too late to be traipsing about in the forest alone, but they were obstinate. When they come back, I'll send them your way."

"No, that's all right. Just give Eldira my thanks. I'll likely have already gone by the time they return." Valhalla smiled in thanks.

Diamantina nodded and patted Valhalla's back in farewell. Valhalla watched as she made her way back to the counter, taking a mouthful of the soup. On her way, a drunk man grabbed Diamantina's arm in one hand as the other found its way to her ass, and grinned sloppily. Valhalla's eyes widened, knowing what would come next.

Sigurdr chuckled. Without a moment's hesitation, Diamantina seized the man by his brightly colored hair and kneed him hard in the stomach. As he let out a loud groan and slumped to the floor, the surrounding patrons roared in laughter. Diamantina then continued on her way and wiped her hands on her apron.

Valhalla snorted loudly and quickly covered her mouth, nearly spitting out her food. She turned back around in her seat and continued eating.

Sigurdr cleared his throat to call her attention, his mouth stuffed with meat. "There'sh an unshettling rumor goin' around that the High Princessh hash been shlain. There'sh terrible talk comin' from the highborn circle . . . what did they coll it? Noblesh Perch? Anyway, no one hash sheen nor heard from the Princessh in weeksh."

Valhalla's brows twitched at the news. "That's quite a rumor, but you shouldn't talk with your mouth full. I can barely understand you." She said, unnerved.

"Suppose yer right." Sigurdr swallowed and wiped his lips of grease with the back of his hand. "From what the silver guards said, the High Queen needs someone to pose as her daughter, to draw out those after the High Princess's life."

Valhalla nodded in understanding. "All right. I'll leave tomorrow morning after the sun breaks the sky."

The two scarfed down the remainder of their meals in silence and washed it down with their drinks. Sigurdr was the first to stand and grabbed hold of his intricate, amethyst decorated silver halberd, which he had named Brihigir. The weapon was hidden behind a square wooden pillar, and he leaned it against his shoulder. "Ye be careful, there feels to be dark forces at work here."

Valhalla agreed and stood up. She reached out a hand, and the two grasped each other's wrists. They clapped hands with their free arms and bowed in farewell. Releasing, Sigurdr walked past her and made his way out the tavern's exit to rest below ground.

Valhalla gathered the empty dishes and stacked them together, lifting them off the table. The tavern had grown quite rowdy during her conversation with Sigurdr.

She danced past the drunken patrons, now singing and dancing themselves into quite the stupor. As she reached the counter, she found Diamantina vigorously washing dishes in a wooden basin, cursing angrily under her breath as she scrubbed.

The Amazon glanced up and, spotting Valhalla, smiled warmly. She returned it and handed her the dishes. Diamantina took them and dropped them into her basin.

"Need anything else for the night?"

Valhalla gently shook her head. "No, I'm going to turn in, I'm . . . well, pretty tired from my last task. Facing an Elder dragon is no easy feat after all." She chuckled softly, hoping Diamantina wouldn't read further into it.

Diamantina's gaze softened lightly with concern. "All right, if you promise you're well, then who am I to pry? Goodnight, Valhalla. I'll come check on you once the tavern has emptied."

Her chest tightened. "You . . . You've been told what happened, too, haven't you?"

Diamantina cocked her head to the side, a brow raised. "Of course, you know Aura always informs us of your adventures. Please," her face grew stern, "don't ever lie to us about how you're feeling or what has happened. I know you don't like to worry us. Trust me, I'm the same way, but we care for you. We love you, and we just wish to know that you're well. We'll always be there to safeguard you if need be, just as you would for us. Don't ever forget that, little sister." Diamantina's face softened once more, a twinkle of warmth in her dark brown eyes.

Valhalla's pulse quickened. She looked down at her hands and squeezed them tightly. The words were familiar, the same she had heard spoken before, but by another who was no longer with her.

She closed her eyes and bowed in understanding. "That's fair, I'll try to keep that in mind, big sister." Valhalla forced a smile for Diamantina, who met it with acceptance.

"Now go rest. I'll have breakfast ready for you before you depart tomorrow."

Valhalla smirked bashfully. "Thank you, Dia. Night."

"Night, my Crimson Amazon."

Bowing her head in farewell, she walked to the stairs and headed up.

Valhalla

Noise was Better than Silence

Valhalla's room was on the fifth floor of the longhouse, which turned out to be quite the climb, though she didn't mind the exercise. It gave her a short time to be alone, the first moment truly to herself since the dark seidr overcame her in Asgard. Besides, it gave her a chance to admire the carvings of Celnor knot dragons decorating the halls and stairways along the way.

Like the mural in the Hall of Valkyries, the carvings told a story. These told of the founding of Alf. They depicted how Vardan fought against the hunters who had imprisoned the dwarves and Diamantina, freeing a young drake before riding it into battle, slaying the hunters with her chakrams.

Other stories were depicted as well, though without firsthand experience from one who was there, it was hard to grasp the intricacies of what really took place. Valhalla had asked both Diamantina and Vardan what happened several times, but they both gave her the same answer, preferring the stories to remain where they belonged, in the past.

She pursed her lips in frustration. The memories were likely painful, and she understood their reservations; however, she just couldn't help but be intrigued. She sighed heavily and continued.

Upon reaching the final floor of the building, she headed toward her room at the back of the hall. She stopped at her door and glanced at Vardan's room across from hers. His door hung open an inch. Flickering lights glowed from within. She carefully tiptoed over and peeked inside.

Vardan sat resting on his bed, reading the letters scattered about him. She scanned his bedside. His eyepatch and recently lit pipe laid on the nightstand, along with his one and a half handed longsword with falcons flying about the guard, he named Sundfoerr, leaned against it. Two daggers in completely different designs rested near the hilt of the sword, one azure and the other violet.

"Can I help you, Valla?"

Valhalla startled back, hitting her elbow against the doorframe. "No! I'm sorry if I'm intruding. I noticed the door was open."

Vardan laughed as he set the letters down and moved to the edge of the bed. His coat and tunic had been folded and set aside. The candlelight danced over his muscular body. Small scars covered his amber-touched tawny skin, the largest of which was a scar over his right eye, stretching from the top of his forehead to the edge of his rugged jaw.

Wrapping around each of his biceps were two black Celnor knots, the left depicting horses and the right, blue whales. He once explained that the tattoos represented the brothers he had lost many, many years ago.

"Diamantina was in here a little while ago, but was needed downstairs. She should be at the bar if you're looking for her." Valhalla shook her head with a small smile, but Vardan just sighed. "All right, are you heading to bed? I heard you had quite the day." He laughed softly.

Valhalla's expression turned to a frown, and her brows knitted together. "A-Aye . . ."

Vardan glanced up to her, seeing the timidness in her posture. Exhaling, he stretched out a hand to her. "Come here."

She interlocked her fingers tightly and lowered her head. Her heart quickened. Valhalla walked over to him and placed her hands on his palm. Vardan rested his other hand on top of hers in a soft caress. The warmth of his hands was soothing.

"Now look at me."

Heat filled her cheeks, and she slowly met his eyes. The left shined with a bright golden hue in the light of the fires. The right had paled since losing its sight and now had a silver sheen. His smile was as friendly as the day she met him.

"I know you don't like it when we worry, but we can't help it. We love and care for you, and will *always* worry about you. Please don't misunderstand, it isn't because we don't have faith, far from it actually." Vardan cocked his head to the side, his hair sliding off his shoulders and his lips stretched wide and proud. "You've grown so much since you were that small girl I met so long ago. You've become quite the warrior and are one of the strongest people I know. You're perfectly capable of taking care of yourself, but you needn't walk this path alone. Please, know that there are many, myself included, ready to come to your aid should you ever need it. Do you understand me, my Crimson Flame?"

Valhalla's pink garnet eyes softened as she nodded. "Yes. I—" She hesitated for a moment. It was as if her mother lived on in all of her friends. Valhalla shook the thought away and gazed at Vardan. "Diamantina said something similar."

"Ah, you already ran into her, and I see my Little Amazon told you too, did she?" Valhalla nodded. Vardan raised a hand to her cheek, cupping it gently. "Then you know how we feel. Please, don't hide yourself or your troubles away from us, that only makes us worry more, all right?"

Valhalla's eyes slowly began to sting, tears rising to the surface, and she closed her eyes. She touched his hand on her cheek "I-I know . . . because of what happened back then, I distanced myself from you all. I didn't mean to. I never realized how much it affected me, I suppose . . . I still don't." She opened her eyes and looked at Vardan again, seeing his smile fade and lips tremble. His brows furrowed as though trying to control his anger.

She knew how angry he got at the mention of *him*. For what he did to her. Or tried to. She should know better than to hide herself, her feelings, from someone who had watched over Valhalla since she was a child. Vardan had been like a second father to her. With lips closed, she silently apologized to him.

"I'll try to do better, I promise."

"I'll hold you to that promise. Now, go to sleep. You deserve some rest." Vardan said.

She thanked him and slid away. Valhalla walked toward the exit and paused in the doorway. Resting a hand on the door, she turned around to Vardan. "I have to wake early and will be traveling to Hilliard. Something is, or has, happened to the royal family, and the High Queen requested my aid. I thought you'd want to know."

Vardan blinked at her, surprised. "Hilliard? What kind of trouble is it? Do you want me to come with you?" He asked quickly, his concern clear in his tone.

Valhalla smiled in appreciation, but gently shook her head. "Thank you, but no, that's quite all right. I'm sure the High Queen doesn't want me revealing what's going on, so I must respect her secrecy. Diamantina plans to make me breakfast before I leave. Please, eat with me and see me off. I'm sure I can handle this task myself." Confidence returned to her eyes. "You have a good night, Vardan."

He smiled, and his posture relaxed. "You as well." Vardan raised his right hand and pressed his index and middle fingers to his lips, blowing a kiss.

She replied in kind and exited, closing the door behind her. Spinning on her heels, she leaned against his door with a small frown. Valhalla apologized for keeping her heart closed off from him. Her oldest friend. She never meant to hurt him. She then sighed, troubled.

"I don't know. I didn't think discussing my feelings would be this difficult. Maybe if I sleep on it, it'll be easier in the morning." She whispered to herself.

Hopping off his door, she crossed the hall to her room. Opening the door, she was surprised to find her room brightly lit by many candles. Smiling and glad to not be welcomed by darkness, she silently thanked Diamantina.

She walked inside, closing the door behind her, and unbuckled her cape. Valhalla gazed about her room, wondering where to place her armor and cape. There was only a wooden desk and chair by her bed, so she placed the fabric and leather armor on the chair and then headed to her bed.

The mattress lay within a decorative wooden frame covered in carvings of dragons about its surface. She leaned down and placed her hands on the fur sheets, letting the soft bristles poke between her fingers. Pushing down on the mattress, it felt thicker than usual. Valhalla wondered if Diamantina restuffed her mattress with sturdier straw. Perhaps she would be sleeping comfortably tonight. She giggled to herself.

Standing, she unbuckled her longsword and belt from her waist, leaning the weapon against the desk. Flopping onto the bed, she basked in its softness with a beaming smile on her face. She then turned over, facing the window before the bed, and stared out to the bright stars dotting the dark sky.

Raising her hand in the air, she waved it once from left to right, snuffing out all but one of the candles in the room, leaving just enough light to dimly cover the place.

Questions began to swirl in her mind about the castle city. How bad were things in Hilliard? Would it be anything like Asgard, or worse? She cleared her head of the dreary thought. There would be plenty of time for worry tomorrow.

Valhalla took a deep breath, exhaled steadily, and closed her eyes. The town of Alf was still as lively now as when she arrived. The sounds of people singing tales and picking fights fill the air.

She chuckled to herself, finding the noise of the town soothing, preferring it to pure silence, and listened to the music playing nearby. Her pulse slowed and her body relaxed, giving in to her fatigue and letting sleep finally take her.

Part
2

13

High Prince

The High Prince's Lament

All was quiet in the golden city of Hilliard. The morning sun slowly crept over the massive exterior walls, which protected the citizens from outside threats. Ostara decorations lined the buildings and castle halls, filling Hilliard with the wonderful scent of spring flowers. The faint sound of sollerets marching against the cobblestones echoed through the castle halls and city streets.

The High Prince, Alistair Hilliard II, should've been resting, sleeping peacefully in his bed after having just celebrated his twenty-first day of birth. Instead, as was becoming more common with each passing day, solitude remained out of reach. Thanks to the Bedr Prael Law, he was forced against his will to bed any of the many noblewomen of the country whenever they sought him out, and last night was no exception.

The noblewoman was of an esteemed family from the castle city of Rjóðr, far to the East. The scent of sea salt and wine invaded his senses, causing his stomach to churn. Her curly, golden blonde hair fanned out across his bed, his pillows scattered across the floor. Her red skin shone in the rising sunlight, and her vibrant blue eyes glinted with hunger. She was a friend of his little sister, sent to remind him of the law and his place in Hilliard.

Alistair tirelessly thrust his pelvis against hers, panting and exhausted. She moaned with pleasure at every thrust. He took no delight in these encounters, and each time the law was invoked, a little piece of his soul was chipped away.

Forcing himself to kiss her neck and collarbone, Alistair hoped to hasten things along to be rid of her. She shrilly giggled against his ear as he struggled to keep what little composure he could muster. Bile crawled its way into his throat. Her sharp, painted fingernails dug deep and scraped across his scarred back.

He hated the law. Hated having to be subservient to the whims of noble women barking commands as though he were a trained dog. Alistair's mother managed to push back the age at which the law could be enforced from thirteen springs to sixteen, in an effort to spare her son for as long as she could. Unfortunately, the vultures circled him until his sixteenth nameday, taunting him, ready and waiting for that not-so-special day. A war spared him for a short time longer, buying him one more year before his living nightmare became real.

Four years had passed since that first time. He hoped that he would grow numb to these encounters, that the revulsion and true powerlessness of being violated so thoroughly would lessen with time. That wasn't the case. Each time was just as terrible as the first.

The noblewoman began her endeavor the day before, pawing at him, tormenting him with the disgusting act that would commence upon nightfall. Once the act had started, she barely allowed him a moment of reprieve. Between sessions of ecstasy, she commanded massages from head to toe until he was able to go for another round.

Exhaustion was setting in. His eyelids were heavy, and his limbs were weak from the effort of holding his body up. Alistair pushed himself upward, desperately trying to catch his breath and wanting nothing more than to be rid of the woman.

His head hung low, eyes closed. He startled as her fingers snaked their way up his muscular arms to his neck, and felt them entangle in his long, dark brown hair. "Don't stop, High Prince Alistair. We're *finally* getting to the best part." Her words dripped with lust in a heavy Leodan accent.

The woman locked her arms around Alistair's neck, trying to force him back down to her. As he resisted, she pulled herself up and pressed her bright red lips against his. Her vile tongue wormed its way into his mouth, tasting of tobacco.

He managed to jerk himself away from her venomous mouth. His anger rose, filling him with renewed energy. He wanted to lift her off his bed and throw her out of his room, barring the door so he could be alone, but knew better than to act on the urge. Instead, he thrusted harder than he had all night. She let out a loud cry of pleasure, locking her legs around his hips, and looked to be lost in the moment.

"Ah! Yes, harder. Make me feel it." She latched herself tightly around his neck. "Make it hurt!" Her head fell back, and her back arched high.

Alistair's spine shivered as the woman revealed her destined desire. With her incessant demand and control over him, her constant mocking and belittling, it was all to make him angry enough to pleasure her a certain way. Alistair's blood boiled. He thrusted as hard as he could, her screams deafeningly loud in his ear. Hopefully, if he thrust hard enough, maybe the woman would pass out and finally give him some peace.

It was the same almost every day. His hateful little sister sent her friends to his bedchamber to torment him. If they were unavailable, she would seek out someone who would order him around as though he were nothing more than a prostitute, desperately doing what they must to survive.

Alistair's anger finally peaked. Unable to take any more, he clenched his crimson silk sheets in his trembling fists and punched his mattress. Alistair lifted himself high, grabbed her arms, and pushed them away. She fell back onto the bed with wide, confused eyes. Grabbing her legs, he shoved them out of his way, sliding himself to the edge of his bed. He leaned down, grabbed his orange silk robe, and stood, slipping the garment on.

Before he could even tie the cincture around his waist, the noblewoman, whatever her name was, he hadn't bothered to learn it, grabbed one of his sleeves and yanked him back to her. Her blue eyes seethed with rage. "I'm not done!"

"Well I am!" Alistair retorted.

"Listen you whore! The law—"

Alistair pulled himself free of her clawed grip and strode to his bathing chamber, intent on locking himself away until she left in frustration. This had worked before, but his shoulders trembled at the memories of the women on the other side screaming and punching at the door. He quickly swallowed the terrible memory and hoped the woman would just give up and leave him be.

He grabbed hold of the handle and pulled the door open, and froze. There, he was greeted by a familiar, yet worried face. "Shu Yen?" Alistair's mouth fell open in bewilderment. Had she been waiting in his bath chamber all night?

His memory of the evening was a blur. He remembered finishing his bath as Shu Yen tidied up, readying himself to sleep when a knock sounded at his door.

Alistair knew he shouldn't have gone to see who it was, knowing full well it was likely to be the woman who had tormented him all day with promises of the night to come. It could've been one of his Queensguard reporting a threat just as easily as the noblewoman here screaming for him to return to bed. For better or worse, it had been his duty to answer, and so he had little choice in the matter. Now Alistair hoped it was a threat, because at this point, that probably would've been easier to contend with than the frustrated noblewoman.

She had barged in and demanded he undress her. The memory of last night was clearing for Alistair now. The noblewoman noticed Daenery and Aegos lying by his bed, and when they growled, she ordered them to be removed. It all happened so fast, he must've forgotten Shu Yen was still there.

His large black, groenendael dogs never liked being far from him, unless otherwise entrusted to a trustworthy friend. One of them walked up and stood before him, the creature's tail wagging beside her. The other sat behind his attendant. Both were visibly eager to greet their companion.

Shu Yen's eyebrows curved heavily over her dark brown monolid eyes. Dark circles marked her eyelids, and she looked to be struggling to keep herself awake. "Shu Yen—"

"Your Grace! Are you even listening to me? I demand you return to bed this instant!"

Alistair's hands flew to his ears and pressed firmly to the sides of his head. He was tired. Rageful. And was just so done with all of this. He cursed inwardly at the woman, wishing desperately that the Leodan would just go away.

He felt a pair of soft hands cover his, interrupting his thoughts, and they gently lowered his hands to his sides. Opening his eyes, Shu Yen's stern gaze was upon him.

"Alistair," she whispered, "I can help. Tell me to get rid of her." She flashed a small smirk just for him to see. "It's my duty as your attendant to follow your command, regardless of the terms of the Bedr Prael. Besides, judging from what I heard last night, I'm sure you've done enough to satisfy the law and deserve a reprieve."

Her words and Weidan accent calmed him lightly. Unique in this part of the world, her vowels were slightly elongated, and shorter words came punctuated by a staccato rhythm. It was fainter now, having lessened over the years, but still present.

"Shu Yen, I—"

"Alistair, I'll NOT stand for this!" The noblewoman bellowed from the bed.

Alistair's dogs, hearing her shout, jumped out of the bathing chamber and growled fiercely, positioning themselves between her and Alistair.

"Look at me, Alistair." He looked down at Shu Yen, standing barely five foot five. "I'm your friend, but I'm also a *highly* skilled attendant. I can deal with her, but I need you to tell me to do so."

Alistair's eyes wavered with exhaustion. He looked away and gently squeezed her hands in thanks, then shuffled past her, entering the bathing chamber. "Please, get rid of her for me."

Shu Yen nodded and walked into his bedchamber. "Of course, my High Prince. She'll be gone before you finish your bath."

Alistair jolted with surprise and turned around. "Wait, you got a bath ready for me?" Looking back, Shu Yen had already closed the door.

He stared at the wooden surface, dumbfounded. She was stuck in the bathing chamber all night, listening to the woman's barking moans and cries, and she still took the time to care for him?

Shu Yen always took care of him, even more so than her responsibilities required. Alistair was her High Prince, supposed protector of this country, but he couldn't even take care of himself.

Almost every day was the same. Be strong. Protect the people by day and play the whore at night. Take it all in stride. Learn to enjoy it. Don't show weakness. Never flinch. Never speak out of turn. Remember your place.

Alistair's heart ached. He raised a hand to his chest, feeling for his late father's ring.

He instantly realized that in all the chaos, he had forgotten to grab it as he got out of bed. His sight blurred, and tears streamed down his cheeks. He looked to the bathing waters. Steam rose as petals of cherry blossoms and lavender floated about its surface.

Alistair stepped toward the bath, stopping at the water's edge, and fell to his knees. He looked at himself in the water's reflection.

He was a child born of two races, a Hillian mother and a Vilzhenian father. The dark brown hair of his father's line fell loose and disheveled from his head. His build was tall and muscular, a trait common to those of the Hillian race.

Alistair's skin was of warm ivory with large splotches of gold, as if someone had permanently painted portions of his body at birth. The gold hue lined his jaw and coated his neck, continuing down beneath his robes. His gaze lowered, looking at the gold stretching across the backs of his hands and ending just over his knuckles, his fingers returning to warm ivory once more.

Folding his fingers inward, he looked back to his reflection in the water, seeing his father's Vilzhenian amber brown eyes looking back at him. His mother's beautiful, clear sapphire shade distinctly marked the iris of his right eye just as a dark birthmark would over snow-white skin.

Alistair believed his sister to be lucky in this regard. Her appearance was fully Hillian, with the exception of her height, standing much shorter than the average. High society looked at her as though she were the perfect Hillian, either ignorant of or disregarding by choice, her callous, crude, and disrespectful nature. The same high society looked at him either dismissively or with open disgust for the apparent mixing of races in his being, as though he could single-handedly ruin their *perfect* society.

The water lightly rippled as his tears met its surface. His throat tightened, and his chest ached. Alistair's breath was shallow. He crossed his arms on the edge of the bath and lay his head down, silently crying for what little peace he had left.

Hilliard, the Castle City of Gold

A rainbow portal sparked to life before a town nestled just outside of one of the several grand gated entrances of the capital city of Hilliard. Out hopped Valhalla atop her companion Edan, and the portal dispersed just as quickly as it had appeared.

She jerked back on Edan's reins, startled by the sight of people scurrying about the main road. The few who had noticed her arrival eyed her curiously before continuing with their tasks. Many were busy decorating their homes and shops for Ostara.

Those not busy decorating instead tended to their fields, delivered barrels full of ale and mead, and went about their daily lives. Children ran and played nearby, wielding wooden swords and staves, pretending to ride toy wooden horses without a care. Valhalla smiled, watching them play as her thoughts drifted to memories of her childhood.

Valhalla, is everything all right? Edan asked.

"Yes," she returned to him, "just reminiscing for a moment."

Valhalla turned to the main road, which led to the city gates in the distance. Her gaze followed them upward, up to the brickwork above the gate's arch, all the way to the top of the outer wall. "Oh my, this . . . Hilliard is a pretty big city, huh?" She chuckled with astonishment.

Valhalla signaled Edan to proceed toward the wide open gates of the golden city, seeing many countryside homes and turf houses all about the town as they proceeded. Reaching the massive entrance, she guided Edan to the right gate door and placed a hand on the wooden surface, feeling the smooth craftsmanship. Dragons and ravens were carved onto the gate's face, flying about in the beautiful mural.

"Can you believe this Edan? It's incredible."

Edan chortled. *I can't believe you've never been here before.*

"You and me both," Valhalla replied with a chuckle.

She and Edan continued through the gates into Hilliard, careful not to bump into the people walking beside them who were eyeing the two with curiosity again. Looking away from the passersby, she was taken aback by the festivities before her in the massive city square.

Weidans danced in perfect harmony, draped in red and gold, and twirled crimson ribbons in celebration as they formed a circle in the square. Bells chimed and drums thrummed melodiously as crimson confetti filled the air. The people cheered in amazement as two papercraft serpent-like dragons entered the square in their own jubilant dance. They were decorated with colorful fabrics, had streaming paper manes, and short horns that twisted like tree branches above their heads.

"Oh my! I didn't know anyone here celebrated the Weidan Lunar New Year." Valhalla watched on in awe as colorful streamers flew overhead. The sweet aroma of baked goods filled the air, and both Weidans and Veerencians celebrated together.

When Valhalla stayed in Weida Long, to the North of Veerence, for a year learning tàijí from a friend of Vardan's, there had been a town near her Master's home celebrating the Lunar Festival for several days before she had to return home. Back then, Valhalla hadn't been allowed to leave the Master's home due to the ruler of the nearby towns' animosity toward Veerencians. For her protection, the Master and Vardan agreed that she should remain in the Weidan's home, as it was just outside of the town's border. Her heart swelled with longing for her Master and his greenery-filled home.

It's quite the surprise, that's for sure. Edan said.

"I'll say." Valhalla leaned down and patted his neck, laughing gleefully.

"Scuse me, miss, might we have a word?"

Valhalla startled lightly in her saddle and turned to her right. Two soldiers of Hilliard, a man and a woman, donning golden armor decorated with dragons, stood at her side. "Yes? Did I do something wrong?"

"Not at all miss, we just need ya to reveal what's under your cloak." Replied the man. "Need to be certain there's nothin' suspect underneath, is all."

Valhalla raised a hand to her cobalt blue cloak, a gift given to her by Diamantina before departing Alf. Dark blue fires decorated the end of the thick fabric. "Nothing like that, I assure you. It was rather cool this morning. In all the festivity, I forgot I had it on." She chuckled.

To avoid causing trouble, she did as the soldier asked and lifted the fabric on her right side, revealing her longsword hanging in its scabbard.

"That's quite the blade for such a young woman." The man exclaimed, now waiting for a response.

"It's only for my safety, I assure you. A woman traveling alone can't be too careful, as I'm sure your compatriot can attest to. She must be quite skilled with her own blade."

With a hearty laugh, the man responded, "Aye, quite right." Grinning, he looked up at her and nodded.

The woman cleared her throat. "Miss, your horse . . . it's—"

"Don't mind him, he's just a little shy around new people." Valhalla patted Edan's neck. "He's actually very sweet once you get to know him. His name's Edan."

The woman looked at her with confusion in her sapphire eyes. "That's not—"

"Is there a reason for your visit?" The man interjected, nudging the woman with his elbow and jolting her from her stare.

Valhalla shook her head. "No, not really. I heard of the grandeur of Hilliard and wanted to see it for myself, is all."

"A-Alright," the woman cleared her throat, "if ya follow this road here," she pointed behind her with a thumb, "there's an inn on the right-hand side of the road called The Violet Tulip Inn. Ya can't miss it."

"Thank you." Valhalla bowed her head graciously.

The gold soldiers pounded their fists against their chests and bowed to her in return. The soldiers then returned to their patrol, making their way around Valhalla and Edan. The woman continued to stare at them as the man glanced back and whispered to her.

Valhalla, perplexed, leaned down to Edan, pretending to comfort him. "What's that all about? Do you think they suspect us of anything?"

Edan chuckled playfully. *This isn't Asgard. If you meant to enter the city without drawing attention, arriving atop a flaming horse may not have been the best idea.*

Valhalla stared at him in bewilderment and then looked around the square. Even with all the commotion of the Festival, she spotted several people staring and pointing at her and Edan with large, curious smiles on their faces.

She groaned, cursing herself for not foreseeing the attention Edan would bring. Valhalla wondered if perhaps this was what spending too much time in Alf had brought her; lapses in judgment. She laughed with embarrassment, scratching the back of her head.

"Well, what's done is done. Come on, let's go check out that inn." Valhalla gently kicked Edan's sides. He continued to laugh as the two traveled along the path toward the inn.

15

Valhalla

Not All was Grand

ARRIVING AT THE INN, Valhalla was taken aback. Flowers of various purple hues surrounded the extravagant, tall longhouse. The cascade of lavender, lilac, periwinkle, violet, and plum filled her nostrils with a sweet scent. She spotted a bright purple sign hanging over the door. The words The Violet Tulip Inn were inscribed across the wooden surface, surrounded by, as the name suggested, violet tulips.

"No wonder the soldier said I couldn't miss it." Valhalla chuckled with amazement.

As she and Edan passed through the archway leading to the inn, Valhalla noticed a stable just to the right of the longhouse. "Here we are, you can wait there while I take care of things inside. How's that sound?"

Alright, but it better not smell as bad as Diamantina's stable. It was so undignified.

Edan neighed in an annoyed tone.

Valhalla chortled as she patted the side of his neck. "I doubt it. With how this place looks, it'll likely smell too flowery for your taste, but at least it won't stink." She laughed as they entered the stable.

The interior was spacious. Most of the pens were packed with horses, at least two within each. The horses stirred lightly, their posture timid, likely due to the flames flickering from Edan's mane, tail, and hooves. With a soft neigh from him, the horses seemed to calm.

"Well done, Edan." Valhalla glanced at her companion, "it wouldn't help us if the horses started to panic."

It's not their fault. It's in their nature to fear fire. They just needed to know I'm a friend.

The two scoured the stable for an empty pen. Finding one, Valhalla pointed Edan in its direction. As they approached the empty pen, Edan stopped and peered inside as Valhalla hopped off his back.

I suppose this'll do. At least I have a view of the road. Could serve me well to get an idea of the city and the people as they pass by.

"See, and you thought this was going to be a terrible experience." Valhalla giggled as her friend rolled his crimson eyes.

She scratched under his chin and raised his face to kiss the side of his snout, then led him into the pen. Valhalla looked out to the road, seeing the sun shining brightly on the cobblestones.

Wait, Edan sighed, *tie my rein on the post here.*

"Are you sure? You hate being tied down." Valhalla looked at him curiously while tilting her head.

Yes I know. It's to . . . play the part of a normal horse, as much as I'm able to at least. It also might serve to dissuade any thieves from trying to steal me. You saw those eyes on me, the vultures. It would be a shame if I had to burn something to the ground.

Valhalla chuckled in understanding. "Alright, alright. How about this?" She tied the leather reins to the post, but left enough slack so that he might free himself if the need arose. "There, that should look convincing to those passing by."

Now go on. Why not get some rest? Edan's eyes scanned her carefully. *We can meet the High Queen later today.*

"You sure? I'd hate to be asleep if you were in need." She said, a hint of worry in her tone.

Yes. I'll be fine. He chuckled as he nudged her away. *Now go. I'll be here if you need me.*

Valhalla smiled in thanks and patted the side of his neck, then turned to leave. As she exited, she stopped and noticed the eyes of a few passersby on her, whispering and pointing, seemingly in a mixture of amazement and curiosity.

She glanced around, a feeling of bashfulness coming over her as her cheeks heated up. At the moment, Valhalla was thankful; the people seemed more friendly than not.

Trying to ignore them, she continued on her way to the inn's entrance. As Valhalla drew close to the door, something lightly bumped into her right side. She felt something quickly slide into, then out of her belt, causing her to stumble back. Regaining her balance, Valhalla turned to see a young boy turning to run away from her. "Hey!"

He looked back with a confident smirk. "Whoa lady! Why don't ya watch where ya goin'!"

Valhalla lunged forward, reached out, and grabbed the back collar of his tattered vest. With a quick pull, she yanked him back to her.

His short, oily, ebony hair flew about his dirty face while his sapphire eyes looked up at her with a brief flash of alarm. He glanced over his shoulder and briefly flailed his arms, trying to free himself, and stopped, his apparent fear now masked by annoyance. "Hey, what are ya—"

"Return the bag of crowns you took from me." Valhalla met the boy's eyes, her expression still and stern.

The boy cleared his throat, composing himself. "What!? I ain't steal nothin'! Let me go." He flailed his arm again, fighting her grasp in vain.

Valhalla raised her hand and tightened her grip on his collar. She presented her free hand, palm up, and waited silently for her bag to be returned. The boy tried to feign ignorance a moment longer before sighing with defeat. He reached into his trouser pocket and returned the bag of crowns.

She released his collar and spun him around to face her. Valhalla knelt down to look the boy in the eye, raised the bag a bit, and reached inside. After a moment, she pulled her hand from the bag, slid her coin purse back into her belt, and took the boy's hand, placing twenty gold crowns on his palms.

As she did, the boy's eyes shot wide, a dumbfounded look upon his face. He looked up at her with his mouth agape. With a soft smile, Valhalla lightly patted him on the shoulder. "Go feed your family, young one."

He took a deep breath, and tears rose in his eyes, then instantly bowed his head. "Thank ya lady!"

With that, he ran past Valhalla in the direction he had come from. She watched as he disappeared into a nearby alley. Valhalla walked to the alley and poked her head around the corner, wanting to watch over the boy a moment longer.

A sudden pungent odor crashed into her nostrils like a ton of bricks. The splattering of the contents of chamber pots against the cobblestones caused her to wince. Homeless men, women, and children rested by the sides of buildings, looking to be malnourished, and as though they hadn't bathed in quite some time. Some begged for money from the soon-to-be patrons of bruised prostitutes hanging close together at the opposite end of the alleyway.

A slow chill ran up Valhalla's spine as she watched. It seemed Hilliard wasn't quite as grand as it appeared to be from the sights of the main road. At least the people of Asgard didn't turn a blind eye to those in need. These people seemed almost forgotten. She suspected this wouldn't be the last surprise awaiting her in her time in this city.

Shaking her head, Valhalla turned back and continued to the inn's entrance. She welcomed the return of the scent of flowers about the inn. Valhalla walked under an archway with bright purple wisterias hanging from the wood, letting her fingers brush against the soft petals, and strolled up to the door. Grabbing the rose shaped door knob, Valhalla lightly cracked the door open, listening to gauge the number of patrons within. Hearing nothing, she peeked through the opening and continued inside.

Looking around the lobby, she found a woman behind the counter and was taken aback by her extravagant appearance. "Welcome to the Violet Tulip Inn, darling." The woman bellowed with a flourish. "Will you be needing a room for the night?" She continued, her voice slightly masculine under an otherwise shrill, effeminate tone.

She was a rather plump woman. Her well-fitted lavender gown and long gloves of the same hue stretched from hand to bicep. It suited her well. Two bright blue and pink bracelets decorated the woman's wrists, with a single beaded band of white between them. A bright pink feather scarf was wrapped loosely around her neck and trailed over her shoulders. Her flaxen hair, clearly dyed due to her visible ebony roots, was pulled back and braided in a tight bun, cascading down her back in waves. The woman's warm ivory skin had been powdered ghostly white, and the bright sapphire of her eyes was drowned out by the lavender makeup adorning her face.

The woman cocked her head to the side, her eyes twitching lightly, and gave Valhalla an investigative stare. Valhalla, growing slightly nervous, answered while trying to convey a relaxed demeanor. "Yes, but my stay may keep me for several weeks." Approaching the woman, a glint of intrigue shone in her eyes.

"Hmm, that's a lovely color you're wearing."

Valhalla looked down, raising a hand to the gold clip on her cloak, assuming the garment to be the item of the woman's reference. "Isn't it? A friend made it and gifted it to me."

She loved the cloak dearly already. Besides it being soft as cotton, it was very cozy and warm. Valhalla reminded herself to find a gift here in Hilliard for Diamantina, as a thank you for the cloak at least.

"Ahh! I know, you must be the Lady Red I've heard rumors about." The woman raised a hand to her chin, her tone oddly cheerful.

Valhalla chuckled, looking down at her red outfit peeking through the opening of the cloak. "Uh, I suppose so. I had wondered how she knew of me." Valhalla grabbed her chin and whispered to herself. "I didn't think my reputation had spread this far West, at least not so much as to be common knowledge."

"She?" The woman at the counter tilted her head with a curious smile, resting on the tip of her index finger.

Valhalla gulped nervously, trying to mask her accidental slip-up of almost mentioning the High Queen. Her invitation from the High Queen was to be kept secret after all. "Oh! I-It's nothing to be concerned about. So, how much for a room?"

"That depends, darling."

"On what?" Valhalla asked, worried she had given something away.

"If you're paying in barvs."

"Barvs!?" Valhalla's eyes widened in shock. "Seriously? Aren't those a rarity here? You must not have many patrons if that's the case."

"They are indeed." The woman winked playfully. "As you may know, ever since the Raven Queen took Hilliard hundreds of years ago, the use of barvs was replaced by crowns."

Valhalla rolled her eyes. "Yes I'm aware."

"Ahh, then you must also know that all transactions using barvs are to be immediately turned over with a rather generous exchange rate." The woman rested her elbows on the counter and her chin on the back of her hands.

"I . . . Oh, so you're trying to help rid the city of barvs for the lucrative incentives then?"

"One person at a time love," the woman shrugged. "And it's not just for the financial benefit. Let's just say I'm forever indebted to the royal family, to the late High King specifically, for helping people such as myself, making life a little safer. A sort of . . . due diligence, I suppose. Besides, with the current state of the city, we do all we can to scrape by."

Valhalla relaxed, seeing no further need for concern. "Alright, I understand." She pulled out her azure coin purse and peeked inside, counting her barvs. Valhalla stopped and looked at the woman again, curious if the woman was a good source of information about Hilliard. "Due diligence huh? Answer me this, then, how many will I need for my stay?"

The woman tilted her head and shrugged with a wink. "If you hand over all your barvs, be they iron, silver, or gold, you may stay as long as you need."

"Re-Really?" Valhalla exclaimed, having expected the woman to haggle.

"Mhmm," the woman nodded, "you do this city a great service. These barvs go toward repairing homes and people's lives."

"Is that so?" Valhalla looked down at the purse and smirked. "With that in mind, I wonder if you can make it worth my while. I've got quite a few barvs you see, and I'd be reluctant to part with them for only room and board, even for such a worthy cause." Valhalla leaned over the counter and rested her chin on the palm of her hand.

The woman leaned in closer. "What do you need, love? I've a number of services I may be able to arrange, assuming what you say is true." She gave Valhalla a small but mischievous smile.

"Information."

"Oh, I know plenty of gossip. I've many ears in many places, ask away." The woman's sapphire eyes twinkled with excitement as she drew her hand back from her hip and placed her elbow on the counter once more. She rested her chin on her clasped hands.

"The state of this city, how bad is it? Really?" Valhalla raised a brow, skeptical of whether the information would be of use.

She then remembered something Vardan told her long ago: *Gossip is rarely reliable, but it can be born of truth depending on its source.*

"Hmm, that's quite the question." The woman straightened herself upright and grabbed hold of her round chin, thinking for a moment. "Honestly, it varies from year to year. If the High Princess is away, the city prospers. When she returns, well, that's when things get more . . . difficult."

Valhalla cocked her head. "Why's that?"

"The High Princess enjoys . . . indulgences, especially when with her friends, her fellow daughters of nobility. Wonderful splendors are plentiful at the castle by her command. The people work tirelessly, providing goods and services to make it so, but with little and sometimes no pay in return." A frown fell over the woman's face.

"And . . . And the High Queen just lets that happen?" Valhalla's brows curved over her eyes, concerned as to what kind of trouble she was walking into.

"The High Queen does as her court says, ruling by committee to placate the nobility rather than by her own ideals. At least, that's the way it seems from down here. I'm afraid the only help the people receive from on high is thanks to the High Prince himself."

"Okay." Valhalla's curiosity piqued. "What can you tell me of him?"

"He really seems to care for the people, taking after his father. He has the respect of many here in the squalor, for all that's worth. It doesn't seem that sentiment is shared among those of higher station, even in the High family." The woman's smile was sadder than anything else.

Valhalla jolted. "A-Are you telling me no one cares about him?"

"I believe the High Queen cares for His Grace, but she certainly prioritizes her role as Queen over being a good mother." The woman sighed as she twirled a few strands of flaxen hair around her thick finger. "That poor boy, no matter what he does for the city, for the people, he isn't taken seriously by his family's court. He's doomed to be the nobilities whore for the rest of his life." The woman's eyes softened, a look of frustration on her face now.

Valhalla was taken aback. "Wait, what do you mean whore?"

"Oh, have you not heard of the Bedr Prael Law?" Valhalla shook her head. "It's one of the . . . I'll call it a *perk*, and I use that term *very* loosely, of being a male royal. Since the takeover by the Raven Queen, the law served to humiliate the men of the royal family. They are required to service ladies of nobility on command in matters of the bedroom. Refusal is out of the question, unless they marry, of course."

Valhalla shuddered at the thought. "Was there . . . even an objection to this?"

"Not at first, no. It wasn't until the men realized they had no real power at court anymore. No say. Nothing. Just like in their bedchambers." The woman sighed. "Many of us citizens hoped the High Queen would abolish the law when the High Prince won the War of Lions at only sixteen, or seventeen Winters old. It's been a while since then. He also stopped what could've been a civil war just last year. In my opinion, that law should've been abolished thanks to everything the late High King did for this city, including his role in that business with his family."

"And what's that?" Valhalla asked with a softness to her voice.

"Grár's Failed Rebellion. I'm sure you've heard of that? When he was still Prince of Grár, he learned of his family's plan to overthrow Queen Valeria the Fourth and sent warning of the attack." The woman crossed her arms loosely over her round belly.

"Sounds like quite the family," Valhalla said as she looked down at her coin purse, contemplating what to do. "Tell me, and be honest, would you aid the royal family? If the situation called for it?"

"Yes," the woman replied plainly, "I would without hesitation."

"Why?" Valhalla tilted her head curiously.

"Contrary to everything I've said, as an outsider looking in, Eilis and Alistair seem to really try to do what they can for the people. You'll see."

Valhalla contemplated the woman's words and those of Aura's before leaving Asgard. If there was truly a plot against the High Prince and Princess, there could also be one against the High Queen. How terrible would it be for the common folk if the Hilliard royal family were replaced? There would likely be infighting among the nobility for power. The people would then suffer until a new ruler was established. Even then, would the people fare any better under such a ruler?

Valhalla took a deep breath and reached inside her coin purse, grabbing hold of every single barv in her little bag, and handed them over to the woman. "That's all the barvs I have. Is that sufficient?"

"Yes, darling." The woman happily took the barvs. "Stay as long as you'd like. Meals are included in your stay." With a light curtsy, she turned around to grab one of the many keys hanging on the board behind the counter.

The key was silver, adorned with a red glass butterfly hanging from a violet ribbon. The woman then returned to Valhalla and handed her the key. "Your room is three B, on the third floor, love."

"Thank you," Valhalla said as she took the key and walked to the stairs on the left side of the lobby. Before continuing up the steps, she stopped, noticing a giant map of Hilliard. Valhalla stood before it and perused the details of each road and notable building.

The map was edged with Celnor knots, each depicting Jörmungandr, the World Serpent, with his head meeting his tail. On one corner, two ravens circled each other, and on the adjacent corner, a drake rested. In large letters was written Commoners Nest, the district encompassing the entire outer ring of the city. There was even a building painted a beautiful shade of lavender. Valhalla assumed it to be The Violet Tulip Inn.

"You aren't thinking of doing some sightseeing already, are you? Your journey must've been quite the distance. Wouldn't you like to rest?" Asked the woman.

"That would likely be for the best, I'm sure, but tell me, if I wished to speak to the High Queen, what would I have to do to get an audience with her Grace?" Valhalla asked, her attention still focused on the map. She examined the roads that would lead her through the Nobles Perch district and into Ravens Lookout, where Hilliard Castle resided, centered on the map.

"Oh, that's an easy one to answer." The woman giggled in a high, shrill pitch. "Once a month, the castle holds an event known as the Gathering. It allows the commoners to speak with the royal family. There you could present an issue, lavish praise on any you feel deserves notice of her Grace, or simply offer a gift to the High Queen. The choice is yours."

Valhalla abruptly turned to the woman. "Perfect, when is the event? Will I be waiting long?"

"You're in luck! Today is the tenth day of the month of Einmánudur. The royal family always hosts the event on the tenth day of each month, even when it falls on holiday festivals. It begins with the fifteenth bell, I believe. The twelfth bell rang not long ago, so the wait isn't too long now." The woman grinned at Valhalla.

"That's good to know, thank you." Valhalla bowed to the woman and turned to walk out of the inn, but the woman called out to her before Valhalla had a chance to open the door.

"Be sure to take that beautiful horse, love. Hilliard is very large. You won't make it if you choose to walk."

"Thank you . . . By Yggdrasil's shade, I forgot to ask you your name!" Valhalla exclaimed. "I'm terribly sorry."

The woman giggled sweetly. "My name is simply Madame, darling. May I have yours in return? Need something to scribble in the ledger other than the Lady Red."

Valhalla nodded thankfully. "Alright, Madame, it is. My name's Valhalla Önníka." She chuckled, waving farewell and exiting the inn.

She headed straight for Edan in the stable, untied his rein, and guided him to the road.

Valhalla, are you not going to rest? Edan asked, perplexed by her sudden urgency as she hopped into the saddle.

"No time, we have about three bells to meet the High Queen, or else we wait a month. We need to head to the castle. I know the way. Now ride my friend."

Edan stared at her a moment longer, but nodded without protest. *A month in this stable . . . No, thank you. I will get you there.*

He reared up onto his hind legs, then slammed his front hooves down hard, swiftly carrying her through the city with her instruction guiding their way.

16

Valhalla

Watchful Eyes

Passing under a guarded portcullis at a trot, the city bells began to ring. Valhalla counted thirteen chimes in total, leaving her only two to reach Ravens Lookout, or else miss the Gathering.

As she looked about, soaking in the scenery, she noticed the cobblestone road was no longer covered in dirt and filth. The stalls that had dotted the Commoners Nest were nowhere to be seen; instead, large shops lined the streets, each displaying alluring finery and trinkets from their windows. Valhalla was sure she had now entered the Nobles Perch, based on all the splendor on display.

Jewelry of various makes and gemstones sparkled in the light. Gowns of vibrant colors and styles were displayed at shopfronts. Exotic weaponry rested on racks, some of which Valhalla had never seen before.

The aroma of delectable sweets filled the air, even catching Edan's attention, who snorted in the shop's direction. The sweets looked as though recently plucked from a master's painting. The extravagant countryside was filled with spring flowers and glittering fabrics. Wooden statues of gods and creatures perched on corners and entryways.

The people were dressed quite differently from those in the Commoners Nest, many wearing vibrant gowns, tunics, jerkins, vests, and capes. Both men and women were ostentatiously adorned with jewelry. Rings, necklaces, broaches, bracelets. All were on display.

Even a brothel, The White Dragoness Brothel, was on full display, not hidden in some back alley, but on the main street parading beauties both elegantly poised and equally decorated. The prostitutes appeared to be from faraway lands with skin ranging from fair to golden, hair and eyes of various colors, and exotic clothing to match.

The people here must be of the social elite, Valhalla thought to herself. Judging by this display, they weren't stricken by lack of means. She assumed there would be those here who wanted for nothing, just as there were those who would never know a moment without wanting. A scowl fell over Valhalla's face.

Traveling on, the number of shops grew fewer and fewer before ceasing entirely to a long stretch of fields on either side of the road and large homes in the distance. She came across the first of many of the grand longhouses of Hilliard. Banners displayed unique insignias hanging from the homes and gardens. Small pockets of soldiers walked the grounds of their respective houses in the garb of their lords and ladies. The homes and surrounding lands were lavish with decoration, furnishings, and vegetation large enough to put some farms to shame.

Valhalla rolled her eyes at the overabundance on display. Of course, *these* homes would belong to nobility.

She leaned forward to reach Edan's ears. "Edan, I don't mean to be rude, but can we please hurry? I'm . . . quite tired of this district. That and I'm not sure how much further it'll be till we reach the castle. I'm worried I'll miss the High Queen at this rate."

Edan laughed. *You wish for speed? Then you shall have it.* He reared up, gave out a powerful neigh, and stomped his hooves down on the cobblestones, jostling Valhalla lightly in the saddle.

His speed increased tenfold, leaving a small trail of fire behind that immediately dissipated. Valhalla ducked behind his neck, shielding her eyes from the stinging wind. The world became a blur around her.

Hearing the fourteenth bell ring across the city, she peeked up to look ahead. She had no idea that so much time had passed already. Edan then began to slow to a stop.

Approaching another set of stores, there was another open portcullis at the end of a large town square. On either side of the square were shops bringing out their wares for the people passing by.

Carts full of people dotted the area, laughing and conversing with one another. Residents of the Commoners Nest gathered at storefronts and walked toward the distant wall, looking to be in awe of the items on display. Many of the nobility passed them by, ignoring their presence here, though a few were clearly opposed to the situation.

Do you think we've arrived? Edan asked as he looked back to Valhalla.

"I believe so. The castle must be just through those gates." Valhalla gestured toward the portcullis. "Many of the people going in look like commoners from the outer district. I was told the Gathering is meant to allow their voices to be heard. Come on, let's find someone on the other side to speak to."

Edan nodded and made his way through the gates, careful not to bump into the people walking about. They emerged into a massive courtyard. The Hilliard castle towered high above them. Valhalla's eyes widened as she took in its grandeur, so unique compared to the other castles she had visited across Veerence.

Many spires jutted from the castle peaks, reminding her of spears protruding from a shield wall. Statues of ravens flew about every corner. Silver armored soldiers adorned with raven crests surveyed the courtyard, some patrolling the area while others stood guard by the castle gates.

Large violet banners, each depicting a black raven, hung on either side of the gate. The raven's wings were spread wide, encircled by white laurels. A sixteen-pointed star shined above its head, and an elegant silver crown rested beneath its wedged tail. Just beneath the crown lay a white banner inscribed with the words, *Fly Free and Proud.*

"Wow," Valhalla whispered in awe.

Edan chuckled at her. *Quite a wonder, huh?*

"Oh come on," Valhalla giggled. "You could at least pretend to be amazed every now and then."

HA! If you've seen one castle, you've seen them all. Besides, nothing here compares to Asgard. He shook his head left and right, the fires of his mane flapping about his neck.

"Now that's not fair. I think each castle is pretty amazing . . . once you've . . ."

A shiver ran up Valhalla's spine. An odd feeling came over her, as if being watched. Discreetly, she looked around.

Many people walked about the courtyard waiting to enter the castle, but none gave her so much as a passing glance. She then spotted a woman to her left hiding in the shadows of the wall surrounding the castle. Valhalla took a deep breath to calm herself as the woman's eyes remained locked upon her.

Valhalla's brows twitched, unsure of the woman's intentions. She was small in stature, around Aura's height, thinly framed, and wore a form-fitting black dress and a white frilly apron. An equally frilly headband adorned her reddish brown hair with bangs cut evenly above her dark brown, nearly black monolid eyes.

She wondered if the woman was from Weida Long. Her pale ivory skin showed in the shadows. The woman's hands clasped together over her waist, seemingly waiting for Valhalla to make a move. Could she be imagining things?

Her brows furrowed lightly over her eyes, unsure of what the woman could possibly want from her. She wondered if the woman worked in the castle.

Valhalla grabbed the edge of her cobalt blue cloak and reached into a pocket, pulled out the scroll from the High Queen, and looked at the wax insignia still tied around it.

She hugged the scroll close to her chest, sure to place the seal on display, and watched the mysterious woman. Confirming Valhalla's assumption, the servant maiden reacted, jolting at the sight. However, the maid paused, hesitating, and looked around, then returned to the shadow of the wall. The woman's eyes locked on Valhalla once more as she discreetly waved a hand, signaling for her to come closer.

Valhalla nodded, understanding the secrecy, and pulled Edan's reins in the woman's direction. Drawing closer, Valhalla hopped off Edan, landed by the wall, and positioned the horse so as to block prying eyes.

"Excuse me, I don't suppose you work in the castle under the High Queen?"

"Yes," she answered, "my name is Shu Yen Ling." Her voice was soft. Hearing the woman's accent and name, Valhalla was confident in her assumption about her being from Weida Long.

"Tell me, is that from High Queen Eilis?" Shu Yen pointed to the scroll.

Valhalla nodded and raised the scroll to hand to her, presenting the wax seal. Shu Yen raised a hand, refusing to take it. "No, it's not my place to take it. Your name, please."

"Oh, um, it's Valhalla. Valhalla Önníka." Valhalla was surprised, expecting Shu Yen to at least inspect the scroll to verify the writing within. Was her name all Shu Yen really needed?

"Thank you, please, follow me."

ShueYen stepped closer to Edan, stopping in front of his face. She stared at him for a moment, her expression not of surprise, but of contentment, then scratched under his chin with a small smile on her face. "You're such a beautiful creature." With that, she continued toward the gate of the castle.

Valhalla stepped out from behind Edan, a perplexed look on her face. She and Edan shared a surprised glance. *Let's follow her.* Edan suggested with a whinny. *Maybe you'll get more answers once inside the castle.*

She nodded in agreement, and the two followed after Shu Yen, doing their best to avoid the ever-growing crowd. Some turned and stared at the flaming steed, but none halted their pace. Valhalla tried to ignore their stares, feeling her cheeks heat up with embarrassment.

The three reached the stairs of the castle, pulling more than a little attention their way. Shu Yen stopped and turned to Valhalla, pointing to a vertical post beside her.

Edan stopped and looked at the post, then to the people around them, fidgeting nervously. *Wait! You can't really expect me to stay here with all these people around me.*

 Shu Yen's eyes widened slightly. "Oh, you speak." She stepped close to him and Valhalla, placing a hand on his nose. "Don't worry. I first need to get your friend to the High Queen. I'll have a friend of mine come to tuck you away in the castle stables. No one will bother you there, except to sate your needs. You won't have to wait long." She giggled earnestly.

Edan looked at her, silent for a moment, and then released a soft sigh. *Alright, but don't let it be too long. I don't like all these eyes on me. It's worrisome.*

Valhalla tied the reins loosely to the post just as she had back in the inn's stable. "Just be patient for me, alright." Edan nodded as she followed Shu Yen up to the castle gate.

They veered to the right of the large entryway and headed to a door far off to the side of the castle. Shu Yen grabbed the thin silver handle and opened the door.

The smells of roasting pork, apple pies, and an assortment of other culinary masterworks wafted from inside. Valhalla looked through the doorway, down the small stairway, and saw many servants' feet rushing in all directions. Orders to prepare this and that rang out.

Shu Yen was the first to walk through the door and down the stairs. Valhalla followed, and her eyes widened and mouth watered as she entered. The kitchen was surprisingly expansive, the walls stretching far to her left and right. Sunlight crept in through the windows near the tall, stone ceiling, bathing the stations in golden light.

On the wall to the right were many stone ovens stuffed full of baked goods, pies, and breads, all cooking to a beautiful golden brown. As the workers pulled the finished delights from the ovens, they drizzled caramel, creams, chocolate, and sprinklings of powdered sugar over the confections.

Large fire pits were placed between the ovens, some heating large iron pots that hung just above as cooks stirred the broth within. Others had spits with large bits of pork and beef slowly roasting over the blazing fires. The meats sizzled loudly as they slowly spun, cooking to a beautiful reddish-brown.

In the center of the kitchen were stone ovens and wooden counters arranged in a circular formation. The cooks there were busy grilling large fish over thin iron racks, periodically turning and prodding the fish with two-pronged forks to ensure they were ready to eat. They sprinkled on black and red spices, and showered freshly squeezed lemons over the scales, which made them shine in the firelight.

Valhalla walked about the kitchen, careful to keep out of the workers' way as her eyes surveyed the dishes around her. She clutched hold of the fabric over her stomach as her belly grumbled lightly. Her jaw tightened as she basked in the aromas filling her nostrils.

She couldn't remember the last time she ate. Valhalla swallowed, and it quickly dawned on her that she hadn't eaten since breakfast, accidentally going without food until well into the mid-afternoon.

Valhalla looked around, hoping to find something to quell her appetite while Shu Yen stopped to speak with one of the many servant maids. Seeing an opportunity, Valhalla looked to her left and found a scullery maid chopping up apples and placing the small bits into a large bowl. Before her rested a basket of bright apples, both red and green.

Her mouth salivated as she slowly approached. It was just one apple. She was sure no one would mind. As she approached the scullery maid, the young woman handed her an apple, surprising Valhalla.

"Here, ya look like yer starvin'." A large grin lit up her face.

"Oh, thank you so much." As Valhalla reached out to take the apple, Shu Yen interrupted and grabbed her arm. Valhalla turned to her. "Yes?"

"Your friend will be taken care of. We need to speak with the High Queen. Now."

Shu Yen hastily pulled her and made their way through the kitchen. Valhalla reluctantly followed while her eyes were affixed on the assortment of delectable foods as she passed them by. Her stomach grumbled in protest.

The two rushed through the kitchen, weaving past the scurrying kitchen workers and servants. Soon, the two reached a wide ramp leading up through a short tunnel. Many bright torches and silver serving carts lined the walls to the top.

Valhalla proceeded through the tunnel toward a bright opening at its end. "Does this lead to the castle? And what's with all this food? Preparing for a banquet today or something?"

"Yes," Shu Yen giggled, "this tunnel will take us to the castle. The servants' entrance is kept far from the main hall to avoid our being seen by those of high society. They expect our services, but complain when they notice our presence." She rolled her eyes. "As for all this food, it's for the people attending the Gathering, silly. Who else would it be for?"

"Oh wow. The High Queen feeds the commoners during the event? That's quite kind of her."

"Not exactly. Both the event and the provided food were the High Prince's idea." Shu Yen's posture softened, and a small smile creased her face. "He thought it would benefit the royal family to learn of the people's plight, to better understand their struggles and priorities, especially those living in the Commoners Nest."

Valhalla's heart warmed at the thought, her pace slowing and her mind wondering just what kind of person the High Prince must be. From everything she had heard about him, he seemed a kind sort, a trait not shared by many of royal lineage.

Her thoughts then turned to the High Queen. She seemed like a conflicted person, torn between being a good mother and a good Queen. No wonder she couldn't do both. From what Valhalla had seen of the nobles, she couldn't imagine they would make ruling easy.

She raised a hand and placed the tip of her thumb between her teeth. Valhalla wasn't sure if the High Queen was worthy of helping. The High Queen seemed to prioritize the nobility, but her son had her ear. That seemed to be a good thing, Valhalla hoped. He sounded like he might actually care for the common people. Perhaps for him it was worth it.

Valhalla removed her thumb from her mouth, her lips forming a heavy frown. There was also the High Princess to consider. She sounded like an awful, spoiled brat, but maybe that was all rumors. At the very least, Valhalla should hear them out, make her decision then. The High Queen sought her out all the way in Alf. To go to so much trouble, the situation must be serious. Valhalla just hoped, whatever it was that the High Queen would ask of her, it would ultimately benefit the people.

"Valhalla, is everything alright?"

Valhalla jolted, now realizing she had stopped. She looked to Shu Yen far ahead of her, the maid's head tilted lightly in confusion.

"Uh, yes, sorry." Valhalla promptly closed the distance and followed Shu Yen.

If Valhalla felt the task might ask too much of her, or not be worthy of aiding, she hoped the High Queen wouldn't be so enraged as to call for an execution should Valhalla decide to refuse. Her spine shivered at the thought. Historically, it rarely proved wise to refuse a King or Queen's request.

Shu Yen and Valhalla exited the tunnel and entered a grand hall stretching far before them. Valhalla looked about her surroundings. The ceiling stretched high above her and the buttresses criss-crossed overhead. The walls were painted in a vibrant violet as tall windows lined the right wall, each with dark azure curtains tied open with silver rope. Between a few of the windows were large raven-black curtains draped along the wall.

To Valhalla's left, there were large, beautifully crafted paintings depicting Hilliard's royal families. Each member shared similar traits. Ebony hair, sapphire eyes, and warm ivory skin, dressed in colors matching the banners hanging outside the castle, violet, white, black, and silver.

The portrait before her seemed older, the style of clothing quite dated compared to today's contemporary fashion. She wondered if the current royal family had a portrait as well. Valhalla looked down the long hall at the many, many portraits ahead. As she started to walk forward, Shu Yen called to her, having Valhalla turn.

"Come," Shu Yen pulled back one of the black curtains, unveiling a hidden staircase, "we need to take these stairs to meet with the High Queen."

Valhalla, astonished, approached Shu Yen and looked up the staircase, which was pitch black within. The hairs on the back of her neck stood on end, and her blood turned cold.

Standing at the entryway, the darkness grew, spreading fast and enveloping her vision. With eyes closed, she jolted back with a gasp, a hand reflexively moving to the hilt of her sword, and the other raised in a blocking posture. She startled as something gripped her raised hand. Opening her eyes with labored breath, Shu Yen's hand was upon hers, looking at her with confusion and a hint of concern.

"Valhalla, what is it?" Shu Yen's dark brown monolid eyes trembled, and her brows curved.

Valhalla stared at Shu Yen in silence, her heart racing. She attempted to calm herself, taking a few deep breaths in vain. "I-I . . . I can't . . . I don't like dark enclosed spaces . . ." Valhalla closed her eyes and lowered her head.

Dropping her arms and gripping her wrist in front of her, Valhalla squeezed tightly to stop her hand from trembling, trying to tell herself that everything was fine. She began to work on her breathing, or at least focused on it to help in controlling the fear still growing within her.

Without realizing it, her grip on her wrist tightened, unaware how numb her arm was becoming. She hoped to finally be rid of this fear. The enveloping darkness. Being trapped under the floorboard. The screams. The terrible, blood-curdling screams. A sword right above her head, and something warm and wet dripping onto her. The nightmares never left her. They haunted her to this day still, and she wasn't sure if it was because she was weak, or if she truly was trapped with those nightmares forever.

"I'm sorry. I didn't know. Wait, I think there's a candle here somewhere."

Valhalla opened her eyes again just in time to see Shu Yen disappear into the shadows. Taking a hesitant step forward, she tried to see the maid, but couldn't. Noises emanated from within, light steps, shuffling and clanking, and ended in a thud, followed by a sigh.

Shu Yen emerged with curved brows. "Unfortunately, it appears I was mistaken. I can't seem to find a candle. I won't be able to light the way for us. If you don't mind waiting, I can run back to the kitchen for a lantern." She said as she folded her hands over her stomach.

"Oh, it's fine. I can take care of it. It just . . . caught me by surprise, is all." Valhalla moved to the precipice, the light fading into the shadows, and took a deep breath. Shu Yen stepped to the side, watching curiously.

Valhalla opened her eyes and looked intently into the darkness before her. Her heart and breathing began to settle, but her muscles tightened. She took a deep breath, filled her lungs, and summoned forth a strong heat within her breast. The darkness had no control over her, she thought. It shouldn't. She wouldn't let it. "Koma 'ortha 'ixan or bruni."[1]

Valhalla raised her hands to her mouth and clasped them together. A gentle breath escaped her lips, the heat within her chest collected and swirled in her palms. Her hands glowed, and vapor seeped from between her fingers. Opening her hands, a sweltering heat flashed and subsided just as quickly, replaced by a pixie of pure flame which floated before her.

Shu Yen jumped back in astonishment, her mouth agape. The little creature fluttered over and twirled around her, causing the maid to giggle and twirl with the pixie in delight.

Valhalla raised a hand, and the pixie flew back to her. The creature was slender in frame with fiery, wispy hair flowing back and forth. Her eyes glowed brightly in a golden yellow hue. Valhalla flashed the pixie a soft smile, finding

---

1   Koma 'ortha 'ixan or bruni is Celnor(Norse) for Come forth, pixie of fire.

her as beautiful as the lady Yggdrasil Herself.

"Amazing!" Shu Yen exclaimed. "You know magic as well?" Her eyes were wide and twinkling with excitement.

Valhalla, astonished, looked at Shu Yen curiously. "As well? Do you know someone else who can wield magic? I was told magic had faded from the people of Veerence."

"Yes," Shu Yen nodded in affirmation, "his Grace, High Prince Alistair practices it. Along with the division of the silver guard under his command. I struggle with the ancient tongue of your ancestors, but I believe they call themselves the Jórsalafarar. They are similar to the Zaragoans' Knighthood of Paladins, though with different magic and beliefs; less zealous. Have you not heard of either?"

"No, I haven't. Are they mages?"

"Sort of." Shu Yen giggled. "More like warrior mages—battlemages, warrior knights who wield both blade and magic. Like you it seems." She pointed to Valhalla's longsword, which was just visible under her cloak.

"Interesting. I had no idea the mages of Midgard had changed so much."

To think mortals of Midgard have learned to practice battle magic as the Einherjar do without the aid of the golden apples. Valhalla watched the pixie dance and twirl about on her palm in excitement.

"Well, I wouldn't say that. The Knighthood of Paladins has been around for centuries, the Jórsalafarar, however, is a recent creation. I think they were formed just after his Grace's eighth or ninth spring in this realm by the late High King." Shu Yen approached the stairway, grabbing hold of the black curtain. "Are you ready to proceed?"

Valhalla took a deep breath, and without command, the pixie flew in, illuminating the stairway. With a sigh of relief, Valhalla entered the stairwell.

As she placed a foot on the stone steps, Shu Yen sheathed the entrance once more beneath the curtain. Valhalla turned to the maid. "If this place is meant to be a secret, are you sure you should be taking me this way? I wouldn't want to be the cause of any trouble."

"It can't be helped now. Besides, her Grace would've brought you here eventually." Shu Yen, having finished securing the curtain, turned and lifted the skirt of her dress and walked past Valhalla to lead her up the stairs.

Valhalla's chest tightened as a feeling of apprehension washed over her in waves. She hoped she was making the right choice in meeting with the High Queen. Valhalla was probably overthinking things. If everyone thought she should try, she would at least hear the High Queen out. She took a deep breath and climbed the stairs, the pixie illuminating their way.

17

The High Queen of Hilliard

The climb was long, but Valhalla and Shu Yen continued their ascent in silence. As they drew closer, Valhalla saw light emanating from an archway at the end of the staircase.

The pixie turned to Valhalla and flew closer. With a twirl, the creature twisted and distorted, becoming a wild flame. Valhalla opened her arms, and with a flash, the flame returned to her and dispersed.

Reaching the open archway, they came to a large circular room. The space was free of clutter and bathed in a mixture of blues and whites as sunlight peered through the windows of the dome-like ceiling. A silver chandelier hung just overhead, each of its lit candles the size of her head. Valhalla walked to the center of the room and twirled on the white marble floor, taking in the beautiful secret chamber, its size akin to a throne room.

It reminded Valhalla of Freya's hall. She pictured the tall, muscular woman sitting upon her throne of gold, looking over her acolytes, and on occasion, Valhalla herself, teaching the ways of prophetic seidr and the sword.

Valhalla took a few steps back, absorbed by the thought, and inadvertently bumped into Shu Yen. She spun to the maid and apologized. Shu Yen, however, raised a finger to her lips and looked ahead with a low curtsy.

Valhalla cocked her head to the side in a moment of confusion. She turned to look in the direction of the maid's focus and saw two women standing upon a tall dais, one a head shorter than the other. Behind them rested a beautiful silver throne intricately detailed with ravens and lilacs.

Valhalla froze, not even breathing, as both women's beautiful sapphire eyes fell upon her. The face of the taller woman relaxed into an expression of relief, though the other continued to watch intensely with suspicion. Both had ebony hair, but intricate braids cascaded in waves down the taller woman's back. The smaller woman's hair was loose and stretched low past the small of her back. Both women were similar in feature and frame, though the taller had sharper features. The taller woman's skin was pale and worn, likely from years of stressful living. The smaller woman's warm ivory skin was vibrant and youthful, though dark rings surrounded her bloodshot eyes. The taller woman's attire was simple yet elegant. She donned a violet azure dress and was adorned with silver jewelry. The whole attire almost reminded Valhalla of Frigg; even when alone and relaxing, the All Mother still flaunted her status. Atop the taller woman's head rested a circlet that spiraled her crown with detailed metal flowers and leaves. A large blue tanzanite was embedded at its center. The woman's circlet reminded her of elven jewelry, striking Valhalla as odd. The smaller woman's dress was simple and black. No sparkling jewels or ornamentation decorated her person. A light layer of makeup elevated each of the women's beauty and matched their gowns.

Valhalla watched the two curiously.

"You may come forth." Proclaimed the taller woman, a gentle smile on her face.

The smaller woman's eyes flickered with hardened anger, turning to her companion at her side. "Eilis please, I implore you, we don't know her."

Valhalla was startled by the name, as Eilis was the name of the High Queen, but why would they be meeting here, of all places?

"I know, but if what the people say is true, she may be able to help us." Eilis took the smaller woman's hands, pulled her in, and touched their foreheads together tenderly. The smaller woman's anger melted away, and she was soon on the verge of tears. "Please, trust me. Why not go for now, wait with the others until this is done?"

"And leave you and Alistair alone!? Not a chance. Eilis, please, he at least should be told—"

"Embla, I will tell him when the time is right." Eilis's eyes turned from understanding to injunction, her tone shifting perceptively.

Embla slid her hands out of Eilis's, staring at her with unrestricted outrage. "When the time is right? He's the head of your Queensguard and your son! She was—"

Eilis's eyes, although shrouded in a veil of stoicism, began to tremble. They took on a glossy appearance as she took a deep breath and placed her hands on Embla's shoulders. She then pulled her in for an embrace. "I know that. I know. It's alright, Embla. She alone may be able to keep you all safe. For that reason, I will take this chance. Please, I've not been a good daughter, sister . . . or mother. Let me try to make amends. Let me do this." She released Embla, her eyes shrouding once more. "Go wait with the others. I'll have Alistair retrieve you when all is finally clear."

Embla remained quiet for a long moment, taking a deep breath. "Will you at *least* tell him your plan?"

Eilis didn't answer. Her demeanor was poised, and her eyes lingered on Embla just a moment longer. Taking a step back, Eilis turned her gaze to Valhalla, their conversation clearly over.

Embla's brows furrowed harshly over her eyes. With a few tears and a begrudged sigh, she turned from her High Queen's side and began down the steps of the dais.

Pausing briefly at the bottom, she turned back to face Eilis. "Honestly, dear sister, if you want to be a good mother, you might start by being honest with your son, lest he discover the truth the hard way."

Eilis's face hardened, her cheeks flushing. After a tense silence, the High Queen gave Embla a single nod, her manner statuesque, save for a momentary fiddling of her silver bracelets.

Embla turned once more with haste and made her way toward the exit. Valhalla locked eyes with Embla as she brushed past, catching a distrustful glare as the young royal left her sight.

That gaze seemed awfully cold. How desperate was this situation to warrant such a welcome? At least the High Queen seemed more amicable.

What was Valhalla getting herself into?

She watched as the woman disappeared into the darkness of the stairway and out of sight, lost in thought.

"Please, don't be offended." The High Queen said with a softness in her tone. "My *little* sister is very protective of me and my son. She means well, I assure you. Recent events have caused tensions to run high as you'll come to understand."

At the clacking of heels, Valhalla returned her attention back to the Queen. Shu Yen walked toward the High Queen, motioning for her to follow. Valhalla did so and joined Shu Yen before the dais.

The maid curtsied briefly to Eilis. "Your Grace, I have brought Lady Red herself." Stepping aside, she gestured to Valhalla as though she were presenting a prized statue to a noble, causing the warrior's cheeks to blush.

With a nervous gulp, Valhalla hesitantly stepped forward. She couldn't understand why she felt so anxious. Valhalla had met royals before, but this felt different. All the secrecy led her mind to wander, each possibility worse than the one before. Just what could've happened here, she thought to herself.

She took a deep breath and bowed low. As Valhalla straightened, she opened her mouth to greet the High Queen, but was interrupted before she could muster a word.

"If the rumors are to be believed, you help those in need, always donning a crimson garb. 'An unmatched warrior of the people.' Is it true fire can't harm you? I wonder." Her red lips stretched into a curious smile.

Valhalla was uneasy, shyly rubbing a hand against her neck. She wasn't aware of the rumors people were spreading about her, just that her reputation had apparently stretched further than Alf. She was, however, curious to know just how fantastical the rumors had become.

She giggled bashfully. "It's an honor to be known by someone such as yourself, but people embellish on the reality of things. I'm not someone with such divinity as to be untouched by the elements. I'm only resistant to fire as it resides within me, my magical element. Flame can't hurt flame."

Cupping her hands together before her breast, she took a deep breath and concentrated on her conjuration. Heat traveled through her veins and emanated from her palms. Wisps of smoke rose from her fingertips. Valhalla slowly pulled her hands apart, palms facing one another as sparks crackled and popped lively with flashes of light. An explosion of fire burst to life.

"Amazing!" The High Queen startled with excitement and let out an astonished laugh. "I had no idea anyone in Veerence, save for those within these walls, still practiced magic."

Valhalla grinned. "It depends on where you look." Dismissing the fire, it disappeared as quickly as it had come forth. "The practice has diminished, it's true, but a few still practice here and there. As for the crimson clothing, it's more of a—cultural thing. I was recognized long ago for my deeds by those very dear to me. So out of respect, I don the color of their family." Valhalla opened her cloak slightly to reveal her crimson attire.

"Extraordinary." Eilis's eyes widened with amazement. "Please, might I have a better look at you?"

"Oh, sure, as you command, your Grace." Valhalla raised her hands to the clip of her cloak and removed the fabric from her shoulders, displaying her crimson garb in full view. Shu Yen stepped forward and accepted the cloak.

Eilis lifted up large folds of her dress and proceeded down the steps of the dais. Valhalla was taken aback as the Queen approached, unaware of just how tall the woman was. The two almost matched in height, which was unusual for the women of this region, but Valhalla was sure the High Queen's heels were giving her a boost.

She watched as the High Queen circled her, carefully inspecting every facet of her body. Worry and doubt showed clearly on Eilis's face.

"I . . . I don't know how well this will work. I heard you're a warrior," she pointed to the longsword hanging by Valhalla's waist. "But I didn't expect your physique to be this well . . . toned." The High Queen chuckled, her tone sounding more than a little troubled.

She stopped in front of Valhalla, still looking her up and down. "I think . . . you may even be taller than her." Eilis turned to Shu Yen. "What do you think? You've been with my children for some time now, you likely know them better than I." She said with a subtle hint of pain in her eyes.

"The warrior is taller than your daughter by nearly a head. Her physique is more muscular, of that I am sure, but their skin tone is similar, if not a little fairer. Lady Red's eyes, though we won't be able to cover." Shu Yen replied matter-of-factly.

"Her eyes?" Eilis looked closer at Valhalla's face, curious, and squinted. The High Queen stepped closer, mere inches in front of Valhalla, and raised her hands to the warrior's face, brushing her hair aside. "Must your face be so covered? When speaking with someone, I prefer to look them—" Eilis let out a sharp gasp and swiftly withdrew her hands, almost as though their proximity had somehow burned her.

"I-I suppose you're not accustomed to those sharing my eye color." Valhalla chuckled nervously, trying to ease the tension in the room, and took a small step back from the High Queen.

"N-No, I'm not. No one shares that shade. Your name, tell me now." Eilis' face was urgent, her tone commanding, and her hands clasped tightly over her chest.

Valhalla's eyes darted back and forth between Eilis and Shu Yen. She then noticed the Queen's eyes were trembling. The maid looked just as confused as Valhalla at the reaction.

She didn't understand the woman's anxiousness, especially as Valhalla had no clue what made her eyes so special to Eilis. Realizing now that she had been silent long enough, Valhalla thought it was best to answer her, if only to appease the woman.

Meeting the Queen's eyes, Valhalla nodded and answered, "Of course, your Grace. My name's Valhalla. Valhalla Önníka of Seeras."

"Önníka!" Eilis's face lit up in shock. "No, you can't be . . . The Önníka family perished thirteen years ago. My late husband confirmed it after we received word of an attack!"

"Your Grace, please, calm yourself. It's true the rest of my family passed. I was there, I saw everything. My parents hid me under the floorboard of our home." Valhalla's heart tightened as the memory rushed through her mind, the anguish she had felt in those early days during and after the attack still a raw, unhealing wound.

Holding back her tears, Valhalla noticed a twitch in her hand, and quickly balled it into a fist, focusing on her breathing to steady her nerves again. "Eventually, I was found by a group of traveling warriors. They were kind and buried the people of Seeras, my parents included. They have taken care of me ever since. I didn't know anyone else had knowledge of my family name, to be honest."

"Where . . . have you been?" Eilis stepped toward Valhalla, startling the warrior lightly.

"Your Grace?" Valhalla's brows curved over her eyes.

"Where have you been all this time!? Tell me!" Eilis grabbed hold of Valhalla's shoulders, squeezing them firmly. Her gaze was intense.

"A-Alf! I've been living in a town called Alf, far to the East of here." Valhalla defensively raised her hands to her chest. Having promised to never bring up Asgard if asked where she called home, Valhalla had made sure always to name Alf instead. It was a half-truth which made it all the more convincing. However, she didn't understand why the High Queen would care at all about her or her family. Did Eilis know them?

"So . . . you've been alive all this time, and we didn't even—"

Valhalla gently grabbed hold of the High Queen's wrists and removed her hands from her shoulders, stepping back, and placing Eilis at arm's length. "Your Grace, how do you know my family? Seeras was a small city far West of Hilliard. I didn't think—"

"I'm—sorry." Eilis turned away and raised her hands to her face for a moment. "It's nothing, it's nothing dear."

"Um, a-about my eyes, you don't have to worry about the color. I know someone who has pills, the magical sort, that can change my eye color to match your daughter's. With your permission, Your Grace, I'd like to meet the princess to get a better idea of her mannerisms and who she is."

Eilis remained quiet for a long moment before turning to face Valhalla. She wore a false, trembling smile. "Please, call me Eilis. I believe we will be spending a great deal of time together. For the sake of time, it would be best to dispense with formalities. Walk with me, please." She stepped beside Valhalla, wrapped her arms around one of Valhalla's, and escorted the warrior up the dais.

Reaching the silver throne at the top, Eilis led Valhalla behind it to a black curtain, similar to the one at the base of the stairway outside. "You should know your request is no longer possible to fulfill." Eilis released Valhalla's arm and stopped in front of the curtain.

A shiver crawled up Valhalla's spine. "What do you mean?" She stared at the curtain, now noticing an ill yet familiar scent coming from within the shrouded chamber.

Eilis fell quiet again and reached for the curtain. She slightly turned to Valhalla, her face only visible in profile, and paused. A single tear rolled down her cheek. Eilis pulled the curtain wide. A cold mist spilled out from the now-open chamber and covered Valhalla's feet.

"I think . . . it's better that I show you." The High Queen turned to face Valhalla, her eyes heavily glossed, and turning red.

Valhalla hesitantly looked past Eilis into the dark room. Her body lightly trembled as she agonized over what she might discover within. She took a deep breath to steady herself before entering, then commanded her tense muscles to take a step, then another, and another.

The interior of the chamber was freezing. Her breath visibly hung in the air, and the hairs on her neck stood on end. Raising her hands to her mouth, she exhaled, followed by a fiery glow emanating from between her fingers. Tapping into her flame seidr, her body temperature rose to combat the biting cold.

Valhalla's eyes finally adjusted to the dim light of the room and, looking up, found a bright column of blue light shining down from the ceiling. Expecting to see a window at the top, she was surprised to find a seidr circle instead. Celnor runes depicting snowflakes were haphazardly scratched into the ceiling, the circle clearly created in a hurry.

Valhalla followed the light down and startled back. A young woman lay still on a white stone pedestal, her eyes closed as though she were sleeping.

She cautiously approached as the realization set in, her heart speeding faster with every step. As Valhalla grew closer, she noticed a strong resemblance to Eilis in the young woman's face. Her skin, however, was quite pale with a faint hint of blueish gray. Ebony hair was combed back and fanned out over the surface of the pedestal. A crimson stain covered nearly the entire right side of her white and yellow dress while a gash was visible on the young woman's neck, the skin and muscle sliced clean through.

Valhalla's hands flew to her mouth, stifling a gasp, and her eyes looked on in horror. The young woman dead on the pedestal was the High Princess.

18

Alistair

Held Back Screams

Alistair's blood was boiling. Barely restrained energy turned his muscles into knots. The loud thudding of his footsteps echoed through the halls of Hilliard's castle. He carefully rubbed his wrist, trying to soothe the rope-chafed skin.

The muscles of his jaw were sore from gritting his teeth, fighting back tears as his heart drummed heavily in his chest. Alistair glanced down to inspect the severity of the bruising, the gold skin around his wrists discolored in shades of blue, purple, and yellow. He cursed inwardly at the two noblewomen who had tied him down on his own bed.

Lost in his anger, he stumbled, tripping over a slightly raised rug. Catching himself and bracing against the painted wall, his throat tightened, and the hollow weight pushing against his chest spread through the rest of his body. Alistair closed his eyes and grabbed hold of the collar of his tunic around his neck, stretching the fabric down in the hope it would ease his labored breath.

Anxiety and fear sent adrenaline through his veins. The thumping of his heart felt like it might burst from his chest. This had been happening more often lately. It started years before when he was kidnapped and raped by two women who were now no longer members of his mother's queensguard. He tried to tell himself to breathe as the terrible nightmare resurfaced. Iron shackles. Rope. Ribbons. If Alistair could ban those items from the queendom, he would, but for now, he had to try and get past the trauma on his own.

Before he knew it, memories of a different night flooded his thoughts. The faces of his abusers flashed before him. Lorna, his own sister. Her friends: Inge. Áse. Grete. Kjerstin. Ebba. "Damn them all," he cursed to himself. Countless others, many of whom he never even learned their name, haunted his memory.

The few times he had fought back, he was reminded of his place. Even his mother, of all people, reminded him of the law. He had to close his eyes, bear the burden, and push through, all for the acts of his forebears. That was when it escalated. Sometimes he was drugged, other times bound. Once even whipped like a dog.

He told himself to breathe. Repeating it like a mantra by this point. Alistair's thoughts turned to his father, how strong and confident he was. He needed to try and be more like him.

Feeling his fury rising, he quickly covered his mouth to stifle a scream. His muscles throbbed, the skin of his palms turning white. His chest was tight, and his heart was racing. He couldn't breathe. The hall's walls were closing in on him, trapping him as his knees quaked, ready to buckle. Alistair's body felt as though it could explode at any moment.

This is going to pass, he told himself, repeating the thought over and over. It had to. If it didn't, it would all come out right there in the hall, regardless of who was around to hear. Rage. Fear. Exhaustion. He was going to let it all out if he couldn't manage to breathe.

Just as he was about to burst, something heavy landed on his right shoulder, making him jump and let out a sharp breath. A hand softly, but firmly, gave him a squeeze.

He turned and was relieved to find his sword and magic trainer, Druoga Drigarrson, standing before him. Druoga was a giant of a man, standing well over a head taller than Alistair. His piercing yellow eyes met his, full of concern for the High Prince.

His mahogany druidlocs were tightly tied back in a ponytail, falling long down his back to his waist. The sides of his head were cleanly shaven and covered in celnor bear knot tattoos, swirling beautifully over his scarred reddish brown skin. The tattoos, a gift forced upon him during his time as a young slave fighting as a gladiator beneath Grœnn, stretched from his head down his neck and continued past the collar of his white and violet uniform and silver armor.

Alistair stared at his mentor and friend, mouth agape, unsure of what to say. "Druoga—" A tear rolled down his cheek. He turned to wipe it away, not wishing to burden his Mentor with his perceived weakness.

"Alistair." Druoga carefully spun the High Prince back to face him. "Ye don't need to turn away from me, don't hide yer pain. It's a strength to admit when ye need help, don't think yerself weak. We all need help from time to time, and I'm here for ye, little brother, ye know that. Come here." Druoga pulled Alistair in and embraced him gently. The scent of cinnamon and leather filled Alistair's nostrils, and his tears flowed unabated, as thoughts of this morning's events ran through his mind.

When he awoke, he was happy, looking forward to finally being free to attend the Gathering after missing it these past few months. Alistair almost missed the Lunar New Year Festival last month, too.

After a hearty meal and dressing for the event, a pair of twins barged into his chamber, demanding he sate their appetites while weilding the Bedr Prael Law as their shield. Moments later, it was all he could do to hold back from lashing out in anger as he was blindfolded, bound to his headboard, and gagged. As the women descended upon him he heard someone barge through the door and demanded that they leave by order of the High Queen. They even threatened the twins if they continued to delay Alistair's appearance for the Gathering.

Alistair eventually recognized the voice; it belonged to Drouga. He knew his Master's words to be a lie, but the twins didn't. No sooner did Drouga finish intimidating them when Alistair heard the twins rush out the door. After Drouga freed him of his bonds, the two sat together a moment before his Mentor left so Alistair could dress.

The memory was short, but painful, just another to add to his collection. Alistair hugged his friend tight, his anger and sadness poured freely in this moment. He released a muffled scream into his Mentor's chest, releasing his pain and thankful for having this briefest of moments.

Alistair's heart slowed, his breath calming. Druoga stepped away and placed his hands on the High Prince's broad shoulders. Alistair focused on his breath as he looked to the floor, wiping the tears from his face.

"Ye feel better, little brother?"

Alistair chortled softly and looked up at his Mentor, seeing a small, warm smile on his rugged face. Taking a deep breath, he exhaled steadily and answered,

"I . . . I suppose I feel a little better. Considering—"

"Don't. Don't think about what could've been. Have ye thought about going elsewhere for a time? How long has it been since ye've seen Prince Daemyn? I'm sure he can use a friend right now, too. With how long it's been since his older brother left for that sea war, it must be hard on him."

"It has been a while." Alistair's gaze dropped to the floor. "A really long while, now that I think of it. However, with Lorna's nameday just around the corner, I don't think Mother will let me go."

Druoga sighed with disappointment. "I don't think it could hurt to ask . . ." He glanced up, his yellow eyes looking past Alistair, and darted about the hall with annoyance.

Alistair turned to see what his Mentor was looking at, only for his heart to sink into his stomach. People of nobility peppered the hall and stretched all the way to the throne room. Some were staring at him with leering eyes while others turned away, whispering to one another.

In his angered state, he hadn't even noticed the others in the hall. His stomach churned into a painful knot. Alistair's hands flew to his silver, raven-decorated circlet, straightening it about his head.

Druoga turned Alistair back to look at him. "Besides, if ye *actually* talk to her, I'm sure she will understand and let. Ye. Go."

Alistair took a deep breath, holding it in for as long as he could, and exhaled steadily, hearing the sense in Druoga's words. However, he couldn't help but have reservations about the decision.

"I'll try to talk to her, but there's no guarantee she'll let me go." He forced a smile to show all would be well.

Druoga stared at him for a moment before nodding in acceptance. "Alright then, come on, lad. I'll escort ye the rest of the way."

Alistair startled. "Wait, you don't have to—"

Druoga gave Alistair a stern yet determined glare, causing him to stop. With a nervous gulp, Alistair nodded for him to continue. He knew better than to try to talk Druoga out of escorting him, especially when the man just wanted to make sure he was alright.

He took a moment to compose himself, still feeling a tremor in his knees, then followed after Druoga. There was no reason to linger under these mocking eyes any longer than he already had.

Following his Mentor down the hall, some of the nobles standing about began noticing him and turned. Some bowed to show their respect to their High Prince, while others continued on with their conversations, ignoring him entirely. A few even snickered, mocking him as he passed by, their voices just loud enough to reach his ears.

"Oh look, it's the Whore of Hilliard."

"Have you lain with him yet?"

"Ugh, no. I'd rather save my virtue for someone actually worthy of me."

Their shrill voices reminded him of cats shrieking in heat. They were giving him a headache.

Alistair did his best to ignore their gibes, trying to walk tall, and kept his face still with disinterest, but that alone wouldn't cease their insults. He couldn't show more weakness, not here. It would just embolden them even more.

His chest tightened. Why did this still bother him? He hoped he would've grown used to it by now. Why could he not just tune them out? Ignore them? Why did it still hurt? Do they truly hate him that much?

Alistair's fingers curled into tight fists. He looked at the broad back of his Mentor in front of him. At least he had people like Druoga. He wished they could always be with him. It hurt less when Alistair was with them. He couldn't even remember what it was like when he was younger.

A pang pierced his heart, hanging heavy in his chest. He wondered if perhaps they had always treated him this way. Maybe Alistair just hadn't noticed because he was a child. If only he were not the High Prince. Perhaps then—No. If it wasn't him, it would just be someone else. He wouldn't wish this on anyone. Alistair had to stay strong.

Be like his father.

Alistair slid a few strands of his dark brown hair over his shoulder and twirled it around his warm ivory fingers, staring at how long it had grown. The rest hung loose down his back, nearly reaching his waist. He'd been close to cutting it short a few times, but every time he came close, he thought back to why he let it grow long in the first place.

The women of high society held most of the power in this city. He hoped that by letting it grow long, by mimicking the women of high society in this way, they might show him some semblance of respect, even if only subconsciously.

Alistair slowly raised a hand to his chest and felt for his father's ring hanging from his neck. He flattened his hand over it, feeling the iron ring under his tunic against his palm, as though his father was standing watch over him. His heart tightened.

He wondered if his father ever doubted himself. If he ever hated what he was. Alistair doubted that. He remembered the confident smile his father had on his face whenever they were out of the castle. How strong he was when he carried Alistair on his shoulder when greeting the people. The kind gestures of his father for the people showed just how much the royal family cared for them.

To Alistair, his father was amazing, and he missed him dearly every day.

Alistair's eyes stung as he returned to the present and looked up before him.

Druoga stood still in the middle of the hall, causing Alistair to do the same. "Druoga, is everything alright?"

His Mentor turned to him with curved brows. For some reason, worry showed in his yellow eyes. Alistair cocked his head to the side in confusion, looked ahead, and sighed heavily in disappointment.

The doors to the throne room were wide open, and the people of the Commoners Nest poured out. "So that's it then, I missed yet *another* Gathering. Some High Prince I am, huh?" He forced out a weak chuckle.

"This isn't yer fault, Alistair, ye know that. Like I said, talk to yer mother, *please*. This life of yers can't go on this way. I worry for ye, little brother." Druoga placed a hand on one of Alistair's shoulders, squeezing it for comfort.

Alistair turned his head away, unable to look his friend in the eyes. He kept his gaze on the floor, feeling a weight pour over him. Alistair sometimes struggled with bearing Druoga's confidence, feeling it had to be misplaced, himself unworthy of it.

"I'll . . . I'll try and talk with her. It's just, I feel like the city herself is against me. Like, she doesn't want me here. No matter what I do for her or the people, there's always something there barring my path."

"And yet ye always find a new way forward," Druoga said as Alistair looked back at him, speechless, his eyes searching. The massive man returned a confident smile to the High Prince. "It's a trial for ye, I know. I see ye try again and again, fighting as well as ye can, and the people see that too. Ye have their appreciation, Alistair. Don't believe me? See for yerself." Druoga stood aside and gestured for him to step forward to the people.

Alistair's stomach churned, but he hesitantly took a step forward toward the people exiting the throne room. Their faces lit up, eyes shining brightly as they conversed with enthusiasm.

"Did ya meet with her Grace?"

"Of course, but I was so embarrassed. Me mouth was stuffed."

Laughter echoed through the hall.

"The High Queen accepted a flower from me daughter, it was so precious."

"Her Grace plans to send someone to check over the Northwest section of the Commoners Nest, per the High Prince's request. She agreed that the buildings could use some fixin' up."

"Do ya think that means we'll need to move out?"

"Nah, it's probably just a check-up, to see what needs to be done. Everythin'll be fine, I'm sure."

The people's excited tones lightened Alistair's spirits. A small smile slowly broke across his face. They all looked so happy. So relieved. All this from simply meeting his mother, or was there something more?

Alistair noticed the crowd began to thin, and he leisurely made his way toward the throne room.

"Oh, High Prince Alistair!"

Hearing his name, Alistair stopped and turned to find an old woman doing her best to curtsy with respect. Many around her followed suit, each of their eyes locked on him.

His cheeks filled with heat as he raised a hand to the back of his neck, rubbing it in embarrassment. Sliding his hand to his chest, he bowed in return. "Please, everyone, you needn't stop for me. Carry on with your day."

He straightened and continued toward the throne room, but before crossing the threshold, a man with light brown skin stepped forward with a nervous grin. "Y-Your Grace, I wanted to thank ya for what ya did for us in the Commoners Nest East Gate area this past month. Fixin' our homes, fillin' the market with fresh produce and meats, and helpin' us keep our jobs." The man's smile turned into a worried frown. "But somethin' is happenin' in our district, somethin' that's . . . spreadin' fast, and changin' folk."

Though perturbed, Alistair was careful not to show his concern in front of his people. He stepped toward the man, keeping his outward appearance as calm as possible. "Do you know what this something is?"

A person behind him stepped forward, a young woman. She clasped her hands over her chest. "It's a drug of some kind, I think. Many of us told the High Queen about it and she assured us it'd be looked into, but, well . . . now that you're here, I'm sure ya can stop it from claimin' any more of us." She spoke with a mixture of fear and hope in her tone, as a soft smile grew on her face.

Alistair looked into their pleading eyes and carefully hid the tremble in his hands. He took a deep breath and exhaled, placing a hand on each of their shoulders, and attempted to exude confidence. "I will do my best to discover what's happening and do everything in my power to stop this, but I must ask for your patience while the Jórsalafarar and I investigate."

"That's all we wanted to hear from ya." The man responded, smiling with relief. "I knew we could count on ya, your Grace."

The commoners curtsied and bowed low in thanks, causing Alistair to smile bashfully. He placed a hand over his heart and bowed low in return. As he stood, the people each thanked him as they exited the castle. He nodded at them graciously, standing at the entrance to the throne room, and waved farewell.

Crossing the threshold, his mother's silver guard proceeded to close the massive doors. He quickly stopped and spun back around, just now remembering Druoga, but the doors closed before he had a chance to call out.

Alistair cursed at himself. He would have to make sure to ask his Mentor to look into that mysterious drug after meeting with his mother. The idea of something like that spreading through his city had him unsettled, but he was confident he and his Jórsalafarar could figure it out.

As he turned back and looked ahead, his heart dropped into his stomach.

19

Alistair

LORNA?

Alistair glanced down the long hall of the empty throne room, seeing how alone he really was. He grabbed hold of his violet tunic, feeling his stomach churn again. Alistair didn't understand why he felt so isolated, especially since he was just going to speak with his mother. He was sure she would listen to what he had to say. She had to.

His lips stretched into a nervous frown. He shook away his doubt and proceeded forward, looking around the long hall, and hoped the scenery would serve as a distraction.

The violet throne room was lit by many candles housed in silver chandeliers and tall candelabras. Large white stone pillars stretched high to the second-floor balconies. Painted celnor knotwork depictions of white dragons and black ravens flew about the wall's surface. Alistair tilted his head up to the paintings. The creatures were beautifully rendered, graceful yet fierce at the same time.

He wondered why the dragons were allowed to remain on the walls. They were a symbol of the Gold Guard. Alistair figured they would have been taken down with the rest of the old heraldry of Gullhyndr by the first Raven Queen. He chuckled lightly to himself, musing that maybe he should've paid more attention to his history teachers.

Alistair looked up near the chandeliers and saw the eight banners of the major houses of Hilliard. Each had a distinct color and heraldry, including unique inscriptions. His brows slowly furrowed over his eyes as he scanned each one.

One. Two. Three. Only three of the great houses supported him. The rest were selfish and in his opinion, were only out for themselves. They all lived in this city together. As far as Alistair was concerned, the least the great houses could do was to donate a portion of their abundant wealth to helping the people. The same people who broke their backs so these nobles could live in their lavish longhouses.

A frown stretched across his face. What more could he do? How could he convince the other houses to help? They would simply ask what was in it for them. Could he convince his mother, knowing it would likely earn her enemies amongst the nobility? What about Lorna? As much as it pained him to admit it, she likely wouldn't be swayed either.

Now that his mind had turned to his sister, he realized that while her friends made her presence felt at night, he hadn't actually seen Lorna in quite some time. It had been over a month at least. It was the same for his mother, likely even longer still. Alistair thought back to the past several weeks, to every attempt he made at spending time with his mother or his family as a whole. Each time, he was turned away. No dinners. No meetings. Nothing.

Alistair wondered if his mother no longer cared for him. His heart ached, and his eyes stung. No, that couldn't be true, could it?

Alistair knew she had been with Lorna, maybe his mother had finally gotten through to her. Lorna's lifestyle needed to change. She needed to think of others, of the common people at least, if not her own brother. He could stomach her animosity if it were to the benefit of the people.

He took a sudden deep breath through his nostrils as his jaw tightened. Lorna would be High Queen someday. Yes, that must be why he hadn't seen his mother. She had to focus on helping Lorna learn to be a better person. A better ruler. He was sure of it.

Alistair blinked back tears and exhaled steadily, continuing down the long hall to the tall dais leading up to the raven and laurel decorated silver throne. Above it hung his family's banner. A raven with its wings spread wide, surrounded by white laurels, a sixteen-pointed star at the peak and a silver crown at its base. Below the crown were the words that always gave him a sense of unease: *Fly Free and Proud.*

Honestly, what was there to be proud of? And what freedom did *he* have?

Alistair's shoulders hung low, deflated. He missed his mother, his aunts, and although she had been cruel to him for so long, he even missed his sister. He took another deep breath and exhaled. His eyes traveled back down to find his mother speaking with several of her advisers, whom were busy reading over scrolls they passed amongst one another.

She hadn't yet noticed Alistair's approach. His nerves threatened to get the better of him. What if she didn't want anything to do with him? If Lorna could be cruel to him, so could his mother. The thought turned the blood in his veins cold.

His eyes glossed and tears breached his attempt to stifle them back. He slammed his hands to his face, cursing himself. Why did he always think such depressing things? Every year it got worse, his thoughts growing ever more bleak. If he didn't figure out a way to stay above it all, he was sure he would be swallowed by the darkness slowly creeping over his mind, and may not be able to break free.

Alistair quickly wiped the tears free of his face as Alistair bent a knee and softly called, "Mother."

He looked down toward the silverish marble floor and heard his mother's conversation end. Alistair struggled to muster the courage to look her in the eyes. His pulse quickened and he tried to ignore the tremble in his hands. He balled his free hand over his knee into a tight fist to hide his concern.

"Thank you, you're all free to go. We can speak again in a few days." The skirt of her dress shuffled across the surface of the dais and the clanking of her heels sounded with every step as she descended the stairs.

"Oh my dear Alistair." Disappointment rang clear in her voice. Was she disappointed in him, or was it something else? He couldn't be sure.

Alistair's heart leaped into his throat the moment the thought had entered his mind. He tried to swallow it back down, but it was all that he could do to simply remain still.

The violet fabric of her gown slid into view. The strong scent of lilacs and sweet peas invaded his nostrils.

Alistair's eyes locked on the edge of her gown, too afraid to look up. The fabric gathered and folded over the floor. Her hands cupped his face, raising his head to meet her gaze.

His mother's face was painted with makeup to match her silver and violet gown. Her raven black hair was beautifully braided under her pointed silver crown, the raven crest staring at him with its amethyst eyes. She smiled warmly, her brows curving upward as her sapphire eyes softened with worry.

"Mo-Mother, I'm sor—"

She pressed a thumb to his lips. "Don't. Don't apologize, Alistair. I had a feeling someone stole your time. I'm sorry, fo-for . . ." Her eyes glossed and tears welled as she placed her hands on his shoulders, helping him stand.

Standing erect before his mother, she seemed to be taken aback, looking him up and down. "My goodness," she released a soft giggle, "have I not been paying attention? When did you grow so tall? Your father wasn't even *this* tall. I dare say he would be looking up to you were he still with us." The two looked at each other in silence, the smiles fading from their faces.

His mother's bright red lips trembled as she raised a hand to his cheek. Her lips parted as though to speak, but the words didn't come. Looking away, she embraced him as tightly as she could and buried her face in his chest. He heard a soft, muffled chuckle as she squeezed him tightly. "I can barely wrap my arms around you."

Alistair remained motionless, hesitant to raise his arms to her.

"Alistair . . ." Her voice cracked. "I'm so sorry."

Alistair jolted at the words, unsure of how to respond, and simply placed his arms around her, hoping the gesture would convey what his lips couldn't. After a moment, he slid his hands to her shoulders and gently placed her at arm's length, seeing her makeup now running down her flushed cheeks.

Was she upset because they hadn't seen each other in so long, or was it him? Was he a disappointment as a son? Should he have tried harder to see her sooner, or should he not have come at all?

His eyes welled up, and tears fell alongside hers. He attempted a smile and cupped her face, wiping away the tears from her cheeks, smudging her makeup. "Mother, what is it? Why are you sorry? Was it something I did, or didn't do?"

She stared up at her son, her eyes darting between his amber and amber-sapphire mixed eyes. "This life . . . you don't deserve it. The pain. You deserve better—"

Alistair instantly wrapped his arms around his mother again, holding her tightly to his chest. In that moment, all his worries cleared away, and he felt ridiculous for doubting her moments before. He took a deep breath before responding. "No matter what, Mother, I love you, and I will always stand beside you. I don't want another life. I've never wished for that. I just want to aid you and Lorna as best I can. Know that I've *never* borne anger for being your son." He lowered his head and kissed her forehead, accidentally tilting her crown askew. The two laughed as she repositioned the crown.

His mother's laughter faded as quickly as it had come. She reached into one of the pockets of her skirt and pulled out a handkerchief, and wiped her face. "By Frigg's guidance, I must look a mess, huh?"

"No, never." He replied, flashing her a playful smile as his eyes met hers.

She gently slapped his shoulder, and the two laughed softly. His mother then took a deep breath and calmed. "Alistair, would you like to have tea? With me, that is. I . . . there are matters we must discuss."

Alistair grinned. "Mother, I would like nothing more than to spend time with you."

With a sigh of relief, she continued. "That's good. Let me check to be sure I haven't left anything by the throne, then we can be off to my chamber."

Alistair nodded as he approached the dais, placing a foot on one of the steps. "You know . . . I've been hoping to meet with you all month. I suppose I wasn't trying hard—"

"I know. I'm so sorry, Alistair. There were things that . . . needed my attention." She interrupted solemnly.

"Right . . ." Alistair paused. His curiosity gnawed at the back of his mind. "Mo-Mother, where's Lorna?"

The Queen stopped halfway up the dais. Fixing the skirt of her violet and silver gown, she turned with her hands resting over her stomach. "What do you mean, Alistair?" She tilted her head askew and wore what looked like a forced smile.

Something about the look felt off to Alistair. Was she on guard? She often wore that same expression when speaking with the more volatile members of the nobility. "Mother please, it's been over a month, and I haven't seen nor heard from her since she returned from Rjóðr. Many haven't. Rumors are even starting to—"

"What kind of rumors?" She interrupted again, her eyes squinting defensively. It almost felt as if she were challenging him to answer.

Alistair gulped nervously. The rumors he heard couldn't be true, but he had to ask. It was his duty to protect her, and that alone compelled him to continue. Besides, he didn't know when next he would get another chance to ask. "That . . . That she's—"

"Dead?" His mother stated plainly. Alistair's breath hitched in his throat. "I figured as much."

"You figured! Mother?" Alistair's eyes widened, waiting, hoping that she would explain.

She raised her hands, trying to calm him. "Alistair, she's—"

"For fucks sake! Can't a woman have a little fun without being pestered by her family?"

Both he and his mother looked up to the voice at the top of the dais. The jingling of jewelry sounded as a figure stepped out from behind the silver throne.

The young woman stopped at the edge of the dais, glaring down at them both. Her usually fair skin seemed unusually pale, whiter than it had been the last time Alistair had looked at her. Her sapphire eyes stared daggers at him, and her face wore quite an annoyed expression. A silver tiara sat atop her head, gaudily adorned with an overabundance of amethyst gems, both forming flowers and dangling down the sides of her raven black hair. Her violet and white dress hugged the curves of her body tightly.

Though it had been a while, something about his sister felt . . . different, but he couldn't place just what it was that felt wrong. "Lorna?" He questioned.

She rolled her eyes and scoffed. "What? You really don't recognize your *own* sister? It's only been a month. Do I mean so little to you that you'd forget me so easily? I suppose I'll just have to make my presence better known." The last words dripped with deadly venom. She then twirled a strand of her hair around a finger, as if bored. "Perhaps your nights have been too restful of late."

Alistair stared at her angrily, the gibe hitting hard, as he had come to expect that from Lorna, but couldn't shake the feeling that something was different about her. His eyes hardened as his brows furrowed. Straightening his posture, his hands balled into fists. He was getting answers, one way or the other. "Tell me, sister, where have you been?"

"HA! It isn't my responsibility to make up for your shortcomings, *brother*. I won't be notifying you of every step I make." Lorna looked away and walked down the steps of the dais, adjusting the bangles around her wrists.

Alistair inhaled deeply, trying to calm his nerves, and focused, standing firm. "It *is* my business. As a Captain of the Queensguard—"

"Captain of the Queensguard?" Lorna stopped at the base of the steps, standing almost as tall as him, and looked on with a sneer. "Please, oh High Prince, don't make me laugh. You're a whore dear brother, nothing more, and don't ever forget that."

"Lorna! You will apologize to your brother." The High Queen commanded.

Alistair and Lorna both ignored her, their stare down unwavering.

A corner of her red lips twitched and formed into a condescending smirk. "Why should I? That is what he is. You made it so, or rather, I should say you did nothing to prevent it. Remember?" Lorna turned to their mother with a snide grin. Their mother took a deep breath. Her eyes glossed as a brief look of regret fell over her face.

Alistair stepped toward his sister, but stopped as she turned to him with a mocking grin, giggling at his gesture. Her eyes watched him daringly.

Lorna was baiting him. She always baited him, pushing him, daring him to act as his forebears acted. Vile. Cruel. Misogynistic. Purists. Alistair wasn't like them. He wasn't a monster. And would never be one.

He averted his eyes and stared down at the ground. Taking a long, deep breath to calm himself, Alistair slid a step back. "Regardless," he said softly, "you need to correct that attitude of yours, before someone——"

"Before someone, what? Kidnaps me? Assassinates me?" She laughed incredulously, waving away his concerns.

"Yes, exactly," Alistair responded sternly.

"Oh please, Alistair, you're too paranoid." She began to circle him as a lioness would its prey. "I'll be High Queen one day. The people WILL obey me, and the nobility WILL bend to my every whim. If not, there are always those who are more . . . *loyal* to take their place. Everyone, and I mean every. Single. One of them WILL bow before me. If not, they'll find their necks wrapped by nooses as I watch their final breaths leave their worthless bodies, my smile the last thing they see in this world." She shrugged, crossing her arms over her chest.

A shudder crawled up Alistair's spine as he stared speechlessly at his younger sister. Lorna then stepped closer, stopping just inches away, and gave him a conniving smirk. She cupped his cheek with one hand, the cold metal of her silver rings chilling his skin. "I suppose you may continue being Mother's bratty, favorite child for now. Go, seek what comfort you may in her warm bosom." Sliding her finger off his skin, one of her clawed rings scratched him as it withdrew.

Tears rolled down his cheeks as he raised a hand to the small cut, watching her in disbelief. He stood as still as stone, speechless, unsure of what to make of who his sister had become.

There was no way that *that* was his sister. His Lorna. Whatever happened to the little girl who loved to play knights and wizards with him when they were kids? He quickly said a prayer to Ódin and Frigg, pleading desperately to know why Lorna had become who she was now.

20

Alistair

My Father's Ring

Alistair sat alone at the edge of his bed. Sunlight glistened off his bare chest and arms, still damp from exiting his bath.

He exhaled softly, enjoying a moment of rest after a long morning of training in the ways of the sword and longbow. Archery had never been his forte, preferring the sword, but Druoga suggested he not neglect the skill as understanding the weapons' benefits and shortcomings could be invaluable, should he one day command the regiment that used it.

His dark brown hair hung braided over his shoulder, swaying lightly as he patted the heads of his black groenendael dogs, Daenery and Aegos. Alistair's eyes glanced to the golden skin of his arms and chest, a frown forming as he stared in displeasure. He couldn't help but wonder how or even why he was born with such an aberration.

Alistair had been born with what was known as second skin, or as the healers called it, Gudrídr, after the first recorded man with the same condition and color variant as Alistair. The Raven Monks of Ódin believed those with Gudrídr were touched by the gods at birth. Gold meant you were Ódin Touched, silver for Máni Touched, crimson for Týr Touched, and so forth.

Although Gudrídr was such a rare condition, there were records of others with similar anomalies, but they were kept within the Hilliard stave temple, under the protection of the High Raven. The thought of being seen in such reverence sent shivers down Alistair's spine. Most members of nobility, on the other hand, used the aberration in their arsenal of mockery.

He was startled from his thoughts by the groaning of his dogs. Their joyous calm put a smile on his face, but only briefly. His thoughts soon turned to his sister's words, nearly a week now passed. Alistair raised a hand to his cheek, feeling the remnants of the small cut Lorna left him in her parting: *If not, they'll find their necks wrapped by nooses as I watch their final breaths leave their worthless bodies, my smile the last thing they see in this world.*

The dogs softly began whimpering and nudged his muscular stomach with their cold, wet noses, prompting him to continue petting them lackadaisically.

His sister really had changed, hadn't she?

He slouched forward and buried his face in a hand. "Dammit, why couldn't I see the signs sooner?" Alistair whispered to himself. "I was sure someone was manipulating you, Lorna, that deep down you were still you, still good. Perhaps I could've stopped this turn before it was set in stone. I fear now that time has passed."

Alistair reflected over her misdeeds, feeling foolish for not accepting the truth long ago. The two worst acts she had committed haunted his thoughts. Were she anyone else, anyone but the future High Queen, the consequences would've been swift and severe.

At the outset of the War of Lions almost five years ago, Lorna failed to send for aid from Svartr and Grœnn. She was only eleven then. Lorna swore she had sent word. That something must've happened to the ravens, but no one saw her in or even near the Ravens' Nest. The event was swept under the rug, explained as being a simple mistake by a girl too young and naive to understand the importance of the task. Alistair knew differently in his heart, but chose to believe the lie. After all, how could his little sister not send him aid, knowing full well he was on the battlefield?

Then there was the time Lorna and her friends tied him down while he slept, already swept away in the hold of the medicaments he had taken to help him sleep. He awoke to the sound of a whip cracking as it hit his back, and pain exploded through his body.

He jolted at the memory. That was harder for him to justify. To look past. Perhaps it was a prank gone too far, or someone had put her up to it. Beneath all of the acts of aggression, he still held out hope that she could return to being the sweet little sister she once was when their father was still alive.

All the signs were there, plain as day, yet he couldn't face it. He supposed he was a failure as a brother, as much as she was a sister.

His chest tightened, recalling that after every *conversation* with his sister, he would avoid her for as long as he could. Her words hurt, piercing his heart as if she were using a blade. He had intentionally avoided her for a long while after she returned home from her trip to Rjóðr. That meeting had been especially unpleasant, but when he eventually sought her out, she was nowhere to be found. That was, until they met again in the throne room.

Alistair slowly opened his eyes and glanced to his left. A chain necklace hung on a small silver tree. He had left it there this morning before setting out for training, and on this chain were three things. The symbol of Óðin, the valknut, three interlocking triangles pressed into an iron medallion. The rune of protection, the algiz, was also pressed into an iron medallion. They were given to him just recently by his mother. Nestled in between them was the third item, a special ring.

Raising his head, Alistair stared at the ring and, after a moment, reached out. He grabbed hold of the chain, placing the ring in the palm of his hand. His father's ring, the Ring of Grár, was a symbol of their heir.

Vultures encircled the iron band as the sharp crown held a large black onyx stone. Alistair could just vaguely remember the colors of Grár's banner.

He then pictured his mother's ring, the Ring of Hilliard. It was silver and decorated by ravens with a large amethyst at its center. That ring would never be his; it instead belonged to the rightful heir of Hilliard's throne. That being his sister, when the time was right.

He remembered his father's story about their family so vividly. The day Alistair's grandfather rebelled against his grandmother, High Queen Valeria Hilliard IV. What the Grár Royal family didn't know was that she had already heard of the plot to overthrow her. She had been warned by Alistair's youngest uncle, Velondr, and Alistair's father, Alistair I.

She awaited their arrival with a much greater force than they could've ever imagined. Her forces took over one of the gates of Grár and waited for their enemy to enter the ravine. Once Grár's entire army was in the ravine, Alistair's grandmother set her plan in motion and trapped them. However, she lost her husband while taking the Grár royal family, but ultimately won the day.

Alistair's father would've been next in line to become King of Grár after King Verdon. Instead, High Queen Valeria IV took both King Verdon and Alistair's father from their home, crowning Verdon's second son, Darien, as King of Grár. She then banished the remaining Grár royal family from ever leaving their region of Vilzhen. Alistair's father was forced to marry then Princess Eilis Hilliard after executing his father, the traitor King Verdon, upon arriving in Hilliard.

Alistair rubbed the cold metal ring between his fingers. He wondered if he should wear his father's ring, but worried his mother would be upset if he did.

Holding the ring steady, he looked into the black onyx head, seeing a small reflection of himself in the smooth stone. His mother gave it to him after his father's death. Alistair didn't wish to wear it as a sign that he was an heir, but wanted to simply display the support and love he still bore for his father. His chest twisted as bile slowly slid up his throat.

He grabbed the thin silver chain and placed it around his neck, taking care to fix the medallions behind his father's ring. Alistair then exhaled steadily, his tension ceasing. The ring was both a comforting memento of his father and the heavy burden of his legacy.

Alistair closed his eyes, breathing deeply, and heard his sister's last words once more. His brows furrowed as he raised a thumb to his lips, placing the tip of his nail between his teeth.

He needed to speak with his mother about Lorna. He knew it needed to be done. Clearly neither of them alone could change her, save her from the path she had chosen, but maybe there was something he could do to help. There just had to be. Even after everything she had subjected him to, he wasn't ready to give up on her. He released a tired sigh.

"I'll just have to ask her." Alistair turned his head and leaned back while resting an arm on his bed. "Shu Yen, are you still here?"

"Yes, your Gra—Alistair." Shu Yen answered.

Alistair chuckled playfully. "You still find it strange to address me by my name?"

Shu Yen stepped out of Alistair's walk-in closet holding two sets of clothes for him. She looked back and forth between the garments, trying to decide which he should wear for the day. "Only slightly." She answered as she looked at him with a smile. Their eyes met briefly before she returned her attention to the clothes. "I've been using your title for so long after all. Since you were a baby." She laid a red and black tunic, a white under tunic, and a long stretch of fabric on his bed.

Alistair gave her a somber look. "I'm sorry. I should've corrected that much sooner." He leaned forward, rested his elbows on his knees, and interlocked his fingers under his chin.

Shu Yen came to Hilliard when she had only seen seven winters, sent along with many others as part of the annual gift for the Raven Queen from the Emperor of Weida Long. She had been with Alistair since he was born. Shu Yen was like an older sister to him, and this was how he repaid her. Alistair scolded himself for taking so long to correct this mistake.

The clanking of her heeled boots sounded as she stepped around the corner of his bed. "My dear High Prince." Shu Yen started softly, taking a seat beside him. Alistair winced as he felt her hand on his. He glanced at her. A pleasant smile rested on her face.

"You should know I hold no resentment. None at all. I may be your friend, but I'm also your servant. When alone, I will happily say your name, but openly, I must respect my position. Please understand, Alistair, I care for you, but this castle is my home, and I must adhere to that standard to keep it."

"You don't think I would sit idly by as you were sent out into the streets, do you?"

"No, of course not, but the choice might not be yours to make. I don't trust most of the nobility here. They would be bound to start talking if they saw us speaking so casually. We must both remember our stations. Isn't that why your mother spoke to you a few days ago?"

"Sh-She . . ." He sighed in defeat. "It did come up." He rubbed the back of his neck with his free hand, annoyed, but understood. "Alright, alright. I'll be careful."

"Thank you." With that, she patted his hand and stood up, straightening the skirt of her dress. "Now, was there anything you wanted from me, *Alistair*?" She asked with a playful smile.

Alistair chortled as he reached out, grabbing his boots by the foot of the bed, and slipped them on. Afterward, he planted a quick kiss on each of his dogs' heads, then stood. "Yes, do you happen to know where my mother is?" Alistair asked as he stepped closer to Shu Yen. She held up his pair of tunics, staring at the bright orange marble floor under them.

Stopping just before her, he cocked his head to one side. He raised a hand to one of hers to make sure she was alright. Shu Yen jumped back, flapped his tunics, and blinked innocently. "Go ahead, turn around."

"Alright." He chuckled and acquiesced.

Alistair raised his arms back and slid them into the sleeves of the tunics. She pulled the fabric up to his shoulders, then paused. His brows winced, and he peeked over his shoulder. Shu Yen's dark brown eyes seemed distant, her lips quietly moving, as though talking to herself.

"Shu Yen?"

With a twitch, she snapped back to attention and gazed up at him with an unusual smile. "What?"

He looked at her and asked. "Is everything alright?" Concern dripped from his voice.

"Yes, sorry. I'm just . . . thinking of my many chores to do today." She chuckled weakly. "Anyhow, last I checked, your mother was in the hidden throne room over by the kitchen."

He nodded in thanks and spun to face her. As he reached up to button his tunics closed, she slapped his hands away with a smirk. "Ow!" He exclaimed, shaking his hands lightly with a chortle as she fastened them closed. "That's interesting. By any chance, do you know why she's been there so often recently?"

Clipping the last button closed, Shu Yen brushed the wrinkles from his shoulders and turned away. She remained silent as she grabbed the long, black fabric and accompanying leather belt. Shu Yen brushed the velvety material, her gaze again glazing as if her thoughts were far away from here in some unknown place.

Alistair tilted his head, confused. "You know, it's okay if you don't know. She's been so distant this past month. I just want to make sure she's alright."

Shu Yen spun to him, her face still. "I'm sorry. No, I'm afraid I don't know the High Queen's business there."

He nodded in thanks and grabbed the long fabric, laying it over his left shoulder as Shu Yen wrapped the belt around his waist and buckled it tightly. Afterwards, she moved to the left side of his bed and grabbed his father's broadsword, Dancingraven, which now belonged to Alistair. She walked back and handed it to him.

Accepting the weapon, Alistair lifted it up, inspecting the elegant ravens of the guard and hilt. The scabbard was a mixture of silver and violet and was also decorated with depictions of ravens. Though it belonged to his father, it wasn't the Sword of Grár. That sword, Reaperskiss, was still in Grár with the rightful heir.

Reaperskiss had belonged to his father before the uprising, but he didn't have it with him at the time of Grár's treachery and wasn't permitted to retrieve it. Dancingraven was a gift from Alistair's mother to his father as a symbol of her thanks for helping keep the peace in Hilliard during his time as the High King, and her husband.

Alistair unsheathed a portion of the blade, allowing the silverish white metal to gleam brightly in the sunlight. A bead of sweat fell down his forehead, and he squeezed the sword's grip.

He thought back to the days when he was young and watched his father swing his sword about during training, trouncing each combatant, one by one as if it had been their first time wielding a sword. The memory was bittersweet. As more time passed the vision of his father's face continued to gradually slip away. Alistair could barely picture the man's eyes, but he remembered one being amber brown and the other as black as ink.

"Everything alright, Alistair?"

He started at the sound of Shu Yen's accented voice. "What? Yes, sorry. I was just . . . Never mind." He clipped Dancingraven to his belt, feeling the weight pull his belt low on one side. He looped and tightened the excess leather around the buckle.

"Alright then, I suppose I'll just have to speak to Mother. Hopefully, she will know of some way we can help Lorna. To stop her from becoming a tyrant."

"Alistair." Shu Yen's dark brown monolid eyes softened, and she looked at him with unusual sadness.

"What, you don't think she can be saved?"

"I didn't say that." She replied, her voice soft. She gently took hold of one of his wrists. "I just don't . . . want you to get hurt."

Alistair slipped his wrist free and cupped her hands. "I know she's frustrating to deal with, but after losing Father, I just . . . I can't lose anyone else. That includes Lorna."

Shu Yen's eyes lingered on him a moment longer, glossing lightly as if about to tear. Her lips curled inward. She took a deep breath and hesitantly nodded. "I-I know. Just . . . be careful, Alistair."

Alistair chortled in confusion. "I'm just going to talk with Mother, it's not like I'm going to battle." He started toward the door of his bedchamber as his pulse quickened and his sight went fuzzy.

Reaching for the door handle, a flash of his time in the War of Lions ran through his mind. He saw the savannah, and his hands were covered in blood. A tremor ran through his body. His breath snagged in his throat, and his knees went weak, sending him slamming into the hard wooden door. Alistair caught himself with an outstretched hand, and he buried his face in the other.

Screams and the clashing of blades surrounded him, while the scent of death filled his nostrils. Bile quickly rose in his throat, and sweat slid freely down the side of his face. The wails grew louder and louder, drowning out Shu Yen's calls and the barking of his dogs. Alistair covered his ears, trying to silence the noise.

"ALISTAIR!"

He immediately opened his eyes and jumped back, hitting the wall by the door. His breath was labored, and his heart pounded in his chest. Alistair's eyes darted around the room, searching, but not recognizing a thing.

"Alistair, it's alright, it's okay! Listen to me, breathe. Just breathe. That's it, just—"

Alistair slammed both his hands to the sides of his head and slid to the floor. Tears streamed down his cheeks. "Wh-What the fuck. Dammit! Wh-Where . . . I—"

Shu Yen grabbed Alistair's shoulders and pulled him close, embracing him, and touched her forehead to his. Her slow, steady breaths gave him something to focus on as she gently rubbed the back of his head. "Listen to me, Alistair, focus. Slow. Steady. Breathe. That's it."

His lungs began to sync with Shu Yen's. Breathing in. Then out. Inhaling, then exhaling. Over and over. Alistair's hands slowly stopped shaking. His heart relaxed. He took a deep breath and let his head fall back against the corner of the room.

Alistair closed his eyes. "Dammit. It's been what? Three weeks? Almost a month?" He let out a choked chuckle.

"The last time it triggered, you were watching the cavalry soldiers running drills in their formations. Were you thinking of something just now? Of your time during the Lion War?"

Alistair glanced at her while trying to control his breath. "I thought of the first day on the field."

Shu Yen's shoulders fell as her brows curved over her eyes. "Oh Alistair—"

"I know. I know. It just happened." He took a deep breath before continuing. "You know it's funny. I struggle to remember my father during the happier times, but I remember so vividly the night he died in my arms. Why is it that the worst memories are the ones that shine the brightest?" A tear crawled down his cheek. "I remember my first day of the war. The sky was so bright, so clear, and it was so fucking hot." Alistair laughed weakly. "Rjóðr's red wall, the one separating Veerence and Eenhide. The gateway was battered, torn down. Bo-Bodies littered the ground around it. It was—"

"Alistair, try not to think of it. I know it's hard, those memories, such horrible things. No one should have to bear such burdens. We can't let them rule us."

Alistair winced slightly. "Have you had attacks like these too?"

"Sometimes." Shu Yen hesitantly nodded. "They come when I sleep, nightmares of my time with the Serpents Blade. I try not to think of it. Come on, why don't you rest for now?"

"If I were to do that, I would only have nightmares of my own." Alistair placed his hands on the wall behind him and pushed himself up off the floor, wiping the tears from his face. "I should go . . . find Mother." He passed Shu Yen and approached the door.

"Wait. Your face is still so pale. Are you sure you're alright?"

Alistair stopped, the door now ajar. He exhaled and turned to her with a small smile. "I'm fine, I promise. Um . . . Shu Yen, you've been very kind and have cared for me all these years. Please, I want you to use this day to tend to yourself. You, more than anyone else, deserve it."

She blushed bright pink in embarrassment and sighed with defeat. "Alright, thank you. You should keep your hair braided today. It looks really nice."

"Uh . . ." Forgetting it was still braided, he softly laughed. "Aye, perhaps." He turned away and walked out of the room. His dogs Daenery and Aegos followed him down the hall, dancing around him playfully.

Alistair stopped dead in the middle of the hallway, holding his braid in his hand. His grip trembled lightly over the braid. His hand clenched briefly in a fist and untied the braid, letting the still-wet strands of hair fall long in small waves down his back. He cursed while calling himself a coward.

His hands fell limp at his sides. Alistair was sure his father wouldn't have been so weak and scared to be himself. He was strong. Stronger than Alistair could ever be.

He blinked back tears and looked at the ceiling. He told himself to take deep breaths. His heart was pounding against his ribcage. Alistair still had a duty to uphold for this city and to his mother.

Taking one last deep breath, he exhaled and looked ahead. He had to speak with his mother. And soon, before it was too late.

21

𝔄listair

Where's My Sister?

ESCENDING through several stairways and passing through many large halls, Alistair emerged near the entrance to the secret throne room. Looking down the hall, there were several curtains draped from ceiling to floor along the walls, the first black, the next blue, and so on, repeating in that fashion, stretching all the way to the far ends of the hall. He then realized he had no idea which one hid the passageway.

Eyes darting to each of the black curtains, he came to the conclusion that he would simply have to check behind each one.

Alistair glanced to his right, seeing all the large portraits of his family, feeling their eyes looking down at him. He walked along the hall, looking at many of the paintings until he stopped, his eyes focusing on a familiar portrait. It had been so long since he had been in this section of the castle. Not since his father's death. The painter had captured his father's features exquisitely. A sudden cold shiver ran through Alistair's body as he stared up at the man. Taking a deep breath, he exhaled slowly and returned his focus to the curtains, trying his best to ignore the paintings.

Approaching the black curtain nearest to him, he pulled it aside, finding only the wall underneath. Alistair continued down the hall, checking one by one, continuing his search, which quickly grew tiresome. Looking behind the fifteenth curtain and again finding only the wall, he raised a hand to the back of his head in frustration.

Alistair gave out an exasperated sigh, not realizing just how many curtains hung through the hall. There were still many more left unchecked. Thinking it over, again, he decided to start at the very beginning of the hall, thinking maybe the secret entrance was there.

Searching and searching, he walked to the end of the hall and looked behind another set of curtains. Again, he found nothing. Alistair let out an annoyed groan. "Seriously, where is it!?"

Giggles echoed and reverberated along the columns. Turning around, he saw a few servant maidens scurrying down the tunnel into the kitchen. Letting out a heavy sigh, he slumped his shoulders and rubbed his face with one hand. "Wait . . . didn't Shu Yen say it's by the kitchen?"

He walked down the hall to where the servants had stood. Startling him, his dogs rushed past him to the kitchen's entrance and began sniffing the nearest set of black curtains. After a moment, Aegos poked his nose under the fabric. His ears perked up with interest; the right being more noticeable as it was whole. The left had a small chunk missing since he was a puppy. The creature then slid his head beneath the fabric, followed by Daenery.

Alistair's breath caught in his throat, and he pushed forward in a hard sprint. "The secret entrance must be behind that curtain."

As he drew closer, the dogs' wagging tails were the only thing sticking out from under the dark curtain. He caught a glimpse of a wall protruding from the building just outside the nearest window, stretching high from behind the fabric.

Alistair skidded to a stop before the curtain and chuckled to himself. "I can't believe I didn't notice that before, but then again, it wouldn't be a secret room if it were obvious."

He reached for the curtain and pulled the thick fabric back, revealing a shadowy stairway stretching high into the darkness. His dogs sat at the base of the steps. Their tongues hung, and their tails wagged wildly. Alistair laughed warmly at his companions. Looking up into the darkness, his breath hitched in his throat. Steeling himself, he exhaled lightly to calm his nerves.

"I hate the darkness," Alistair whispered as he began forward through the threshold and closed the curtain behind him, shrouding him completely. "Uh oh, it's much darker than I thought."

Alistair took a step back and accidentally bumped his shoulder against something hard. "OW! Dammit, wha—" He spun and raised a hand to feel for what it was, but banged his hand into whatever it was. "FUCK! Come on!" Alistair stood as still as possible, careful not to knock into anything else and acquire himself more bruises.

He slowly raised his hands again to feel for the sturdy hidden object. "Is this a shelf? I wonder . . ." Alistair slid his hands across the flat surface, hoping to find something to light his path, but found nothing. "Okay . . . now what?"

Alistair stood there in the darkness for a moment, thinking of what to do. He heard his dogs whimper lightly, and the patter of their feet circled about him. They nudged him with their heads as if they too had no love for the dark. Alistair raised his hands in front of himself and felt a twitch in his fingertips.

"Perhaps . . . I've been studying to wield light magic since I was eight, but it's quite taxing and there are quite a few stairs here." Alistair looked up into the darkness and could just faintly make out a sliver of light coming from the secret throne room above. "Well, it can't be helped. At least I won't fall."

Alistair balled his right hand into a tight fist and pulled it to his chest. With a deep breath, he recalled the Celnor incantation needed for such a predicament. "Kveykva."[1]

The magic surged through his chest, then poured into his arm, and finally into his hand. A bright white light shone from between his golden-tinged fingers. He winced as his eyes adjusted to the light and stared at it briefly in awe. The light steadily grew brighter until it illuminated most of the stairway.

Alistair looked up at the stairs and back at the light in his hand. What now? Conjuring the light was one thing, but he couldn't hold it while moving.

After a moment, an idea came to mind. He thrust his hand toward the top of the stairway. The light flew from his palm and rose several feet above his head. It halted and hovered in place, casting its light throughout the surroundings.

His lips stretched into a large grin. "I can't believe it, I did it! That was easier than I thought." He took a few steps up the stairs and clapped once in excitement as the light followed. "Amazing! Alright, here we go. Come on you two." Alistair waved his hand, signaling Daenery and Aegos to follow. They both barked excitedly and accompanied him.

He couldn't believe how much easier the lantern spell was to conjure

---

1   Kveykva is Celnor(Norse) for Light or To Light.

compared to the Skjald-borg[2] or the Kveykva Hjálmrǫdull[3] spells. Perhaps that was his problem. Alistair chortled to himself. Druoga was right after all; Alistair should've started with the basics. Now he wanted to start his lessons over from the beginning. He was sure Druoga wouldn't mind.

Although starting his magic training quite some time ago, Alistair had been impatient and tried jumping straight into offensive and defensive magics instead of focusing on the basics. Druoga told him learning the basics would make it easier to conjure the stronger spells, but Alistair was adamant on prioritizing the stronger ones immediately. It was under the guise of keeping his family safe, and he didn't have time to learn the basics when they could be attacked at any time. It was a good excuse, he thought at the time, but now he knew better.

He chortled at the memory. Alistair felt he had been such a brat back then. He couldn't believe Druoga let him fumble on his own for so long. Maybe his Mentor wanted him to discover his mistake on his own. Alistair made a mental note to apologize to his old friend when he saw him again.

Reaching the top of the stairs, Daenery and Aegos waited patiently with tails wagging. He stopped at the entrance of the secret throne room and looked up to the floating sphere of light before him. Alistair grew curious as to how to extinguish the light.

"What was the spell again?" Alistair raised his hands and cupped the ball of light. "Sl-Sløkkva?"[4] He said, more a question than a command, but the light slowly dimmed.

He shuddered as the energy flowed back through his hands and arms, causing his skin to tingle. Alistair hadn't realized his magic could return to him like that. He let out a shaky breath and pushed himself forward into the hidden throne room.

Entering the large, circular room, he glanced ahead to the dais and froze. His mother was there, but was speaking with Lorna. Alistair's shoulders slumped, and he let out a nervous sigh. His mother's brows seemed to be deeply curved over her trembling sapphire eyes, and concern was etched on her face.

Alistair wondered if the two were arguing. His mother crossed an arm over her stomach and placed a finger to her bright red lips. Her demeanor seemed nervous, which struck him as odd. He hoped everything was alright.

Bracing for another inevitable confrontation with Lorna, he started walking toward them. As he approached, his mother glanced in his direction and was noticeably startled at the sight of him. Lorna turned around as well, and her eyes

---

2   Skjald-borg is Celnor(Norse) for Shield Wall.

3   Kveykva Hjálmrǫdull is Celnor(Norse) for Light Blades.

4   Sløkkva is Celnor(Norse) for Extinguish.

widened, looking uncharacteristically uneasy.

"W-What in Ódin's name are you doing here!?"

Alistair winced, but continued forward, uncertainty building within him. Lorna had never referred to Ódin by name. Ever. She always preferred Freya. Something had to be wrong.

Their mother quickly grabbed hold of one of Lorna's arms and turned her around, her back now facing Alistair. Their mother then quietly chastised his sister.

Her voice was harsh, but his mother's eyes betrayed her guise, looking more rattled than anything else, verging on panicked as they darted between Lorna and him.

Daenery and Aegos rushed past him to his mother's sides. Both turned to Lorna with hair bristling and teeth bared. They growled defensively and caused Lorna to startle back.

Alistair jolted forward to stop his companions, filled with confusion. As much as his dogs had never been fond of Lorna, they would never lash out like this. "Come on now, what's gotten into you two?"

Struggling to gain control of the dogs, he glanced at Lorna. Fear was plain on her face, and her eyes were trembling, but something was amiss. Lorna's eyes had always been a deep shade of blue. This woman's eyes were pink!

His eyes slowly widened as the realization set in. "Oh no!"

Alistair's hand flew to the hilt of his sword. Without a second's hesitation, he drew it from its scabbard and rushed at the imposter, swinging the large blade wildly at his foe. The imposter startled back, just barely dodging his blade by a hair, but slipped on the fabric of her dress and fell flat on her backside.

Seeing the opening, Alistair stepped forward, ready to strike. She looked up at him, seemingly terrified, and attempted to crawl away in vain. Her flat shoes lacked traction and continuously slipped on the fabric of her lavender, pink, and white dress.

Helpless and scared as she was, rather than strike her down, he fought back the rising fury in his heart and pointed Dancingraven toward her. "Who are you and what have you done with my sister?"

Her breath caught in her throat. "Wait, how did you—"

His mother gasped behind him. "Valhalla, your eyes!"

Alistair startled, pausing as his mother's concern for the intruder was clear in her tone. Confusion clouded his thoughts. He glanced back at her, eyes searching for an answer. "Mother, you know her?"

A sweltering heat called his attention back to the unknown woman, and as he turned, he found her still on the floor, but a torrent of flame whirled between them. Its light was so bright, he was forced to raise his free arm to shield his eyes lest he be momentarily blinded. He could just barely make out her visage through the gale of fiery fury. There, she stretched her arms out wide, then dismissed the flames. In her hands, she now tightly gripped a hand-and-a-half longsword. Where moments before she seemed a fearful, harmless thing, now knelt an unflinchingly dauntless opponent, her gaze steeled and exuding an essence of one not to be taken lightly. She swatted away his sword with the face of her blade and rose.

"Dammit! She knows magic?" He hopped back as the imposter shoved the fabric of her dress to one side and raised her sword defensively.

He tightened his grip on the hilt of Dancingraven and his brow furrowed hard over his eyes. His anger reignited as he realized he had been kept in the dark. Something regarding his sister had been kept from him by his own mother, no less. Where before he had no outlet for his anger, he now had just the circumstance to let it all pour forth. His father's horrible death. The memories of war haunted his dreams. The nightly torments visited on him by his sister and others of the nobility, while his mother stood idly by. As his fury reached its crescendo, he forgoed restraint and attacked. He would have answers. Now.

Alistair lunged toward the imposter, his sword raised high, and swung down on her with all his might. To his surprise, she was much faster than she had been when caught off guard. She planted her feet and swiftly blocked the attack with ease. The edge of his blade slammed down on the face of her sword. The sound of the strike rang out and echoed about the hall.

Without a moment's hesitation, she forced him back with a hard shove. Finding his footing once more, he attacked again and again, unleashing a volley of strikes with each signaling a death knell for his opponent. She gracefully dodged and blocked each of Dancingraven's strikes, but not once did she raise her blade to strike back.

His heart raced as his breath was heavy. Sweat slid down his face, and his palms ached. Alistair's knuckles turned white as he squeezed the hilt in anger. Alistair's teeth ground, and he snarled through a clenched jaw. His body was tense with agitation, and the same questions repeated over and over in his mind. Who was this impostor? Why did she look like Lorna? What was his mother's connection to this? What in the realm of Helheim was going on here?

As Alistair continued his relentless assault, the two fought at a stalemate, and they both eventually began to tire. His attacks slowed, as did her deflections. His muscles ached, but the years of pent-up rage fueled him. All the while, her unwavering, determined stare followed him.

Feeling his body giving way to exhaustion, he refocused his attacks, forcing her to favor her left side in the hopes that she would falter first. Strands of her long, raven black hair stuck to her sweat-filled face. As she twirled about, her step heavied and the sound of their blades sang through the hall.

Alistair swung a powerful attack aimed at her hip, forcing her again to step aside. She attempted another twirl to position herself behind him, but it seemed Alistair's strategy had paid off. Her foot landed on the fabric of her dress and she slipped, sending her falling to the floor.

He turned to her, tired and arms numb, but his anger kept him going. As she struggled to pick herself up, his feet set firmly, and all the strength he had left gathered for a finishing strike. Now was his chance. Alistair raised his sword high in the air and brought it down upon her.

She quickly looked up and braced to defend. His sword smashed into hers. At the moment their blades met, her sword twisted, catching the brunt of the attack again on the flat part of the blade.

Had his attack struck the edge of her blade, the fight would have been over. The power of his attack would have driven her own sword into her chest. Instead, the sudden shift of her blade and her positioning of one hand on her hilt and the other on the blade, she dispersed much of his attack through a wider area and survived, but was now pinned down. Struggling to hold him back, he forced all his weight down onto the sword.

The imposter's arms trembled wildly as she bared her teeth. Her pink eyes darted between his fiery stare and her blade as he forced it closer and closer toward her neck. His blood boiled, jaw sore from gritted teeth, and snarling with fury. He swore to Ódin that if anything happened to his sister Lorna, no matter how monstrous she had become, he would make the imposter pay. One way or another.

"Alistair, STOP! She's not our enemy. This I promise you!" His mother screamed out, her tone both an order as much as it was a plea.

Alistair glanced at his mother, her words piercing the veil of his blind wrath, then returned to the woman below him, who was literally bearing the weight of his anger. The worry clear on her face struck him as an arrow, causing him to startle. Tears welled and fell from her eyes, but didn't seem to be for her own well-being. He had seen that countless times during his time at war. These seemed to be tears of sympathy, understanding, and regret.

His breath caught in his throat as he pulled his weight back and withdrew. She let out a sharp gasp, breathing heavily, and didn't take her eyes from him. He felt his body fiercely tremble as fury and confusion swirled within him. Alistair looked at his free hand, which shook uncontrollably.

He wanted to ask—No, demanded to know what was going on? Where was

Lorna? Did something happen to her? And who was this pretender? How long has his mother been lying to him?

Alistair's jaw tightened, teeth grinding, and his eyes locked on his mother, silently pleading for answers. He slid his hand through his sweat-drenched dark brown hair, pushed the loose strands from his face, and wanted to rip them out. The questions repeating over and over in his mind were like torture?

He took a deep breath and screamed, releasing all his anger and frustration in one massive roar, feeling years of anger leave him. His scream echoed through the throne room and probably down the secret stairway.

Alistair's breath finally relaxed, his heart steadying, even though his throat was tight and in pain. He stood himself upright and took one last deep breath. He then sheathed Dancingraven. His hand lingered on the weapon's hilt, squeezing it tightly as he tried to extinguish the burning anger within him, and just managed to let go.

He turned to his mother, and she startled as their eyes met. Recalling memories of a previous conversation, a scowl formed on his face. "You promised you would never lie to me again. Never deceive me. Do you remember!?"

His mother's eyes glossed, heartache clear in her stare. She remembered.

Alistair pointed to the imposter who was slowly rising from the ground, her body trembling from exhaustion. "What's going on here? Who is she and where's Lorna!?"

His mother stared back at him with tear-filled eyes. Her painted lips parted, but no words came forth; instead, she clutched her hands tightly over her chest.

"Mother, please!?" Alistair pleaded, searching and impatiently awaiting answers.

Feeling heat behind him, he turned to the imposter. She dismissed her longsword in a whirl of fire. Her eyes lingered on the floor briefly before meeting his and looked past to his mother. The woman's expression caught Alistair off guard, seeming a mix of compassion and concern. "Eilis, I think . . . it's time that you told him what happened."

Alistair glanced back at his mother. A few small tears fell from her sapphire eyes and ran down her flushed cheeks. In silence, she closed her eyes and turned to walk toward the dias, toward her throne.

He followed her with his gaze. "Mother?" Alistair called softly as she continued on, disappearing behind her silver throne. His brows twitched as he stared on in confusion.

Glancing at the imposter, she nodded once, silently suggesting he follow after his mother. A hollow pressure began to build in his chest. Why wouldn't they just tell him what was wrong? Why the silence? The secrecy?

A pit of molten lead formed in his stomach. His nerves flared. He looked to where his mother disappeared and followed after her.

Each step felt heavier than the last, weighed in uncertainty, and steeped in anxiety. Although growing closer to the answers he sought, his vision narrowed, the image of the throne seeming to extend further and further in the distance.

Alistair jolted as something cold and wet rubbed against his hands. He looked down and found his dogs, Daenery and Aegos, whimpering beside him. In all the commotion, he had forgotten they had come with him.

He placed a hand atop their heads, feeling the soft, black fur rub against his palms. "Stay here and wait for me, alright." Daenery and Aegos sat, looking up at him, seeming just as concerned as he felt. "Don't worry, I'll be fine." Alistair flashed them a weak smile and continued to the dais.

Once there, he climbed the steps up to the silver throne, his throat drying the higher he climbed. An invisible weight pressed against Alistair's shoulders. His mind raced with all the possibilities of what awaited him. What answers would he find, and why was he stricken with this unbearable sense of dread?

The ache in his gut and the worry of what lay ahead felt as though he was tethered to an immovable anchor, fighting to hold him in ignorance, but he continued forward, knowing he couldn't remain in the darkness any longer.

His fingers slid along the throne's cool silver surface. Alistair could hear weeping just ahead. He walked around to the back of the throne, and there his mother waited, tears flowing freely down her flustered cheeks and holding back black curtains leading into a darkened room. Alistair glanced down beneath the curtain and saw a faint, cold mist flowing from within.

He stepped closer to his mother, who watched him in silence. The room was obscured by the hanging fabric. As Alistair readied himself, he stepped forward, but paused as his mother spoke. "Alistair, I'm so sorry for keeping this from you." Her soft voice cracked, straining to finish her sentence.

Alistair's trembling eyes watched her, his heart sinking. He didn't know what she meant. Why would she be sorry? His thoughts paused on one possible answer, the only logical answer, but he refused to accept it. Without hesitation, he ducked under the curtain and walked through the entrance.

The room was freezing. The hairs on the back of his neck stood on end. He raised his hands to his biceps, attempting to warm them as his body shivered. His breath puffed in small whisps as he breathed. Why was it so cold in this one room alone?

Alistair looked about and saw a bright blue light shining down in the center of the room, coming from a circle of runes carved into the ceiling above.

A chill crept up his spine as he slowly followed the light down to the very center of the room. Alistair stopped, his body was as still as stone and his eyes widened in horror. The thing he feared most of all lay before him. A young woman lay motionless on a white marble pedestal. Her white and yellow dress was heavily stained with blood, but he recognized the gown beneath the carnage. It was the dress his sister wore the last time he had seen her.

Alistair's breath caught in his throat. "Mo-Mother?" He tried to turn to his mother; however, his eyes were transfixed on the young woman.

Alistair slowly walked toward the pedestal, hoping beyond hope she was simply sleeping. Perhaps this was some sort of coma or magical state of suspension. He stopped before her, staring down at the young woman.

Her pale skin was now a bluish gray, and a long, deep cut stretched across her throat from one side to the other. Raven black hair fanned out beneath her. He followed the trail of blood down her gown and found a second wound on her right side.

Alistair raised a hand to one of Lorna's, lying flat on her stomach. As the tip of his finger touched the back of her hand, he pulled away lightly, shocked by the icy bite of her flesh. He reached out again and grabbed hold of her hand, feeling the painful cold against his warm grip.

"L-Lorna . . . Lorna?" Tears fell from his eyes while disbelief and guilt set in. "No no no . . . No. No! Lo-Lorna, you can't be—" His free hand flew to his trembling lips, looking her over as feelings of anger, sorrow, regret, and hopelessness flowed over him all at once.

Memories of his sister flooded his thoughts. As a baby, she had such tiny fingers. They looked so small, grabbing hold of his hand.

His vision flashed before him. He remembered Lorna learning to walk as he helped guide her forward, step by step.

Everything blurred. Pink ribbons adorned her hair as a little girl. She chased him through the Crimson Garden with a wooden sword in hand, pledging to save Alistair from some evil sorceress as they played.

His heart tore as though he were peppered with arrows. He failed her. His sister. And he felt so incredibly sorry that he did.

Alistair fell to his knees, breath heavy, and body shaking. Touching his forehead to the cold marble, the world around him crumbled away as he gave in to anguish and despair.

22

Alistair

LORNA LOVED NO ONE

Alistair was forced to go about the day as though nothing was wrong, as though he hadn't just seen the deceased body of his little sister. He wore a forced smile for those who had shown him and his family nothing but kindness, pretending that everything was alright, when really, all he wanted to do was scream and cry.

However, beneath the pain, deep down, a small part of him felt comfort in the thought that he would no longer be haunted by the looming dread of what torment Lorna would visit upon him next, and that her absence would likely ease the burdens she placed on the common people. The thought turned his stomach and only served to add guilt to his dour state of mind.

Alistair visited the Crimson Garden for a short time, hoping to find guidance in dealing with his grief. Memories of his sister, both good and bad, enveloped his thoughts, but the garden offered little in the way of respite. There was just too much history here, and the only insight he gained was to do as his mother had told him. Wear the guise of the dutiful High Prince. Conceal the heartache. This was already something he was well accustomed to doing, but Lorna's death hit differently. The spark of hope that one day she would see reason and return to the loving little sister she had once been was cut out of him. The finality of death meant that her legacy was carved in stone. She would always be known for her deeds in her final years.

He passed through the door of his bedchamber, but stopped as he looked out his balcony, and for a moment watched the sun as it set on the city of Hilliard. His favorite colors painted the sky in a beautiful array of deep orange and red. Alistair's dogs Daenery and Aegos ran inside and headed to the balcony. Their tails wagged too and fro, their faces happy, and they propped themselves up on the stone railings.

Alistair continued into his bedchamber, when his breath caught in his throat. The room began to spin. He stumbled forward and slammed the door shut behind him, then fell back against its wooden surface.

His heart raced, and his muscles spasmed. He wasn't sure what to do. Alistair raised his hands to his chest, clutching his father's ring as tightly as he could, and let his head fall back. Breath flowed uneasily as short bursts through his nostrils. Tears welled up under his eyelids. Try as he might to hold them back, it was of no use. The dam had broken, and hot streaks flowed down his cheeks.

Old memories of his sister bombarded his mind, coming in flashes. Moments. The images flooded his mind so quickly that he couldn't distinguish from one to the next. His jaw tightened, and his teeth ground against each other. He hesitantly pushed himself off the door, struggling to walk straight, but his vision blurred. Doubling over, he clawed at his chest as his throat tightened and struggled to breathe.

Croaking out Lorna's name, he tried to apologize for not being there to protect her, but found his words wouldn't come. He felt like he was trapped in a whirlpool, sinking deeper and deeper into the void. The ability to breathe was nearly lost to him as he cursed in frustration.

He grabbed for his belt, fumbling to remove the constricting accessory. As the buckle unclipped, it and the sword both crashed to the floor with a loud, echoing clang. His hands flew to his ears, trying to drown out the sound while the now loose black fabric draped over his shoulder slid off and fell to the floor. He looked up to his balcony, desperately wanting to feel the fresh air against his two-toned skin.

Alistair hobbled toward the opening, but he only got as far as his vanity. He nearly gave way to gravity's pull but slammed his hands hard on the wooden surface to catch himself, panting. Alistair opened his eyes and stared at the mahogany surface, watching the tears as they dotted the smooth wood. Questions gnawed at the edges of his mind. Why did his mother keep Lorna's death a secret? They hadn't shared many words after he stumbled onto the truth. Just an apology and a command to act as if all was well. She should have told him sooner. Why had she left him out of whatever plan she had concocted to find the one responsible? Lorna had many enemies, but who would have had the gall to act?

Alistair startled as he heard the door to his chamber creak open.

He glanced through the disheveled dark brown strands of his hair to spot Shu Yen in the doorway. Her eyes were bright with confusion. She looked back and forth between him and Dancingraven on the orange marble-tiled floor. "Alistair, what happened? What's wrong?" She rushed to him without a moment's hesitation and placed a hand on his back. Her caress was gentle, and her other hand grasped his muscular arm. "Talk to me, Alistair, what troubles you?" Shu Yen asked in her light accent.

For a long moment, he could only respond with a look. His lips trembled, and tears still flowed down his cheeks. He began to wonder if his friend knew of Lorna's death.

"Tell me, Shu Yen, did you know?" He asked. Shu Yen tilted her head curiously at him and seemed to be waiting for him to elaborate. The words came with great difficulty, but he managed; he needed to know. "Of Lorna's death, I mean."

Shu Yen's hands jolted away. Her caring, dark brown monolid eyes were filled with surprise and turned away. When she met his eyes again, he could see the regret plain on her face.

"That answers it then." His heart hurt. His mother had trusted Shu Yen before her own son with this secret. He was one of the many left out. "Did you all think me a nuisance? Is that why you kept me in the dark?"

"No! No, Alistair, we never thought that at all."

"Then why?" Alistair's eyes trembled, and his words bit. "Why did you all keep me out of this?"

"I-I don't know." Shu Yen's eyes shook with remorse. "You know it isn't my place to ask questions. I just . . . I just follow your mother's commands."

Alistair narrowed his eyes for a moment, but before he could respond, the door to his bedchamber opened once more. The tapping of shoes sounded and was promptly followed by a young woman entering the room. Alistair startled with a jolt. Of all the people he would've expected at that moment, he never would've named the impostor to be the one to visit, especially after their earlier confrontation.

He straightened his posture and quickly wiped the tears away from his face. Glaring at the floor beside him with hands tightly closed into fists, he searched his thoughts for how to proceed.

She was still dressed as his sister Lorna, which ignited several conflicting emotions within him. Logically, he assumed it was the only way she could really meet with him. It wouldn't be proper for an unknown stranger to freely walk the castle, let alone visit the High Prince's bedchamber. She wasn't a noble, as far as he was aware, so the Bedr Prael Law didn't apply to her. Lorna, on the other hand, had full access to him. The imposter also likely needed to regularly make appearances here and there to keep up the guise that Lorna was still alive. As much as it made sense, he still didn't like it. His emotions were still raw.

Alistair took a deep breath, hoping to calm himself before letting his anger get the better of him. He turned to the imposter with a stern stare in his mixed colored eyes. "Why—" He started but instantly stopped himself, his voice already elevated. It was all he could do not to unleash a string of curses at her, none of which she deserved. Alistair's eyes remained closed, and he kept his head turned from the woman, unable to look at her as she was in this form. "Please, whatever your reason for being here, the least you can do is remove that damn disguise while in my presence."

The room was quiet for a long moment. Alistair wondered how she would respond. Would she acquiesce? Would she be angered by his outburst, or bear him ill will for their earlier confrontation? He then heard a long sigh, followed by the click of the door and the imposter's surprisingly soft voice. "I understand. Shu Yen, can you help me with the wig?"

He listened to the clanking of her heels and the jingling of her jewelry as the two women removed the disguise. As he opened his eyes, he first saw Shu Yen holding a wig in one hand and a circlet in the other. His gaze then panned over to the woman who had been keeping up this charade, for how long he didn't know. He wondered if it were actually her, and not Lorna, whom he had spoken with in the throne room just after missing the Gathering about one week ago.

He was taken aback by her appearance. Her short, raven black hair reached her shoulders. She had soft, porcelain white skin and beautiful pink eyes. The only thing he could remotely relate them to was a pair of pink diamonds his mother had worn a few times during the springtime festivities, but even those paled in comparison. For some reason, he couldn't shake the feeling that he had seen those eyes before. They were familiar to him, but he wasn't sure where from.

His heart fluttered in his chest.

Alistair cleared his throat, hoping that it would free him of the strange, yet warm feeling. The two silently stared at each other. She raised a hand to her forearm, and a look of discomfort formed on her face. Alistair wondered if it were an injury he had caused during their fight. Everything had happened so fast that his memory of their duel was blurry at best.

"Well," Alistair finally broke the silence, "why are you here?"

"I—Oh, right." With a hand, she grabbed some of the fabric of her white, lavender, and pink dress, and curtsied low to him. "My name is Valhalla Önnîka. I was summoned by the High Queen to aid her in finding who took the High Princess's life."

"And . . . how long have you been at this?" Alistair asked, his brows curving over his trembling eyes. He felt overcome by a feeling of dread as he waited for her answer. Would he feel better if she had just begun? Would it be worse if she had been at it for a long while now? And if she had been here, deceiving him for a long time, how could he not have noticed sooner?

"Not long. A week, maybe two at most. Your mother . . . the High Queen, thought it best that I train for a month to learn the ways of your sister's—"

"A month!? Lorna has been dead for a month!?" Alistair stared at Valhalla with wide eyes. His outburst had made her visibly uncomfortable. Regret shone in her eyes.

He eyed her closely as she took a deep breath and seemed to struggle at holding his gaze, which only served to aggravate him further. "I-I'm her son. A Captain of the Queensguard, charged with keeping the High Queen and her heir safe, and-and . . ." His eyes blurred, and his throat tightened. "She asked for you, a complete stranger, to aid in this threat against *my* family!?"

"Your Grace, I can only assume—"

"Don't! Don't even fucking—NGH!" Alistair buried his face in his hands, stomped over to his bed, and slumped down on its foot.

The only sound filling the room was from the wind blowing outside and the pounding of his heart. Alistair took a few deep breaths, which did nothing for him now. His hands slid up and balled into fists over his forehead, accidentally grabbing hold of some of his long hair strands. In his frustration, he nearly pulled them out.

He could hear footsteps slowly coming toward him, and after a moment, a hand wrapped around one of his wrists. As his fist was pulled from his face, Alistair opened his eyes and found himself faced with Valhalla. She was kneeling down on the floor and looked at him with concern.

"Listen to me, your Grace, issues of trust were not why the High Queen came to me instead of you. I'm sure it was fear, though she would never admit it. Please, I'm sure her Grace wanted to come to you about this, but . . . from what High Princess Embla explained, it seems the High Queen is not . . . thinking clearly." She spoke her last words with hesitation.

Valhalla then looked away from Alistair and pulled out a large white leather journal from somewhere behind her. She placed it softly on his lap. His eyes darted back and forth between her and the journal. Confused at first, he opened the book and read the familiar handwriting within.

"Is this—"

She nodded. "It is. This is High Princess Lorna's journal. Everything I needed to know about her is written here. How she felt about people, her duties, her family . . . it's all here." Valhalla fell quiet and glared at the journal, which startled him.

"What is it?" He asked.

"Her Grace has . . . many unkind words about you. Your family. Even your friends." Valhalla stopped for a moment, as though considering her words carefully. "I know about the many arguments the two of you had. She even gloated about causing you to walk away in tears. So, why?" Valhalla looked up at him, curiosity crossing her face.

"Why what?" His eyes shuddered.

"Why would you shed tears for someone like your sister?" Her brows pushed hard against each other.

He stared at his sister's journal. Alistair slid a hand across one of the pages, trying his best to ignore its contents as his chest tightened. His eyes blurred. "Fo-For a long time I . . . longed for the return of my sister, of who she was before our father's death. I still remember when she enjoyed my company. We played together, snuck food out from the kitchen and ate while hiding in the many gardens of the castle, only to eventually be found and scolded later on." Alistair chuckled weakly, but instantly frowned again. "I just . . . was holding out hope—" His voice cracked as he spoke. "That my little sister would come back to me, but . . . I suppose the person she became is—" A few tears flowed down his cheeks. "Is who she really was, wasn't she?"

Alistair didn't want Valhalla to answer. Not really. He didn't want to know the answer, but in his heart, he already did.

Valhalla looked away. "I'm sorry, but I don't know who she was before your father passed. I only know her thoughts from after, but if Lorna did change," she grabbed chunks of pages and flipped them to the very first one, "it may have been due to a lie told to her by Lady Berenice Drigun Rosa."

Alistair's eyes widened. "What lie?"

"It seems . . . Lady Berenice convinced your sister that the High Queen never loved her and that she favored you, her son, over a daughter, and that any affection you showed her was a lie to further your own gains."

"What!? No, we . . . we would never—"

"The timing couldn't have been worse, Your Grace. After your father passed, you and your mother succumbed to your depression. Your lack of wanting to be with anyone convinced the High Princess . . . that you two didn't care for her." Valhalla looked at him.

Alistair could only stare at her with trembling eyes. His mouth hung agape, unable to say a thing in protest.

Valhalla's eyes softened. "I'm sorry, your Grace." She stood up and walked to Shu Yen.

His friend helped Valhalla put on the wig and circlet once more, making sure to hide her short, raven black hair underneath. Valhalla thanked Shu Yen and glided toward the door of his bedchamber.

"Wait." The word escaped his lips before he knew how to continue. She stopped as soon as she grabbed the door handle and glanced back at him, as though knowing what he was about to say. Alistair steeled himself and gathered his thoughts, then continued. "I will be a part of this investigation. But know this, whoever we discover to be my sister's murderer, whoever is threatening *my* family. Don't. Get. In. My. Way."

Valhalla smirked. "I had a feeling you would want to take part, but remember, her Grace still needs us to act the part. So please, whatever you do, don't hinder your mother's plan."

Alistair glared at her for a moment but nodded. "Don't you worry, I won't ruin a thing."

23

Alistair

Impatience and a Lead

I t had been five days since Alistair found out about his sister's death. Five long days, he hadn't been allowed to mourn. Five days pretending everything was fine. He continued the charade, arguing with a woman who looked like his sister in front of all who needed to believe she was still alive. It had been exhausting, and they were no closer to finding Lorna's murderers. Alistair's patience was wearing thin.

He sat, forlorn, on the steps of the dais in the secret throne room and read a newly released romance story, hoping for a temporary escape from the events unfurling around him. Instead of finding enjoyment in the substance of the pages, his mind kept wandering elsewhere.

His mother temporarily ceased the Bedr Prael Law, claiming an incident had befallen him in training, leaving him with a *weakened constitution*. Alistair adopted a subtle limp in his gate to support the claim. This was met with a not-so-surprising amount of ire from the nobility, especially those whom he counted as enemies, but was ultimately accepted as a necessity. The excuse also gave his mother the excuse she needed to place guards about him at all times without raising suspicions.

The newfound freedom felt odd at first, but gave him the opening needed to begin his investigation into his sister's death. As much as he hated the Bedr Prael Law, he had grown accustomed to his torment, and its absence left him unsure if he could let his guard down. He barely spent the first few nights, awaiting the knocking on his door that never came, but by the fourth night, he was finally able to rest.

In his mission to uncover the facts about his sister's death, he spoke with every one of Lorna's backers, careful not to give away his reasoning for the questions. He simply claimed he was doing his duty as her protector, cataloging her goings-on of the last several months. He had to keep the timeframe wide, starting long before the time of her death. He didn't know when the plot had started and needed to know her everyday habits to establish a baseline so that when something unusual occurred, he could make note of it.

They treated Alistair just as he had expected, like he was worthless, no more important than a raven's droppings. They ignored and mocked him, acting as though they were better. He gleaned little from them and so sought out Valhalla. Seeing her parade around as his sister for some reason made his blood boil. Through no fault of her own, she had become the living embodiment of his failings, a reminder of his guilt. He feared taking out his anger on her and so avoided the possibility entirely, keeping his distance unless absolutely necessary.

He kept their conversations brief. He demanded that she give him any information she found, and he shouldn't have been surprised by her responses. She seemed hesitant to speak with him. He wondered if she feared him. Alistair controlled his anger as best he could, but occasionally his composure slipped, which he regretted. The information Valhalla had found didn't seem directly linked to Lorna's death, but she had discovered a shocking number of the noble houses secretly backed Alistair. Only a select few were outspoken about it, but apparently, many felt that he had proven himself to be a much-needed pillar for the people, both noble and peasant alike.

Rattled by the information, he shook lightly away the thought and tried to focus on the book in his hand, written by Erma Friggtadottir. Books were only ever penned and published when ordered by those of high society. Authors made their rounds in commoner sections of cities, telling their tales to any who would listen in the hopes of being noticed by one with the means to fund their work.

Alistair was gifted this copy just a few days ago by his aunt Embla. Thinking of her, a smile snuck its way onto his face.

He stared at the page before him. The love interest of the story was confessing her feelings to the main character: *I love you, do you hear me, Imera? When the sun has been eaten and the moon devoured. When the sea has turned to poison and the sky cracked. When the world is nothing but darkness and all is forever lost, I will still love you. Don't ever forget that, my Imera.*

Alistair's cheeks blazed with heat as he read the words. His heart fluttered and raced. He hoped to one day find love like that. Someone to tell him that they love him and that they would be there for him, no matter what.

Music began to sound, pulling his attention from his book. He looked up to see his mother busy teaching Valhalla the dances known in Hilliard. For some reason unknown to him, Alistair found himself at the same time enthralled and frustrated with Valhalla. He was sure it was largely in part due to her being disguised as his sister, but there was more to it. She willingly stepped into this situation, a stranger, knowingly putting herself at risk of harm with little to gain from it.

Folding a corner of the page, he looked away from Valhalla and leaned back on the steps, placing the book on the floor next to him. Alistair tried to think of all the angles he could've missed in his interrogations in trying to discern who could've killed Lorna; however nothing fell into place. His brows furrowed frustratedly over his eyes.

"I don't think this is working as well as I'd like. Alistair, can you come here, please?"

Alistair looked up at the sound of his mother's voice, and the music ceased. He pushed himself up from the steps and made his way to her. She met his eyes and gestured at Valhalla. "Do you mind dancing with Valhalla? I think this would be easier if she had a partner."

Alistair groaned. He wasn't in the mood for this. With everything going on, how could they focus on dancing of all things?

His mother, seemingly noticing his aggravation, crossed her arms over her chest and continued. "Alistair, please, like you, Lorna was a great dancer. Valhalla must learn these steps before tomorrow, or she may be found out."

Alistair's shoulders fell back, and he released a strong exhale in protest. Begrudgingly, he stepped beside Valhalla and raised a hand to her. He could see the hesitation clearly on her face, and her brows curved over her pink eyes.

She raised her hand, slowly and cautiously, sliding her fingers across his palm. As she grasped his hand, a strange warm feeling crawled its way up his arm, making the hairs on the back of his neck stand on end. His brows twitched uneasily, but he shook the feeling away. Once they assumed their positions, Alistair's mother clapped her hands, signaling for the musicians to begin anew.

The melody started slow and at a hum, like birds just beginning to stir on a spring morning. Alistair stepped gracefully away from Valhalla, crossing his legs, then straightened. They held their arms aloft at their sides, hand in hand. Moving his arm in a quarter-circle arc, he guided Valhalla around to his front.

As if moving on its own, his body pulled her toward him. It was as if lightning had surged through every fiber of his muscles and caused his arm to retract, his hold on her hand firm and unwavering. He could've, should've been more gentle, and at the time didn't know or understand what had come over him. Her eyes widened with surprise as she barreled into him.

He cursed under his breath, angry with himself, but pretended it didn't happen. Alistair placed his free hand on her hip and held his other hand outstretched to one side. He stared into her eyes, her beautiful, rare eyes. The strange, warm sensation filled his chest. His heart fluttered wildly, and his breath escaped him.

Alistair tried to focus on the task at hand but found himself distracted. Valhalla was beautiful, but what of it? Why did his thoughts cloud over and his focus grow wary the greater her proximity came? The feeling gnawing at the forefront of his mind was familiar but distant, and he found it both distressing and unwelcome. He needed to focus on something else, anything else. It wasn't like he didn't have more important concerns.

Valhalla paused for a moment, looking at him with clear apprehension. A pang of guilt ran through him as she took a handful of the folds of her bright blue and white, butterfly-decorated dress, and placed the other gently atop his outstretched forearm. Forcing himself to find his composure, Alistair began to guide Valhalla to the rhythm of the music.

The two twirled and stretched themselves about the floor. Valhalla moved in perfect harmony with him, gliding gracefully to the rhythm of the music. Her arms swayed with the fluidity of water sliding over the bedrock of the tempo.

Alistair found himself surprised at how well she was keeping up with him. She was quite gifted. Confident. Graceful. A skilled dancer in her own right. Most of all, she progressed through the lesson effortlessly.

He found Valhalla to be impressive. In public, she encapsulated Lorna perfectly. In private, she had shown herself to be quite kind. She took care in her choice of words, especially when speaking of the late Princess, never once speaking ill of her in front of him. Instead, she only mentioned facts. She also asked him how he was holding up, but never pressed the subject. He was surprised at just how dutifully she dedicated herself to the role while not once forgetting their true goal.

As drawn to her as he was, she was still disguised as Lorna, which did little to ease the conflict within him. Images of Lorna's cold, still corpse flashed through his mind. His eyes hardened. His lips tightened and curled inward as his frustrations grew. They had no leads. No clues to go on whatsoever. Nothing. And here he was, dancing.

As Valhalla was emerging from a twirl, he abruptly grabbed hold of her wrists. His jaw clenched, and muscles burned. His anger nearly got the better of him, but as his eyes met hers, he quickly let her go and stepped several feet back. The music came to a screeching halt. His hands flew to his hair as a storm of emotions swirled and bubbled to a breaking point.

"What in Helheim are we doing!?" He screamed out.

His mother jolted at the outburst. Her mouth fell open, but no words came forth. Her silence only served as fuel to his fire. "Here we are teaching *her* how to dance when we are no closer to finding Lorna's killers!"

Alistair turned away, struggling with the mixture of shame and anger that filled him. He shouldn't have yelled; he understood that. Why did he yell at her? She had to be just as frustrated as he was. He took a deep breath and heavily sighed.

Alistair turned around, about to apologize, but Valhalla spoke first. "I . . . have a hunch as to who killed the High Princess, or at least . . . who might've planned the assassination."

"WHAT!?" Both he and his mother exclaimed in unison with wide, disbelieving eyes.

Alistair immediately approached Valhalla, hands raised. Seeing her step back defensively, a bit of fear flashed across her face, which made him pause. He forced himself to stop, needing to regain his composure.

He looked at one of his hands, turned it over, and watched as his palm trembled. Alistair closed it into a fist and dropped both arms to his sides, taking a deep breath. After a moment, he steadily exhaled and tried again. "Why didn't you tell us you had a lead?" His words had softened but still held an edge.

"Because I'm not certain yet and wouldn't want to accuse an innocent man."

"Tomorrow is Lorna's nameday ball! What more could you——"

"Alistair, please." His mother placed a hand on his shoulder and pulled him away from Valhalla. "You said man. So you already know their name?"

Regret was rising in Valhalla's face. It was clear she felt uncomfortable with giving a name to her suspicion, but for Alistair, this person could bring closure. For him, she didn't have much of a choice, and he wasn't about to let this go.

"Give me the name and we will plan accordingly." The High Queen stated plainly. "No harm will come to them should they prove to be innocent. Regardless of whether he took action against Lorna or helped to plan it, he may know something. There's a chance that he, and quite possibly others, will try again. Emboldened by their last attempt, they *might* use Lorna's nameday ball to strike. Now, give me the name, Valhalla."

Alistair's brows twitched as his mother's gaze hardened. Both stared at her, awaiting her answer. Valhalla took a hesitant step back. Alistair wondered if perhaps she wasn't accustomed to people being angry with her, or perhaps it was the fact that they were royals. The consequences for angering a lowborn were one thing, but the ire of a Queen could shape the lands themselves. He understood her predicament.

Valhalla glanced around the room, seemingly seeking a way out of the conversation, but Alistair knew his mother well, and she wasn't one to go unanswered in matters of family.

Valhalla nervously rubbed her wrists and, after a long moment, took a breath and answered. "Alright. Lord Ing Favrine, a Viscount of Hilliard."

Alistair started at the name. His mother's body went rigid and struggled in protest, "Th-That can't be."

"You're lying." Alistair blurted out. "You have to be!"

Ing had been an ally to his family, even a dear friend to him. The man aided Alistair many times throughout his life, even more so since his father passed away.

"I have witnessed him in conversation with other nobles, and the topic always turns to Lorna. He has even shown a special interest in the night of her murder. He was the only person who seemed surprised when he first saw me—as the High Princess, walking about as though nothing was wrong."

Alistair shook his head, unable to accept what Valhalla was saying. "But . . . But he can't . . . He can't be involved. He's always, *always* been there for this family."

"Has he really been there for this family, or you?" Valhalla's brows curved inquisitively over her eyes.

He was taken aback at the insinuation. No. No, he helped by issuing trade agreements with the other surrounding countries. Ing even helped Alistair in ending a budding civil war within these very walls just last year. His actions were always to the benefit of the family. Of course, Ing had been there for them. Hadn't he?

24

ℌlistair

Night of the Ball

Alistair stood alone, concealed and peering through a large, violet curtain. On the other side of the curtain was one of his mother's many silver, raven, and laurel-decorated thrones. The hour was late. The nineteenth bell rang in the distance, and as the chimes subsided, the nobility of both Hilliard and some from across Veerence began pouring into the fifth-floor throne room. In no time at all, they partook of the wine and many delicacies provided for the celebration of Lorna's Nameday Ball, each dressed in the luxuries afforded only to those of high society.

The throne room was decorated with an abundance of red and white roses. Lorna's favorite. They choked every pillar. Petals were strewn about each of the tables and across the floor.

The food was fresh, and steam slowly rose from each dish. Stuffed pigs and grilled fish. Chocolate and caramel drizzle lathered over an assortment of sweet-smelling breads. Colorful cakes, pastries, cookies, and other baked goods. It was a scene fitting of a painting.

Alistair scanned the floor, inspecting each guest, and watched for Ing. As per usual, the people of nobility donned their most gaudy, outlandish attire. The colors and fabrics were vivid and many. Each hue clashed against the next in the sea of rainbow splendor. Sparkling jewels twinkled in the firelight flickering above the crowd set in low-hanging chandeliers. The trinkets decorated the people's fingers, wrists, earlobes, and necks. Their coiffures ranged in styles from all across the continent. Elaborate curls, intricate braids, lacquered and combed. Alistair wondered just how long it must have taken them all to prepare for the event.

His eyes darted left and right, faster and faster, looking at every face in the crowd, but there were too many. New guests poured in by the dozens and filled the throne room. Alistair's grip on the curtain tightened. Where was Ing? He knew the man was planning to show; Valhalla had confirmed earlier in the day.

His anger slowly bubbled within him, his blood smoldering. He winced as he heard the clanking of heels thumping behind him.

"Alistair?"

He turned around to find his mother exiting her dressing room, standing tall and poised in the colors of his family's banner. Violet, black, and white. She was also adorned with several silver accessories. Raven and lilac designs decorated her gown as they swirled about the bottom of her skirt and dwindled as they neared her corset. Her silver raven crown rested atop her black, braided hair, and her silver Ring of Hilliard was displayed proudly on her right middle finger. Its amethyst jewel shimmered faintly in the firelight.

He glanced to the right and spotted Lorna, or rather, Valhalla, dressed in colors much more vibrant than his mother's. Roses and ravens peppered her gown. A silver tiara sat upon her raven black wig, and tiny white and lavender buds dotted her braids. Both women's faces were lightly painted with makeup to match their gowns.

Alistair glanced down at his outfit, grabbed his loosely braided hair, which hung over his shoulder, and tossed it behind him. He didn't realize how differently he stood in contrast until now. His garment was mostly black, with some violet ravens scattered here and there. A raven-decorated, silver circlet crowned his head. He hoped his darker attire wouldn't be a problem.

Alistair raised his gaze to Valhalla, who stood close to his mother, her hands clenched tightly within each other. She seemed to be fidgeting quite a bit.

She looked him up and down with wide eyes and pursed her lips. Clearing her throat, Valhalla greeted him, "Umm . . . y-you look handsome, your Grace."

As much as he wished to appreciate the compliment, he couldn't, not when she resembled his late sister. He could feel his face harden as his body went stiff. Alistair stood still in silence, staring at her, unable to reply with a thank you and compliment he knew he should offer in return. After a moment of awkward silence between the two, both shifting uncomfortably left and right, he turned around and looked back through the violet curtain, returning to his search for Ing.

"Alistair."

He could barely bring himself to glance back. His mother's tone was bitter with a hint of forlornness. Alistair knew he had been rude. Valhalla didn't deserve his silence, but seeing her in disguise had not grown easier since their first meeting. Besides, if everything went well tonight, he hoped she would no longer need to continue the charade and they could start anew. He sighed and turned around to face his mother, and was startled at just how close she was to him.

Before he could respond, she wrapped her arms around his neck, forcing him to bend down a bit. Her lips drew close to his ear. "Try to remain calm and clear-headed, Alistair. Everything'll be fine, I promise. Remember to fly free and proud." She whispered.

Alistair was taken aback. She rarely said aloud their family motto to him. Why was she saying it now?

His mother then released him and slid a hand onto his cheek. Her thumb brushed gently across his jaw, and before he could say a thing, she slid past him through the curtain to greet her guests, leaving his mouth agape.

He glanced at Valhalla, who stood nervously before the curtain, her gaze fixed on the white marble floor. His heart began to flutter. Alistair raised a hand to his chest, grasping for his father's ring beneath the layers of fabric composing his doublet, demanding his heart to calm down.

Alistair shook his head and grabbed hold of the curtain. He found himself hesitating, unsure as to what stayed his hand. He knew he should return to searching for Ing, but something within him, not more than a whisper, told him Valhalla was on edge.

He looked at her and found her nervously rubbing her hands together. Eyes closed and breathing deeply, she seemed frightened by what the performance demanded of her. If she were trying to conceal her woes, she was doing a poor job of it.

His brows twitched, surprised at her demeanor. He didn't know her all that well, but in public, she had always put on a convincing show of being Lorna. Her hands raised to her biceps and squeezed as if she were comforting herself. Before now, he had thought this deception had come easily to her.

"Are you nervous?" He asked, his voice soft.

"S-Sort of. I'm just . . . I'm ready to end this damn facade." She replied with more than a hint of disdain in her tone.

Alistair tilted his head to one side and raised a brow. "Why do I feel like there's more you aren't telling me?"

She opened her eyes and looked back to the floor. Her body trembled lightly, as if cold. His eyes slowly widened as a realization dawned on him, thinking back to each of their encounters. "Are you afraid of me?"

Valhalla jolted and took a step back. "What!? N-No, of course not." Her now sapphire eyes raised to him as she massaged her right wrist.

Alistair's brows twitched again, and he cautiously stepped toward her. He reached for her wrist and cupped it in his hands, feeling her tremble at his touch. He brushed a thumb against her soft, warm skin.

The aroma of her perfume mixed in the air: roses, his sister's favorite, and wisterias. A dull ache crept into his heart. "I hurt you yesterday, didn't I?" He asked softly.

"I-It . . ." She started with a sigh. "It was just as we were finishing our dance . . . you squeezed my wrists pretty tight. It didn't leave a bruise, but it made the joints sore."

His eyes shook, feeling ashamed for acting out as he had. He closed his eyes, took a deep breath, and exhaled steadily through his nostrils. "I'm sorry, I shouldn't have held you like that," Alistair said and let her go.

"I mean, you were angry yesterday. I know you've had a hard time with everything that's been going on." Valhalla raised a hand to her chest as she glanced away with bright pink cheeks.

Meeting her eyes, he took a deep breath, ignoring the pang of guilt stabbing at his heart. "That's still no excuse. I've treated you poorly. I should know better. I should be better." Alistair stated flatly, finding himself perplexed by the concern in her expression.

Valhalla raised her other hand to her chest, grasping her wrist again, and held it there. Her cheeks reddened, bringing warmth to her otherwise porcelain white skin. "Thank you."

Alistair bowed his head low and stood beside Valhalla, waiting for his mother to call them.

The silence hung heavily between them. Alistair looked away from the curtain and impatiently tapped his fingers against his thigh. Questions slowly roamed his thoughts.

"Why—"

Both Alistair and Valhalla started in unison, catching each other by surprise, then both chuckled softly at how silly they must look to one another.

"You go first," Valhalla said as a small smile broke her face.

"Are you sure? I have two questions." Alistair smirked.

"Well, I only have one." Two started to laugh, unsure as to why.

Catching his breath, Alistair asked, "Wow, where did *that* come from?" Alistair clutched his stomach with one hand, tending to a cramp residing in his ribs.

"I don't know," Valhalla answered through a deep breath. She gently brushed the hair of her wig over her shoulder with the tips of her fingers and stared at the curtain before her, her smile remaining. "Maybe we've finally realized just how silly we've both been with each other. Myself especially."

"I don't think you've been silly," Alistair stated warmly, his cheeks turning bright pink. With a roll of his eyes, he added, "Me on the other hand, I must look like a horse's ass."

Valhalla burst out laughing, having never expected the always serious prince to say such a thing. She doubled over and embraced her stomach. Tears gathered on her eyelids. "N-No, don't make me laugh like this! I'll ruin my makeup." She took a deep breath, raising her fingers to the sides of her face, and tried to blink them back.

"Sorry." Alistair chuckled. "How about this, as I think we still have time, I'll ask my first question, then you ask yours, and I'll finish with my second."

She pulled out a small mirror from a hidden pocket in her dress and hastily checked her makeup. Glancing at him, she nodded. "Alright, ask your question then."

"Why," he started, the smile falling from his face, "did you agree to help my mother?"

Valhalla was visibly taken aback. She turned away and stared at the curtains before them. After a long pause, she took a quick breath and sighed. "I don't really know. To be honest, I just want to help people. I think it's just in my nature. When I first met Her Grace, although she would never admit it, her eyes shone with a deep sadness. How could I possibly say no to someone who wanted to protect the rest of her family, to make sure no one else would be lost?" When Valhalla finally looked back to him, the caring warmth in her eyes caught him by surprise.

In that moment, he knew she too understood the insatiable ache of loss. Alistair's eyes softened, and his warm smile returned. "Thank you."

She tilted her head, her expression turning curious. "For what?"

"For—being there. Helping my mother. I spoke with my aunt Embla. She was just as frustrated as I was for being left out of this." He raised a hand and rubbed the back of his neck, feeling his frustrations returning.

"Your mother does this often?" Valhalla played with a strand of her hair while keeping her eyes attentively on him.

"Sort of." Alistair shrugged. "Any time my mother senses that we might be in danger, she places mountains between us as a way to keep us safe. However, she always tries to solve the danger on her own." He groaned loudly at the thought. "Also makes it so that we can never help, taking on the burden alone. It really pisses me off." His words hung in the air. His tone then softened, concern surrounding his words. "No matter how many times I tell her to include us, she doesn't listen."

Valhalla chuckled softly. "You're quite honest, aren't you?" She asked with a smirk, causing his cheeks to heat up. Embarrassed, he glanced away but nodded.

"It's a flaw of mine. Gets me into trouble more often than not."

"I don't think it's a flaw. After the time I've spent here, it's actually quite refreshing. Well, anyway, are you satisfied with my answer?"

He looked at her, surprised and nodded.

"My turn then . . ." Her smile faded and she was quiet for a moment, glancing away once more.

He stared at her curiously, wondering why she had gone cold. Just what was it that was on her mind? What could be troubling her so? The seconds stretched long and the tension between them became unbearable. As she opened her mouth to speak, a chill ran down his spine.

"Why—" She sighed. "Why do you care so much about your sister, especially after everything she's done to you? I just want to understand." Valhalla glanced at him guardedly, as if waiting to see how he would react.

His heart dropped into his stomach. Alistair had a feeling she would ask him that very question for a while now, a question he had asked himself many times. The answer had eluded him for a long time, a feeling nearly impossible to put into words. He returned his gaze to the curtain before him, gradually falling to the floor as he reached for his father's ring under his doublet. He remained quiet as he gathered his thoughts, trying to finally find a way to describe the turmoil that had been festering within him all these years.

"I'm sorry," Her words were soft, just barely above a whisper, "I shouldn't have asked."

"No, it's . . . as I said before, a part of me just wished, or rather, hoped that one day the Lorna I knew before our father died would come back to me. We were really close once. I never could let go of the spark of hope that a flicker of that part of her still existed. No matter what I did for her, helped her, lifted the stress of her duties off her shoulders, my efforts only ever seemed to have the opposite effect. The people of our court never helped, often comparing my deeds to hers, as if it were some damned contest. I just . . . don't understand what happened. " He answered quietly.

"Did you not read the High Princess's journal?" She asked inquisitively, tilting her head to one side.

"I-I couldn't bring myself to read it." His stomach churned; the idea of Lorna's true thoughts now resting in his bedchamber made him sick to his stomach. "Every time I tried to open it, I grew so angry that I wanted to cr—" He slammed his hands to his lips, stopping himself from saying something that would normally bring mockery.

Valhalla seemed taken aback. She reached for the hand over his mouth and lowered it. He refused to face her gaze, but allowed his hand to remain in hers. Her words were not what he had expected, but brought him some level of comfort. "Finish what you were going to say."

Alistair's lips curled inward, sliding between his teeth. He wanted to bite down, but blew out his bottom lip. "I managed to read a few pages, but . . . the words brought me to tears. I was angry. Furious at myself for not being there when she clearly needed me most. She, she was five . . . only five—" His throat tightened and voice cracked. He held his eyes tightly shut, hoping to stop the tears he could feel bubbling to the surface, but they flowed unabated, and his lips quivered.

"That-That *fucking* family!" Alistair's jaw tightened as his head fell back. His teeth ground together. "The Rosa's always hated me and my family. I could *never* understand why—" He felt a tug, jostling him from his anger.

Alistair looked at Valhalla, confused as to why her shoulders were raised, and her bright red painted lips were thinly closed. He looked down at his hand still cupped in hers.

He started to pull his hand away, but she held firm. "I'm sorry, I don't—"

Alistair paused, watching as Valhalla slid her arms over his shoulders and around his neck, embracing him warmly. He was taken aback. His trembling eyes shot wide. Should he hug her back or withdraw? She squeezed him gently, her head by his and resting on his shoulder, sending gooseflesh about his being.

"I don't know how you feel about hugs, but a warm embrace given by someone I care about helps when I'm upset."

Alistair chuckled softly, and his shoulders relaxed slightly. He felt a sense of relief from her gesture.

"You know, you're free to ask your second question. If you still want to."

A sudden laugh escaped his lips. Valhalla then released him from the embrace and stood at about a half arm's length apart, holding each other, hand in hand. As his soft laughter quieted, she flashed him a warm smile. He quickly wiped the tears from his face and smirked in return.

"Thank you. Ugh, I must look like a mess."

She laughed and answered. "Not at all. We all need moments to just let it out from time to time."

Nodding in agreement, he swallowed, then began, "My question. I don't know . . . maybe I shouldn't ask." Alistair's expression wavered as he looked away to the curtain before them, the sounds of the crowd just outside still building.

"It's alright, just ask. Hopefully, I can answer it in time. I'm not sure we have much time left." Valhalla responded as they both turned to face the curtains together. Laughter erupted, and they could hear his mother continuing her address.

"Alright," he sighed begrudgingly, "I just wanted to know, are you certain of your suspicions of Lord Ing?" Alistair asked.

Valhalla's smile faded. "I am. Honestly, I don't know if it was intentional on his part or if he truly was being careless, but as I said before, he has had several candid conversations with others of nobility. Most troubling," she swallowed, "they all happened near Lorna's chamber . . . His interest in her goes far beyond any other reasoning I can come up with."

The discomfort in her tone was clear. Alistair glanced her way as an unsettling thought crept into his mind. "Valhalla, why was Ing near my sister's chamber?"

Valhalla remained quiet, pursing her lips as she stared at the floor. With a sigh of defeat, she answered. "Maybe it's good you didn't read your sister's journal. The details—Well, I will just say that Lord Ing was one of the High Princess's *many* paramours."

His eyes widened with disbelief. "P-Paramours!? Lord Ing is half her age! How many did Lorna really have?"

She looked at him with unease as she tapped one of her heels against the floor anxiously. "More than any child, royal or otherwise, should have." More than a bit of judgment seeped into her tone, and her cheeks pinkened. "Judging from Lorna's words . . . most of them didn't seem to know of each other." Valhalla wrung her wrist and her face scrunched in disgust.

Alistair's brows twitched, his interest turning momentarily from Lorna to Valhalla. "Valhalla, have you never lain with anyone before?"

Her cheeks went so bright red that for that one moment, she could've been indistinguishable from a tomato. Her eyes shot wide, and her posture straightened, obviously put off by his question. "I don't see how that's any of your business!" Her voice was just shy of a shriek. Were it not for the roar of the crowd, they certainly would've drawn attention to themselves.

Alistair laughed softly and placed a finger on his lips, causing her to fluster even more.

"What's so funny?" She asked in a demanding yet quieted tone.

"I'm sorry, I promise I'm not laughing at you. I just didn't expect that." Alistair replied.

"Didn't expect—I'm sure virgins are not *that* uncommon here in Hilliard." She looked away with pursed lips, arms crossed tightly over her chest.

Alistair couldn't be certain if her arms had crossed to keep from hitting him but dared not to ask. He struggled to stifle his chuckle and couldn't pry away his eyes from her, looking at her with warm delight. "I suppose that's true. It's not like every story of conquest echoing the walls of the Dragon and Raven Knights Tavern can be believed, but even still, most have crossed that bridge when they come of age. Besides, here we're all pretty open with each other about our sexualities, or in your case, a lack thereof. It's incredibly rare for one of your beauty to have not done so." Alistair turned to her with a sincere smile. "Haven't found the right person yet?"

Valhalla slowly met his gaze and her glare faded into a bashful smile. She playfully rolled her eyes and answered. "No, I-I haven't met the right man, but simply being right isn't enough." Her cheeks were still a bright pink but her natural color was returning. She twirled a few loose strands of hair between her fingers.

Alistair tilted his head with curiosity. "So what are you looking for then?"

"A connection of sorts. I don't know, it's hard to explain, but just feel like your first—" She paused and a flicker of guilt crossed her eyes. "I'm sorry, I'm the last person you should talk to about this."

He laughed with confusion. "What do you mean?"

She looked at him for a moment and opened her mouth, but before even a sound escaped, she turned away.

Alistair considered pestering her about her sudden silence, until the thought dawned on him. "O-Oh, right, that law."

"I'm sorry—"

"No. No, don't be." Alistair gazed at Valhalla with a weak smile. "Honestly, it would've been nice to find someone special to have spent that moment with, but I understand my role in this city. For this family. I have to do what must be done, even if," he sighed, "if that means appeasing the highborn daughters of this country."

She turned back to him with a look not of pity or sadness, but of held-back outrage. Valhalla opened her mouth but was interrupted. Alistair forced a smile and placed a hand on her shoulder, hoping that the gesture would convey that everything was fine. That he was fine, even though he was anything but.

Valhalla seemed to understand and sighed with defeat as she turned away from him, clasping her hands together over her waist. After a moment, Valhalla spoke with a subtle tremble in her voice. "Have any of them . . . been kind to you, at least?"

"Rarely." Alistair shrugged. "I think the last woman who was kind to me in that circumstance was Lady Violet Streamborn. She's blind and never thought she would draw the affections of a desirable partner. She was curious about the desires of the flesh and asked to lie with me. She was one of only a few who didn't outright demand it of me." Feeling the need to bring some levity back to the conversation, lest he begin to dwell on dour memories, he continued. "I've also gotten many offers from men. They promised to be kind, pledging to *save me from the clutches of those harlots*." He chortled with a roll of his eyes.

Valhalla giggled with a small shrill and smirked playfully. "Couldn't connect with them?"

"No, I just . . . don't have that sort of interest in men. Besides, I doubt many of them sought more from me than my royal influence. I'm no fool, at least, not in that." He laughed to himself.

He jolted and straightened, hearing his mother call out their names. Alistair offered her his hand. "Come, my mother just announced us."

Valhalla's smile faded, and they both stared resolutely at the curtains before them. "Alright," she said with a whisper, "let's get this over with."

25

Alistair

AN ANXIOUS DANCE

Valhalla placed her hand in Alistair's. As they stepped forward, the curtain slid open. They rounded the silver throne, and as they entered the firelight, a roar of applause from the crowd washed over them both. The two made their way forward, Alistair leading with Valhalla beside him, toward his mother.

The closer they came to the edge of the tall dais to join the High Queen, the more his stomach churned with revolt. He figured after eleven years he would have grown accustomed to standing before such a gathering, but that hadn't yet been his experience. The nobility's eyes bore down upon him. Though their smiles were on full display, he could just imagine the murmurings likely being uttered under their breaths. His shoulders slumped with every step.

Alistair's heart quickened while bile clawed at the base of his throat. He choked down the urge to vomit. He wanted nothing more than to run back to the relative safety behind the curtains and hide from his family's court, but he had to persevere. Tonight was his best shot at finding justice for Lorna's murder.

His breathing heavied and palms moistened. A tremor ran up Alistair's spine. He tightened his free hand into a fist, not realizing he was squeezing Valhalla's as well.

Just then, Valhalla's hand twitched, and she pulled her hand free from his. Had he been so absent-minded that he squeezed her hand as well? Confirmation came just as quickly as the thought occurred to him. She rubbed the sides of her hand, then brushed her palm across the fabric of her dress. To his surprise, she never once dropped the act and added a subtle sneer in her expression. At least he hoped it was part of her act.

The two took their places at his mother's sides, he to her left and Valhalla at her right. The applause soon died down, replaced by a dull hum of whispers filling the quiet air of the throne room. Valhalla, or Lorna now, wore her usual smug smirk as she stood with unearned confidence, but there was something more to her posture. There was a sensuality about her. She balanced a hand on her slightly up-tilted hip, a pose that for many seemed pleasant, but for Alistair, always made him cringe. Even though she had only come into her adolescence a few years before, she had mastered the art of weaponizing her femininity.

His eyes drifted to his mother, surprised to find her looking at him, but she smiled kindly, which helped him find some ease. She raised a hand to the exposed portion of her chest between her heart and necklace, then drew an invisible circle.

Alistair nodded once, knowing and understanding the meaning behind the sign. His mother taught it to him in his childhood. It was her secret way of letting him know she would forever love him.

It was a sight he had thought lost to memory. His eyes began to tremble. She hadn't made that sign since sometime before his father died eleven long years ago. He never would've guessed such a small thing could bring him to the verge of tears, and as simple a gesture as it was, it meant the world to him.

He released a soft sigh of relief, as if a weight had been lifted off his shoulders. She nodded once, then returned her attention to engage the crowd. His fingers twitched as a shudder ran from his shoulders, down his wrists, and into his hands. He immediately hid them behind his back, grasping one of his wrists and squeezing hard, hoping to hide his shaking. His momentarily sincere smile turned forced.

"Now that my Lorna has come of age to marry her betrothed, Prince Daemyn of Svartr, tradition would mark this occasion for His Highness to take my daughter for their first of many dances to come. Unfortunately, such a moment must go unfulfilled, set aside for such a time where our merriment could be shared throughout all of Veerence. The thoughts and prayers of Hilliard are with our brothers and sisters of Svartr, whose hearts are with their Prince Albrecht Svartr and all those brave sailors who have journeyed overseas, far from our resplendent lands, to aid Zarago with the Gran Mar War, a war that has raged on for three long years now. The Svartr royal family awaits the destined return of their heir, as should we all. In his absence, Prince Daemyn has taken his siblings' responsibilities upon himself, shouldering the burdens of both brothers. His vigilance and dedication to his home are something we should all aspire to. In his place on this night will stand my son Alistair. He will accompany Lorna on our first dance of the night."

His mother took a step back and spread her arms out wide, presenting her children to the crowd. Alistair startled back to the present, realizing he had wasted his opportunity to search the crowd from this vantage point and cursed under his breath. Nervousness had gotten the better of him. He gulped to steel himself and stepped toward Lorna, offering his hand to her.

A contemptuous expression crossed her face, her nose scrunching in disgust. With a modest curtsy, she flicked her wrist upward and then delicately placed her hand in his. She only gave him the tips of her fingers, acting as though the act of touching him would inflict her with the Fúna Plague. "Fine," she exclaimed, "if I must." Following her not-so-veiled display of contempt, the crowd buzzed with whispers and hushed tones.

Now it was his turn, and Alistair sighed heavily. Valhalla was incredibly convincing in her ruse, and though he knew it was only an act, her actions stung all the same. He guided Lorna to the center of the square hall, his still expression barely masking his insecurity. The people parted, spreading to either side to clear a way toward the center of the room.

"Pretend it's just us," Valhalla whispered.

Alistair was taken aback. Her support was unexpected and at that moment, dangerous to their plans. He glanced her way but found Lorna's annoyed scowl staring back. It seemed she hadn't dropped the guise entirely, and thanks to the hum of the crowd, he knew no one else could have overheard. It was the first time in all his life that he was gladdened to have his sister's scornful glare. It was an unusual sensation, to say the least. His brows twitched for only a moment, fighting to ease the pounding of his heart, and slipped on the practiced stoicism his father had used as a shield for many of his years as High King.

The momentary thought of his father, which usually brought him strength, had been a mistake. His father was a goodman. A strong, kind-hearted man. He cared greatly for the people and was the foundation of all of Alistair's beliefs, but for all his vigor, he was still susceptible to the void. He had met a violent end to a foe who had once belonged to this very group. The last image of his father's face was in that moment forever seared into the bedrock of his soul. He struggled to keep his face still. He couldn't show any weakness here. He had to keep up appearances. His heart thumped hard, again and again.

Alistair nearly walked past their mark but felt a pull on his arm. He immediately stopped, crossed his legs, and looked at Valhalla. There was concern in her eyes, but she played it off with mock laughter.

He pulled her forward, guiding her in a semicircle to his other side, then posited her before him to begin their dance. Stretching out an arm, he waited as she placed one hand on his forearm and with her other hand, slid her middle finger through a thread ring hidden on the fabric of her lavender dress so she could lift the skirt of her gown when needed. His free arm found its perch at her waist.

The two stood, frozen in place, waiting for the music to begin. His eyes darted to his eyes left and right, staring at the people around them. His stomach churned once more.

Alistair told himself that he could do this. He had to. He had danced numerous times before. His skill wasn't in question. Given his station, he had practiced with many masters of the art over the years. He just needed to gain control over his nerves. So much was riding on his performance, the weight of it all bore down on him like an anvil to an ant.

He looked at Valhalla, and she, right back at Alistair. A small bead of sweat rolled down her face, and he wondered if she was just as nervous as he. Her mouth was slightly parted, and her eyes flitted between his. She may still be a stranger to him, and their first dance had been cut short thanks to his impertinence, but he knew they could pull this off. The two had clashed swords, and both came out alive. That act alone was far more intimate than any dance could be. He understood how she moved, the nimbleness and balance in her steps. If he was going to fool anyone into believing the two had danced together as he and Lorna had, she was the best partner he could have asked for.

The music finally began. Its rhythm was slow and methodical. Alistair took a deep breath, and as he moved, so did Valhalla.

The two twirled and shifted their bodies about, Valhalla moving in perfect sync with the music and Alistair keeping pace. As the tempo sped up, the song becoming more energetic, Alistair began to struggle with his footing.

Whispers mixed with the music, judgmental and mocking. His heart pounded so hard he thought it would stop at any moment.

"Alistair, can you not handle crowds?" Valhalla whispered quickly with curved brows.

"What? I-I . . . Is it that obvious?" He took a deep breath, but held it in for a while before answering her. "No. It's not crowds per se. Ever since my father's death, I find myself terrified to be before *them*, the nobility."

They weren't a trustworthy sort. Alistair couldn't go more than a few steps without one of them whispering hurtful things just loud enough for him to hear. About him. His mother. His family. Even the few friends he had. He hated them. Every single one of them.

"Alright, I don't think saying not to worry is going to work, so instead just . . . pretend you're helping me dance in private."

He let out a dry laugh. "You mean like yesterday?"

"No, not like yesterday. This is a new day. I'm Valhalla, not your sister. I just look like this and . . . Damn, I'm making this worse, aren't I?" She chuckled nervously and hid a smile.

His heart fluttered as he let out a trembling breath. "Well, at least you're trying." He shrugged.

As they continued, they reached a part of the dance requiring a bout of endless twirls. Her hands flew through the air, and she looked like a beautifully sculpted statue. The fabric of her dress and the long strands of her raven black wig swirled and flowed in a tornado of movements.

The familiar scent of his sister invaded his senses, causing his mind to whirl. He grasped hold of her hands, crossed them over her stomach, and pulled her close so that her back pressed against his chest. Another wave of gooseflesh flooded over his skin. Her warmth washed over him like a warm blanket.

Alistair's chest swelled. Valhalla was now at the forefront of his mind, the crowd of vipers fading to the back of his consciousness. She turned her head and glanced just over her shoulder. The two looked at each other, their eyes locked. Her eyes were the sapphire of his sister's, but at that moment it didn't bother him as it had before. He only saw Valhalla.

She then broke their contact and stepped forward with a twirl. He was startled for a moment but regained his composure. As she came out of the spin, she held an arm bent at an angle between them, and he immediately did the same, their arms locking together at the elbows. They danced in a circle, folding their arms upward and intertwining their wrists around each other. Valhalla's breath then caught in her throat ,and her eyes flickered with recognition.

She whipped her head to Alistair while keeping in rhythm with the music. "He's here!"

Alistair narrowed his eyes curiously at the statement, still captivated by the moment. "Who is?"

"Lord Ing, he's here."

26

Alistair

To Do Nothing, or Strike?

Valhalla whispered, her words just loud enough for Alistair to hear.

His eyes widened, and he immediately scanned the crowd, and there, to the right of them, stood Ing. He was garbed in colors of emerald and sapphire. His raven black hair was pulled back in braids with a few gray strands woven in between. Ing's expression seemed stuck between disinterest and confusion.

His sapphire eyes stared intently, following them like a wolf stalking its prey. No, not them, Alistair realized. His attention was locked on Lorna. Ing's lips stretched into a thin, unreadable line. A small scar marred his smirk, the same scar he had received aiding Alistair in Hilliard's civil war just a year ago. Alistair's woe instantly turned into anger at the sight of the man whom he at once considered a friend.

"Alistair, you're losing rhythm!" Valhalla whispered with a disquieted tone. Her words doused his rising rage, and he forced himself to focus on the dance.

The two twirled about the dance floor for a time, moving as one, not a step out of place as the music commanded their movement and their bodies responded without hesitation. As their breath became labored and weariness started to set in, the tempo slowed, and the end was in sight. Alistair felt a renewed sense of vigor and twirled Valhalla as he positioned himself behind her. He placed a hand on her waist and held the other outstretched. As her hand raised and their hands met, the two kept pace with the final crescendo, and with one final spin, they stopped at the center of their square.

The two stood as still as stone, soaking in the moment. Alistair then bowed, and Valhalla curtsied low in return. The throne room exploded with applause and cheers. The two straightened, still out of breath, and just then, Lorna flashed Alistair a snarky sneer. "I suppose I'll take my leave of you now, oh Prince of Light."

Alistair's heart skipped a beat. Had Lorna complained about the nickname in her journal, or was this simply an embellishment on Valhalla's part? Either way, the moment was over. She was fully Lorna now, as she needed to be.

The Prince of Light was not a title he gave to himself. Ever since taking it upon himself to learn light magic through the help of Druoga, then teaching it to his Jórsalafarar in the silver guard, others had taken notice of his ability, slow going as it was.

Next thing he knew, the silver and gold guards began calling him by the moniker, along with a few within the nobility. The name even stretched to the Commoners' Nest, where the people there truly embraced it. They were more likely to use that title than even his birth name. Variations of the title popped up from time to time, but the one which came up most with the common people was The Light of Hilliard. Lorna caught wind of this, of course, but he wasn't sure if the anger that glowed in her eyes was due to the title's use or simply the flames of hate that had been consuming her as she matured.

Valhalla flashed him a brief apologetic expression but quickly took a deep breath and returned to the act. She forced a smile toward someone behind Alistair, "Ugh! I thought that dance would never end." Then pushed past him.

"Eeek! I can't believe you actually had to touch him. Who knows where his vile hands have been?" A young woman's voice answered. The two cackled as they walked to join a group of Lorna's friends huddled by one of the tables on the right side of the throne room.

Alistair's stomach churned tightly as his eyes fell on the group. He wrung his hands and tried to steel himself. "And the mocking begins."

He spun on his heels to find his mother standing by her dais, speaking with several of the nobility from her court. Alistair began to approach them, hearing the roar of the crowd start to drown out the music.

"Ugh, can you believe all this splendor wasted on that greedy bitch of a Princess?"

"Someone should tell her that bigger doesn't mean better." Some answered with a laugh. Alistair glanced around and found the source, the man's eyes locking with Alistair's as he continued. "Oh look, it's the Whore High Prince of Hilliard."

"What a disgrace. Did you hear he cries like a child?"

"Oh! How humiliating. Maybe if he weren't whipped like a disobedient dog, he would act like a real man. Pity." The people cackled, the sound like a knife scraping against a glass table.

With every step Alistair took, the hall seemed to stretch, the floor tilting under his feet. His head started to spin with discomfort. He glanced around, his mouth dry, and the people's faces shifted into something shadowy and grim. Their smiles were wicked, and their eyes glared judgmentally.

He raised a shaky hand to his face, rubbing his forehead with distress. Massaging his brow, he let out a slow groan. The voices around him grew louder. He worried they would swallow him whole.

Alistair raised his other hand to his chest, feeling for his father's ring tucked safely under his doublet. He wanted to cover his ears, to drown out the hateful voices swirling all around him, but knew it would only feed them.

All of a sudden, he found a familiar, smiling face in the sea mares. His heart leaped for joy at the sight as he watched the man approach.

"My little nephew." He said with an accent that was almost as melodious as an Aoldearians accent, but with less intonation.

The man grinned over his bronze skin. He had amber brown eyes, the same color as Alistair's father, which shone brightly in the firelight. His garments were awash in shades of azure and ebony. Raven designs flew about the fabric. His dark, wavy brown hair was pulled back into a loose ponytail, and a thick mustache hovered over his lips.

Alistair's breath caught in his throat as elation gripped him. "Uncle Volundr!"

He rushed to join his uncle, his late father's youngest brother from Grár, and embraced him warmly. A chuckle then escaped Alistair's lips, realizing now just how much he had grown since last seeing Volundr. His uncle was taller than him and, while having a rather lean build, was still imposing in his own right, but now Volundr's chin just barely rested on Alistair's broad shoulder.

"Well, you're not so little anymore." His uncle mused. "It's been five long years since I last saw you, and boy, look how you've grown." He said, patting Alistair on the back a few times before releasing him, then eyed his nephew up and down.

"When people said I surpassed my father in height, I thought they were being kind. Mother especially, she's been saying that a lot recently."

"Well, you do have Hillian blood running through your veins. That's good, though, your Hillian height and Vilzhenian muscle are a strong combination for a great warrior. I'm certain that's what saw you through the War of Lions." His uncle gripped his shoulder, a proud twinkle in his eyes and a jubilant smile on his face.

Alistair felt his own fading and tried not to show his embarrassment. He wasn't ashamed of his parents per se, but the years of mockery for being a *half breed* from the nobility had taken a toll on his feelings about his lineage. His hand slid up to his chest and rested over his father's ring again. His eyes alone were a beacon of his ancestry. The mention of the war didn't help his nerves. His body wanted nothing more than to retreat from the persecution he had come to expect. Though he knew his uncle would never speak ill of him, this wasn't a logical response. His lips curled inward, trying to hide his discomfort, but Volundr had always had a keen eye.

"Alistar, are you alright?" His uncle's head tilted inquisitively as a brow slid over one eye.

"Uncle, I—"

"High Prince Alistair, you and your sister danced splendidly. Ever the graceful pair, as is to be expected from our high royals." Lord Ing stepped beside Alistair, jostling him from his thoughts. The man's tone was full of respect as he bowed.

Alistair took a deep breath as his blood bubbled with righteous fury, wanting nothing more than to tackle the tall man to the ground and beat him until he confessed to his part in the tragedy that had befallen his sister.

A tremble ran through his arms and he balled his fists at his sides, his knuckles white with fury. He needed to calm down, to stick to the plan Valhalla had devised. It was the only way to be certain, and as much as Alistair needed to find the culprit to be free of the anger threatening to consume him, he would never forgive himself if he attacked an innocent man. He didn't fully agree with Valhalla's plan, using herself as bait to bring out his family's enemies, but he had no choice. They had no alternative.

He placed a hand on his chest and bowed in return, finding his composure. "Thank you, Lord Ing. You're too kind."

Ing stood himself immediately straight. "Please, if you don't mind my prying Your Grace, what befell your sister? She disappeared for nearly a month after having returned from Rjóðr. It was . . . peculiar not to find her spending those hard-earned crowns of hers as she is wont to do."

Alistair's brow twitched. The man was already vying for information? His directness proved his impatience. He was either being careless, which was not an attribute he was known to have, or he was planning something. Were he innocent, this could be the simple curiosity of a jilted lover, but if he were truly behind Lorna's murder, it could mean he was growing desperate.

"You couldn't ask her?" Alistair asked with a raised eyebrow, daring Ing to explain himself in the hopes he would overplay his hand.

"It seems your mother felt she needed additional guards, and very persistent ones at that. I couldn't imagine what could've happened to necessitate such measures that she couldn't even be visited by a friend. So no, I wasn't able to ask your sister much of anything." He answered and flashed Alistair a frustrated smile, causing his brows to twitch again in agitation.

Valhalla was right; he could feel it in his gut. Ing was either being overly careless or he was overconfident, toying with Alistair in this game of secrets. Regardless, he knew he needed to choose his words carefully.

"Are you so certain it was my mother who placed the guards between you two? It's just as likely that Lorna simply wished for quieter evenings as of late, to rest after her long journey. Besides, she's become quite fickle. It's just as likely that she wished for a change of company. Unfortunately, I don't know myself. Lorna's not one to share anything with me . . . not anymore. You should know that, my Lord." Alistair's heart swelled with pain, struggling to accept how distant his sister had become from him and hoped it didn't show on his face.

Ing's lips twitched, as though irked by Alistair's reply, but if his gibe had landed, it was difficult to tell. Ing's expression remained flat as he acquiesced. "Of course. Your sister does love her *secrets*. I should've guessed you wouldn't be privy to the inner workings of her machinations, nor those of our distinguished High Queen. I apologize for squandering your time. Please, enjoy your evening as best you can Your Grace. I feel a change is coming to this country . . . hopefully for the better." He bowed quickly and took his leave toward the right side of the hall, vanishing into the crowd.

Alistair's heart jumped into his throat. What did he mean by that?

"Alistair, is everything alright?" His uncle asked, placing a hand on his back and startling Alistair from his thoughts.

"What? Yes, everything's fine. I'm sorry, uncle, I don't seem to be present tonight."

His uncle's eyes widened, his brows heavy and all but the fiery glint dancing upon his irises fell lost to shadow. Alistair had forgotten just how imposing Volundr could be when he wanted to. He hadn't felt this nervous from a look since the first and last time he ventured down into the dungeons below the castle. He had been only six or seven springs young. There, he happened upon his uncle's tools. A tray held several teeth and an assortment of fingernails. Metallic instruments of varying shapes and sizes rested on a lined cloth draped over a wooden bench. A fresh coating of blood and what appeared to be clumps of flesh left little uncertainty as to their purpose.

Volundr stepped into the room, looking as though he had just finished washing up, rubbing a small cloth between his hands. That was the first time he saw this particular look. As punishment, his uncle kept him there, describing to the young boy in vivid detail how each tool aided him in his journey for the truths most men and women would otherwise keep hidden. It terrified him. It was several nights later before the comfort of sleep found its way back to him. Since then, Alistair promised to never disobey Volundr. He would never again venture into the places he wasn't supposed to go.

"Alistair, you know you aren't a very good liar, right?"

Daggers of ice ran down Alistair's spine. He let out a nervous chuckle as he ran his fingers through the loose strands of his dark brown braided hair. "Maybe with you, but I've been able to fool others just fine."

Alistair forced a smile as he straightened and tried to convey confidence before his uncle. He had succeeded in spreading the lie that Lorna still lived to the people of his mother's court, which was more than he thought possible of himself before all of this had begun. That was a feat in its own right. Many who comprised the court were skilled in deception, and in his heart, Alistair knew it was likely he had only succeeded thus far due to their underestimation and general lack of acknowledgement of him as a whole, but this was Volundr. In his uncle's presence, it was everything Alistair could do not to simply crumble under his stare.

His uncle's thin lips then turned into a proud smirk, his demeanor relaxing. "Fair enough. Maybe it's the . . . stuffiness of the air in here. So many in our present company have their heads firmly tucked up their asses, it's no wonder the only thing coming out of their mouths is shit. At least that would explain the need for the excess of perfumes throughout the hall."

A burst of laughter escaped Alistair as he quickly covered his mouth to stifle the sound with a snort. His uncle chortled in return. "Come. Why don't we go outside and get some fresh air? I think that would do you some good."

Alistair regained control of himself as his laugh quieted to a soft chuckle, rubbing his chest to catch his breath. "Uncle, how is it that you always know just what to say to help me feel better?" He asked with a grin.

Volundr patted Alistair on the back, laughing gently, and nudged him toward a balcony situated to the right side of the throne room. As they started through the crowd, his uncle, while maintaining an air of exuberance, discreetly took hold of Alistair's arm and pulled him close, leaning into his ear and whispering. "No matter what, Alistair, I will always be there for you, to keep you safe as best I can. Even if that means spiriting you away to Grár."

A sinking sensation came over Alistair. He stared at his uncle, confusion clear on his face. Where was this coming from? "Uncle, what do you—"

Volundr patted Alistair's shoulder once more, shot him a disarming smile, and gently pushed him forward toward where his mother was still making small talk with her court. Concern began to fester in the pit of his stomach. As they caught his mother's eyes, she waved at them cheerfully.

Alistair glanced at his uncle beside him. He couldn't shake the feeling that Volundr knew something he didn't. As much as Alistair wanted to understand what was going on between his mother and uncle, there was a plan that still needed tending to. If all went well, events would unfold and hopefully lead to the truth.

Alistair engaged Volundr with a smirk of his own. "Uncle, why not meet with Mother. I'm going to eat something, then I'll rejoin you. I'm feeling a bit peckish. Would you like anything?"

"No, thank you, Alistair. I had a bit of a bite before coming. Don't worry about me, go enjoy yourself, alright."

Bowing his head in thanks, Alistair watched his uncle saunter off. He then turned his attention to the tables close by, all elegantly stocked with foods on display for his sister's nameday ball. It seemed to him that the kitchen staff had outdone themselves for the event. Foods from every corner of Veerence were prepared and laid out in such a way that each dish complemented the one adjacent. Alistair wondered if it were a subtle reminder as to how each region was made stronger by their neighbor. The sight seemed perfectly suited for a painting, but regardless of how wonderfully the smells intermingled or how deliciously mouthwatering the food likely was, Alistair wasn't at all in the mood for any of it.

He walked in front of the tables, feigning interest in the delectables spread across each surface. Stopping in front of a roasted pig so large it took up most of a rather sizable table, Alistair reached out to pick a plate when a figure stepped beside him. He glanced to his left to see who it was and froze. It was Lorna, or rather Valhalla, staring at the table with a heavy frown on her face.

"What are you doing!? Lorna would never scowl like that in public." He whispered, his tone harsher than he had wished.

Her brows hung heavily over her eyes as she responded. "I just threatened to parade one of your nobles through the streets. His family would be hung by their wrists on the walls of their home, forced to watch as I whipped the man . . . like a dog until he passed out from pain or death." For a brief moment, her mask entirely slipped away, and the depths of anguish in her eyes seemed an endless and everlasting pit of regret. "I-I can't. I can't keep doing—"

Alistair reacted as fast as he could. He went for a tray of dressed eggs and slid it off the table, causing it to fall between them. The silver tray crashed to the floor, clanging with a metallic cacophony of pings as the eggs splattered with a series of wet squishes, somehow just missing their shoes and her dress entirely. The music stopped, and the people's chattering immediately ceased. All turned and stared at him, and little to his surprise, not a soul looked at Lorna.

She startled back, her breath heavy as her eyes looked to the food on the floor and then glanced back up at Alistair. Confusion, anger, exhaustion, all flickering as a wildfire in her eyes. He could clearly see it, plain as day. Alistair, on the other hand, contorted his face into a look of shock. He stiffened his posture to help sell the facade and glanced behind her, spotting Ing amongst a group of nobles. His were the only eyes that seemed to not be on him. No, his attention was fully locked on Lorna, and in them he saw scorn and conviction. A heavy glower darkened the man's face.

Hopefully, this fake outburst would work, the spark which would force the man into action, Alistair thought to himself.

"Are you really doing this now?" He pleaded, meeting Valhalla's eyes. He glanced at Ing again, then returned to Valhalla, hoping she understood his reason for the impromptu ploy. The urge to apologize made his teeth itch. She needed a moment of comfort, and instead, to keep their plan alive, he forced her to withdraw back into the persona that clearly pained her. He promised himself that he would make this up to her later, somehow, but for now, this was necessary. If it worked, then they *both* could be done with this charade for good.

She took a moment, frustration visible on her face, but instead of screaming as was clear from every fiber of her stance, she instead adopted an annoyed smirk, tilted her head lightly, and lowered her shoulders nonchalantly. "Of course," her words bit, "a dog is expected to eat off the floor, not from a table."

Lorna, without breaking eye contact, reached for another tray of food and with a swift, elegant flick of her wrist, slid it off the table. As it glided toward Alistair, he jumped back, and the plate just narrowly missed him, splattering even more delicacies across the floor. "Enjoy." She sang in a taunting tune. She then turned and walked away, making her way in Ing's direction, and with a hard right, turned toward one of the balconies behind him.

Alistair reacted as he would be expected to, a look of shock and frustration on display as he ignored the usual judgmental whispers thrumming from the surrounding crowd. He then glared after her, chest puffing in anger and hands balled into fists.

Once sure the crowd had lost interest in his sulking now that the incident had concluded, he turned his attention back to Ing. He scrutinized the man carefully. Ing's concentration seemed locked on Lorna as she disappeared beyond the violet curtains of the balcony, annoyed fury building in the man's sapphire eyes. He returned his attention to the nobles beside him and said something Alistair couldn't hear over the crowd. To his surprise, the group dispersed. As each of the nobles vanished into various corners of the throne room, Ing made his way after Lorna.

Alistair's stomach churned wildly, not due to fear of the plan's failure but for Valhalla. He took a long, deep breath and whispered to the gods to watch over her, wishing her Heimdall's protection and Thor's strength. If their suspicion was correct, as tough a warrior as she was, she might still need it.

27

Valhalla

A Ballad so Quaint

Valhalla rushed to the edge of the balcony, eyes stinging, and trying to hold back her anger. Her heart pounded in her chest, and her hands clenched into fists.

Reaching the stone railing, she slammed her hands down upon the hard surface. Valhalla's breath was heavy, tears brimming in her eyes, and she wanted nothing more than to scream in outrage. She desperately wanted to be done with this charade. To move past the part she must play. Who she *must* be.

Her hands squeezed the railing, and she threw her head back. The fresh night air filled her lungs. She held her breath for as long as she could, and as she felt she was about to burst, her lungs on fire, she finally exhaled.

She hated this place. The people. Everything about it. Valhalla hated what this city represented. So much for the *glory* of Hilliard, she thought. These high society bastards were hoarding crowns so far up their asses their greed could rival the dragons of old legends. They taunted, mocked, and kicked people when they were down. They laughed off the concerns of those born less fortunate as if they were simply lesser. What kind of place could breed such callousness? She had witnessed human cruelty before, but these were a different sort. Each would eat those around them for even the meagerest of gains.

Just then, startling her from her thoughts, Valhalla felt a cool tingle envelop her eyes, similar to the sensation of a cool breeze kissing her skin on a warm day. Energy was fading from her irises. It was the magic from the auga pills. The magic masking her eye color was ending.

She raised her left arm and peered beneath her silver bangles sparkling in the moonlight. Pressing down on her skin to make space between her arm and bangle, she counted the remaining auga pills given to her by Lady Freya Nerthusdottir. Although the Goddess of Love and Beauty, Freya, had other gifts she bestowed upon the realms. One such gift was the birth of seidr. Since its creation, Seidr spread to all nine realms, changing and blossoming in ways unique to each race that wielded it. Freya herself nurtured seidr in Asgard by combining runes with herbs, berries, and even blood, concocting various potions, elixirs, powders, and pills which could be used for healing, poisons, changing appearances, and many, many more practicalities. The auga pills were one such creation, allowing Valhalla's eyes to change color.

Only four remained.

Depending on how the night went, she feared she would have to slip away on another trip to Asgard to retrieve more. Valhalla grabbed one of the pills between her index finger and thumb, placed it in her mouth, and swallowed it whole.

She closed her eyes for a moment and awaited the magic. "One, two, thr—"

A burst of energy swirled to life in her chest, traveled up her body, and into her eyes. Valhalla then opened them and blinked a few times to try to clear the odd tingling sensation away. She hoped the pill would stay in effect long enough for their plan to play out, to whatever end.

Footsteps then sounded behind her, causing her to jolt with a start. The thumps of the footfalls were close. Was it Lord Ing?

"By morning of summer. By night of winter. The lady in violet—"

Valhalla forced a giggle, interrupting the Lord, recalling that Lorna hated romance ballads. She especially hated those whom Alistair had a particular fondness for. She had even used her status as Princess to ban a few from playing within the walls of Nobles Perch or Ravens Lookout. If he wanted to see the plays, she thought it best for him to crawl through the squalor of the Commoners Nest.

"Will stare into the sunset for her true love to return, riding a white dragon. Ugh! I hate that ballad." She said with a sneer.

Valhalla felt Ing's presence drawing ever so closer to her, sending shivers up her spine. His essence emanated a venomous warmth. "Why, because it's one of your brother's favorites? It's not his fault that he's a helpless romantic."

She attempted a scowl to mask her discomfort. "Because pining for a woman like *that* is pathetic, though I suppose it's why he's drawn to it."

Ing trailed a hand slowly up her arm. Her throat dried, and her eyes widened. She demanded her nerves to remain calm, but an old memory invaded her mind. *He* touched her that way, she remembered. It was an echo of her past, but even so, it took all of her will not to let her defenses crumble. Ing and the phantom of the boy were not the same person, and she was not in this moment Valhalla. She was someone else. She conjured images of her impression of who Lorna was, flooding her mind with the princess's secrets scribbled away in the safety of her journal, concentrating on depicting herself as the spiteful young woman. Erecting new barriers within herself to seal away the bloody wound she believed would never truly heal, Valhalla allowed Lorna's persona to worm its way into the very fibers of her being. She forced herself to remain still, to endure Ing's romantic gestures, for now.

"Tell me, Lorna, where have you been? I met with you on the day you returned from Rjóðr, and then, nothing."

Valhalla's brows twitched. She didn't know Lorna and Ing had met after she came home. That was information Eilis would find interesting. That was the day Lorna had perished. Ing was one of the last people she met with. He might have been the last person she saw. Ing could even have been the one who—No. Valhalla needed to pry more from him before jumping to conclusions.

She took a moment to find the best response, searching for Lorna's voice, how she might answer such a thing. "Did we meet? Mother forced me to hide away in the castle for over a month so she could . . . *fix me*. As if I need fixing." She said with a roll of her eyes and a long groan of annoyance, hoping Ing would buy her deception. "I even had to use a double to bring me news. As if anyone could simply replace me, only an idiot would fall for that, and can you believe the fool got themselves killed? Some coward actually sent an assassin after me!" Valhalla allowed her voice to elevate with outrage and slammed a fist down on the stone railing, her gaze never leaving the city skyline. "They could have at least sent someone not so dense as to fall for a decoy. Must have been blind and stupid."

"Is that so?" Ing grabbed Valhalla, wrapping his arms around her tightly and trapping her between the railing and his well-toned chest. His lips crept up against her ear. Valhalla's muscles tensed, and her heart skipped a beat, unnerved and fighting the urge to send him hurtling over the railing toward a quick death.

"What are y—"

"You're sixteen summers old now, eligible to marry the soft-hearted fool from Svartr."

Valhalla's eyes trembled as she glanced at him, her lips turning into a thin line. His touch made her stomach queasy. She had stayed quiet for too long; she needed to say something quick, to keep him talking.

"I don't want to marry some Oceanan. I won't have anyone who isn't a pure-born Hillian to rule beside me . . . you know this." Valhalla's heart beat so hard against her chest that she worried she might break a rib. She tried to control her breathing, but adrenaline was pumping through her veins, every instinct telling her she was in danger.

Ing was quiet for a brief moment, and she was unable to see his face. His grip held fast, and he stood as still as stone, not giving her any indication of which way this conversation would lead. His silence took a toll on her nerves. She tried to focus on every possible means of escape available to her, but knew that was a worst-case scenario. She needed a confession before she could act and hoped it would take the form of words instead of action. He then let out a soft chuckle. "Stupid girl, what makes you think anyone wants *you* to rule?"

Her eyes slowly widened as the implication of what would follow settled in. "Wh—"

Ing quickly covered her mouth with one hand and revealed a blade with the other. It was a stiletto, its blade long, thin, and deadly. "When you die, Alistair will be the ruler. He is who this country deserves, who it *needs*."

He pulled his stiletto back and readied to plunge it into her side, but Valhalla had what she needed from him. Unlike Lorna, she was not helpless. She didn't have many options. She had little time and was still pinned between him and the rail. Moving as fast as she could, she caught the blade in her hand and gripped it tightly. The action clearly caught Ing by surprise. He hesitated and gawked with confusion, his attention on the blade in her bare hand.

With his attention elsewhere, she raised her opposite arm and jammed her elbow into his gut with all of her pent-up frustrations powering the blow. He groaned and faltered back. Valhalla shook herself from his grasp, grabbed the fabric of her skirt with both hands, raised it high to her waist, and drove the heel of her foot into his face. The kick smashed him square in the jaw.

With a spin, his body fell to the floor with a loud thud. He was dazed but not yet unconscious. The stiletto was no longer in his hand, likely tossed somewhere on the balcony in the commotion.

A sudden rush of fire soared from her hand and ran up her arm, causing her to shriek and double over. With all the adrenaline dulling her nerves, she hadn't realized the blade had slid clean through the meat of her palm and pads of her fingers. She stared at her hand as the warm, red liquid flowed from the wounds and down to the floor.

"Shit! I should've—" Valhalla jolted, the adrenaline spiking again as she heard rushed footsteps coming toward the balcony.

Valhalla looked up, ready to fight off another attacker, but was relieved to see Alistair approaching. His sword Dancingraven now hung from his waist. She had forgotten Shu Yen was here, hiding and watching with their weapons should they prove necessary. Valhalla stood herself upright, and as Alistair closed the distance between them, she was surprised to find concern growing in his gaze as he looked from Valhalla to her bloodied hand.

His eyes immediately widened, and his hand reached for her. "Val—"

She instantly hid her hand behind her back, pretending not to be bothered by it. "It's nothing. I'm fi—"

Another groan poured from Ing as he rolled to his back on the floor beside them. Alistair and Valhalla both reflexively turned as he tried to push himself up off the ground. The man startled and froze as his eyes fell upon Alistair standing before him. "A—Ngh! Your Grace, how—"

Alistair unsheathed Dancingraven from its scabbard as quickly as lightning and brought the point of the silver blade to Ing's throat. For a moment, all of the man's bluster melted from his face. Alistair's breath quickened, and his eyes lightly glossed, his glare fixated on the man on the floor.

He looked to Valhalla as though he were barely staying his hand. "Are you—" Alistair's voice cracked. He attempted a deep breath and blinked back his tears. "Are you the one . . . who killed my sister?"

Valhalla found the question ill-timed but not exactly surprising. It would have been better to secure Ing's capture before questioning him, but she understood what this meant to Alistair. He needed the answer just as much as she needed to be free of Lorna's personage. She glanced at him before looking back at Ing. He stared at Alistair, regaining his smug arrogance, and glared silently at the prince. After what felt like a long stretch of quiet, a smirk flashed across his face.

Alistair's eyes widened as he jolted forward toward Ing. "Wait!?" He screamed out as he reached for Ing, but he had been moments too slow. Ing raised a hand, a strange ball in his palm, and slammed it down into the ground. A large puff of gray smoke exploded before them, concealing everything in a thick, dense cloud.

Valhalla's eyes stung and teared in the haze. The substance filled and dried her throat, forcing a harsh series of coughs to stall her pursuit. A chill wind and rumble of thunder came out of nowhere, so strong it nearly forced her to the ground. In moments, the smoke cleared and her breath returned to her lungs.

She attempted to open her eyes, but what little she could see was a blur. Blinking, she tried to clear the stinging pain from her teary eyes to no avail.

All she could discern were two figures fading into the crowd of the throne room, most likely Alistair giving chase to Ing.

"Your Grace—" She started, but all that followed was another series of harsh coughs.

She could barely make sense of her surroundings through the haze of whatever had been in Ing's concoction. Valhalla took a few cautious steps toward the throne room, the light of the fire setting the world aglow before her.

She could hear the hushed whispers of the confused crowd inside, but their words seemed somehow fuzzy and indistinguishable. A single repeating sound stood out from all the rest, the clanking of heels emanating from somewhere to her right. Valhalla's muscles tensed, and she took a defensive stance. "Who's there?" She asked, her tone more a command than a question.

"Valhalla, drop your head back!"

A rush of relief washed over her, recognizing the woman's voice. "Shu Yen?"

A hand pressed gently to the back of Valhalla's head, and the sensation she acquiesced to the instruction. Now, looking at the ceiling, a cup came into view, and a cool stream of water poured down over her face. A series of gasps sounded from the nobles in the throne room. Valhalla took a few steps back and blinked several times until her vision finally cleared.

"Hear, drink this."

"Thank you so much, Shu Yen," Valhalla replied coarsely as she took a tall cup of water from the maid, the same one used to splash water on her face. Without a moment's hesitation, she emptied its contents down her throat and swallowed every last drop. As she lowered the cup, she spotted Eilis emerging from the crowd and stepping onto the balcony.

"Lorna, what is going—"

"It's Ing." Valhalla blurted out. "I need to hurry after them."

Eilis stopped dead before Valhalla with eyes wide, while Valhalla handed the cup back to Shu Yen, who in turn handed her a cloth napkin to dry her face. She vigorously wiped away the remains of the water and most of her makeup, leaving only faint smudges suggesting it had been there at all.

"Please, Valhalla, tell me what has happened." Eilis said.

"He made his move against me. Ing revealed his intentions, then abruptly tried to stab me in the same place he had Lorna. I stopped him, and Alistair gave chase, alone."

Eilis remained still, save for a slight tremble in her expression. Her gaze then slid down. "Valhalla, your hand!"

"It's fine, I just ne——Ngh!" Another shot of pain went flying up Valhalla's arm as she attempted to wrap her injured hand with the cloth napkin she used to clear her face.

Eilis stepped forward, taking the cloth and assisting, wrapping it several times around the wound, then fastened it with a knot and cupped the hand. "Please, protect my son."

Valhalla watched as Eilis met her gaze with a vast, endless sea of worry shining in the pools of her sapphire eyes. Valhalla stared back and steeled her face with determination. "Of course."

A scream rang out from the throne room, startling the trio. They spun, and just beyond Eilis's personal guard, one of the women in the crowd was pointing at Valhalla's dress. "Blood on the princess!" In moments, the peoples whispers turned to a roar of fear.

"Was there an attack!?"

"Here!? In the castle!? I thought we were supposed to be safe here!"

"If there's been an attack, I'll not stay here a moment longer!"

The people began congregating toward the doorway of the throne room.

Valhalla's brows furrowed hard over her eyes as she took a step into the hall. "I don't think so. Rjóðr angwedh binda inn crumguru!'"

Valhalla raised her uninjured hand high and, in a swift motion, thrust it down and slammed her hand to the floor. Energy flowed through her arm and rushed out through the marble surface, spreading out in many directions like snakes through tall grass.

Just as the crowd of faces started turning to confusion, she closed her hand, and crimson chains exploded into existence in a fiery spectacle. The people jolted and screamed in terror. Valhalla then pulled her fisted-hand up to her chest. The chains wrapped around twenty——No, thirty of those in attendance, forcing them to the floor. Were any of the nobility not already panicking, they certainly were now.

"What . . . did you just do?" Eilis asked, stepping beside Valhalla with confusion and a hint of worry in her voice.

---

1   Rjodr angwedh binda inn crumguru is Celnor(Norse) for Red chains bind the guilty.

Valhalla released a tired breath. As she stood straight, she felt a pang of anger at just how many had been ensnared. "That was a lot more than I expected. I bound all who conspired to murder your daughter. The spell wouldn't have worked without a clear link to at least one of them, in this case, Ing."

Grabbing hold of the wig and tiara atop her head, she pulled them off, allowing them to fall to the floor. Then she placed her index finger on the corner of her eye. "Taka.²" Valhalla felt the energy leave her eyes, returning them to their original state. With a quick turn to Eilis, she curtsied. "If you'll excuse me, your Grace."

Without waiting for a reply, Valhalla rushed away and ran through the crowd of people. They all scurried away from her in a panic. With their newfound fear of her, it made it easy to reach the doorway of the throne room. There, she found a few members of the silver guards rushing in.

Valhalla immediately stopped before them. "Please, whatever you do, don't let anyone else leave unless the High Queen says otherwise."

One of the guards began to ask. "And who might you—"

"Of course, my lady." The second guard answered, cutting off her subordinate. The first woman looked at the second with a glare but seemed wise enough not to press the matter. "I promise I'll explain later." The second said to the first, then addressed Valhalla again, "Before you go, where is her Grace?"

Valhalla pointed to where Eilis stood, now speaking with Prince Volundr of Grár. With that, the two guards stepped aside. Valhalla exited the throne room, emerging into the fifth-floor main hall. Several more guards passed her by, none of whom gave her a second glance. She looked to her left and right but didn't see any signs of the High Prince or any traces of where he and Ing might have gone.

"Dammit." She knelt down and placed her uninjured hand flat on the floor. Valhalla closed her eyes and pictured the High Prince. She focused on his face, his physique, and his essence. To her surprise, a light flutter, no stronger than a butterfly, filled her chest. She shook off the sensation and whispered, "Leita.³"

Energy swirled through her arm and down to her hand. A sweltering heat filled the space between her palm and the marble below. As she opened her eyes, a bright, fiery glow burst forth and created a trail ahead of her. Fiery footsteps etched themselves into the floor at her right. Valhalla stood and raced forward. "Please be alright."

---

2   Taka is Celnor(Norse) for Remove.

3   Leita is Celnor(Norse) for Find/Search For.

28

Alistair

My Resolve

Alistair ran after Lord Ing, chasing him through the halls of his family's castle. He forgot how spryly Ing could move for his age. After everything the man had done during the Commoners' Uprising the year before, Alistair chastised himself for underestimating his opponent.

With a huff of frustration, Alistair continued his pursuit. His lungs burned, and his heart pounded hard. Sweat soared down his face, the salt stinging his eyes as he blinked the sensation away. Ing was in his sights, and Alistair wasn't going to let Lorna's murderer get away.

The man threw smoke bomb after smoke bomb in an attempt to mask his escape, but the High Prince rushed through each blast with eyes closed and breath held so as to avoid the noxious concoction.

Alistair's legs were beginning to wobble and ache from all the exertion. He screamed at Ing to stop, but the man seemed to increase in speed. No matter what, Alistair wasn't letting Ing escape. Alistair had to keep going. He just had to.

A memory of one of Druoga's many lessons on magic then crossed his mind. He wondered if he had enough energy to use his magic to stop Ing. Could he conjure it quickly enough to ensnare the man? He decided the risk was worth it and skidded to a stop. Magic had long been a struggle for him, only able to conjure a couple of spells over all his training, but there was one he had mastered even better than the sphere of light.

One hand remained on Dancingraven, should he need it. The other hand, he raised it to his face and concentrated on his palm. Alistair remembered Druoga saying he could send light through objects. He glanced at the wall beside him and swiftly placed his palm flat on its surface.

Alistair closed his eyes and recalled the word to summon his light barrier. "Skjald-borg[1]."

A strange tingling sensation rose from within his chest, traveled through his arm, and exited through his palm.

Alistair immediately opened his eyes and let out a loud gasp. He felt as though he had been held underwater nearly to the point of passing out. A short distance beyond Ing, he saw a wall of sparkling white light flash into existence, blocking two pathways, but Ing disappeared down a set of stairs toward the fourth floor.

"SHIT!" He pushed himself forward, continuing after Ing, only for his knees to buckle under his weight. Alistair caught himself on the wall by the stairs. With a deep breath and no small amount of willpower, he forced himself down the steps after Ing, thankful the man hadn't gone up. At least this way, gravity was on his side. Alistair ignored the fire in his lungs and the aching screams of his limbs.

The man continued past the fourth floor and went onward toward the third. Alistair let out a tired breath and slammed his hand on the wall of the stairs. "Skjald-borg!" He screamed out the spell, summoning another light shield, and blocked the entrance to the third floor. Undeterred, Ing flew past the barred path and headed down to the second floor.

Alistair's vision blurred in and out of focus. The world spun before him as he stumbled and fell onto the iron railing. He grabbed on quickly before just narrowly avoiding crashing to the floor.

He glanced to his right and saw Ing at the bottom of the stairs. It seemed Ing, too, had grown weary. The two stared at each other, out of breath. Although

---

1   Skjald-borg is Celnor(Norse) for Shield Wall.

Alistair's eyes had hardened in a mixture of anger and betrayal, Ing stared back at him with fiery conviction embedded in his steady sapphire eyes.

It made Alistair's blood boil.

Ing then took a deep breath and continued running down the steps. Alistair commanded his body to move. There would be time to recuperate, but it wasn't now. He pushed himself up and gave chase once more.

He had trusted Ing. After everything that transpired in the time following Alistair's father's death, from a conspiracy to dethrone his mother, to the economy almost crashing, and the rising tensions between high society and the commoners, Ing had been right there to help mend the cracks. But what was all of that even for? Did he do all of that simply to get close enough to his family to strike?

Alistair stumbled and slipped off one of the steps, sliding down and tumbling end over end several times before abruptly stopping as he hit the wall. Dancingraven landed with a clang on the step beside him. He groaned through gritted teeth, and his body ached. A range of emotions compelled him upright, ignoring the pain, pleading for him to remain still. Rage. Duty. Justice. Revenge. Anguish. He didn't really know which was driving him on, but it mattered little. Alistair cursed at himself for falling behind.

He slammed a hand down on the floor of the stairs and summoned as much energy as he could muster to conjure more light shields and sent it through the stones. "SKJALD-BORG!"

Alistair blocked the rest of the openings of the stairway, stopping Ing from going further down. If the man reached the bottom floor, it would be all but impossible to stop him from getting away. A single hallway remained open to Ing, and the man fled out of sight.

Pushing himself off the ground, he picked up Dancingraven and hobbled after Ing. Alistair was out of breath. His lungs raged with fire as he wiped the sweat from his forehead. Rounding the corner of the hall, Ing came back into view.

Alistair then noticed something about the hall. He passed the castle library to his right, lit by many sconces on the walls. The windows were left wide open to let in the moonlight, revealing white callunas decorating the hall. This place led to the White Garden.

He stumbled forward, his limbs weak. His legs were exhausted from running, and his hand could barely keep its hold on Dancingraven. His eyelids were ready to close, and he wanted nothing more than to allow his body to fall forward to the cool floor. Just then, the sting of tears caught him by surprise.

Alistair couldn't understand why his sister had to die. To him, she was all talk. She was always just talk. Lorna wasn't a threat, at least not yet. Alistair was sure of that much. There had still been time before her crowning, time for her rebellious streak to end and for her to snap to her senses.

A sudden burst of adrenaline coursed through Alistair's veins, gifting him a much-needed second wind. He sprang into a run and continued his chase after Ing. Reaching the entrance of the White Garden, he halted and scanned the area.

Green foliage engulfed most of the threshold. The vines crept a good way into the castle hall, and moonlight softly lit the garden. He cautiously took a few steps inside. The garden had no walls; instead, four pillars held the ceiling of the floor above and were wrapped by vines of ivy.

He searched the massive garden, white flora and green leaves filling his vision. Four large ponds dotted with lily pads and stor nøkkerose rested in the corners of the garden. In the very center of the pavilion lay one of many treasures of the Hilliard castle, a tree with silverish white leaves. Its trunk was as black as ink. The flowers strangely grew in the shape of a peacock's head, twisting into a sharp point like a thin beak. The open end was circular, and out from it came white stamens.

Beyond the tree, by the white stone railings surrounding the garden, stood Ing looking out over into the night, likely searching for another way to escape the castle, but there was none. He had trapped himself in a dead end.

Alistair stared at the man and the quiet city before them. Though still out of breath, Alistair was starting to regain his composure. While weakened by the excess use of magic, he would simply not allow himself to faint until his deed was finished.

A soft metallic clang sounded by his side, catching him by surprise. He glanced down and then realized it was his sword. The tip now rested on the stone. His strength had waned more than he had expected. Ing had jumped at the sound as well and now looked directly at Alistair. Fortunately, he too seemed out of breath and heavily fatigued from his flight.

He fully turned himself around to face Alistair. The two stared at each other almost as if daring the other to make a move. Ing's eyes blazed with resolve and more than a little agitation. Alistair's brows curved sternly over his eyes. confusion, sadness, and anger swirled within him like a hurricane.

This was the same man who had been there for Alistair, helping him secure trade deals with other countries, appease stubborn nobles who refused to donate to causes of safeguarding the city, raising funds to improve the city and its people's lives, and helping stop the civil war brought on by heavy taxation. People were starving and losing their homes. Whether the tactics used were barbaric or tactful, the end result was the same. This man defended Alistair against nobility from his mother's and sister's court. So, why did Ing kill Lorna?

Alistair took a few steps toward Ing, the point of his blade screeching against the white cobblestone path with each step.

Ing flinched at the sound, but stood himself firm, his hands turning into fists. "Dammit, Alistair, I'm not your enemy!"

Alistair stopped and fell deathly still. "Not my . . . You murdered my sister! After lying with her, only gods know how many times! How could you not be my enemy?" His breath hitched, and his eyes burned with tears.

"I did what I had to, Alistair, but I'm no fool. I had another to do that deed for me, a prostitute from the White Dragoness Brothel, selected for their similar build to me after learning what that . . . *child* was scheming for our country."

Alistair's mouth fell open. "What do you—"

"You and your mother made your choice long ago. You both either decided to ignore who she was or, in your ignorance, truly didn't know everything that Lorna had done. You both were ready and *willing* to accept a tyrant on the throne!" Ing's brows furrowed, but he exuded conviction.

Alistair shook his head lightly. "You don't-You don't know that."

"Oh, but I do." Ing took a few cautious steps toward Alistair. "The amount of information she divulged to me was . . . startling, to say the least. Allying herself with corrupt nobles and traders from foreign lands. Lorna is the one who convinced the late Princes of Eenheid into war with us, promising that if she killed you on the field, they would be rewarded with Rjóðr."

Alistair jolted, nearly losing his grip on Dancingraven. "You-You lie!"

A few tears rolled down his cheeks as old memories of Lorna flooded his mind once again. His body trembled with uncertainty. "No . . . No, you're wrong," he said as he shook his head, "she would've been great!"

"She would've run this country to the ground, and you know it! Her cruelty would have been unshackled, and you and your mother would have been powerless to stop her."

Ing's retort caused Alistair to jump in place. His heart raced, and his breath quickened. He curled his free hand into a fist, squeezing so hard his knuckles went white.

His body moved as if he were possessed by a demon. He rushed Ing, raising his arm back and flung it forward, punching Ing right in the jaw. The man fell to the ground with a crash and a loud groan. "Lorna-Lorna was problematic, I get that, but she was no monster!" More tears fell as he grabbed hold of Ing's doublet and raised Dancingraven. Alistair pulled the man high enough to look him in the eyes, but there again, he found only resolve.

Not a single ounce of remorse or fear shone through his sapphire eyes. It made Alistair shake with anger. It was not an anger born of Ing's actions, not of the treason he accused Lorna of committing, not even of his part in murdering Lorna. No, this was an anger sparked by the seeds of truth Alistair had actively spurned all these years. His mind flickered back and forth between hearing the sense in Ing's argument and wanting it to be nothing but honey-covered lies to save himself for the fate that assuredly awaited any who would commit regicide. He loved his sister for who she had been growing up, not who she had become. Alistair was disappointed in who she was becoming, and sometimes even hated her for the things she had put him through, but he could never have given up on her.

"Alistair, you're the one who reunited the seven castle cities through acts of friendship, not Lorna. You even made connections with other countries, strengthening our Queendom. Lorna, your so-called sister, was going to destroy all of that. She would toil away in her lavish parties while our enemies chipped away at *our* resources until there was nothing left of our lands. She chose this course of action simply because *you* had brought us together. She hated that. She despised you because the people love you, and not her."

Ing, still on his knees, stretched himself upright and puffed out his chest. His eyes seemed to dare Alistair to argue. "She planned to sell you off as a slave to some desert kingdom, I can't remember the name, but only after framing *you* for the death of your mother. I believe she planned to use poison."

Alistair's breath hitched in his throat as tears streamed unabated down his cheeks. His eyes widened with horror as he slowly lifted his sword with a trembling hand.

No, his heart protested. Ing was lying. He had to be. "Sh-Shut up!" Alistair bellowed. "She . . . Lorna was my sister! She would ne—"

"Alistair," Ing spoke softly and with understanding in his tone, "your sister died alongside your father eleven years ago. She stopped being your sister when those vipers' words slithered their way into her ears."

He stared up at Alistair for a long moment, then raised a hand to his High Prince's wrist, which rested over his chest. "I understand your heartbreak, Alistair, I really do. Strike me down if you must, take your vengeance. Lorna could've burned down an entire district, and you would still care for her. Stare on in horror, perhaps, but love her still, you would. I don't think you could ever bring yourself to stop her. To do what was needed. You have too much heart to do the deed, but then again, that's why we are here, that's why *we*. Follow. You. Why *we*. Choose. You."

Ing squeezed Alistair's wrist as the words stuck in his mind. "With nary a word, with only your actions to speak for you, you command loyalty and respect. You show true leadership and friendship, Alistair, you show trust. You showed it to Veerence during The War of Lions, and you showed it to Hilliard during the Commoners' Uprising."

Ing grabbed Alistair's shoulders and brought him closer, the two nearly nose to nose. "So strike me down. Pierce my heart if you must. Let my blood, and only my blood, be on your hands. By Forseti's witness, I did what I had to do, what I felt was right, because I knew you would never be able to. I will become a martyr, Alistair, but in time you'll understand, so let my blood show you the way if it must. Trust me when I say that I'm glad to have ended that monster's reign. I did it not only for you, or your mother, but for this country. We'll rejoice in secret so that you may grieve in peace, but know that what was done paved the way for you, my High King."

Alistair jolted as his heart dropped into his gut. "High King! I'm not fit to be High King, and that was never my goal! I just—" His mind spiraled out of control. The insinuation was too much to bear.

The color flushed from Alistair's face. His heart thumped heavily and caused his chest to ache. He was unable to look away from Ing's gaze. His breath went heavy, and he no longer knew what to do. If Ing's words were true, and Lorna was guilty of the things that could no longer come to pass, he had done the city a great service but at a cost Alistair could never accept.

"Why . . . Why do so many believe I should be High King!? I've only ever wanted to help my sister and Mother. I never sought the throne—Never wanted it!" Alistair pulled Dancingraven back, and the tremor in his hand ceased. The blade came to a statuesque stillness as Alistair prepared himself to do what he felt was necessary. He thrust it forward towards Ing's chest with a powerful roar.

"Alistair stop!"

The point of his sword flinched and stopped a mere inch before Ing's heart. The man hadn't lifted as much as a finger in his own defense. He simply stared up at Alistair with a serene assuredness of what he had done, and the prince starred back in utter confusion.

What was Alistair doing? Why had he stopped? Ing deserved to die. Alistair knew he should carry out the sentence. So why? Why did Alistair stop?

"WHAT AM I SUPPOSED TO DO!?" Alistair exclaimed, feeling like his sorrow, anger, regret, and every negative emotion would swallow him whole.

"Your Grace, please, just stop."

Alistair stood frozen in place, this moment a crossroads leading to unforeseen futures. Was sparing Ing the right choice? His very bones ached for justice. For vengeance. What consequences would arise from executing the man? Did those possibilities outweigh the harm of the future he would face were he to stay his blade?

"I know you're filled with so much anger and hatred right now, your Grace, but hear me now. If you kill this man before he can give us the information we need, High Princess Lorna's death would be for nought. There could be more to the plot than we know. There could be more conspirators than those who attended Lorna's nameday ball. They may even have been so bold as to plan to attack your mother next."

A tremor wormed its way through Alistair's body. "E-Easy for you to say. You've never felt helpless to save someone you cared about. To stare the killer in the eyes!"

The garden was silent for a long moment. Not a murmur filled the garden, save for the soft blowing of the cold winds rustling the leaves of the tree. Then a few steps broke that quiet. It startled him at first, but with every step, his breath lessened to follow the relaxed patter of the cadence.

"But I do know, your Grace. No matter how many times you may wish it, or even demand it from even Hel herself, killing Lord Ing . . . won't bring your sister back."

Warm hands wrapped around him, holding firm to the cold hilt of Dancingraven. He slowly turned and saw Valhalla by his side, no wig and no sapphire eyes, just her own. She looked at him with such worry, he then wondered if she knew what it was to feel the anguish he was struggling with at this moment. Beneath her expression, he could sense the shared heartache as a glint of fear entered her strong pink eyes.

He forced his grip to relax from the hilt, a needling sensation rushed down his forearm, and covered his hands. He hadn't realized until now just how tightly he had been holding Dancingraven, and allowed Valhalla to take the blade from him, making his choice to spare the man.

A short breath escaped his lips. Making the decision caused his head to grow light as the strength in his limbs gave way to the fatigue that had plagued him since the stairwell. He faltered back onto a white stone bench.

His breath was heavy, and his sight was fuzzy. Alistair held onto his doublet, feeling for his father's ring, wanting so badly to feel his father's presence and hoping beyond hope that he had made the right choice. Tears flowed freely now with no regard to whether he wanted them to or not.

Alistair's jaw tightened, and a lump lodged in his throat. He took a deep breath and let out a scream of anguish which echoed through the garden and down the halls of the castle.

His dark brown hair that had earlier been tied back in a braid fashioned by his mother now fell over his face like a broken waterfall. Alistair kept his head down, letting his tears fall as rain upon his lap.

The clanking of heels called his attention from his dreary thoughts. He glanced up as Valhalla stabbed Dancingraven into the soft grass. She watched Ing as he slowly rose to his full height, and to Alistair's surprise, she rushed at him with fist raised, and struck him in the nose with so much force that the hit was followed by a crack, and then he crumbled to the ground. He landed hard on his back and let out a croaked moan.

Ing had once been described as having a stately profile due to the prominence of his rather considerable yet distinguished muzzle. Alistair had no idea why the thought crossed his mind, but he couldn't help but feel his spirits lift slightly as he watched the blood flow from Ing's nostrils, which would likely never be the same.

A sizable contingent of metal footsteps then reverberated from the castle hall, causing Alistair's heart to skip a beat as he wondered who was leading the Silverguards. He hesitantly turned his head to find his mother leading a slew of the Queensguard soldiers. A fleeting sense of relief came to him as their eyes met. She looked to be out of breath, and in her eyes burned an energy he hadn't seen since before his father's passing.

He withdrew from her gaze, and shame began a string of questions bombarding his mind. Had he made the right call? Should he have killed Ing? Maybe it was the right choice to keep the man alive, at least for questioning? But if his mother simply ordered Ing's execution, then what was the point of Alistair's hesitation? Would she chastise him for it?

"Arrest that man on the ground and place him with the others." His mother ordered.

The clanking of sollerets rushed past him, and the noise sent his mind swirling. A curtain of violet and lavender then slid into view. He jolted back but stopped as his shoulders bumped into the stone behind him. He was filled with fear. Fear that his mother would yell at him, punish him for . . . What? Not killing Ing? Not saving Lorna? But why would his mother be angry with him? He knew there was no logical reason for him to be feeling the way he did, but all the same, the fear was there.

He slowly raised his head to face his mother, only to be taken aback. Her sapphire eyes were heavily glossed as if she were trying to hold back tears. His fears ebbed away at the sight, back to the recesses of his mind.

Alistair released a trembling breath, reached for his mother, and grabbed large swaths of the fabric of her dress. He pulled her to him, burying his face against her stomach, and embraced her waist tightly. She then wrapped her arms around him and gently caressed his now tangled hair. He could hear her softly sobbing alongside him, and there, the two were finally free to mourn the future that had been stolen away, the daughter and sister, the person Lorna could never become.

29

Alistair

Traitor's Confession

"**W**ell, I don't suppose you'll tell me why you killed the High Princess, or will I have to bloody my hands a bit first?" Alistair's uncle mused. He stood looming before Lord Ing with arms crossed loosely over his chest, now dressed in black garb, his preferred attire for torture.

"Not at all, Your Highness. I have no qualms with answering your questions. I feel no guilt for my part in her death, nor would I seek to hide my conspirators. We did what was needed and understood the consequences should we be found out." Ing answered, his voice betraying no sign of fear or any other emotion. Though fully bound to the chair from head to toe, his posture was poised, and he showed no discomfort with his current predicament. He was the very definition of stillness, and his expression remained a blank canvas. No smirk. No pride.

Nothing.

"Then talk." His uncle commanded in a low tone.

Alistair watched and listened from his position leaning beside the door of the stone chamber. The faintest of torchlight illuminated the room, chasing the shadows to the corners of the small room and bathing the visible area in a dull yellow-orange hue. He hugged his arms about his torso and fought to mask his discomfort, wearing a stillness about his face even though his insides churned into painful knots. As Ing glanced his way, a chill crawled up Alistair's spine, forcing the faintest of frowns to form on his face.

Squeezing his body tighter to hide the tremble, Alistair wondered if he could do this. Ing's stare, his mannerisms, and the casualness with which he held himself were unsettling. The conviction was too much. The man acted as though he was prepared for any outcome and welcomed it as one would a cloudy day, with total indifference. That, paired with the knowledge of Volundr's techniques and what he knew of what transpired within the depths of these walls, gave Alistair all the more reason to listen to his unease.

Why had he agreed to come here? Alistair asked himself that question over and over.

Ing's sapphire eyes remained locked on Alistair, unblinking for what felt like an eternity. Alistair wondered for a moment if his uncle could sense his anxiety, but he already knew the answer. Of course, he could. Volundr had honed his skills for longer than Alistair had been alive. He was a true master of his craft. He hoped that at the very least, Ing didn't share Volundr's ability. Then, with a deep breath, Ing pulled Alistair from his thoughts, then looked back to his inquisitor.

"First, I want you to understand I don't believe I am a righteous man for removing the High Princess from the board. She was . . . an obstacle, to say the least. One that, if left in place, would truly have brought this country to ruin."

"So, what? Were you hoping to take the throne yourself?"

Ing chuckled softly at the idea. "Your Highness, if I wanted the throne for myself, I would've married Lor—"

"High Princess, or her Grace. You've lost the right to speak her name." Alistair's uncle growled.

The Lord stared at Volundr silently for a moment, his small grin fading back into obscurity. With a shrug of agreement, he continued. "Fair enough. Anyway, if I wanted the throne, I would've married her, and I believe my actions show that I very much didn't care to do that."

"Then why?"

Ing glanced at Alistair again, causing his lips to thin and curl inward, retreating between his teeth. His body went cold as he recalled Ing's words in the garden, but his uncle stepped in between them before Alistair's discomfort forced a visible reaction. "Don't look at him, he will not help you," Volundr stated flatly. "Now tell me why you murdered the High Princess. And I warn you, should you drag this out any longer than needed, I shall compel you to hasten your answer." His uncle's voice rose, his patience fading.

Alistair shifted and peered around his uncle, trying to get a look at Ing. The Lord glanced up at Volundr, and as their eyes met, a confident smirk creased the man's face. "To make way for someone better."

Alistair's heart dropped into his gut at the implication. His body froze, and his eyes went wide. Several seconds passed before he realized he had stopped breathing.

"Many of the fools in my circle bickered about the roles forcefully bestowed upon the men and women of this city. Short-sighted as they are, I never fully trusted them with all the details of my plan, but the one thing I agreed with is that there needs to be a change. What lies between a person's legs should not alone a ruler make. Anyone of any gender should be of consideration. To limit that role simply for the sake of tradition and to ignore what is right before our very eyes is folly. Good rulers are as common as bad ones, but a great ruler, one who can see beyond their station, is a rare find. I hoped to live long enough to see such a ruler in my lifetime, but I'm doubtful that will be the case."

Ing glanced at Alistair, and as their eyes met, he bowed his head in respect. Alistair ducked himself back behind his uncle, unable and unwilling to hold the man's gaze. He feared that if he allowed himself to consider the meaning behind Ing's words, he might acknowledge the wisdom there, and in doing so, understand his actions. By doing that, by giving any part of the events that led to Lorna's murder credence, he too would be guilty of what transpired, and he couldn't allow that.

"I only want what's best for this country. We need a ruler who would put the people above all else. To me, Alistair is that ruler, and is the one I am certain who will prove to be the very best Midgard has ever known. I'm sure of it. He has the potential to surpass not only the High Queen, but even his late grandmother, as an unrivaled champion of and for the people." Ing groaned from deep within his throat as he struggled against his restraints.

Alistair clutched his father's ring, holding it so tightly he could feel the metal embedding itself into his palm. His fisted hand rested against his bare chest between the unbuttoned folds of his doublet. His jaw muscles ached, and a bead of sweat rolled down the side of his face.

Why? Why did Ing do all of this on his behalf? What had he done to instill such a belief in the man? What act drove him to commit treason?

Alistair had only ever done what was needed to support his mother and sister with their duties. Trying to lighten their load where he was able. He had never aspired to be more. The line of inquiries caused his every act as Prince to play out in his head, second-guessing his every choice in the hopes of isolating the spark that had ignited the flames of treason in so many.

Why had this been done in his name? His eyes stung, and his temples throbbed.

"Eilis is . . . a decent ruler, to put it bluntly. She has made for a good puppet to the wills of a number of those in her court, but now, with my actions, I'm sure we will see a change for the better very soon. I also doubt her Grace will continue to be so accommodating to those who strive to steer her, and thus our country, toward ruin. She will no longer turn a blind eye, isn't that right, your Highness?"

Alistair could hear the triumph in Ing's voice, every self-important word becoming a knot in his stomach. Bile rose in his throat, and his mouth tasted of acid.

The chamber began to spin, and his head felt faint. A few tears flowed down his cheeks. Alistair couldn't stand it anymore. He couldn't hear another of Ing's platitudes.

He immediately turned toward the door beside him, grabbed the handle, and threw it open. Wasting no more time, Alistair fled the chamber before his uncle could mutter a word of protest and slammed the door shut behind him.

Alistair stopped, frozen before the door, his head hanging low and eyes set on the stone floor. The firelight danced around him, his shadow flickering about his feet.

His heart pounded away against his chest. He raised his hands to his face and tried to steady them, but to no avail. He watched, the rest of his body as still as the stones around him, as his hands convulsed with the thumping in his veins. Was it fear or anger? He didn't know. After an endless moment, he buried his face in his palms to stifle the tears.

Apologies ran over and over in his mind. To Lorna. His mother. His people. To anyone he felt had been and would be affected by Ing's actions. Though he hadn't been involved, he couldn't feel he was the cause. The man had stated as much, and surely if Alistair had come to such a conclusion, so too would his mother, his uncle, and likely many who already openly opposed him in court.

Lost, he was unsure what to do. How should he continue? If only he had foreseen what was happening before him, seen Ing as a threat, things would be different. He was a Captain of the Queensguard after all. It was Alistair's duty to keep his family safe. The High Queen and her heir. His mother and sister. He felt like a complete and utter disgrace for not being there for them as he should have been. Lorna was gone. He failed her completely, no second chances, but his mother yet lived. He couldn't—wouldn't fail her again.

Alistair's fingers curled inward, and his head lowered until his face rested on his fists. He let out a shuddering breath and allowed his arms to fall to his sides. Walking away from the door, he traveled down the hall, wanting desperately to get away from this place and never, ever return.

After walking in a daze down the barely lit hall, he eventually came upon a few screams echoing from a far-off room somewhere behind him. Jostling from his sadness, he glanced back and wondered what horrors awaited at the source of the commotion.

He questioned how it was he let his uncle talk him into coming down into this decrepit place. Down deep beneath the castle. It was a dungeon like many others, of misery and torture. Of inescapable and excruciating pain. Alistair's uncle knew damn well how much he hated this place and yet somehow still talked him into coming here.

Alistair had never had the stomach for torture. At least in war, you are facing a soldier on even footing, but here, there is no fighting back. No honor to be gained. Only pain to inflict and secrets to be surfaced. The methods came at a cost Alistair couldn't bear. So why did he follow Volundr?

His uncle always argued that what he did was for the sake of the Queendom. It was for protection, the royal family and the people, but Alistair just couldn't bring himself to accept such methods as were practiced here. He continued on with a much faster pace.

As the sounds of misery grew quieter and quieter in the distance, a different sort of screaming erupted beside him, making him jump. He looked to his right and saw the source of the disturbance. There, a door hung lightly cracked open.

Keeping a safe distance, Alistair peeked inside to find a room similar to the one he had just fled, although a bit smaller. The only furnishings were a table and two chairs. It was most likely an interrogation room, or so he assumed.

He stepped closer and startled when he spotted Valhalla. She was dressed more comfortably now, no longer wearing the guise of Lorna. She wore trousers, a fitted tunic, and a vest overtop. A Lord he vaguely recognized was chained to the table, Balder Selfora, if Alistair recalled the name correctly. He was of a minor house here in Hilliard, known for their iron trade, which reached all the way to Hvítr. The man was the source of the commotion, screaming and berating her with such fury and lack of wit that, were Alistair a child, he might have mistook the man for a troll.

"She would've destroyed everything! We've done nothing wrong! She was the real threat, not us!" Balder bellowed and flailed, causing his chair to knock from side to side. Valhalla rubbed her uninjured hand across her face and looked exhausted.

Alistair's eyes narrowed as he released a long, steady breath from between his lips. "So, he too believed Ing." He whispered.

A hand then patted him on the shoulder, startling him, and as he turned, he found his uncle looking at him with a troubled frown beneath his thick mustache. "Alistair, how are you doing?"

Alistair hadn't the words to answer the question. He could only stare back as a faint sense of shame clawed at his chest. Wishing he had the strength to remain at the interrogation of Ing, Alistair tried to control the queasiness bubbling in his belly and searched for an answer to his uncle's question. In his heart, there were many seeds of doubt he had let fester and bloom over the years, and the events of late felt all too familiar to ignore the aching in his soul. He took a few steps back and turned his gaze to the floor, hugging his biceps softly.

"I . . . I don't know anymore. It's—" He forced himself to raise his head and took a long, deep breath. His eyes remained tightly closed as he fought back tears and struggled to force the question that had been circling his thoughts out into the open. "It's father all over again, isn't it?" Alistair asked weakly. His voice cracked as though the words physically pained him as they came out.

The memory of his deceased father plagued him. The man lay in Alistair's tiny arms. It was his tenth nameday ball, and all had fallen deathly quiet. The King's bronze skin was so pale, gray as stone. An inky black liquid flowed from his father's every orifice. Dark eyes stared blankly at the ceiling as Alistair cried. The people stood around him, not one approaching. Whispering began to fill the room, no louder than a dull hum. Young Alistair yelled, pleading for his father to get up, to move again, to look upon him. To do anything.

His breath hitched in his throat. The memory of his father's death was always with him, appearing every time Alistair closed his eyes. His memories, even the happy ones, turned into nightmares that crept upon him every now and again. They served as a constant reminder of what he had lost, and of what was likely lying in waiting for his family should he not be careful.

Alistair brushed his fingers through his dark brown, knotted strands of hair. Noticing Volundr had remained silent, Alistair opened his eyes and looked at him. His uncle's grip on his shoulder tightened as a strained smile worked its way onto Volundr's face. He then released Alistair and moved to the door, leaning beside it against the wall, and glanced inside.

"She's a remarkable young woman, that one." Volundr gestured inside with his thumb, then crossed his arms casually over his chest. "Knows a few fire spells too. Those flames of hers were a great help in prying answers from some of the more stubborn highborns last night. No amount of torture I can employ could cause such a spectacle, that's for sure."

"She what!?" Alistair's eyes widened as his brows furrowed, baffled by the insinuation.

His uncle rolled his eyes and chuckled. "Oh, relax, Alistair. She didn't have the stomach to actually hurt them with her fire. Fear of pain can sometimes be more powerful than pain itself. I just needed her to scare them into talking, and scare them she did, but after a while, I saw the method was taking a toll on her, and that is why I instead stuck her with those who would easily break. All she has to do now is sit and wait. For some, all that is needed is a little patience. Sure, they'll bark and posture, but once they've worn themselves out, they'll tell you what little they know. She doesn't even have to say a word." Volundr chortled with self-satisfaction.

Alistair's muscles relaxed, and he let out a sigh of relief, not exactly sure why it had bothered him in the first place, but he was glad that she wasn't like his uncle. He loved Volundr to death, but his uncle terrified him. And he was pretty sure his uncle knew it.

His eyelids grew heavy, feeling the toll setting in as he was sure Valhalla must be feeling as well. Alistair had been up all night at the request of his uncle. He said it was to allow his mother to rest. Something about knowing Alistair was safely accompanied by him and that they were working toward uncovering every little secret these villains held to breast. Alistair was already tired after they had captured Ing, and his thoughts were distracted, so he acquiesced and did as his uncle requested. At this point, though, there was an invisible weight on him. It took everything he had not to simply collapse to the floor.

He rubbed his eyes with a thumb and finger, feeling the fatigue hitting him with the strength of a horse's kick. Alistair winced at the thumping he thought was coming from inside his skull, then realized the sound had been Volundr knocking on the door and waving for Valhalla to come out.

Alistair heard the wood of her chair screech against the stone floor, followed by her footsteps coming closer. He stepped back to allow Valhalla some space when exiting. She stopped just short of the doorway as Lord Balder called out to her again, embers glinting in her eyes as she scowled and looked back at him.

"Wait, you were the one disguised as the High Princess, right?" He asked as if the thought had just dawned upon him. "You must've learned who she really was. How can you stand there and judge us to be wrong?"

Though Alistair could no longer see her face, he could feel an indescribable heat coming from where she stood. "Whether or not your justifications have merit is not the issue. She wasn't only your future High Queen. She was a sister and a daughter. She was also still in the chrysalis of adolescence. In time, it's possible she could have seen the error in her ways, understood the ramifications of even the tiniest of her actions, and maybe even grown into one deserving of her station. You and yours robbed her of that in your short-sightedness, stole her from a loving brother and mother, and now we will never know what future she would have brought."

Alistair watched in stunned silence as she exited the room and closed the door behind her. Balder, as if not understanding a single word she said, continued yelling as if anyone could make out the muffled belligerence spewing from his mouth on this side of the door.

Alistair knew the night up until Ing's capture had been more difficult on her than himself, but her weariness caught him by surprise. Tired as he was, he could see she had little energy left to give. She cupped her injured hand, and her eyelids obscured all but a sliver of her pink eyes. Dark rings shrouded the area encircling her eyes. She slouched forward and seemed to be propping herself upright by sheer force of will.

Valhalla sighed and took a few steps away from the door, looking as though nothing would please her more than placing distance between her and the man in the cell. She headed to the nearby stairs, which led up and outside. Alistair looked past her, his eyes drifting up the steps to the top where sunlight peeked through the iron bars of the locked gate. He squinted as the light glinted off one of the upheld swords of a guard standing just outside it.

Looking back to Valhalla, she had stopped mere feet from the steps and flopped herself against the wall with a heavy sigh. Her head dropped back and rested against the stones. Valhalla rubbed her face wearily, her brows trembling with exhaustion.

"Amazing, truly . . ." She stated flatly. "It's all the same. Every one of them, even those I had . . . *spoken* with." Valhalla rolled her eyes. "They all despised the High Princess. 'The High Queen and Prince were blind fools to trust her and were ignorant to what she was.' They just kept repeating that same sentiment."

"So it really is true?" Volundr asked.

Alistair let his gaze linger on the ground. He could feel Volundr's gaze boring into him, but he was unable to look his uncle in his amber brown eyes. His lip quivered as the cycle of self-loathing began anew and latched onto one of his biceps. Alistair hesitantly nodded as he dared not speak.

His uncle sighed and rubbed his face, most likely feeling just as tired as he and Valhalla. Volundr then walked up to Alistair and placed a hand on his shoulder, garnering what little attention he had to spare. "Go to sleep, Alistair. We can talk about this with your mother after we've all had a proper rest."

Alistair looked up to his uncle, feeling what little energy he had left escaping him, and nodded. Volundr then turned toward the stairs. "Valhalla, can you please help my nephew to his chamber? I'd appreciate it if he makes it there in one piece and would only entrust him to you."

She nodded in agreement. "Of course."

Valhalla pushed herself off the wall and walked up to Alistair. She placed a hand on his back and the other on his forearm. The two stared at each other with tired eyes, and there he took comfort in the warm smile spreading across her face. He was glad to finally see the woman for who she really was. Since he had first met her, he had his guard up, and his mind was too distracted to really give her the attention she deserved. In that moment, he wanted more than anything to tell her thank you, to tell her how much her help meant to him, and to apologize for every slight he had given her, but he was simply too exhausted.

"Let's go, your Grace, let's get you in bed."

Alistair could only nod in response, and as the two left their ordeal behind them, the warm sun washed their troubles away.

30

Valhalla

I've Gained a New Friend

Valhalla placed a bracer on her right forearm, and while attempting to thread the straps through their buckles, she struggled with keeping it in place. She was so used to having the aid of one of her friends that she had rarely ever needed to do this on her own.

"Damn you, hold still." She growled through gritted teeth. Try as she might, the bracer slipped from her hand, and as it tumbled to the floor of her inn chamber with a thump, she groaned.

"Wait, how did Aura say to do this again? Oh, right." She picked up the bracer and again held it to her arm. Raising a foot to the edge of a chair, she folded her right arm over her thigh and tucked her forearm between her stomach and leg. Pulling the straps through the buckles, she smirked and whispered a quiet thanks to the Valkyrie.

As she pulled tight on one of the straps, a sudden twinge of pain surged up her arm, causing her to wince and her fingers to twitch. "Dammit." She looked down at her wounded hand with a scowl. White linen bandages stretched from her wrist down to the middle of her fingers. Valhalla lamented having to leave her glove for that hand back in her bedroom in Alf, but she was warned her wound needed to breathe, so she had to go without. Valhalla would have welcomed the padding of the glove should she need to grasp onto something, giving her a much-needed buffer against any impact the wound might need to endure, but for the time being, she would need to avoid putting such a strain on the hand. She tried to curl her fingers into a fist, and as the muscles around the cut stretched and pulled, the pain flared, and her lips curled into a thin line.

"I'll need to meet with Eldira after getting back to Alf. This really fucking hurts."

She did her best to finish tightening the straps on her bracer, then made her way over to her cobalt blue cloak, which lay across her bed. Taking the cloak in hand, she twirled it over her shoulders and clipped it firmly over her chest. Taking a final look out the window, she realized just how barren the streets before the Violet Tulip Inn had become.

A small number of red and white roses were strewn about the cobblestones, as was the custom in the event of a death in the royal family. The practice was a display of respect for the fallen, and though Valhalla had no way of knowing with any certainty, she felt as though the people had only observed the practice in sympathy for the High Queen and Prince, and not to honor Lorna. Every now and then, she spotted one of the common folk hurriedly passing by, likely running errands, and noticed not a one minded their footing. Many of the flowers had been trampled or otherwise damaged.

"Discourteous." She whispered with a sigh. "But I suppose I understand."

Turning away from the window, she grabbed the red glass butterfly and silver key from a wooden table and headed toward the door of her room. Valhalla grabbed the handle and paused before pulling the door open, allowing her eyes to drift over the quarters one last time. The space was considerably cozy. The decor was a beautiful shade of lavender and purple, adorned with an assortment of white flowers all about.

Valhalla's shoulders slumped with disappointment. "If only I could stay here a while longer, but I suppose it can't be helped. Who knows, maybe another time." She then took her leave, closing and locking the door behind her. Taking the stairs down to the lobby of the inn, her feet fell lazily as she soaked in the warmth of the residence, stretching her departure out as long as she could.

Arriving on the ground level, she found Madame, who was busy wiping down the countertop. An assortment of recently collected, colorful butterflies and silver keys hung on the wall behind the counter.

Madame was dressed in muted colors, and Valhalla mused that if it were her way of observing the somberness of the day, the sentiment hadn't affected the amount of makeup that caked her face. Her ebony dyed, flaxen hair was decorated with so many braids around her head that Valhalla couldn't tell where one began and another ended.

The rotund woman glanced up at the sound of Valhalla's footsteps and flashed her a kind smile. "Afternoon, darling. I hope your stay was a pleasant one." She cocked her head to the side and rested an arm on the counter.

"The room was wonderful. I made use of it as often as I could whenever I could escape my . . . task." Valhalla smiled weakly, the previous night still weighing heavily on her shoulders.

She approached Madame and handed over the silver key, watching as the woman hung it beside the rest. Madame then spun around, her face now taking on an apologetic expression, which took Valhalla by surprise. "I did so wish you wouldn't have to leave on such a sad day. The city is a much warmer and livelier place when we aren't stricken by such news. Ostara may have come and gone, but Endispretta is just around the corner. I wonder if the city will pick itself up by then? I certainly hope so."

"Endispretta? Oh, is it the festival to celebrate the end of spring?" Valhalla asked with a shrug. "I completely forgot about the holiday. Who knows, perhaps the people will come up with something to help lift the High Queen's spirits. I hope so, at least."

Madame nodded in agreement. "I'm sure they will. You take care, darling. There's a chance the High Queen will request your aid again *very* soon."

Valhalla's brow twitched with curiosity. "Wait, how would you—" She stopped herself, holding her hands up. "Never mind. If that's the case, I'll happily accept."

"Oh, made up your mind about our High Queen, have you?" Madame smirked.

"She's . . . an interesting woman. The High Queen has her flaws, as we all do, but she loves her family dearly, and she does her best to be a good ruler. You take care, Madame." Valhalla finished and bowed farewell. As Madame waved goodbye, Valhalla took her exit.

The city glowed with a radiant orange tinge as the sun slipped toward the horizon. "With Edan's speed, I should be able to reach Alf by nightfall . . . After such a long stay here, he should enjoy the ride," Valhalla added with a chuckle, making her way onto the cobblestone streets and turning toward the stable to retrieve her companion.

As she stepped through the threshold of the stable, she was surprised to be greeted by the pleasant aroma of flowers instead of the pungent mixture of horses and hay. Valhalla scanned the interior and found Edan to her left, drinking from the trough within his pen. She made her way to his side and patted his neck. "Hey, sorry I took so long. Did I make you wait?"

Not at all, I'm just glad to be leaving this place. He answered with a snort and shook his head from side to side.

"Didn't like the stables here?" She smirked playfully.

They were alright, but look at what little space I have, it's ridiculous! I can't even turn around or stretch my legs. I don't know how these creatures do it. They are lucky I didn't have an itch; otherwise, I'd have burned the place to the ground just trying to scratch it.

Valhalla rolled her eyes with a soft chortle. "Oh, come now Edan. If you were really having that much difficulty, you should've left for Asgard. I would've called for you when I was ready to leave." She giggled as she took the leather reins in hand and guided him out of the stable. "But I'm glad you were here for me. Come on, you silly horse."

Once the two had made their way out onto the streets, Valhalla placed a foot in the stirrup and climbed into her crimson saddle. Trying to reacclimate herself to the seat, she shifted about in search of a comfortable position. Once settled, the two started on their way. Their course was set. Out through the East Gate, then past the boundaries of Hilliard, and once the city had finally vanished from view, it was just a quick bifrost to their destination of Alf.

Their trip was mostly uneventful as they traversed the streets, passing a few of the citizenry and garnering surprisingly little attention, and it wasn't long until they reached the East Gate. The massive doors were left wide open, revealing the town outside the wall and the grand plains beyond. Valhalla sighed, her eyes lost in the beautiful pinks and purples of the sun setting sky, soon to be blanketed by deep oranges and crimsons, and finally, the endless black of night.

"Valhalla!"

The call caught her by surprise. The voice was familiar, but she struggled to match it with a face.

Valhalla looked around and noticed what few people who had been about the square were now all past her. Turning around as best she could in her saddle, her heart skipped a beat. Alistair was riding in earnest toward her atop his white and black clydesdale.

She immediately pulled on Edan's rein, causing him to spin around, and rode to meet the High Prince. As they met, the two slowed their horses, and

Valhalla came to a stop at his left side.

"Your Grace, you and your horse look ready to collapse." Valhalla chuckled. Her heart fluttered nervously, though she fought to ignore the feeling. Had he pushed his horse so hard just to catch her before she left, just to say goodbye? No, she thought, there must be some other reason. Perhaps the Queen sent her thanks, or mayhap there was more to be done. Whatever the reason, she was heartened to see Alistair once more before leaving. She reached out to pat the side of the poor creature's neck; it panted heavily, and its eyes were weary.

"I know. I know. I know——" He answered, leaning forward and embracing his horse's neck.

Valhalla retracted her hand, dumbfounded as to why she had done so with such haste, but was glad to see Alistair hadn't taken notice.

"Thank you so much, Beor." Alistair continued with a grin. "I promise I'll give you all the apples in the Queendom for getting me to her." Alistair laughed, and as he did, his horse neighed happily as if it understood his pledge.

Alistair struggled to sit himself upright on his saddle, trying to soften his breathing by taking long, deep breaths as he continued to laugh. "Aye, I-I don't even know why I'm out of breath, I w-wasn't even the one . . ." He stopped as his eyes drifted down and began to widen as they set upon Edan. He raised a hand and rubbed his eyes vigorously, then opened them again as if in complete disbelief. "Your horse is on fire . . . Your horse is on fire!?"

Valhalla burst out laughing, the tension that had been building in her chest dissipating at the silly expression hanging on Alistair's face. "I don't know why that reaction gets me so, but yes, Your Grace, my friend Edan is on fire. He's a magical horse, but I'm sure this isn't why you rode all the way from your castle and tired your poor steed, right?" She raised a brow at him with a playful smirk.

In the dusky light, he seemed to glow; his warm ivory skin blending and turning gold at his jawline, spreading down his neck and beneath his white top.

His cheeks blushed a soft pink as he chuckled bashfully, pulling away from her and running his fingers through his silky, dark brown hair. She absentmindedly gave him a quick once-over, taking in his appearance. Valhalla was pretty sure he was still wearing his night clothes and wondered if Alistair had just awoke before rushing his way here.

"Right. Anyway, I rode here to see you because——" He paused for a moment, staring at her with a soft, apologetic look in his mixed eyes, eyes that she found to be quite beautiful. They were unlike any she had seen on another living being. They were mostly amber brown, looking to her like a field of wheat touched by the blazing warmth of the setting sun, but the explosion of sapphire in the bottom left corner of his right eye was as striking as the brightest star in the night sky. Realizing she had allowed herself to get lost in them again, she looked away.

Her heart thumped hard, and each beat came more rapidly than the last. The sensation startled her as she inconspicuously raised both hands, cupping them together atop her chest. Every time. She wasn't sure when it started, but every time she saw him now, her heart reacted so. She didn't understand what it meant or why it was happening. She had never had such a reaction to someone before. Burning cheeks. Dry mouth. A tightening in her chest. Whatever it was she was feeling, it was beginning to scare her.

Alistair released a heavy sigh, bringing her attention back to the present. As she met his eyes again, he was the first to speak. "I want to apologize."

Valhalla was taken aback. "For what?"

"For everything. For how I have acted. How I treated you——"

"Your Grace, you didn't do anything wrong." She tried to smile, but thanks to the surge of adrenaline coursing through her veins and the unshakeable unease building in the back of her mind made it difficult to manage anything above a shallow grin.

His gaze remained on her, his brows curving deeply, and a look of guilt shrouding his face. "I attacked you in the secret throne room. I even hurt you."

Valhalla's mouth fell agape. She was momentarily speechless. Finding some semblance of composure, she sighed. "Listen, you reacted the way anyone would in your position. You didn't know me and recognized I was an impostor. You moved simply to protect your mother. I don't hold what happened against you. Not any of what you did. Those circumstances would have proven difficult to anyone, and you handled it as best you could. Besides, you already apologized for my pained wrists." She tilted her head to rest on her shoulder and tried to convey as much warmth and sincerity as she could with every word.

Alistair's lips thinned momentarily. "I . . . Hmm, then how about this, thank you. For all you've done for my mother and me. You risked your own life to help my family." He gestured at her injured hand, and as he did, she raised it to inspect the bandages.

The corner of Valhalla's lips twitched, and she let out a soft giggle. "Don't tell my friends I did that, or they will have a field day with me again."

Alistair's brows winced with curiosity, but also a hint of concern. "You risk your life often, don't you?" She answered by simply shrugging her shoulders, feeling embarrassed. "Still, thank you, Valhalla. Will I . . . see you again?"

Heat flooded her cheeks, and she was unsure if she had heard yearning in his voice. Valhalla quickly cleared her throat and pushed away the thought, nodding in affirmation. "Of course, your Grace. Despite everything, I quite like Hilliard, and there's still much of the city I haven't had a chance to see. Besides, if you ever have need of me, look for a dwarf named Sigurdr Sirginson in the town of Alf between here and Rjóðr."

Alistair's brows pushed against each other, and an expression of skepticism crossed his face. A giggle escaped her at his reaction. "Don't be silly. Trust me when I say dwarves are *very* real. Once we've gotten to know each other more, I'll introduce you to them." Valhalla winked playfully.

He looked at her curiously and released a soft sigh. "Alright then, I hope when we meet again it's under better circumstances, and as friends." Alistair stretched out a hand to her, and her heart nearly leapt from her chest.

Valhalla reached out to take his hand and was taken aback as he stretched his arm further, passing her hand, and gripped her wrist. Alistair then cupped her hand against his forearm and bowed his head low. His forehead nearly touched their hands.

She stared at him wide-eyed and wondered how it was that he could believe dwarves to be mere myths and yet execute their greeting so perfectly. Alistair sat himself erect on his saddle, and as he did, his smile faded back to confusion when his eyes met hers.

"How . . . do you know that gesture?"

His head tilted lightly, and then he answered. "It was taught to me by Master Druoga. Why? Have you met him?"

"Well, no, but——" She stopped herself and shook the thought away. "Never mind, don't worry about it. Till we meet again, your Grace." Valhalla released her grip on Alistair's wrist. As she pulled away, their fingers brushed together, and a strange spark ignited from the tips of their fingers.

Her hand flew to her chest as her cheeks heated again. Being this close to him left her feeling breathless. By the end of their dance the night before, she had felt so dizzy she worried she might pass out and ruin their plan. Fortunately, that hadn't been the case. Valhalla's chest filled with a warm, swelling sensation that sent tingles through her body. What was going on with her, she wondered.

"Valhalla?" She jumped in her saddle, remembering Alistair was still there. "Is everything alright?"

She grabbed hold of Edan's reins, her mouth dry, and nodded. "Yes, don't worry about me, your Grace."

Valhalla gently kicked Edan's sides, signaling for him that it was time to take their leave. She guided her companion around the High Prince. "Focus on tending to your mother. She'll need you now more than ever." She said quickly. "Remember, if you're ever in need, ask for me in Alf. Ride Edan!"

Edan reared as soon as they faced the East Gate with a happy neigh, stomped his front hooves down with a loud clatter, and began to gallop.

It was nice to meet you, Your Grace! Edan exclaimed as they sprinted through the gate at great speed.

Fire trailed behind them as the wind whipped through her hair. Valhalla, surprised at Edan's outburst, peered back and saw a look of sheer shock on Alistair's face. She patted her friend on the neck in thanks and was glad to be putting distance between herself and the city, hoping the ride would calm her rapidly pounding heart.

Part
3

31

Valhalla

A Message from a Queen

Valhalla breathed in deeply, soaking in the scents of apples and pines that mingled with the salty sea air. Opening her eyes, the morning's rays greeted her, piercing through her large open window. The sound of trees rustled outside. Sprawling across the bed, she stretched the morning stiffness from her limbs and was thankful for the comfort of the coziness that was her bedchamber nestled in Fensalir, otherwise known as Frigg's hall, the All Mother's home hidden away from everything.

Wrapping herself tightly beneath the furs, her sleepy eyes scanned across the spacious room. Wooden panels stretched from floor to ceiling, where a wide gold chandelier hung at the center. From the look of the candles, they had not burned for quite some time. The wax was firm, and no remnants of smoke lingered above the wicks. The fireplace across from her bed was also in a state of disuse, the hearth blackened, and only a pile of ashes remained where the night before had been kindling. A sliver of sea air brushed against her feet, sending a shiver up her limbs. She could just barely hear the waves crash against the nearby beach.

A sigh escaped her lips as she sat up. Lightly tapping into her fire seidr, she let out a breath into her cupped hands to chase away the chill. The cold was eerie. The realm was well within the warmer months of spring, nearly summer, yet the bite of winter was still upon them. There was no way the gods would've allowed the seasons to fall into disarray, so whatever was happening must've even been out of their considerable power to affect. Dropping her arms on her knees, she stared out the window, watching the leaves dance in the wind. It was probably nothing. Just a long-lasting winter. It had to be. After all, if something were wrong, the Gods would've said something. If not to her directly, to the realms as a whole. Hopefully, it was nothing.

Valhalla startled from her thoughts as the loud flapping of wings breached the ambient tranquility of her lodgings. A few heartbeats passed before an eagle perched themself on her windowsill. The creature was far larger than any normal eagle; an offspring of Verdrfolnir. Long ago, Yggdrasil created Verdrfolnir, one of Her earliest creations, coinciding with the birthing of Ratatoskr and Nidhoggr, serving as a flying scout to keep the Great Tree safe. Until one day, in a state of desperate loneliness, he requested that Yggdrasil create him a mate whom he could love and care for. Yggdrasil, wanting the best for Her children, obliged and created a beautiful eagle to serve as Verdrfolnir's companion. Their deep affections spread across the realms in the form of thousands of their offspring, most of which now serve as messengers for the Æsir.

Tilting her head in acknowledgement of the creature, the eagle bowed. *Greetings, young one*, the creature spoke through a mental voice, just as Edan, the feminine pitch clear in Valhalla's mind, *I bring a message from Queen Hel of Helheim.*

"A message? What is it?" Valhalla threw her fur coverings to the side and scooted herself to the edge of the bed.

Her majesty wishes to meet with you. She claims it to be urgent. The eagle shrugged her wings. *I'm afraid that was all.*

"Oh. Umm," Valhalla stood, trying to process the request. What it was Queen Hel would want with her, she didn't know. Of all the things she expected this morning to bring, this was far removed from expectation. She glanced at her walk-in closet. "A-Alright, I'll see her as soon as I'm able to. I mean, sorry, I'll be quick!" She slammed a hand to her face, trying to rub the exhaustion from her eyes, and mumbled, "What is wrong with me?"

The eagle laughed. *I'll just tell her majesty you're on your way.*

"Thank you."

Just as the eagle withdrew and took flight, Valhalla rushed to her closet and began searching for some clothing suitable for her unexpected destination. She wouldn't be fighting, at least she hoped she wouldn't. Helheim wasn't exactly Vahalla's favorite realm, a desolate wasteland of ice and little else. There were the dead, sure, but they were usually kept at bay by ice and snow. It wouldn't be like last time. She would be fine. Of course she would be fine. She had to be.

Valhalla fought away the memories of her last visit to the wretched place, but her heart quickened nonetheless. Bony hands sprang from the ground, clawing and grabbing at her legs, pulling her down, down, down.

She gasped, tripping and stumbling forward, just barely catching herself on the frame. Her body trembled violently. Valhalla focused on the present. She was still in Fensalir. Still safe. Shaking her head, she cursed for allowing the old fear to resurface. It was one of many. Too many. She needed a distraction.

Looking down at the blue and white travel garb in her hand, she slipped off her nightgown, dropping it into a wicker basket, and grabbed a few other items for the trip. Chestwraps to tie down her breasts, an under tunic, leggings, and trousers. Where she was going, warmth was in short supply. She also plucked out a pair of thick socks, winter boots, and a cloak lined with thick furs.

The cloak was held fast by a pair of clasps connected by two strings of colorful beads, which rested just below her collarbone. The cloth draped over her shoulders and fell long down her back. Valhalla stood before her mirror, taking one last discerning look over her garment. Once she stepped foot out the door, there would be no turning back. Was she ready? Valhalla wouldn't be fighting, she repeated in her mind. She would be fine. She had to be.

Her hands went cold at her sides. Gloves. She needed gloves. On her way out of the closet, she grabbed a pair of leather gloves, slipped them on, and left her room.

No one else seemed to be awake. Just across from her on the second floor, Frigg was still asleep or at the very least hadn't yet left her chambers. Syn, her guardian, leaned against the door, arms crossed and eyes closed. Even asleep, Syn had proven to have a keen alertness of her surroundings, like a hungry bear waiting to catch a fish in mid-jump.

Valhalla stepped as quietly as she could. There was no need to wake anyone, and doing so would only cause alarm if they learned of her destination. She had almost made it to the top of the stairs before a door opened beside her. There stood a familiar thirteen-year-old boy, sleepily rubbing his eyes, his dirty blond hair swaying over his face from the motion.

"Valhalla? What are you doing up?" The young boy, Hermódur, asked.

Valhalla leaned down and rested her palms atop her thighs, flashing him a playful smirk. "I could ask you the same thing, little brother."

Hermódur, like Valhalla, had been adopted by Ódin and Frigg. The All Mother was present on the day of his birth, and while he was born strong and in good health, sometimes the doors into our world swing both ways. Hermódur's mother was lost in the process. Such a thing was a rare occurrence here in Asgard, and in his case, with there being no father to claim him, Frigg, with Ódin's blessing, adopted little Hermódur as her own. From that day, Valhalla and Hermódur had grown up together.

The boy let out a wide-mouthed yawn. "I heard loud flapping noises outside, so I came to see what it was."

"Ah. Sorry, an offspring of Verdrfolnir visited with a message, but he's already gone. That's all." Valhalla shrugged, hoping he wouldn't press for more information.

"Oooooh, trying to sneak out to meet a boy?" Hermódur leaned in with a whisper, causing Valhalla to snort with surprise, then quickly shielded her mouth.

"No, of course not! Why would you ask that? I've never snuck out to meet a *boy*." She grinned with an uptilt of her head, curious as to why that would be the first place his mind would go.

"Oh. Really?"

"Yes, really. Hermódur, where's all this coming from?" She chuckled.

"Nothing. Nothing. It's just, well, where are you going?"

Valhalla raised a brow at him. "Hermódur." She said with an accusing look.

Hermódur sighed with defeat. "Fiiiiine. While you were gone, Mother was really excited about you meeting some Prince in Midgard. She said you two looked cute together. Or something. I don't know, I lost interest when her, Lady Freya, and their handmaidens started gushing about this Alistair guy." He made a face while twisting a portion of his hair into a small braid.

"Oh no." She breathed a heavy sigh.

If the Goddess of Love and several other things Valhalla had no current interest in were involved, then . . . well, she didn't know exactly what that meant. Anticipating the motivations of the gods was anything but straightforward. Anxiety brought on a familiar tightness in her chest. With a shake of her head, she decided that now wasn't the time to dwell and wallow in what might be.

"A-Anyway," she rubbed her forehead and straightened, "Can you keep a secret?"

Hermódur sparked with curiosity. "Of course!"

Valhalla raised a finger to her lips. "Shh. I'm going to meet with Queen Hel."

He stared up at her, blinking. "Queen Hel. As in *the* Queen Hel? Of Helheim?"

"The one and only."

"But-But Father said—"

"Hermódur," Valhalla placed a hand on her little brother's head, disheveling his hair, "I'm well aware of the All Father's decree concerning that place, but I wouldn't be surprised if he already knew of the message I received. In fact, my escort will probably already be waiting for me at the Bifrost by the time I arrive. I'll be fine."

Hermódur sighed. "Alright, but caaaaan I at least see you and Edan off?"

"Absolutely, I was just about to offer." Valhalla giggled as she offered him her hand, which he gladly accepted.

They both made their way down the steps and took their leave of the long hall of Fensalir. Emerging into the woodsy surroundings, the warm golden glow of the morning sun bathed everything in its light. Valhalla wasted no time in bringing a finger and thumb to her mouth and let forth a great whistle.

In his excitement, Hermódur began bouncing on the balls of his feet, a grin growing across his face. He pointed ahead to a spot on the earth where the soil bubbled and grass hissed. Moments later, a stream of lava sprouted and congealed, forming into the shape of a clydesdale with a black coat, crimson eyes, and a fiery mane.

Valhalla's little brother threw his arms up in the air and proclaimed, "Edan!" He then rushed toward the horse as Edan trotted to meet them with a happy whinny.

And here I thought I was going to sleep in today. Edan chuckled as Hermódur wrapped his arms around the horse's lengthy snout.

"Sorry, old friend, Queen Hel wants to meet. Can you take me to the Bifrost?" Valhalla asked as she patted his neck.

Edan looked her up and down, his hooves clomping rhythmically in place. *Helheim? Are you—*

"As I've told Hermódur, I'm going to the Bifrost and will wait there to see what happens next. I don't expect I'll be traveling alone." Valhalla said, hoping to head off his protests. She followed with a small smile. "It's alright, Edan, I'm taking this one step at a time." She added as she climbed up into the saddle, situating herself into a comfortable position.

A weight tugged at the hem of her cloak. It was, of course, Hermódur who was looking up at her with icy blue puppy dog eyes. "You promise you'll be alright? I worry about you." His brows curved, and his face shifted into an expression that made her heart melt.

"I'm older than *you*, you know. I'm the one who's supposed to worry about you." She answered and took his hand in hers, brushing her gloved thumb across his knuckles. It was then that she noticed the small scarring now formed between his fingers, no doubt from combat and seidr training. She felt a swell of pride in the man she thought her little brother was growing into. "I know I'm not Asgardian, but you have nothing to worry about, Hermódur. Trust in me."

"I *do* trust you!" He pressed himself against her leg, latching onto her with his free hand. "I just don't always trust in the Norns," Hermódur whispered, as if scared the sisters of fate might hear his words of doubt.

Valhalla's smile weakened. "The fates don't plan, they simply interpret the many possible paths our lives may take." She leaned down and kissed the top of his forehead. "Only once a moment comes to pass is it written." With that, Valhalla took the leather reins in hand and snapped them with a mighty hyah. Edan spun around once, then raced off, leaving little Hermódur behind.

She didn't want to leave him that way, but if Valhalla had lingered any longer, it would've proven all the more difficult for her to leave. He was still young, still small enough for fears of the dark and the unknown to rule his judgment, but soon he would grow and be brave enough to face whatever was to come. There was still time for him to grow, to be stronger than she ever could be.

With a deep breath, she tried to stamp away her own fears. Edan raced through the slowly waking streets of Asgard. The shops and stalls blurred as they raced by. The people exited their homes and inns with the promise of a new day, while others emerged from brothels and taverns, still in the throes of revelry from the night before. The morning scents of kitchens filled the city air and sent her stomach into a fit of yearning. Valhalla then regretted not grabbing something for the journey, hunger not making for the best travel companion.

As Edan rounded a corner, Heimdall's Bifrost came into view dead ahead. All that was between them was the massive, glittering rainbow bridge. To her left was Heimdall's hall, Himinbjorg. It stretched as tall as it was long, and many knotwork carvings of ravens, bears, and seals decorated the wooden building. The shining sun gleamed upon its surface in vibrant glory, a stark contrast to the terrible darkness within. While it was true there was nothing malicious within, it was what the darkness stood for, a symbol of the burden of purpose. It was as a cave whose forest had long departed, never to return

Heimdall rarely left the Bifrost, not to visit family or friends, nor to eat or rest. She had heard the Guardian of Asgard had been bestowed with the keenest of senses long, long ago, but to never rest or take refuge in his own home seemed more a punishment than a gift. Valhalla didn't know his reason but supposed that whatever it was that kept him there, ever alert and at the ready, Heimdall found it to be of the utmost importance. And while he never complained about his constant vigil, she couldn't help but worry for the Æsir.

The heavy clomping of Edan's hooves against stone abruptly changed to a soft thump as he continued across the rainbow bridge, sounding reminiscent of rain droplets against stained glass. Shortly thereafter, Valhalla and Edan arrived at the golden spherical hall of the Bifrost.

Edan slowed as his hooves tapped against a marble floor. Valhalla lowered herself from the saddle and found herself before the eight golden gates which lead to the various realms inhabiting the vastness of all space. Her breath hitched as she took in the grandness of it all. The hall's dome ceiling arched high above her and was completely covered with intricate golden knotwork of the various creatures who represent the gods of Asgard: Ravens, boars, snakes, wolves, swans, cats, and so many countless others were given representation here but without the ability to fly, many were simply lost in the intricacies and height of the structure.

Patting Edan's neck in thanks, Valhalla bid him farewell and continued deeper into the Bifrost, listening as his hooves trudge in the opposite direction. She had known him long enough to see the signs of his concern, from the change in the rhythm of his stride to the flick of his ears. Valhalla wished there had been something she could've said or done to assuage his concerns, but he was right to be concerned. Had she any say in the matter, he would've stayed. A message from the Queen of the Damned wasn't something to ignore, no matter how badly her stomach twisted in knots. She had to go. With a heavy breath, she walked on. Heimdall stood at the center of the Bifrost on his tall, cylindrical dais, adorned in all his usual gold and white splendor.

"Lord Heimdall," Valhalla began, "I—"

"I know." Heimdall chuckled as he glanced back at her, his golden eyes shimmering in the sunlight. "Huginn and Muginn arrived before you with a message from my father, *the* All Father. He would like you to wait until he has gathered a proper escort for you. He doesn't want you in Helheim unprepared." His voice was deep and velvety smooth, somehow calming like a tender hug or a warm bath after a long day. Heimdall then laughed. "Come, you may join me while we await your companions. Keep this old Æsir company." He playfully winked and returned his gaze out the large circular opening to the endless golden shimmering sea. His hands rested atop the hilt of his golden sword, Gullhrafn.

Although Heimdall called Ódin father, their familial ties differed greatly from the conventional method. Heimdall, like Hermódur and Valhalla, had been adopted by Ódin, but they shared a blood bond. He had been created by nine Jotunn völvas, sacrificing their lives to birth him into existence. Through the use of the Urdar Fountain's waters beneath Yggdrasil's tree, Heimdall was birthed into existence through the use of Seidr. Many ingredients were involved in his creation, and one of the more potent of these was none other than the blood of the All Father himself, given freely. Through Heimdall's creation, a bargain was struck to allow Jotun refugees passage into the Æsir camp during the very first Æsir and Jotunn war centuries ago. It is said that traces of the nine Jotunn völvas were carved into the knotwork of Heimdall's halls, but which symbols are meant to represent each of the women was known only to Heimdal himself. Valhalla was gladdened to know Asgard's Guardian had honored his mothers in such a way, but it made her all the more saddened that he was never able to venture there to be with them.

"You know what, I think I'll do just that." Valhalla straightened her back to walk as tall as she could and headed over to the dias, then promptly plopped herself down on the steps.

She cursed at the fears encroaching on her thoughts once more. For Valhalla, the idea of returning to Helheim held all of the appeal of being bound in chains and thrown to the seas. She had visited the freezing realm first when she was nine years of age, and that one time was enough to imprint an indelible addition to the nightmares that plagued her.

Dead. There had been so many dead there. Hands clasped like cold iron around her ankles, thighs, wrists, clothing, anything they could get their bony mitts on and pulled her into the freezing realm to join them for eternity. Valhalla let out a trembling breath and dropped her face into her hands. The memory was so vivid. Why was the memory so vivid? She had been tasked with guiding Yggdrasil's chosen through the realm, to Her tree that had been planted there centuries ago. Things had gone relatively smoothly until Valhalla arrived at the sister tree. The dead, all of the dead, awoke. The scent of life radiated from her, and by the time she had reached the tree, the scent had spread, and the dead could no longer ignore her presence. Hel herself couldn't keep the dead at bay. The ghouls surrounded them, seemingly appearing from nowhere, and in a flurry of agitation, grabbed, clawed, and pulled Valhalla down to join them in the cold. Down into the ice. Down into the darkness.

"Keep shaking your leg like that and you might send a tremor through all of the nine realms." Heimdall laughed softly, startling Valhalla from her memories.

She looked down at her legs and found one was indeed bouncing like Ratatoskr bounding across the great tree. Slamming her hands against her knees, she managed to stop the bouncing but had no certainty they would stay that way.

"Valhalla."

Valhalla glanced back to Heimdall, his expression curious.

"I know you have no love for that realm. Why not have another go in your stead?"

She let out a long sigh, her shoulders hanging. The thought had crossed her mind. "Because Hel doesn't like intermediaries. In her words, 'tales dilute as they travel and have a way of losing their original meaning.'" Valhalla shrugged.

Heimdall let out a hearty laugh, which caught her by surprise. "Truer words have never been spoken. I swear she is so much like her father in that regard. He required his messages to be delivered in person as well. Either he would tell you himself, or would have them written down with seidr to ensure they couldn't be tampered with. I swear, ever since he learned how tales of us had been distorted in your realm of Midgard, he simply refuses any other way of communication. His mouth, or his letter. No lazy messengers. No other way." Warmth radiated from the Æsir as he spoke, the sensation chasing away her worries.

"Is that so?" Valhalla tilted her head. "Tell me, Heimdall, how is it that Queen Hel became Loki's daughter?"

Valhalla

The Children of Loki

"**D**id she have a birthmother like me? The tales say it's Angrboda, if they are to be believed. Or," Valhalla gave Heimdall a curious look, "was she born as you were?"

"Ah, an interesting question, that. One, I would've expected the Wolf or the Serpent to have answered instead of I." His head tilted over a shoulder, raising a quizzical eyebrow at Valhalla.

"Well, I did. It's just," her expression softened, recalling the one and only time she had mustered the courage to ask them. Both Fenrir and Jörmungandr had seemed almost physically pained by the question. "They both just seemed so sad. I couldn't bear the thought of making them answer."

"Hmm, they do miss their father dearly," Heimdall said, stroking his neatly trimmed beard.

Valhalla just nodded.

"Why not?" He said rather abruptly, "We still have time to talk." Heimdall slid his golden helm from his head, his long gray curls falling in a low tied ponytail, then placed it on the hilt of his sword. The mingled scent of pine and sea air grew as he descended the dais, his expression turning rather sad. "The way Loki left," his words came low and troubled, "still baffles us to this very day." He stopped and planted himself beside her on the steps, letting his arms drape over his knees.

"I heard his scroll from the Norns went missing when he left."

"It was, but so was Ildri's." Heimdall's eyes narrowed at the floor, and his attention turned inward.

Valhalla winced, sensing an unusual aura of agitation from the Æsir. "Vitalia's middle child?"

Heimdall nodded, then met her gaze. "After her death. Just after his parting. Both scrolls went missing. None of the Norns know how it happened," he closed his eyes and sighed deeply, "we had no suspects until Kiara's betrayal. Then her's too went missing."

"You think she has the scrolls?" Valhalla asked in a hushed tone, feeling the gravity of the insinuation.

"I don't think, I know. Aside from Loki and Hodr, Kiara is incredibly proficient with dark seidr. She could've easily shadow walked in and out without anyone noticing. Do you understand?" His expectant look made her breath hitch.

Unable to find the words, she simply nodded, and then he continued.

"I know that Vitalia, Ódin, and Frigg have each forbidden you from seeking or facing them, but should you happen across where Kiara and Loki are hiding, please, you must find and retrieve those scrolls. We need to know what happened to him."

"Him?"

"Loki. Chaos or no, I knew him before the change. He loved his tricks," Heimdall's lips slid into an affectionate grin, "but he was a gentle soul and one who endured so much for the sake of his kids."

Valhalla was taken aback. "Please, would you tell me about them?"

Heimdall chortled and nodded. "Well, their origins were a curious case, but no, Hel, Jörmungandr, and Fenrir were not born in the manner that you were. Nor did they come into being as I did."

Valhalla's eyes widened, and she sat upright.

"Hel was the first Loki discovered within Yggdrasil's roots."

"What?"

Heimdall laughed heartily, most likely at her stunned expression. "He was ten when he—How did Loki describe it again? When he heard her call to him. Like a whisper carried by the winds is how he described it."

"She was just . . . there? Hiding in the roots?"

"That's right. Encased in stone."

"Wow. And they were each found in such a state?"

"Mhmm, Hel at the time was a frail, sickly looking baby. Jörmungandr was in a large egg. And Fenrir was a wolf pup. All three in a stony, petrified state. They were somehow freed after he picked them up. Both Sigyn and Angrboda had been present for each."

Valhalla released a short breath. The story was so very different from the tales spread around Midgard. "Were they . . . received well? After Loki found them, I mean."

Heimdall raised a hand to the back of his neck, rubbing it so fervently that his bright umber skin reddened. "Hel was received well enough, but Loki and the girls were reprimanded for trying to care for such a frail child on their lonesomes for nearly a week. Ódin and Frigg were frightfully worried for the child when they saw her."

Valhalla winced. "Would Queen Hel have died if they hadn't found out about her?"

He nodded. "Yes. Dark seidr or no, she was still an infant. Angrboda was only a healer in training at the time, and there was only so much the three of them could do without Frigg's expert hand."

"Oh my." Valhalla clasped her hands around her knees, recalling one of the tales told of Hel in Midgard, how it had been Ódin to cast her into Helheim, seemingly to be rid of her. There had to be more to it. "So Hel being cast into Helheim, did it have something to do with saving her?"

"Yes," Heimdal answered. "Frigg and Ódin saw the child's connection to Helheim and posited that she would regain her strength therein, and so they shepherded her there as swiftly as they could.

"Her majesty Hel must've really been important for the All Father to bring her there himself?"

"Oh yes. Hel's very nature is to watch over and control the very flow of death. Helheim was quite literally created for her to oversee the punishment and rehabilitation of the damned. She's like a warden to a prison."

Valhalla tilted her head in curiosity. "So, who originally created Hel?"

Heimdall didn't answer, only shaking his head in refusal.

"Oh. Alright then, um, what about Jörmungandr and Fenrir? What was early life like for them?" She asked, wincing at the anticipated answer.

Heimdall shrugged. "Could've been worse. Jörmungandr spent five years in his serpentine form, until all of a sudden, he became aware of the ability to transform into an Æsir. He was about the size of a python at that time, but even back then, he was a quiet boy and took his studies very seriously. No one really paid him any mind, and while I'm sure that may have been lonely from time to time, his days were peaceful. Fenrir, though," the Æsir paused with a sigh and a grin, "he was the most energetic, playful pup you could've ever met."

"Really?" Valhalla's lips slid into a grin, picturing a fluffy ball of wolf pup bouncing on its hind legs.

"Yes, he was a little troublemaker, but in a good way. He made many of us smile, even mister surly, Tyr."

"No way!" Valhalla laughed.

Heimdall joined her in the thralls of jubilation, but then his smile fell from his face. "Yes, but unfortunately, not all good things last, I'm afraid." His golden eyes twinkled with a keen sadness. "Fenrir remained in his animal form for nearly twice as long as Jörmungandr, and was still growing."

"How big had he gotten at the time?"

"Fenrir was the size of a pony, and it was he who our people took notice of. The unrest grew rapidly and eventually became so severe that Tyr suggested for Loki, Fenrir, and Jörmungandr to start training in combat should they need to defend themselves one day. He hoped that through their training, people would recognize their discipline and self-control. Jörmungandr was no fan of combat, but he put up with it well enough for his family."

"Well," Valhalla rested a cheek in her palm and smirked, "for someone who hates to fight, he is *clearly* very good at it, judging from the way he wields his daggers."

Heimdall snorted. "Yes, I know," he sighed again, "but Fenrir, like most children, preferred to play rather than train. He quickly became trouble, but what raised the most concern was his random bouts of aggression."

"Oh?" Valhalla's chest tightened.

"You already know where this tale is headed. One day, when the three of them were busily training with Tyr, something just . . ." Heimdall stilled and his eyes drifted from the here and now, lost in a distant memory. "I'm not sure how to put it into words. I don't rightly know what happened. *We* don't know the why of it. It was as if something just snapped; his mind reduced that of a vengeful beast. Fenrir just attacked, lashing out at anyone and everyone." He glanced in Valhalla's direction but seemed to be watching the unseen memory as he spoke. "Even Loki."

She sucked in a breath, her mouth open in shock and disbelief. She had heard records of the day but never from a firsthand witness.

"He was trying to stop his son from attacking the other Einherjar, when Fenrir lunged at him with fang and claw. Loki stood frozen with fear, and that's when Tyr jumped in—"

"And lost his right hand." Valhalla softly added.

Heimdall nodded, his face sullen. "Exactly. Tyr's scream is what snapped Loki from his stupor. He jumped atop Fenrir's face and fought to free Tyr. Loki was so terrified of how Ódin would respond to Fenrir's outburst that he used his dark seidr to travel himself and Fenrir to Helheim in the hopes of snapping his son back to normal. Once there, Hel stepped in and tried to chain him down, but Fenrir wouldn't be bound, and as his raging seidr swelled, her chains broke."

The Midgardian tales once again swept through Valhalla's thoughts. They told of how Fenrir broke each and every restraint the All Father tried. Even thick iron and steel gave way beneath the wolf's might.

"Hel's chains creaked and snapped faster than she could rebind her brother. For three days straight, the two worked to undo whatever had come over him. Loki uttered every spell he knew that might subdue the chaos inside of Fenrir, but nothing worked. Each spell slid off him like water over an otter's fur. Not even tales of their lives together worked. Loki recited every moment the two of them shared, and none of it swayed Fenrir's wrath. That's when Ódin arrived with a small mahogany box."

"Fenrir's runic bindings," Valhalla said, leaning toward Heimdall, her heart racing.

"Yes. With help from the dwarves of the Amethyst Clan, Ódin came to Loki with a way to silence and lock away the chaotic seidr while still allowing him to keep his freedom. Hel and her hordes of undead did their best to keep Fenrir in one spot, as it was the only way for the runes to work. Two things were needed, blood belonging to the one who would be bound and the one who would cast the enchantment."

"Ódin wanted Loki to cast the runes?" Valhalla raised a brow curiously.

"Ódin felt Loki needed to prove to all of Asgard that he was capable of doing what was necessary. He, above all others, needed to show that he could control Fenrir. In the end, I suppose everything worked out." Heimdal then leaned back against the stairs, his posture relaxing as he swiped some errant gray curls behind his shoulder.

Valhalla crossed her arms over her thighs. "Life is full of challenges, I suppose."

"Not always, but it's wise to expect some push back every now and then." He then stood and held out a hand to her, his lips creasing. With thanks, she took his hand and stood. "And once those challenges reveal themselves, you face them head-on with all the strength you can muster. Life is like the sea. You may be gifted with many calm, peaceful days, but in an instant, the winds may blow, the bedrock shifts, and all the beauty before you turns to abject horror. Come what may, be prepared as best you can." Heimdall winked at her and climbed the stairs of his dais, tilting his head toward the Bifrost's entrance.

Valhalla turned and found two familiar young men waving at her. "Narfi? Nari? What are you two doing here?" She rushed to join the twin brothers, arms wide and beaming.

The brothers' faces were nearly identical, but their styles couldn't have been further apart. While the brothers both had curly auburn hair, Narfi, the warrior, had his brushed lazily to one side where it fell like a waterfall crashing on his shoulder. Warbraids decorated the opposite side of his head. Nari, the völur, typically wore his curly hair pulled back in a tight bun, but today it was loose and framed his face as a lion's mane. Both had blue-green eyes, which shone like gemstones. Narfi's brown skin was covered in knotted tattoos of wolves all about his body; Nari's brown skin, on the other hand, was clear of any such marks or piercings. The brothers were eighteen years of age, like Valhalla, and while they were handsome enough to draw a fawning crowd of men and women alike, she was simply glad to call them brothers.

Narfi wrapped his arms around her waist, lifting and twirling her in a circle, then hugged her even tighter before finally letting go. "We came to see you off, along with these three." He pointed behind him with a thumb, and there, Valhalla spotted Sigyn leading both Jörmungandr and Fenrir their way.

"Hello, dear." Sigyn greeted with a small curtsy, which brought heat to Valhalla's cheeks.

She was a beautiful woman, and like all Æsir, towered over her. Sigyn's curly hair was a dark brown, but in the right light was easy to mistake for black, matching the color of her eyes. Patches of creamy white dotted her otherwise brown skin like abstract brushstrokes on a perfect canvas. The mark it created over her left cheek resembled a white fire swirling over her skin. Elegant, graceful, an incredible healer, the Goddess of Loyalty and Trust, and mother to Narfi and Nari, it was nearly impossible to not be enamored in her presence.

Valhalla couldn't suppress the urge and marched right up to Sigyn, embracing the woman. The Æsir let out a hearty laugh and hugged Valhalla in return. "By Yggdrasil's shade, I feel like it's been forever since I've seen you lot," Valhalla said.

"It may as well have," Nari answered, his voice sweet as he tucked a few curls behind his ear, "it's been almost six months since we last saw you."

Valhalla winced. "Has it really been that long? I'm sorry."

Narfi nudged her with an elbow. "Don't worry about it. I'd be busy too if I were running errands for the Valkyries."

"I wasn't running errands!" Valhalla pursed her lips poutily. "A lot has happened, alright."

As the twins and Sigyn began to laugh, she turned her attention to Fenrir and Jörmungandr. From what Heimdall told Valhalla, they had no blood relation to one another, and yet the pair bore a striking resemblance when in their Æsir form. They even shared some similarities to Loki, their adoptive father.

Jörmungandr and Fenrir shared eyes of a blue-green, not unlike the twins. Their hair was black, and their skin tawny. Fenrir was also an exceptional warrior like Narfi. His lupine instinct and power made Fenrir deadly swift and vicious in a fight, even though he had a gentle soul. Jörmungandr was a völur, like Nari, but he always held himself in quite a stern manner. Some even considered him to be quite cold. The reality of it, though, was that he was just too dedicated to his studies, always seeking new ways to help his family, to better their lives, and relieve them of undue hardship. Valhalla was happy to call them friends.

"Do we get a hug too?" Fenrir asked meekly, and even had Valhalla not already been planning to hug the pair, the question and look would've spurred her into action.

"Of course you do!" She rushed over and wrapped her arms around his torso with a tight squeeze. "I can't believe you even feel like you have to ask."

Fenrir blushed as Valhalla turned her eye to Jörmungandr standing quietly beside them, a rare smile on his face almost imperceptible. She grabbed him by the collar, startling him, and pulled him closer. "Come here, you!"

She gave the brothers one last squeeze and released them, taking a small step back. "Don't tell me, are all of you coming with me?"

"No, not all of them."

Valhalla startled at the sound of the new yet familiar, silky smooth voice. Jörmungandr and Fenrir quickly stepped aside, their expressions turning downtrodden. At the entrance stood the All Father himself, Ódin, with Thor and Aura in tow.

The air in the Bifrost grew dense. The sensation sent an anxious pang through Valhalla's stomach. She stood herself as tall and took a proper stance as the King approached. His golden spear, Gungnir, was gripped tightly in one hand. Huginn and Muninn, his black ravens, rested atop each of his shoulders, and Geri and Freki, his black direwolves, flanked his sides. Each of the great wolves stood tall enough to reach the All Father's waist.

Looming and statuesque, Ódin's face was stern and had a glimmer of surliness that boded of ill tidings. Valhalla's breath always seemed to labor when in his presence. It was as if a great weight pushed against her chest. Today, his white hair was done up in tight warbraids, and his beard, also sporting more than a few intricate weavings, fell over his chest. A gold metal patch was bolted over his right eye. His left was a deep, almost dark green that seemed to pulse with purpose. The King of Asgard's robes elegantly flowed in swirls about his being, concealing and yet allowing freedom of movement should action need be taken. The Æsir's appearance was that of an aged, wise elder, but that didn't mean he was frail. He was anything but. The Æsir's muscular build was sterner than stone, and his shoulders and chest so broad they could rival even that of his son, Thor.

"Jörmungandr and Fenrir will act as your escorts in your journey to meet with their older sister. Aura will also be going as your protector with light seidr—"

"And I'm coming as your protector as well." Thor interrupted. "I won't let the events of last time happen again." The Æsir's meaty hand patted his hammer Mjölnir, which was attached to his belt, Meginjörd. His was no ordinary belt. The accessory served to double the red-haired god's strength. Valhalla's brows twitched as she noticed he had also donned his iron gauntlet Járngreipr, too, another rune-carved item to further alter his already significant prowess.

She wondered if Thor really needed so much protection. Even with what had happened to her on the last trip, this seemed overkill for one such as him.

Ódin let out a low rumbling grunt as he glanced at his son with annoyance.

"Yes. Thor is going because he doesn't trust Hel, despite my advocation's." The All Father then raised Gungnir a few feet in the air and abruptly slammed its end against the marble floor. The sound boomed and echoed in the domed hall. "Now go. Whatever Queen Hel needs doing, it can't be a good sign of things to come."

"Lord Heimdall, the portal to Helheim if you would," Thor said, somewhere between an order and a request. He then took his leave of his father and moved to stand before one of the gates which led to Helheim.

"It shall be done," Heimdall answered as he grabbed hold of the guard of his weapon, Gullhrafn, and pushed the blade deeper into the cylindrical pedestal before him.

A loud clunk emanated from deep within the hall, and the Bifrost itself began to spin to the right. The Æsir turned his golden sword in unison with the hall. Valhalla counted six turns before the hall began to pick up speed. In no time, the loose strands of her hair flicked about her face, and the fabric of her clothes flapped in the rising winds.

Valhalla's heartbeat like a drum against her ribcage, keeping tempo with the magics at work. It was almost time to go, to leave and venture deep into the freezing realm of the dead. Out of the corner of her vision, she spotted both Jörmungandr and Fenrir embracing Sigyn, saying their farewells to their mother.

The twins embraced Jörmungandr and Fenrir as well. They were all more than simply brothers in arms after all. While Narfi and Nari were the only biological children of Loki and Sigyn, Jörmungandr and Fenrir too called them Mother and Father, with Angrboda also serving as a mother to the pair. This made the twins and the foundlings kin, regardless of any blood ties. Besides, all of them had their father's eyes.

Valhalla jumped as she felt a hand on her arm. Looking down, she found it was Aura. "Are you alright? The portal is opening."

A thunderous boom shook the walls of the Bifrost as the spinning began to slow. In one of the eight gates which lead out to the separate realms, a white light formed at its center and instantly exploded into a swirling rainbow portal. Valhalla sucked in a breath. It was time to go.

"Valhalla?"

She glanced behind her, to the All Father who was staring at her with his stony expression, but there, in his one green eye, she spotted something unfamiliar. Was it . . . concern?

"The Wolf and the Serpent know their sister's realm better than anyone. Should you feel doubt, trust in them. Should you ever feel fear, ask for their courage. And should you find yourself lost, seek them out. Good luck."

A trembling breath was all she could muster as a response. Ódin had rarely, if ever, wished someone luck on a quest. Had something changed in him, she wondered.

Noticing she had been silent for far too long, Valhalla swallowed and, through some effort, forced a nod in thanks, allowing Aura to pull her rigid body along toward the portal. As she drew close, Thor outstretched an arm. "Ready to go, Princess?"

The simple gesture and warmth of his words melted away some of her trepidation, and Valhalla found herself chuckling softly. Accepting his arm with a roll of her eyes, she grinned and answered. "Oh, shut it you."

The group stood before the sixth circular gate of the Bifrost, the gate of Helheim. Its surface was covered in knotwork depictions representing the essence of the realm and what awaited them. At the very top of the circle was a being bearing a sharp, pointed crown atop her head, Queen Hel. On either side of her outstretched arms were wolves. They served as her protectors, and Valhalla hoped to be fortunate enough to avoid their gaze. Encircling the entirety of the golden gateway were the dead, each reaching toward their lady, not with the intent to harm, but rather seeking her guidance in the hopes of a peaceful afterlife.

The depiction sent a shiver up Valhalla's spine. A sudden, cold bite touched her hand, sending a jolt of momentary fear which tensed every muscle in her body, but it only lasted a moment, and she calmed when realizing it had only been a brush of Thor's gauntlet. He then squeezed her hand for comfort. "You ready?"

She took a deep breath. "Yes. Yes I thi—"

Pure white electricity exploded over the portal's surface, shrieking and changing the air around her, followed by a terrible grunt from behind. They all turned to Heimdall, his face contorted with pain and his pauldrons trembling.

"Heimdall? Son, what is it?" Ódin exclaimed as he rushed to the dais.

"I-I must move you away from Hel's fortress!" He glanced at Valhalla. "Garmr is fending off ghoul and draugr attacks at the entrance."

"Dammit, of course he is," Thor growled.

"Then move the portal!" Ódin commanded with a wave of an arm and heavily curved brows. "They'll make the trek to Hel if they have to. The brothers know many routes to their sister."

Heimdall nodded and closed his eyes in concentration. Valhalla then realized what was happening to the Æsir. Ódin's father, Borr, had placed a protection spell over Gullhrafn and the Bifrost pedestal. Should a portal ever be opened near danger, pain would shoot through the one controlling the Bifrost. It would only cease once the portal were moved or sealed.

Valhalla had never seen it in action and so felt caught off guard. She kept her eyes on Heimdal, finding such a thing distasteful even as a precaution, and now grieving the fate dealt to her oldest brother. Heimdall shouldn't be forced to endure such a thing, no matter the reason, she thought to herself.

It wasn't long until Heimdall's body stopped shaking and his expression relaxed. He straightened and released a long breath. "Alright, I found a spot to drop you off, but be warned, it is deep within the Ironwood Forest, and Hel's denizens are stirring."

Valhalla's pulse quickened. "Oh no." She whispered softly.

"Tsk! I wish she had better control over her dead." Thor growled, hugging Valhalla close and turning back to the gate.

"Hel has as much control over her realm as the All Father does over Asgard. Not all rulers are as omnipotent as you would like." Jörmungandr said with no discernible expression. Thor only sneered in response. "Anyway, Fenrir and I will go through first. Get a feel for the realm. Valhalla, once you're ready, you and Thor may follow. Aura, do you mind holding the rear?"

"Not at all, head on through," Aura replied, and Jörmungandr nodded.

He shared a momentary look with his brother, then they both leaped into the swirling rainbow portal.

Valhalla's heart thumped in her ears. Her mind raced with memories of the last time she visited the freezing realm. The gaunt faces. Bony hands. Terror-inducing wails. She felt like she was being squeezed from the inside out. Her grip tightened around Thor's bicep. Valhalla could feel him looking at her, but she couldn't bring herself to face him.

"Valla, are you re—"

As her fear spiked, she turned around. "Heimdall?"

"Don't worry, your Highness," Heimdall said in as soothing a tone as he could, "thanks to your status, I'm allowed to pick you up if you find yourself in danger."

Her lips parted, but she hadn't decided just what she wanted to say. She hated bringing pain to those she cared about, inadvertently or not. The electricity had clearly been more than a discomfort, and while he would never have even considered it to be her fault, she couldn't help but feel it was. Valhalla needed— No, wanted to rectify this. "I promise to make this up to you. How can I?"

Heimdall laughed and placed a hand on his hip. "I would tell you not to worry about it, but I know that would only fall on deaf ears. So, that being the case, I hear Nidavellir's Crimson Dragon Ale is quite delicious. I'd like to try it, and I'd like you to try it with me."

"Deal!" She forced a smile. "I'll be sure to bring you the largest barrel they have. That's a promise."

With that, Valhalla had made her peace and found an ounce of courage. She spun back to the portal, took a deep breath, and held fast to Thor's hand. It was now or never. She and Thor leaped into the rainbow portal.

33

Valhalla

Helheim

Icy winds cut into Valhalla's bare face and even bit through her garb. While the garments offered some protection from the cold, this place was unlike any in all the realms. The cold was much more severe, as if traces of magic flowed through the very makeup of the elements. It felt like being struck by a thousand tiny razor blades all at once, never quite letting up and only lessening between gusts.

The winds howled through the forest, the place known as the Ironwood. The pocket of forest where she and her group emerged was dark. It wasn't pitch black of night but rather a dim gray that was cast over the world as though the sun were blotted out by the ever-present cloud cover, which was all the more exacerbated by the canopy of the forest. The trees were thick and grew close to one another, huddled together for what little warmth that might provide.

From her previous visit, she knew the sky to be a deep violet, regardless of time of day, which washed the realm in a bluish lavender hue. The absence of that gentle coloring made her worries only grow. Thunder boomed overhead as if to punctuate her building dread.

A chill drew up her spine with the force of a dagger. The trunks of the trees were so wide that a single felled tree could've supplied the lumber needed to build a structure as large as the Violet Tulip Inn and likely have much left over. As useful as that might sound it wouldn't be such an easy feat. The deep gray bark was covered in sharp thorns. Dark sap spurted forth from small fissures in the bark, sometimes freezing upon breach, leaving long frozen tendrils resembling sickly amber outstretched arms. When the substance didn't freeze outright, the sap clumped around the roots and released a sharp burning odor not too dissimilar from a blacksmith's forge tinged with decay. The trees were a species of pine which only grew here in Helheim, known as Járn pine. Even its leaves were off-putting. They were dark, needle-like things so sharp that in the absence of a weapon, one leaf would make for a decent substitute.

As she stared up into the trees, a flash of light illuminated the leaves, and for the shortest of moments, she spotted a gaunt face staring back at her. She let out a sharp breath and took a step back. Before her foot could settle back to the ground, a sudden blast of cold wind crashed into her, nearly toppling Valhalla to the snow below. Her body violently shivered. The beating of her heart thumped rapidly against her breast. In response to the cold and her rising fears, she tapped into her fire seidr, quickly warming her body. Her eyes darted about, reacting to every snap of a twig or crunch of snow.

"Valla."

She jumped, and before she could place a face to the voice, an ear-piercing wail shattered the quiet of the forest. Valhalla's hands flew to her ears. Something, or someone, then took her in a strong embrace. Somehow, she knew not to fight it. She had just enough sense to realize the arms belonged to one of her companions. Allowing herself to be guided into their chest, the pair knelt low to the ground. The scent of earthy forest and grapes filled her nostrils. Some of the tension left her shoulders as the person's image finally came to her mind. Slowly opening her eyes, she looked up and was, in that moment, thankful for Fenrir's company. He was as a shield over her, his furrowed gaze locked behind her. His hand was firmly guarding her head, which made it impossible for her to turn to see what it was he was looking at.

He then leaned in close, a hair's breadth from her ear, and whispered, "It's a hlakka."

The tension came flooding back to Valhalla's muscles. Hlakkas were ghoulish women who used their terrible screams to instill fear in their victims, immobilizing them and driving their victims into madness so as to devour their life essence without a fight, leaving only a shriveled husk behind as nourishment for the animals of the wild.

Jörmungandr then kneeled slowly beside them, a finger to his lips, and a hand near the ground, palm facing up. His gaze, too, was fixed on a point behind her. Something shiny and black slithered from beneath his sleeve and raced off in the direction both brothers stared.

After a moment, bushes rustled and another piercing cry rumbled through the forest. This time, the cry sounded more distant. A timeless quiet passed before, finally, both Jörmungandr and Fenrir exhaled in relief.

Fenrir then slid his hands to Valhalla's shoulders, gently adding distance between them, and said, "It's safe. We're safe, Valla."

Muffled, hasty footsteps sounded, and Aura slid in beside her, placing a hand on her back. "Valhalla, are you alright? Can you stand?"

"What the fuck was that?" Thor snarled. "I don't remember anything like *that* existing here before!"

"Everyone, please," Jörmungandr said much more gently than Valhalla would've expected given the situation. Everyone, safe for Fenrir, who was busy keeping an ear out for threats, turned to look at him with curiosity. "We must remain calm. This realm and everything within it will play into your fears. Your doubts. Even your regrets." He said this while pulling something round from his pocket and holding a book close to his chest. "Everything will be alright, so long as we don't attack every little thing that moves."

"Little? You call whatever that thing was *little*?"

Jörmungandr ignored Thor's outburst while inspecting the round thing in his palm. Valhalla squinted her eyes to try to get a better look at it, and to her surprise, it seemed to be some sort of compass. He held the object out to the left, then ahead, and back to the left again. With a nod, he returned to Valhalla. "If we travel this way, we should make it to the River Gjöll. From there, we can make our way to Hel's fortress."

"Wait," Thor pointed ahead, head turned and looking deeper into the Ironwood Forest, "why don't we just keep going forward, find Helvegr Path and take the road to the fortress?"

"You're underestimating the forest," Jörmungandr answered. Thor rolled his deep green eyes as Jörmungandr stepped past him, his own eyes still on the compass. Fenrir and Aura helped Valhalla to her feet.

"Oh, come on, I'm here with Mjölnir. Nothing will come near *my* sister." Oh no, Valhalla thought. Here we go.

Aura wiped her hand across her face, and Fenrir sighed. Each of them knew what was coming, and none had any way of stopping it.

Jörmungandr stopped dead in his tracks and turned to look at Thor with eyes narrowing. The stare radiated annoyance. Since Valhalla had known the two, they had never gotten along. It was prophesied that Thor and Jörmungandr were destined to one day have a battle so grand as to be felt across the nine realms, culminating in each of their deaths. She often wondered if their bickering had been caused by the prophecy. If they hadn't been told of their eventual fates, would their relationship have been different?

Thor planted his hands on his hips and leaned toward Jörmungandr with a raised brow. "What, got something to say?"

"Now that you've asked," Jörmungandr forced what looked to be more of a bearing of teeth than a smile, "Fenrir and I know this realm like the back of our hands. We know every creature that lurks beneath the dark freezing sky. Every enchantment these creatures can conjure. And instead of listening to us, you wish to stand there and argue like a child. If I didn't know any better, I'd say your choice of coming wasn't just because you don't trust Hel," Jörmungandr stepped right up to Thor, staring unblinkingly up into the Thunder God's darkening, seething face, "but because you don't trust Fenrir and I. You've NEVER liked us!"

"How could I? You know what's to come between us, between your brother and my father." Thor exclaimed.

"That's enough!" Aura commanded. Her voice was stern and her expression hard as she stepped between them, placing a hand on Jörmungandr's chest and shoving Thor back several paces to his great surprise. "You know *damn* well that's not fair, Thor. Especially after everything they've done for us. No one knows how a prophecy will play out, and I would expect a child of the All Father to act with wisdom, not to seek out his fate before it's meant to come to pass."

Thor looked away, hiding his reaction, and waved her away. "Whatever."

Valhalla fidgeted in the cold, an uncomfortable moment of silence stretching between the group. They had only just arrived and yet were already off on the wrong foot. She cleared her throat. "Well, I see the edge of the forest to the left of us. If the river is a straight shot to Hel's Fortress, and it's devoid of danger, then we should take it. Jörmungandr, could you lead the way?"

The grimace on his face softened as he sighed, then answered, "Yes."

"Perfect." Valhalla clapped her hands together with approval. "Then it's settled. Fenrir, would you be so kind as to take up the rear? Let us know if you sense anything unusual."

Fenrir shrugged. "I could, but with Garmr at the gate, I should probably take the lead. I can calm him . . . well, enough to let us pass."

"Sounds great. I trust you. *Both* of you." Valhalla glanced at Thor. His shoulders hung slumped. Good, he heard the sense in their words and was feeling remorseful, not that he would ever say so out loud, but Valhalla had known him long enough that his silence was all the confirmation she needed. If he still objected to the plan, he would've said as much. She then turned her gaze to Aura and held her hand outstretched. "Please, stay beside me."

Aura chuckled and took her hand. "You don't have to tell me twice, little sister."

Valhalla gave the valkyrie a half smile, then returned her attention to Thor. With her free hand, she placed it atop his shoulder and pulled him to face her. "Thor, I'd like you by my side as well. Please, *promise* me you won't pick a fight with Jörmungandr, Fenrir, OR Hel." He glanced away with lips pursed, clearly weighing if that was even possible. Thor, for all his faults, was keenly aware of the trouble his temper could bring. More than once, it had driven him into otherwise avoidable fights. His needling of Jörmungandr stemmed from his anger at the prophesied battle to come and wasn't an issue he could easily set aside. Still, his fondness for Valhalla had sometimes been just enough to outweigh the Æsir's fundamental instincts.

His contemplation dragged on, and with annoyance, Valhalla rolled her eyes. "Thor, I trust them with my life, just as I do you and Aura. Despite what's happened, or what may eventually come to pass, they have *always* been good to me. Their character alone should be enough to convince you that at this moment, they. Are. Good." She then held her hand out to him. "Promise to behave yourself or go back to Asgard, but know I feel safer with you here."

Thor stared at Valhalla's hand and for the briefest of moments looked as though he might leave, but to her relief, he accepted her terms and clapped his meaty hand into hers. "Good. Oh, and by the way," she smirked, "you're not having any of the Crimson Dragon Ale."

"What!?" His dark green eyes widened with disbelief.

Valhalla shrugged. "Apologize to Jörmungandr and Fenrir, then *maybe* I'll reconsider."

"I—But—AAGH!" Thor slammed his hands against his face, rubbing it with a groan of frustration. Aside from his fighting prowess, Thor was also known for his equally mighty thirst. He preferred special and rare ales, meads, and wines, and Valhalla thought perhaps he enjoyed them a little too much. His hands fell to his sides, and he frowned dejectedly. "Fine." He spared Jörmungandr and Fenrir a quick glance. "Jörmungandr. Fenrir. I'm sorry for being as welcoming as a pair of goat's shit."

Jörmungandr's expression remained stern, but with a shrug, he began making his way toward the river.

"I suppose that'll have to do," Valhalla said. "You can have some of the ale, but only AFTER asking Heimdall for permission."

With that, the Æsir straightened and a triumphant grin wormed its way onto his face. Even after being forced to admit he was wrong, which he never cared to do, it seemed the promise of ale had lifted his spirits. "Sounds good to me. Let's go."

"Honestly, this would've been so much easier if Sif were here. She would've set him straight." Aura chimed in with a wink.

Valhalla and Fenrir shared a chuckle, and they all finally began their trek to the River Gjöll.

The forest was eerily quiet save for the crunch of snow underfoot. As they continued on, Valhalla found herself missing the sounds of birds, foxes, deer, and other creatures which were generally found in such environments. She then wondered if any such creatures might live in such a place. If so, would they be as their kin in Midgard and the other realms, or would they be as the other nightmarish dead found herein? Her mind filled with flashes of what could only be described as horrific possibilities. Oozing and decayed creatures of feather and fur, silent as death and filled with the yearning for a life they could never have again. She hadn't seen anything of the sort on her last foray, but that did mean they weren't here.

Valhalla found herself clinging ever closer to Aura, taking her bicep in one hand and squeezing the Valkyrie's hand with the other. She mused to herself that she must've made for a sore sight, a warrior clinging to another who was a full head shorter than herself. At least there were no judgmental eyes here in their present company.

A sudden realization then dawned upon her. Glancing to the small warrior, she found Aura had forgone her armor, instead only wearing her violet and white travel garb. While the garments were extravagant, they offered little in the way of protection. Compared to Thor's choice of attire, it struck her as strange. Was it optimism that caused her to travel so light?

"Aura?" Valhalla called softly. "Where's your armor?"

"Back in my chamber still," Aura answered, keeping her gaze ahead. "It's very cold here, and I worried my armor would only slow me down. Don't worry," she patted Valhalla's hand and gave her a small smile, "if the time comes, I'll call it here. Besides, if we play it safe as Jörmungandr is, I won't have need of it."

The answer brought some comfort to Valhalla. To have one such as Aura by her side was a much-needed warmth in this bitter place.

Just ahead, the trees seemed to thin, and she could just faintly hear the sounds of rushing waters. Reaching the mouth of the forest, Valhalla looked up and found the sky obscured by thunderous clouds. Lightning shrieked and illuminated various patches of the vast gray expanse. The lands before her were dark, but there were glowing ice spires here and there, jutting from the ground and bathing their surroundings in soft blue light.

In the distance were jagged mountains of rock and snow. As the lightning storm flickered across the snowy vista, what seemed at first to be shadowy outcrops of rock revealed themselves to be figures, both humanoid and otherworldly things encased in ice. They almost looked to be moving in the bursts of illumination, and Valhalla found herself hoping it was only a trick of the light.

The boom of lightning striking rock nearby sent her whirling in a panic. Turning as a shadow fell over her, she looked up and to her right, a jolt of adrenaline screamed through her veins. Her eyes shot wide at the sight of the massive, decay-riddled corpse of a bear. It was as if her imagination had become real and now towered before her. Its matted fur was caked in a slick black substance. Sores surrounded its nose, mouth, and eyes. Her feet moved on their own as she crashed into Aura, the commotion alerting the rest of their group.

Brief moments passed, and yet nothing happened. The creature didn't move. It wasn't until another flash of lightning brightened the beast that she found the answer as to why. It was frozen stiff. She felt a pang of sadness for the creature as she recognized the anguished expression on its lifeless face. It looked to have likely starved, which would've explained its skeletal frame. As tragic a fate as that was for any living thing, Valhalla couldn't help a small sigh of relief. Facing an undead human, elf, or dwarf was bad enough. She couldn't imagine the power an undead bear might wield and was glad it was frozen in place. Still, to know with complete certainty that animals too ended up here, bode ill for their journey, for there were much worse things to be found throughout the realms than bears.

"I think," Jörmungandr stared inquisitively at the corpse, "wherever this cloud coverage blots out the sky, it freezes the roaming denizens of the realm in place."

"Is there not always cloud coverage here, though?" Valhalla asked. "I remember seeing a glimpse of the deep violet sky the last time I was here, but it was still terribly cloudy."

"You're not mistaken," Fenrir interjected. "There's always cloud coverage, but some days you can see glimpses of sky through the haze as you described. On those days, it's safe for the denizens to walk freely outside their havens without fear of being frozen."

"Then is it safe for us to be out and about right now?" Valhalla looked around with curved brows, beginning to worry that her fire seidr might not be enough to keep them from befalling a similar fate to the bear.

"The heavy blizzard usually comes in the mornings. It's like the strongest hurricane you've ever experienced mixed with a sandstorm so dense it could swallow a castle in an afternoon. If we were caught in it, well, best to avoid that. Besides, the storm has already passed for today. What you see overhead is only the remnants of what came before." Jörmungandr explained without pulling his eyes from his compass. "Anyway, we're at the river, so where——"

"Already lost, little snake?" Thor gibed, palpable annoyance in his tone. Valhalla shot him a glare, stunned that he was already back at this?

Jörmungandr's jaw muscles tensed and turned just enough so that the big Æsir could see his device. It was housed in a mahogany frame, and the face was quite like any other compass Valhalla had ever seen, except for the fact that it only had one arrow pointing north. "It's my very own vísa. I made it myself, and yes, I made sure it *worked* before we left. I tell it what I want and it shows me where to go. So no, I'm not lost and——I don't even know why I'm bothering. It's not like you care." Jörmungandr focused back toward the dark river, staring at his vísa in silence.

Fenrir walked past them and as he did, shoved Thor with his shoulder, which absolutely wasn't going to make things any better. As expected, the Thunder God began seething for a fight. Lightning danced across his fingers, and his bulk grew in size. Valhalla quickly grabbed his wrist. It was like trying to wrap fingers around a great oak. He looked at her with a brief snarl before recognition and surprise set in. Were she anyone else, that might've been the spark to ignite the powder keg that was his fury, but she wasn't just anyone to him. She steeled her gaze and squeezed his wrist as tightly as she could. "You promised, Thor."

She wondered if he could see through the false mask of strength she wore on her face, if he could see beneath it to the dread forming in the pit of her stomach. If Thor's senses gave way to the berserker within, it was unlikely that the combined might of Aura, Fenrir, Jörmungandr, and herself could stop him. Jörmungandr would be forced to transform into his serpentine self, and were he to do that, not only would it be incredibly unlikely for anyone in the surrounding area to survive their battle, but the commotion could draw the attention of hordes of undead to their presence. Fortunately, Thor still had control of his senses, and his body relaxed into a slouch. The electricity in the air around him dissipated as he pursed his lips in a pout and mumbled an apology.

Just as Valhalla was about to scold him, she caught notice of Fenrir sniffing the air. "The scent of the dead covers everything. There's no way I can locate the Ferryman."

"Ferryman? You actually intend for us to traverse *that* river?" Thor pointed at the murky, turbulent waters speeding by. The rapids crashed against rocky banks.

"The Ferryman can calm the River Gjöll with the runes carved onto their boat," Jörmungandr answered. "With them, the river would be perfectly safe."

"Then we must be missing something," Aura said as she made her way a short distance to the group's left, looking down the river's west end. "What does it look like?"

"The boat's appearance is no different than any simple row boat, but is much larger so as to accommodate as many passengers as might be needed. A hooded figure would be standing at the bow. You really can't miss them."

Valhalla went to look in the opposite direction. She climbed up a small boulder, hoping height might give her an advantage. In the far distance, she spotted what looked like a large wall of stone and ice, stretching far in the direction of the mountains on her left. To the right, the forest obscured her view.

As she scanned the river through the darkness, a flash of lightning illuminated a small dock which was tucked into one of the river's more treacherous turns that had been impossible to spot from the ground. At the far side of the pier, just as Jörmungandr had described, was a figure standing on a longboat. Valhalla pointed and called out, "Is that the Ferryman?"

Her companions rushed to join her, Jörmungandr hopping up to her side atop the boulder and the other three circling around its mass lodged in the snow. "It is!" Grinned Jörmungandr. "Come on." He then hopped down the boulder and reached up, taking her by the waist, and helped Valhalla down. Once on the ground, Jörmungandr clapped his hand in hers and cautiously guided her to the dock.

As they all reached the dock and carefully approached the Ferryman, Thor pushed his way to the front of their group. He looked the Ferryman up and down, but the figure remained completely still.

The Ferryman was hooded in a plain set of black robes that stretched well past their feet and bundled about the longboat's floor. They held a long, thin oar cradled in their bony, gray hands, which vanished into the inky waters below. Sure enough, the waters were calm and gently lapped against the runes, which glowed violet around the boat's rim.

Leaning close to the Ferryman, Thor tilted his head, looking confused. He then turned back and shrugged, unsure of how to proceed.

"You have to get into the boat," Jörmungandr explained. "Only then will the Ferryman awaken."

Thor stepped into the longboat, causing it to bob up and down, and even though it wasn't tied to the small dock, the boat remained in place. "Alright then. Come, Valla." He reached out, but before she accepted his hand, she spared another look into the dark waters.

It was as black as ink and the surface still as the dead, but there was a strange violet hue to it. Small bubbles then began agitating the river. They came slowly at first, one, then another, then several. More and more, they came. The bubbles grew in size until finally one as large as a pumpkin swelled and burst.

Valhalla sucked in a breath, bumping into someone behind her, and their hands clapped onto her shoulders. She stared at the surface, and yet, nothing. The bubbles came as if from a creature beneath the water, but it must've been her imagination. It could've just as easily been underground gases simply escaping through the soil.

"Valhalla," She jumped at the sound of Thor's voice. His hand was still outstretched and his gaze determined, steadfast, and singularly focused on her. "I promise you will not come to harm while I—*we* are with you. Just take my hand. Everything will be alright."

Staring at his hand and fighting to keep what little composure she had, Valhalla took a hesitant step forward. The person behind her stepped to her side and squeezed her shoulder. Turning her head to them, she found it had been Fenrir, a pleasant smile resting on his face.

With a deep breath, she accepted Thor's hand, and he pulled her aboard the longboat with one tug of his arm. She crashed into his broad chest, and the scent of rain and leather wafted over her. With his strong hand pressed against her back as he guided her to a bench where she sat, blinking at him, speechless.

Thor, seemingly amused, gave her a wink. "See, that wasn't so hard."

Valhalla pursed her lips, but couldn't quite be annoyed with him at that moment. His causality made her cheeks burn, but she was simply too thankful to him and all her companions for accompanying her. There was simply no way she could do this without them. Aura was next to step into the longboat, gently pushing Thor out of her way as she took the seat on Valhalla's left. Jörmungandr then approached, and to Valhalla's great surprise, Thor proffered a hand to help him into the boat. She hadn't been the only one stunned by the big Æsir's offer. Everyone was staring at him.

Thor sighed. "I promised that I would try. So . . ." He grunted, "Just take my hand before I change my mind."

Jörmungandr feigned indifference as he slid his book into his satchel, but Valhalla spotted the smile tugging at his lips. After stepping into the longboat, he took the seat at her right, and Fenrir plopped himself on a bench behind her.

"Alright," Thor started as he turned to the hooded Ferryman, "now what? Do I talk to it or something?"

"Try tapping the Ferryman's shoulder. There's no smell, so I don't think they're awake yet." Jörmungandr answered. This caused Valhalla to tilt her head, but before she could voice her question, Thor beat her to it.

"Smell?" He asked and eyed Jörmungandr wearily.

"Oh, don't worry, you'll see," Fenrir answered with a shudder.

Thor cautiously turned back to the Ferryman, and just as he was about to tap the figure's shoulder, Thor froze and let out an awful sound of disgust. He immediately tucked his nose into the crook of his elbow and stepped back.

Just as the Ferryman began to turn, the scent assaulted Valhalla's nostrils. Her body went taut. The smell of ancient decay filled the air. Once, years before, upon returning to Alf, she found the place overcome by a foulness so odious that the residents considered relocating the entire town. No one knew where the smell had come from. It had come on faint at first, only noticed here and there, carried on the wind, but none had been able to discern its origin. Valhalla's search eventually led to an abandoned shop that had collapsed in an earthquake several weeks prior to the onset of the odor, and there, beneath the rubble, she found a collapsed wall in the cellar, which gave way to a passage where the scent thickened the air. The walls were cramped and seemed to have been naturally formed by the shifting of the earth. At the end of the passage, she found the source of the smell. It came from a long-forgotten mass grave where it seemed hundreds had been sealed inside. The quake had unsealed the tomb, and the stench had finally been freed. This new aroma dropped that experience down to the second-worst thing she had ever smelled.

The Ferryman's black robes twisted around its legs as it came to face them. A wide V cut in the fabric revealed his masculine chest and skin, dry and gray as stone. His breathing came in hoarse rasps. Raising his head, the Ferryman's face came into the light, and the figure became all the more unsettling. His lips and eyes had been sewn completely shut.

I am Kaledvrishoth, a Ferryman of the River Gjöll. His masculine voice pierced Valhalla's mind like shards of glass scraping stone. Her head shrank into her shoulders, and her hands clutched fistfuls of her skirt. *To ferry you to her Majesty's fortress, a payment must be made.*

Thor cleared his throat, and though the urge to gag still assaulted his voice, he managed to choke out a few words. "Payment? What kind of—"

"I have it!" Aura spoke up, holding a handkerchief over her nose as she reached inside her skirt pocket. "Mother gave it to me before we left, just in case." She pulled out a black leather pouch and withdrew her handkerchief from her face. Both her hands rummaged through the pouch, and soon Aura pulled free a handful of pure white bones.

"Bones?" Valhalla exclaimed with teary eyes.

Aura returned the pouch to her pocket and stood up, bringing her handkerchief back to her nose. "Eight bones should be sufficient for five passengers if I'm not mistaken." She said as she dropped the bones into Kaledvrishoth's hand.

His gangly fingers curled in around them. *Eight is more than enough.* Kaledvrishoth spun to face back toward the river, and to everyone's relief, the scent lessened. The Ferryman straightened his body and positioned his long oar.

"Wait," Thor looked at Aura, a raised brow and the beginning of a sneer on his lip, "where did—"

Aura rolled her amethyst monolid eyes and took her seat once more. "They're animal bones, Thor. You know, the same ones used by Valas in fortune telling?"

Jörmungandr planted his chin on his palm and rested an elbow on the longboat's edge. "Hel uses them to populate the realm with raised animals. Says it brings some normalcy to this frozen place."

Thor's expression seemed a mixture of annoyance and skepticism. "Normalcy? The souls that find themselves here have done terrible, unspeakable things. This place is anything but normal?"

"Souls who regret what they did in life. Most seek only forgiveness." Jörmungandr said with a glance in Thor's direction. "You'll see once we reach my sister's fortress."

The big Æsir shrugged. "Whatever you say." He added as he sat himself on the bench opposite Valhalla. Not long after, the longboat began to move, gently gliding through the waters toward their goal.

Valhalla

Hel's Guardian

Though surrounded by her friends, Valhalla couldn't quite get a hold of her nerves. The constant unease left a quivering discomfort in her gut. The ever-present threat of attack did nothing to lessen the hostility of the realm.

Flashes of lightning painted the land in bursts of shadow and illumination. Thunder rumbled with a sound not dissimilar to an army on the move. The Ironwood Forest was now a distant thought, a speck on the horizon. Their vessel flowed through jagged ravines between ice spires of spiral configurations, which jutted from rock and water alike. Every time she allowed herself a moment of rest, a frozen corpse trapped in the ice would materialize almost as if the wastelands were singularly focused on feeding her fears.

The squeal of something scratching at the bow jolted Valhalla to attention.

She scanned what she could of the waters, yet only the inky depths lapping against the wood. The sound came again, this time from the opposite side of the longboat. It came a third time, dragging on long and pronounced. Each of her companions was as alert as she, their gazes peering over the sides but finding no more than snow, rock, water, and ice.

Valhalla grabbed Aura's hand. "What was that?"

Aura shook her head as she straightened in her seat. "Pay it no mind, Valla. It was likely only debris beneath the surface. Besides, whatever it was, it's pa—"

A dark figure exploded out of the river, latching onto the edge of the longboat and dragging the side toward the darkness below. The sudden shift threw everything into chaos. A flash of white light appeared beside Valhalla. Aura was now sheathed in her protective white and gold armor, and a round buckler covered her left arm. She looked prepared to attack, but a blur crashed into her and sent the valkyrie falling back with a grunt.

"Aura—" Valhalla's cry was cut short. Something wrapped around her neck in a hold stronger than iron. Its touch burned with cold, assured death. All she could manage was a choked shriek as it pulled her forward. In moments, she was face to face with a shriveled corpse. Black liquid oozed from each of its orifices, and its skeletal features stretched into a hungry grin. Her bowels turned to liquid.

"It's your fault he was on you." It gurgled as its grip tightened. *"You just lied there. You could've fought him off, but you didn't!"* Valhalla whimpered and gagged. Her lungs screamed for air. *"You're no victim, just a—"*

Valhalla then found herself falling, the blackness around her vision receding. She hit the floor, just barely managing to land on her feet, and as she looked toward the creature, she found Jörmungandr standing between them, his black daggers buried deep in the corpse's chest. He was inches from the creature's face, blue-green eyes seething with rage, but his expression otherwise still.

"Return to the river where you belong." His words were quiet and restrained.

Fenrir then stepped beside his brother, taking the corpse by the scruff of its neck and hurling it far behind them, where it landed with a splash. "And stay there!"

Valhalla labored to regain her breath, but air only seemed to come in shallow bursts. As she brought her fingers to where the thing had wrapped around her neck, a bloom of searing pain spread down to her collarbone and up to her jaw. Her vision blurred as she struggled to keep conscious, and she was faintly aware of something crawling beneath her skin. It was as if worms of fire were wiggling and burrowing into her flesh.

"Aura, are you alright?" Thor's voice echoed as if through a void.

"I'm fine," Aura responded with a huff of breath, "but damn that thing punched harder than I . . ."

Everything went quiet for some unknown reason. Valhalla's thoughts were growing fuzzy. Perhaps the corpse had damaged something inside her neck? That would explain the trouble breathing. The notion should've been worrying, yet it came and went as a leaf carried on a breeze. The world tilted. Her eyelids were impossibly heavy. Sleep. Perhaps some sleep would do her some good. The idea spread through her limbs and enveloped her in warmth.

"Wait, is my armor—" A voice gasped.

"It's decaying!" Another answered.

Hands seemed to rummage about Valhalla's body. Her shoulders and face. Her arms and hands. The world shifted again. Someone was holding her in their arms, and whoever it was had an earthy scent about them, which she found not unpleasant. The faces of her friends came in and out of focus almost as if they were apparitions, there one moment and evaporated the next. A wave of sensation blossomed on the right side of her neck and spread like a weed throughout her being, igniting her every nerve with such overwhelming force that there simply wasn't a word in all of the realms sufficient enough to describe it. Had she made so much as a whimper or her body trembled, she didn't know. Were a comparison to be made, running bare through a thousand miles of bramble bushes while shrouded in dragon's fire would've been as a warm bath after a hard day's toil.

"Shit! Shit shit shit! It's rot! Hel warned me of such a thing, but I didn't know it could act so fast." The panicked voice belonged to Jörmungandr.

Something again touched her neck, but this time, no pain assaulted her body. The thing was wet, yet surprisingly warm. It wrapped around her neck.

"Valhalla. I-It's alright. It's going to be alright. We're going to fix this!"

"How are we supposed to fix THAT!" Thor roared, and the world shifted again. "If you knew something like this could happen, then why didn't you—"

"Take your hands off him NOW!"

Valhalla's eyes parted, something in Aura's fury giving her strength. It was Fenrir who was cradling her, and his expression was pointed forward in worry. Following his gaze, she found that Thor had Jörmungandr's collar clutched in hand and Aura had taken the Thunder God's wrist in hers. The anger on Thor and Aura's faces didn't bode well for what was to come next.

"You have light seidr, why don't YOU do something to help her!" Thor growled.

"This is death seidr you dumb ass!" Aura snapped. "My light can't repel death no matter how hard I try."

"Then what good are—"

"STOP IT!" Valhalla shrieked. The pain came in waves. Even swallowing hurt. Thor jolted and turned to look at her. Aura glanced away. The three remained in each other's hold, but some of the fight seemed to drain away. "I-I don't know what's going on," her voice came hoarsely, "or what's gotten into you, but we are in this *together*. If you can't trust one another, then you shouldn't be here."

Fenrir hugged her closer, and she got the sense that he approved. It was a small comfort, but at that moment, she was glad to have it.

"Hel," Jörmungandr paused, sucking in a breath. "Hel has the power to remove the rot. So long as we keep it covered, the ointment will stay its spread and she. Will. Be. Fine."

Valhalla lightly touched the fabric covering her neck and felt something squishy underneath. "What exactly *is* wrong with my neck?"

In truth, she didn't really want to know. Fear often made people act foolishly, and in this case urged her to remain naive, but doing so wouldn't help solve her predicament. To understand the situation would better prepare her on how to solve it.

Jörmungandr pried Thor's hand off, freeing himself from the Thunder God's grip, and climbed over a bench to kneel down beside her, and took her hand in his. "That corpse, a River Ghoul, unfortunately touched your skin with its bare hands. Because of that, it infected you with decay that will spread and kill you if we don't get to my sister in time."

"Oh. Is that all?" Valhalla sighed and slumped into Fenrir's arms. A series of coughs made the pain swell and the cold made her tremble. She could feel her grip on her fire seidr weakening. A small gust of wind stung like hail. "I-It's too cold. Making my neck hurt." She managed to say through chattering teeth.

"Here," Aura turned and held out a hand. With a flash of sparkling light, she summoned a thick white scarf and handed it to Jörmungandr, "will this do?"

"I hope so." Jörmungandr answered, accepting the garment and gently looped it around Valhalla's neck as Fenrir helped her up into a sitting position.

"Are you sure?" Thor asked, his voice soft but deadly serious. His dark green eyes were shaky and fixed on the wound about Valhalla's neck. "Are you sure that Hel can help her?"

Jörmungandr nodded. "This realm was made for her after all."

"Hel can undo any curse the dead can inflict," Fenrir added.

"Alright then." With that, Thor slumped down on the bench where he sat before the attack, interlacing his fingers and rubbing a thumb across his knuckles. "To Hel's Fortress then."

"Promise, again, to behave yourself with Jörmungandr and Fenrir?" Aura planted a fist to her hip, giving Thor a stern glare. He nodded but didn't speak, a guilt-ridden shadow passing across his features. Seemingly finding his response to be adequate, Aura then sat herself beside Valhalla and gave her a small smile. "We'll be at Hel's Fortress soon, Valla. Just hold on a little while longer." The valkyrie then glanced at the brothers. "Can you two watch over her?"

"Yes," Jörmungandr replied, his hand tightening around Valhalla's as he did.

Fenrir repositioned himself and pulled Valhalla to lie against his chest. "Just rest, Valla. As she said, we're almost there." He adjusted her cloak to be sure it covered her as much as possible.

The freezing winds were ceaseless as they continued down the River Gjöll. Each of her companions remained quiet, still, and vigilantly alert for any signs of another attack. The boat drifted and swayed in the current. Lightning flashed across the sky and thunder boomed, but Valhalla no longer found it disconcerting. The rumbles of the sky and soft hum of the wind no longer seemed so threatening. She wasn't sure if it was because she was tired, an effect of the curse lulling her into complacency as it ravaged her flesh, or some unknown spell woven into the scarf given to her, but she finally felt at ease for the first time since entering the realm of the dead.

She stared out into the frozen wastelands as the boat drifted down the river. She couldn't see much from within the shallow ravine, and of what she could make out, little variety was to be found. Snow. Ice. Rock. More snow. She felt herself gazing over, and her sight drifted, not focusing on anything in particular until eventually the river split. The longboat continued on its course, but in the gap as they passed it by, she spotted a stone bridge which stretched across the open span, upward to meet large stone walls on the other side. She saw it only briefly before the branching path vanished behind the rising edge of the ravine.

Her eyelids became terribly heavy as they traveled on. The rhythmic thumping of Fenrir's heart beat combined with the steady rise and fall of his every breath, becoming the totality of her focus. Slowly, she rose and then fell. Two beats up. Three beats down. Sleep called to her, and as the passage of time turned to sand slipping between her fingers, she found little reason to resist. Hel's Fortress could've been just around the next bend, or several hours still downriver. How long had it even been since the attack? Her eyes closed of their own accord.

"Valhalla!" Jörmungandr exclaimed with a strong tug of her arm, forcing her upright and startling her to wakefulness. "You have to stay awake. If you fall asleep, there will be no waking you up. The curse will take hold and . . . Please keep your eyes open, alright?"

She attempted a swallow and winced at the pain in her throat. After a few deep breaths, she gave him a nod and repositioned herself to sit atop folded legs. Fenrir leaned forward and softly rubbed her back, his gaze full of worry.

"Good," Jörmungandr continued, "because we're here."

A massive shadow enveloped the boat. Looking up, the drowsiness faded away, and Valhalla's eyes shot wide. Hel's Fortress loomed above, as intimidating as it was oppressive. The fortress stretched high into the sky and nearly scraped the thundering clouds above. Its walls were a combination of black stone and spiraling ice spires that spread as wide as the fortress was tall. Frost, ice, and snow coated every surface. New elements which had not been part of the structure on her last visit were peppered about and did nothing to make the place more welcoming. Valhalla's stomach twisted into knots as she surveyed countless bodies of every mortal being found within the nine realms, which were strung about like some sort of twisted ornamentation.

Humans, elves, dwarves, fae, Vanir, and Jotunns were suspended by iron chains bound about their wrists. Fresh and stale, frozen blood alike was strewn in a masterwork of horror. The ichor dripped from various wounds across each of the figures, spilling over flesh, stone, and ice, leaving a spectrum of hues across everything in sight. It looked as though a painter, long since lost in the throes of madness, had toiled in crafting a battlefield, meticulously using each and every color of Asgard's rainbow bridge in their work. The bodies were stripped as a newborn babe. Muscle, bone, sinew, intestine, organs. It was all on full display. Bile rose in her throat. The scene had taken her so off guard that she hadn't even realized when the longboat had stopped.

"Valhalla?"

Valhalla jumped and turned to the valkyrie. Aura was standing and staring at her with confusion.

"Is everything alright? We've arrived."

"Y-You don't see that?" Valhalla's voice came shrilly as she pointed to the bloody mess before them.

"See what?" Aura asked as she and the others scanned the castle. While fields of gore from battle's aftermath were not unfamiliar to her companions, still, if they too could see what Valhalla was seeing, surely they would've responded. Yet each of them looked on unperturbed.

Valhalla vigorously rubbed at her eyes, and upon opening them in the hopes it had only been a terrible daydream, the corpses remained. How could they not see it? There was much about the realm she didn't know. Perhaps the scene was some sort of response triggered by her deep-seated fears and anxiety. Or maybe it was a consequence of the curse on her neck? If it were the latter, reaching Hel and removing the curse would be an even greater relief. If not, well, she would avoid returning at all costs.

"Come on, Valla," Aura called, reaching out a hand.

As the Valkyrie helped her stand, Valhalla's legs quivered beneath her weight. Her body was heavier than it should've been, and simply remaining on her feet felt like a monumental task. Before the affliction, she would've felt less fatigued from a full day's training in sword or seidr. Cold bit at her limbs and chest. Aura's face flushed from worry to panic. Her monolid eyes went wide, unsteadily shifting between Valhalla's.

"Give her here."

The voice was Thor's. He now stood just outside the boat by what looked to be the bottom of a stairway leading up to a courtyard. Valhalla's sight blurred in and out of focus, the big Æsir's red hair now looking like actual fire in barely restrained warbraids. The brothers had also taken their leave of the longboat, Fenrir now standing at the lead at the top of the steps with Jörmungandr beside him.

With Aura's help, Valhalla inched over to the Thunder God, the world tilting with every step. Thor wrapped his fingers around her hand and gently pulled her forward. He then wrapped his muscular arms around her waist and lifted her out of the boat, but her foot hooked the boat's edge, which sent her tumbling into him. The scent of rain washed over her as she landed in his embrace.

With eyes closed, she felt his hand touch the back of her head. "Valhalla, how are you feeling?"

"Like I want to throw up." Valhalla blurted out. The pain in her neck spiked, but as it fell away, she sighed and added, "Let's just go."

Thor slid her to his side, an arm around her back and a hand holding her bicep. At his lead, the two carefully climbed the stairs. Each step gained multiplied the invisible force pushing her downward. Her muscles screamed for her to stop. It wasn't the burning fatigue of hard strain that usually accompanied heavy labor, but a deep numbing sensation, like a voice's last cry before being forever silenced. She wasn't sure how much longer she could keep going, but she knew she had to try.

As she and Thor neared the top, she realized Fenrir and Jörmungandr hadn't stopped simply to wait for them. They didn't even acknowledge her or Thor. Their gaze was locked ahead, Fenrir with hands clenched at his sides and Jörmungandr unreadable from behind. Valhalla peaked between the brothers and found what had them so distressed. The scene before them was carnage, pure and simple.

Black wolves with white skeletal armor battled against the undead denizens of the realm. Simple ghouls, shrieking hlakkas, and even battle-hardened draugrs were amongst the fray. It took Valhalla several long moments before she vaguely recalled Heimdall's words. Garmr had been fighting just outside the fortress. It was why they had entered Helheim through the forest, and now, it seemed that conflict had spilled inside the gates.

The courtyard hummed with the sound of battle. Whimpers, growls, and the howling of undead and wolf alike reverberated off the circular walls, but the clamor came to Valhalla's ears as if her head were under water. Her vision fared little better. Of what she could make out, she found blood peppered about, staining stone and snow in black. Blurry streaks of fur flew and crashed into the horde of dead, digging fang and claw through rotted flesh. Ghouls were simply outmatched in this fight and only stood a chance due to their numbers. Draugr, though, held their own. Their blades shredded tissue and cleaved through bone. The hlakkas' screams didn't affect the wolves as they did other living beings, yet it bought them a few moments by stunning the wolves. More than enough time for them to strike, boring their clawed fingers through the softened tissue where their limbs met chest and hind.

Valhalla's stomach squirmed like a mass of angry snakes. "What is even going on here?"

"It's a fucking mutiny, that's what it is," Fenrir whispered, his words taking on a deadly edge. "If any of these dead manage to breach the castle itself, they'll attack the Helheim tree. Thor—"

The Æsir's muscles tensed and swelled as he slipped away from Valhalla, Mjölnir already in hand. Sparks of blue electricity swirled and lashed outward with every step he took. Valhalla's hair went weightless, and her skin tingled with gooseflesh. The air turned sharp and bitter. A sour, metallic taste filled her mouth. A rattling in her lungs made breathing more difficult. Her older brother's might continued to grow and radiated outward, catching the attention of friend and foe alike.

Aura rushed up to take Thor's place at Valhalla's side, keeping her on her feet. The Valkyrie's shield was gone, and her hand wrapped around Valhalla's torso. The support was most welcome. Even through the haze assaulting her senses, she was keenly aware of her declining state. Meeting Aura's gaze, the warrior gave her a nod, and the two watched as Thor made his way past the brothers.

Fenrir's face instantly washed with concern. "Wait, not the wo—"

In an instant, Thor thrust Mjölnir high into the air, summoning lightning from his very being and sending it skyward like a beacon slicing through the clouds. Lightning shrieked and flashed as though the heavens had been lit ablaze, and before the count of three, an instant of violence turned everything white. Countless deafening bangs left an intense ringing in Valhalla's ears. Even with her eyes closed, she saw dizzying stars.

Screams were cut short with every bolt. As the banging ceased and color returned to the world, Valhalla opened her eyes. Charred remains were all that was left of the dead. Steam rose from cracks where they had stood.

The wolves, to her great surprise, were completely fine. Fenrir let out a deep sigh of relief and looked to Thor in stunned silence. He simply shrugged and twirled Mjölnir at his side. "What? Give me some credit, I'm not *that* bloodthirsty."

Fenrir raised a brow but didn't argue. He, too, had expected the worst. The wolves were dazed and looked about in confusion before their eerie violet eyes finally found her group. Their mouths pulled back in snarls, black stained fangs promising violence.

They moved quickly, dashing through the courtyard and closing in on their new targets. Valhalla nearly lost her footing, but Aura managed to keep her steady, lowering her to a knee and taking a defensive position between her and the charging beasts. Thor readied another current of electricity, and the momentary triumph was almost replaced with sorrow. Luckily, they had Fenrir.

"STǪDVA!"[1] He raised a hand and commanded in the Celnor language. His tone of voice was laced with strength and assuredness.

The wolves had closed the gap incredibly fast, but stopped their charge just a few sword lengths away in a half circle of threat. They all stood ready to pounce but didn't move. Were it not for the rumbling of their growls, they could've been mistaken for statues.

Just then, a deep guttural sound, something between a snarl and a chuckle, drowned out everything in the courtyard. Valhalla's entire body shook. She glanced to her left and spotted an entrance she hadn't noticed before. The stones were shaped into a tall arch, and inside, all light ceased to exist. Her eyes were drawn there by a presence, and as she stared into the blackness, the sound came again.

Two brilliant violet spheres, each with a dot of black at their centers, blinked open, each the size of a human head. The eyes stared back into Valhalla's for several heartbeats before raising high toward the peak of the arch. A creature cloaked in shadow then emerged, claws scraping and paws causing small tremors with each step. It stopped just outside the opening, not once taking its eyes away from her. An electric shudder ran up Valhalla's spine. There stood Hel's

---

1   Stǫdva is Celnor(Norse) for Stop/Halt.

guardian in all his terrifying glory. Garmr, the great wolf of Helheim, had made himself known.

To say he was large for a wolf would be an understatement, like comparing Mjölnir to a mason's hammer. His size was so great, Valhalla imagined that had he seen them as a threat, it wouldn't have taken him more than two bites to swallow her entirely. As with his offspring, he wore white skeletal armor, but his wasn't fused to his body. Garmr's black fur shone in the faint glow of the ice spires of the courtyard. His mane bristled and lips curled, showing off his broadsword-length fangs.

As Valhalla slowly stood, Garmr chuckled once more. *Oh my, the human actually came.* His words flowed into their mind, his voice a cacophony of tones.

Aura held her arm raised in defense. Her amethyst monolid eyes glared at the great wolf. "And why wouldn't she?"

Garmr scoffed, causing his offspring to snap their jaws. *Well, humans are weak little cowards after all. They only bring misery.* He said with a nudge of his snout toward the charred remains of the dead, most of which had once been human.

Thor's grip tightened around Mjölnir's hilt, lightning dancing across its surface. "Not. Her." He responded, a warning in his tone of voice. As it seemed he was readying for a fight, Valhalla felt a surge of adrenaline and with the strength it brought, pushed herself to the front of her group.

Fenrir quickly grabbed her wrist before she could get more than a step past and shook his head. Leaning close, he whispered, "Stay close. Just because he hasn't attacked doesn't mean we're safe."

She knew better than to argue and nodded in understanding. Returning to Garmr, she attempted another painful swallow, her mouth dry and breath shallow. "Queen Hel—" Valhalla winced. "H-Has called for me. Is s-she here?" The world tilted, but she kept herself upright, sensing now wasn't the time to appear weak.

Garmr's lips relaxed, and he turned his head upward in the direction of Hel's Fortress. His pointed ears twitched and flicked, listening to something she couldn't hear.

When he turned back to her, a hungry grin spread across his face. *Her Majesty waits for you in the throne room. Take the lift, but you'd best hurry, the dead know you're here.* Garmr let out a laugh laced with menace but stepped aside, allowing them entry through the ominous archway behind him.

The great wolf's offspring parted but watched hungrily as she and her companions passed. Fenrir wrapped a hand around Valhalla's arm, holding her close.

Valhalla leaned into him, thankful for the support, and whispered, "You made a really scary wolf, Fenrir."

His cheeks glowed bright red. Garmr had, after all, been his creation. With Jörmungandr's instruction, Fenrir studied and used conjuring seidr to create the guardian in an attempt to prove his loyalty to Asgard. And his fear of Garmr was a testament then, that just because something or someone came to be by your own hands, doesn't mean that act alone will afford you its undying devotion. "I know, but Garmr is what you get when my sister's cauldron serves as a womb."

"Well, at least he's a good protector."

He sighed. "That much I can agree with."

Nearing the entrance, Valhalla wasn't sure if it was the darkness of the path ahead or fatigue, but shape and form lost their meaning. She began to sway backwards and heard Fenrir curse as he caught her. He wrapped his arm around her back and hugged her close, his strength taking away some of the burden from her shaky legs. Each breath came with a worrying wheeze, but they continued on until they emerged into the second massive courtyard.

She sensed an army of dark figures on the periphery of her vision, but couldn't make any distinction between them. Each was a blurry silhouette, a nondescript shape in a sea of shapes.

"What are these? Statues?" She heard Thor ask.

"Don't touch them!" Aura responded swiftly, some urgency in her tone. "These are the souls who've proven their worth to Hel. Once she has enough of them gathered here, Hel calls upon my mother to collect them so they may be shepherded to Valhalla."

"Y-You can . . . find wo—" Valhalla's knees had had enough. They buckled, and she fell. The world was as black as pitch, and she didn't know if it was her vision that had failed or if it were her eyelids no longer responding as she strained to lift them open. She felt cold. Numb. That's when she stopped breathing.

35

Valhalla

TRANSFERENCE OF POWER

A KEEN AWARENESS CAME OVER Valhalla. She was dying, but that knowledge wasn't as frightening anymore. Why was that? It wasn't like she wanted to die, but she had done everything she could, pushed herself as far as she could go. Besides, she knew what came after. Someone squeezed her tight, probably Fenrir. It smelled like him. Weightlessness followed as she lay against something hard.

"Shit! Jörmungandr, she's—"

There was panic in Fenrir's voice. Valhalla felt a pang of sadness and wanted to comfort him, to tell him it was alright, but her body was done moving. This wasn't his fault. It was no one's fault. It just happened. Often, death came from happenstance.

Footsteps shuffled all around her. Warm palms pressed against her cheeks and lifted her chin. "Valhalla." It was Jörmungandr now. "Valhalla, can you hear me? Come on!"

"What are you doing?" Thor exclaimed. "Let's get her to your sister!"

"She needs to be conscious or it won't . . ." Jörmungandr didn't finish the thought but she expected she knew. She'd be dead. That wasn't far off now. No one spoke for several long moments, that which was left unsaid somehow more powerful than had it been spoken aloud.

"Thor . . . you have to . . ."

Silence again. Chirping then sounded. So much chirping. Like thousands upon thousands of birds had descended to where she lay, all screeching in bloody horror. For a moment, she thought it a dream. There was a soft tap against her chest. The sensation that followed was another first for her since this expedition began. Where the ghouls touch brought untold anguish, this was pure, untamed exhilaration. Power so great it was as likely to reshape the world as it was to destroy it. Cold ceased to trouble her. Every inch of her body tingled. Valhalla awoke with a gasp, vigor coursing through her veins, but it was too much. It was as if someone had taken the raw, destructive force of a dragon and channeled it into a mouse, or so the folktale went. For a few moments, that mouse was said to be the most powerful creature in all creation, and then it exploded.

She curled in on herself up to a sitting position with a moan, then a shriek. Her bones rattled, and the faint scent of undercooked meat stuck in her nostrils. "Wh-What did you—"

"I transferred some energy into you." Thor hastily answered, his eyes wide and clear surprise on his face. "To revitalize you. Lightning is," he scratched the back of his head and frowned apologetically. "A gamble. It sometimes works on other Æsir, but I've never tried to revive a mortal before."

"What's important is that it worked, and what Thor gave you should be enough to get you to Hel," Jörmungandr added. He took Valhalla's wrists and lifted her to her feet. "Come on, the faster we get you to my sister, the sooner she can heal you."

Just as he was about to pull Valhalla after him, Aura grabbed his coat and stopped him in his place. "Jörmungandr, be still for a moment. Please."

Aura gestured to Valhalla, forcing him to look at her. Valhalla's muscles spasmed, and she rubbed her biceps, fiercely trying to remove the thousands of invisible ants rampaging under her skin. "I-I . . . Maybe we don't do that ever again?" She growled, which caused her friends to chuckle.

Jörmungandr, on the other hand, sighed. "I understand and I'm sorry, but Thor's the only one of us with transferable seidr."

She had heard of the concept before. If someone was losing energy, be it seidr or their own life force, very few elements could be channeled in such a way to sustain them. Lightning was one such element. Fire was another, but Valhalla had no idea how to do it. It took a lot of energy, and too much could mean death for the invoker.

"N-No, it-it's fine. It was that or d-die and I'm g-grateful, really. I j-just need a m-moment." Valhalla replied, just then realizing her teeth were chattering.

The jitteriness from the transference did eventually fade, albeit far slower than she would've liked, and her body finally lulled into a state of mild agitation. As she waited, she looked over the army of figures which had eluded her understanding in her once blurry haze. The figures were corpses. Of course, they were corpses. These, however, each existed with a surprising amount of poise, as still as sculptures carved with reverence for those they reflected. Each sat on folded legs, their heads bowed, and hands raised as if cupping water in their palms. The corpses lined either side of the path her party walked, granting those who were deserving entry to Hel's Fortress. Their numbers seemed as though they could be endless.

"There's so many of them, and each is worthy of entry to Valhalla?" She asked, turning to Aura.

"Yes, it was part of a new agreement struck between Hel and Ódin after her resurrection by Loki's hands." The valkyrie replied, a small smile creasing her lips and arms crossing as she inspected the corpses nearest her.

"New?" Valhalla questioned.

"Ugh!" Aura rolled her eyes. "Do mortals still think you have to die in *valiant* battle to be accepted into Valhalla? It doesn't matter how great a warrior you are in life, so long as you are a good person. True, honorable, and kind-hearted. Those are the traits one needs. That's when my sisters and I will find you, to send your soul to Valhalla." She then shrugged. "The rest come here."

"Where their will and resolve are tested," Jörmungandr added, "and they may work their way toward forgiveness and servitude. Or, they try to fight against death to force their way into Valhalla, apparently." His eyes glanced back to the courtyard they had come from, where so many dead had fought against Garmr's wolves.

"Huh," Thor huffed, outwardly impressed as he inspected a corpse next to him, "so why this posture?"

"To show respect and to say thank you for finding them worthy of a second chance," Fenrir answered, rolling back on the balls of his feet and seeming a bit anxious to move on. "Big sister petrifies them during their wait for Lady Vitalia, and based on the amount here. . . clearly it's been a while."

"Yes," Aura said flatly, her eyes narrowed as she scanned row after row of petrified corpses. "I'll have to speak with my mother when we return to Asgard." She then looked pointedly at Thor. "After all, your father still demands souls to pack Valhalla."

"I bet he does," Thor murmured with a roll of his eyes, nonchalantly making his way across the courtyard toward the fortress.

Fenrir then placed a hand on Valhalla's back. A frown marred his face. "Are you well enough to continue, Valla?"

She let out a soft sigh and stretched her shoulders back. "Yes, I think so." Valhalla's voice cracked, the pain coming again. "At least, I certainly hope so."

"Come on then. I can't imagine how that curse must feel, but you've always been strong." With that, he gave her a soft nudge forward and walked with her, remaining at her side as they walked.

She wanted to tell him thank you, that his words of encouragement meant the world to her, and that just his presence brought her comfort, but it hurt too much to speak. Instead, she nodded. Her skin stung as it stretched with movement. Thor's energy had chased the darkness from her eyes, yet it still clung to the edges of her vision. She could already feel her strength beginning to ebb. Frustration bubbled in her gut, but it was almost over. The Queen of Helheim was close. Just one step at a time.

As the group reached the end of the courtyard, they came upon a semicircular indentation on the surface of the stone building and a circular platform at their feet. On the left stood a tall corpse, nearly as large as Thor, resting in a position that, to Valhalla, seemed uncomfortable. It loomed over a wheel which had many handles.

"I remember this," Valhalla croaked, "we just need to stand in the center of the lift and they will awaken to turn the wheel."

The group allowed her to take the lead and followed her to the center of the round stone floor. It wasn't long before the corpse stirred. Valhalla wondered if in life it had been a Jotunn or a Vanir. Decay had long since taken its toll on the being, and now it was impossible to identify. It lifted itself off the wheel and grabbed hold of one of the handles, pulling the wheel back. The floor jostled beneath them with a loud clunk. The chains jingled and creaked, but held as the round floor began to carry them up into the sky.

It was slow going at first, but gained speed as it climbed. Valhalla's legs strained from the extra force. She wasn't going to be able to hold herself up for long and knew she needed to conserve what little stamina she had. At least she wasn't going to be fainting, she thought. She lowered herself to the ground, accidentally startling her friends.

"Valla?" Aura called in an almost motherly tone.

"I-I'm fine. Promise." Valhalla assured, folding her legs beneath her. "I just needed to rest my legs." She gave them a half smile, hoping they might not see through the deception, and gathered the furs of her cloak around her neck to shield away the cold.

Aura sighed and looked to accept her words at face value. "Alright then, I'll join you." She knelt beside Valhalla as Fenrir did the same opposite her, gently rubbing Valhalla's back.

Thor and Jörmungandr stood at the edge of the lift. The Thunder God crossed his arms over his chest and stared out at the vastness of all of Helheim. Valhalla couldn't help but look out as well. An entire realm of ice, snow, and stone. A vast forest could just barely be seen at their left, and mountains to the right. The sky in all directions was choked by the same thundering clouds that had greeted them. It's no wonder mortals didn't wish to come here after death, and they had never actually seen it as Valhalla had, twice now. She counted herself among them.

"This place is something, isn't it?" Valhalla said.

"I'll say," Thor responded, his shoulders relaxing and planting his hands on his hips. "You know, it's odd how much this realm reminds me of Niflheim."

"Both realms are basically wastelands of snow and ice," Valhalla answered, tucking her raven black hair behind an ear. "Ice spires and stone mountains abound, not to mention the corpses."

"HA! That's probably it." Thor chuckled. "Maybe that's why humans get the two realms mixed up."

His laugh brought a grin to her face. "Some think both realms are one and the same."

The group jostled as the lift shifted and slowed. Looking up, they found they would soon reach the top of the fortress. Hel's throne room was now just above them. Fenrir stood first, reaching a hand out to Valhalla, which she accepted. With a heavy grunt and several deep breaths, she stood on wobbly legs, her sight starting to blur once more.

Dammit, she silently cursed to herself. She wasn't sure just how long Thor's energy would last and doubted she would survive another surge. We're almost there, she told herself.

The lift finally came to a complete stop, and as she spun around to enter Hel's throne room, her breath caught in her throat. Valhalla's eyes went wide. The floor of the circular hall before them was almost completely covered by snow white hands sticking out of the floor, like wheat in a field, each desperately reaching for one thing. Her.

36

Valhalla

The Queen of Helheim

Claws scraped and slammed against the floor, stone against stone. A wave of cold spread across Valhalla's skin. Of all the things she had expected to await her at the top, this wasn't quite the worst thing she had imagined, but it was a pretty close second. The last time she was here, there had been no field of hands, but there had also not been hanging bodies down below or a horde of dead attacking the castle. There appeared to be a clear path, at least, just wide enough for two people walking abreast.

Something slid its way around her shoulders, causing her to jolt. As she looked to make sure one of the hands hadn't managed to free itself from the ground and somehow made its way behind her, she was relieved to find Thor staring back at her. His jaw was set, and his expression filled with determination. "Valhalla, you can do this. Just stay close, alright?"

She nodded quickly and clung to his side as the two proceeded to enter. Valhalla had feared Hel since first they met, but thinking back on it now, she may have unfairly judged the mistress of death. The woman's appearance had been terrifying back then, and was likely even more so now, but she dwelt in a realm filled with horrors. The place had been made for her, sure, but that didn't mean Queen Hel was a cruel goddess. Looking back, Hel had never taken action toward her to justify the presumption. It was possible that she let her fear of the undead and the realm itself color her perception.

Valhalla couldn't, no, shouldn't keep fearing the Goddess, or death itself for that matter. It was simply a part of life. Something to face head-on. Every life had an ending. Denying that would be like denying the beauty in life. She would face the ruler of this underworld and, for the first time, was determined to view her with unbiased eyes.

Keeping her back straightened as best she could while in Thor's embrace, she took step after step. Her pink eyes were fixated on the hands as they grasped for her and her companions, but she didn't let fear freeze her in place. As she watched the hands, a realization set in. They weren't the color-drained, frozen skin of ghoul hands. They weren't flesh at all. They seemed to be made of alabaster stone, which struck her as peculiar, but so too was this realm. Each of her companions kept pace, carefully avoiding the flurry of seeking fingers, until Thor abruptly stopped with a grunt.

The big man growled and rubbed his nose with annoyance. He glared ahead and raised a hand to the air, rubbing it across an invisible surface.

Jörmungandr squeezed between Valhalla and Thor and touched his hand to it as well. With a heavy sigh, he said, "Sister, please, it's just us. Remove your barrier so that we may speak."

Valhalla looked ahead, and even with her renewed sense of courage, she startled. She hadn't realized Hel was actually in the throne room with them. The revelation freed her focus and allowed her to take in the rest of the room. The interior was surprisingly beautiful, in a grim sort of way. The great hall was circular. Its walls looked to be mostly made of black carborundum stone, the distinct black surface shining with various rainbow hues as it caught the light. Black melanite geometric pillars dotted the area, each shining with a spiderwork of golden hues beneath the crystalline surface. Beneath her feet were marble-like black blizzard stone tiles.

Nine-tiered iron chandeliers hung in a circular pattern from the massive dome ceiling. The stone offered a nice contrast to the rest of the room. Its surface was largely white, with a bit of an ice-like quality, and was peppered with plant-like black fractals which shimmered in the light of pale blue fires. Her time with the dwarves gave her a strong appreciation for the scene. For a moment, it took Valhalla's breath away.

In the very center of the circular hall stood a tall figure. White, stringy hair ran down their back, stopping a blade's width above the floor. A black, iron spiked crown from which linked chains draped about their neck and shoulders, rested atop their head. Queen Hel herself. Black furs streaked with gray were bundled about her shoulders. Just beneath the fur fell a cape which flooded down her back and spilled onto the floor. Black plates and dark beads hid beneath the furs caught in the firelight as she turned. Hel stood in profile. Her thin, bony frame was all rigid angles, which barely held up her faded violet gown. Skin of a pale gray clung to her nearly visible bones. She was gaunt and looked so deeply ill that a pang of worry struck Valhalla that the Queen might just keel over and die at that very moment.

A cloth covered Hel's eyes, the color a perfect match to her gown, save for two painted white runes. They were the othala and tiwaz runes, home and justice, which Valhalla wholeheartedly felt a connection to.

The Queen looked toward them, and while it was impossible to know where her gaze found rest, Valhalla had the sense that it was she who was Hel's singular focus. A moment later, she raised a hand and waved for Valhalla to approach. Thor raised his hand again, and his expression hardened to pure aggravation.

Valhalla followed suit and raised her hand in the air. "How does she expect me to——" She stumbled forward, hand passing clean through empty air, and was instantly hit with the strong scent of decay.

Just as she began to gag, Valhalla felt a tight grip and strong tug back on her right arm. She crashed to a stop against Thor's chest, the scent of death somehow gone, and she sucked in a breath of the freezing fresh air.

"I don't fucking think so!" Thor exclaimed with a snarl, jostling her in his vice-like grip. "Hel, take down the barrier, or I will." He threatened, sliding Mjölnir from his belt, Meginjörd. Lightning shrieked across its silvery iron surface as if to make clear he was willing to follow through.

Valhalla's eyes widened in concern, and her body moved of its own accord, leaping and bringing her full weight down against her older brother's arm, keeping Mjölnir lowered at his side. "Thor, stop!" He looked down at her with a raised brow, as though he didn't understand that if he were to act, the already tenuous situation would fall apart. "I know your solution to everything is to just hit the problem with Mjölnir, but please, think for a moment."

Thor blinked a few times at her, stunned. "Well, it usually works." He said defensively.

Taking a breath, she forced a weak smile up at him. "I need to do as she wishes. If Hel can help me, then who are any of us to question her?"

He stared at her in silence for several long moments before relenting. As his expression softened, Thor let out a defeated sigh. His eyes shone with understanding, but winced as they glanced down to her neck.

The decay had spread up to Valhalla's jaw, worming its way in frosty tendrils to coat her skin. A flicker of concern sparked on his face, and in that moment, he looked as though he might grab hold of her. Reflexively, she hopped backward out of his reach, passing through the barrier, and again the stench of rotting flesh washed over her.

She managed to hold her smile, ignoring the bile rising in her throat. "Do-Don't worry, everything will be alright."

Now wasn't the time to hesitate. If she did, the curse would take her. She could feel it beneath her skin. Corrupting. Damaging. Eating away at the tissue. It left a foul taste in her mouth that was only getting worse. She spun on the balls of her feet, took a breath, and approached Hel. The smell grew thicker with each step, and it became clear the Queen of Death was its source.

Old memories of Valhalla's long-lost home bubbled to the surface of her mind's eye, but she shook them away as quickly as they came, forcing them back down where they belonged. This wasn't the time nor the place to reflect on such things. If she allowed them to take hold now, she would be accepting her demise with open arms. Summoned instead a barrage of the happy memories she had made since then, picturing her friends and family of Asgard.

Just as she reached the tall goddess, Aura's scream broke her focus. Valhalla's heart fell into her stomach as she turned to find the hands had managed to surround and subdue her companions. They clung to limbs and fabric alike. Her friends fought and struggled to free themselves, but somehow the hands held fast. It seemed that the more they struggled, the tighter the grip became. Even Thor could do nothing to break their hold. It was then that Valhalla realized the true extent of their plight. Her friends weren't simply bound. They were being pulled down, sinking into the very floor where they stood.

A jolt of adrenaline burned through her veins as she turned back to face Hel with pleading eyes. "Your Majesty—"

Hel moved impossibly fast. Her hand shot forward and took hold of Valhalla by the back of her neck. The Queen's hold was far too powerful for the image she portrayed, sturdy as a mountain and as inescapable as a dragon's maw. Valhalla yelped. With a jerk, she found herself face to face with the Queen of Helheim. Hel's icy breath softly caressed her cheek. Valhalla's eyes scrunched closed as Hel forced her head to tilt back, causing Valhalla to gasp. The sudden gush of breath filled her lungs, and to Valhalla's surprise, the stench of decay was gone.

She was instead infused with the scent of blood oranges and hellebores.

Slowly, Valhalla opened her eyes and was instantly taken aback by Hel's new visage. Her skin was no longer gray, but was now as white as alabaster stone. The Goddess's hair was now full and lush. Hel's face and body were fuller, healthy and soft. No longer did the violet and silver gown barely cling to her form. She was beautiful, like the sparkling snow at daybreak when the sun peeked over the rim of the waking world.

Releasing Valhalla's neck, Hel straightened, and the goddess smirked. "You don't even remember why you feared me, do you?"

Valhalla was taken aback by the question. Hel's words carried no malice or malicious intent. She almost sounded pained by the question. Her breath then hitched in her throat. Had she wounded Hel by fearing her so? She had treated Hel poorly by judging her by those who dwelt in Helheim. The realm was dark, freezing, and altogether violent toward the living. Somehow Valhalla had conflated that with who Hel was. In her time in Midgard, Valhalla had met many wicked souls and had never seen them as a reflection on their kings or queens. Hel had deserved the same courtesy, yet Valhalla had inadvertently spurned her.

Hel gently took Valhalla's chin between her finger and thumb, bringing Valhalla back to the present. The Queen lifted a single finger, its nail long and painted black. There, an unfamiliar rune glowed in violet. Hel then moved the sharp point of the nail to Valhalla's neck, where she could feel the scarf slide down and a tingling shiver spread about her being.

There was a strange tug on her skin. Her body went instantly rigid, and her jaw set. The tug turned to a steady pull. Something was desperately trying to cling to her. As the pull grew, it felt as though her skin would rip free from muscle. She whimpered from the pain, grinding her teeth and tears streaming from burning eyes. An instant later, something tore free, sending her into a breathless stumble.

With Hel's help, Valhalla steadied herself. As she raised her gaze to the glowing nail, she spotted what looked like a translucent sheet of gray matter disappearing within the rune. She flung a hand up to her neck, and although it was left a tad sensitive, her skin felt normal. Relief crashed over her. The curse was gone.

A flash of white flooded her vision, and a state of disorientation followed for several long moments, but as she opened her eyes, her friends were no longer bound and vanishing beneath the floor. The white hands were gone. It was as if they were never there in the first place.

"You will have to excuse me, young one, but I placed illusions throughout the realm. To test you." Hel said as she clasped her hands and set them to rest over her stomach.

Jörmungandr sighed heavily, a disturbed scowl on his face and a hand on his hip. "Of course, it was *you* leaving things for only her to see."

"Wait," Thor's eyes darted between them, his expression growing agitated by the moment, "test her? Test her for what?" He stomped over to her, brandishing Mjölnir in hand, lightning again screeching across its surface.

Aura stepped forward to grab him, but Hel raised a hand, which stopped the Valkyrie in place. Thor stopped and stood before Hel, the two both towering figures in their own rights. One with bulging muscles and a scrunched snarl marring his face. The other, stoic and patient, seemingly unbothered by Thor's proximity.

"To see if she is ready to face them. The dead. The illusions were necessary for what is to come next." Hel answered, then turned her head to Jörmungandr and Fenrir. "Brothers, you should have *known* better than to take a semi-mortal through the River Gjöll."

Valhalla's brow twitched. What did she mean, semi-mortal? Her lips parted, but before she could ask what the Queen had meant, Fenrir cut her off. His hands hung clasped together at his waist, and his eyes were on the floor, his face dejected.

"We're sorry," Fenrir responded, his tone oddly timid, "Heimdall dropped us off all the way in the Ironwood Forest."

"My vísa claimed the river to be the safest route." Jörmungandr added, also wearing a mask of shame, coloring his face."I was careless. It will never happen again."

Hel's lips curled into a half smile as she walked over to join her brothers. Raising a finger to Jörmungandr's chin, she lifted his eyes to meet hers and cupped his cheek. "My little serpent, I'm not mad, but you must be more cautious in the future, should I ever have need of her again, that is." She touched her palm to Fenrir's cheek as well. "Do you both understand?"

Fenrir's frown faded as he leaned into her touch, then nodded. Jörmungandr's features relaxed, the corners of his lips seemingly holding back a smirk, and he nodded as well. She then spread her arms, inviting their embrace, which instantly followed.

Thor sneered at the display. "How can they stand to be around her with that smell?" He grumbled, but Valhalla couldn't help but raise a brow at him.

This caught Valhalla by surprise. She recalled the scent of rotting flesh which had filled the chamber, but that was no longer the case, at least not for her. She glanced at Aura standing behind him, and the valkyrie playfully waved a hand over her eyes, before resting it back on her hip.

Valhalla gave her a curious look, working out what the gesture had meant. Her eyes drifted back to Hel, and part of the answer formed in her mind. The version of Hel which greeted her, the thin, gaunt, sickly visage. Was that who Thor was seeing? But why? And most importantly, how?

"Come, young one, there's something I must show you," Hel said, releasing her brother and making her way to the center of the room, to the Well of Foresight.

The well was strikingly similar to Vitalia's in Asgard, though with Helheim's charm giving it a distinctness all its own. Hel's well was held not by ten angelic figures, but by ghouls. The stone was ebony instead of white. Its rim just reached the goddess's waist, and out poured white mist that fell like a waterfall and pooled around her feet. Valhalla hurried to stand at her side, anxious to know just what it was the Queen of the Damned had in store for her.

Hel dipped her hand into the mist and slowly moved it about in a circular motion, causing an opening to reveal itself where, within, a silver liquid rested beneath. Its surface rippled seemingly of its own, to and fro, Valhalla's reflection receding and slowly being replaced by something else, a place. It was several long moments before familiarity began to sink in. A city of black stones sat on a cliff's edge overlooking a glittering sea, but the setting was unsettlingly dark, as though a soot and smoke-tinged sky had choked out the sun's light, except there was no fire, no columns of smoke, no sign of siege or plight. The winds blew with the ferocity of a hurricane. Then she spotted the herald of a bright blue leviathan on black banners and knew which city she was seeing.

"Are you—" Hel started but stopped, silently looking to something at Valhalla's rear, not more than an arm's length from where she stood.

Valhalla turned to see what it was that pulled Hel's attention, and as she found it, her heart leaped into her throat. A shambling ghoul had entered the throne room, and for a moment, she expected it to attack. Its hands quickly raised to show it meant no harm, and had its face enough structure left to make a readable expression, Valhalla got the feeling it would've been a mix of anxiety and fear.

"I will be just a moment," Hel said flatly, stepping around Valhalla and approaching the ghoul.

The being fell to its knees and bowed low in her presence. "My apologies for interrupting, your Majesty," it said with a hoarse moan, elongating some of its syllables, "but I bring news of those that once laid before the great tree."

Hel's hand twitched at her side, but her face betrayed nothing. "I had a feeling they would soon wake, but I thought I had more time. Do you know where they've gone?"

The ghoul nodded, not daring to meet her eyes. "Yes, your Majesty. They've entered the fortress. I believe they are coming here."

Hel then raised a hand to the ghoul's head. It flinched but managed not to back away. Finding its composure once again, it straightened. Her hand hovered in place, and Hel's being grew very still for several long moments before life seemed to return to her, a pleased smile rounding her cheeks. "You've done well. Thank you." Hel said and straightened herself as the ghoul bowed. "Take refuge behind my throne until I have seen to my guests. Then you'll have your reward."

"Oh, thank you, Your Majesty, thank you. You are too kind." The ghoul just barely rose before shambling away, silent as a mouse.

Hel then swiveled back to her well, her covered face locked on Valhalla. "We must be quick now." She pointed to the image within the silver liquid. "I trust you know this place?"

Valhalla looked at the image again, waiting until she was absolutely certain before answering, then nodded. "This is Castle Svartr. The city of black stones. Vardan took me there when I was very young. I don't remember its streets all too well, but I believe he still has a place there."

"That'll do. My task involves this place." Hel looked into the liquid, her jaw clenching and words coming in a staccato bite. "Something, or someone I should say, has disturbed the flow of death. There have been many killings there. I've felt them, one and all yet no souls have been delivered forth."

"Wait, what do you mean, your Majesty?" Aura approached and stopped on Hel's opposite, her brows furrowed with concern.

Hel looked at the Valkyrie. "It doesn't make any sense. It's like something stopped the natural flow of things. I thought if anyone might know what's . . . you—" Hel was facing Valhalla in less than a heartbeat. The Queen loomed over her, and within the breadth of a single heartbeat, Hel's hand shot forward and came to a stop on Valhalla's chest. The speed of the movement should've knocked the air from her lungs, but landed with the gentleness of a dying breath.

"Y-Your Majesty?" Valhalla called softly, looking at Hel and trying to not be afraid. Lightning crackled across the floor as Thor stomped over. His meaty hand grabbed hold of Hel by her wrist, and he pulled the Queen, but she didn't move an inch. Hel's face took on a clear anger as she met Thor's growl, and Valhalla said a silent prayer that things wouldn't unravel further.

"Let. Go," Hel commanded.

"Not until you explain yourself! Why were you reaching for Valhalla?" Thor's deep green eyes were alight with the promise of violence.

"For a moment, I sensed something that shouldn't be. You'd do well to heed my warning, child of ill temper."

"Or maybe you were trying to prematurely steal her soul!" Thor growled, his free hand finding the hilt of his hammer.

A blur of movement obscured Valhalla's vision, and Fenrir had joined the fray, his hand clamping down on Thor's wrist at his side. His blue-green eyes were wild and seething, but as his eyes flicked to her, then back to Thor, there was a glint of an apology. He didn't want a fight any more than Hel or herself.

The air smelled of rain, and the spark of energy made Valhalla's skin prickle.

Hel, with an aura of ease about her, leaned in so close to Thor that their noses nearly came into contact. When her voice came, it was smooth and filled with sincerity. "I don't keep worthy souls. And your sister's is by far meant for a destiny greater than anything Helheim could ever offer. Jörmungandr, if you would."

Jörmungandr approached and placed his hands on his brother's shoulders, pulling him away from Thor. Both brothers remained ready to protect their older sister if need be, but stepped back to give her space. Hel then withdrew her arm from Thor's grasp, and in the gap, Aura stepped in and grasped the collar of Thor's jerkin, pushing him away. Neither Hel nor Thor removed their gaze from one another.

"The valkyries and I have an understanding, which is more than I could ever say of you and I." Hel's face then took on a dour sneer. "Tsk! Balder and you would be a menace if either were ever given the throne. Balder, with his head so safely nestled within the warmth of his illuminated posterior, and you, so earnest and full of potential, could just see past the prison built by promises of an unknowable tomorrow."

Valhalla watched as Thor's anger faded and his demeanor turned sullen. Had Hel's words actually sunk in? The idea took Valhalla aback. It was unlike the big Æsir to hear reason from one he had deemed an enemy, and if Hel were able to reach him, but she was glad of it. Thor took another step away from Aura and turned his gaze to the ground.

"Your wife must be a being of incredible patience." Hel started as she turned back to her well, leaning against the rim, her gaze fixed on Svartr. "A trait I often aspire to, but we're running out of time. I had hoped the valkyries were simply finding it difficult to keep up with the demand Midgardians place on their duties, but now I'm starting to believe otherwise. Something more is transpiring where I cannot see. This has been building for several months, and I lament not summoning you sooner, and by the time I asked of you—"

"I was in Hilliard." Valhalla finished.

Hel cocked her head to Valhalla and nodded. "Correct. I need you to find out what scheme is at play and stop the one who's disrupted the natural flow. Use your swords to end this."

Valhalla's fingers twitched, and her expression turned serious, dread turning her blood cold. "My swords?"

Hel straightened to her full, imposing height, her entire attention singularly on Valhalla. "Yes. Any being amongst the living struck down by the sword of a Valkyrie, whether in defense or aggression, will be sent immediately to me—"

"Or Valhalla," Aura added, crossing her arms and looking displeased.

"Exactly," Hel answered. "I have no doubt the soul in which we speak will come to me. I'll bring judgment as surely as the coming night snuffs out the last light of day, clean and final. They will be punished for the woes they have wrought. Life and death are a balance. It must be kept. I'll not suffer a disruption on my watch."

Valhalla's mind raced with the possibilities of what punishment might be dealt to one who slighted the Queen of Death. Not only was Hel asking her to end someone's life, but to also doom them to untold horrors which would likely last for more than her remaining lifetime. The weight of such a request seemed almost too much to bear. Valhalla found her next words spilling out before she could stop them. "B-But I've never killed before. I don't think I have it in me to do it."

Hel then lowered herself down to match Valhalla's height, placing her hands on her thighs and leaning close. "Should you require motivation, the High Prince of Hilliard is currently on his way to Svartr and will arrive in several weeks' time. Countless others have had their lives cut short already. Don't let your inaction add his to the pyre."

Valhalla's heart leaped into her throat as a flash of Alistair's face floated into her mind's eye. "Wait, *the* High Prince? Why would he—"

"Trust me, Valhalla, when I say he's destined for greatness, but his paths all converge on this place. The Nornir see his many ends, one of which is at Svartr. He. Can't. Die. at Svartr. Only you can see to that." Hel's words were soft. There was compassion there, but even more so, conviction.

A blood-curdling howl rang out. Each of her companions looked toward one of the openings about the chamber and readied themselves for an attack. One then became two, and soon a symphony of undeath drowned out the quiet. Valhalla's spine went rigid as she spotted the first shadows of the writhing crowd of corpses appearing just outside the throne room.

Thor was instantly at Valhalla's side, grabbing her wrist. His expression was not that of anger or the thrill of battle, but of a deep worry. "You got your message, now we need to leave!"

"You two as well," Hel said to her brothers.

"What!?" They replied as one, clearly uncomfortable at the idea of leaving their sister to fend them off alone.

"The Mark of Yggdrasil brings a powerful scent of life which they cannot ignore. You two are not safe here. None of you are. Even with me. Now go!" Hel waved a dismissive hand to Jörmungandr and Fenrir, but neither brother moved. They stood there, eyes trembling and brows knitted.

They loved their older sister dearly. Valhalla knew as much. It was clear in how they spoke of her. Like Valhalla, Hel too was a Mark of Yggdrasil, but it seemed her powers over the dead were greater than the pull of the Great Life Tree. She could protect herself, but it seemed that was the extent of it. She couldn't extend that protection to others.

Jörmungandr was the first to act. He grabbed Fenrir, and the two followed after Thor and Valhalla. The group rushed back the way they came, heading for the lift. Aura took the lead, having already summoned her glittering white horn, pressed it to her lips, and produced a boom which must've carried for miles.

Struggling to keep up with Thor's stride, Valhalla chanced a glance back, fearful for Hel. She nearly lost her footing when her eyes found the horde of ghouls spilling into the throne room. They came through every doorway, bodies contorting in wet pops just barely audible beneath their wails. For a brief instant, she felt the urge to turn and assist the Queen of Death, but it was a fleeting notion.

"Remember what I said, Valhalla Önníka," Hel's voice sounded above the commotion, "stop the disruption. By any means necessary."

The ghouls parted like a school of herring and swarmed past their Queen, racing after Valhalla and her companions. The dead bottlenecked at the opening of the hall, slowing them only slightly. Thor pulled at her arm hard, keeping her from losing her balance, and they all ran as swiftly as their feet could carry them.

Just as they reached the center of the circular contraption, Valhalla looked up and saw something bright and colorful hurtling toward them from the sky. Heimdall had summoned the Bifrost. Relief fought with the fear raging in her gut. The howls of the dead weren't far behind. She turned to watch their approach, nothing left to do but wait to see how things played out. Just as it seemed they had been too slow, that the dead would crash into them and the best she could hope for was a swift death from the fall, the rainbow pillar enveloped Valhalla and her friends. She felt an instant tug and soared into the sky of Helheim, into the cosmos, and was back in the golden realm of Asgard.

37

Queen of Svartr
Lies

A violent shiver woke Ayunli. Her body ached, and a terrible pain throbbed in the back of her neck. A fit of coughs shot lightning down her back, and then, there was only blackness.

As she came to, she had no idea how long she had been out. The world around her was a dim blur. Her knees were sore from bearing her weight. She was pressed against something cold and hard. Perhaps stone. She groaned as exhaustion coursed through her body. With effort, she raised a hand to inspect her neck, but something stopped her. It was solid, whatever it was, and was fastened about her neck. Running a finger across the surface, it was coarse, and she traced a groove, then another. A sharp sensation bloomed on the tip of her finger. A stockade, maybe.

She tried to blink away the haze obstructing her vision, took a breath, and slammed her hands against the wood. Another shot of lightning. Her body tensed, then went slack, but to her credit, she hadn't passed out.

Her hands slid around to inspect the device which bound her, and she counted two wooden slabs and a small circle at the center where her neck was trapped. Support beams ran parallel to her legs, and a beam ran vertically on either side of those that held her in place. Her heart sank with realization and confusion. Surely this was a nightmare. She would wake soon in the comfort of her bed, all of this a distant horror fading into the obscurity of the day. She couldn't cling to the delusion. The pain was real. This was real.

Slowly, she turned her body and neck, gritting her teeth through the pain of the movement, trying to see what she knew in her gut was waiting above. Dread told her to stop, but she pushed on. She could only see a sliver of it. A glint off the metal's edge. Ayunli closed her eyes and turned forward again, allowing her head to sag. She fought back a sob. She had her answer. Ayunli was locked in a guillotine.

Heart racing, pounding with bursting ferocity against the prison of her sternum, despair clawed at her insides. What was going on? Why was this happening? Where was she?

That's it.

She could at least figure that out. She knew the palace inside and out. Lifting her head again, she scanned the room. It was small, and shadows obscured much. Her flaxen hair draped loose over her eyes, which didn't help. The floor, ceiling, and walls were all bare stone. It was a cell, but unfamiliar. That was a start, she thought. A terrible stench of decay and iron lingered heavily in the air.

As the Queen of Svartr, Ayunli knew the prison cells beside the castle well, and this was no that. An eerie violet light added color to the room, dim as it was, and whatever was casting the light, she couldn't see. All she knew was that it came from far to her left.

"H-Hello?" She called through chattering teeth. "Is anyone there? Please, Aegir, where are you?"

Only silence responded.

Ayunli sifted through her memories, trying to remember her last memory before waking in this place. Her breath hitched. It had been late. Everyone was asleep, and she was running toward Daemyn's bed chamber, to her son, to warn him of Lord Tamanna Gadhavi, her husband's Steward. She had reached the door and could see the surprise in his face, but her words died in her throat, and the world went dark. And now, she was here.

There had to be more. Some flash of recollection between then and now. If not, had something happened to her? She wouldn't just black out. Of all the issues she faced, health had not been one of them. But if that was true, she had reached her son. Daemyn. A new fear crept into her mind, stronger than those about her present state. What had happened to Daemyn?

"Daemyn, are you here? Please, say something, my little snowflake!" She pleaded, trying and failing to mask the panic in her voice.

"I assure you, our son isn't here, Ayunli."

Ayunli jumped, the pain flaring again at the sudden movement. The voice was all too familiar and had come from her right. She turned her head to look, glancing from the corner of her eyes, and found a figure had stepped out from the shadows. The violet glow bathed her husband's features and did nothing to ease her worry. Aegir Svartr stood tall, statuesque and imposing before her. His arms were crossed over his lean chest, and his expression bored.

"Aegir, what is this?" Her voice cracked. Tears stung her eyes, and her heart broke. "Why am I bound in this place? Why are you treating me so, my love?"

"Those who conspire to overthrow me are to be immediately, without exception, executed." His voice was deep and velvety, and his words came as though he were reciting the law to a petty thief.

A surge of adrenaline spiked and sent Ayunli's mind racing. "What!? My sweet, what do you mean? You know I would never—"

"You've been skulking around in the late hours, conspiring with the *nobility*. You were caught trying to convince our son to turn against me. Against Albrecht." Aegir's eyes darkened, and his tone turned deadly. "I won't let you pit our sons against each other. I won't let you start a civil war." He said with a growl, stepping beside her.

Ayunli's eyes widened as she watched, almost as if time slowed to a crawl, as he placed his hand on a lever. After everything she left behind in Blár, for him, all the comforts, friends, and family she had ever known. After everything the two had been through, plagues, storms, sending Albrecht off to war. Why would Aegir believe she could ever betray him? Why would he think she could ever bring him or their sons to pain?

"Any last words, traitor?" Aegir asked, his face lost in shadow.

She let out a sharp gasp as tears stained her face. Her body was frozen. "A-Aegir, please!" Ayunli sobbed. "I swear to you, as your wife, as the mother of our wonderful sons, on *our* love, I swear to Njörd himself, I've done no such thing! It's Tamanna, he isn't to be trusted. This is him! Go to his chamber, I beg you. He has a strange journal on magics I've never seen. He's the one who plots to overthrow you, I promise. Please!" She cried, desperation the only thing she could cling to.

Her husband remained quiet for what felt like an eternity. She couldn't see his face, and his posture gave nothing away. His hand remained on the lever and didn't so much as twitch with indecision. What was he thinking? Had her pleas fallen on deaf ears? Her thoughts drifted through their years together. He was always a stony man, difficult to read no matter the situation, but she alone had a knack for chipping through that exterior. She could always make him smile. A memory of relaxing in the rose garden just behind the castle brought to mind his expression. He played with the boys while she painted. Aegir couldn't have forgotten their love for each other. He would never throw away what they built. Family was everything to him, to them both.

Through the tears, the pain ravaging her body, and her nails digging into the palms of her fisted hands, the serenity of that memory brought her the strength to smile up at him the way she had on their wedding day. "Aegir, please, I love you. I have always loved you."

She stared at where she knew his eyes to be, and the years of a life spent with one another allowed his features to show through what couldn't be seen. With a soft click and the faintest idea of movement, she had his answer. He had thrown the lever. Down slid the cold metallic end of her world, but she didn't feel bitterness or anger for what he had done. Her last moment was one of sorrow. Sorrow that she couldn't help him, that she would never again see her boys, kiss their foreheads, or see who they would grow into.

And then she was gone.

Part
4

38

Alistair

Svartr, the Black City by the Sea

Alistair was alone in his carriage, standing at the window. He stared out into the vast, bright blue sky above. Gravity pulled him to and fro as the vehicle swayed on the uneven turf. Steep hills made traversing the grasslands an altogether unpleasant endeavor. The road, a generous term for the dirt path distinguishable only by the well-trodden lines of wagon wheels, snaked between the greater of the hills and over the shallows to make the trip as expedient as possible. This did little to make the trip relaxing, and he found himself glad that motion sickness was not something that troubled him. The route to and from Svartr, the capital city of the region Oceana, truly mirrored her people. Simply put, they were made of sterner stuff.

A chill wind drifted through the window, and he slumped against the wall in an effort to escape it. He sat himself down on a cot built into the carriage body, the frame big enough for two, and traced a finger across several knotted raven designs, which brought a small smile to his face.

Clutched in his opposite hand was a letter. A dear friend, one not heard from for far too long, had written to him, and the thought of their reunion gave Alistair hope that better days might be ahead.

It had been over three years now since he set foot in Svartr. Three long years since his friend, Albrecht Svartr, was sent in his stead to take part in the Gran Mar War. A decision that was forced upon Alistair, which he had little choice but to accept.

His eyes drifted down to the letter written by Daemyn Svartr, Albrecht's younger brother. Its contents filled him with uncertainty. It had ever since the day the letter arrived and he set out on this journey, twenty days past. But regardless, he was going to see his friend, and that was reason enough to look forward to whatever awaited him.

It wasn't a short trip, traveling from Hilliard to Svartr, and if it called for a high royal's attendance, there must've been a good reason, and in this case, both Alistair and his mother found it to be just such. In a separate letter, delivered to his mother, the High Queen, it announced the return of Prince Albrecht and the end of the war, resulting in victory for the combined forces of Svartr and the island country of Zarago. He was to serve as a representative of Hilliard.

He tilted the letter which had been delivered specifically to him, and read over the first line. Again.

Alistair, this may not be the best time, especially with what happened to you and your family, but after you arrive, can we talk about the possibility of an us?

He sighed and stopped, having already read over the remainder countless times. He rubbed his face tirelessly. "Daemyn, you were just engaged to my sister."

Daemyn was still a young prince of only seventeen winters, which made him five years Alistair's junior. Their parents had met long ago and soon came to the decision that Lorna and Daemyn would be wed. Each had only been a few years old at the time, their births only months apart. Their joining was conceived in the hopes that it would strengthen the bond between the two regions and houses. His heart twisted at the thought. The arrangement would've been forced upon them, and neither party was excited at the prospect. Lorna had made it clear in her journal that she despised Daemyn, and Daemyn, polite as he was, paled whenever the topic came up.

"Your Grace?"

Startled, he quickly folded the letter and glanced up to find one of his silverguards peering through the window of the carriage.

"We're nearly arrived, your Grace, but the Captain wanted to warn you of the dark clouds looming over the castle city. It might rain soon."

"Oh?" He stood, curious to see just how bad it could be. Looking out the window, it was just as the guard said, dark clouds hung above the city in stark contrast to the clear blue at either side. He could just barely make out the faint sound of thunder.

As with Hilliard, a town brushed right up to the outer gates, the longhouses and countryside homes fanning from the entrance as if the city had been filled to bursting and the buildings here had poured from the gates and spread as water from a breeched barrel. Farms edged the town, but their plots were smaller than Hilliard's due to the hills. This would've and likely did cause shortages in wheat and vegetable stores before the trade agreements between the two cities had been struck. Now the Oceanans enjoyed the bounty of Hilliard, and the Veerencians indulged in the exotic flavors of the sea.

"It seems the castle city has been set upon by a storm." The silverguard said.

"Not surprising really," Alistair crossed his arms and rested them on the windowsill, "it is the summer season after all, though you wouldn't guess it with this chill in the air." He chuckled softly as he rubbed the cold from his bicep. He wondered if perhaps the cold was due to Svartr's placement in the North, the cooler winds being carried across the seas beneath the cliffside at Svartr's back. "Many storms are common here. If the Captain doesn't mind, could we hasten our approach? I'd like to beat the rain before it falls."

"I know I wouldn't mind, your Grace." The silverguard replied with a grin and bowed her head.

Returning to the confines of the carriage, the silverguard vanished from view, racing to deliver the request to the driver and Captain. With the snaps of reins, the horses' hooves pounded, and the carriage sped up.

Alistair stood there and squeezed Daemyn's letter in his hand, trying to figure out what to do. What was he to say that wouldn't injure their friendship? He stuffed the parchment into his trousers' pocket.

"I'll just have to let him down gently."

With his arrival growing near, it was time to properly dress for his meeting with the Svartr royal family. Stepping over to his chest, which was filled to the brim with a variety of clothing, from travel to casual meetings with nobility. Should he have need of anything fancier, that would need to be procured within the city itself. Upon opening the chest, he sighed.

"Dammit, is there even a way to let someone down gently?" Alistair groaned and planted his cheek on a palm, glancing over the clothes in the chest.

He slid his other palm lazily over the clothes, feeling the soft silks and hand-stitched embroidery. His tunics and jerkins were lovely, but he just now realized how dark they all were. Deep crimsons, azures, emeralds, and even those fashioned with the colors of his house. The colors were all too dark for such a joyous occasion.

Pulling a violet tunic from the stack, he looked it over. Black ravens flew about the thick fabric, and after several long seconds, he tilted his head with a smile. "I think this'll do."

He removed the jerkin and under tunic he had been wearing and laid them beside the chest. Sliding the new garments on, he glanced back into the chest and spotted a matching shoulder cape poking out from beneath several other items. Alistair reached in and pulled it out, unfolding the fabric before him. He startled at a clang, as something hit the floor.

Thinking it might've been a belt, he held the cape aside, and as his eyes found the object which had fallen, a deep sigh emanated from his chest. It was his raven circlet. He distinctly recalled not packing *that* with Shu Yen, but his Aunt Embla had looked over his belongings before he took his leave and must've placed it within.

Alistair couldn't help but chuckle. His cheeks heated as he knelt down to the circlet. He never felt comfortable wearing it. Lorna had found a way to turn it into a reminder of the Bedr Prael law, calling it the symbol of the Whore High Prince of Hilliard. His stomach hung heavy with the thought, and guilt soon followed. He wasn't glad for her death, but a part of him was happy she was no longer around. It meant freedom from her constant harassment. Unfortunately, his conscience conflated the two ideas, making him feel as though the joy of the absence of being berated somehow meant he was equally joyous of her death. As much as he tried to logic the notion away, the guilt remained.

A sudden jostle of the carriage as it came to a stop cost him his balance. He was now cast in the shadow of the black stone wall surrounding Svartr. Voices sounded outside.

"State your business." An unfamiliar voice bellowed, most likely belonging to a member of the city's blackguard.

"We are escorting his Grace, High Prince Alistair Hilliard II, to welcome home his Highness, Prince Albrecht Svartr." That voice was undoubtedly the Captain of Alistair's charge.

After a few moments of silence passed before a response came. "Alright, he was expected later in the day. You made good time. You may pass."

Clanking metal and thundering hooves announced the carriage's movement once again. The gate, which opened into Sailors Reef, a section of the city not unlike Hilliard's Commoners Nest, passed by through the window. They had entered the outermost district of the city.

Once through, he returned his attention to the circlet still lying on the floor. Alistair lightly chewed the tip of his thumb. As he stared at it, something his aunt had told him drifted to the forefront of his mind. *No matter what, Alistair, you must show who you are. Represent your family, your home, with honor and without shame. Trust the people to show you the same respect you give yourself.*

Alistair took a deep breath, held it to the count of three, and exhaled through his nostrils. His lips were tightly sealed, but a smile found him all the same. Grabbing his circlet, he placed it on his head, ignoring the knots which had likely formed in his long, dark brown hair, sliding the strands back and down his back. He then returned to the business of clasping his tunic closed and buckling the cape over his right shoulder.

"I came here in my role as a friend, not as the High Prince, but as my family has reminded me all too many times, I have to show confidence in myself." Alistair then fixed his sleeves, checking that his under tunic hadn't bunched underneath, and paused. He closed his eyes and exhaled again. "I can do this. Despite the loss, the people need to see we are strong."

Doubt lingered at the edge of his thoughts, like a quiet fox stalking a hen house. The sensation made him feel a bit queasy, but he needed to have courage. After all, one of his best friends was coming home, and that was reason to celebrate.

He walked to a window and leaned forward, his arm resting against the top of the frame. He wanted to look out, to see how much the city had changed since the last time he was at Svartr. The city was strikingly different from Hilliard, from little things like how the people dressed, bundled up to combat the chilly sea winds, to larger things like how closely the buildings had been packed together.

Oceanans were bred to ride the seas. Some were tall, others short. Many were lean with tawny skin, dark hair ranging from bright brown to black, and varying, subtle hues of brown marked their eyes. There was, however, something odd about the people. One glance his way sent parents scooping up their kids and retreating inside their homes. Dark bags hung heavily under the citizens' eyes, and many held their heads low.

"Is everything alright here?" He asked, to no one in particular, scanning to his left and right, looking over the people going about their day. "What has them so terribly spooked?" He was then taken aback as another large shadow swallowed the carriage. They had passed through another gate and, by the looks of things, had reached Nobles Bay.

As with Hilliard, the homes of upper society exuded grandeur. They were several times larger than that of the common folk, but were still closely knit. The manor's designs drew from various periods and regions of Celnor architecture, angled roofs, knotwork inscriptions depicting creatures of the sea, and sported a vast array of colors, standing in stark contrast to the buildings within Sailors Reef, which were mostly just black stones. The one thing both sections of society shared was the decorations for the upcoming celebration of Midsummarblot, a festival to welcome the coming of summer and, for this region in particular, the brightest time of the year.

The scent of the sea wafted through the carriage. As it hit Alistair, he sucked in the scent and found it utterly relaxing. A wave of nostalgia sent him reminiscing about his time as a child playing on the black sandy beach at the base of the cliff, Daemyn and Albrecht, both his constant friends. They swam and splashed, not yet burdened by the responsibilities of their titles, while their mother and Queen, Ayunli Nealfire Svartr, watched. Those were much simpler times, Alistair mused.

Once again, a large shadow came and went, this time passing through to castle black, home to the Svartr royal family.

"Leviathan's Cove." He muttered, head falling back and enjoying another salty breath. "Here we go."

He stood himself straight and smoothed out his clothes, doing his best to ignore his churning stomach. As Alistair slid a hand up his chest, he found his father's ring beneath the fabric, bringing a small smile to his face. For the briefest of moments, he could almost feel his father's presence standing beside him.

Alistair released a long breath. "It's fine. At least now, I'll finally have some answers."

Since Lorna's death, Svartr had remained unusually quiet. He had found it rather odd, especially when considering Daemyn and Lorna's engagement, which had been the King of Svartr's idea in the first place. The letter regarding Albrecht's return and the subsequent letter holding Daemyn's confession had been the only correspondence between their two houses since Albrecht left for the Gran Mar War.

Memories of King Aegir Svartr began to play in Alistair's mind. The man was stern and notoriously stoic, save for a broody scowl which seemed to be a permanent fixture of his heavy brow, and Alistair had a faint recollection of Queen Ayunli once joking that that had simply been how her husband's face looked at rest. He could almost hear her assuring voice saying it was due to his being distantly related to a troll, which caused him to snort. The only time Alistair could recall seeing that look lift from his face was when he had suggested the pairing, which begged the question: Why was King Aegir so silent? Surely he would've felt the loss, but he was never the kind of man to hold that against Hilliard. He wouldn't have been angered by the loss of a political union. Instead, he would've felt a sorrow akin to Alistair's or his mother's. The loss of a member of the family. He had never once shown himself to be petty or spiteful, but then why the silence? Perhaps Alistair had misjudged him, or something could've changed over the years.

Alistair shook the thought away. "No. No, he isn't that kind of person." He groaned while letting his head fall back. "Fuuuuuck! Why am I so nervous? I know it's been a while and . . . and a lot has happened to both our cities since then."

His finger frantically tapped against his thigh.

"I must seem deranged, talking to myself and jumping to faulty conclusions."

A final shadow loomed over him as the carriage rounded a bend and came to a stop. Out the window, all he could see was a wide set of steps.

He pounded his fist gently against his chest, just below his father's ring. "Alright, here I go. Be confident and poised. *Be* confident and poised."

The driver of the carriage rushed to open his door and bowed. With a deep breath, Alistair stepped forward and climbed down the steps out of the carriage. He smoothed out his cape, and as he looked up, he was taken aback. Alistair had forgotten just how imposing castle black was to behold. At a distance, it towered, but when standing right in front of it, it was something else entirely.

The entire structure was of precision-cut black stone. Countless spires stretched into the sky, and as Alistair stood there, he felt as though a mouse might if standing before a legion of soldiers with swords raised high. Colorful stained glass windows of various colors dotted the surface. Violets, blues, and whites about a canvas of black.

Banners of house Svartr flapped against the castle walls, a bright blue leviathan with azure fins upon a field of black. The creature encircled the symbol of a stone etched with white, and the beast's tail was wrapped about a sharp crown of silver. Beneath the crown, the following had been inscribed: *Land is Temporary, Sea is Eternal.*

"Intimidating, yet strong," Alistair said, mostly to himself.

"I see you remembered what I said." A familiar voice boomed down at him, the accent brisk with clipped tones, not unlike most Oceanans.

Sliding his gaze down the castle, Alistair found a familiar figure standing atop the stairs, a confident smirk on King Aegir's face.

It had been such a long time since Alistair last saw Aegir, it took a moment for the face to register. The man's striking brown hair, which was pulled back in a tight low ponytail, was now streaked with gray. His vibrant tawny skin had paled as well, as if he hadn't spent time in sunlight for a good while now. His highly decorated, black and crimson garment was inlaid with gold, and a blood red cape flowed long down his back. A pointed crown as black as night rested on his head, the depiction of a leviathan at the front, its sapphire eyes glistening in the faint sunlight. However, there was something unsettling about Aegir's eyes, and Alistair couldn't quite place what it was.

Shaking the thought away, Alistair's lips stretched into a grin as he hopped off the final step of his carriage. He readied to rush over and embrace the King, but stopped as the man raised a hand. Glancing to the right, Alistair found a familiar young man, one who had grown much in the last three years, Prince Daemyn Svartr.

Alistair was taken aback by his young friend's growth. Daemyn's flaxen hair was tied loosely at the base of his neck, bangs blowing softly in the chilly wind. His blue eyes were so clear and bright they could rival the beauty of the summer skies above Hilliard. He looked so much like his mother, Ayunli. His once vibrant tawny skin also looked to have paled. Alistair began to wonder how long it had been since Daemyn last went sailing.

Daemyn's attire was just as Alistair had pictured it to be, vibrant, a stark contrast to his father's. He wore colors of blue and crimson, his coat inlaid with silver, and beneath it a ruffled shirt. His fingers were adorned with rings set with various gems of pinks, purples, and blues. The only thing that seemed to not belong was the simple black circlet adorning Daemyn's head. It was so unlike his friend to wear something that plain. The younger prince seemed to take notice of Alistair's perplexity and shrugged a shoulder.

Aegir proceeded down the steps of his castle, Daemyn at his side, and stopped before Alistair. With a flick of his cape, he and Daemyn knelt and bowed their heads low.

Alistair's heart fluttered as he realized, far too late, that he had completely forgotten the traditional greeting he was to do as the High Prince of all of Veerence. It had been years since he last went through the motions, and so, with a soft sigh, he bowed and hoped the gesture would be sufficient.

"Your Grace, we're honored to have you visit. I trust your journey wasn't too harsh?" Aegir asked, head still low, and as Alistair opened his mouth to respond, Daemyn snorted a restrained laugh.

The young Prince clearly wasn't taking the meeting as seriously as tradition demanded, and for that, Alistair was glad. Daemyn had always been quick of wit and dismissive of the notion of following proper conventions. Alistair's lips tugged into a smirk as he considered just what quip was struggling to break free in Daemyn's mind.

Straightening and clasping his hands behind his back, Alistair smiled at the King. "Not at all, your Majesty. Please rise, King Aegir and Prince Daemyn. I'm overjoyed to see you both."

"Ugh, fiiiiinally! Cobblestone is absolute murder on the knees. If you know what I—OW!"

Aegir tapped his knuckles against Daemyn's temple. The young Prince quieted, pursing his lips and rubbing the side of his head. A chortle escaped Alistair's lips, but he quickly recovered, clearing his throat and forcing down the urge to grin.

The two stood erect, and as Aegir's eyes fell on Alistair, he felt his knees grow weak. In that moment, he felt like a kid again, staying with the Svartr royal family just after his father's death. He didn't remember the King's eyes being so black, but it had been many years since he had seen the man and brushed it off as a failing of his younger self's memory. Alisatir was now the same height as Aegir.

A lump formed in his throat. "King Aegir, I-I've come to—"

Aegir raised his gloved hands and set them atop Alistair's shoulders, pulling him into a gentle embrace. The gesture caught Alistair completely by surprise, and after a stunned moment, he reciprocated. The man had never been a hugger save for the few moments Alistair could remember when the Queen had coaxed him into it. On that thought, he realized she wasn't there, which was unlike her. Ayunli had always been full of whimsy, but never shirked her duties. Just where was she? And why was the scent of sea and pine so strong with Aegir? The smell was beyond overpowering and caused Alistair's eyes to sting.

As Aegir finally released him, rubbing a few tears from his eyes, Alistair found the King smiling. His facial hair was rugged, brown, and peppered with gray. Aegir then stepped away, and as he did, a blur of flaxen hair crashed into Alistair, and had he weighed any more, the force might've sent them both toppling. Alistair let out a hearty laugh as he embraced Daemyn as tightly as he could.

Daemyn stood on the tips of his toes, one arm around Alistair's neck and the other clutching tightly to his back. His friend's shoulders were trembling, and Daemyn squeezed him close. "I'm sorry to hear about your sister, Alistair. I truly am, but I'm glad you and your mother are safe." He then placed himself at arm's length, sliding his hand to his shoulder, and slammed his other hand onto the opposite, smiling up at him. "Also, thank you for being here to welcome Albrecht home. I know he'll be happy to see you again."

Aegir chuckled as he placed a hand on both of their backs. "Well, come on then, no use standing around in the cold." His eyes again drifted to Alistair. "Why not rest before Albrecht arrives. There's still time."

A giddiness rose within Alistair that he hadn't anticipated, but he tried his best to hide it. "Is he here? In Veerence, I mean."

Aegir nodded as he clasped his hands behind his back. "I received word just as you approached the city. Knowing him, he'll be here soon enough." He said, laughing heartily and bringing a warm smile to Alistair's face.

Alistair nodded and looked back to his silverguards still standing by their horses. "I'd like you lot to rest for the day. I'm sure the Svartr Kingsguard can look after me until tomorrow." Alistair said with a bow of his head, his tone gracious, causing them to smile with pride and appreciation.

The Captain, donned in silver, raven-decorated armor and a purple cape, bowed his head, and the remaining guards followed suit. "Thank you, Your Grace. You're too kind."

"One of my captains will escort you to your living quarters," Aegir said with a wave toward a soldier adorned in black and silver armor, which was decorated with leviathans all about the metal surface. A black cape flowed behind her. She stepped forward and pounded a fist to her chest. "From there, you can plan out the rest of your stay."

Just as Aegir placed his hand against Alistair's back once more, nudging him up the stairs, a servant rushed to Daemyn with a purple and silver cane in hand. It was beautiful, its body twisting and swirling with ornate detailings of snowflakes from top to bottom; however, Alistair questioned why his friend might need such a thing. He wasn't limping and had no visible injuries. Knowing Daemyn, it was likely just an accessory, and it was quite lovely, but still seemed odd for someone so young.

Daemyn took his place on the opposite side of his father and flashed Alistair a brilliant smile. As Alistair returned it, the image of Daemyn's letter flashed in his mind, causing something in his chest to constrict. The letter was safely tucked away in his trousers' pocket. It was something best not put off, and he hoped they would have the chance to speak in private sooner rather than later. It was best to get things out in the open, to discover what was going on, and make things right if Alistair could.

"Now then, Alistair," Aegir said, pulling his attention away from Daemyn, "let's take you to your chamber."

"By any chance, is it the same one as last time?" Alistair asked, his mind a whirl of memories, not all of which had been pleasant. The room was nice enough, but it carried the weight of the past within its walls.

"Of course. A window view of the beach below the cliffs. One of our finest. Now go rest," Aegir patted Alistair on the shoulder as they disappeared through the entrance of castle black, the King smiling all the while, "I have a feeling it's going to be a long night."

39

ℱlistair

Awkward Stalling

Alistair and Daemyn wished Aegir farewell and continued toward the fifth floor in companionable silence. A pair of blackguards flanked them. Servants scurried about and on more than one occasion nearly collided with the pair of Princes, busily readying for the night's festivities.

As they neared the fifth floor, he couldn't help but stare at Daemyn's purple and silver cane gently tapping away against the marble floor. With a soft clearing of his throat, he asked, "Daemyn, what's with the cane?"

"Hmm? Oh, this!" Daemyn lifted it in the air before him, tracing the silver swirls about the shaft with his fingers. "Mother got it for me on my sixteenth nameday. Aaaaand, get a look at this," he stopped and spun to him. His thumb pressed against what Alistair had thought to simply be a part of the ornamentation, an amethyst gem nestled beneath the handle.

With a click, the swirling silver top popped up, and Daemyn slid a hand to a divide between the swirls. His fingers wrapped around the center bar, and a grin spread across his face. His arm jerked upward with a twirl, and Daemyn thrust it forward, revealing a shining silver blade.

He let out an astonished laugh. "It's a hidden rapier?"

"I know, right?" Daemyn beamed up at him, his voice wreathed in excitement. "I won so many of the fencing competitions last year, Mother said she wanted to get me a new blade. One that just *screams* me. Her words, not mine." He laughed giddily, pulling the sword and cane close to his chest.

"That's amazing, and congrats, but what's with all the snowflakes?"

"Oh, um," Daemyn slid the blade back into the cane, tracing his fingers now to the silver snowflakes dancing over the cane, his cheeks turning a shade of bright pink, "you remember the nickname Mother gave me, right?"

"Um, well, it's been a while." Alistair looked to the floor, placing a hand to his chin.

"Come on, don't make me say it." Daemyn pleaded.

Alistair shot him a playful smirk. "Oh, that's right! Her little snowflake."

"Ugh, PLEASE don't go there!" He demanded, eyes rolling and mouth pursed. It was faint, but Alistair could just barely spot the corner of Daemyn's lips twitching upward. He was fighting back a smile.

"Don't go where?" Alistair asked, leaning down and gently poking at Daemyn's cheek. "*Little* snowflake."

Daemyn immediately swatted his hand away with an elbow, a smirk betraying his mock outrage. "Get off, you raven's ass." He laughed, promptly rushing down the hall and to the right.

"No wait, come back! I'd hate to incur the wrath of *the* little snowflake." Alistair chuckled and gave chase.

He missed this, missed his friend, missed having someone he could just be himself with instead of worrying over his every word.

Daemyn skidded to a stop before a pair of mahogany doors and leaned an elbow against them, giving him a sly smile. "Tell me, do you *really* want to rest?"

Struggling to breathe through his laughter, he came to a stop before his young friend. "Not even a little."

Seemingly overjoyed by his answer, the young Prince hopped off the door and bowed with a flourish. He wasted no time grabbing the handles of the doors, pushing them open, and entering. It was Daemyn's bedchamber.

Before following, Alistair glanced over to his right, to the doors which, if he remembered correctly, led to the chamber where he would be staying. He wondered if he should check it over, but shook the thought away. Everything would be fine.

As he entered the chamber, the blackguards closed the doors behind them. Daemyn hung his coat and circlet on a coat rack by the doors while Alistair fiddled with the buckle of his shoulder cape. It caught in the fabric, pulling a string of thread with it. Alistair grunted with annoyance and struggled to free the buckle without tearing the garment, then suddenly Daemyn was there, sliding his hands out of the way.

"Here, let me." He chuckled.

"Wait, Daemyn,"

"It's alright, I don't mind." Daemyn smiled without looking up.

Alistair's heart sank as he remembered Daemyn's letter. He forced a gracious smile, but if anyone could see through it, it would be Daemyn.

With a triumphant Ha, Daemyn slid the cape from Alistair's shoulder and draped it over his arm. He then raised a hand and gave Alistair a look as if expecting something.

Alistair only blinked, confused. "What?"

"Have you worn it so many times you no longer notice it on your head?" Daemyn asked.

"My—Oh!" Alistair said as he slid the silver circlet off his head and handed it to Daemyn. "Right. It's a perfect fit, so aye, I actually did forget it was there."

Daemyn just shrugged, his expression was gentle and genuine, and turned to hang the cape and circlet on the rack by his own. Alistair took the opportunity to turn away, racking his brain for the right way to broach the subject of the letter. He wrung his hands raw. He needed a distraction, something to calm his nerves before bringing it up.

Looking about, the chamber was lit by what had to have been half the candles in the Kingdom. There were even candles on the crystal chandelier at the center of the chamber. The walls were lined with mahogany, every large panel covered in knotwork carvings of leviathans and creatures from the sea. As he scanned the walls, Alistair spotted several paintings he didn't remember being there when last he visited. They were bright with a gentleness in the brush strokes, colorful, and quite beautiful. Each was a portrait, some of men and some of women, centered on the canvas. Flowers, fish, birds, butterflies, and other assortments of things were seamlessly blended into the depictions. Droplets of paint purposely punctuated the subjects, forms falling into indistinct silhouettes of color against the canvas.

"Daemyn, these paintings are amazing," Alistair said in awe, his mouth agape as he inspected them one by one. The colors were akin to spring flowers, vibrant and natural. He'd never seen anything quite like it.

Alistair stopped before a painting still clipped to an easel. On it was the depiction of a familiar woman. She looked to be in a garden, roses of various hues in hand and surrounding her. Her bluish white skin was soft, accented by a few watery residual splatterings of a similar color. The woman's flaxen hair was twirled in large curls over a single shoulder, and white dots resembling snowflakes decorated the strands. The liberties with form and abstract color placement were present throughout the piece in a style that evoked a stirring of serenity and joy in Alistair's thoughts.

The woman had a striking resemblance to Daemyn's mother, Ayunli. She looked so real and yet surreal at the same time. Alistair unconsciously reached out a hand and was about to touch the canvas when Daemyn's breath hitched. He nearly leaped to catch Alistair's hand.

"I wouldn't! That is, I'd appreciate if you didn't. It's new and still drying."

Alistair jerked the hand back and stepped to a safe distance, seeing Daemyn's shoulders relax for the gesture. "Right. Sorry." He chuckled. "I heard there was a style of painting with watercolors. Many of the nobility of Hilliard were in a frenzy to get their hands on the new works, but I never got a chance to see one for myself, and I didn't know who the painter was." He then gave Daemyn a curious smirk, pointing at the painting. "Are you the cause of all this?"

His friend's cheeks heated to a bright red as he laughed with embarrassment. "Aye, I was NOT expecting it to explode the way it did. And neither did Mother."

"How did you get these colors?"

Daemyn sighed with puffed cheeks. "A *lot* of trial and error." He laughed as he stepped beside Alistair to look at the painting. "I was tired of all the dark, muted, and downright dreary paintings I was told to make. I needed a change. I wanted to make something that just seemed more,"

"You?" Alistair finished with a grin.

"Aye, I suppose. It took a while to discover this style when Albrecht left. Without him, we were just not quite ourselves, so I wanted to paint something to brighten our days. This is what I came up with. The first paintings I made were of him, and when I showed them to my parents, Mother was so giddy she wanted to show them off to all the famous painters."

Alistair's brows shot up. "Of course. And your father?"

Daemyn was quiet for a moment, his smile lessening just a bit. "He said he was proud of me, but I think it made him more sad. He rarely wanted to see my paintings after that."

Alistair was taken aback, not exactly surprised that the King would be upset at seeing Albrecht, but that he would have such a reaction in front of his own son. "Daemyn, I'm so sorry."

Daemyn shook his head, his smile more sad now. "Don't be. Father loves Albrecht more, I should've known better."

"Daemyn, your father doesn't—"

The young Prince grabbed Alistair's shoulder, catching him by surprise. "Alistair, it's fine. I know my place in this family. Albrecht is the heir. I just need to not be an embarrassment."

Alistair's heart shattered. Daemyn's words were all too familiar to his own, to what he had told Valhalla. It was crushing to think Daemyn felt the same as he had all these years.

"Anyway," Daemyn shrugged, "despite everything, can you believe I actually didn't get many takers in the beginning?"

It was clear Daemyn was trying to move away from the subject of his family, so Alistair obliged, at least for the time being. "Daemyn, modesty doesn't suit you."

Daemyn chortled. "No, really. The Svartr painters were complete snobs about the whole thing. They nearly had me believing the style would never take off." He took a deep breath, eyes drifting down to the floor as he rocked on the balls of his feet. "That was until Father called on the painters from Blár and Rjóðr."

And there was Alistair's counterargument. Aegir never would've gone to the trouble if he didn't care. Something on his face must've given away what he was thinking because Daemyn glanced up at him and shrugged.

"Anyway, they were captivated by my paintings. They even asked for a demonstration. Some merchants commissioned paintings in the new style to hang in their shops, selling tales of simply wanting to share it with the common people." Daemyn raised a perturbed brow. "Of course I fell for that. I realized too late their plan to just hike up the prices of my earlier works."

"Of course." Alistair rolled his eyes.

"Aye, but a letter to the royals of the respective cities put a stop to that. My paintings should be available to anyone of any income. I know it's a small gesture in the grand scheme of things, but if one of my paintings brings some happiness, they shouldn't have to choose between it and feeding their family. Other painters can do as they wish, and the nobility can pay out their asses for all I care, but a farmer or maid deserves a taste of the comforts we all take for granted." Daemyn winked at Alistair. "Just like you and your needlepoint work."

The two laughed, and Alistair's cheeks burned a little.

"Oh!" Daemyn continued. "But I did inspire a few of the artists from Grœnn to try creating new styles of their own. Our realm would be much better off if we stopped copying one another! At the very least, it would be more interesting." He smirked and slumped back, feigning a collapse which made Alistair laugh.

"What of Hvítr and Grár? Were their artists snobs as well?"

Daemyn blanched, looking as pale as a ghost, but cleared his throat. "Despite the invitation, Grár's artists never bothered to show. Hvítr's on the other hand found my style *nice*, but couldn't come to a consensus on whether their people would love it or hate it."

Alistair snorted. "Tell me you're joking? I think Princess Amarantha would love it."

"Oh, she did." Daemyn took a seat on the arms of one of his two lavender couches, a pleased expression on his face. "She took the first chance she got to visit and subsequently commissioned me to paint a portrait of her. Her other siblings, though, well, for better or worse, they wanted to see the gods in my style."

"No way! Did you?"

"Well, it was interesting painting my take on Tyr, but so far, no complaints." He shrugged.

"That's amazing, Daemyn." Alistair returned to the painting on the easel. "This is your mother, isn't it?"

"It is," Daemyn answered, his voice soft and taking on a dour note.

"Well, speaking of, where's Ayunli? I was surprised she wasn't with you two earlier. If she's here, I'd love to say hello." Alistair said, and to his surprise, Daemyn's demeanor shrank. His smile faded, and his bright blue eyes glossed over.

Daemyn looked away, twisting one of the silver rings on his index finger. It was a habit he had had ever since he was a child, something he would do whenever nervous or scared. "She-She's ill, Alistair. No one's allowed to see her, not even me, and . . . I'm really worried about her." His voice cracked as he spoke.

To say Alistair was stunned felt like an understatement. He couldn't believe Ayunli could've fallen so ill. If that were truly the case, why had Aegir not called on Hilliard's healers? What could've befallen her that she would need to be hidden away from even her family? A chill set in his gut.

"It's not the Fúna Plague again, is it?" Alistair asked, his eyes widening.

The thought of its return nearly sapped the strength from his legs. In its time, the Fúna Plague spread like wildfire. Black bruises were the first sign, as it wreaked havoc on one's insides. Fever, chills, blindness, and a bloody cough drained the body of strength. Necrosis would spread, and by the time the pain set in, organ failure was soon to follow. The sickness popped up every other century, brought on by swarms of rats fleeing the mines below Svartr. When it struck, it washed across the city, and when that happened, you survived or you didn't.

Daemyn shook his head. "No. No, it's not that. My late grandfather took measures to ensure that dreaded disease would never return. Since the rats were the issue, satchels of mint were spread throughout the mines as a deterrent. They really hate the stuff. So it's not that. From what Father told me, it-it's something else entirely, though what that could be, he hasn't said."

The frustration in his friend's voice was palpable. Alistair stood before Daemyn and placed a hand on his shoulder. The young prince wiped a hand across his cheek, likely trying to put on a brave face, and as Daemyn brought his gaze to meet Alistair's, the look on his face shot a pang of sorrow through his heart.

"Hey," Alistair started, not really sure what he could possibly say to reassure his friend, "no matter what this is, I'm sure Ayunli can beat it. She's always been strong. And, if her symptoms get worse, Grœnn is only a week and a half's ride from here. I'm sure Queen Adsila would be more than willing to send one of her healers to help your mother. Herbal medicines and ointments are their specialties after all. I'm sure they can solve it no problem. I could also send for one of our healers to assist. It's a long journey by horse, but a raven could have them working on a solution in only a few days."

Daemyn was quiet for a bit, his lips quivering to hold back sobs, but eventually he swallowed and let out a tired sigh. "Aye. Aye, you're right. I-I just miss her, is all. It's been several weeks now since Father placed her in isolation. I miss hearing her voice." He laughed weakly, but Alistair could see he was just trying to hide his real feelings. Alistair had all too much practice doing the same.

"I can imagine. Ayunli has the most amazing singing voice. I wouldn't be surprised if she were blessed by Bragi herself." Alistair said as he glanced past Daemyn to the other side of the bedchamber. There, he spotted a few more paintings hanging on the walls and several stacked on the ground against it.

Some were of Ayunli in her gardens and at the beach. Parasol and without. Holding a flower and a bundle. She was never surrounded by the same set of colors. Each was as beautiful as the last. He then noticed one major change to the room.

"Huh, that's new. What happened to the mahogany piano?" Alistair asked, straightening and walking over to an instrument which seemed in every way more beautiful than the one he remembered. The new piano was covered in intricate details of ornate woodwork. It was a great ebony beauty nestled between Daemyn's bed and second couch.

Daemyn sniffed as he looked it over, remaining where he stood. "Oh, that thing was so old, I was having trouble keeping it in tune. It was originally my great-great-grandmother's." He shrugged. "Father caught me waist deep in the thing, trying to fix it. So, one day while I was out visiting an orphanage in Mother's stead . . . he got me a new one. Donated the old one to a piano maker who said he thought he might be able to restore it. I think he just wanted it for parts."

"And here you thought your father was playing favoritism." Alistair challenged, but Daemyn only pursed his lips.

"Just because Father is nice every now and then doesn't make what I said any less true."

Alistair could only sigh at that. Seeing that further arguing the point would be fruitless, he conceded for the time being. "Anyway, it's too bad about the piano. It was a nice color." As he pulled back the lid to reveal the keys, their pristine white gleamed in the light. "I suppose this one is just as nice." Alistair then shot Daemyn a playful smirk. "Your father's taste will never change."

He placed his hands gently on the keys, spreading his fingers in imitation of a professional. Taking a deep breath, he pressed down firmly, and the instrument bellowed in response, the tune long and wild. In truth, he had never picked up the skill and so could only achieve a melody akin to cannon fire. It was nothing short of unpleasant.

Daemyn burst out laughing. "What was that?"

"I've always been envious of your skill with the piano." Alistair straightened, grinning at the instrument and then back at Daemyn. "A cat running across the keys has more talent than I. My fingers always stumble over each other. Lucky you inherited your mother's melodious touch." He laughed and wiggled his fingers at Daemyn, who doubled over in a fit.

Task accomplished, Alistair thought, but as he went to close the lid over the keys, the image of Daemyn's letter flickered in his mind, feeling now like an unbearable weight in his trousers' pocket. "Dammit." He groaned, sliding a hand within and grabbing the letter.

"What's wrong?" Daemyn asked between heavy breaths, swiping at his eyes with the base of his palms.

"Daemyn, I think we should talk about this." Alistair turned to face his friend and raised the letter for him to see. Daemyn's body went rigid, as if he had just been struck by a bolt of lightning. His expression slid into something resembling immense distress with a touch of fear.

"You . . . You actually got it." Daemyn didn't form it as a question, but his reaction perplexed Alistair.

"Well, aye. It was given to me just as I was getting into the ca—"

Daemyn sprang into action, vaulting over the couch between them and plucking the letter right out of Alistair's hand. He then immediately turned his back to Alistair. "Dammit, you were never supposed to see it!"

He instantly crumpled the letter into a ball and paced in a fit of frustration. Alistair had expected this conversation to bring out strong emotions, but this reaction was far worse than anticipated. He wanted to tell Daemyn that it was alright, to hug him and tell him that while he didn't share the same feeling, it wouldn't change anything about their friendship. Daemyn then stopped and dropped his face into his fisted hands.

A lump formed and twisted in Alistair's gut. "I-I wasn't?"

"No!" Daemyn heavily sighed. "No, you weren't. I was doing one of those," his hand flew in the direction of his desk at the corner of his bedchamber, but he didn't continue. Instead, he walked over to his fireplace and chucked the letter into the blaze, quiet as he watched it burn.

After several long moments, Daemyn gave out another heavy sigh. "One of those . . . write a letter to yourself and then put it away forever, kind of things. The one time I forgot to put it away, one of the servants found it lying on my desk, saw your name on the letter, and took the initiative to send it. If she had just asked first," He buried his face in his hands again.

Alistair felt like he had just been kicked by a horse. How could he have thought Daemyn would choose now, right after Lorna's death of all times, to bring this up? He felt like a fool. But now the secret was out and needed to be addressed.

Raising a hand and rubbing his neck, he cleared his throat. "I see. Umm. Daemyn, I-I'm so sorry."

To his surprise, Daemyn let out a soft chuckle. "Why are you sorry?" He asked, finally turning to look at Alistair with a slight shrug.

"I—Well, were you ever going to tell me?"

"That depends, were you all of a sudden going to be interested in men?"

"Uh, no." Alistair lowered his head apologetically.

"And there's your answer. AGH!" Daemyn threw his hands in the air with a heavy groan.

Alistair watched as Daemyn trudged over to his balcony, pushing the doors open with a heavy thud, and slumped against the iron railing overlooking the crashing ocean waves below. The dark sky thundered above.

40

Alistair

DON'T SHOULDER the REALM ALONE

Alistair's stomach was heavy as he approached his friend on the balcony, stopping within the doorway. He wrung his hands as anxiety spiked his adrenaline. His heart thumped, again and again, like the quickening beat of a drum. What could he possibly say to make things alright between them?

For years, he had no clue how Daemyn felt toward him. He had been too oblivious to ever notice, though in hindsight, it should've been obvious. As children, Daemyn was always clinging to him, holding his hand as they explored the city, and sitting beside him when the opportunity presented itself, but Alistair assumed it was just because of how close they were. Albrecht always teased his little brother. It was never as bad as how Lorna had treated him, not nearly so, but even light-hearted teasing can bring about a rift. Their interests simply never overlapped. Where Albrecht took after his father, Daemyn took after his mother. Albrecht was the firstborn, the heir, and he was strong. That alone meant they had never been on equal standing, even though Albrecht had never been the kind of person to hold such things over his brother. With Alistair, however, there had not been such barriers. They were on even footing.

He sighed, regret spreading over him like waves crashing against the coast. He was stupid and blind for far too long. Daemyn's arms were crossed over the iron railing, the chilled salty sea air sending his flaxen hair flittering wildly about.

Daemyn cleared his throat. "You know, this is about as close as I'll ever be to the sea."

"What do you mean?" Alistair asked, finding his courage and stepping beside his friend. His hands found the railing, and the cold bite of the metal sank into his palms.

"Since Albrecht left, I took it upon myself to see that his tasks didn't go unfulfilled, and let me tell you, he has . . . a *lot* to do, more than I had realized." His shoulders sagged, and he stared out toward the horizon. "Father got so frustrated with me for doing so much that Mother felt she needed to step in to help. Then she got sick, and someone needed to see to her tasks, so I took that on too. I saw to many meetings with various people, local and not, spent so much time at the orphanages around Svartr that I know most of the children by name, ensured trade continued without issue, tended to the servants of the castle, placated the nobles so their squabbling wouldn't spill into the streets, anything and everything that came about. It . . . was too much."

Daemyn's gaze fell to the beach below, and his arms wrapped around himself, still leaning over the railing. "Father noticed the state I'd allowed myself to fall into this morning and has barred me from taking part in his Council meetings for a while. I just, I didn't want your or Albrecht's return to be hampered by worries of things that needed doing. Unfortunately, some things have fallen through the cracks . . . and they are not trivial matters. There's a string of murders. I've been trying to solve them for the past three months to no avail. Father got wind of them. You should've seen his face, Alistair, he looked so disappointed in me."

"Daemyn," Alistair took his friend's shoulder, hoping he would turn to him, but he didn't, "I'm sure your father wasn't disappointed. He was likely worried about you. You've always had a bad habit of taking on the world and never asking for help." He tilted his head with a playful smirk. "Remember when you were eight winters young? Aegir placed you in charge of the castle's stable because you *demanded* to be given some responsibility so you could help. You gave those poor horses the wrong feed, and even the sailors anchored a league out could smell it."

Daemyn jolted, his cheeks burning red with embarrassment. "Is that your idea of consoling me?"

"Then there was the time you begged Ayunli to put you in charge of preparation for the Thorrablot festival when you were eleven winters—"

"ALRIGHT I GET IT!" Daemyn lightly shoved Alistair and dropped his face into his hands. "You're terrible at this!"

Alistair softly chuckled. "The point is, you shouldn't have taken on so much without asking for help. You may be a Prince, but that doesn't mean you can do everything on your own."

A smile slowly broke across Daemyn's face. He dropped his hands and let them dangle at his sides. "You mean like you do with your sister's duties?"

"Actually, my Aunt Embla helped me with that." Alistair felt a pang of melancholy at the thought of Lorna, and it must've shown on his face because Daemyn's smile waned.

Daemyn ran a hand across his forehead. He spared a guilty glance at Alistair before returning to watching the waves. "I'm sorry, here you've come from a funeral and I've made everything about me."

"Your mother is sick with something no one here has ever heard of, I accidentally forced you into confessing your feelings, the people are scared and hiding in their homes for gods know why, and a storm hangs above your doorstep." Alistair waved at the thundering clouds while lightning danced across the sky, as if to acknowledge the statement. "I'm surprised you were able to see me at all."

Daemyn stiffened, and his eyes shot to Alistair. His face went pale, and his demeanor took on a nervousness Alistair had never seen in him before. His bright blue eyes trembled, and as he spoke, Alistair thought he heard fear. "You noticed too?"

A knock at the chamber doors sounded, making Daemyn nearly jump. Alistair narrowed his eyes questioningly, but as Daemyn looked up and his mouth opened to speak, he clamped it shut. The Svartr Prince then rushed back inside.

"Your Highness, are you in? I knocked on his Grace's door, but there was no answer." A feminine voice sounded from outside the doors. It was most likely a servant of the castle, Alistair thought, though there was something strangely familiar there.

"Oh damn, one moment." Daemyn hurried across to the doors as Alistair walked back inside, carefully watching his friend.

There was something more going on than Daemyn had let on, but if that was the case, why was the young Prince keeping quiet about it? For now, Alistair decided he would be patient. Either Daemyn would come clean on his own, or Alistair would force the matter should the need arise. He sat himself down on one of the couches with a clear sight of the chamber's doorway.

Daemyn went on to open the doors, and there stood a servant maiden. She was taller than him and held a silver tray on which was an assortment of food. "I'm sorry to bother you, Your Highness, the Head Chef prepared some food for you and His Grace. He thought you both might be hungry." She said with a kindness twinkling in her eyes.

"Oh, I'm hungry." Daemyn looked over his shoulder. "What about you?"

"I could eat. Thank you." Alistair answered with a bow, noticing he was wringing his hands. He had been doing that a lot lately. It was a habit which he knew would need breaking.

Daemyn smiled at the servant maid and stood to one side, waving her in. She curtsied, then entered. On her tray, there were several thickly sliced portions of bread, a bowl of mashed crab meat and chives, and a side of honey lemon tea so aromatic that Alistair knew what it was without needing to ask. The servant maiden set the tray down on the small table between the two lavender couches. She busied herself with removing two small plates, each with an upside-down porcelain cup, and positioned them one in front of Alistair and the other across from him, where Daemyn was taking his seat. She then took the matching teapot in hand and held it out to Alistair. He flipped his cup upright and watched as the wonderfully scented amber liquid poured in.

"Will that be all, your Highness?" The servant asked.

"No, I'm alright, thank you," Daemyn answered.

She then turned to Alistair, holding the teapot delicately in her hands. "Your Grace?"

He found himself staring at the young woman's features. Something there felt terribly familiar, but he couldn't quite place it. Her raven black hair was held back by a white band. Her cheeks were round, and a slight bump gave character to the bridge of her nose. Her skin was the color of porcelain, and her eyes were a rich brown.

There was a sudden hard poke against his forehead, and he withdrew, rubbing the spot with a hand. "OW!" Alistair yelped. Daemyn was leaning over the table and looking at him with an irked grin.

"I get it, she's pretty, but try *not* to openly stare at her, it's impolite."

Alistair's lips pursed, and he shot his young friend a glare which softened as he saw the disappointment on Daemyn's face. "That's not why I was . . ." He stopped, taking a moment to compose himself, then started again. "Shit. I was staring, wasn't I?" He met her eyes and found she hadn't even flinched, still patiently waiting with the teapot held outstretched, and so he raised his cup. "I'm so sorry. You just reminded me of someone. For a moment, I thought you *were* her, but I must've been mistaken."

She giggled sweetly and gave him a subtle shrug. Even the trill of her laugh was familiar. "That's quite fine, Your Grace. Believe it or not, I get that a lot. I'm used to it." She answered, filling his cup. As she placed the teapot on the small table, a loud boom sounded, followed by a bright flash which briefly brightened the room.

Alistair spun in his seat to look out the balcony. The winds whistled as a powerful gust sent the curtains wildly flapping about and snuffed out many of the candles about the room. Even the flames in the fireplace died under the gale.

"Oh my!" The servant maiden exclaimed as she rushed toward the rattling balcony doors.

Just as she stepped outside, the winds increased and knocked her off balance. To her credit, she didn't fall, instead dipping low and spearing her arms forward, grabbing hold of the handles. She struggled for only a moment before wresting control of the doors, then pulled them closed, flipping the lock with a huff. Wiping a few droplets of sweat or rain from her forehead, she proceeded to relight the fireplace and followed up with the candles.

Alistair was unsettled at just how fast the darkness had descended. "By the gods," he whispered, "who pissed off Thor?"

"I think you meant the god Aegir."

Alistair glanced back at Daemyn, thinking his comment to be a joke, but his friend's eyes trembled with a fear born of something more tangible than mere superstition. Daemyn's brows furrowed as he stared into the raging sky. The skies brightened with a flicker of lightning, and Alisatir's lips parted to ask if he was alright.

"A storm could just as easily be that. A storm." The maiden said, lifting a pole to the crystal chandelier above, concentrating on lighting the candles within. "If this storm was of Aegir's doing, it would've started on the waters, but the waves are as gentle as ever. Phew! Done." She lowered the pole and snuffed out the small fire at the tip, then placed it back with the tools beside the fireplace. "I still can't believe the late King named your father after the God of the Raging Seas."

Daemyn let out a soft chortle. "Aye, Father said it was in the hope that the god might bless his way on the open waters. It must've worked, though, given his boasts about always sailing through calm seas." He grabbed his chin, glancing away for a brief moment before sliding his eyes to Alistair with a wink, making him snort.

"Anyway," Daemyn started as he returned to his seat on the couch, "thank you, Emera. Do you mind waiting here until we're done with the food?"

The servant, Emera, curtsied. "Of course, your Highness." She then made her way to an empty spot by a wall and stood in waiting, grasping her hands over her lap.

"Now, as much as I'm just *delighted* by the setting, last I checked, you weren't overly fond of the dark." Daemyn focused his gaze on Alistair. "You alright?"

Alistair flashed him a small smile. "I've actually gotten much better about it since Father's death." He poked at the food on the table. "I don't get scared like I used to, but the darkness is still far from something I would consider a friend, even though I no longer hold any animosity toward it." He finished with a laugh.

Alistair's stomach grumbled impatiently. He needed to eat. Reaching out, he picked up a thick slice of bread and the knife-like spreader beside it. He stabbed the spreader into the crab meat and plopped a large helping onto the bread. Alistair could feel the smile spreading across his face, and his mouth began to water.

"Alistair?" Daemyn called.

"Hmm?" Alistair answered, unable to peel his eyes away from the food as he folded the bread in half to keep the crab in place.

"Be honest with me, how are you fairing with your sister's death?"

41

Alistair

Tell Me How You Really Feel

I t was the question Alistair had been dreading since he first set foot in Svartr. He wasn't sure who would be the one to ask it or when it would be broached, but the subject of Lorna's death was sure to come up eventually. The words, hidden away in her journal, brought a sour taste to his mouth that no amount of bread, or meat, or tea, would wash away. There, he learned the true depths of her hatred for him.

Lorna had started the War of Lions. Everything had been orchestrated as a means to be rid of him. Then, when things didn't go as intended, she wrote in exquisite detail of her annoyance with the now late Princes of Eenheide of whom was to capture and swiftly execute Alistair. Reading over her words brought on a painful clarity which he had fought long and hard to deny. Alistair had held on to the notion that perhaps one day their relationship could've been salvaged if only she had lived. Her words, written by her own hands, destroyed that small flicker of hope completely. But somehow that hadn't been the worst of it. The content near the tail end of her journal somehow cut deeper.

Feeling a sneer coming on, he stabbed the spreader into the crab meat and took a large bite of the food before him, stuffing his mouth so full that no expression would be able to shine through. He chewed with malicious intent, as if punishing the meal might quell the bile rising in his throat. As he swallowed, he reached for his tea and swirled the amber liquid, allowing the honey and lemon aroma to fill his nostrils.

"Tell me, Daemyn," Alistair started, taking a long sip of his tea, "how would you feel if you discovered your brother was planning to kill your father, take the throne, and then blame you for his murder?" He let the silence stretch between them for several long moments. As he set the fragile cup back down on its saucer with a loud chink, he let out a deep sigh and added, "She was going to sell me off to slavers and call it a kindness, exile instead of execution."

Alistair's brows furrowed. A deep scowl darkened his face, and he wanted so badly to lash out, to punch the table, and to scream, but who would that do any good for? Would it make him feel better, lessening the burden of what he now knew? No. He would feel the same, only gaining a sore hand in the process, not to mention likely scaring the servant maid and further troubling Daemyn, who had always been burdened with empathy. So Alistair sat there and waited for someone else to speak.

Eventually, Daemyn made the first move. He reached out, not to Alistair, but to the food on the table, gathering a portion of the snack together. The young prince raised a piece of bread lightly covered in a layer of crab to his lips. Before taking a bite, he paused, and for the first time since Alistair had posed the question, met his eyes.

"Honestly, I would be quite stunned. Not because of the plan, though, because it would be completely out of character. Albrecht isn't that cruel and is much more imaginative." Daemyn's lips slid into an apologetic smile.

Alistair found himself surprisingly lightened by the comment and chuckled softly. He could always rely on his friends to lift his mood, even if only a little.

Daemyn playfully shrugged, taking a bite and washing it down with a sip of his tea. "Lorna, on the other hand . . . that sounds like an average after-brunch activity, something to fill the time between skinning cats and poisoning orphans."

The statement brought on a terrible pang in Alistair's chest. Had he really been the only one blindsided by Lorna's cruelty?

His entire body trembled, not from sadness but anger. Anger for all the time he spent trying to push through the horrible things she said and did to him, to show her kindness and find ways to help her as if he had been the one who somehow wronged her, only to have her spit in his face. Here, he had done everything he could conceive of to keep his sister happy, to assist her so that she might not feel so overwhelmed in her duties. It had always been for not, and yet he never allowed himself to see it.

His half-eaten food trembled in his hand, dangerously close to becoming a victim of his rising rage. Just as he started to lift his arm to throw it across the room, he stuffed it in his mouth. At least that way, he might not say something he would come to regret. Alistair's cheeks were puffy as he tried to chew. He knew he must've looked boorish, but it wasn't something Daemyn would hold against him, and he could always apologize to the servant maid when his temper wasn't running quite so hot. Swallowing, he washed down the remaining food in his mouth with hot tea, the flavors mixing surprisingly well.

A stretch of silence followed between the two, the sounds of thunder and the crackling of fire in the hearth giving the room an eerie ambiance. Alistair had the urge to feel for his father's ring hanging against his chest, but decided against it. Instead, he planted his elbows on his knees and let his hands hang limply, sighing with a heaviness in his heart.

"Then I suppose I was just a pathetic fool who longed for the return of who she was so long ago." He said as he reached for the teapot and poured himself another cup.

Daemyn, with his elbows on his thighs and a snack in hand, had a worried look in his eyes. His cheek rested against his free hand, and when he spoke, his tone was soft and quizzical. "You mean when she was still five springs young and very impressionable?"

Alistair's brows twitched. He slammed the pot on the table and found it difficult to look his friend in the eyes. He wasn't angry with Daemyn; far from it. He was thankful, or knew he would be sometime in the future when the wound wasn't quite so raw, that he had someone he could be honest with and would be honest in return. He needed the help to confront the reality of who Lorna was.

She had been far too young when their father died. She didn't understand death and didn't know how to grieve as he and their mother had. In that state, it likely only took a few clever words at the opportune moment to sway her, to turn Lorna against her family. Odin knows there were plenty of kind-faced snakes amongst the nobility who would've seen her for the opportunity she must've seemed at the time. The High Queen shut herself away. Alistair was shipped off to Svartr. And Lorna, the rightful heir, was shipped off to Rjóðr. It must've seemed easy.

His chest rose, a sudden deep breath to suffocate the rageful roar building within. He choked it back and reached for another slice of bread, retrieving the spreader still in the crab meat.

"Alistair," Daemyn spoke up, "you're probably going to be upset with me for what I'm about to say, but it needs to be said all the same. Your sister was never the same after your father's death. I don't know how or why, but something broke in her, and what came after was a reflection, similar in appearance but deeply wrong. Attempting to let you die in the Lions War should've been your first clue."

The words sparked something in Alistair's memory. Ing had said something similar. His jaw muscles tightened as he sat in silence, eating. Daemyn's words were painfully true. He should've realized it then, but he didn't. Entertaining the possibility that Lorna was too far gone was more painful than anything she could've subjected him to. Even if he had managed to see it, what then? Would he have just allowed her to continue down the path she'd chosen? Were he strong enough, could he have done something? Had he acknowledged what was happening, faced her head-on, would it have made a difference?

Shoveling the last of the food into his mouth, Alistar wiped the buttery residue from his lips with a thumb. Overwhelmed by the direction his mind was headed, he found that at some point he'd clasped his hands and dropped his forehead to rest against his knuckles.

"You're right." Alistair raised his gaze to find Daemyn looking back at him with surprise. "I should've acknowledged it during the War of Lions, and if not then, when she and her friends gifted me the horrid keepsake on my back."

The storm of resentment and sorrow churned in his chest. Holding it back seemed to only feed the emotions he'd denied all this time. He still blamed himself, now for different reasons, but finally was ready to acknowledge the truth. There was no denying that he had played a part in allowing her transformation. It was ultimately her choices which guided her actions, and so she bore most of the blame; yet, his blind eye was his sin to own. He wept openly and allowed the dam within to crumble. His face felt hot, and every fiber of his being tensed with white hot fury.

"I was a stupid shit, allowing her to skulk about the halls of our very castle, whispering of treachery so thinly veiled she might as well have been flaunting it openly. A larger Queendom. The removal of one of the houses. Taking the gods' forsaken throne! I could've done something, but I didn't. Perhaps that's why—"

Alistair's breath hitched in his tight throat as he stared at Daemyn through blurry eyes. His pulse pounded between his ears and his hands shook. He was ready to face another terrible truth, one that had been teasing the recesses of his mind, the reason for Lorna's death.

"Alistair?" Daemyn called quietly.

Alistair released a trembling breath as he looked at the palms of his hands. His mind raced as he struggled to find the strength to continue. Saying openly what he'd felt in his heart for a long while now, putting the guilt into words said aloud made it somehow more real and thus, all the more painful to bear.

At that moment, something his aunt had once said floated through his thoughts. What needed to be said didn't always need to be said. It was sage advice at the time. In the politicking of nobility, sometimes it was better to remain quiet, to see how things played out, before making one's move. It also applied well to relationships. Just because you needed to say something to cleanse your conscience didn't mean it was wise for what needed to be said to be heard. He nearly bit his tongue at the remembrance, but as he considered the circumstance, if he kept the emotion to himself, it would fester as a wound. Of all the people he could confide in, Daemyn was the one person who could hear his confession without judging him or thinking less of him, and wouldn't use this information against him or his family.

It was now or never.

"The night she died," he started with a whisper, "Lorna cornered me in the White Garden, I was her guard. She stopped and said it was time to really speak aloud, in no uncertain terms, her *feelings* toward me." His jaw tightened, and he squeezed his hands into fists, watching as his golden knuckles turned white. "She spoke of how our mother didn't love me, only pitied me for being a High Prince within a society that preferred me on my knees rather than standing beside *them*. Told me I'm useless, worthless, even as a cock, and that she hated me for hiding the monster that I truly am. She said she was looking forward to the day I met the same fate . . . as our father. Said I deserved it."

Alistair heard Daemyn gasp, but if he dared meet his friend's gaze at that moment, he was afraid of what he might find there. Afraid that he might not be able to continue. Might break down completely or worse, see a glimmer of agreement in Daemyn's eyes, even though intellectually he knew better. More than likely, he would find pity there, which was equally unappealing. What's worse, the anger that had arisen within him was now falling away, replaced by an anguish which lodged in his throat.

"Lorna had said many terrible things about me in the past, and much of it to my face, but that night . . . I hit my limit. I was done. After she dismissed me, claiming she would be meeting one of her friends and didn't need me stinking up the place, I left. I left her there, Daemyn. Alone. Not once looking back." Alistair mustered his courage and looked his friend in the eyes. Whatever he was going to find there, so be it. "I left her there to die!"

"No. There's no way you could've known that at the time. You aren't to blame." Daemyn said, his words laced with concern and opposition.

"Yes, I do, because when I was barely even halfway down the hall she called out to me."

Daemyn straightened, a look of shock plain on his face. It only lasted a single heartbeat before he busied himself with adjusting the food on the tray, his eyes glancing over the table's surface as if mulling over the new information.

"I didn't even glance back. I was so angry that I overlooked the difference in the tone of her voice. I just shook my head and kept walking. Went straight to my chamber, took a couple of sleeping pills, and went to bed. Even then, I laid there for a while as rage and concern haunted me. I imagined what it was she wanted to say. Was she not done berating me? Was something wrong? I didn't know, and honestly, didn't care. It wasn't until morning that I realized it was fear in her voice, and when I asked of her, I was told she didn't want to see me, but now I know that was a lie." His voice cracked as his eyes fell to the floor, lips trembling and tears unending. "She died because I turned my back on her, Daemyn."

The two sat in quiet for a long while. Alistair glanced up from time to time, wanting his friend to say something, anything, but every time Daemyn's eyes were locked on the far end of the table, and he didn't know if his friend was lost in thought or disgusted with him and simply waiting for him to leave. The idea hurt, and he didn't want to believe it had come to that, so he waited.

Eventually, Daemyn raised a hand to his face and dragged it down to his chin as his eyes moved to the opposite end of the table. What in the nine realms could he be thinking? The possibilities were driving Alistair mad, but he dared not be the first to speak.

"No." Daemyn suddenly said with a shake of his head. "No! Ravenshit. Horseshit. Sharkshit! Whatever, all you spouted was shit, Alistair!"

Stunned, Alistair could only manage a word. "What?"

"You mean to tell me that you've been carrying the guilt of your sister's death all this time, *knowing* full well that her actions and her words were what got her killed? You mean to tell me that no one has made that clear to you. You couldn't have saved her. No action you could've taken would've saved her, Alistair."

Alistair's breath grew heavy. Daemyn spoke with absolute conviction and sincerity, and the quietness with which he spoke Alistair's name unbalanced him. "I could've." He whispered feebly.

"No, Alistair, you couldn't." Daemyn smiled matter-of-factly, and Alistair felt all of his arguments slip away like grains of sand between his fingers.

He could've saved Lorna. He was sure of it. Alisatir was close by. He should've run back. He could've.

"Even if you ran back to her," Daemyn continued, his voice gentle, "had you held the wound closed and shouted for help or carried her as fast as you could've to the Healing Wing, which last I checked, the White Garden was on the *other* side of the castle, either way Lorna would've bled out regardless. She still would've died, in your arms no less, and you would still be sitting across from me, blaming yourself for not doing enough, or not having the foresight to see it coming. Even if you hadn't walked away from her, she chose to belittle you, to distract you, and in that state, you couldn't have seen the attack coming in time to stop it. You might've caught them after the dagger struck, but the result would've been the same."

A shiver ran through Alistair's body. The sureness of Daemyn's expression shook him to his bones. Was this the same young man he hadn't seen in over three years?

Slowly, his friend's eyes became glossy, and soon both of them were crying when Daemyn continued. "You've done everything in your power to be supportive. Not only for Lorna's sake, but for your family. You've shed literal blood, sweat, and tears, and that *bitch* was *never* going to acknowledge that. Never. She resented you for being what she should've been; for being good."

Alistair jolted, stunned. Daemyn seemed to notice and immediately looked away. The hint of a thought crossed Alistair's mind. "You knew of her paramours, didn't you?" He asked softly.

"Oh please, Alistair, how could I not?" Daemyn answered with a roll of his eyes as he relaxed into the couch, arms splayed across the back. "It's not like her *friends* kept it hidden from me. Besides, if she wasn't going to keep true to our parents' engagement, it meant I didn't have to either." He let the silence linger between them for several seconds, then cleared his throat, his eyes on the ground and brows furrowed. "Mother found out. She found out how angry I was and how I wanted *nothing* to do with Lorna."

Daemyn's eyes focused and met Alistair's. A flicker of something shone in Daemyn's eyes, but just as quickly as it had come, it vanished along with whatever it was he was about to say. Daemyn shook his head and continued.

"Anyway, she was going to help me convince Father to abolish the engagement."

"You were really going to abolish it?" Alistair exclaimed, genuinely surprised, but in Daemyn's face, he saw conviction and had his answer, not that the marriage mattered now.

"Aye." He answered with such rigidity that for the first time, Daemyn sounded like his father. He then softened into his usual self and smirked. "What, did you think Lorna might stop her wickedness once we were married?"

Alistair sighed defeatedly, his body slouching, and then he too fell back against his couch. Frustration rose within his chest, but without heat. He pressed his palms into his face and snuffed out the exhaustion setting in. "You're right. You're right!" He let his hands fall to the couch and stared up at the ceiling. A surprising numbness came over him like a blanket. "You're right, I'm sorry. I shouldn't have been surprised."

Daemyn chuckled. "I sometimes worry you have too much heart for this life."

Alistair's body shuddered again. Ing had said much the same. Perhaps it was true, he thought, but it did little to comfort him.

His head lolled to the side, and his gaze landed on the servant maiden. In the heat of the moment, he had forgotten she was even there. She fidgeted uncomfortably under his gaze. Emera glanced at him, her expression soft and her eyes surprisingly filled with concern. Was she worried for herself, having been present for such an open conversation? Nobility generally didn't disclose such things in front of others lest the information be used against them, and it was common for those who overheard such conversations to go missing. He would have to apologize to her for putting her in such a situation. But there didn't seem to be fear in her concern. She was worried for him, for them both, he and Daemyn. Again, there was a familiarity there he couldn't place. As soon as she noticed Alistair staring, she startled and tilted her gaze away.

Finally removing his eyes from Emera, he looked back to the ceiling again and brushed his fingers through his dark brown hair. "And here I was worried about you."

"Well, I suppose we are both broken Princes. We'll just have to survive this shit place we call Midgard together." The honesty in the statement brought a soft laugh from them both.

Alistair then glanced at his friend, who was turning his attention to his prepared snack. Daemyn then reached for another slice of bread and placed it on top of the crab meat. Confused, he asked, "What are you doing?"

"What do you mean, what am I doing? I'm finally going to eat. Despite all this misery, my stomach is growling." Daemyn's lips slid into a wide grin, coaxing a curious raised brow from Alistair.

Taking the two pieces of bread in hand, Daemyn gently squeezed them together, causing the crab meat to squish and expand at the edges. He then raised it before Alistair, holding it as if it were a grand heirloom or prized possession.

"And here you have it, your Grace. I present to you a sandwich."

"A what?" Alistair chuckled as he looked at it both with curiosity and confusion. Emera snorted a laugh but quickly hid behind a hand and turned away, finding a sudden interest in the painting beside her.

"A sandwich," Daemyn answered with a showy grin. "Several weeks ago, I was making my monthly rounds through Sailors Reef when I spotted some folks playing cross and pile in the corner of one of the squares, and they introduced me to this remarkable yet simple concept." He held the sandwich between his fingers and thumb. "Makes it easier to eat while on the go."

Alistair just burst out laughing. "You've got to be joking."

"No, seriously, it's great. It's much easier with a solid filling, like chicken or pork. I got a little carried away and tested it with all sorts of things. Honey and mashed potatoes make a huge mess." Daemyn chuckled, holding the food with both hands now.

"Don't forget when you tried it with soup." Emera chimed in.

"We don't talk about that!" Daemyn blushed.

Alistair raised a brow at him. "Really?"

"Aye, now shut it and watch how amazing this is." Daemyn took a large bite. His eyes rolled up in satisfaction as he pulled away with a moan of delight. "By Njörd's catch, that's good crab." He mumbled as he chewed.

Swallowing, Daemyn turned the sandwich in inspection and as he reached the back, he nearly jumped up out of his seat in triumph. "Aye! I've finally mastered the consistency." He celebrated with another bite, his expression gleeful and ravenous. Alistair doubled over in a fit of laughter at the display.

His friend only shook his head, seemingly disinterested in how silly Alistair found this all to be. "I don't know why you're laughing, I struck real gold here!"

A series of quick knocks rapped against the door. "Your Highness," a masculine voice sounded, likely belonging to another of the castle's servants, "I bring news of Prince Albrecht!"

Emera, without hesitation, rushed to the doors. Daemyn busied himself drinking his tea to wash down the mouthful. As the door opened, a man dressed in the attire of a Svartr Gentleman of the Bedchamber entered, taking several wide strides, then bowed low to each of them.

"Prince Daemyn, Prince Albrecht was just seen riding into town near Sailors Reef. Because of his Highness' return, his Majesty wishes you to join him in welcoming Prince Albrecht in the throne room." The Gentleman's words came fast through panted breath.

"Of course!" Daemyn laughed, but seemed unusually nervous as he stood. The Gentleman grabbed his circlet and coat off the coat rack, about to place them on Daemyn as the young Prince glanced at Emera. "Please tell the chef that the food was delicious as always for me."

She curtsied low. "The chef will be delighted to hear your compliment, Your Highness."

"Alright,"

"Wait." Alistair interrupted, causing everyone to stop and look at him. He wasn't exactly sure why he had said it, and now that he had, he wasn't sure what to say.

The entire conversation played backwards in his mind and came to a rest on his friend's confession, on the letter. Daemyn's feelings for him and his response felt insufficient, and he didn't want to leave him with the wrong impression. He wanted to make sure they understood one another and that their friendship would remain as strong, if not stronger, than it had ever been. There was every chance that Daemyn had been battling those emotions for a long time and was likely still struggling with them. The last thing he wanted to do was to make his friend uncomfortable, but as Alistair opened his mouth, he couldn't find the words. Besides that, their moment of truth and sincerity had passed. They were no longer alone, and what needed saying felt wrong in the company of others.

Daemyn tilted his head at him and raised a brow. "Alistair?"

He decided it was best to wait. "Uh, you go ahead. My throat feels a bit dry, so I think I'll have some more tea, then meet you in the throne room." It wasn't a lie; his mouth was uncomfortably dry. There would be plenty of time to reassure Daemyn, he hoped. For now, they needed to welcome his older brother home.

The Gentleman assisted Daemyn in putting on his coat, then backed away as the Prince of Svartr placed his black circlet on his head. "Are you sure? I don't mind?"

"Go on." Alistair laughed, enjoying the giddiness in his friend's bounce. "Honestly, I don't mind. I swear you look like you're about to soar out of here, and I don't want to weigh you down."

Daemyn brushed his bangs out of his face, his bright blue eyes twinkling with excitement. He was blushing, and Alistair was unsure if it was just the joyous anticipation of reuniting with his older brother, or if it was the now open secret they shared of Daemyn's crush on him causing it. Daemyn let out another bout of nervous laughter, and Alistair hoped his friend was going to be alright. He couldn't shake the idea that something was wrong, that Daemyn might be keeping something from him, but since he had no proof other than the feeling in his gut, he chose not to ask.

"Oh, come on, can you blame me?" Daemyn asked with all the excitement of a boy half his age, then his expression softened and his brows curved worriedly over his eyes. "But seriously, are you sure? I can wait."

Alistair gave him a small smile. "Yes, I'll be fine. Promise."

Grinning back, he nodded graciously and backed into the hall. "Thank you, but you *better* not take long. I'll send half the guards if you're late." He said with a wink, then took his leave. Two of his blackguards turned to follow while the remaining two remained to accompany Alistair when he was ready to go.

Just as the Gentleman moved to gather Alistair's belongings from the coat rack, Alistair stopped him. "No, thank you. If I need any assistance, I'll be sure to send for you." He then gave the man a thankful bow, and the Gentleman, returning a bow of his own, left Alisatir and Emera alone in the room, closing the door as he went.

The servant maiden stepped forward, ready and waiting for the confirmation to collect the food and drinks from the tray. Looking at her, he recalled he had told everyone that he was thirsty, so Alistair took up his cup and drank its contents. The liquid had cooled, but was still warm and tasted just as wonderful. Out of the corner of his eye, he caught Emera tilting her head quizzically to one side.

"Sorry." Alistair placed his cup back on the saucer and stepped to the coat rack. "I promise, I won't waste any more of your time."

"I swear, your Grace, you're no waste. You needn't speak so negatively about yourself. Especially for someone as kind as you." She answered, carefully stacking the used dishes on the silver tray.

Plucking his circlet from the rack, he paused. She had seemed so familiar, and now, the inkling tugging at the back of his mind blossomed, giving rise to a keen suspicion. The image of another who had disguised herself came into focus. In their time apart, her image had grown fuzzy, but now that Alistair knew what to look for, the resemblance was uncanny. "How would you know that? We've never met." He slid his circlet on his head and grabbed his cape, sure to keep his eyes on her and watching for the act to slip.

"Well, I've heard stories of you, your Grace." She looked at him with a grin and innocence written across her face.

"Hmm." Time for a change of tactic, he thought. "You know, with this dreadful weather outside, I hope Albrecht makes it in safely. What do you think, Valhalla?"

"Hmm?" Her eyes widened, and she accidentally dropped the pot onto the tray. The look of surprise lasted only a moment as she scrambled to make sure the tea didn't spill and then straightened back into practiced composure. "I think His Grace is mistaken."

Alistair couldn't help but laugh. "Oh, come now. You can change your eyes and your clothes, but not your face. I knew you looked familiar!"

Valhalla quickly held her hands before her, trying to calm his excitement, her expression full of worry. She buried her face in her hands and shook her head. "By Vidar's secrecy, your Grace!" She took a deep breath and let her hands fall back to her sides. Her eyes drifted across the floor and to the doors. "I was . . . really hoping you wouldn't notice me."

Alistair's brow twitched, but he managed to retain his smile, trying to convey that he wasn't upset about the deceit. She must've had her reasons after all. "And why is that?"

Valhalla didn't respond, hugging her arms about her torso, her gaze locked on the doors. His smile wavered, and where delight had filled his chest, a seed of worry crept in.

Alistair looked back at the doors and remembered the blackguards standing just outside. Consciously lowering his voice, he returned his gaze to Valhalla and asked, "Valhalla, why are you here? Please tell me it has nothing to do with my friend's family? Tell me they aren't in danger."

Her response was silence again, but it was clear from her shifting stance that Valhalla was struggling with whether or not to involve him. She started to say something as her mouth fell open, but no words came out. Alistair closed the distance between them, careful not to unnerve her, but close enough so that outside ears couldn't hear their conversation.

"Valhalla, you're seriously worrying me. Is Daemyn's family alright?" He tried not to let his worry show, but he felt his body stiffening.

Moments stretched between them until finally, she took a deep breath and raised her false brown eyes to his. To his surprise, even under the weight of his building dread, he found himself missing the vibrant pink of her natural irises. She licked her lips, and her words came so softly that even at this distance, he could barely make them out.

"Even if I told you, I doubt you would believe me," Valhalla said.

"If my friends are in danger, I'm open to any possibility. Besides, after what we went through in Hilliard, I'd hear you out no matter how outlandish it may sound." He forced a chuckle, hoping to hide his nerves and possibly calm hers, but it didn't work.

Valhalla's stare was unsteady and darted between Alistair's eyes. "You have to promise. Hear me out *fully* and *completely*. No interrupting, answering only when I ask you something, no matter how wild this is going to sound."

He raised a hand to his heart and swallowed. "I swear it. You have my word."

After a deep exhalation, she started. "Alright, so what do you know of Helheim and its Queen?"

42

Alistair

The Return of the Svartr Prince

Alistair's heart pounded. He stood at the left side of the dais where sat the Svartr throne. It was unique as far as thrones went. Its surface was an impossibly deep ebony which caught the light if viewed at just the right angles, looking almost as if the builder had managed to shape it out of the starless night sky itself. On the backrest was a vicious carving of a leviathan, a most terrifying sea serpent which shared little in common with the Midgard Serpent, save for its monstrous girth, held aloft by various sea creatures which spread down the seat and to the floor. Seahorses, sharks, whales, jellyfish, and countless others were intricately detailed, so many that it would've taken an entire afternoon to catalog each, and even then, many would likely still be lost within the design.

The thunderous booming in the skies continued, ominous and arrhythmic as ever. Alistair turned and looked toward the throne room's gates, which were still shut tight. There was no sign of Albrecht, and his worry grew with every moment.

His thoughts were heavy with the knowledge of what Valhalla had shared. Asgard. Helheim. Even Queen Hel herself. They were all real. The young woman kept a steady face the entire time, not once wavering or giving any sign that she didn't wholeheartedly believe the words pouring from her mouth. He had hoped that at the story's end she would confess to only be joking, to deliberately trying to unnerve him in jest, but her conviction was as solid as stone. Valhalla truly believed everything she had said, and thus, she must've been telling Alistair the truth . . . Right? She had already proved a trustworthy ally and seemed of sound mind, but if what she said was true, then at the very least, they were all in grave danger.

He glanced to his left, to Daemyn and Aegir occupied greeting noble after noble, most from here in Svartr and a scattered few from elsewhere in Veerence, like him. He eyed the royal family warily, wondering what it was that they could be hiding, *if* even they were hiding anything. Valhalla's suspicions lay more with the King than Daemyn, and from what she witnessed of his rule already, the instilling of a curfew, people vanishing without a trace, and a willingness to forgo trials for dissidents, made her stomach churn nervously.

Then there was the issue of dark magic, or dark seidr as it could be called in the old tongue, which Valhalla seemed more accustomed to using than he. It was so much to simply accept all at once, and he wasn't sure if he even could, given enough time. He raised a hand over his eyes and massaged his temples with thumb and middle finger.

Music startled him from his thoughts. It started playing somewhere off to his right, and its rhythm was something he had never heard before. He found the musicians quickly enough. They had brown skin and were dressed in colorful attire; all sat close together on the floor. One had a pair of what looked to be hand drums before him, while another had a longer, singular drum lying on its side. Two others wielded string instruments, one that distantly resembled a lute, though much longer, and the other, an instrument like a cello, but smaller. Together they created an almost otherworldly sound which seemed to yearn for his full attention. In front of the four musicians were five other seated women, and as if on cue, the one in the center began singing.

Her voice was lyrical and gentle, her words in a language he didn't understand. The group twirled their hands in slow and deliberate motions. Their fingers flowed from one intricate shape to the next. Their bodies remained steady and straight, with only their arms moving to the tempo of the song. The melody and their movements slowed and softened into a quiet, statuesque pose, lasting only a heartbeat, and then everything burst with energy again. The dancers hopped up onto their feet in one swift motion, and Alistair found his worries melting into the back of his mind.

He watched in awe as the music picked up, the dancers and musicians all collectively chanting with the lone singer. The dancers and singer moved with fluid precision, fanning and contracting, threading their arms from pose to pose, never quite stopping. Their bare feet lightly thumped against a large crimson rug, which he now realized had been brought in solely for this purpose. Tiny round bells jingled around their ankles in harmony with the sound of the instruments.

With a twirl, the chanting ended, and again the lone singer continued her song. Everything about them was different than anything Alistair had beheld. Their clothing was bright and vivid, the colors of crimson and a white so pure it made the clouds look filthy in comparison. Their skirts bloomed with every twirl and were edged with gold. Their accessories, necklaces, and earrings, were adorned with rubies set in gold. Of particular interest was the single red dot at the center of four of the five dancers' foreheads. The singer had a gold accessory hanging over hers, and Alistair wondered if beneath it, she too had the marking. What was the meaning behind the mark? Was it religious in origin, or had it some other explanation? Each of them had dark hair tied back into tight buns, circled by white flowers. Their tops and trousers hugged their frames, and a lone gold scarf draped over a shoulder, held fastened at the waist by a satin belt.

He got the feeling that a story was playing out before him, and yet, no matter how closely he watched or how keenly he listened, the meaning behind it all remained a mystery.

"You're staring again."

Alistair jolted and looked down beside him to see Daemyn, smirking curiously up at him. "Stop sneaking up on me. And stop making me out to be a pervert!" He glared at his friend with what must've looked like an annoyed pout, which only made the young Prince laugh.

"Don't worry. I'm only teasing. Here," Daemyn said, holding out a black chalice of wine.

Alistair looked down at it and hesitated. He wasn't sure if he wanted to drink at the moment, especially as Valhalla's story drifted back to the forefront of his thoughts. A knot twisted in his stomach, but as Daemyn tilted his head at the hesitation, Alistair immediately took the chalice. Best not to disrespect his host. Still, getting drunk would be a mistake, so he planned to take only minor sips.

"Anyway, their dance is beautiful, isn't it?" Daemyn asked, more a statement than a question, while watching the spectacle unfolding before them.

"I'll say. What's this dance called?" Alisatir asked as he forced a sip of the surprisingly earthy wine, finding it a bit too strong in taste and smell for his liking.

"The ladies you see before you call it Kathak. They hail from a place called," Daemyn snapped his fingers a few times, seemingly searching for the word, "what was it again? You'll have to excuse me, Alistair, I have to get it right." He chuckled bashfully. "It's Maha——"

"The kathak dancers are from Mahaanbrahma, your Grace. As is yours truly."

Turning to find the source of the voice, Alistair's eyes landed on a man whose features resembled those of the kathak dancers. His brown skin was of a softer tone than the women's, and his black hair was pulled loosely back in a ponytail. His garb was of a similar fashion to any noble of Oceana in hues of ebony, yellow, and orange. He wore half a smile that didn't suit him, and in his dark brown eyes there shined curiosity and a deeply insatiable hunger, but for what, Alistair hadn't the faintest idea. Alistair wasn't sure if it was his imagination mixing with the dread plaguing his thoughts, but under the man's gaze, he got the impression of being a mouse standing before a viper.

"O-Oh, Lord Tamanna Gadhavi, I didn't hear you approach." Daemyn said, taking on a sudden interest in the contents of his chalice. He too must've felt the imposing presence of the man.

Tamanna placed a hand over his heart and bowed to the Princes, and to avoid appearing disrespectful, Alistair bowed his head in return.

"My apologies. If I startled you, it wasn't my intent." He chuckled softly with a shrug. The man's accent was thick but honeyed. "I came to—Oh! It appears the ladies are almost done with their dance. You should watch. We can speak after."

Alistair and Daemyn acquiesced and returned to watch the kathak dancers as they twirled and jabbed their hands into the air. Their movements were quick and precise, their footfalls landing perfectly with the music. Soon, the dancers made their final bout of twirls, each larger than the last until, as if of one mind, they all stopped. The dancers held their final pose, the music turned to silence, and the singer standing erect at the center of her dancers with arms raised squarely by her head.

Once it was clear they had finished their performance, the Princes, along with those that gathered in attendance, erupted in a round of cheers and applause. The dancers, though out of breath, curtsied in their own way, each wearing a humble grin.

"That was amazing." Said Alistair, turning back to Lord Tamanna, pushing past his first impression of the man and forcing himself to relax. "Will they be performing another dance?"

"They have told several stories already, Your Grace, and as I'm sure you understand, the performances can be rather taxing. They need a break."

"What kind of story? The song was beautiful, though I couldn't understand the words." Alistair's mixed colored eyes twinkled as he spoke.

"My, aren't you a curious one." Lord Tamanna laughed. "Much like Veerencians, Mahaanbrahmans tell stories through oral traditions, but that isn't the only way. My people also do so through dance. And sometimes what is sung parallels what is portrayed, two stories sharing commonalities, similar themes and lessons meant to be learned, or simply two opposing angles to the same tale. Like your people, we tell stories of our great gods such as Krishna and Vishnu, and of our heroes such as Karna and Abhimanyu."

"Amazing, truly! Can you tell me where your country of Mahaanbrahma resides? I would very much like to visit. It seems an incredible culture, and if we could establish a friendship with your ruler, perhaps both our peoples could benefit."

Lord Tamanna tilted his head at Alistair and raised a brow, seemingly pleased to hear this. "Actually, Mahaanbrahma is a city, the capital of the region, much like your Hilliard of Veerence. Raseela is the name of my country, and it lies beyond the Desert of Khufu, as the Eenhiedians call it."

Alistair's jaw fell open. That was quite a distance away. "You crossed that desert? I've heard that traveling the Desert of Khufu means death. I didn't think it was possible. What could've driven you to make such a journey?"

Lord Tamanna spread his arms wide is a showy gesture, his grin turning genuine for the first time since they began speaking. "For knowledge, and to expand our countries' hands in friendship, just as you said. I, too, believe we have much to benefit from one another. Besides, I'm quite the scholarly explorer, Your Grace. How could I pass on such an opportunity?" He shrugged.

"Then I gladly accept your hand." Alistair held out an open palm and grinned welcomingly. "However late in coming this may be, welcome to Veerence, Lord Tamanna Gadhavi."

The Lord took his wrist with a small smirk. "Thank you, Your Grace. I'm *so* honored." He then released Alistair and stood to the side, allowing both Princes a line of sight to King Aegir. "Before I forget, his Majesty has asked for the two of you to join him. He would like you both at his side when Prince Albrecht arrives."

"Thank you, Lord Tamanna. We're going." Daemyn quickly grabbed Alistair by the arm and pulled him up the dais to his father.

Alistair blinked at his friend, confused by his haste. "Daemyn, is everything alright?"

"It's nothing. Just . . ." Daemyn paused. When he looked back at Alistair, his brows were deeply curved, and his eyes trembled. When he spoke, his voice came low, just above a whisper. "Whatever you do, watch yourself around that man."

Alistair's heart leapt into his throat. He inspected his friend's unsettled features, hoping he might say more, but as it became clear that Daemyn wouldn't, he nodded. It was just one more in a growing list of questions he would have to ask Daemyn about later.

His young friend nodded approvingly, then turned back toward his father.

Aegir tilted his head at them as they approached. "Everything alright? You both look a tad startled."

"Aye, Father, I'm just . . . suddenly tired. Probably just the weather." Daemyn flashed his father a weak smile.

"Or perhaps you both should've slept and saved your reacquainting for the morrow, but patience is not for the young." Aegir laughed and took their chalices, placing the cups on a small round table beside his ebony throne.

"Even if we had rested, I doubt it would've been enough." Alistair chuckled.

"Too true, but if you had, then you might've noticed your closet full of Oceanan clothes for the occasion," Aegir smirked and raised a brow. Alistair winced as he only then noticed he had completely forgotten about his Hillian garb. "I remember you used to get so uncomfortable if you stood out too much."

Alistair's hand drifted over his chest. He had gotten so preoccupied with his thoughts and worries that he hadn't even thought to change. At least that, too, had kept him from falling victim to his insecurities.

"Thank you, Aegir, I think after all that traveling, I was just so glad to be rid of the carriage that I forgot." He forced a laugh, hoping it didn't sound too fake. "I'll be sure to rest tonight and will make good use of the clothes you've so generously provided tomorrow." Alistair smiled and as he looked into the King's eyes, Valhalla's concerns came flooding back.

A loud screech, followed by the groan of the massive doors which led in and out of the castle, pulled everyone's attention. The time had come. As the opening was just wide enough for a single person to squeeze through, a figure emerged from the darkness, and the firelights of the throne room chased the shadows away. He waltzed in with an air of confidence befitting one suited to the line of kings. His posture was straight, shoulders rolled back, and head held high. A red cape billowed behind him.

A wave of whispers consumed the crowd in an instant. The people huddled close and watched with wide eyes. Many bowed or curtsied while some were simply too awestruck to follow the custom. The man briefly bowed his head to one and all in acknowledgement, and soon everyone was showing their respects.

"I know it's been three years, but I can barely recognize him," Daemyn whispered, his expression a mix of guilt and happiness. He had only been twelve, nearly thirteen winters young, when his older brother left.

The young man, two years Alistair's senior, was growing ever closer. His features were strong, and he wore a proud smirk on his chiseled face. He was handsome, nearly the spitting image of his father, save for his tawny skin and bright brown hair, likely bleached from his time on the sails. The color of his eyes was a perfect match to Daemyn's, to their mother's, a striking sky blue, but that's where the resemblance ended. Where Daemyn's eyes were generally filled with whimsy, his older siblings' gaze was battle-hardened like forged steel.

Prince Albrecht Svartr had returned home.

"He kind of looks like your father when he was young, doesn't he?" Alistair asked, trying to push past his worries. Just then, the last memory of him and Albrecht crashed into his mind.

His chest felt like it was caving in. Three years. Three long years, Albrecht had gone from war to war. First was the War of Lions, and soon followed the Gran Mar War, leading all of it alongside Zarago, all by himself, because Alistair couldn't accompany him due to the wounds inflicted by Lorna. At the time, Alistair had been all but immobilized, not to mention the trauma the experience had left him with and how that might've affected his mental state. He was in no condition to make the hard calls that war necessitated.

Would Albrecht be angry with him?

Despite the bloodshed, Albrecht had been more put together than Alistair during the Lions War, but that could also have just been a show he put on when he was around Alistair. Only the gods knew what he could've been thinking and feeling when alone.

Alistair's stomach twisted into a knot of guilt, bile creeping up his throat. He took a deep breath and exhaled steadily. Looking Albrecht over, examining how his friend had grown and changed since the last time they saw each other, he found himself pleasantly surprised. Outwardly, his friend seemed about the same.

Sure, Albrecht was broader and taller, but he was still thinner than Alistair, and from a distance, they seemed to still be about the same height. His friend's garb was similar to his father's. The crimson wasn't quite as deep, and it had a few extra accents, gold buttons and chains decorating the coat and vest, but otherwise, they were a match. The ebony Ring of Svartr on his right hand glistened in the firelight. It was the ring signifying him as the heir to the throne.

Alistair's memory of the detailing of the ring was fuzzy now, time washing away all but the most basic of forms and shapes. What he could recall was that the band was a leviathan. A crown held a black stone, the same as that which built the city of Svartr all those centuries ago. His brown hair was pulled back in a tight but low ponytail, held by a thin black ribbon. Alistair was surprised to find he didn't don his circlet and wondered if it might've been lost, another casualty of the war.

The dark glint of something tucked within the confines of Albrecht's coat then caught Alistair's eyes. His lips twitched in excitement. It could only have been one thing, the Sword of Svartr, Roaringserpent, as beautiful an instrument of war as there had ever been. The sword, from blade to hilt, was as black as midnight. The face of the leviathan made up the entirety of the weapon's guard, its face frozen in a constant, ferocious roar, hence the name. Just as the ring, it too was a symbol of the heir.

"Alistair?"

Alistair turned to find Daemyn staring at him and replied, "Hmm?"

"I asked how you would know what my father looked like when he was young?"

"Oh! Aegir's old paintings, remember? You showed them to me when we were little. Your mother mentioned that Albrecht was looking even more like your father day by day, just as you are her." Alistair answered with a grin, nudging his elbow with his own. Daemyn's eyes shone with remembrance, and he turned his head to look up at his father.

"Oh wow, you're right," Daemyn whispered as if he had somehow forgotten.

It seemed Aegir had been listening in on their conversation, as if on cue, and without breaking his gaze on Albrecht, the King raised an arm and wrapped it around the young Prince's shoulders, pulling him close and jostling his hair. The two shared a laugh while Daemyn wrapped an arm around his father's waist, his cheeks turning a bright shade of pink. Alistair watched as father and son shared a moment of genuine affection and felt a small pang for the loss of his own father, only to be all the more gladdened for his friend. After Daemyn's assertions about his father's feelings toward him, it was nice to see a display like this.

Albrecht was now nearing the dais. Alistair released a shaky breath. His friend had both changed and not changed since last they saw one another. The only news Alistair ever received of him were buried in reports of the war effort, and most of those only mentioned his deeds, nothing of the man himself. They never told him what he really wanted to know. How was he holding up? Had he been hurt or lost anyone he cared about? Did he have anyone there to watch out for him? But those weren't the sort of details one could safely place in a letter, nor were they of particular interest to many who would be reading them.

Despite the warnings Valhalla had given, the ever-present gloom which shrouded the whole of the city, Alistair decided he was going to use the time he had to make up for all they had missed, to learn everything he could about the lives of his friends while they had been apart. He wanted to see who they'd become in these three years. He got a glimpse of Daemyn earlier, and much of it was as he had expected, but he knew there was more still to discover, layers of defenses and pretext to peel away to uncover even the most minor of changes to who they were. All people, especially those with even a fraction of power, kept a part of themselves concealed lest it be used against them. This was true of him and had been true of both brothers, and he wanted to know them as intimately as he had once known them, those few and many years ago.

Albrecht stopped at the base of the dais and knelt to one knee. His red cape flared at his back, and he bowed his head low, placing a hand over his heart. "Father, I've returned a conquering hero, and done so unharmed," his voice was accented and as velvety as his father's. He spread his arms wide, revealing the whole of himself, and grinned, "Naturally."

A chorus of amused sounds came from the crowd of nobles within the throne room. Alistair felt himself stifling a chortle as well. This overconfident heir of Svartr was exactly who he remembered. Albrecht had always been gifted at working a crowd, and this man beamed with the pride of one who had earned his confidence. He was loud, charismatic, and strong. Inspiring people was something he did as if it were no more difficult than breathing. When they were young, Alistair had wanted to be more like him and mused that he likely hadn't been alone in that.

Albrecht laughed along with the crowd, but the revelry faded. His expression hardened to an unreadable mask, and the entire room fell silent. It was as though his shift stole the joy straight from the crowd's throats.

"You know, Albrecht, you make it difficult to ignore when something is on your mind. Three years may have passed, but you still struggle to hide your thoughts." Aegir flashed his oldest son a small smile.

Albrecht returned the look half-heartedly. "I suppose I haven't." He immediately stood and met his father's gaze, shoulders squared and jaw set. "Father," Albrecht paused, a flicker of concern on his brow.

"Son, whatever the concern, I'm always willing to listen. Rarely do I turn away the woes of my sons." Aegir stated, hugging Daemyn a little closer.

Albrecht's jaw softened, and after a deep breath, he continued. "Father, regardless of my successes in the Gran Mar War, there were heavy costs. I . . . regret to say a great many men and women paid for this victory with their lives.

Most were lost to the sea. Zarago was kind enough to prepare proper send-offs for those who could be accounted for, but it's my hope that despite her times of ire, that the Goddess Ran takes good care of them within her husband's hall beneath the sea." His expression hardened once more, fists tightening at his side. "We may have won this war, but it's my greatest shame to return with fewer than I left with, and worse so, without the bodies of those who were lost that their loved ones could at least say their final farewells."

"Aye, but you brought back as many sailors as you *could*, my son. The families who've lost someone will appreciate that you *tried*, and the fact that you grieve with them, I'm certain, is of great comfort."

"I suppose." Albrecht shrugged. "But not all will find that to be enough." The depths of Albrecht's guilt hung on every word.

Aegir's smirk vanished, and his expression became that of granite. He released Daemyn and stepped forward to the edge of his dais. "Until time immemorial, we will be criticized for every action we take. It's how we handle said criticism that makes a true leader."

His son forced a nod. "Father, I would send compensation to the families of those sailors who didn't make it home."

A surge of shock ran through the crowd, their murmurings all too familiar to Alistair's ears. This was not a request they would welcome, and to follow through could bring dissent. But as far as he was concerned, he found nothing wrong with such a request. If anything, it was the right thing to do. While nothing could replace the loss of a loved one, it was likely that hardship would fall upon those who were left behind. For many, a soldier's earnings kept an entire family afloat, and with that now taken from them, it was likely their lives would be forever changed, and not for the better. Had they farmland or other means, they would still struggle, but for those without, starvation was a distinct possibility.

"That sounds more like a statement than a question," Aegir said, flashing his son a challenging smirk.

"That's because it's something you—No." Albrecht shook his head, closing his eyes momentarily. "It's something we must do. These sailors, their lives, were my responsibility. I let them and this city down by not keeping them safe."

"My dear Albrecht, I've told you this during the War of Lions, and evidently I must tell you again. You've not let *anyone* down."

Albrecht's eyes shone, but he held his father's gaze, listening to every word.

"Albrecht." Aegir's voice was gentle. "You've not let our sailors down. You've not let this city down. Loss is an inevitable reality of war. Even the best leaders in all of history suffered losses. It isn't something that can be wholly avoided, no matter how badly we wish it to be different."

Alistair glanced at Aegir, and his heart flipped, finding the King's gaze meeting his own. It seemed that, unlike Albrecht, Alistair couldn't yet hold the weight of his stare and looked away. His heart pounded as he realized the man's words were not only meant for Albrecht. They were for him, for Daemyn, and likely all in attendance. His words, spoken in this moment, were certain to spread through the city, to be heard by every ear, and thus any who might've spoken in anger for the loss of family or friends would now be silenced by the weight of the word of their King.

"So long as you return with those still under your care at the battle's end, you haven't failed. And if I've heard correctly, you managed to return with over eighty ships worth of sailors. To them, I guarantee you haven't failed. Remember and honor the dead, but also think of the mothers, fathers, sisters, brothers, sons, and daughters who tonight will be reunited. That alone is enough to make anyone proud, especially your King." Aegir's smile widened and radiated pride. "Of course, I'll allow for compensation, for *all* our sailors. Those who've made it home, and those who haven't. Once our sailors have settled, we'll meet with them and their families within the fortnight. In the meantime, letters will be sent to the families of our fallen. We will meet with them as well. I'm sure you've collected their names." He said knowingly.

"Of course, Father. Thank you." Albrecht bowed graciously, and with that, the hall exploded in applause.

The cheering became all the louder as Albrecht straightened and turned to the crowd of highborns. The Prince's large grin softened as he bowed his head, and to Alistair's great astonishment, many offered shares of their own coffers to be given to the families affected by the loss of someone during the war. Even still, he was skeptical. He would believe it once it happened.

Aegir then raised a hand in the air, and soon silence came over the crowd. His face grew serious. All eyes turned back to the King.

His hand turned into a fist, and he placed it over his chest. All mimicked the gesture. "Land is Temporary, Sea is Eternal!" He bellowed.

The crowd joined him in the chant, repeating the cherished Svartr motto. Their words echoed and lingered in the air, and once they finished the chant, all bowed their heads in a moment of silence for those now gone, returning to where they believed every Svartr babe had truly belonged.

Once King Aegir stood himself erect, he climbed down the steps of his dais to join his eldest son, the two embracing without a moment's hesitation. Albrecht's shoulders trembled. His father cupped the back of his son's head in one hand. Daemyn, still by the throne, took a deep breath and followed after his father. Alistair remained close by, watching over his young friend to make sure he was alright.

"I'm so glad that you're home, Albrecht," Aegir said softly, and kissed his son gently upon the temple, causing Albrecht to bashfully let out a chuckle.

"It's good to be home." The Prince responded with delight written across his face.

Daemyn suddenly stumbled on the last step of the dais, Alistair catching him well before he hit the floor, and the young Prince tried to pretend as if nothing had happened.

"Daemyn?" Albrecht asked, releasing his father, mouth agape.

Aegir laughed. "He's grown into quite the young man, hasn't he?"

"I'll say. By the gods, look at you!" Albrecht rushed to his little brother, and the two wrapped their arms around one another.

"You're one to talk," Daemyn's voice croaked, "I almost didn't recognize you."

The two laughed softly. Albrecht then held his brother out at arm's length. "Daemyn, the last time I saw you, you were barely thirteen winters. You were so much smaller!" He pinched Daemyn's cobalt blue coat between his fingers, inspecting the garment with a knowing smirk. "I see you still prefer flashy, bright colors," Albrecht said with a playful wink.

Daemyn rolled his eyes and pursed his lips, causing his older brother to laugh. Albrecht then cupped the back of his little brother's head, and the two touched foreheads. It was a gesture the two had shared all their lives. Tears rolled down Daemyn's cheeks, and the two stood there like that for a long moment. Daemyn, of course, was the first to break it.

"Fuck you, you're just jealous that I just know how to look fashionable." With a sniffle and a smirk, he pulled Albrecht in for another embrace. When he spoke next, it came as a whisper. "I'm so happy that you're back, brother."

Alistair's heart swelled at the sight. Not wanting to interrupt the moment, he started to withdraw, intent on vanishing into the crowd. He only managed a few steps before Albrecht's gaze found him, as if sensing his thoughts. Alistair froze.

The elder Prince of Svartr squinted at Alistair, recollection slowly blooming and warming his features. "Alistair? By Ódin's fucking grace!" Releasing Daemyn, he rushed to Alistair and within an instant had him wrapped in an embrace.

Of the reactions that had filled Alistair's expectations, anger, apathy, and mistrust, this possibility hadn't once occurred to him. It seemed that after everything Albrecht had been through, even with all the pain, loss, and hardships he had faced, upon seeing Alistair, the one emotion that beat out all the rest seemed to be, by all accounts, joy.

The salty scent of the sea and earthen hints of pine clung about Albrecht. The tension that had been clinging to Alistair's shoulders seemed to fade away. With a long sigh of relief, he lifted his arms and wrapped them about his friend. The moment was pleasant, but unfortunately short-lived. His friend's hands clapped down on his shoulders, and as he had Daemyn, Albrecht pulled back and held Alistair at arm's length, looking him up and down. The Svartr Prince's eyebrows raised. "You've gotten big as well." He laughed with an expression that seemed almost impressed, and Alistair couldn't help but feel slightly embarrassed.

As Albrecht glanced at him and his smile faded, Alistair's heart raced. The Svartr Prince then cupped the side of his neck, forcing Alistair to look solely at his friend. "The news reached me as soon as I stepped foot on the docks of Flotnar. I . . . never cared much for Lorna, especially for the way she treated you, and for that I can't say I'll mourn her loss, but she was still your sister, and it's for you that I'm sorry. My heart aches for what you and your mother must be going through." Albrecht leaned forward and touched their foreheads together, the gesture common in Svartr but reserved only for members of the same family, leaving him frozen and breathless.

Albrecht had made it clear, years ago during the War of Lions, that he had no love for Lorna, and his dislike for her turned all the more bitter when it became known that she was to wed Daemyn. After Hilliard had received word from Zarago, requesting their aid in beating back the invading forces bombarding them with cannon fire, Alistair immediately took up the call. The timing couldn't have been worse, though. Lorna and her friends had left their marks upon his back just days before the message had come. He wanted away from her. Away from Hilliard, and even with the bloodied state they had left him, the Gran Mar War seemed the best way to achieve that goal. He had only just arrived in Svartr with full intent on leading their forces when Albrecht caught wind that something had happened. Alistair was forced into a fight where his wounds were instantly revealed.

It was then that Albrecht offered to go in Alistair's stead, to represent Veerence to aid Zarago. Had it been up to him, he would've refused, but his older friend hadn't offered this to him, instead proposing the idea to his father, King Aegir. Alistair tried to argue; it should've been him after all. If he died in battle, less would be lost. He was heir to nothing, not like Albrecht. His arguments, while sound, were likely hindered by the simple fact he was making them while doubled over in pain from the contest with the older Prince. Aegir, of course, deemed him unfit due to his injuries, and so things played out as they had.

He had been forced to reveal how he came by his injuries and then was compelled to remain in Svartr. He stayed long after Albrecht left, time enough for his wounds to turn to scabs and then the beginnings of scars. It was because of those events he knew all too well how the Svartr heir felt about Lorna, but even still, he felt a pang of sadness for her loss and was thankful for his friend's sincerity.

Alistair's eyes stung with tears, his throat tight, and he managed a forced smile. "Thank you, Albrecht. My feelings on the subject are . . . rather complicated."

Albrecht grinned and then released him. Aegir then stepped up beside his son, placing a hand on his shoulder, bellowing an announcement to the crowd, "Come now, it's time to celebrate. Our Prince and heir has returned home, some music please!"

Aegir waved to the Raseelan musicians to continue, and with a nod, they picked up their instruments and began. It was a new song, and the dancers took their positions, following the woman who had been singing in their previous performance in yet another intricate, precise dance.

The King seemed to relax as he watched them for a time. He looked over the crowd, at the nobles enjoying the performance and chatting amongst their typical associates. His gaze then locked on something, or someone, at the far right of the hall. Alistair glanced as discreetly as he could to see what it was that held the King's attention. There, before a door which led out of the room, hidden half in shadow, hands behind his back and expression flat, almost lifeless, was Tamanna.

"Albrecht," Aegir turned his back to the crowd and leaned in close to his eldest son and Alistair, his expression as dark as a grave, "as much as I wish we could spend your first evening back together, I'm afraid some things have come to my attention that must be handled immediately."

"Things? What things?" Albrecht asked with shock and confusion clear on his face. Alistair felt the same concerns, Valhalla's warning resurfacing in his mind.

Aegir rubbed his chin in thought and then, with a reluctant sigh, straightened. "It would seem there's been some talk of rebellion. Some of our highborns think it wise to try to overthrow me, and by extension, you."

Albrecht was understandably taken aback by the news. Alistair looked at Daemyn and found his friend's eyes trailing the floor and twisting the rings about his fingers. The rings seemed rather large on him, and Alistair wondered if there was a significance to that. He looked Daemyn over more carefully, taking in the details he had missed or dismissed before. There were small dark patches under his eyes. His garments, while well-tailored, seemed a bit too wide at the shoulders and waist.

Had he known? Was this rebellion what he had been hiding as well?

Aegir continued to speak, looking annoyed all the while. "I meant to squash such nonsense before you arrived, but like fleas on a rat, they can be difficult to find."

"But, Father,"

"Albrecht, you just came from a war, and I'll not thrust you into another. Don't worry, my boy, I won't be long." Aegir cupped his oldest son's cheek and smiled warmly. "Enjoy the festivities. Catch up with your brother and Alistair." He briefly touched his forehead to Albrecht's, then took his leave, joining Tamanna and disappearing into the castle.

Albrecht stared after his father, his bright blue eyes swirling with conflict, while Daemyn seemed to withdraw into himself. Alistair was about to check on the young Prince, but Albrecht stepped in front of him, stopping him in place. "Did you know of this?"

Alistair was shocked at the accusation thinly veiled within the question and shook his head. "No. I've only just arrived today, and while Daemyn has told me of some of what has been happening, I knew nothing of this. I doubt he knew either. He told me he was removed from his father's council so—"

"What!?" Albrecht exclaimed, his wide-eyed gaze turning to his younger brother.

"I-I was doing too much. Father ordered that I take a reprieve when—" Daemyn quickly covered his mouth, clearly hiding something, and Alistair assumed it was to do with their mother. It was possible Albrecht hadn't been told of her illness to avoid distracting him from the war effort.

Alistair's breath quickened as he realized they were drawing attention. He had to do something, and fast. The last thing he wanted was for gossip to bring further trouble to the Svartr royal family.

Albrecht's face was hard, and a growl rose in his throat. "Dae—"

Alistair forced a smile and slammed his hands on Albrecht's shoulders, turning him about to face the crowd. He could feel his friend's ire, but there would be time to apologize later.

"Albrecht, I promise we'll talk, clear everything up, but not here." He whispered into his ear with a wave to the crowd. "Besides, there are many here who wish to greet you, Your Highness."

For the briefest of moments, Albrecht's stern expression looked so much like his father's, but to his credit, he seemed to understand. The smile that crept onto his face sent a chill down Alistair's spine.

"Fine," Albrecht answered, clapping a hand on Alistair's shoulder. His grip was tight, making it perfectly clear that he was anything but accepting of the situation. "I'll play along. For now."

You're Not a Disappointment

THE EVENING GREW LATE. Dark clouds blotted out the sky, making it impossible to determine the exact time, but night drew near. Rain pelted the walls of the castle. Alistair and Daemyn were busy escorting a rather inebriated Albrecht on their way to the fifth floor, where their chambers awaited. The eldest Prince's arms were draped over each of their shoulders, and he swayed with every step. Having lost the ability to keep a single thought to himself, he laughed between boasts of his victories, slurring all the while.

At least he seemed a jovial drunk, Alistair thought.

Daemyn let out a huff in exertion, his older brother seemingly too heavy for him. As he looked over to Alistair, all the High Prince could do was shrug, flashing him a smirk followed by a quiet chuckle.

"Oh, you should've seen the battles," Albrecht swayed and leaned in close to Alistair, the smell of wine less pungent than he had expected, "the sea battles were glorious! Cannons roaring and water spraying everywhere." He let out a hearty laugh. As he did, Alistair thought he caught him glancing behind them, and it hadn't been the first time. As they reached their intended floor, all was quiet. It seemed for all the crowds below, this area of the castle was devoid of people, save for them. The absence of guards caught Alistair by surprise, but he shrugged it off. It was possible they were simply on patrol after all. Albrecht sucked in a deep breath, and his weight sagged, forcing Alistair and Daemyn to stop or risk dropping him.

Albrecht peered to the left and then to his right and suddenly straightened. With a deep exhalation, he lifted his arms from Alistair's and Daemyn's shoulders and patted the two on the back. "Good show, lads." Stretching his neck to one side, he walked ahead, leaving them both in stunned silence. "I swear I don't know how braggarts keep it up. That was exhausting, and you two were no help. I ran out of material by the second floor and just started making things up."

"You dick!" Daemyn was first to respond, trying to catch his breath.

Alistair blinked at his friend and, after several long moments, found himself laughing. "Seriously? All this time, you were faking just to get out of your own welcome back party? How are you not drunk?"

Albrecht glanced back with a mischievous smirk. "Oh, come now, Alistair, I'm a sailor. Besides, did you forget what I told you when we were young? Act how your subjects expect, give them the opportunity to underestimate you, then surprise them when the time's right." He said with a wink.

Clasping a wrist, armed resting behind his back, Albercht turned to his side and looked at them. He stood tall, statuesque, and his expression turned serious. "Well? Start talking, you two. What's been going on in my absence?"

Alistair and Daemyn shared a glance, their smiles fading. The younger prince was visibly nervous, and Alistair felt for him. Daemyn's gaze roved over the floor as if there he might find a way to answer. Alistair wondered what it could be that had Daemyn so pent up. He struggled to think of what he could do or say to reassure Daemyn, to help him find the words to explain what was on his mind, but nothing came. The truth was he knew very little. Daemyn had given little away in their talks, and what Valhalla had told him was cryptic at best.

They stood in uneasy silence, and Albrecht clearly wasn't going to budge. To his credit, he had waited patiently until now, but it seemed there would be no more of that. Alistair, feeling the weight of the silence bearing down on him, decided that he might as well speak on the little he knew. "Albrecht, I—"

"It's alright, Alistair," Daemyn interrupted, grasping Alistair's wrist, "can you lead the way to my chamber, please? Better not to speak in the open."

Daemyn hadn't looked up, but at the very least, he found a way to push through his fears, and while he was clearly afraid, he had spoken up. Honoring the request was the least Alistair could do, and so he answered, "Of course." He then moved past Albrecht and took the lead as the group made their way toward the end of the hall where Daemyn's bedchamber lay.

With a deep breath, the young Prince began explaining what he knew of the happenings within Svartr during the past few months. He didn't know much of the rebellion. The topic had been largely avoided in his presence. From what he knew, there had been little more than whispers of descent, a noble or two griping about this and that. It was rumored that some people had gone missing, but that seemed speculation more than anything else. Several of the names had been discovered on ship manifests or had booked passage by cart, and so the matter had been dismissed. Aegir suggested the weather had something to do with the people's woe, believing the storm and superstitious imagination to be the source of the people's worries.

Daemyn also spoke of taking up Albrecht's duties in safeguarding the city and its citizens. Sailors Reef had become a place he frequented often, meeting with the common folk, merchants, and farmers alike, to make sure that they had what was needed so that trade continued between the great and minor cities. There he had learned of a few discrepancies in trade, but those had been dismissed as poor bookkeeping. A storehouse had caught fire, and many records were lost. On inspection, there were no signs of foul doings, simply an accident caused by a farmhand who erected a fire pit too close by who was now laboring to rebuild the structure.

The mood darkened as the subject turned to Daemyn's mother.

"Mother fell ill with . . . something, and when that happened, I didn't know what to do!" Daemyn said with a croak. "I didn't want her work to fall behind. So, I took up her duties as well. Checking on the kids in the orphanages around Svartr, making sure the healers were stocked up with the herbs, ointments, and medicines, and checking on the castle's staff. Everything." His words came with exhaustion and poured out like a dam breaking. "It was more than I—"

Albrecht laid a hand on Daemyn's shoulders to stop him, his little brother turning his head away. Albrecht's lips thinned, and he pulled Daemyn close, wrapping his arms around his brother. The young Prince's eyes were wide, and it was clear he hadn't expected the gesture. Alistair smiled knowingly. He could sympathize with Albrecht's position. Even being an older brother himself, he imagined how he would've felt were Daemyn his younger brother in Lorna's place.

Albrecht had never really been much of a hugger; even in his saddest moments, he seemed to confront the emotions alone. When they were younger, Daemyn was found in tears like many boys his age, and for all sorts of reasons; being bullied by other kids or a favorite toy breaking. Every time, Albrecht just stood there, stiff and unsure of what to do to console his sibling. He eventually came to the conclusion that the best course of action was simply grabbing Daemyn by the wrist and dragging him to their mother. She had always known just what to do, and while she comforted Daemyn, he set about fixing the toys or ensuring those who dared harass his little brother would think twice in the future.

"A-Albrecht?" Daemyn stiffened in his brother's arms.

"You fool," Albrecht said sweetly, "you damn fool." He slid his hands to Daemyn's shoulders, placing him at arm's length, and smiled at his younger brother. "I'm not good at this, not like Mother, but here I go." Albrecht cleared his throat. "Father wasn't disappointed in you. You aren't lacking in skill. Whatever you set your mind to, he and I both know you'll succeed. We've always believed in you. But when you split your focus, again and again and again, eventually something has to give. You aren't at your best when you're so clearly exhausted. This is true of you, me, all people. Even Father." He chuckled and patted Daemyn's shoulders. "You care so much about the little details and yet miss the bigger painting. Do you remember what Mother told us? After the um, *incident* with the stable all those years ago?"

"W-What?" Daemyn's cheeks turned bright pink.

"Of the two of us, you held the larger basket, but when it was full, you kept filling it, and when it could hold no more, it burst at the bottom. You should *never* overwork yourself, Daemyn. Take a step back, breathe, and *rest*. You're no good to anyone in such a state." He cupped his younger brother's cheek. "You're always so good at taking care of others, yet forget to take care of yourself, and that's why our parents worry about you. That's why Father stripped you of your duties. If someone doesn't force you to rest, you won't."

Daemyn stared back at his older brother, his sky blue eyes trembling and filling with tears. Dropping his head forward, he fell into his brother's broad chest and the two embraced. Alistair leaned against the wall before the entrance of Daemyn's bedchamber, crossing his arms and smiling proudly. His heart swelled.

"For someone who claims to not be very good at this, that wasn't bad," Daemyn said with a tight throat. "You're such a barracuda at times, but dammit, did I miss you."

Alistair snorted but slammed a hand over his mouth. The nickname had been one Daemyn gave Albrecht a long while ago. His older brother was known to be aggressive when the need arose and dominated in combat training. Albrecht never let up, even when facing his younger brother, but every single time,

Albrecht would check on him when the match was done to make sure that he was alright. He even snuck Daemyn sweets he'd procured from the kitchen's when the servants weren't looking.

Albrecht chuckled as he looked at Alistair and winked. "And I missed you, my little guppy."

Watching the two, Alistair's mind flashed to Lorna when she was younger, back before his father's death. His smile wavered. They had been close like this once. How had everything gone so horribly wrong? As happy as he was that his friend's family was whole once more, he couldn't help but feel a pang of jealousy, followed by shame.

Pushing off the wall, he stepped to Daemyn's bedchamber and raised a hand to knock, when Albrecht called to him. "Alistair?"

Albrecht released Daemyn and smirked. "Come now, what's with that face? Do you need a hug too?" As he spoke, he stretched his arms out wide and waved, inviting Alistair in.

"You know," Alistair started with a weak smile, "I'm glad you two have each other. Not many siblings, or people for that matter, can say the same."

Daemyn wiped the tears from his face, and though he still had the shadow of a pout about his expression, his gaze steadied. "Alistair, what happened to Lorna wasn't. Your. Fault."

Alistair's heart twisted. He wanted to believe Daemyn, but there was no logicing away the sense of guilt which haunted him. Taking a deep breath, he pressed a hand to his chest in the ritual which he had been repeating more frequently of late. His hand found his father's ring nestled safely under the garments, and he let out a long sigh. "You say that, but I can't seem to convince myself of it."

Footsteps sounded in the hallway, startling the trio. Alistair glanced about but found no one. Turning back to his friends, he found Albrecht inches away and was wrapped in a tight hug before he could process what was happening. His breath caught in his throat.

"I wish I knew what to say, what words might help you move past this grief, but I don't. So for now, just take the damn hug." Albrecht said with a chuckle.

Alistair stood there as dumbfounded as Daemyn looked, but after a moment, he felt some of the tension in his shoulders and back melt away. For all the ways Albrecht was the same as he had been before the wars, there were some distinct differences. He had grown warmer, more sincere, and Alistair welcomed the change.

"This is so odd," Alistair chuckled as the two let go of one another, "you rarely hug, no matter the circumstance."

"Ah, well," Albrecht raised a hand to the back of his neck, blushing slightly, "I may have . . . met someone. She challenged me to be more compassionate, I think is the word she used."

"What?" Both Alistair and Daemyn exclaimed.

Daemyn slid up beside his older brother, eyes twinkling with excitement. "Who is she, and when can I meet her?"

As Daemyn began peppering his sibling with questions, Alistair returned to his task and knocked on Daemyn's doors. Albrecht had never had any interest in the women of nobility about the city of Svartr. When pressed on the matter, he generally waved the subject off, saying they would only be interested in him for status, and to his credit, that was likely true. If they were anything like the nobility in Hilliard, Alistair considered, they would be more likely to seek out a partner to increase the power of their name over anything else. Marriages of convenience. Besides, due to their treatment of him, he was glad to see Albrecht avoid the matter. But now, to have been busily waging war and to have found a woman who could shatter that barrier, well, she must've been someone truly impressive.

"I promised and," Albrecht said, reluctance entering his voice, "agreed to keep her identity a secret. For now, at least." Albrecht looked away. His tawny cheeks reddened, the bashful expression unsuited to his features.

"Why?" Daemyn asked with a tilt of his head. "Since when do you keep secrets from me? We always share." A mock hurt came over his face.

Albrecht grinned at his little brother's ploy. "How did I *know* you were going to bring that up?" Placing a hand on Daemyn's shoulder, he leaned in close. "I know we share many things with each other, little brother, but allow me to keep this secret. Please? If news got out before either of us were ready, she worries her father might try to put a stop to it." He said pleadingly.

"Oooooh, her father is one of those. Hmmm." Daemyn pinched his chin in thought for several long moments, then raised his hands in defeat. "Alright, fine, but I'm at least allowed to guess who it is."

"By all means, little brother," Albrecht tousled his younger brother's neatly tied flaxen hair, "I'll give you one guess. Besides, you *and* Alistair have already met her."

"We have?" The two said in unison.

Albrecht answered with a nod just as the doors of Daemyn's bedchamber opened. Before Alistair stood a familiar servant maid, Emera, as Daemyn knew her.

She curtsied low to them in greeting. "Your Grace. Your Highnesses. Welcome." Standing aside, she gestured for them to enter. "I'll be attending to you tonight, so if there's any——"

"Hello, Valhalla." Alistair interrupted with a wave. "Best we get to it."

Valhalla stood there slack-jawed, frozen with astonishment. Her still brown eyes glanced over to the Svartr Princes and then back to Alistair. It was clear in her features that this hadn't been part of her plan, and Alistair felt a pang of guilt for having been so careless. His cheeks burned as he dipped his head in apology.

"O-Oh. Of course." As if struggling to decide how to respond, she clasped her hands before her and looked away.

Daemyn stepped beside Alistair, joining him as they walked through the threshold. "Um, her name's Emera. Did you hit your . . ." He then glanced at Valhalla and froze, eyebrows raising. Guilt was written across her face as brightly as a torchlight at midnight. "Your name's Emera, isn't it?"

Valhalla winced with a shrug. Alistair placed himself between her and the two rightly suspicious Svartr Princes. "Remember, during the festivities, when I said I had some things to discuss with you both?" The brothers nodded hesitantly. "Well, it involves her. She's . . . not who she says she is." Alistair laughed, realizing in the moment that it had been foolish to not plan any of this out. He was tripping over his words, and a sense of foreboding settled into his gut. If he didn't fix this fast, they were going to think she was a threat.

Daemyn, understandably confused and a look of concern growing in his tense features, tried to peer around Alistair to look at her. "Should I be worried?"

Albrecht then stepped forward, and his expression darkened, hand resting uncomfortably close to the hilt of his sword. "Alistair, who——"

"I know I'm doing a terrible job at explaining, but please trust me. You have nothing to be concerned about. I promise. She's a true friend. That said, there's something you should be aware of. Come on," Alistair waved for them to close the door, "allow her to explain."

Both Daemyn and Albrecht shared a look, shrugged, then made their way further into the chamber. Valhalla, very clearly upset, pushed Alistair out of her way and closed the door.

She spun around to him, brows furrowed, cheeks flustered, and a flicker of murder in her eyes. "Your Grace!"

He raised his hands in front of himself, hoping to calm her annoyance. "I know, I know, I'm sorry! I honestly don't know what happened there. I just got so overwhelmed." He pinched the bridge of his nose. "Listen, if what you say is true, then they have every right to know what you know. Please. Tell them. Trust them as I trust you." Her expression softened a bit at his words, and so he continued. "Again, I'm sorry. I'll try to be more," he half shrugged, "subtle, next time." He finished with a chuckle.

She stared at him for a moment and then reached out a hand. She seemed to be waiting for something, and then it dawned on him. She'd acted as a servant for all this time, and even though her identity had been brought into question, her duties had likely become routine, and thus, whether intentional or not, she intended to carry on in her responsibilities. It seemed like a good idea to him. Acting as expected might help to ease the situation and help make the brothers more receptive to what they were about to hear. He slid the silver raven-decorated circlet from his head and handed it to her. Accepting it, she then walked to Daemyn, where he, too, handed her his. As she stood before Albrecht, he just shook his head. She stared at him for a moment, then spoke. "My apologies, Your Highness." With a bow, she rushed to the coat rack and deposited the circlets on two separate hooks.

Looking at his friend, Alistair noticed Albrecht wasn't wearing his circlet and he raised his hands to his cape's buckle with a chortle. "No circlet today—"

"Don't," Valhalla said firmly.

Alistair flinched and looked at her, perplexed.

"It's my responsibility to gather your things, Your Grace. Please wait a moment until I come to you." She then turned away and began helping Daemyn out of his coat.

"I see you still aren't comfortable being dressed by servants," Albrecht said with a wide grin.

Alistair's cheeks heated with light annoyance. "Ever since my father taught me to dress myself, it just felt odd having others do it for me." He shrugged.

Valhalla slid Daemyn's coat from his shoulders, and as she went to hang it over his circlet, the young prince crossed his arms and looked at Alistair with a tilt of his head. "I wonder why that is exactly."

"Why what?" Alistair asked.

"Why your father taught you how to dress yourself? You're the High Prince." Daemyn answered, rolling lightly on the balls of his feet as Valhalla approached to remove his cape.

Alistair sighed and turned his gaze elsewhere, feeling the melancholy of the memories of his father wash over him. "Honestly, your guess is as good as mine."

As Valhalla began to remove his cape, working open the clasp on his right shoulder, he glanced at her and their eyes met. Features were soft, warm. His mind traveled back to when she had still been disguised as Lorna, their investigation into his sister's death deep underway and her identity exposed, when she had comforted him with a hug. They were still largely strangers, but she felt for him. She'd offered him more warmth than he had felt in a long while. He found himself longing for that. Valhalla then placed a hand on his shoulder and squeezed it gently with a smile that was as sincere as it was comforting. Unsure of what to say, he simply nodded his thanks.

A laugh then escaped Albrecht's lips, drawing Alistair's attention. "Well, if we follow custom as tradition states, Daemyn and I should be the ones to dress you, being High Prince and all that."

Alistair rolled his eyes and scoffed. "Ugh! Please don't remind me. Daemyn already did that when I first arrived, and trust me when I say that isn't less awkward."

As the brothers laughed at Alistair's expense, Valhalla placed his cape over his circlet on the hook and approached Albrecht. She gave him a bow, and though he eyed her warily, eventually he spread his arms at his sides, allowing her to remove his cape and coat. Once everything had been hung, she spun around to them and seemed to pause, an uncertainness about her expression and shoulders.

She cleared her throat and, with a meekness in her tone, asked, "Do you wish to keep your sword, your Highness?"

He looked down at Roaringserpent, hands crossed at his back. His eyes traveled down to his weapon, and his brows furrowed. In a swift, smooth motion, Albrecht unclipped the blade from his belt and held it before him. He stared at it for several heartbeats, his expression so serious, and as he brought his gaze up to Valhalla, answered with a single word. "Aye."

He then walked over to one of the lavender couches and took a seat. Valhalla released a sigh of relief, and the tension in Daemyn's shoulders eased. Alistair turned to both of them. "Remember, he just came from a war. He needs time to adjust. No matter how many battles a person has been through, each leaves its mark."

They both nodded, seemingly understanding, or at the very least, knowing better than to question his surliness, and proceeded to follow after Albrecht's example and took seats on the couches. The Svartr Princes sat together on one couch, Roaringserpent in clear view leaning against Albrecht's crossed legs, and Alistair sat at their opposite. Valhalla stood herself before the small table where earlier she had served their refreshments. She stared at the wooden surface and wrung her hands, her porcelain white skin turning a shade of pink.

"Well," she breathed deeply, "where should I begin?"

44

Alistair

Conspiracy of the King

Valhalla stared at the Svartr Princes, seemingly waiting for their answer. Albrecht raised a questioning brow at her, and Daemyn looked to be doing his very best to blend into the couch. Each was as uncomfortable as the rest, and none seemed to know just what to say. Daemyn knew little, or at the very least, if he did know something, it clearly hadn't occurred to him that whatever it was, was important enough to lead with. Albrecht had just arrived home and knew nothing of what was going on. Alistair only knew what Valhalla had told him already, which admittedly he hadn't yet fully wrapped his head around. She then turned to look at him, her fingers twiddling and her gaze pleading for help, but what should he suggest? The gods. Who she was. Helheim. Dark seidr. King Aegir and Tamanna? It was all just too unbelievable, and he felt a pang of guilt when all he offered was a shrug in response.

"Oh!" Valhalla exclaimed with a little too much enthusiasm, given the tension in the room. "A drink! Are any of you thirsty? I also have snacks if that's something you want."

Albrecht's sigh carried the warning of a lion's growl, his hands clenching into fists over his lap. "Would you kindly,"

"Aye, please." Daemyn interrupted, stealing a brief glance at his elder brother before returning to the relative safety of Valhalla's equally concerned stare. "There's a bottle of the Great Queen's Road on the top shelf of my bar. Middle cabinet." As he pointed in the bar's direction, Valhalla wasted little time in bowing and retreating to gather the glasses, tray, and bottle of scotch.

Great job, Daemyn, Alistair thought to himself, alcohol usually made tensions lessen. Albrecht also seemed to think this was a bad idea as he turned to his little brother with a raised brow and a shake of his head, silently asking why. Daemyn shrugged and flashed them both a small smile. "Well, a promise is a promise, remember?"

Albrecht tilted his head, gazing at him through confused, narrowed eyelids. Daemyn then, to everyone's surprise, laughed. "I told you when you returned home that the three of us would drink one of the best scotches in all the queendom. So naturally, I got us the best." He grinned with excitement.

With a twitch of his lips, a reluctant smirk grew on Albrecht's face. "You're not old enough to handle The Queen's Road."

Daemyn scoffed in exasperation, feigning offense. "I'll have you know Father says I can handle it just fine . . . One glass at least." His words became mumbled there at the end, and with that, as absurd as the timing of his joking was, a lighter sense came over the room. Alistair and Albrecht found themselves laughing as the young Prince giggled at himself.

Valhalla returned with the bottle, glasses, and a small bowl of flower and star-shaped cookies coated with chocolate at their undersides. Albrecht wiped his eyes. "Alright, alright," he gave in, never able to say no to his younger brother, "a glass wouldn't hurt."

"These look excellent," Alistair said with a gleam in his mixed colored eyes, reaching out and taking a few of the cookies for himself.

"Seriously?" Albrecht questioned as he reached for the glasses and The Great Queen's Road. The black bottle had a violet label and a distinct depiction of an open-winged raven painted on the glass.

"Fuck you," Alistair answered, a jovialness in his tone as he popped one of the cookies in his mouth, savoring the fruity crunch of the cookie and the sweetness of the milk chocolate underneath, "they're delicious and Svartr is the only place to get them."

Albrecht attempted to steady his hand to pour the scotch into the glasses, but that proved too difficult as the three continued to joke and laugh and enjoy each other's company, the purpose of their conversation temporarily out of mind. As Alistair calmed from a fit of laughter, he looked up and was taken aback to find Valhalla watching him, a sweet smile on her face. With a breathy, shrill giggle, she bent down and plucked the bottle from Albrecht and filled the glasses with the bronze colored liquid. She set a glass before each of them and adjusted the bowl of cookies until it was perfectly nestled in the center of the table. Standing herself erect, she waited quietly as they enjoyed the delights of the late evening, and Alistair found himself grateful that she would allow them this moment before things again turned to darker topics.

Wrapping his fingers around the glass before him, Alistair took a large sip. The amber liquid coated his tongue, the rich vanilla and notes of lavender smooth and malty. A pleasant warmth spread across his chest and settled into his belly. Exhaling, his muscles loosened, and as much as he wanted to immediately take another swig of the beverage, he knew the last thing he needed was a spinning head once the conversation was in motion. So, he placed the glass back on the table and made do with popping a few more of the small cookies into his mouth.

He didn't want Valhalla to have to do this alone, but no one knew her findings better than her. First things first, he needed to make sure the brothers trusted her. After a swallow, he took a deep breath and looked up to his best friends, his expression growing serious. "Listen up, you two. Valhalla has found some . . . troubling things going on in the city. I understand that you don't know her, but all I ask is that, in honor of our friendship, take her word as if it were mine and hear her out completely. Alright?"

"How can I be certain I can trust her?" Albrecht asked, his expression suddenly stern.

Glancing up toward Valhalla, Alistair caught her gaze. Her brows were curved over her still brown eyes, and he found himself missing the true pink hues that should've been there. Her hands were clutched together, and she took a silent gulp. She was nervous.

With a deep breath, he nodded softly to her in confidence and met Albrecht with all the confidence he could muster. "She's the reason Lorna's murderer was found and then quickly captured. By my word, yes, you can trust her."

Albrecht stared back at Alistair for a moment, silent. Alistair hadn't realized he was holding his breath until his friend finally nodded, seemingly satisfied with Alistair's response. Albrecht then took on a more relaxed position on the couch, leaning back with his glass of scotch in one hand and the other resting on his lap. "Well, the floor's yours then, Valhalla."

Valhalla rubbed her bicep vigorously, still hesitant to divulge the purpose of her mission. Alistair then realized that while he had managed to convince the brothers to give her their trust, he had done nothing to convince her of them. It was a mistake he needed to rectify swiftly.

Leaning forward, he softly called to her, "Valhalla." When she met his eyes, he continued, "I swear on everything we went through, you can trust them. They're my dearest friends. Besides, no one knows this castle better than them. I doubt even your mysterious friend in the city knows this castle better. There are things only someone in the royal family would know about."

Valhalla looked at him, and for a moment, it seemed she wouldn't back down, but then she took a deep breath and let out a long, steady breath. Hesitantly, she began to speak. "Alright, but I'm still not sure where—"

"Valhalla," Alistair interrupted and tapped the corner of one of his eyes, "why not start here? Allow them to meet the real you, as I did."

"O-Oh, umm, alright." Valhalla closed her eyes and raised a hand to the side of her face, touching the pad of her middle finger to the corner of one of her eyes. "Taka.[1]"

The brothers seemed taken aback as they heard the words of the ancient Celnor language. As Valhalla opened her eyes, just as Alistair had witnessed in Hilliard, the brown of her iris faded outward. After a few blinks of her eyes, they had turned from an average brown hue to a wonderful shade of pink. The color shone in the firelight, and a familiar flutter came into Alistair's chest.

Clearing his throat, he stole a look at his friends and chortled at their bewilderment. Daemyn was openly in awe at Valhalla's transformation. Albrecht, on the other hand, was more reserved in his response to the change. His brows knitted as he glanced her over warily, as if not sure of how to accept what he had just seen.

Valhalla turned to the brothers and bowed her head. "My name is Valhalla Önníka, I'm," she quieted, her face contorting as if searching for the words. Raising her hands before her chest, a small gap between palms, "Perhaps it's better to show you." A small orb of fire sparked to life and hung in midair, causing the brothers to gasp. "I'm a fire mage, and as His Grace said, I aided his family in uncovering who was responsible for the murder of High Princess Lorna."

"OH!" Daemyn exclaimed, his excitement getting the better of him. "Are you the Lady Red I've heard so much about?" He asked, an actual sparkle in his sky blue eyes.

---

1   Taka is Celnor(Norse) for Remove.

Valhalla, visibly surprised by the question, dismissed the flame with a wave. If the look on Albrecht's face was any indication, he, too, was surprised by the question, and a moment later, he asked, "Lady Red?"

"When I visited Sailors Reef and the homes outside the city, I heard tales of a woman clad in crimson, who could wield fire and who aided people all throughout Veerence. I wasn't sure I believed it at first, but there were far too many accounts of her deeds to have been purely fiction." Daemyn then turned his gaze to Valhalla, smiling. "Are you her?"

Valhalla's cheeks matched the shade of her irises, and she looked mildly uncomfortable with what he had said. She raised a hand and ran her fingers through her raven black hair, twirling a few loose strands between her index finger and thumb, then nodded.

Was she actually embarrassed, Alistair wondered with surprise. He'd known she wasn't one to gloat, but still.

"I-I am. But now I'm beginning to worry that my notoriety has become too high." She said while not meeting any of their eyes.

"You shouldn't be!" Daemyn declared. "You should be honored! You saved an entire town from draug—"

"Wait, what?" Albrecht interrupted, looking at him in disbelief. "Surely you weren't going to say draugr."

"Daemyn," Alistair called, "you can't be serious?"

"Mhmm. Now I know neither of you believes in that stuff, but I like to keep an open mind, and when our citizens said they were being attacked by draugr, I felt it needed to be looked into, even if it ended up only being bandits. So, I hurried over to the Shillphirian Ambassador,"

"Oh come now, Shillphirians are superstitious at the best of times and always make out banditry to be attacks of werewolves and the like," Albrecht said dismissively.

"Yes, well if we assume draugr are real, who better than to ask?" Daemyn replied with a question. "His knowledge of draugr matched what the village detailed about the attacks," his face turned serious as he returned to Valhalla, giving her a thankful smile. "I left at once, but worried I wouldn't make it in time to help. But, when I arrived, the town people were safe. They assured me that a woman in crimson and a man in ebony had dealt with them using fire magic and incredible skill with a sword."

"That doesn't confirm any—" Alistair began but was cut off.

"I sent my soldiers patrolling and soon found stragglers skirting the edge of the town. We dealt with what remained much the same as you did, minus the magic." Daemyn laughed. He then placed a hand over his heart, grinning.

"Thank you for helping the people of Hildr. I honestly don't know what I would've done if you hadn't been there in my absence. We only faced a few, and if their original numbers are to be believed, I hadn't brought nearly enough men and surely would've been counted amongst the dead."

Valhalla returned a soft smile. "I remember the town. Although we were supposed to just be passing through, my friend and I were happy to dispose of the draugrs. I honestly don't know——"

"Alright, well, your knightly deeds are all well and good, but Alistair said you had troubling information about *my* city, and I believe that's a more pressing matter. Don't you think?" Albrecht crossed his arms tightly over his chest. His jaw was set, and a thinly veiled yearning for action seemed to threaten the idleness of their conversation.

Alistair was taken aback. He considered scolding his old friend for the outburst, but one good look at Albrecht told him doing so would only make matters worse. A tremor ran through Albrecht's arms. His leg bounced anxiously. They had stalled too long. Experience told him that once Albrecht got like this, it would be difficult to calm him.

Valhalla and Alistair shared a stare, and it seemed she, too, had noticed just how the mood in the room had soured. Swallowing, she forced a nod. "R-Right, my apologies, your Highness." Then, taking a deep breath, she began. "I was . . . charged with looking into some strange happenings going on in Svartr."

"What strange happenings and charged by whom?" Albrecht's eyes narrowed, his tone giving the impression this had become an interrogation. Despite Alistair having vouched for Valhalla, his friend held fast to his suspicions.

This wasn't good.

"I, ugh,"

"I charged her!" Alistair interrupted, and Valhalla gave him a look of surprise. For a moment, Albrecht too seemed shocked before the glare set in. Alistair's heart raced. Despite what Valhalla had told him, there was no way Albrecht would believe she came on behalf of the gods. Alistair wasn't even sure if *he* believed her. But he trusted her, and that was enough. "I've heard tell of strange happenings in the city, and so I asked Valhalla to look into these matters. Discreetly."

His heartbeat pounded between his ears. Stealing a glance at Valhalla, she seemed almost disappointed. Alistair cursed. He would need to apologize to her later, but there was no time for dwelling on that now.

"Explain." Albrecht eyed him warily.

His brow twitched, and he struggled to force down the growing lump in his throat. Had Albrecht seen through his lie? If not, he likely would if given enough time. Alistair opened his mouth, hoping an explanation would flow from his lips, but he was far from well-practiced at subterfuge. He needed to say something, anything, but nothing was coming to mind. Glancing about, he caught Daemyn's gaze and held it for a moment. Surprisingly enough, there was no judgment in his eyes. He seemed tired. Alistair cursed again.

Valhalla dropped her arms to her sides, hands clenched into fists. Closing her eyes, she took a deep breath and exhaled through her nostrils. Her eyes didn't open when she spoke. "Your father may be behind Svartr's troubles."

Albrecht went rigid, and for a moment, he almost looked as though he would rise from his seat and lash out, but with a breath, he sat forward, and his words came with a growl. "Mind how you speak of my father."

"I understand that he's your father, but his actions lately don't match the man his history paints him to be." She lifted her head and met his stare. "I don't really know how else to tell you this but to put it plainly."

"Think carefully on your next words!" Albrecht snarled.

"Albrecht, I—"

"No, fuck you, Alistair!" Albrecht instantly stood. "I come home to find rebellion plotting against my family, and now I learn you've been spying on my father?" He exclaimed, pain skirting the edge of his voice. It hurt Alistair more than words could describe. This was his second family. He was closer with them in many ways than he was to his family by blood. This hadn't been how he wanted this conversation to go. At every turn, he felt he'd screwed it up, and now, it sounded as though Albrecht believed him a betrayer.

"Your Highness, please. I'm trying to tell you—"

"What?" Albrecht turned, his rage promising violence were they to make another misstep. "What could you possibly be trying to tell me?"

Valhalla startled back a step, but quickly regained her conviction. Her brows raised at the center. Her jaw muscles tensed, and shoulders squared. "That there's no rebellion!"

Were the room any larger, the silence that followed would've been drowned out by the echo of her words.

The anger that had been clouding Albrecht's sky blue eyes turned to confusion. His lips trembled. "What are you saying?"

"I'm saying that the people of Svartr are terrified. Many are too afraid to even leave their homes. The servants dare not even walk the halls of this castle. Your father accuses, arrests,"

"And execute them."

Daemyn's voice was small, a whisper in the wind, and yet his words rang with the crack of thunder. His eyes were wide. The color of his skin drained away, and he was terrified, staring blankly at his half-empty glass of scotch.

"Daemyn?" Albrecht called to his brother, but he didn't respond. The younger Prince's eyes roved across the table surface.

"There's more."

Albrecht and Alistair returned to Valhalla, but she didn't look at them. Her focus was on Daemyn, and Alistair's gut churned. The concern in her features warned him of where the conversation was going, and dread spread through him like a sickness.

"It's about Queen Ayunli."

"I've heard enough." Albrecht snapped. "Next you're—"

Daemyn grabbed Albrecht by the wrist, stopping his older brother like a sword to the heart. The younger Prince's face was obscured by his flaxen hair, but the twitch of his shoulders and sound of his sobs diffused all the anger in the room.

"Daemyn?" Albrecht questioned.

"I need to hear what she has to say," Daemyn said through choked tones, placing his glass on the table, "please, Brother."

He didn't say any more after that. Albrecht visibly deflated. He gazed down at Daemyn's hand and hesitantly reached for it. Albrecht cupped it in his palm and sat beside his little brother.

Alistair caught Valhalla's questioning expression, then nodded for her to continue. She had an uncertainty about her, but with a hesitant nod, she continued all the same.

"I visited the tower where your mother was supposed to be kept, but she wasn't there. No one was." Valhalla's voice was measured and gentle.

Albrecht winced, his expression still teetering on distrust, but the worry for Daemyn kept him from voicing it. "W-Where is she then?"

"That's the thing," her head shook from side to side, raising a hand to the back of her neck, "I don't know. I've searched this castle from top to bottom, and I can't find any trace of her. I also haven't found where your father could've imprisoned the people who've vanished. The castle cells are empty. My friend searched the city, and even he had no luck."

Quiet stretched between them for a time. Seconds, minutes, Alistair wasn't sure. Albrecht stared at Valhalla, disbelief and concern warring in his eyes. Daemyn's trembling grew worse. He seemed to be suffering the effects of his own personal blizzard. Albrecht watched him intently, feeling his forehead for the warmth of a fever, then squeezing Daemyn's shoulder. "Daemyn, what's wrong?"

Daemyn released a shaky breath. "I-I . . . Lately, I've been having dreams. I'm walking down a long, dark stairway. Mother's asleep in my arms. There's an eerie violet light behind us, but when I turn, I can't remember what I've seen. The stairs seem to stretch on forever, but eventually we reach the bottom." He squeezed his brother's hand and let out another sob. "Then, we passed through a door, and there I—" His breathing quickened, and his last words came ragged. "I lock Mother in a guillotine." His free hand slammed into his face, and tears streamed between his fingers, falling to the floor with a soft patter.

"Daemyn, come on," Albrecht gently shook his brother's shoulder, "however terrible, it was just a dream."

Daemyn raised his tear-streaked gaze to Albrecht, fear clear in his features. "How do you know? What if my dreams are trying to tell me something?"

"Calm down," Albrecht chuckled with what was likely an attempt to relieve the tension in the room, "for starters, you were able to carry Mother. She's a tall woman."

"That's not funny. I've grown while you were away. There are plenty of things I can do now that I couldn't before!" Daemyn screamed. "Please, Albrecht, I need to look into this. I need to know."

Albrecht paled, clearly surprised by the outburst. "W-Why?"

"Because I'm terrified of our Father every waking moment!" Daemyn stared at his brother, pleading in his choked words. Albrecht could only stare back, stunned.

Bright blue eyes, glossy and trembling, Daemyn removed his hand from Albrecht's and turned his attention to Valhalla. "There's a place your *friend* couldn't know of, known only to those of Svartr royal blood."

"Alright," Valhalla answered gently, "Tell me where and—"

"No." Daemyn shook his head and stood, his back straightening and shoulders rolling back. "I'm *taking* you there."

Valhalla's head started to shake in protest, her mouth agape as if words would pour forth to dissuade the young prince from his decision, but she said nothing. Unfortunately, in her role as servant, even though it had only been a guise to gain her entry to the castle, she couldn't seem to bring herself to reject a royal. At least that's the conclusion Alistair reached. It was that, or something in Daemyn's plea had swayed her, which was equally likely. She turned to Alistair, and he had his answer. The expression she gave him was one seeking aid, hoping he might convince Daemyn to let her go it alone, to find the answers he sought, and to spare him the sight of what they might find there. The Queen had been missing for a long while, and if there was some truth in Daemyn's vision, well, he dared not imagine it. Still, he understood the need to go, to be there for whatever they might find. Alistair shrugged with an apologetic smile.

Turning to Albrecht, Alistair hoped he hadn't lost all of his friend's trust and steeled his expression. "Albrecht, I'll go with Daemyn and keep him safe. I know you want to go, but at the moment, all of this is speculation. Were you to go and your father come looking for you, we would be found out. Should we find the prisoners, or Ayunli, we'll be able to learn what's really going on, and I'll tell you everything. I swear to you, we're just looking for answers. Trust me, please." Alistair hoped his sincerity might win his friend over. He meant every word. They did need answers. Surely there was some sort of misunderstanding, and once Ayunli was found, everything would make sense. Things would be alright.

Albrecht's once concerned expression slowly hardened. "Fine, but just so we're clear." He stood and walked straight to Valhalla. She startled as he grabbed her by the collar and shoved her hard against a wall by Daemyn's bar, pinning her in place. His ferocity and her sudden shriek caught both Alistair and Daemyn by surprise.

Alistair reached out to stop Albrecht, but paused as the heir of Svartr held out a hand.

"Listen to me, and listen well," Albrecht raised a pointed finger to a now wide-eyed Valhalla, "if anything happens to my brothers, I'll hold you *personally* responsible. Do I make myself clear?" Albrecht growled, less a question than a statement.

Valhalla stared back in disbelief. She kept her body and hands flat against the wall. The only sound she made was a groan. Within moments, he released her. She seemed about ready to collapse to the floor and let out a shaky breath.

Albrecht marched straight to the doors leading out of the chamber, ignoring his things on the coat rack, and swung the doors wide. He suddenly stopped, planted dead in the center of the threshold. His hands briefly clenched and then relaxed at his sides. Spinning back to Daemyn and Alistair, his brows were knitted, and while his anger still seethed, Alistair spotted the concern etched in his bright blue eyes. "You two *better* be careful." Then, with that, he disappeared into the darkness of the hallway.

After a moment of silence and shock, Alistair rushed to Valhalla and was immediately followed by Daemyn. As he touched her shoulder, she flinched, and the look on her face was abject fear. Had Albrecht truly terrified her so, or was there more to it? In Hilliard, she had struck him as someone not so easily shaken, and seeing her now, he wasn't sure what to say.

His expression softened, and he knew the only thing he could offer was an apology. "Valhalla, I'm so sorry. I-I didn't—" Alistair shook his head and forced his hands to his sides, daring not to touch her again. "I'm sorry, I didn't expect him to treat you like that."

"Emer—" Daemyn knelt and held his hand outstretched, "Valhalla. Are you hurt?"

"I'm fine!" She exclaimed, and Daemyn flinched. She closed in on herself, grasping her wrist over her chest, and closed her eyes, taking several deep breaths.

She didn't seem to be panicking. Alistair had enough experience with doing that on his own to know the difference. She was trying to calm herself. So, Alistair tapped Daemyn on the shoulder, and as his young friend gazed up at him, Alistair signaled for them both to step away. She needed space, and so she would have it. He couldn't help but watch her, scanning Valhalla for signs of injury. However, by all accounts, she seemed to be alright. He took a few steps back and grasped his forearm to wring out his concerns. The two waited a short distance away while Valhalla regained her composure.

After a few more deep breaths, the tension seemed to leave her body, and her eyes opened, trailing the floor. "I'm sorry, I just . . . I wasn't prepared for that." She turned to Alistair with upturned brows. "I honestly thought he had calmed, but I suppose the thought of you both in danger just brought that out of him."

Alistair shook his head. Even if that were the case, it was no excuse. "Again, I'm so sorry, Valhalla. He's always been a tempest, but I thought," he sighed, "I hoped my approval would've been enough."

Valhalla shook her head at him as well. "I don't think it was a lack of trust, Your Grace. I accused his father of doing terrible things. He just returned from seeing countless horrors. This was meant to be a place of peace, and was instead welcomed home by nothing but more troubles. While I don't excuse his outburst, I understand it."

Alistair let out a sigh as he dragged his palm down his face. "You may be right. Let's get this investigation over with. The sooner we find these prisoners and Ayunli, the better. There must be something we're missing." He then turned to Daemyn. "Where do we need to go?"

"Just follow me and you'll see." Daemyn's hands were clenched at his sides, and his face was full of worry. "However, we *have* to remain quiet while roaming the halls. Albrecht's tired, so he'll be heading to his chamber, but . . . it isn't safe. Do you understand?"

"Of course we'll be quiet, but why the concern?" Alistair asked, cocking his head in confusion.

"Father placed a curfew over the castle, and let's just say," Daemyn let out a shaky breath, "you *don't* want to know what happens to those who disobey."

45

Alistair

The Secret Stairway

Alistair and Valhalla followed closely behind Daemyn, the three of them moving as quietly as possible. None dared speak a word as they crept through the dimly lit halls of the castle. It seemed odd to Alistair that so many of the lanterns would be left unlit, though with the curfew in place, it wasn't as if the servants would be going about their duties. Perhaps a draft had blown them out, he considered, though was unconvinced.

As they descended, Daemyn regularly stopped to peer around corners and stairways, making certain the way was clear before continuing. He moved about as a mouse trapped in a den of vipers. His caution made Alistair nervous. Just what punishment had Aegir put in place to make even his own son fear being caught? They were sneaking around like thieves, and everything about it left a bad taste in Alistair's mouth.

Soon, the three of them arrived at the second floor. Daemyn's pace suddenly quickened. It appeared as though they were close to their destination now. In heartbeats, they reached the sky hall, which connected the castle to the cells next door. Alistair thought back to his first tour of the castle as a child. If memory served, these cells were specially used for prisoners of war and others deemed important by the ruler of Svartr. It was similar to the cells beneath his own castle. Any whose incarceration was too important to the safety of the realm would be housed here.

As the trio proceeded through the sky hall, Alistair glanced to his side, to the wide windows where he should've found a beautiful view of the castle courtyard, but instead all he found was complete darkness. He stopped in his tracks, which seemed to catch the attention of Valhalla. "Your Grace?"

Daemyn then noticed, already several paces ahead. He turned to look at Alistair with furrowed brows. The concern in his bright blue eyes was palpable. "Alistair, we don't have much time?"

"I understand, but," Alistair started as he stepped toward the window, placing a hand on the glass, "it's so dark outside." He turned to Daemyn, confused. "Has it always been like this?"

"Not usually, no," Daemyn answered with a quick shake of his head, "this is recent." The young prince then spun away and continued down the sky hall. "Come on, we can't be caught."

Valhalla immediately followed after Daemyn, but Alistair lingered there a moment, something souring and weighing heavily in the pit of his stomach. There was a question he needed to ask. "Are the punishments really that bad?"

Daemyn immediately stopped, his hand outstretched toward a handle of one of the doors leading to the prison structure. His demeanor tensed all the more, and he seemed reluctant to answer. Eventually, his hand dropped to his side, and he turned to face Alistair. His eyes shone with tears. "One night, I was in my chamber but wasn't tired. It was after Father placed the curfew. I never questioned why he did it and until that night, it hadn't concerned me. I was restless, so I decided to take a stroll through the castle, heading to Mother's Rose Garden, hoping the scent of her flowers would relax my mind and help me sleep. This was also after Mother fell ill and had to be kept in seclusion. Perhaps, I simply missed her and wanted to be near something that reminded me of her."

He looked away, his shoulders quivering.

"There was a servant maiden attending to me at the time. Logír. I asked her to accompany me. Understandably, she was concerned and brought up the curfew, but I told her that so long as she was with me, she would be fine. I promised." His eyes closed, head tilting down, obscuring his face. "I was wrong." He finished with a croak.

A chill prickled Alistair's skin. His thoughts jumped to several conclusions, none of them good, and so he waited until Daemyn was ready to continue.

"We were about halfway through the garden before Father found us. With him were four of his Kingsguard. I was unsettled at first, I'll admit. It was Father, but he looked so . . ." Daemyn shuddered. "Anyway, shaking off my apprehension, I greeted him as I usually do, but he immediately cut me off with a line of questions. Why was I out and about? Why would I disobey his order? Was I trying to. . ." He paused and took a deep breath. "I answered him honestly. I told him I couldn't sleep and that Mother was on my mind. Father understood, at least he said as much. Unfortunately," he returned to Alistair, wiping away a tear rolling down his cheek, "even though I was the one who convinced Logír to accompany me, he said she had no excuse. Can you believe that?" Daemyn asked, glancing from Alistair to Valhalla, and back again. "He ordered two of the guards to bind her and the other two to hold me back."

Alistair's heart twisted, and his fingers climbed toward his father's ring.

"You're right to worry, Alistair," Daemyn said flatly. "I begged Father to let her go. I pleaded to not punish her, that I was the reason she was there, that I promised she would be safe and that if he needed to punish someone, it should be me. Do you want to know what he said?"

"I'd rather not guess," Alistair answered, heart racing.

Daemyn nodded once in understanding. "He said, let this be a lesson. When someone of his status gives an order, he expects *everyone* to abide by it. It was my one and only warning. I was then dragged back to my bedchamber with no knowledge of what would befall Logír. I didn't sleep that night." He let out a troubled sigh. "The next morning, Emera, or should I say, Valhalla, came to get me. Mistress Lilianna needed to see me, I believe, is how she worded it. She's the head Servant of the castle, and so I hoped I'd see Logir and could apologize. Valhalla took me to the Servants' Quarters. I thought if Logír was injured, I would pay whatever was necessary for her to see a healer." Fear and rage twisted Daemyn's features. "Instead, when we arrived, Lilianna ushered us to a room where I found out what fate my father deemed *appropriate* for my slight. Logír was dead on the floor, beaten and flayed. A letter was nailed on the wall above her remains, warning everyone of what would happen if they disobeyed curfew again, and that even the Prince would be powerless to protect them."

Alistair's breath caught in his throat. How could such a punishment be warranted? Why would Aegir torture his son like that? This wasn't right. Aegir had never been someone to do such a thing in the past. Just what was going on here?

Ignoring another wave of nausea, Alistair cleared his throat. "Daemyn, I—"

"It's alright." Daemyn shook his head and turned to the doors before him. "Since then, the castle staff have been cautious around me, and I've made sure to not insist on anything that would put them in danger." Opening one of the doors ever so slightly, Daemyn peeked inside, the conversation dying with the creak of the hinge.

Alistair gazed at Valhalla, her back to him. He leaned in close to her and whispered, "Why didn't you tell me?"

"It wasn't my story to tell. I was one of the few who volunteered to attend to His Highness. Since that morning, the other staff have been afraid of being around him. They blamed him for Logír's death. Most did, but a sparse few didn't, myself among them." Her hands perched about her waist. "It was an accident. A terrible one, yes, and none have punished him for it more than his Highness has himself. I did what I could to care for and soothe his nerves, and to his credit, he's treaded carefully around his father ever since."

Relief spread through Alistair's chest. "Thank you, Valhalla, for being there for my friend."

She nodded once, the warmth of her smile softening the twist in his gut. "Of course, your Grace. I've done what I could, I just wish he hadn't had to suffer through so much, but by this point, I suppose we all have, in our own way." Valhalla shrugged.

Sighing, Alistair nodded in agreement. Albrecht had just returned from war. Daemyn was terrified of his father. Alistair lost his sister, and he, too, had seen war firsthand. Then there was Valhalla. For as much as he trusted in her, he really knew next to nothing about her. Her words and deeds spoke volumes of her character, but he knew nothing of her hardships. What he knew for certain was that she constantly put herself in danger to help others. Just as he opened his mouth to speak, Daemyn groaned with frustration.

"Dammit, it's too dark in there." Standing before the small opening, Daemyn looked beside him to a hanging lantern by the doors. His hand reached for it, then froze, a heavy sigh escaping his lips, followed by the slumping of his shoulders.

"What's wrong?" Alistair asked.

"If I take the lantern, Father will think a servant was out tonight," Daemyn answered, shaking his head. "I can't do that to them, not again." He began agitatedly spinning a ring around his finger. His nerves were fraying.

Alistair smiled and placed a hand on Daemyn's shoulder, squeezing it gently for comfort. "It's alright, I understand, why don't I—"

"You two are precious," Valhalla said with a chuckle.

As Alistair and Daemyn turned to her, a tiny ball of flames no larger than a pebble ignited and hovered over Valhalla's cupped palms, a playful smirk creasing her face.

Daemyn slapped a hand to his face. "Dammit, how did I forget *you* could do that? Oh, wait," he turned and slapped Alistair square in the chest, "you know light magic, why didn't you do that?"

Alistair rolled his eyes. "For your information, I was *about* to. She just beat me to it." Placing a hand to the side of Daemyn's head, he nudged him out of the way, and the younger prince chuckled as he stepped to the door. It felt good knowing he could make his friend laugh at a time like this. Now, they needed to solve the mystery of what was going on with Aegir.

As Alistair pushed the door open, it dawned on him just how dark the castle cells truly were. He could just barely make out a dark shape, likely iron railings lining the walkways. "Well, this is dark. Daemyn," he spun to his friend, "seeing as Valhalla doesn't know the way and she's our source of light, you should stay beside her. Is that alright?" He turned to Valhalla for her response, but was taken aback. She seemed shaken by something. Her eyes were wide, staring past him into the darkness.

At first, he wasn't sure if it was a trick of the light, but the slight tremble in her cupped hands worried him. He tilted his head, debating reaching out to reassure her, but thought better of it as she took in a breath and exhaled, expression softening. She wasn't completely at ease, a flicker of fear still visible in her pink eyes, but seemed steady enough to press on.

"O-Of course," Valhalla answered, "it's not a problem."

Alistair trusted her, believed her well enough, however for the sake of caution, wanted to be certain. "Is everything alright?"

"I'm . . ." Valhalla swallowed nervously. "I don't love the dark." She replied, her voice soft and taking on a shroud of emotion he'd never heard from her. Was that shame, he wondered?

"That's alright," Daemyn walked up beside her and wrapped his arms around one of hers, seemingly not even noticing the height disparity between the two of them, and shot Valhalla a warm smile. "Just stand by me, I'll keep you safe from the darkness, my Lady. Let's just not get caught." He waved an arm forward with a flourish as if to punctuate his words. Alistair rolled his eyes, thinking the gesture a bit much, but it seemed to work on Valhalla, if the sweet trill of her giggle was any degree of measure.

"I swear you're such a silly young man." She said, then proceeded into the darkness with Daemyn at her side, leaving Alistair to close the doors behind them.

"Eh, I try." Daemyn stifled a chuckle and guided Valhalla to the right. A deathly quiet filled the space, their breath and the tapping of their footfalls gently echoing against the stone.

Following after his friends, Alistair could barely make out his surroundings. Valhalla's light only illuminated the space within an arm's length of its source. At least the place was empty, or at least seemed to be, though that brought little comfort. Sure, it meant they wouldn't be spotted by a loose-lipped captive, but the absence of residents was at odds with the rumors of disappearances. It unsettled Alistair. If there had been threats made against the Svartr royal family, those accused would've been taken here.

Alistair kept close to the light, inspecting what he could see of the empty cells as they moved through the structure. Each cell seemed fairly large, able to hold a couple of prisoners at once. Iron bars stood between him and the interior. Most of the building was made of the same black stone as the castle, save for the wooden floors both within and outside of the cells. Unused cots dotted the corners of each cell, and occasionally, an iron-barred window, only visible thanks to the glint of the firelight reflected from metal, would add some variety to the otherwise flat structure. Everything was unusually clean.

"The stairs should be right here." Daemyn's voice pulled Alistair's attention ahead.

The group made their way down the stairs to what Daemyn said was the ground floor, where wood underfoot became stone. A shiver ran through his body as a surge of cold hit him. The change in temperature was so abrupt it was like waking aboard a boat to find yourself underwater. Alistair brought his arms to his biceps and tried to rub some warmth back into them. "Is it usually this cold?"

Daemyn and Valhalla huddled close, and the younger prince answered. "In the winter months, aye, but this doesn't make any sense." His words came with a chattering cadence. "Come on, I think it is this way, Valhalla, can you stretch the firelight a bit further?"

With a nod, she stretched her arm out, and the flame grew. Light spread, revealing several more empty cells and a distinct gap up ahead.

"Aye, there it is." Daemyn pointed and quietly hurried to the opening.

Valhalla and Alistair jolted and rushed after him. As they reached the young prince, Alistair was surprised to find the space was about the same size as the cells. There were no bars blocking the entrance to the square area, but otherwise it was unremarkable. Valhalla stepped into the center of the space and held her fire aloft, letting the light soak over the area. She then looked to Daemyn. "So what're we looking for?"

Daemyn stared, confusion twisting his features for a moment, then shook his head. "Sorry, there's usually more here. A table, chairs, other trappings, and at least one guard at the entrance. I expected the guards to be gone given the curfew, but still, it's just odd seeing it so empty now."

He approached Valhalla, searched the space, then continued past her. Daemyn stopped before a wall of stone bricks and placed a hand on its center. His hand ran slowly across the surface. "Where is it?" Placing a second hand on the wall, he examined, but for what exactly, Alistair wasn't sure. Just looking at the wall, the brickwork gave away no hint of its secret. "Father's taller," Daemyn continued, "but it shouldn't be *that* high."

Alistair and Valhalla walked to either side of Daemyn, scanning the walls, but nothing stood out. Valhalla raised her fire higher. "Your Highness, what're you looking for exactly?"

A groan emanated from the young prince's throat. "Sorry, it's just been a while. One of these bricks has a small engraving of my family's crest on the face. I know it's on this wall, I just don't know where!" Daemyn pushed the wall in frustration, as if that might actually solve the problem, only managing to push himself back several feet.

"Alright then—Ngh!" Valhalla winced and brought a hand to her right shoulder, massaging the muscle and rolling the shoulder back as she inspected the wall. Alistair and Daemyn gave her a look and then shared a knowing glance. No doubt, Albrecht had injured her when he shoved her against the wall earlier. "The bricks are small, but if we—"

"Wait," Daemyn took her hand from her shoulder and turned her to face him. "I know this is poorly timed given our current surroundings, but I know I didn't say anything earlier, after my brother placed his hands on you the way he did, and I should have. I'm sorry, Valhalla, I-I wasn't expecting any of what happened. I was taken by surprise and froze. Still, I froze, and you paid the price, and for that I'm ashamed. I swore I wouldn't let anyone else get hurt because of me, and I've already failed in that."

She blinked a few times at him, but then, to his and Alistair's surprise, a smile grew on her face. She glanced at Alistair, and as their eyes met, his breath hitched in his throat. Feeling the shame built in his gut, he looked away. Neither he nor Daemyn stopped Albrecht when they should've. By the time he looked back at her, she had returned her attention to Daemyn and touched her hand to his bicep. "Listen to me, the *both* of you, as I said before, I'll not excuse what Prince Albrecht did, but I understand it. His Highness had been through a lot. War changes everyone, and he's not the first I've seen become quick to aggression. He may continue to be unpredictable for a time."

She gazed at Daemyn for a long while. "During the festivities, many of the castle staff witnessed Prince Albrecht acting unusual. A few times he snuck away, likely needing to be alone, to drop the act, so to speak." Daemyn and Alistair rightfully startled at that. "Some witnessed his Highness's breathing go ragged, heard sobs and curses, apologizing to the dead."

Alistair's breath caught in his throat. "Why didn't he tell us he was struggling with what he went through?"

"Because it's just how that big *idiot* is!" Daemyn cursed with tightness in his throat. "He's *always* kept things bottled up, never wanting to *burden* anyone. He thinks himself a lone wolf, which by the way I've reminded him isn't a thing. They travel in packs after all, but he doesn't listen. I swear he's worse than Father!"

Valhalla let out a soft sigh and cupped his cheek, waiting for him to look up at her. "In my experience, we just need to be patient with him. When he's ready, he'll come to you. Just be there for your brother when the time comes. The moment might be faint, and you dare not miss it."

Daemyn let out a troubled sigh and mumbled, "I doubt it."

Valhalla was visibly taken aback, and Daemyn shook his head, sliding away from her touch. He rubbed the back of his neck in frustration and let his head fall back, face upturned to the ceiling with eyes closed. "If this is anything like The War of Lions, Albrecht will bottle everything up until he can't hold it in any longer, then explode like cannon fire." He slowly opened his eyes, and Alistair sensed the sadness flowing from him. "I witnessed it, and honestly, it terrified me then as it terrifies me now. But," his hands fell to his sides, "Mother was there to help him. Anger, crying, fits of fear, and apologies. But most of all, she bore his confusion. He didn't know what to do with himself after the war ended. Mother contacted someone from Hvítr who specialized in healing the mind."

"Who better to turn to than a castle city that for ages has specialized in warfare and raising surprisingly resilient soldiers," Alistair said, coming out as more of a statement than a question.

Daemyn nodded in agreement and shrugged. "It was a process, of course, but Albrecht eventually became himself again, though I suppose the aggression never entirely left."

"Then that's what you should do," Valhalla said matter-of-factly. "Seek out this mind healer from Hvítr and convince your brother to meet with them. If it helped before, then his Highness is sure to see the benefits of speaking with them again. Trauma is a terrible thing to let be."

"You know," Alistair started with an agreeable smile, "I think that's a good idea. Once we find Ayunli, we can ask her to help with the problems facing

Albrecht, Aegir, and this city. With her knowledge, I'm sure things can be straightened out." He walked up on the other side of Daemyn and placed a hand on the wall. "So let's return to the task at hand. Valhalla, what were you about to say before we got sidetracked?"

"Oh, I was going to suggest that we split our search. You take the left side of the wall. His Highness can search the center, and I'll take the right." Valhalla flicked her right hand upward, tossing the flame to float in midair.

Alistair and Daemyn gaped at the display for a moment. "Sounds good," Alistair responded with a chuckle, then turned to Daemyn. "We're just looking for a brick with your family crest, right?"

"Aye. Hopefully, it won't be too hard to find. We just need to feel around for it. It should be about chest level for the both of you." Daemyn answered as he turned to start his search.

Alistair nodded and began his search as well. Running his hands across his section of the wall at the far left. Several long moments passed as the three searched in quiet. Even with the light, it was difficult to spot the engraving. He had paused at several stones, thinking that he had felt a small dip in the surface, but each had turned out to be nothing.

Inching ever closer to Daemyn's search area, he worried he might've missed it and would need to start back at the beginning, when suddenly his thumb brushed against a spot that differed from the others. Sliding his fingers slowly over the spot to inspect it further, each of the lines felt too precise to be anything other than what they had been searching for. It was located at chest level, just as Daemyn had said, and so Alistair bent down and leaned to one side to better utilize the firelight. Sure enough, there embedded in the stone was a familiar sea serpent within a ring.

"Daemyn, I found it." He said a little too excitedly, a sentiment clearly shared by Daemyn as he slapped the wall in triumph.

"I had a feeling it was close by! Go ahead and push the stone." Daemyn pointed to it, and Alisatir obliged with a nod.

Pressing on the spot, he was surprised at just how easily it slid into the wall with only the faintest sound of stone rubbing against stone. A loud clunk followed from somewhere inside the wall, and after, a mechanical ticking, rhythmic, like gears stirring from a long sleep. Alistair's heartbeat a little faster as he stepped away, unsure of what to expect, then Daemyn laughed. Alistair rolled his eyes and pursed his lips, feeling a little foolish. Valhalla stepped beside him, eyes locked on the wall, possibly sharing his concern.

After a long, breathless moment, a section of wall moved out just enough to cast a vertical line of shadow from floor to ceiling. Daemyn punched a fist in the air, reveling in the small victory and likely excited at the idea of finding his mother, then walked toward the opening. "Valhalla, could you bring your fire closer?"

"Of course, one moment." Raising her hand toward her fire, she summoned it back with a twirl of her wrist and stepped around Daemyn, the light washing over the area.

"Here it is! Now, I just—NGH!" Sliding his fingers around the protruding stone, Daemyn pulled, but nothing happened. His cheeks reddened and puffed as he tried again, but clearly the wall was too heavy for him alone.

Alistair rushed beside him and ran his fingers down the edge, finding small recesses which could be used as grips. Sliding his fingers into position, he latched onto the surface and pulled. The stone began to grind, moving away from the rest of the wall.

"Woah!" Alistair's jaw dropped. "You have a hidden passageway?"

Daemyn chuckled through a grunt. "Less talking, more pulling!"

"Right!" Alistair said as the two put all their strength into moving the door. His muscles tensed and veins pulsed. Eventually, they managed to pull the door open just enough to see a darkened stairway inside. It led down into complete blackness, and as he stood there, peering into the void, the hairs on the back of his neck stood on end.

46

𝔄listair

A Terrible Stench

Both Alistair and Daemyn heaved in heavy breaths as Valhalla warily inspected the entryway of the secret tunnel. Alistair's hands burned from exertion, and after a few deep breaths, he let out an exhausted laugh. "Well, I definitely wasn't expecting that."

Daemyn joined in, his laughter catching between breaths. "I know, right? This was made loooooong before my time. Father told Albrecht and I that if the castle were ever breached, we had to come here to flee. There are some hidden rooms below. It's a safe place to hide, and should the need arise, we could follow the path further. It leads into a cave which opens to the sea."

"Was this built after Gullhyndr invaded?" Alistair asked as he stood himself upright, stretching his sore muscles.

"Pretty much." Daemyn shrugged.

Alistair grinned at that. "Well, it's impressive, but it's pretty far from your rooms. Wouldn't it be safer to use the secret passageway behind that painting at the back of the castle?"

"Either is fine, but it never hurts to have a backup plan. Besides, who would expect us to flee toward a dungeon? Now come on, let—" Daemyn stepped to the opening and froze, slamming a hand over his face. "Ugh, what the fuck!?" He exclaimed and stumbled back.

"What is it?" Alistair asked, stepping beside Daemyn and Valhalla, it hit him. An odor crept up the stairway and into his nostrils, familiar as it was horrible. A shudder ran up his spine. The foul stench brought him back to the aftermath of the War of Lions. Mounds of bodies littered fields where crops once grew and children played, left as carrion for rats and crows.

Alistair's body went taut. He stared wide-eyed into the descending darkness and a knot formed in his gut. Valhalla leaned back against the wall beside him, a hand over her nose and her eyes wide, trembling. Was she familiar with this scent as well?

"It," she swallowed, her voice a shallow whisper, "It smells of death."

Alistair stared at her, perplexed. "I-I'm afraid to ask how you know that smell."

"Then don't." She growled, avoiding his gaze. "The last thing I want is to relive those memories."

His body shuddered at that, understanding completely. Any memory that surfaced with the smell of death was a memory most unwelcome. He didn't need to know her demons to empathize with the sentiment. Nodding in understanding, he attempted to swallow the lump in his throat and replied, "Agreed."

"Sh-Should we turn back?" Daemyn asked.

Looking at his friend, Alistair found the young Prince's eyes brimming with tears, possibly from fear of what they might find, or simply due to the smell. Probably both.

Alistair shook his head gently. "I have a terrible feeling we've found those missing prisoners." His stomach churned.

Alistair lingered there a moment longer, holding his breath, and then took a shaky step. His booted foot landed on the first stair step, followed by the second, and then the third. He cautiously allowed himself to take another breath, and death filled his lungs. Bile raged up his throat. He slapped a palm over his mouth and held his breath. His back slammed against the wall beside Valhalla and seemed to startle her.

Thump. Thump. Thump. His heartbeat in his ears. Adrenaline surged like lightning through his veins. Something shifted in his gut, and pain immediately followed. His lungs burned for air.

Closing his eyes, he focused on keeping the vomit down and reluctantly breathed again. The decay and rusty iron stench wafted out of the stairway, but the smell was so much worse only a few steps into the smaller space. Both Daemyn and Valhalla watched him as if he might know what they should do. After several moments of searching for his composure, Alistair gazed at his palms through bleary eyes. His gaze lingered on the sleeve of his under tunic, faintly poking out from beneath his violet garment.

He rubbed his watery eyes, then ran his hands down the length of his buttoned tunic, and an idea took shape in his mind. He grabbed for his under tunic, rubbing the cloth between his fingers. "It just might work." Using his teeth, he made a small tear near the bottom of the white tunic, then, using his hands, made a much larger tear.

On and on he ripped, his companions watching with curiosity and confusion. Soon Alistair had freed a large strip of fabric and placed it over his face, tying it in the back to create a makeshift healer's mask. Once certain the knot was snug, he tucked the excess fabric into the tops of his tunics, hoping the new garment would lessen the smell.

Finally raising his eyes to his companions, he shrugged. "This is the best I can do."

"Oh!" Daemyn exclaimed. "That's not a bad idea, but I'm not ripping my clothes." He reached into one of his trousers' pockets and pulled free two handkerchiefs, one pink, decorated with colorful hand-stitched flowers at one corner, and the other bright blue with snowflakes, also stitched into one of the corners. He turned to Valhalla and handed her the pink one.

She took it, but gave him a perplexed look. "Thank you, but why do you have two?"

Daemyn used the handkerchief to cover his nose and mouth and pointed to the pink one in her hand, "That one belongs to my mother. I found it in my room the day I learned she was quarantined. I've been holding onto it for her. Please, don't lose it."

"Of course, your Highness, thank you." Valhalla tightened her grip on Ayunli's handkerchief and mimicked Daemyn, placing it over her mouth and nose with one hand, and holding out the fire with the other.

They both turned to Alistair, and he gazed back into the darkened stairway. Dread clung to his heart, fearing what he might find once they found the source of the smell. With a deep breath, he said, "Daemyn, I'll walk with Valhalla the rest of the way, alright?"

"What about the door?" Valhalla noted with a tilt of her head.

"I'll close it once we're through. If we hear it open, we'll just have to hide in one of the rooms Daemyn mentioned." Stepping into the stairway, he tested a breath and to his relief, the smell had lessened. "Come on."

He reached out a hand to Valhalla. She placed the ball of fire above her shoulder and took his hand in hers. Warmth bloomed once more with her touch, sending his heart fluttering, which in the moment seemed strange, but not entirely unwelcome.

He was glad his face was obscured by the mask, as he was certain the look on his face must've been a strange mix of revulsion and something else, an emotion he wasn't sure how to put into words. It was likely just her fire magic causing the sensation anyway. Alistair pulled her toward him, and as she passed by, he caught the faintest scent of wisterias and revebjelles filtering through the rotting stench.

Valhalla gazed at Alistair, her eyes darting between his, with brows curved upward in confusion. He glanced down at their hands and immediately understood. He let her go and squeaked out an apology through his tightening throat.

"Everything alright?"

Alistair jumped, having momentarily forgotten about Daemyn. "Aye, just . . . It's nothing, come on." Waving his friend in, Alistair was certain he saw a hint of a smile crease Daemyn's eye as he walked past, but shook the thought away.

Alistair grabbed hold of a large iron handle bolted on their side of the secret door and pulled. To his surprise, it was much easier to close than it had been to open. With a loud clunk, the door shut. Gears began to whir inside the walls, followed by a click, and then silence.

"Alright then," Alistair said as he returned to Valhalla, "let's find out what's going on here."

"Let's hope I don't vomit on the way down." Daemyn groaned, hugging close to the wall as the three started their descent.

"Just breathe slowly in through your mouth and out your nose. There'll be a terrible taste, but it should help with the gagging sensation." Valhalla said matter-of-factly.

Deeper and deeper they went, the smell growing all the while. Valhalla suddenly stumbled forward, and Alistair jolted to her side. She was hunched forward, face contorted, and body trembling. An arm rested on the wall beside her, and hand clenched in a tight fist.

Gently, he touched her back and arm. He felt her tense, but she didn't pull away. "Valhalla?"

She let out a gasping breath, as if she had been holding it in, and shook her head. He spotted a few tears rolling down her cheeks. Her eyes closed and her brow lined with worry, but before he could say anything else, she answered, "I-I'm sorry. I'm sorry." Her voice cracked with strain. "Unwanted memories flooded to mind. Dammit. Why do they always resurface?"

Alistair's breath hitched in his throat; the question one he had often asked himself. Softly rubbing her back, he leaned close and said, "I won't pry, and I won't force you to continue on."

Valhalla shook her head, her eyes opening. They were glossy in her firelight, and a stern expression came over her face. "I-I have to—" She swallowed, "I have to keep going. I'm not about to abandon the two of you." Forcing herself to stand, she took a deep breath and nodded at Alistair to continue on.

Alistair slowly stepped away, inspected Valhalla. "If you're sure."

"I am. Please, your Grace, press on." Her beautiful pink eyes blazed with determination.

She had gone through something terrible in her past. He was certain of it. What that could have been, though, he wasn't sure. As much as curiosity pressed him to ask, he would honor her wishes. Besides, now wasn't the time for it anyway. Looking at Daemyn, he was also clearly struggling, be it from the smell or the surely gruesome scene that awaited them ahead . . . probably both.

"Daemyn, what about you?" Alistair asked, hoping to spare the young Prince of such a sight. He might, after all, be thankful for the opportunity to return to his room and wait for their return.

Daemyn shrugged. "I'm not having the best of times," he replied through heavy breaths, "but I can keep going."

"That's good," Valhalla responded, "because it appears we've reached the bottom."

Alistair turned past her and, just at the edge of her firelight, spotted the bottom of the stairway. To his surprise, a small flicker of relief spread over him. It was better to have the truth than the dread of what might be. He rushed down the remaining steps and staggered at the bottom as the smell hit him. It was somehow so much worse all of a sudden. Valhalla was behind him, hugging her side of the wall a few steps up, and handkerchief clamped to her face.

Alistair reached up his hand to her, and she quickly took it. He guided her to stand at his side, holding her gaze and silently promising he would be there for her should she need it. She seemed to understand and nodded.

Daemyn was several steps up, looking like he might pass out. Alistair reached out as he had for Valhalla and said, "Come on, Daemyn, we're almost done."

The younger Prince seemed to drag himself forward and soon found the bottom. "Dammit, how can you withstand this stench?"

The question chafed. The truth was that Alistair's two years fighting in the War of Lions served as good preparation, but it wasn't something he knew how to put into words. By the end of the war, he could walk through a field of corpses without so much as a handkerchief over his face, but now, well, time had passed, and he was out of practice. It wasn't a skill he ever wanted to hone again anyway, and were it within his powers, future generations would never need to either.

Alistair placed a gentle hand on Daemyn's back and his other on the young Prince's bicep, feeling more muscle than he would've expected. Daemyn wasn't as big as Alistair, thin of frame and shorter by a head, but still, what muscle was there was firm as iron. Perhaps this was the benefit of training with a rapier, thin but strong and probably faster for it.

"Alistair, I-I'm so sorry. That was insensitive."

"Don't be. I just hope you never have to experience such a thing."

"I know. I think that's something you and Albrecht both share." Daemyn said with a soft chuckle, followed by a cough. His expression then changed, turned worried, and his eyes looked past Alistair. "Valhalla, wait!"

Alistair spun around to see her hand on the handle of a door, and before he could react, she pushed it open and both her and her fire disappeared.

The sound of her coughing and a loud shriek was all they had to guide their steps. Both princes slid to a stop as they caught sight of the fire. Daemyn stood just behind his shoulder and him in the doorway. Valhalla's back was against the inner wall just by the door. Both hands clung to the handkerchief. A myriad of expressions warred on her face, but the strongest among them was revulsion. Her body shook with fear, eyes locked on something before them. Alistair's entire being screamed for him to take her and Daemyn by the hand and run, to flee from this wretched place and to deliver them both to the safety of Hilliard. But he didn't.

His body carried him a step further, and as his head turned to see just what it was that had elicited such a reaction from her, he instantly stopped dead in his tracks. Regret filled him like an endless carafe of wine to a chalice, spilling over the rim and flooding everything in sight. His heart sank, and something in his gut ached. He couldn't breathe. Legs, arms, bodies, all severed and piled in a heap before him, a mass of horror and sin.

47

Alistair

A Bloody Memory

T he pile of bodies was stacked up to Alistair's chest. Some were decomposed for what could've been months, others so recently added to the collection that they could've been killed that very evening. Some seemed largely to be intact. Many were dissected and so completely dismembered that even kin would likely find it impossible to spot where their loved ones began and ended. Their clothing was completely soaked in blood. Several bodies hung suspended above the pile, held aloft by intestines. Their skin had been completely stripped away. It was impossible to know who they were in life, but in death, they had become a madman's or a mad King's gruesome marionettes.

The downward pull of the world seemed to shift and caused Alistair's body to sway. He felt himself helplessly falling backward, yet strangely, the ground never left his feet. His stomach churned. He braced, expecting the wall to come crashing into his back any moment, yet it never came. A breeze, hot as a forge, brushed his cheek. The bright sun was blinding overhead, and sweat beaded his brow.

Just what in Helheim was going on?

Dizziness plagued him. The savanna before him stretched in all directions, and within moments, he knew where he was. The air was tainted with the stench of iron. His head felt heavy, and he reached up to run his hand through his hair but flinched at the sensation of metal against his skin. It was warm and slick as if wet. Something slid down the side of his forehead. Holding his hand to his face, he realized he was wearing his old Hillian, raven-decorated armor. It was coated in blood, his gauntlet dripping with gore.

His vision refocused, and he found himself surrounded by the bodies of the fallen. They were the warriors of Hilliard, Rjóðr, and Eenheid. All dead. There were so many. Something foul built in his stomach, then within moments, it shot up into his throat, and the acidic taste floored his mouth. He vomited. "No. No, not again!"

Alistair's body heaved, and he violently shook his head, demanding for all of this to stop. He wasn't here, couldn't be here again. He drew in ragged breaths. Wide, dead eyes stared back at him. A sinking feeling enveloped him as the world turned again. The ground turned to quicksand, and he was drowning in the sea of bodies. Metal plates hung loose from leather armor straps, fabric frayed to thread beneath. Purple-black bruises covered the bodies of various skin tones, weaving a tapestry of these people's last days. Alistair's jaw clenched, veins straining as a scream tried to tear its way free from his throat.

A faint sound carried on the wind. Was it a voice? It came again, softer and vanishing into the din of moans from the dead and dying. Alistair climbed to keep his head above the bodies; however, his legs were locked in place. Listening for the sound to come again, he recognized it. It was a voice, certainly, and though he couldn't place a face to it, he knew it was his salvation. The words were too quiet to make out, but it was calling to him.

What was he doing? Where was he again?

The bright sky grew dark. Ash fell all around. Blood and decay mixed with fire and dust. His body heaved to vomit again, but there was nothing left to expel. He wanted to collapse into sleep; however, the fear of never waking kept him from giving in. "No. No, stop this." Hot tears rolled down his cheeks, and he shut his eyes. "I'm sorry. I'm sorry, I can't do this!"

Everything went silent. The moaning dwindled to nothing, and fires snuffed out. He listened, waiting for something, anything, but dared not open his eyes again. Time stretched on like that for hours. Days? He didn't know.

Then suddenly, deafeningly, the voice returned, "Alistair, open your eyes!"

Alistair startled, eyes shooting open as he remembered where he was. Daemyn stared up at him with hands clamped tightly about his shoulders. Alistair's body shook as violently as if he were freezing. He was back in the stone room again, the same dark pit of death. The pile of bodies lay somewhere behind Daemyn, but his eyes couldn't, or wouldn't, focus on anything but his friend.

Tears stained Daemyn's pale tawny skin. Alistair struggled, but raised a hand to the young Prince's face, and Daemyn startled. As gently as he could, he wiped away the streaks with a thumb. "Daemyn?"

Daemyn let out a deep sigh, relief on his face. "Thank the gods, Alistair. What the FUCK happened to you?" His grip tightened on Alistair's shoulders. "Valhalla fell against the wall and-and I don't—"

The young Prince fell into Alistair's chest, his sob surprisingly loud in the quiet of the space. Alistair let out a trembling breath and brought his arms around Daemyn, hugging him close. It had been a long while since he experienced one of his episodes, and hoped he was past it. To have one surface here, of all places, he found it deeply concerning. Had they been in danger, he would've been helpless. "Daemyn, I can't explain it right now. I just . . ." he took a deep breath and slid his hands to Daemyn's shoulders, "I need a moment, please?"

Daemyn latched tightly to Alistair's tunic, holding onto it firmly as if, should he let go, he might fall away forever, "I don't know what to do!"

"I know, and you don't have to do a thing." With that, Alistair let go of his friend and looked behind him to where Valhalla sat crumbled on the floor. "Like I said, we all just need a moment."

Memories of old clung to him like a spider's web. His feet were unsteady, and his thoughts laced with fear. Alistair needed to fight this; he knew that, and he had to regain control lest he and his friends never make it out of this terrible place.

He stumbled over to Valhalla, each step a feat in and of itself. Alistair wanted—needed to check on her. It was an urge as vital as breathing. Her pink eyes stared blankly at the filth-covered floor, hands hanging limply between her knees. The fire over her shoulder dimmed and diminished, now no larger than a candle's flame. It flickered as if it too was overwhelmed by the oppressive nature of their surroundings.

After more time than he would have liked had passed, Alistair reached Valhalla and threw a hand to the wall to steady himself. His body fought his commands, and he was reminded of a memory from his youth. Just entering his adolescence, one of his instructors felt he should learn of the many poisons of the realm so that he might be better prepared for his role as Prince of the Veerence.

He had been careless in handling one of the vials and experienced a numbing paralysis not too dissimilar to how he felt now. Attempting to kneel, one of his legs gave out, and he fell hard to the floor beside her with a groan.

"Alistair?" Daemyn asked and stepped toward him.

Alistair held a hand up, gesturing that he was fine and forced a small smile, which he hoped was visible through his mask. "I-I'm fine. Promise."

"But I don't understand what's going on with you two. Please, just tell me how to help." Daemyn pleaded.

Alistair shook his head softly. "When you've lived through something that shakes you to your very core . . . some people," he let out a troubled sigh and searched for how to explain, "see things, relive the experience. Like I said, it-it's hard to explain."

"A—Oh. I'm sorry." He replied, quieting.

Alistair nodded in thanks and returned his attention to Valhalla. He raised a cautious hand to her cheek, but paused a finger's span away. With a breath, he turned his palm toward his face and sighed, glad to find it was somehow free of blood. He was fine, or would be, which was good enough given the circumstances. They would all be fine. They still had a mystery that needed to be solved, and unless they conquered their fears, they could not return to safety.

He closed his eyes and tried to rally himself, and when he opened them again, he found there was still a tremor in his fingers. A pang of disappointment filled him. This was going to be a process, it seemed, but at least he shook less than before.

Alistair went ahead and brushed his fingers across her cheek. Her porcelain white skin was soft and warm. Valhalla's hot breath came in slow exhales and sent gooseflesh up his arm. Running his thumb across her skin, Alistair carefully cupped her face and turned her to look at him. After a moment, her eyes blinked and focused, seemingly returning to the here and now. The fire on her shoulder danced back to life, its warmth chasing away the chill.

"Your Grace?" She asked softly, brows pinching.

Like a hand wrapping around his heart, he felt a pressure tighten at the question in her tone.

"It's alright, Valhalla," he answered gently, "you're—Everything's alright now."

Releasing a trembling breath, Valhalla nodded and brought an unsteady hand to his, pulling his palm away. "Alright, I-I just need a moment."

"I think we all do." He replied, squeezing her fingers for comfort. As he stood, the room seemed to right itself. His body was still sluggish, feeling as though he were moving through water, but the effect was lessening.

Alistair was getting control of himself.

Shutting his eyes, he counted each beat of his heart, and on the count of ten, searched about the room. As gruesome as it was, if Daemyn was correct about the origin of these rooms, they had been meant to save life rather than end it. Iron chains were bolted to the walls, but numbered few and seemed quite a new addition to the space. There was barely any wear or rust about them. Bloody tools of torture rested on a servant's cart, which was too fine a thing for such instruments. To the side of the pile of corpses, he found an overturned table resembling those he'd seen at Albrecht's return celebration back in the throne room. Even the straps around it were those meant for trousers, not restraint.

"This place was repurposed," Alistair said, then went on to explain his reasoning. He approached the corpses, brows furrowing, and unease settling in his bones.

"Alright, but . . . to what end?" Daemyn asked.

Alistair shook his head, struggling to focus on the details of each and every body in the pile. As he scanned them over, he tried and failed to discern anything about them other than how they had died. All he could conclude was that he was correct in his first assumption. While many had been here long enough to rot to the point of becoming unidentifiable, some at the top were newly added. Many of the bodies were destroyed and their faces disfigured. He got the sense that, should he and his friends linger, they might find themselves added to the stack.

"The ones at the top of the pile," he swallowed, trying to keep from throwing up again, "they're recent. Daemyn?" He stretched a hand back, waving his friend closer.

"A-Aye?" Daemyn answered, his pitch high like a yelp.

"I know this sight is unsettling, but do you recognize any of their faces?"

"By Njörd's seas, Alistair!" Daemyn exclaimed with a disgusted frown.

"I know, I know, but I don't know who's been missing. You and Valhalla are the only ones here who might tell us who they were, and she's—"

"FINE!" Daemyn grumbled. "Fine, just give me a moment, please."

"Of course." Alistair waited patiently, watching his friend's face shift as a battle took place in his mind. He was likely trying to will himself forward, much the same as Alistair had needed to do. Eventually, Daemyn took his place beside Alistair and what lay before them.

He held his handkerchief tight to his nose. His eyes grew wider the longer Daemyn stared. Daemyn raised a hand to his chest and clung to his vest. His body went taut. "By the very gods, I can't tell by their faces, but I know the crests on their clothing and jewels. Segane, Merlo, and even a Tridon are here. Some are from Svartr's major houses. I," His eyes narrowed, as if confirming before continuing. "I didn't even know my father had accused them,"

Daemyn suddenly paused, causing Alistair to turn to him. "Daemyn?"

His friend stared off to the left and soon began walking in that direction. Alisatir looked at him with confusion until he saw where Daemyn was headed. On the other side of the room, he spotted something that shouldn't have been able to fit in such a room. The ceiling was far too low, and yet, there it was, a guillotine.

The device had been modified, standing about half the size of a normal guillotine. The blade was buried at the bottom of its track. Blood stained the metal and block, but it was dry. Old. As his gaze turned to the body beside the contraption, time stopped. Recognition pierced his heart, and everything in the world became wrong.

The body was dressed in a frilly lavender nightgown. Dark stains marred the patterning of the garment, but it was too fine a thing to be in such a place. A large puddle was on the floor surrounding it. Clumps of thick, curly, flaxen hair stuck out of the pool.

No, this wasn't possible, Alistair thought, and yet knew it to be so.

He stared at Daemyn, wishing somehow they were back in his room, that they had fled this place moments earlier, and that this last secret could've remained out of reach. Something lay before his friend's feet. More flaxen hair shimmered in the firelight. Alistair couldn't see the face from where he stood, but that brought no comfort. He could see her face in pastels. It's how he wished Daemyn to remember her, though he knew in his heart that this was the image that would forever be at the forefront of his memory.

Daemyn dropped to his knees, his image the embodiment of sorrow. He reached out to the head and cradled it with both hands, fingers brushing the hair from her hidden features. The young Prince turned her to face him. Dots of red speckled dingy gray skin. Her striking face and nose were unmistakable. Daemyn had finally been reunited with his mother, Ayunli Nealfire Svartr.

Daemyn's breath came in labored gasps. Tears fell down his cheeks like a burst dam. All the color in his face drained away. When he spoke, his whispered tones cracked, and the words came almost as if a question."I-It's Mother. It's Mother!"

Alistair stood there, frozen in place, unsure of what to say or do. Why was Ayunli in such a place, and what had led to her death? Only one person could've condemned her to this, but the thought was too much to bear, and he dared not speak his fear aloud.

He turned to Valhalla, hoping there he might just find a hint of reason in any of this, but as his eyes met hers, he saw she was just as lost. Her eyes were wide, and her hands were firmly clasped over her mouth. Valhalla clearly had no knowledge of this, not even a hint that something so horrible was even possible. It was plain to see on her face. She had been trying to find Ayunli since the Queen had been isolated, and seeing Daemyn's mother now, several weeks must've passed since her death.

A clunk sounded in the distance, sending adrenaline pouring through Alistair's veins like molten fire. He and Valhalla startled and turned toward the sound. They stared out the open door, back into the hidden passageway to the shadowed base of the steps. The whirring of gears thrummed down the stairway and was followed by the grinding of stone. Muffled voices faintly drifted down.

"Shit!" Alistair growled through gritted teeth. "Valhalla,"

"I got the door," she quickly whispered, "just get his Highness."

As Valhalla rushed to close the door, Alistair grabbed hold of Daemyn's wrist and pulled. Ayunli's head rolled softly back to the ground. "Daemyn, we need to hide!" He whispered and heard the panic in his own voice. Daemyn shook his head and protested, trying to free himself from Alistair's grip.

"NO!"

Alistair clamped a hand over Daemyn's mouth, fearing they would be discovered. As Daemyn continued to revolt, dread built in Alistair's gut. Seeing no other option, he forced an arm around Daemyn's body and attempted to pick him up off the ground.

"Dammit, Daemyn, I'm sorry, but we need to hide!" He gritted, but his words fell on deaf ears. By all accounts, Daemyn seemed to be beyond caring about stealth.

A soft click behind them made Alistair's muscles tense, just the jolt he needed to gain control over Daemyn. Valhalla then appeared beside them, her brows curved in worry. Trying his best not to drop Daemyn, Alistair turned to her, jaw clenched. "Where sh—"

"Behind the table, quickly." She whispered, and although she moved swiftly with practiced grace, fear still laced her voice.

He nodded to her, then dragged Daemyn toward the table. The distance was short, but Daemyn's thrashing sent Alistair stumbling more than once, and he considered knocking his friend unconscious; however, this was no time to fight.

Reaching the table, Alistair fell with Daemyn locked in his arms and grunted as his right shoulder took the brunt of their landing. Daemyn flinched, then stopped moving. Valhalla flew to them and inspected the two for injury.

"Shit." Alistair groaned. "I vomited!"

"It's been dealt with," Valhalla answered, dropping a rag where they knelt. With a wave of her hand, the fire on her shoulder dissipated, and they were plunged into darkness. Alistair adjusted his position, sure to not lose his grip on Daemyn, managing to sit up and lean against the table. Each of them was breathing hard. Daemyn leaned against his chest. Alistair took a deep breath, and he felt his friend do the same, the pair falling into a rhythm. Perhaps he was coming out of his hysteria.

Leaning close to his friend's ear, he said, "Listen to me, Daemyn," keeping his voice low, "I know you're distraught, I know! But we need to be smart. We may be able to learn who's behind this. All of this. So, please, just call—"

The door began to creak, and Alistair went silent, holding his breath. Footsteps tapped and faintly echoed through the room. An eerie violet glow illuminated the wall before them, and then someone groaned in disgust.

"Ugh! Disgusting, perhaps I should have the bodies burned. The smell's starting to reach the cells above."

Alistair's blood went cold. He knew that deep, velvety voice all too well, and the name he'd dared not voice came flooding into his mind. Aegir Svartr. Could he really be capable of all this? Of Ayunli's death? Alistair couldn't see Daemyn's face, but was sure that no matter how terrible all of this seemed to him, for the younger Prince, it was all so much worse. He glanced at Valhalla in the faint violet light. Her hand was clenched, resting on her thighs, the other holding the pink handkerchief over her face. Her brows were curved in an apology. She hadn't wanted it to be Aegir, but she was right in her suspicions. She just hadn't known the depths of the depravity with which they now found themselves.

"It's alright, your Majesty, I'll be sure to burn them once your sons have taken to rest for the night."

Alistair jolted, recognizing the second voice. Although they had spoken only once, the man had made quite the impression. It had to be Lord Tamanna Gadhavi. Alistair was certain of it, but dared not gamble on peeking round the table for fear of being found. Valhalla seemed to be just as confused as he was. Just what in Helheim was going on? What was Tamanna's role in all of this?

"Be sure to burn Ayunli last," Aegir said, a hint of grief in his voice. "Her treachery is still fresh, but I'll soon need to tell my sons something."

"Why not tell them the truth, Your Majesty? She was conspiring to assassinate you and would've likely killed your sons as well. She wanted the throne for herself, I assure you. This was necessary."

It took Alistair every ounce of will he had to keep his silence. The shock of what he was hearing outraged him. Ayunli seeking the throne for herself? That wasn't who she was. She never sought out power. If that wasn't the biggest load of ravenshit Alistair had ever heard.

He still remembered the story Ayunli had told of meeting Aegir for the first time. The marriage arrangement had been agreed upon by Blár and Svartr, sealing the trade alliance between them. Timber, ice, and gems found only in Aoldear would be traded for seafood, salt, and the much sought-after pearls of Oceanna. The rulers of Blár had no daughters, so Ayunli, a woman of one of Blár's six major houses, was chosen instead. She agreed to leave everything behind, her home, family, and friends. The comfort of the Northern winter winds and snow. All of it she sacrificed to create a bond between the regions, for the promise of prosperity for all. How could Aegir believe such a person would throw all of that away for his throne? What was to be gained?

This didn't make any sense.

"They may take some convincing." Footsteps sounded again, receding back toward the doorway of the room. "They both loved her dearly, Daemyn especially," Aegir said softly.

The violet light faded, and with the thump of the door closing, the three of them were swallowed again by the darkness. Alistair's mind was swimming with questions, trying to make sense of any of what he heard. Aegir was executing people, driven by the assumption that he was going to be overthrown, and Ayunli was involved?

No. That was impossible.

The stench of the dead, of the blood and rotting flesh, smothered his senses. He couldn't think straight, not in this place. The three of them needed to leave. They needed to do so fast, before Tamanna came back to burn the bodies. Whatever the truth was, it was clear there were still a great many pieces missing.

48

ℱlistair

Nightmares Made Real

Alistair lay in his bed, beneath the silk sheets, and stared into the canopy above. Every time he closed his eyes, he saw images of the night before. Sleep had been as elusive as it was unwanted. Alistair considered, for a time, taking the sleep aid he'd brought with him on this journey, but decided against it. He was certain his dreams would bring him back to that scene of horrors and held little interest in returning there so soon. He rested an arm over his forehead and the other by his side. A chill nipped at his skin. Either he was cold, or his body was still in shock. Perhaps both.

Turning his head idly toward the fireplace to his right, he found nothing but glowing cinders and a large pile of ash beneath the grate. Even the candles in the chamber seemed dangerously close to flickering out.

As much as Alistair wished things could go back to the way they were before the grizzly discovery, to pretend that last night had simply never happened, a terrible nightmare and nothing more, that was impossible. The pile of dead bodies, the stench clinging to everything it touched, the image of Ayunli's severed head in Daemyn's arms, those things couldn't be denied.

Sometimes, when recalling a battle, trying to remember the details of his time in war, events would come flooding back in a blur. Flashes of recollection could be glimpsed, but much of it was hazy and bled together. He found himself wishing the night's journey into the depths could return to him much the same, obscured by the fear and adrenaline he had in that moment. However, this had been different. It was too personal to be glimpsed as shadows and frayed edges. The memory returned to him in vivid detail. He saw it clearer than the walls and furnishings surrounding him now. Alistair couldn't escape what happened.

Worse than what he had seen was the knowledge that Aegir, his second father, had been behind it all—No, that wasn't right. That couldn't have been right. Aegir wouldn't—Couldn't . . . Did.

What was he supposed to do with this information?

His thoughts then drifted to Valhalla and Daemyn. He could still feel the ghost of Daemyn's limp weight against him. His friend was completely shaken. And who could blame him? Daemyn had thought his mother simply bedridden, ill, and tucked away, but alive. Had she succumbed to sickness and they found her at peace in bed, that would've been terrible enough, but to find her as they had, likely tortured, then beheaded, left to rot where she fell; it wasn't something for a son of seventeen to see. It was a wonder Alistair managed to get Daemyn to his brother's bedchamber.

Valhalla, too, was quiet after Aegir left. Something significant had happened in her past, that much was plain to see, given her reaction to the bodies. They had unsettled her just as badly, if not more so, as they had him. She likely had also felt guilt for being proven right about Aegir. She hadn't said as much, but Alistair was sure of it. Both Albrecht and Daemyn loved their father, and had he at least been innocent in all of this, at least that would've been a small silver lining. However, that wasn't the case. He murdered his own wife. The whole ordeal was unreal.

"And yet," he found himself thinking aloud, "she knew exactly what to say to convince us to not confront him . . ." Alistair began massaging his forehead, feeling a wave of pain and confusion thumping between his ears. "How would we even go about confronting Aegir?" He pressed his hands into his face, suppressing a frustrated groan. "What in Ódin's name are we supposed to do?"

Noises came from just outside his bedchamber, startling him. Looking to his balcony at his left, Alistair could see nothing but darkness through the rain-spattered glass. There was no way of telling if it were the dead of night or early morning. He cursed in frustration.

The door into his chamber opened, and he propped himself up on his elbows. He was taken aback to see Albrecht standing in the doorway, still dressed in his night clothes and speaking to someone.

"Are you sure, Your Highness?" A masculine voice asked, no doubt a Gentleman of the Chamber assigned to Alistair for his stay in Svartr.

"Aye aye, don't worry," Albrecht said with a chuckle. "Unfortunately, he's still shy about being tended to. Daemyn and I will look after Alistair for the remainder of his stay."

Daemyn? Where was the young Prince? Alistair craned his neck and could just barely make out the young Prince standing beside Albrecht. His posture could've been mistaken for fatigue, a longing for sleep, but Alistair knew better.

"As you command, your Highness." The Servant replied. "If either of you needs assistance, just pull the string by your bedside and we'll come to you."

Alistair glanced to his right and found the string the Servant mentioned hanging above the nightstand. This castle was massive, and it occurred to him just how long that string had to be. It was an impressive feat.

"Of course, thank you," Albrecht answered as he grasped Daemyn's shoulders and guided him into Alistair's chamber, closing the doors behind them. He then returned to his little brother, gripping his shoulders again, and gave him a gentle smile. Daemyn just stood there, his posture exhausted, and blank eyes fixed on the floor. "Daemyn, why not sit down for now. It's alright."

Daemyn didn't answer, but made his way toward one of the orange couches centered in the chamber and slumped down onto the cushion. He, too, was wearing his night clothes, brightly colored, befitting the rest of his wardrobe. His flaxen hair was long and unruly, looking as though he had just gotten out of bed. It covered most of his downcasted face, but Alistair could see the dark rings forming under Daemyn's bright sky blue eyes.

Albrecht let out a sigh, calling Alistair's attention, and then strode across the room to meet him. His eyes too shone with worry. Alistair wasn't sure what to do or say. He could still picture his friend's expression as they told Albrecht of all they saw and heard. He was stunned, then furious, and for several long moments, Alistair thought he might fly from the room to confront his father then and there, but to Albrecht's credit, he didn't.

In the end, it was Valhalla, finally breaking her silence, who made the elder Svartr Prince see reason. They didn't know the whole story yet, and she reasoned that it would be better to give her the time she needed to piece it all together. What was Aegir's motive? What was Tamanna's for that matter? They only had a few pieces of the puzzle, and they needed to think before they acted.

Albrecht slumped down on the bed beside Alistair. He seemed lost, the look so foreign to his usual steadfast bravado that Alistair found his heart breaking once again. To see his friends, brothers hurt in this way, it was maddening. And here Alistair was, completely unable to do anything about it.

"Hey." Albrecht broke the silence.

"H-Hey." Was all Alistair could think to say back.

Alistair wove his fingers together about his knees, staring at his older friend. Albrecht's eyes remained on the floor. His brows were furrowed, and some of the color had drained from his tawny face. He must not have slept either, Alistair considered.

Eventually, Albrecht let out a long sigh and stood. "Breakfast is just about to be served. Could you join us?"

"Yes. Yes, of course." Alistair answered, sliding his sheets off and moving to the edge of his bed.

"Thank you." Albrecht stood and met his eyes. Where there was warmth in his words, none showed on his face. As his eyes seemed to focus, his head tilted, and his expression flickered with a hint of sentimentality. "You didn't sleep last night, did you?"

Alistair's shoulders fell. He recalled his first morning in Svartr long ago, just after his father's passing. Albrecht had greeted him much the same. At the time, he'd thought no sorrow could be greater than that tragedy, but now he was coming to understand the folly in that thinking. One tragedy can't outweigh another. His misery then was no greater than what Daemyn or Albrecht felt now. His father's passing was not more painful than the grief he suffered for the family who accepted him as one of their own. It was, in a way, simply different. He let out a trembling breath. "How could I?"

"Aye." Albrecht rubbed his eyes with the back of his hand and made his way to a dresser nestled between the fireplace and the walk-in closet.

Albrecht opened one of the top drawers, but didn't reach inside. He simply stopped, resting his hands on the edge with his head bowed. A slight tremble moved through Albrecht's arms, and then he spoke. "Say what's on your mind."

Alistair was taken aback. His heart began to quicken, and he swallowed a nervous lump in his throat. Just what was there to say? Every apologetic mutterance he'd received when his father fell brought little comfort. What he'd needed at the time was something to do, to occupy his time, a goal to pour his frustration into. Daemyn and Albrecht had been there, filling his days with all sorts of tasks. He had his nights to grieve, but his days had purpose. Were he able to give them that now, he would, but just what was there to do? He had no idea how to proceed and slumped in defeat.

"I . . . I'm worried. I'm worried for you both, but I just—"

"Don't know what to do." Albrecht finished.

Shame fell over Alistair like a wet blanket. He looked into his friend's sky blue eyes and hated how right Albrecht was. "Yes."

His thoughts ran in circles, searching for anything he might be able to offer, any comfort he might be able to give his friends. An image of Valhalla came to the forefront of his mind. He hoped Valhalla was safe, wherever she was, whatever she was doing. Recalling what he'd told Albrecht of her, the lie of her mission given by him, he was stricken with regret. All he had to offer was the truth. To be true to Daemyn, to Albrecht, to hide nothing. It wasn't much, but he would no longer add his voice to the lies the brothers had already endured. With a breath, he readied himself. "Albrecht, there's something you should know,"

"You lied about sending Valhalla here, didn't you?" Albrecht asked as he plucked a plain white nightshirt from the drawer.

Alistair stared at his friend, mouth agape in surprise. "How did you—"

Albrecht glanced over his shoulder and shot him a critical, but not judgmental, look. Alistair's shoulders raised as he sucked in a breath, then slumped. He had already resolved to tell them the truth, and so he meekly nodded and answered. "Yes."

The eldest Prince closed the drawer and turned around to face him, leaning against the dresser, a small smirk crossing his face. "Despite what you might think, you're actually a terrible liar. Don't get me wrong, you're much more subtle now than you used to be, but your tell is still there."

"W-What?" Alistair's eyes shot wide. Certainly, he hadn't been *that* obvious, he thought. He'd spent nearly a week lying to his mother's court about Lorna's death, and not once did anyone question what he'd said.

"You look away when you lie. Here." Albrecht tossed the folded nightshirt at Alistair, who completely fumbled in catching it. The garment came completely undone and fell across his lap.

Alistair's cheeks burned. "I do not!"

"Oh, I count that as one of the best benefits of being your friend AND brother. I can see what others can't." Albrecht said as he placed a hand over his heart and leaned forward, likely trying to be playful. His smirk then faded from his face. "But when we confront my father, and we *will*, I need you to be better at it, because if it's obvious to me, you can bet that Father will notice as well. Remember, Alistair, we were your family for over a year."

A deep ache came over Alistair's heart. Of course, he remembered. His father was poisoned on Alistair's tenth name day. When his family should've come together, instead his mother sent him off to Svartr and Lorna to Rjóðr. He didn't know why she had done that, perhaps to allow herself time to grieve alone, but with the clarity of hindsight, it had been their unmaking. Week after week, Alistair had expected to hear from her, to receive a summons home, or to, at the very least, let him know that he was in her thoughts, but as time slipped by, he lost hope that word would ever come. His mother was devastated after his father's passing. Alistair understood that, but so was he, and perhaps Lorna as well. He had yearned for the comfort of family, and it broke his heart to endure the loss of a second parent to distance and silence. However, in the end, some light came of it. The Svartr family rose to the occasion and became that for him. They did what blood apparently couldn't.

"I . . . Of course I remember," Alistair said softly, for some reason unable to meet Albrecht's eyes.

"I know. Now come, put on the shirt while I fetch your slippers." Albrecht said with a renewed sternness in his tone and stepped to the closet.

Alistair slipped on his nightshirt without argument.

There was no point in protesting. Albrecht was right, after all. They would eventually need to confront Aegir with what they found, and if he truly needed to grow more persuasive in the deceptive arts, then he would, but it didn't mean he had to like it.

Albrecht swung the doors wide open, bent down, picked up a pair of bright orange slippers, and handed them to Alistair. A small smile snuck its way onto Alistair's face. He loved the color, reminding him of the sunrise and sunset.

Alistair slipped them on, then noticed Albrecht standing still before him, looking as though something was on his mind. Rather than venture a guess, Alistair chose instead the straightforward path and asked, "What's wrong?"

"I-I need your help with Daemyn, he . . ." Albrecht paused, took a deep breath, and tensed. "He's struggling with what you found last night."

Alistair turned his attention to Daemyn, who just sat there quietly, as still as stone on one of the couches. Had he not been consumed with worry all night, he might've completely forgotten that his young friend had entered his chambers at all. A look of pure dejection was etched into his face. Flashes of their journey passed through his mind once more. He could still smell the stench of the dead and worried if the odor had clung to his skin.

It was clear that Daemyn was somewhere between shock and grief. Alistair knew deep down he wasn't faring any better, but how was Albrecht handling the news? He was obviously angry. How could he not be? But still, he seemed completely focused on his brother, and Alistair wondered if he had taken any time to process things for himself. After all, he too was a victim in all of this. So, before he thought better of it, he asked, "And what about you?"

"What *about* me?" Albrecht snapped, his brows furrowing into a scowl that could've easily been interpreted as a threat not to press the matter.

Alistair ignored the warning. He stood up to look his friend in the face, but softened his tone. "Albrecht, please, you're a brother to me as Daemyn is to you. I'm worried. This is a lot, too much, more than any person should have to."

Albrecht closed the distance between them in the blink of an eye, startling Alistair back into his nightstand. The elder prince stood almost face to face with him. His glare promised violence, and his eyes shook like a predator when backed into a corner. "This. Is not. The time."

Albrecht was imposing, and when his anger got the better of him, it was difficult to not feel at least a little intimidated. Still, this needed to happen sooner than later. Leaving his friend to deny his own feelings would only lead to them spilling out in other ways. And that might lead to their being found out, which would benefit none of them. Swallowing his nerves down, Alistair pressed, "When, then?"

Albrecht's glare darkened as several silent heartbeats passed between the two. Then, without saying a word, he turned and stepped out of Alistair's space. A sharp breath escaped Alistair's lips, only then realizing he had been holding it in. His hand drifted up to his chest, searching for his father's ring, but found only the soft silk of his nightshirt. His pulse quickened with a jolt of fear. Where was his father's ring?

Fighting back the encroaching panic, Alistair looked about the bed and recalled dropping the necklace on the nightstand as he had lain to rest the previous night. Turning and swallowing the lump in his throat, his eyes darted to the spot, and relief poured over him. There, on the mahogany surface, his father's Ring of Grár rested atop the valknut and algiz medallions. He sighed and scooped up the necklace.

"Come on, Daemyn, how about we get some food in you?" Albrecht's voice came with a softness that contrasted oddly with the anger which had been on his face moments prior. Alistair gazed at him and found a small smile on Albrecht's face. The elder Prince reached for Daemyn's shoulders and helped him to his feet, guiding his little brother to the doors of the chamber.

Seeing his moment now gone, he used this chance to turn away and secretly hugged his father's ring to his chest. His words no greater than a whisper, he began, "Father, I know it's been a while since I last spoke to you, but please, give me the strength to help my friends through this terrible darkness. I want to aid them in whatever way I can. Please, don't let me falter." Alistair then raised the ring to his lips and gave it a quick kiss before sliding the necklace back over his head and tucked it safely beneath his nightshirt.

Hearing the click of the door as it opened, he rushed after the brothers, following them into the hallway. There, between Daemyn's room on one side of the hall and Aegir's on the opposite, was a round table. It wasn't a grand thing, only able to seat six or seven at most, and left just enough room in the space for servants to see to those occupying it when in use. The sight had caught Alistair by surprise at first. He had completely forgotten about the custom. It had been the idea of the now late Queen Ayunli, that no matter how demanding any one of their roles might become, that they may join together in the birth and death of every day as a family, not as King, Queen, Prince, or Heir, but as dutiful Father, loving Mother, and cherished Sons to share a meal and moment of their time. The table and seats would be arranged every morning and evening, then taken away and stored until their next use. It was a time to come together as a family, and few had been invited into the ritual. Alistair was one such individual. On his last stay, this had been a thing of warmth, one of the best parts of the day. But now, the idea of sitting with Aegir, with their wounds raw and emotions high, it seemed like a powder keg, and each of them was a torch.

Servants shuffled about, preparing the table with white ceramic plates adorned with sea creatures swimming about the edges of every dish. Glass chalices were carefully placed by each plate, accompanied by crimson cloth napkins and ebony cutlery. The scent of sea salted scrambled eggs, bacon, and fruit was carried on the air, making Alistair's stomach grumble.

Alistair noticed Albrecht hug Daemyn closer and caught a glimpse of his smile, a mask he wielded like a blade, as he acknowledged the staff busy with their work. Each in turn bowed or curtsied to the trio, wishing them a good morning, then returning to their tasks. Albrecht tilted his head in thanks, guiding Daemyn to the table.

Just as Albrecht pulled free a chair, a servant maiden squeaked a call for his attention. "Oh! Pardon me, your Highness, please save an empty chair between you and the youn' Prince. His Majesty wishes to enjoy both of your company this mornin'."

Albrecht froze in place, the mask slipping as he stared at the young woman. Alistair cursed to himself. The young woman had no idea what she was asking. It was going to be hard enough to act as though nothing was wrong. For him and Albrecht, it was possible Aegir might not notice, but Daemyn had to be terrified.

The servant maiden tilted her head curiously as concern played across her features. Fortunately, Albrecht immediately gathered himself and renewed the act. "That would be lovely. Sorry, I'm struggling to find my footing. Too much celebrating, it would seem." He laughed with warmth and charm, seemingly convincing the servant maidens, who all giggled with delight.

As Albrecht helped Daemyn down into his chair, he glanced at Alistair and then to the seat beside him. Alistair understood. With Albrecht unable to be at his little brother's side, Alistair would need to be his support if they were going to make it through the meal to come. With an inconspicuous nod, he took his seat in the empty chair at Daemyn's left. Aegir's empty seat was at his right, and beside that would be Albrecht.

Alistair got his first good look at Daemyn since the night before, and now, being so close to him, he could see the toll their experience had taken on him. His generally bright blue eyes were dull and surrounded by red, no doubt from crying himself to near dehydration. Dark half circles sagged beneath his eyes. Daemyn seemed as if it took all the energy he had left just to remain awake. A faint, constant tremble presented in his hands and shoulders. His pale tawny skin was drained of color and took on an almost imperceptible blue hue. Alistair's heart twisted with worry. "Oh, Daemyn—"

Alistair reached for one of Daemyn's tightly fisted hands resting on his lap, but was interrupted as a Gentleman of the Bedchamber knocked on Aegir's door, and pulled his hand away. "Your Majesty," the man called out, "everything's set and the Princes await your Kingship."

After a brief moment, the door of Aegir's chamber swung open and out stepped the man, fully dressed with the ebony crown atop his head. It struck Alistair as odd. He glanced at Albrecht, who seemed just as put off by it as he was.

"Thank you," Aegir said as he performatively soaked in the many scents filling the air, "the food smells wonderful, and if it tastes even half as good, it'll still be fit for a," He gestured to himself and grinned at the staff.

They all grinned at the jest and quickly bowed. A short stretch of quiet followed, none of the servants daring to speak, and lingered just long enough to be unnerving. Alistair had the faint sense that they were all hostage to a madman, though he wondered if that was just his imagination. Without the knowledge their small group had discovered, nothing about the moment would've rang as anything other than jovial. Still, gooseflesh spread about his skin.

"Ah, F-Father, there you are," Albrecht greeted, standing beside his seat and spreading his arms to his father, "I was worried we would be eating without you this morning."

Albrecht's smile was forced and his stance stiff, as if unable to reconcile what he'd been told with the father he'd known all his life. That, or Alistair was projecting his own feelings on the elder Prince. He couldn't be sure.

"A shame we couldn't dine together last night, between the party and the unpleasantness there after, well, I wasn't going to miss your first breakfast back, Son." Aegir closed the gap between them and embraced Albrecht, who hugged him in return. The King squeezed his son tight, and Alistair could just barely make out the words he whispered into Albrecht's ear. "I won't let *anything* happen to you, I promise."

The words seemed to catch Albrecht by surprise, his mask slipping again. It bothered Alistair as well. Just what had gotten into Aegir? Did he truly believe someone was plotting against his family? Certainly, there would be whispers of opposition, such a thing existed in every land with rulers and subjects. It was the nature of people. No King or Queen could placate everyone, but rarely ever grew to more than the toothless mutterings of a few behind closed doors. Did he really believe things had escalated to the point of attack?

Alistair's jaw ached, and he realized he was grinding his teeth. They needed to find answers, and fast, before anyone else was added to the pile down below.

Aegir started to release Albrecht when he noticed Daemyn's downtrodden state. "Daemyn, are you alright? You look terribly pale." He continued past Albrecht, grasping his younger son's shoulder, and caused Daemyn to jump in his seat.

Alistair's words poured from him on instinct. "My apologies. It's my fault. We may have overdone it a bit last night! Daemyn, well, tried to keep up with Albrecht and I, but he hasn't a sailor's constitution just yet. He's quite hung over." Forcing a bashful chuckle, he rubbed the back of his neck. "I admit, I'm also a little worse for wear. Albrecht bested us both."

"Ah, if that's the case, then this breakfast is just what you both need. Go ahead and serve the meals." Aegir waved at the servants, who all quickly set to the task of grabbing plates and filling them with scrambled eggs, salmon, thick-cuts of bacon, tomatoes, and sausages. The plates were then placed back on the table, accompanied by bowls of chopped fruit and a glass chalice of orange juice for each of them.

Some of the tension in Alistair's shoulders loosened. He shared a knowing look with Albrecht and then forced down some of the food in front of him.

"Now eat, Son," Aegir said as he brushed away some of Daemyn's flaxen hair and tucked it behind the young Prince's ears. Daemyn looked away with an expression of discomfort, but Aegir continued speaking as if he didn't seem to notice. "The last thing you need is for everything to come back up." He let out a hearty laugh and pulled his chair back, but before sitting, he pointed at Alistair, and his face turned serious. "I'm glad the three of you are becoming acquainted, but do remember Daemyn is only seventeen. He looks up to the both of you, and as you so well pointed out, he will do everything he can to not fall behind."

Alistair's throat went dry. Aegir's care for his family was clear as day, his words standing in contrast to the monster he'd heard in the depths of the castle. "Y-You're right, of course." He gently grasped Daemyn's shoulder, squeezing it and hoping his young friend would feel comforted. "I promise, we'll be very careful with how we spend our time from this day forward."

Aegir nodded, looking to be satisfied with his answer. "Don't act without considering who might face the consequences. That's all I ask of you, Alistair." He then sat, grabbed the crimson napkin from beneath his fork, tucked a corner into his shirt, and began sectioning the food on his plate. "Albrecht, I assume Daemyn has explained the condition of the city?" Aegir asked and slid a portion of salmon into his mouth.

Albrecht sat as well, gently placed his utensils beside his plate, and folded his arms to rest atop the table, his eyes remaining downcast. "As much as he *could*."

"That's good," Aegir dabbed his napkin over his lips and turned his full attention to the elder Prince, "Because of the situation, I'll be indisposed for a time." He picked up a strip of bacon and tore at it with his teeth, chewing with noted frustration. "Also, thanks to the storm season coming early, the three of you are forbade from sailing." The King sat silent a moment, staring out into the darkened sky, and sighed disappointedly. "Before you protest, I understand that Daemyn has been cooped up in this castle for far too long as it is, running himself ragged as is his tendency, and I'm sure Alistair misses the sea, would I be correct in that assumption, High Prince?"

Alistair was in the middle of sipping his orange juice, and choked with a start. "Oh, y-yes." He coughed, struggling to calm himself. "I would love to sail again, but there will be plenty of time for that. I intended my stay to be a long one, with your permission of course, Aegir. I wouldn't wish to impose."

The King took a sip from his chalice and smiled warmly. "Of course, I wouldn't have it any other way."

"Yes, so, um, perhaps we can all go together then? After the storm has passed, I mean."

"Then it's settled. The three of you will remain within these castle walls, where you'll be safe until the storm passes. No roaming about——"

"Father," all eyes shifted to Daemyn. He had barely moved since sitting, and his food was untouched. "How's Mother?"

Alistair's blood froze. It was all he could do to not let the fear show on his face. Albrecht, too, had noticeably stilled. Aegir didn't so much as flinch. He took another sip from his chalice and placed his utensils on his plate. Cupping

Daemyn's hand, his face turned sorrowful. "I'm afraid her condition remains unchanged, Son."

Daemyn deflated in his chair, but stared at his father's hand around his. "O-Oh, I just thought—" His voice cracked, and a shudder ran over his shoulders. "Maybe Mother would like to see Albrecht, o-or I could let her know that he's home."

Alistair's heart ached. The sight of Daemyn cradling his mother's head in his arms rushed to the forefront of his mind. He wanted to leap from his chair to embrace Daemyn, to tell him that everything would be alright, that this was all a horrible nightmare, and that when he awoke, his father wouldn't be a monster and his mother would be alive and well. He glanced up to Albrecht, the man inconspicuously shaking his head with furrowed brows, likely sharing his frustration. Alistair cursed to himself and remained impassive.

"Of course she knows Albrecht's home," Aegir answered, leaning close to Daemyn and squeezing his hand, "in fact, she wanted me to tell you something. She wishes for you to look after him and Alistair, to take care of them as you have the servants."

Daemyn didn't answer, didn't even look up to meet his father's eyes, and Aegir watched him with a tinge of concern. "Daemyn, are you sure you're alright?"

Hesitantly sliding his hand free of his father's, Daemyn attempted to stand on shaky legs. "I-If you'll all excuse me," he shuffled around his chair and made for his chamber, "I'm not feeling well."

"Oh, alright then." Aegir turned to one of the gentleman servants beside the table. "One of you make certain he's comfortable, and light the fires in his chamber."

"Of course, your Majesty." They all bowed their heads, and a few started after Daemyn, who opened his doors and stumbled inside. They all shared a worried glance, then one placed a finger to his lips and disappeared inside.

"Perhaps I should—"

"Now, now, Albrecht," Aegir waved for him to remain in his seat. Albrecht shot him a critical look, but before he could protest, Aegir continued, "Let him rest. As I said earlier, Daemyn has been running himself ragged to keep this castle AND this city in top shape for your return home."

Albrecht turned away with furrowed brows. He mumbled something in frustration, but what it was, Alistair couldn't hear.

"Anyway, eat your fill and then bathe. Everything we don't eat is going to the castle's staff and families." Aegir then returned to eating, clearly finished with the topic of conversation.

Alistair sat there a long moment, then slid his gaze down at Daemyn's plate. Not even the utensils were disturbed. His heart raced with worry for his friend, and he found himself speaking before he knew fully what it was he would say. "Aegir, he didn't eat a bite."

Aegir stopped to look at Daemyn's plate, then grasped his chin contemplatively. "You're right. I'll make sure Madame Lilianna makes him her priority for the day. He will not go without." He turned to Albrecht, rubbing his temples. "After your bath, check on Daemyn for me. If he's awake, plenty of food and water. When your brother busies himself, he easily forgets about his well-being. Be his reminder."

Retaking his utensils in hand, Alistair turned to Albrecht, hoping his friend would meet his eyes. He couldn't help but dwell on Daemyn's state of mind. The idea of leaving him to ruminate alone knotted his stomach. Alistair cleared his throat, and Albrecht shot him a glance of warning, quickly tapping the edge of the table two times. Alistair's breath hitched, and his eyes slid back down to his plate. The signal had been one of several they had thought up years before. Albrecht was telling him to wait, to not press the matter. It didn't sit right with him, but he understood. They needed to move with caution. Alistair raised his fork and tended to his meal.

The three sat there for a time, eating and conversing as Aegir questioned them about this and that. They had to keep up the facade. As unpleasant as it was, it was necessary.

Alistair then wondered what Valhalla was doing. Was she safe? Might she be checking on Daemyn? Had she learned anything? How long would it be until they could speak? His mind drifted between worry and forced pleasantries as he stared out into the storm, dreading that the worst was yet to come.

49

Valhalla

Held Back Tears

Valhalla MARCHED UP THE STAIRS toward the fifth floor of the castle. It was now her shift, her responsibility to serve the princes through the rest of the afternoon and the evening beyond. It had been difficult going about her day as if the events of the previous evening hadn't been at the forefront of her mind. She stumbled, again picturing the pile of bodies, but managed to catch herself on the mahogany wall beside her.

She forced several deep breaths and rubbed her eyes. Valhalla was exhausted. Her heart raced as the new memory mingled with the old, the moment she'd buried long in the past. Her parents. Her city.

No.

With a shake of her head, she sneered with frustration. "Dammit, why can't I be rid of these terrible nightmares?" After several long moments, she regained her composure and swallowed, straightening her garments, then continued up the steps.

Sleep had eluded her, and so she had spent much of her time gathering her thoughts. As much as she wished to bury the new horrors with the old, there were still too many things left undiscovered. History was being written, and she couldn't simply turn her back to let it play out without doing what she could to lessen the burden the princes would need to bear. In her mind, she retraced their steps, picturing the journey downward to where grief and tragedy waited to be found. She lingered a long while on the image of Daemyn holding his mother's head in his arms. His devastation was plain to see, and she did nothing.

Placing the tip of her thumb between her teeth, she swore she would apologize to Alistair as soon as she met up with him. Her other hand slid into her dress pocket and grasped the soft fabric within. Daemyn's mother's handkerchief. Two people to apologize to.

Valhalla regretted that her hunch had been correct. That King Aegir had been involved in the disappearances. She had hoped for Daemyn's sake to be wrong and was as surprised as the others to discover Queen Ayunli's fate. There had to be more to this than just suspicion over a revolt, but if there was, Valhalla still hadn't seen any proof.

Vardan had been largely surprised by Valhalla's findings. Early that morning, before returning to bed, she had found him at their meeting point, and she told him everything that had transpired. What she described left him questioning if she was certain it had really been him. Apparently, the King Aegir he had known could never have committed such deeds. Vardan, for his part, had spent much of his time listening to the mutterings of the townsfolk. If he was to be believed, they had all loved him until recently and now lived their days in fear. He questioned her if it was possible that the King had fallen under another's control, in the same way Loki had been, and while it wasn't out of the realm of possibility, what reason would Kiara have to do such a thing?

A more likely culprit was the mysterious Lord Tamanna Gadhavi. Valhalla knew next to nothing about him except that he came from a land beyond Eenheid. Of his past and what had brought him here, she had found nothing. He was certain to have a role in all of this, but the what or why of it was yet unknown.

Breaking from her train of thought, she found she had already reached the Prince's chambers. Perhaps she was too familiar with her role as Servant Maiden, she mused. To her right, the dining table had already been assembled between their rooms, and dinner would be starting soon.

First things first, she needed to check on the Princes.

Scanning each of the three doors, Valhalla wasn't sure which chamber the three Princes would be waiting in, assuming they were even together. Rather than barging in, she decided to press her ear against the doors, listening for signs of life within. Albrecht's door was silent. Moving on to Daemyn's, she heard music playing within, that of a piano.

For a mere moment, she questioned whether she would find Alistair with Daemyn, then thought it was a rather silly question. Of course, Alistair would be with his best friend. After everything, why wouldn't they be together?

Valhalla knocked on the door. "Hello, your Highness, it's—"

The sound of rushing footsteps caught her by surprise, and suddenly the doors swung open. Alistair's wide eyes stared at her for only a moment before she was pulled inside. It had happened so fast she nearly lost her footing, and in no time at all, she was inside, the door closing behind her.

He was garbed in orange Oceanan clothes. After a moment, he sighed and grabbed her shoulders, a pained look coming across his face. "Valhalla, where have you been? I've been worried sick!"

Valhalla was stunned. "You were?"

"Of course. After what you told me of what happened to Logír, I thought Aegir might've captured and hurt you too." Alistair's grip on her shoulders tightened, and she realized then it had been foolish not to come sooner.

She had essentially disappeared on them after informing Albrecht of what they found. Of course, Alistair would worry. Clasping her hands over her chest, she pushed back a pang of guilt. "I'm-I'm so sorry. Because of everything, I spent my free time trying to sleep. I tried, *really* tried."

He sighed again. "So you had no luck either, huh?" Alistair's eyes softened.

Shaking her head, she relaxed under his grip. "No, last night was . . . a lot."

"You would do well to check in more often," Albrecht stated flatly. She hadn't noticed him until then, and the similarity of his voice to that of his father's sent ice through her veins. He sat on one of the lavender couches and gave her a dour look.

Valhalla jumped in place. "Y-Yes, your Highness." She grasped her forearm, keeping her gaze low. Her lips curled between her teeth.

Since she had entered, Daemyn hadn't stopped playing the melody on his piano or even glanced in her direction. His flaxen hair draped over his face, making it difficult to see how he was holding up. Something about the song he was playing struck her as familiar, but in the moment, she couldn't place it. The tune was soft, gentle even, like a winter morning's breeze under a clear sky.

She looked back to Alistair, and he gave her a look that suggested he was growing exhausted with Albrecht's attitude, that or he was simply exhausted, and she was projecting. He rubbed at his biceps, wrinkling his shirt a bit.

"Oh, are you cold?" Valhalla asked, and he gave her a soft nod. "Let me get the fire started again. It's surprisingly dark in here."

He nodded in thanks, and she responded with a smile. She stepped past him, but paused at the small table between the two couches. Sure to avoid eye contact with Albrecht, Valhalla searched about, wondering why it was so dark. She then realized no one had lit the candles on the hanging crystal chandelier above.

Valhalla considered retrieving the pole she would need to light the candles that high up, but since the Princes were already aware of her seidr ability, she decided on the faster approach. Spacing her hands half a foot apart before her chest, she closed her eyes and reached within herself, calling for the fire. Her chest felt alight as the heat grew, spreading down her arms and into her hands. "Eldr[1]." A flame sparked to life between her palms, its heat brushing against the skin of her face.

Opening her eyes, she watched the fire dance and swirl in the air. With a light toss, the flame arched upward and exploded into twenty small balls of fire, each about the size of a coin. Each landed on a candle's wick, and soon the room brightened considerably.

Alistair stared up with a look of awe on his face. He slowly planted his hands on the back of the couch. "That's amazing."

Valhalla smiled bashfully, feeling the warmth building in her cheeks. Bowing in thanks, she then made her way to the fireplace by the balcony. The fire had nearly died out. What logs remained were charred and blackened. She grabbed hold of four new logs and a handful of tinder and sat them beside her. Taking the shovel from its resting place on her left, she set to work removing the excess ash, pushing it to the back of the grate. Once content with the work, she placed the tinder and new logs into position, careful to not snuff out the dwindling glow of the used wood. Now it was time for her fire spell.

She hovered her palms over the charred log, eyes set on the orange glow, and took a deep breath, "Bjartr[2]." Fire burst to life and spread across all within the fireplace, roaring anew and sending warmth into the chamber.

Smiling, Valhalla stood, noticing many of the candle holders on the walls and shelves held only melted wax. It seemed like she would be replacing most of the candles.

Valhalla caught Alistair watching her, and as their eyes met, he smiled and gave her a thumbs-up, appreciation written across his face. Albrecht remained as he was, quiet with fingers interlocked over his mouth. Daemyn was still playing

---

1   Eldr is Celnor(Norse) for Fire.
2   Bjartr is Celnor(Norse) for Bright or to Brighten.

the piano, though now the tempo was growing faster and the once-gentle melody was turning unbearably agitated.

With a deep exhale, she calmed her rattling heart and returned the shovel to its stand. Gathering a new set of candles from within the bag hiding behind the stand, one by one, Valhalla placed them in the empty holders and lit their wicks with fire seidr. In no time at all, the chamber was illuminated once again.

The last candle was atop Daemyn's desk by his grand piano. In moments, she found his extravagant, silver candle holder and placed the candle within. Then, with a snap of her fingers, a flame sprouted on the wick. She stood there for a short time, watching Daemyn play. His fingers danced across the keys with a speed and ferocity that brought to mind the image of a swordsman moving from one form to another, each press of a key akin to a perfectly positioned thrust. She had never seen him play like this before and grew worried.

With a deep breath, Valhalla approached, careful not to move too fast. His face remained mostly hidden behind his loose flaxen hair. She found it odd. Valhalla couldn't recall a day when Daemyn didn't have it pulled into a ponytail or braid of some kind.

Walking around the piano, she hovered the candle closer to him, lighting the keys up. "Here, so you can see better." She said softly, trying to mask her concern.

Daemyn didn't respond, but continued playing, the intensity growing more and more. "Your Highness?" Valhalla reached out, lightly touching his shoulder, and the moment she did, she was flooded with regret. He startled and fumbled the keys, ruining the song.

His body trembled, and he slowly raised his head. Daemyn's sky blue eyes were wide and surrounded by darkness. His eyelids hung wearily in their sockets. A quiver came over his lips. In moments, his hands began to shake, and before Valhalla could say another word, Daemyn began slamming his fists into the keys in a fit of rage.

Valhalla jolted as he cried out. Albrecht leapt over the couch and rushed to his younger brother's side. Wrapping his arms around Daemyn, he pulled him close and grabbed hold of his wrists. Daemyn's hands dripped with blood.

Letting out a sharp breath, Valhalla turned to Alistair and found him standing beside the couches, frozen in stunned silence just as she was. Daemyn's sobs filled the room, his ragged apologies coming between breaths, over and over.

Albrecht hugged his younger brother with one arm and closed the lid over the keys with the other. Daemyn fell forward into his crossed arms atop the piano and wept.

"I-I'm sorry. I'm so, so sorry!" Daemyn repeated again and again.

Albrecht took a few stumbling steps back, raking his fingers through his dark brown hair. His eyes were wide, and the color drained from his face. Valhalla wasn't sure what she could do for him, let alone Daemyn; just standing around would solve nothing. She decided she would start with something small. The least she could do was bandage the young man's hands.

She turned and placed the candle holder back down on the desk, then reached into her apron pocket, pulling out linen wraps and medicinal ointments.

"You." A voice growled.

A shiver crawled up Valhalla's spine. Footsteps thundered toward her. She turned around and found herself face to face with Albrecht, his fingers wrapping around her neck.

50

Valhalla

Just Unleash

"**T**his is all your doing, ADMIT IT!**"** Albrecht snarled and pushed Valhalla hard into Daemyn's desk, making her shriek. She latched onto the man's wrists, but his grip was too strong and growing tighter by the second.

Black and white spots flooded her vision, and she gasped for air. Albrecht's bright blue eyes shone with rage. It seemed he was convinced everything was her fault. His mother's death. Daemyn's anguish. Even King Aegir's actions. Somehow all her doing. The shock of everything must've been too much. He had returned to his home, full of thinly concealed anguish and seeking peace, but found only more hurt. He was lashing out, and she was the only outsider, the perfect scapegoat for his anger. Knowing this, though, was of little help. Valhalla had no idea how to convince him she was as innocent as he and his brother.

Her knees quaked under her weight, and her mind spun. Valhalla felt her consciousness slipping through her fingers. Much more of this, and she would pass out. Then what, would he choke the life out of her or be content in letting her collapse to the floor with the knowledge that he could've killed her here and now? She needed to act, to be free of him without making herself a threat.

Alistair and Daemyn suddenly slammed into Albrecht from behind, each trying to get him off of her. "Albrecht," Alistair exclaimed, "what the fuck are you doing? Let go of her!"

"Can't you see you're hurting her!" Daemyn pleaded.

Both Princes pulled at Albrecht's wrists, loosening his grip just enough that Valhalla managed a small breath, but the rageful brute held firm. Valhalla didn't want to hurt any of the three, even Albrecht, though he might deserve it. However, she saw no other choice.

Valhalla pressed her hands together at her navel, then with all the force she could muster, thrust them up into Albrecht's forearms. The impact, combined with the efforts of Alistair and Daemyn, gave her an opening. Valhalla's arms shot forward and found purchase on the collar of Albrecht's vest. Grabbing hold of the fabric, she pulled him toward her and jammed her knee deep into his gut. Albrecht groaned and stumbled. In an instant, Alistair was between them and threw his fisted hand into Albrecht's jaw, sending him to the floor.

Daemyn caught Valhalla as she fell to her knees. Her throat ached, and she coughed uncontrollably. As he rubbed her back and held her steady, she looked at him in surprise. Given the state he had been in just moments ago, she hadn't expected him to come to her aid, and yet, there he was. The young man's face was red and tear-streaked, and the look he gave her was filled with sorrow and guilt.

The crack of knuckles against skin brought her attention back to the fight unfolding before them. Albrecht flew back and crashed into the corner of Daemyn's piano, twirling and falling to the ground with a thud. His breathing was gruff, and he snarled as he slowly sat up. Alistair stood firm before Valhalla, feet planted and ready to fend off another assault.

"Albrecht, come on!" Alistair chided. "You're acting like a damn fool. Valhalla's trying to help you. To help us! Blaming her isn't going to solve anything, and it sure as fuck won't bring your mother back!"

Albrecht glared up at Alistair and wiped away a trickle of blood falling from the corner of his mouth. Without a word, Albrecht picked himself up off the floor and lunged at Alistair. Daemyn started toward the pair, but Valhalla grabbed hold of him, fearing he would only get himself hurt were he to get between them. He struggled for a moment, then screamed for them to stop, his voice hoarse.

Wrapping his arms around Alistair's waist, Albrecht forced the High Prince back, the two of them crashing into the lavender couch beside them. Alistair groaned through gritted teeth. Albrecht seized the opening and grabbed hold of Alistair's vest collar, pulled a fist back, adopting the move Alistair had used moments before, and struck the High Prince in the jaw. The blow dazed Alistair, and as he tried to recover, Albrecht threw another punch, this time into Alistair's stomach, causing him to double over with a gasp.

Valhalla and Daemyn winced. Daemyn struggled again to free himself from her grip, but she held him fast. Her throat ached, however, breathing came easier now.

Alistair coughed and held his gut, but Albrecht didn't let up. He grabbed Alistair and, with a quick turn, lifted the High Prince over his shoulder and slammed him hard on his back.

"Albrecht, please!"Daemyn pleaded.

"Wait." Valhalla interrupted, not pulling her eyes from Albrecht and Alistair, and had a realization. The look on Alistair's face was all the confirmation she needed. She had seen him fight in anger, and this wasn't that. He was allowing Albrecht to vent his frustrations on himself.

The damn fools, she thought to herself.

"What? Why?" Daemyn stared at her with wide, confused eyes.

"Because," she spat, "they're both idiots. His Grace is fighting with his Highness to help him. He's allowing Albrecht an outlet for his anger. Don't worry," Valhalla sighed and turned to Daemyn, "if it does go too far, I'll step in and knock the fools on their asses. Just help me up first, if you could?"

Daemyn's brows curved up in surprise, then his expression settled back into sadness. After several moments, he hesitantly nodded. "I understand. Of course, but please, I'm going to help when that time comes, alright?"

Valhalla didn't want the young Prince to get further injured, but reluctantly agreed. Just as Daemyn helped her to her feet, Valhalla stole a glance at Alistair, and her breath hitched in her throat.

Albrecht knelt over Alistair, holding a fist full of his shirt in hand and rearing back, readying another blow. "As if you could understand what I'm going through." He growled as his fist plummeted downward.

Valhalla prematurely winced in anticipation of the strike; however, to her surprise, Alistair caught Albrecht's fist in mid-air. Where Alistair's face had been calm before, he now radiated outrage.

"Seriously," Alistair growled, "I don't know?" Alistair kicked Albrecht's feet out from under him, and as he landed, Alistair wound himself on top.

Daemyn shrank into Valhalla. This was likely the first time he had ever seen

Alistair this angry before and given his feelings toward him, it was probably all the harder to stand by and do nothing.

"I don't know what it's like to lose someone I care about!?" Alistair threw a jab into Albrecht's jaw, the outrage pouring out of him. "You don't think I know what it's like to see the body of someone I care about lying dead before my very eyes? To have a parent lie to my face!?" Alistair threw another punch, followed by another, and another, each connecting. Albrecht flailed in an attempt to defend against the barrage, and a glint of fear crossed his face now that Alistair was fighting for real. The High Prince bellowed his rage. "Tell me, Albrecht, how would you feel if you saw your sister lying dead on a—"

Just as Alistair thrust another fist back, he gasped and froze.

Valhalla hadn't realized Lorna's death still troubled him so. After everything she had done to him, everything she had planned to do, he still felt her loss as keenly as he had when he first learned the truth. But of course he would, Lorna was his little sister. Despite everything, he still clung to the memory of who she was when they were young. It was going to take time for him to finally let her go, to come to terms with her hatred toward him, the pain she inflicted, and the nightmares he suffered as a result. Terrible wounds always take time to heal.

Albrecht stared back, splayed under Alistair, something like regret starting to edge its way onto his tawny face. "A sister, huh? Well, I would certainly have some questions for my father." He said flatly, his expression unreadable.

Alistair shook his head, the jest sinking in. "You're joking after what you've done?"

"I know." Albrecht sighed, seeming tired for the first time since Valhalla entered the room. "I know." He then tapped at Alistair's fist, still clenching his shirt collar.

Alistair immediately let him go, turning his gaze to the trembling in his hands. Neither man moved from their spot. Seeing that the two had calmed to an extent, Valhalla released Daemyn and cautiously walked toward the dejected Princes. Slowly kneeling beside Alistair, she wrapped her arms around one of his. As he turned to her, he seemed so confused, his mixed colored eyes darting about the features of her face. Doing her best to ignore the rapid beating of her heart, Valhalla took a deep breath and aided Alistair up to his feet.

She leaned him against the couch, allowing him a moment to catch his breath and calm his mind. Valhalla then turned to Albrecht, who was still sprawled on the ground. Daemyn was now beside him, lightly examining the bruises forming on his face. As upset as she was with Albrecht, the man who laid his hands on her not once, but twice with clear intent to harm, she couldn't just leave him on the floor. With another deep breath, she stretched out a hand at him and clenched her jaw with brows furrowed so he wouldn't mistake the kindness for anything other than the small olive branch that it was. Valhalla didn't want him to confuse the act with forgiveness.

Albrecht eventually glanced down at her hand hovering over his chest and, with a deep sigh, clapped his palm into hers. Valhalla pulled him onto his feet. His hand stayed fixed in hers, and a hint of worry edged into her heart. She watched him carefully, and while she didn't want to fight, she was prepared this time. His furrowed gaze was downcast to the floor beside him, and with another deep breath, he spoke. "I'm sorry, Valhalla. I-I lost myself there. I . . . I never should've attacked you like that, and, well, I'm sorry. There. I said it. Please forgive me."

Albrecht bowed his head, and moments stretched on where she felt she should've said something, but the words didn't come. His demeanor was different now, and she wanted to believe there was sincerity in his words; however, his tone was as sour as ever. She hadn't realized she was scowling until it was too late.

He looked up and raised a brow at her. "What? I'm trying to apologize."

"Do you always sound so condescending?" Her words came out wrong, but she was still angry with him, and they just slipped out. Valhalla's neck was still sore. Perhaps that's why she couldn't just swallow her pride and accept with grace. Judging by his expression, her answer had landed with as disarming an effect as if she had simply struck him in the nose.

Alistair burst into a fit of laughter. "He does! Albi always does." He doubled over against the couch in a display that had to have either been genuine surprise or perfectly calculated to diffuse the situation. Either way, it seemed to have worked. Valhalla snorted in an attempt to hold back her laughter, and Albrecht groaned with embarrassment as his bright pink cheeks were any indication.

"Shut it, you, and don't call me that! I swear, Daemyn called me that once when he was a toddler, and you never let it go." Albrecht waved a dismissive hand toward Alistair; however, it only served to heighten the High Prince's laughter. "And as for you," he returned his attention to Valhalla, "will you forgive me already?"

She gave him a long, hard stare as the idea of turning him down floated in her mind. Still, he was a brother to Alistair and Daemyn, and they clearly loved him. There had to be redeeming qualities there. She considered the situation and determined things would go smoother with the two of them on better terms, though she wasn't sure she would ever grow to like the man, and cleared her throat. "I'll forgive you, *this* time, but you seriously need to do something about that anger of yours. You . . . could've killed me, and there for a moment, I thought you might."

Alistair's laughter quickly faded at hearing the exchange. Albrecht turned away. "I know, and-and I will. You have my word." He then bowed low, which caught her utterly by surprise. As a Princess of Asgard, the gesture itself was something she was accustomed to, if only seldomly, and yet none of them knew that. Even stranger, here was a Prince and Heir, bowing to someone he thought to be a servant maid. Perhaps there was some humility there after all. Still, if he attacked her again, she was going to light his shoes on fire.

Feeling a touch uncomfortable, Valhalla glanced around the room for a way out of this conversation. "Very good, then, um," she noticed Daemyn bending down to look at the medicinal ointment and linen bandages she'd apparently dropped during the commotion. He reached out to touch the bottle and startled at the state of his hands. "Your Highness, please, allow me." She said and rushed over as fast as she could, retrieving the medicinal ointment and linen strips. Her other hand frantically rummaged through her apron pockets for cotton swabs and rubbing alcohol.

Daemyn stared in seeming bewilderment at the blood and bruises covering his hands. "What happened?" He glanced up at her with curved brows and glossing eyes.

Valhalla opened her mouth, forming the start of an answer, but found the words didn't come. How do you tell someone that they self-harmed while lamenting the loss of a loved one? If he didn't even remember what he had done, words felt too small a thing.

She gently took his hands in hers, feeling his soft knuckles against her palms. There was no way to know what he had been thinking or feeling when he hurt himself, so the best she could offer was to explain what led to the injury, but when she reached the moment where everything had gone wrong, she faltered. "Something overcame you, and this was the result." It was the closest she could come to explaining how he attacked the piano, the fear she felt as it happened, and the helplessness that sucked the air from the room.

"What? That can't be." He said with a croak.

Valhalla took a deep breath and held his eyes. There was no escaping it. He needed to hear what he had done. "I think it was the shock of your mother's passing. I didn't think when I called to you, touched your shoulder, you fumbled the keys, and when the melody broke, I think something inside you did as well." She carefully turned his hands so that both of them could see the damage. There were many deep cuts and small gashes. Blood slowly coagulated around the wounds and bruises, darkening the swelling skin. "You began slamming your hands against the keys, all the while crying out an apology. Fortunately, your brother stopped you before you broke more than skin."

Daemyn released a trembling breath and stared down in disbelief. "I didn't—I couldn't. I had no idea."

"I know. It's alright. You. Are. Alright. We're going to figure this out together." She glanced at Alistair and Albrecht, and both nodded in agreement. "Now come on, let's get you off this floor so I can tend to your wounds."

Valhalla then helped Daemyn up, cradling the medicinal items in one arm and leading Daemyn with the other over to the closest lavender couch. The two sat down, turning to face one another, and Valhalla began her work. She pressed a cotton swab to the rim of the alcohol and tilted its contents onto the swab, then placed the bottle on the table beside them. "I need to clean the wound. This'll sting, your Highness." He winced as she lightly dabbed away the blood and cleaned the cuts, and to his credit, he didn't once pull away.

The two sat in silence for a time as she worked, and as Valhalla finished with the first hand and started to let go, Daemyn suddenly closed his fingers around her hand, taking her aback. "Your Highness?"

"What happened to cause you to react as you did last night?"

The question came as such a surprise that for a moment, she thought her heart might've stopped. Images of her past came in a volley. The experience likely only lasted moments, but the tragedy played out in her mind as it had all those years ago. Her lungs refused to work, and her breath hitched. Darkness spotted her vision, and she felt the room tilt. Suddenly, Alistair and Albrecht were there beside them.

"Daemyn," Albrecht chided, "it isn't your business to pry into someone's past!"

"I-I'm sorry, I just wanted to understand." He answered, now looking away.

As the burst of adrenaline faded, her breath returned, and she exhaled shakily. Her muscles relaxed, and whatever frightful expression had brought Alistair and Albrecht over passed from her face. Alistair gave her a worried glance, and she forced a smile. She then took Daemyn's other hand and returned to cleaning the wounds.

An unbearable silence hung in the chamber, and her mind wandered. Should she explain her past? Valhalla had kept all of that buried for so long now that the thought of bringing it all back to the surface was about as welcome as the idea of being stranded alone in Helheim. She had thought—or rather hoped—that if she didn't talk about it or think about it, those terrible nightmares would fade into obscurity. Recent events proved that to be a falsehood. Valhalla had already frozen up once and didn't want to do so again. Maybe revisiting her past here in relative safety would stop that from happening again. Besides that, telling them might go some way toward establishing the trust the four of them would need if they were going to get through this ordeal. She knew the outline of their suffering. Perhaps opening up would prove to be a good thing.

By the time she had made up her mind, Daemyn's second hand was clean. She stuffed the pink swab into her apron pocket and closed the small bottle, putting it away as well. Valhalla then retrieved her ointment, a gift from Eir, the Goddess of Healing, and one of Frigg's many handmaidens.

"My birth city was small." Valhalla started, sliding a finger across the ointment's surface, and began lightly covering each wound with the green slime-like substance. "We lived modestly. Our greatest resources were found through mining. My father, on most days, would enter the crystalline caves and dig for minerals and the like, while my mother looked after the people on the surface, meeting with dignitaries and running services for our gods in the temple built within our home, carved into the mountain. We didn't have the resources to build a stave in the heart of the city. One day there was—"

Her breath caught, and her throat tightened with grief.

Clearing her throat, she began again. "There was an attack . . . no one else made it. I only survived because my parents hid me under the floor with our emergency stores, between the grain and salted meats. That was moments before they died." Valhalla's voice cracked.

Her hand hovered trembling over Daemyn's, her parents' screams a distant echo, and the sight of their bodies becoming more vivid as she spoke.

"Some passing warriors happened by and found me still crouched where my parents left me. That's when I-I saw the aftermath."

A tear rolled down one of her cheeks, the sensation startling her. She quickly wiped it away and closed the jar, stuffing it back in her apron pocket, and pulled out two gauze strips, pressing one of them carefully onto the side of Daemyn's hands. "I was five falls young, at the time."

"That-That's terrible!" Daemyn stared at her with mournful eyes as she wrapped linen bandages about each of his hands.

"It was," she said softly, "but those warriors were kind enough to bury my parents and my people." She clipped the bandages closed.

He brought his hands to his chest, rubbing them and not turning his eyes away. "Have you . . . tried to visit since?"

Valhalla tucked the rest of the items away in her apron pocket. She had never even considered returning. What exactly was there for her to return to? Her hiding place? The spot where her parents fell, or their final resting place just outside their home? Perhaps to see how the ruins fared now that they were retaken by the wilds? Returning would only serve to add finality to what was lost.

She shook her head. "No. I tried visiting once, years ago, to . . . I don't completely know, bury the memories of my parents? I hoped returning would help me move past that terrible turning point in my life, but I could never bring myself to do it, choosing instead to leave it all behind, I suppose." Valhalla shrugged and turned away, unconsciously wringing her hands.

"It's never easy to move on," Alistair said gently, and the clear comforting sentiment was welcome. He, of those present, knew something of what she was going through. Daemyn and Albrecht were a raw, open wound, both in the shocked stare of grief. Alistair understood the years it took to come back, to rebuild yourself into something no longer whole, yet tempered by the experience. From his father dying in his arms to the complexities of what he was going through with Lorna. For reasons she was unable to explain, she hesitated to look at him.

Valhalla could feel Alistair nearby. Taking a deep breath, she glanced behind her and there he was, leaning on the couch. His eyes were filled with understanding. Her lips parted, wanting to say something, but nothing came to mind, so she remained silent. As if somehow sensing what she was feeling, he reached a hesitant hand and laid it on her shoulder, giving it a gentle squeeze. Gooseflesh prickled her skin. It was a simple thing, and yet, in that moment, she didn't feel so alone. She raised her hand to his. Her vision grew watery as a lump formed in her throat. The grief was threatening to burst forth, bending the barriers she had erected in her heart and mind; however, she focused her thoughts on Alistair. His gentle smile. The colors of his eyes. His soft touch. The trust he had in her. The feeling soon passed, and he squeezed his hand in return, hoping he wouldn't notice the light tremble in her grip.

"Fucking bandits!" Albrecht sneered. "I swear they're the bane of our existence."

The corner of Valhalla's lips perked. She hadn't said they were bandits, but perhaps it was good he came to that conclusion. Bandits were simple, motivated by greed and personal gain. Allowing them to believe that would be easier than explaining it had been a god who was the author of her anguish.

The sound of shuffling behind her ended the moment, and soon Albrecht walked around the couch and took a seat opposite her and Daemyn. Crossing his legs one over the other, he leaned forward and rubbed his chin.

Releasing a tired sigh, he asked, "If no one minds a change of subject, how exactly are we going to deal with my father?"

No one seemed to know what to say to that. Valhalla tapped a finger against the back of her hand. Daemyn rested his elbows on his knees and rubbed his bandaged palms together. Alistair gripped the top of the lavender couch, his face scrunched with irritation, and let out a loud groan. "I honestly don't know!"

Alistair said in exasperation. His fingers sank into his dark hair as he paced back and forth. "I still can't wrap my head around everything that's happened."

"Based on what I've uncovered," Valhalla turned to Albrecht, "I can only speculate. Last night was the first definitive proof I've found, but the reasoning behind everything is beyond me."

"The Steward . . ." Daemyn whispered softly, his demeanor shrinking.

Valhalla glanced at him and considered; there was definitely something about Tamanna that felt off, and the man clearly terrified the young Prince. Maybe he knew something she didn't? She slowly reached for his hands, cupping them in hers. "Your Highness, is there something you want to share?"

Daemyn took a long breath and hesitated, as though he was second-guessing saying anything at all. Conflict and fear mingled on his face for several long moments before his lips parted and he continued. "I know you've looked into my father, but what about Lord Tamanna? Have you looked into him?"

"Well," Valhalla dropped Daemyn's hands and wove her fingers together, brushing the pads of her thumbs. All eyes were on her, and she felt the pressure to say something, give them any answer to go by, but what was there to say?

"What is it?" Alistair asked, coming around the couch and sitting beside Albrecht. Looking at the Princes across from her and she noticed the bruises developing over their jaws and cheeks.

Standing, she walked over to Daemyn's bar and gathered two cloth napkins, placing a sphere of ice at the center of each. Valhalla returned to the pair and placed the cold bundles against their cheeks. Both gave her a confused expression, but held the napkins and ice where she had placed them.

"It's not that I haven't tried," she finally answered, returning to her seat beside Daemyn, "it's just been difficult getting into his chamber. Lord Tamanna keeps the door locked tight. No one is allowed inside, per his request."

"But what about when he has food brought to his room?" Alistair asked with a raised brow.

"When we bring him food, we're told to place the tray on the table beside his door. Later on, we return to retrieve the empty tray from the same spot."

"You never thought to pick the lock?" Albrecht asked incredulously.

"I, uuh," Valhalla's cheeks burned as she pulled back her ebony hair. She had never learned how to pick locks, had never needed to know how. Besides, it had always just seemed morally wrong to intrude on others like that.

Albrecht chortled with a playful smirk. "You don't know how, do you?"

"Well, no, do you?" She retorted, annoyance tugging at her brows.

He just shrugged. "I've been known to dabble."

"Wait, what?" Alistair spun at him, stunned.

"Blame the woman I've been with. She's a bad influence." Albrecht said in jest. " In all seriousness, I had one too many brushes with capture during the Gran Mar War. So, she demanded I learn how to free myself should I ever wake up in a cell. That said, I assume a cell is a bit different from a chamber door, at least compared to the ones here in the castle."

Alistair sighed and shifted the ice to the other side of his face. "Well, I'm just glad you made it back home in one piece. Now, about—Wait!" Alistair exclaimed as he turned to Valhalla. "Didn't you say you have a friend in the city? By any chance, can *he* pick locks?"

She nodded and thought back on the tales Vardan had told her of his travels. One memory stuck out beyond the rest. It had been a rescue mission that sent him on board several disguised slave ships. He had to pick the locks of their shackles. "I think so. I'll be meeting with him shortly, so I'll ask."

"Alright, now what about Tamanna?" Albrecht asked, looking from Valhalla to Daemyn. "How often is he in his chamber?"

"H-He spends most of his time with Father, only leaving to eat and sleep as far as I know." Daemyn cleared his throat and pulled on the ruffled cascade collar. Worry shone in his bright blue eyes. "You could likely get into his chamber right now. He should be busy with Father going over the weekly reports with the council."

Valhalla nodded in thanks and stood. "Then we have a plan. I just—"

"I?" Alistair interjected. "You don't expect us to let you go alone, do you?"

"I do, actually." Her response made Alistair wince. Her tone had been harsh in its abruptness. He was only worried for her safety, and so with a sigh, she continued. "Please understand, your Grace. I can walk around the castle alone as a servant and not raise suspicion, but add you into the mix and people *will* notice; begin to talk. It has to be me. Don't worry," she smirked confidently, "I'll be fine. I visit my friend, learn how to pick a lock, then slip in unnoticed. If push comes to shove, despite that quarrel of ours in Hilliard, trust that I can hold my own when I need to." Valhalla snapped her fingers, and a flame appeared on the tip of her index. She then drew a straight line down, the fire following her finger and slowly forming a sword. With a wave of her hand, she winked, and it disappeared.

Alistair's cheeks turned a deep shade of red as he cleared his throat, and he forced a nod. With a bow, she walked to the chamber doors, and as she grabbed hold of one of the handles, a thought came to her. She turned back to Alistair. "If you're still worried for me, why not hold Lord Tamanna's attention while I scour his chamber. When I'm done, I'll come straight here to wait for you. How does that sound?"

Alistair released a hesitant sigh and nodded. "Alright, we'll do this your way."

"Thank you, Your Grace." Valhalla opened the door and stepped into the hall. The walk back to the castle's kitchen was long, but it couldn't be helped. She needed to see Vardan.

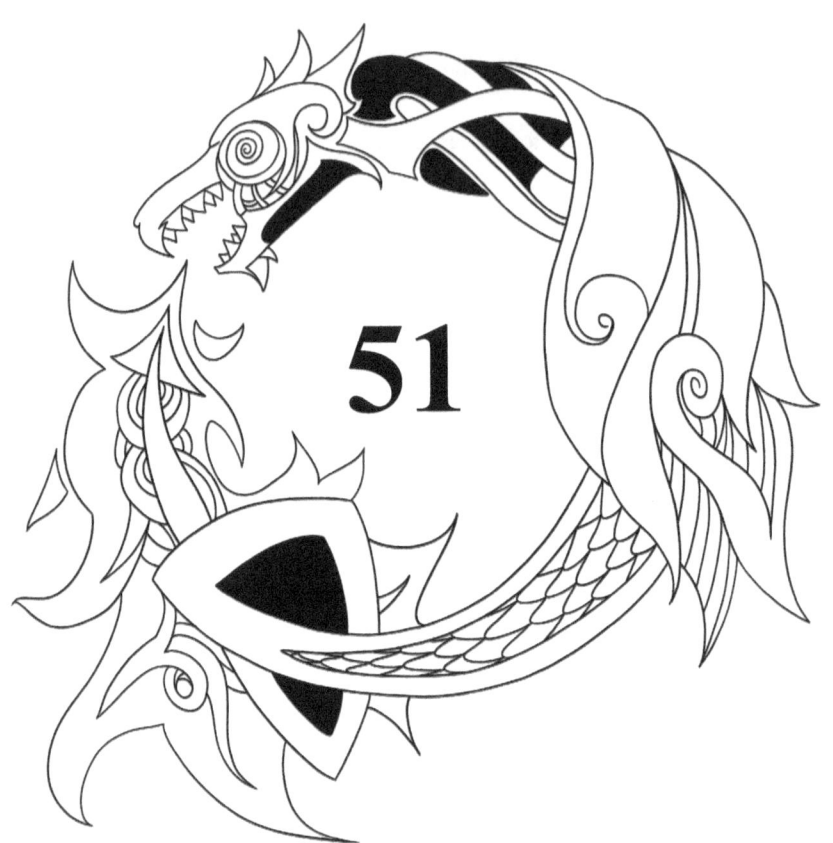

51

Valhalla

Tamanna's Journal

"**A**RE YOU SURE I NEVER TAUGHT YOU how to pick a lock?"
Vardan asked and held up a lantern.

"Yes, I'm sure. It's not like any of us thought I would ever need to learn such a skill anyway." Valhalla waved the notion away as she led Vardan through the Svartr castle, moving as silently as they could. After leaving the Princes, she had found him in the kitchen, hood raised and seated in shadows. Valhalla had asked him to teach her. Several of the longest minutes of her life passed as she tried and failed to convince him he had never shown her how to do it. In the end, he hadn't relented and told her that even if he wanted to teach her here and now, there just wasn't any way she'd be prepared enough in such a short time for whatever type of lock they were up against. There were just too many different locks in the world. Their only choice was for him to accompany her, and to her great frustration, he had yet to drop the subject.

Lord Tamanna's chamber was in one of the highest towers and far from any of the castle's entrances. If Valhalla were discovered here, it would be difficult enough to explain, but for Vardan, even being friends with the head of the castle's staff, they would be in a bit of a predicament. They had made it this far largely by luck and by sticking to the servants' pathways. The climb up the stairs was tiring, but the man's chamber wasn't far now.

"I suppose. But if I didn't teach you, which I'm not saying I agree with, I was probably just waiting for you to ask." Vardan shrugged with a mischievous grin. "I've been waiting for you to ask me to teach you *many* things, actually. Like sailing, for instance. To be honest, I'm a little hurt you've never asked." He held a hand over his heart, his expression turning into an exaggerated frown.

Her lips twitched upward at the corners, but she didn't want him to win her over so easily. Instead, she scrunched her face into an equally ridiculous pout. When she spoke, she added pain to her voice. "How could you forget I get seasick?"

Despite loving the sea, the smell of salt, the rolling waves, and the rhythm as they crashed into the hull, her body simply was not built for it. Traveling on a shallow river was one thing; however, when on board a ship in the open sea, she became little more than a wretch. The sense of balance was the first thing to betray her, followed by her vision, and then her stomach.

"No, I remember perfectly well. So does my lap. Those were my favorite trousers after all." He laughed a bit too heartily, the sound echoing off the walls. Fortunately, they hadn't seen a soul in this part of the castle, and there were no signs anyone would be waiting for them above. "I'm just saying, you won't get used to the motion if you continue to avoid it. OH! You also never asked me to teach you how to fish!"

"Shh!" She spun and pressed a finger to her lips. "We're here." She pointed ahead. At the very edge of the lantern's light, a mahogany door and a small round table came into view.

With hurried steps, she moved to the door and pressed her ear to the smooth wooden surface. All inside seemed silent. "I don't hear anything, but better to be safe." She said with a whisper, then knocked. "Excuse me, Lord Tamanna?"

No answer came.

"Alright, we're in the clear. My Lord." Valhalla spun to the side with an exaggerated bow and gestured to the door handle. He rolled his one golden eye. He had long since renounced his role as a Duke of Svartr and disliked the continued use of his title, which of course she knew and found rather amusing. It was one of the few ways she could tease him and actually get a response.

"You know, if you start referring to me by title, I'll be *forced* to do the same to you, Your Highness." He smirked in challenge.

She hadn't been particularly fond of her title either, given the weight of the memories tied to it. It generally didn't bring on much discomfort these days, but with how all of those memories and emotions were being dredged up, today she found it as welcome as salt on a wound. With a sigh, she shook her head. "Why do we reject titles so easily?"

"I don't reject my title, it's just . . . I left it behind centuries ago. It belongs in the past." Vardan closed the gap between them and cupped her cheek.

It was easy to forget just how long he had walked in the light of the living. He had been alive since a time before the Oceanans sailed from lands across the great span of the Nadr Ocean. The trip across the vast ocean was no easy feat by today's standards, and he had done it at a time when it would've been unthinkable. Valhalla wondered what would have compelled his people to make such a journey. What kinds of hardships had Vardan experienced in all that time? How many people had he grown to care for, then be forced to watch as they grew old and passed away as he continued on, ageless as he was.

"Titles are just words, my darling Valla," he said, her cheeks warming at his sweet tone, "they hold only the weight you give them. They hold power, yes, as all words do, and that power can be used for good just as easily as they can for ill." Sliding his hand away, he shrugged and reached inside his coat, searching for something. "But if that power goes to one's head, the wielder could likely one day find themselves confronted by those they turned it against, facing the reality that the foundation of that power can crumble as quickly as it was built."

He pulled out a small, rolled-up piece of leather and knelt on the ground, placing his lantern on the floor beside his knee and pulled back his hood. As Vardan unrolled the leather, Valhalla looked over the array of thin tools and tilted her head at him. "Even the just have faced revolt, though."

Vardan picked up two of his tools and sighed. "I know. Being a leader isn't easy, and I don't envy those who try." Sticking two tools into the keyhole of the door, he began twirling them about, occasionally flicking them up and down, waiting, waiting, and waiting.

She crossed an arm over her chest and dropped her cheek into her palm, watching as he worked and the moments ticked by. "So, what are you doing exactly?"

"Are you sure I never taught you how to do this?" He answered her question with his own, but left no time for her to respond as he continued. "I'm just feeling around the inside of the lock . . . Dammit, I was fucking close! Anyway, I'm tricking the lock into thinking this is a key."

A smirk slid onto Valhalla's face. "Tricking the lock? Really?"

A sneer edged its way onto his rugged face as he concentrated; however, his tone was playful when he answered. "Hey, until you know how to do this, don't question the explanation." Vardan managed a chuckle, and then his brows set. His eye narrowed, and with each motion, the tools slid a little deeper into the keyhole.

Curling her lips between her teeth, she continued. "You know, if you can't do it, I could always use my fire seidr to blast our way in."

His shoulders slumped as he looked up at her, his expression critical. "Seriously? You brought me all the way up here so we could do this quietly, and now you want to do that? Is stealth that boring for you or are you just itching to fight the entire Kingsguard?"

For a moment, Valhalla thought he hadn't realized she was joking, but then his lips tugged upward into a knowing smirk. Vardan returned to the lock. "It would make for quite an announcement, though. Stairs are narrow too. We might stand a chance of surviving the night."

She giggled again. "Probably shouldn't. Wouldn't want to worry the friends I've made here. Please, continue."

"Yes, shrilly."

"Shrilly?" She raised a confused brow at him.

"Aye, you might not have noticed, but those giggles of yours are pretty high in pitch." Vardan leaned close to the door, and she stared at him with mouth agape.

"My giggles? I don't—"

"Listen, when you finally meet someone who isn't bothered by it, that's how you know they're worthy of you."

Valhalla's cheeks burned, and she turned away. Her mouth opened to argue, however, then she heard a loud click and her attention shot back to the door. Vardan removed his tools and twirled one around his fingers, grinning. Sliding the tools back into his leather kit in one easy motion, Vardan rolled the pack up and stood. His hand grabbed the handle, and with a push, the door cracked open.

"Ta da." He bowed and gestured into the violet and mahogany chamber.

Her eyes widened with triumph. "Thank you, Vardan!" Valhalla pushed the door open some more and was taken aback by the state of the chamber.

"What's wrong?" Vardan asked, picking up the lantern and pulling his hood back over his head. It was important that he keep himself hidden from prying eyes after all. He was written down as deceased in the Svartr archives long ago. If someone were to spot him and recognize who he was, as unlikely as that might be, it was a situation best to be avoided.

"It's so . . . tidy." Valhalla stepped into the firelit chamber. The curtains were pulled and tied in the corners. Through the window, the dark hurricane flashed as lightning streaked across the sky, thunder cracking seconds later. The floor was swept clean and the bed neatly dressed. Flames dotted candles here and there. Even the fireplace was left burning. There wasn't a spot of dust in sight. Tamanna must've been doing his own cleaning, which was uncommon for one of his station.

"Maybe this Tamanna fellow's particular about his environment." Vardan shrugged and leaned against the doorframe.

Valhalla nodded in agreement. "Possibly. It just feels too clean, you know?"

As she surveyed the circular chamber, a desk with a stack of books to her left caught her eye. On the desk, she found a leather-bound book and a single lit taper candle beside it. Rounding the desk, she also discovered an open ink bottle and feather quill pen, its tip covered in dried ink. She picked up the book from the center of the desk and opened it.

The very first page was covered in Enskr and Futhark runes, with pronunciation notes scribbled beside each as if someone had been studying them. Carefully flipping through the next few pages, Valhalla came upon a dated entry from just over four years ago.

The 18th of Gormánudur 1244

It has taken longer than expected, but I've finally mastered the Enskr language and even the Veerencians Futhark runes. Their magic, or seidr as it appears their ancestors called it, was used in all aspects of life. The runes were used to speak with nature, their gods, the elements, and even gave them advantages in battle. I must get my hands on more of these tomes. These runes are vastly different from those in my home of Mahaanbrahman, and I've found hints of something called dark seidr. I've scoured these lands and uncovered all of their secrets. The time has finally come. If I'm to learn more, I must leave Eenheide and cross the border into Veerence.

She released a sharp breath. "I think I've found Lord Tamanna's journal. It seemed he was in Eenheide before coming to Veerence."

"Valhalla?" He called for her, but she was too engrossed in the journal to look up. She continued on, scanning the entries for any clue as to why the man was in Svartr and why he was so interested in Seidr. Page after page, she flipped through the man's obsessive notes until she stumbled across a familiar name. Her blood went cold.

"Valhalla." He called a little louder, but whatever it was, it needed to wait.

"Just one moment. I think Lord Tamanna has met with Kiara, but why?"

The 3rd of Góa 1245

A woman dressed in Veerencian black and violet approached me with something very peculiar. She claimed it was a crystal imbued with dark seidr, and that it would allow me to do anything I wanted with the dark arts, from mind control to even manipulating death itself. The crystal looked like an ordinary black sphere, but when she tightened her grip around it, the sphere glowed violet, and the very room where we met went dark. It was as if the sun itself was devoured and only the light of the orb remained. She was an interesting woman and claimed she wanted nothing in return for the crystal, but I'm no fool. I'll need to tread carefully with this Kiara. She clearly has her own goals, but this opportunity is too great. I will accept this gift and experiment with this seidr crystal, and should the time come that she crosses me, I will be ready.

She struggled to breathe. The room was growing colder around her, and the air itself was dense. Kiara was involved with this man for some reason, and wherever she went, tragedy followed.

Looking through a few more entries, it seemed Kiara was the reason that Tamanna turned his eyes toward Svartr instead of crossing the Rjóðr Gates into Veerence as a whole. He even orchestrated a mercenary attack on Daemyn and Ayunli while they were riding their horses on the beach below the castle's cliffside to get in Aegir's good graces by *saving* the King's family. The entries only grew more disturbing from there. Tamanna used the crystal to mind-control people and animals alike, testing out the limits of his newfound seidr, and even successfully raised the dead.

Valhalla swallowed, feeling the dread forming in her gut. Gooseflesh spread on her porcelain skin. Tamanna could force people into nightmarish sleep, craft illusions, even make the recently deceased look as though they were still alive, puppeting them to his will. It seemed the crystal itself was expanding his knowledge, teaching him everything he had desired, but still, he wanted—needed more.

Then she found it, the answer to the question forming in the back of her mind. Her breath grew shallow as the words hit her like arrows.

The 21st of Tvímánudur 1246

It's done. Aegir accepted my invitation to tea in my chamber. The fool drank the poison and didn't even notice until it was too late, but I was careless. The poison shouldn't have shown any physical abnormalities, but the black roots and graying of his skin is going to be a problem. I'll have to place an illusion over his being every time he sees someone other than me. I was also mistaken about how painful the death would be. Aegir was very noisy. It's fortunate I picked this spire for my chambers. I mustn't be so careless in the future. The small collection of runes on the man's forehead can be easily hidden beneath his crown. I must work quickly. With my black candle finished, controlling others will be much simpler. They just need to be within the light of the flame. Aegir will wake soon. His wife needs to be moved to another room. I'm sure a simple lie of working late to seek out rebel rousers should suffice, but if she proves to be a problem, I'll have to get rid of her, as I have others.

"By Yggdrasil's shade, King Aegir's—"

"Valhalla!" Vardan raised his voice, making her jolt. Hearing the strain in his voice, she looked to him in a panic.

"What?"

"Tamanna has marked the floor with seidr!"

Her eyes slowly widened as his words sank in. She shifted her gaze down to his feet, spotting the runes glowing with purple energy, and followed them all the way around the edge of the chamber. "Oh no."

The hairs on the back of her neck stood on end, and a terrible shiver spidered its way up her spine. He visibly startled, looking past her, and reached out. "Come on!"

She suddenly felt a strange presence behind her. Her breath caught in her throat. She spun around, ready to confront whatever was there, but instead of finding a person, she found a giant eye staring right at her. Its image was in a mirror which hung on the wall just above a table with a porcelain bowl of water on its surface.

If this was a form of dark seidr, she didn't know it. She made a mental note to bother Hodr about it, should they survive their stay in Svartr. He was her brother and the renowned God of Darkness after all. If anyone would know what it was they were looking at, it would be him.

Taking a step back, she fumbled on her heel and toppled into Tamanna's desk. She stared at the open journal below her, gritting her teeth in frustration, and without a second thought, grabbed it and ran.

She cursed at herself for being so careless. Why hadn't she examined the doorway before just waltzing into the man's chamber? It couldn't be helped now. Tamanna had seen her face; she was sure of that, but she hoped he hadn't seen Vardan's.

Rushing into his outstretched arm, he turned and slammed the door shut behind them. Her body trembled. The eye in the mirror unsettled her, but it paled in comparison to what she learned in Tamanna's journal. She needed to meet with the Princes and needed to do so now.

As she pushed herself off of Vardan, he grabbed her wrist, his expression stern and his golden eye shining with worry. "I'm getting you out of here." He pulled her hard as he started toward the stairs, but as much as she understood his concern, she couldn't leave. Not yet. The Princes needed to be warned about Tamanna, and needed to know about the fate of their father.

She rushed in front of him and shoved the leather journal into his chest. "Vardan, listen to me, please. If anything happens to me, please give this to High Prince Alistair and Prince Albrecht. Can you do that for me?"

He snarled in outrage. "Are you crazy?"

She slammed herself against him, embracing him about the waist and nuzzling her face into his neck. His body went still, and she was sure a war of emotions was raging within him. He was a father to her, after all, and given the danger they were in, it was a testament to his respect for her that he hadn't scooped her up and continued down and out of the city.

She squeezed him a little tighter, her way of thanking him for his worries and for waiting to hear her out. "Please, this is important. I know you're worried about me, but," she straightened, looking at him with as much conviction as she could muster, "your home needs you. Your friend and his sons need you. I know this will not be easy, but please, I'm asking you to choose Svartr over me. Can you do what I ask?"

His eye trembled as he stared at her, but eventually, begrudgingly, Vardan accepted the journal wedged between them. With a deep breath, his nostrils flared, and he gave her a single nod. "Fine." He replied in a low growl, visibly struggling to respect her wishes. "My longhouse isn't far from the castle. I'll hide the journal there, but once it's safe, I *will* come back to help you. Is that understood?"

Valhalla smiled graciously. "Perfectly." She cupped her hands behind his neck and touched her forehead to his. This act was sacred to the people of Oceana, and to those of Svartr especially. It was a sign of love, friendship, and care saved only for those you would die for. Valhalla rarely performed the gesture, to not cheapen its meaning, and realized in that moment it had been quite some time since she had performed it with Vardan. She vowed to rectify that once this task was complete.

After a moment, Vardan closed his eyes and exhaled deeply. His lips shook, and when he spoke, his voice was tight. "Please be safe, my Eldr[1]."

---

1   Eldr is Celnor(Norse) for Fire.

The corners of her lips stretched into a grin. "You as well, Father." With that, Valhalla released him and rushed down the stairs of the tower to warn the Princes of what she had learned. With any luck, they just might believe her.

All of this, the deaths, the false rebellion, it was all just so Tamanna could see what he could do with seidr? This was beyond madness. Then there was Kiara's involvement. Just what did she hope to gain? What use was Tamanna to her? He had to know more than what was written in the journal, and she hoped to get those answers; however, first things first, she needed to get the Princes away from the Steward.

52

Alistair

The Steward

Albrecht leaned against a set of double doors with the left side cracked open. He peered into the hall and watched for movement at Aegir's door. Daemyn rested his back against the wall beside his brother, fiddling with the ruffles of his shirt out of boredom and trying to not make eye contact with Alistair, who just completed the forty-second turn of his constant pacing.

After Valhalla left on her mission to sneak into Lord Tamanna's bedchamber, Albrecht suggested they move into his own chamber. His room was across from his father's, and so keeping watch would be a simple thing. So, with nothing else they could do, the group moved into position and waited. It wasn't a bad plan, none of it was, but Alistair couldn't help the feeling that something was going to go wrong.

"Alistair, you need to stop pacing, it's making *me* nervous," Albrecht said flatly, not averting his gaze.

"Is the meeting done?" Alistair asked with urgency and stopped dead in his tracks.

"I would've said so if that were the case." Albrecht chided, then with a deep groan, Alistair resumed his pacing.

Turning for the first time since they settled into the room, Albrecht shot Alistair a glare. "Are you serious right now? You need to stop!"

"What?"

"Valhalla will be fine, put some faith in the woman, will you."

"For your information, I *do* have faith in her!" Alistair shot back, then cooled. "It's just, I don't know. There's just been a . . . feeling in the air. Something isn't right."

"How about a distraction then," Daemyn suggested in a surprisingly jovial tone. He had a curious look on his face

"Um, alright then?" Alistair shrugged, unsure what his friend had in mind.

"What's this about a fight between you and Valhalla?"

Alistair was taken aback by the question. "Oh. Uhh," he cleared his throat, trying to gather his thoughts, "Very few know this. Only Valhalla, my mother and aunts, Shu Yen, perhaps one or two others, but before the official announcement, Lorna had been dead for over a month."

Both Albrecht and Daemyn's eyes widened. "Wait, seriously?" Albrecht asked, surprise clear on his face.

Alistair quickly nodded. "Yes. Mother requested Valhalla's aid in the matter and trained her to pose as Lorna. I . . . didn't know about it. Any of it. When I saw Lorna, or who I thought was Lorna, things were as they usually were. We had our usual arguments, but something about her chilled me to my bones, and after a week or so, I worked up the nerve to speak with Mother about her. When the opportunity came, Lorna was there, and the two of them were talking. It was when they turned to me that Lorna's eyes met mine. Valhalla forgot the illusion concealing her true eye color, and when I realized it wasn't Lorna standing before my mother," Alistair sighed, feeling shame at the memory, "I attacked her, thinking she had fooled my mother."

Both brothers stared at Alistair, blinking and quiet as they took it all in, until Albrecht snorted in amusement. "So you see Lorna with different colored eyes casually chatting with your mother, and you assume she didn't notice? Not only that, you thought she was tricking your mother tooooo what, exactly? Leave the confines of her castle?"

Alistair rolled his eyes, annoyance equal only to his embarrassment. "I panicked, alright. I didn't know her, and I didn't know what she was doing with my mother. After everything that's happened, I'd appreciate it if you didn't laugh at me!"

"Who won?" Daemyn asked through his brother's laughter, his face turning serious.

"What?"

"Your fight with her, who won?" Daemyn asked again.

"Oh." Alistair glanced away, feeling awkward about how things had played out. "I suppose I did, but it wasn't that simple. She was wearing a gown and not really fighting back, only defending."

"Oh." Daemyn shrugged. "I'm sure if it was a fair fight, Valhalla would've won."

"What makes you say that?" Alistair asked, chagrined by the remark.

"Simple," he glanced back with a challenging smirk, "she's faster and better with magic."

Alistair was at a loss for words for several long moments. No doubt, Valhalla was a trained warrior, but it had been argued that he was the best fighter in Hilliard. He would, at the very least, be capable of providing Valhalla with a fight worth remembering.

Alistair felt a vein twitch in his neck, and he narrowed his eyes at Daemyn. "If she wants a rematch, I would happily oblige." He then crossed his arms and straightened his back, "I'm not so petty to refuse—"

"Shh! Shut it, you two," Albrecht demanded, glancing at them before turning back into the hall.

Alistair hurried up behind him, wanting to see what was happening but only able to hear hushed voices outside. "I suppose they're done. You both ready?" Albrecht nodded, and Alistair looked at Daemyn. His young friend rubbed his fingers together, and his posture slumped. Daemyn was nervous, but more than that, he seemed to be genuinely afraid. "Daemyn, you alright?"

His friend's mouth fell open, but he didn't speak. His lip quivered. Alistair wanted to press the matter, but before he could, Albrecht tapped his shoulder and pulled the doors open.

Shuffling away from Aegir's chamber was what was left of his council. Normally, the mass of bodies would've been ten people strong, yet here, there were only four. Alistair didn't recognize the men, but their dejected, hollow expressions filled him with dread for what exactly was going on in the King's chamber. He wasn't able to linger on the idea for long, though, as Aegir and Tamanna stepped out just behind the group.

Albrecht saw his opening and quickly stepped out as well, his charming smile already plastered across his face. "Father." He called out warmly.

Aegir turned to him and seemed genuinely relieved to see his son. Tamanna, on the other hand, if he had felt anything at all, his face did not portray it.

"Something occurred to me while I was catching up with these two." Albrecht gestured behind himself to Alistair and Daemyn with a thumb. Alistair gave a little wave, and Daemyn stood timidly behind him. "I know next to nothing about Lord Tamanna, and if he's to stay here, and willing to transition once it's my time to reign, I thought it prudent we get to know one another."

"I'm honored, Your Highness," Tamanna said with a smile that didn't quite reach his eyes, "but I'm *quite* hungry."

"Then let's eat. We can do so right here, in fact." Albrecht gestured to the dining table beside him and, before Tamana could object, waved at two servant maidens as they rounded the corner heading toward the group. "Excuse me, you two, if the cook is preparing our dinner, mind sending it this way? We'll be dining together."

The women curtsied low. "Of course, your Highness." Giggling softly, the pair turned and headed back toward the stairs to the kitchen.

"There," Albrecht clapped his hands together, garnering everyone's attention, "the matter's settled. Come." He made his way to the left side of the table, Alistair and Daemyn taking their seats on either side of him. His older friend's smile was so innocent and inviting that had Alistair not known better, he would've mistaken it for genuine. Albrecht had always been the approachable one after all.

Aegir sat himself opposite Daemyn. Tamana, with no way left to refuse, let slip a tired sigh and sat opposite Albrecht. As his back fell flat against his chair, he rested a leg over his knee and locked his fingers over his stomach. "So, your Highness, what do you wish to know about me?" His words were full of false warmth, and Tamanna's smirk was half-hearted at best.

Albrecht leaned over the table and touched a hand to his forearm. "Alistair and Daemyn tell me you come from Mahaanbrahma, Raseela, beyond the Desert of Khufu past Eenheid. That's quite a distance. Why journey so far to come here?"

"Knowledge, your Highness," Tamanna answered, a curious glint in his dark eyes. "I'm a scholar, you see, one who seeks that which is yet unknown."

"What kind of information, if you don't mind my asking? Perhaps in my travels, I've come across something which could contribute to your quest." Albrecht tilted his head, eyes watching the man like a hawk.

"Magic."

Alistair was taken aback at how fast Tamanna answered, but what unsettled him wasn't just the abruptness with which he answered but the answer itself. Why magic? Even Albrecht seemed surprised. The two stole a glance at each other, and Albrecht subtly shrugged, returning to Tamanna.

"So, you came to Svartr?" Albrecht asked. "Our history has very little to do with magic. You would've a better chance going to Grœnn, Blár, or even Hilliard, for that matter."

"I know," Tamanna waved a dismissive hand, "but your people's history fascinated me all the same, which is why I stayed."

"Alright, so what led to you becoming a Steward for my father?"

"Oh, did Daemyn not tell you?" Aegir asked as he turned to eye Daemyn, and he wasn't alone. All eyes turned to him, causing the young man notable discomfort.

"Tell me what?" Albrecht's brows furrowed as he glanced back at his father.

"Honestly, I'm not surprised he didn't tell you. The ordeal gave him such a fright, he started avoiding the beach."

"What happened?" Albrecht asked, his tone turning serious.

"Daemyn and your mother went out riding and got attacked by bandits."

"What!?" Albrecht exclaimed in outrage, making Alistair startle in his seat. "Where were the guards?"

"Calm yourself, Albrecht." Aegir raised a hand to his oldest son. "Daemyn challenged your mother to a race, and the guards fell behind. Unfortunately, Daemyn suffered an arrow to the leg and fell from his horse when the creature spooked."

Albrecht whipped his head to his younger brother, his eyes questioning and angry, but Daemyn didn't meet him. The younger boy's gaze was elsewhere, and he shrank into his seat.

"After he fell to the black sands, your mother hopped off her horse and shielded him from the bandits with her body. Luckily, no more harm came to them. Tamanna happened to be nearby and appeared wielding magic, and scared the brigands off. He even healed Daemyn's leg with the magic of his country." Aegir's lips stretched wide, and the look on his face was genuine appreciation, but while he seemed to believe the story well enough, Alistair couldn't help but think it all sounded . . . rehearsed.

Albrecht's hand clenched tightly around his wrist. His jaw was set. "And yet Tamanna can't heal mother's illness?"

Alistair's heart skipped a beat, shocked at his friend's brashness, but the question, a thinly veiled accusation, seemed not to bother Tamanna. The man didn't so much as bristle. His expression was unreadable.

"I'm afraid I can only heal injuries, not illnesses," Tamanna answered flatly. His lips then stretched into a false smile. "However, as Grœnn specializes in such matters, we're taking steps to consult them for aid in healing the Queen. Don't you worry, your Highness." Tamanna's words seemed to take on a bite, and based on the twitch in Albrecht's brow, he had noticed as well.

"So, you asked Tamanna to be your Steward because he saved Daemyn and Mother?" Albrecht asked, moving the topic away from the sensitive subject of his mother.

"No no, not right away," Aegir chuckled and waved the question away, "after speaking with Tamanna, learning of him and his former homeland, I thought his Stewardship might prove a step toward friendship with Raseela. However," he grasped his bearded chin and lines formed on his brow, "we are yet to receive a response to the letters we've sent. In truth, I'm worried for our carriers. Perhaps they merely got lost along the way, but I fear the worst." Aegir grimaced. "I'm going to reach out to Rjóðr for aid in meeting with Raseela. Through their friendship with Eenheid, the distances shouldn't prove such an issue."

Alistair and Albrecht shared another glance. Leaning back in his chair and dropping his hands below the edge of the table, Alistair traced a circle in the air, signaling his friend to keep the conversation going. He couldn't be sure how much time had passed since parting with Valhalla, but she wasn't back yet.

"Alright then, would you mind telling me about Raseela?" Albrecht asked, a smile returning to his face, and resting his cheek on his fisted hand. "I've heard the name but know next to nothing about the country."

Alistair released a breath he didn't know he was holding. Albrecht tactfully kept the questions coming, each designed to elicit long responses. As the conversation continued, Alistair kept a discreet eye out for Valhalla while trying to appear engaged in the conversation, offering questions of his own here and there.

As Albrecht started another question, Tamanna reached inside his gray coat and pulled out a round and flat item from within. It was bronze with a thin chain attached to one side, and it popped open on one hinge like a compact for powdering one's face.

Alistair raised a curious brow at the item and interrupted Albrecht's question with one of his own. "What's that?"

Tamanna's brow twitched, and his head tilted slightly to one side. "Hm? Oh this, it's a mirror."

"I didn't know mirrors came that small," Alistair answered, but Tamanna said nothing, just staring intently into the object. "Is everything alright, Lord Tamanna?"

"I don't know," Tamanna's voice trailed off as he closed his mirror with a snap and slid it back inside his coat, "you tell me, your Grace." His dark eyes locked on his and sent a terrible chill up Alistair's spine.

With a small swallow, Alistair asked, "What do you mean?"

Tamanna smirked and rested a cheek on a relaxed hand, turning his attention elsewhere. "You've been very quiet, Prince Daemyn." The mention of his name caused the younger prince to squirm, and Tamanna continued, "Are you alright?"

"A-Aye, why do you ask?" Daemyn brought his hand to his chest. He grasped his shirt and attempted to sink deeper in his chair, a nervous scowl on his face.

Was Daemyn alright? Why did he fear Tamanna so?

"My goodness, whatever happened to your hands?" Tamanna feigned worry. Aegir now noticed as well, and his eyes widened.

"By Njörd's patience, what happened?" Aegir abruptly stood and shot a judgmental look at Albrecht. The King looked at his son for a long moment, and his eyes squinted, then shot open as if really seeing the trio for the first time since they took their seats. His gaze drifted between Albrecht and Alistair. "And why are *both* of your faces covered with bruises?"

Alistair and Albrecht looked at one another guiltily. Alistair then saw the black and purple blotch just under his friend's right eye, accompanied by several peppering his jawlines. He winced as he brought his hand to his face, realizing he likely had several of his own. They had been so preoccupied that he had completely forgotten about the fight in Daemyn's chamber. How could he have been so stupid?

Both of them fumbled over their words, trying to come up with a lie, until Albrecht turned to his father and spoke. "We were in Mother's Rose Garden. I was showing them a new defensive style I learned in Zarago." His words came rushed and without pause.

Aegir stared at him, looking his son over critically. "Why would you three go there when it's pouring outside?" As if to punctuate his question, the storm raging outside pelted the windows with rain, and the winds howled.

"I wanted to see how Mother's roses were fairing in the storm," Albrecht answered. "When I saw that they were indeed fine, I went back to telling them about this new style. I asked Alistair to try to hit me, and as I began the demonstration, we slipped. Unfortunately, momentum carried us into Daemyn, who fell into one of the rose bushes, injuring his hands on the thorns. Alistair and I kissed the cobblestone on our landing. It was a lapse of judgment on my part, and they paid the price."

Alistair blinked at his friend. There was no way Aegir would believe that, but at least the explanation was plausible.

Aegir stared at Albrecht, his expression flickering between anger and disappointment. He let out a tired sigh as he rubbed a hand across his face. "Albrecht—"

Daemyn suddenly let out a pained scream. The young man slammed his hands against the side of his head and practically curled in on himself on the chair. Aegir dashed around the table and knelt beside his son, eyes wide with concern. "Daemyn, what's wrong?"

"M-My head, it feels like it's splitting open!" Daemyn screamed and doubled over. Aegir caught him before the young man fell, rubbing his trembling shoulders.

Albrecht stood stunned beside his brother, looking unsure of what to do, how to help. As he raised a hand to his little brother, rushing footsteps rounded the corner. "Prince Daemyn!" A servant maiden closed the distance and slid to a stop. Alistair recognized her immediately. It was Valhalla, a look of shock on her face, and panting out of breath.

Daemyn let out another scream, and Aegir hugged his son close. Looking up to Valhalla, he stood, still holding his son. "Emera, was it? You've spent time with my son. Please tell me you know what's going on with him?"

Out of the corner of Alistair's eye, he noticed Lord Tamanna still sat in his seat, seemingly unconcerned about what was happening. No, not unconcerned. He practically glared at Daemyn, the man's hand buried deep within his coat. His brow twitched as if realizing he was being watched, and he withdrew his hand as he stood.

Just what was he doing?

"I, um," Daemyn spoke, suddenly jerking himself away from his father and interrupting whatever it was Valhalla was saying. He shoved Aegir away as he stood up. "I'm fine! It's passed." He stepped back from his father, but stumbled and fell into Albrecht, who caught him.

"Fine?" Albrecht exclaimed. "Daemyn, you were screaming. That isn't fine!"

Daemyn's breath was ragged, and he didn't say anything in response. Albrecht held his little brother at half an arm's length to look at him, but Daemyn kept his head low, arms dangling at his sides. "Daemyn, tell me what's wrong, please." He said softly.

The younger Prince's face was scrunched, and his lips curled with a tremble. When he opened his eyes, he held his gaze on Albrecht's chest. "It started shortly after Mother . . . went ill. I've seen a healer about it, and he's provided medicine. I take it every morning. With all the excitement of your return, I probably just forgot these past few days, that's all." His voice was quiet. There was more to this, Alistair was certain. Tamanna was behind this, but he had no proof.

Aegir, brow wrinkled, looked at Daemyn with concern for several heartbeats. With a deep breath, the King exhaled loudly and rubbed his forehead just below his crown.

Something about that struck Alistair as odd, but he couldn't place it.

"Alright, if you've already spoken with a healer, I'll let it be, for now," Aegir said as he walked up and placed a hand on Daemyn's shoulder, turning him a little to see his son's face. "However, if this continues to persist, please come tell me about it?"

Daemyn glanced at his father's hand on his shoulder. With a slight twitch of his lips, he silently nodded.

"Your Majesty," Tamanna stood by Aegir's chamber door, "might we speak for a moment? I'm afraid something has come up." A half-hearted smirk creased his face as he gestured toward the doors.

Aegir groaned gruffly. "Ngh, what is it now?" He looked again at Valhalla. "Is there any word on our dinner? Our food has yet to arrive, and I'm developing quite the hunger."

"Oh!" Valhalla quickly curtsied. "Yes, the food is taking longer than expected, and the cooks send their apologies. They're encountering issues with the stone ovens. In the meantime, we've prepared a bath for all of you to share, if you'd like."

"Ah, if that's the case, once done, tell the servants to send my meal to my chamber." He rounded the table and joined Tamanna. "I have a feeling this *won't* be a short conversation. The boys can bathe together if they wish."

"I'll eat with you, your Majesty, and I promise," Tamanna shot an eerie glare at Valhalla as Aegir opened the door and entered his chamber, "it won't be long."

Valhalla's body went taut, tentatively looking back at the man, a bead of sweat sliding down the side of her face.

"That's fine, in the meantime," Aegir spun around and pointed a finger at Albrecht and then at Alistair, "you three better behave yourselves. I'll not hear anymore shenanigans about defensive moves and the like. Do I make myself clear?"

"Aye, Father," Albrecht answered, holding Daemyn close.

"Yes, Sir." Alistair lowered his head in apology.

Aegir nodded in approval and disappeared within his chamber. As Tamanna grabbed the doors, he gave Alistair the same eerie glare he had given Valhalla, causing the breath to hitch in his throat. Did Tamanna know something he didn't? Everything about the man felt wrong. The Steward then closed the doors, his gaze not wavering from Alistair's until gone from view, and as the four of them were left alone in the hall, the air around them turned terribly cold.

53

Valhalla

Everything Answered, Well, Almost

Valhalla nervously tapped a finger against the back of her hand as she escorted the Princes to a bathing chamber on the second floor of castle black. Her mind raced through recent events, Tamanna's chamber, the journal, the eye in the mirror, his knowing glare at her, and . . . Alistair?

No, that had to have been her imagination. Surely Tamanna didn't suspect that the two were working together. How could he?

As they stepped onto the second floor, she glanced back to check on the Princes. Albrecht was doting on Daemyn, helping him down the steps. The younger Prince stared dejectedly at the ground and hadn't made so much as a peep since they parted with the King. Hopefully, he was just reserving his strength and not reverting to the state in which he had been before lashing out at his piano. It seemed odd, though, that his attacks would return all of a sudden. She hadn't heard Daemyn scream like that in quite some time now, not since Logír was murdered by the King and the nightmares which followed.

Her eyes then moved to Alistair, his brows firmly drawn in a look of foreboding over his mostly amber-brown eyes. His hands fidgeted against his thigh, apparently as shaken as she was, no doubt. She was curious to ask if Alistair caught Tamanna's look and what he thought of it, if anything. As if summoned, his eyes slid up to meet hers, and she quickly turned back ahead.

Valhalla too hadn't said a word since parting with the King and Steward, partly worried her fear would seep into her words, but also because the halls were far too open a place to speak about what she found. Rounding a corner, she spotted the violet tassel hanging on the door, marking it for royal use only.

"This is it, your Highnesses and your Grace." She gestured, pointing at the door of the bathing chamber.

"Valhalla, you don't—" Alistair started, but she had already taken the handle and pulled the door open.

"Perhaps it would be wise not to use her real name until we are in the privacy of the bath," Albrecht said, giving Alistair a flat look.

"R-Right," Alistair answered, looking more than a little chagrined.

Hot steam wafted over her face as she stepped inside. The chamber was made of black marble and stone from the ceiling to the floor. Ten hanging lanterns decorated with leviathans burned brightly. The tub was built into the floor and filled with hot water.

Valhalla sighed in exasperation. "Oh, come on, there's nothing in the water." She searched the single wooden shelf, which stretched almost all the way around the bath along the walls, for Daemyn's usual oils and petals, but as she found them, the young Prince walked up beside her and tapped the back of her hand.

"Valhalla, please wait."

"What's wrong?" She asked, relieved to hear Daemyn speaking and hopeful that meant he was going to be alright.

He leaned in close, shielding his mouth from the others. "Albrecht isn't into the flowery stuff like myself and Alistair. Why not let me handle this?" Daemyn smiled sweetly, and in that moment, she was so glad to see him back to his senses that she couldn't possibly say no. Besides, he reminded her of her younger brother, Hermódur, which made him all the more endearing.

She looked to Alistair and then to Albrecht. Alistair smirked knowingly and shrugged. Albrecht, on the other hand, placed a hand on his hip and glanced at each of them with a raised brow.

Valhalla chuckled. "Are you sure?"

"Aye, of course." Daemyn shooed her away and began scouring over the bottles while also gathering those which he favored.

As she walked toward the wide changing rooms, hugging the back of the bathing chamber, she remembered something and turned back. "Before I forget, Your Highness, your hands are still healing. Try not to get them wet, alright?"

"Aye." He sang, which was surprisingly lovely for something so simple. "We'll be in the water shortly, then you can come out."

She rolled her eyes and turned toward the changing area.

"Wait, where is she going?" Albrecht asked, visibly confused.

Daemyn snickered. "She always hides because she's never seen a cock before."

Valhalla's cheeks burst with flame, and she spun back around. "For your information, I absolutely *have* seen a cock and I'm quite certain it was twice as impressive as anything you lot might be packing!" Heartbeats ticked by as she realized what she had just yelled and then mumbled, "I'm just trying to be modest."

Then, while the Princes were still stunned, she grabbed the white cloth curtain of the changing room and threw it closed. She was keenly aware that doing so didn't quite have the same effect as slamming a door closed, but hoped they might not notice.

The Prince's laughter was as swift as it was humiliating. She hid her face in her hands, feeling utterly embarrassed. A flurry of insults and inappropriate names came to mind, but she chose instead to groan in frustration and not make things worse.

"Oh fuck," Albrecht said with a sigh of relief, "I needed that. Come on, let's get this bath over with. Do your thing, Daemyn, and while you're at it, explain to me these head pains and why you chose not to tell us about it."

Daemyn had been looking over the various bottles to use for their baths, the glass clinking as he rummaged about, then suddenly stopped. Silence hung for three long breaths after Albrecht spoke, then Daemyn let out a tired sigh, and when he answered, his voice came softly. "I just . . . there are more important things right now."

Something slammed down with a thump on the wooden surface around the bath, making Valhalla jump in place. She grabbed hold of the white curtain and peeked out to make sure everything was alright. A flicker of relief shot through her when she saw both Albrecht and Alistair still had their trousers on. They stood with their backs to her, and their shirts seemed to be unbuttoned and hanging loose at their sides. Albrecht leaned over a wicker basket, head hanging low and hands balled into fists.

The older Prince was clearly frustrated, and as he turned to Daemyn, his bright blue eyes were glossy with tears. "Dammit, Daemyn, why are you doing this to yourself? You ignore your own pains to focus on others. Do you want to collapse dead on the floor?" He exclaimed, nostrils flaring.

"Albrecht, come on,"

Albrecht pointed a finger and cut Alistair's words short. "You're the same! You both pick up *everyone else's* shit. Just leave it be for once. Let those assholes slip and fall. Focus on yourselves." He leaned over the shelf again, breathing heavily as he slid a hand over his face.

Daemyn stood before the bath, holding a few bottles, he and Alistair both staring at Albrecht. Valhalla understood when they didn't have a response. She had witnessed both burden themselves with the responsibilities of others. For Alistair, it was his sister, and Daemyn, his brother and mother.

"Should we just let you fall, then?" Alistair asked, a gentleness in his words causing Albrecht to chuckle half heartedly.

He stood himself up and let his head fall back before facing Alistair. "I don't see why not. Just be there to help me back up."

A small smile grew on Alistair's face. He was clutching something hanging from his neck, but Valhalla couldn't tell what it was from where she stood. As he turned and slid off his shirt, her eyes shot wide at the state of his back. She trembled with disbelief. The scars crisscrossed, looking more like they were caused by claws than that of a whip. The pigment of the healed flesh was so light against the golden and warm ivory of his unmarked skin. The scars reached from the nape of his neck all the way down to the very tail of his vertebrate and expanded like wings across his body. Her breath hitched, the sight sending a terrible chill down her spine.

"I'm sorry," Albrecht said, sliding off his own shirt. A few scars peppered his tawny skin as well. He dropped the garment in his basket and continued, "I don't know why I'm like this with you two, especially lately, well, make that three, I suppose." He laughed and did a double-take as he too spotted Alistair's back, apparently as nonplussed as Valhalla. While the High Prince was busy removing his boots, Albrecht reached out to his friend's back and caused Alistair to flinch.

"Maybe you just need someone to talk with about what you're going through," Daemyn suggested as he finished pouring the oils into the water and placed the bottles back on the shelf.

Albrecht chortled and squeezed Alistair's shoulder before turning to his brother with half a smile. "So, if I contact my mind healer, would you speak with him too?"

Daemyn returned his brother's gaze, held it for a moment, then looked away. "Maybe."

"I'll reach out to him in Hvítr, AFTER this business with Father is settled." Albrecht then tapped Alistair's arm, brushing his long, dark brown hair back over his shoulder. "Listen, I noticed—" He paused mid-sentence, finally sensing Valhalla's eyes upon them. With a nudge of his chin, Alistair turned in her direction, and she immediately slid the curtain closed.

Valhalla stepped back, her hands over her stunned lips. Alistair's scars had shaken her. She couldn't believe Lorna did that to her own brother. Reading her journal, poring over her malicious words, hadn't prepared her for the sight. She bragged about marking him and truly reveled in the experience, in hurting him so. The madness on those pages gave her nightmares, but Alistair had lived through the experience firsthand. Valhalla couldn't believe it and felt ashamed for staring. Why was she staring? That was so rude.

Her heart raced impossibly fast in her chest. It was pounding so hard it actually hurt. Her eyes stung with the beginning of tears. She startled as she heard the soft footsteps of bare feet drawing closer. Fingers then slipped around the curtain's edge and slid it open.

Alisair stood there and was naked from the waist up. The golden hues of his skin turned to warm ivory just below his pecs. The gold wing shapes on his back poke around his sides, their edges stopping just above his hips. She had no idea just how much of the gudrídr's golden skin enveloped his body. It covered both of his arms and stopped just shy of his knuckles. His palms and fingers were ivory. The gold also stretched up to line his jaw.

Valhalla gasped as she realized she was staring again. He flashed her a warm smile. Why were her cheeks so warm? "I'm sorry, I shouldn't have. I didn't mean to—"

He raised a hand, calming her as he chuckled, the sound as sweet as the golden apples of Asgard to her ears.

What was wrong with her?

"Valhalla, it's alright," he reached out and took her hand in his, rotating it palm up, "that's not why I'm here." He then brought his hand up to his neck and grabbed hold of a thin, silver chain necklace, then slipped it over his head. The item was surprisingly heavy as he laid it on her palm, his hand shielding it from view. "Can you hold this for me, please?"

When Alistair withdrew his hands, Valhalla gazed down and found three items on the chain. The first was an iron ring. The second was a medallion with Ódin's valknut pressed into the metal. The third was another medallion, this one with the Algiz rune of protection pressed into the medal. Valhalla tilted her head at the three items and found her curiosity piqued by what significance the ring might hold. She traced the iron ring with her finger, inspecting the brilliant, yet terrifying, details. Vultures encircled a sharp crown holding a black onyx stone. A soft gasp escaped her lips, and realization set in. "Is this your father's ring?"

Alistair nodded, his smile turning sad. "Yes. I normally leave it with Shu Yen when I'm bathing, but seeing as she isn't here, you're the only person I trust not currently in the bath. I've—" He stared at the ring, and his eyes shook lightly. His hand drifted to rest over his heart, fingers twitching as if missing what was now in her palm. "I've never felt comfortable leaving my father's ring without a caretaker, and there are precious few whom I would entrust it to. So, can you keep him safe for me? Only until I'm done bathing, of course."

Valhalla stood before him, open-mouthed and more than a little shocked. The weight of his request bloomed in her chest, and she was surprised at just how much it meant to her that he would share this with her, to trust something so special to her care. "O-Of course." She slipped it over her head and tucked it beneath her black dress.

Alistair exhaled heavily.

"What's wrong?" She asked.

"I . . ." He started with a shake of his head, his smile turning pleasant again. "Nothing. It's nothing."

She returned the expression. "Alright then, I have to retrieve a new set of clothes for you and the others to wear tonight, unless you prefer your sleepwear?"

"Before you leave," Albrecht interjected, "tell us what you've found in Tamanna's chamber." He was in a similar state of undress as Alistair. His expression turned stern, and he crossed his arms over his muscular chest, making it clear he wouldn't budge until she answered.

"I uh, right. Where to begin?" Valhalla stalled, rubbing the side of her forehead.

There were many things written in the journal, and while Valhalla hadn't been able to read all of it, what she did read painted quite a disturbing picture. It seemed Tamanna was behind every terrible happening going on within these walls. The disappearances, the death of the Queen, all of it. She wasn't sure how they would take it, and what concerned her the most was what she discovered about Aegir. Daemyn was putting on a brave face. Albrecht had already lashed out at her, and while she was working on forgiving him, there was no reason to think he would control himself now. Alistair would likely believe her, but he could be swayed by his friends.

Albrecht tapped a finger against his bicep. He was growing impatient. With a long, troubled sigh, she hugged her sides to hide the slight tremble in her hands. "I'm still processing it. I found the man's journal. It documented many of the atrocities he's committed, but I couldn't read it all before——" She let the words trail off, internally scolding herself for not being careful and missing the enchantment in the chamber.

"What is it, Valhalla? Please, I can't take this anymore, just tell me what you found." Albrecht's expression surprised her. She'd expected anger, but when she gazed at him, all she saw was worry.

Valhalla took a deep breath. She owed him an explanation and wasn't going to let her trepidation deny him that. "In my rush to enter his chamber, I didn't think to watch for wards."

"Meaning?" Alistair asked, his brows curving downward.

"Meaning he knows I was in his room and read his journal," Valhalla answered plainly.

"May Ódin help us," Alistair whispered, his gaze falling to the floor. Daemyn walked up beside him, shirt unbuttoned and boots off. He didn't say anything, but seemed as though he wanted to.

Albrecht grabbed his chin. "That would explain the look he gave you." He glanced at Alistair, concern deepening. "And *you*."

Alistair nodded.

Valhalla startled at the insinuation. "Wait, no! How would Tamanna connect his Grace to me? He was with you when I was caught. We were rarely even alone together. Tamanna shouldn't have linked us together."

"He probably hasn't. It's more likely that because of you, Tamanna might speed up his plans. If he's as obsessed with magic as he seems, he may pin Father against Alistair to make himself an opening for Hilliard."

"Even after everything Aegir has done for me?" Alistair asked, skepticism seeping into his tone.

"Remind me again, Alistair," anger and hurt punctuating Albrecht's words, "whose body did you find?"

Alistair winced at that. "I'm sorry. Say no more. Point taken."

Abrecht took his friend's shoulder, squeezing it and softening his voice. "I'm sorry too. It's a raw wound, but we'll figure something out, I promise. In the meantime," he returned to Valhalla, "tell us what you found in that monster's journal."

With another deep breath, Valhalla acquiesced. "From what I could read before we fled, Tamanna is behind much of what's happening in the city. He hired the bandits who attacked Prince Daemyn and Queen Ayunli. He ordered her death along with many others. I believe he's using them to practice necromancy and likely other dark magics. He even——"

A lump formed in her throat as she looked at Daemyn, then Albrecht. Should she tell them? Would they believe her? Aegir was dead, and yet the three of them just sat across from him at the table. Could they believe Tamanna was controlling their father's corpse like a puppet all this time? Would they understand if she told them of her promise with Queen Hel?

"What? Valhalla, what is it?" Albrecht grabbed her by the arms, his eyes wide with pleading. "What's Tamanna doing to my father? Tell me what you know!"

"Albrecht, calm down!" Alistair quickly grabbed his friend's shoulder and wrist. He was about to pull him away, but glancing at Valhalla, she gently shook her head. She was fine. Albrecht wasn't hurting her, this time. He was just scared. They all were.

"I—The King is . . . being controlled by Tamanna." She finally answered, avoiding saying aloud that Aegir was dead. She just couldn't bring herself to do that to them, not yet. Raising a trembling hand, she tapped the center of her forehead. "He, um, his Majesty has a rune painted here. It's what is allowing Tamanna to control and influence the King."

Albrecht's eyes steadied as he released Valhalla. His hands clenched at his sides once, twice. He then straightened, looking at her with knitted brows. "How do we free him?"

"I—" She paused. "I'm sorry, I don't know, not yet. As I said, I had to flee Tamanna's chamber, and what I gleaned was only through skimming."

"Then," Alistair hugged himself and looked away, "that would explain it. Something about him struck me as odd, but I couldn't place it until now. He *always* wore his crown. Tamanna needed a way to hide the rune and so commanded Aegir to never take it off."

"I've noticed that too." Crossing an arm over his chest and tapping a loose fist against his lips, Albrecht walked several feet away, thinking. He stopped about halfway across the room and pinched the bridge of his nose. "Maybe if I—"

"You will bathe and remain in your bed chamber while *I* figure this out." Valhalla interrupted, surprised by the sternness in her own voice. Albrecht's gaze darkened, but she was unwavering. She felt Daemyn and Alistair watching her, but they weren't the ones she needed to convince.

"And why should we?" He growled.

"Because I won't ask you to raise a sword against your father."

The bathing chamber went quiet, save for the sporadic drip, drip, drip of the faucet. Albrecht, to his credit, loosened his arms and let them fall limply to his sides. His expression softened. "You said raise a sword to my father, not Tamanna."

Valhalla chided herself. Her words betrayed her, and she wasn't ready to break their hearts, not here, not now. But she needed to answer, even if it wasn't the entire truth. "Tamanna will make us go through your father to get to him. A son shouldn't have to face his father like that."

"And you think you can?"

Valhalla's heart clenched in her chest. She'd never raised a sword to end someone's life before, and there was no outcome where Aegir could be left in undeath. Even if freed of Tamanna's influence, he was no longer the man he was in life. The dead can only spread more death. Left unchecked, he would be a blight to the realm. How could she tell Albrecht and Daemyn that their father was already gone and that there was no hope at the end of this path, only tragedy?

"Valhalla," Albrecht called, "I understand what you're trying to do, I do, but your eyes are no different from my brother's. You've never killed before, and if what you say is true, Tamanna will order him to kill you."

She couldn't hold his gaze. Albrecht thought he understood, and while he was correct on this, he didn't know the whole of it.

"It's not a bad thing if she hasn't," Alistair answered for her.

"I never said it was."

Valhalla couldn't take it anymore and walked straight to the door, intent on leaving. As her hand wrapped around the handle, she stopped. She tried to force herself to leave, terrified to say anything more, but she couldn't.

"Valhalla." Albrecht called with a tightness in his throat, "You know more than you're telling us."

Her hand trembled. She wished she were strong enough to tell them about their father, but the words just wouldn't come. "I left Tamanna's journal with my friend. He's instructed to give it to you if anything were to happen to me. One way or another, the truth of it will find you." With that, Valhalla swung the door open and left, closing it swiftly behind her.

She fell back against its surface, lips curling and holding back tears. Valhalla felt terrible for keeping Aegir's death from them, but they were still reeling from the loss of Queen Ayunli. Telling them might break them. That was the lie she told herself. Daemyn surely would crack at the strain, but Albrecht and Alistair, she thought they might be capable of seeing things through, but she didn't wish that for them. They already had enough burdens to bear. They didn't need to kill a father.

The sound of sobbing reached her, and for a moment, she thought it was herself. It came from within the bath chamber. She pressed an ear against the surface, and when she heard Daemyn, she too let her tears fall.

"I'm sorry, Albrecht." Daemyn's voice cracked. "I'm so sorry, I failed you. I failed to keep them safe!"

Valhalla scurried away, unable to endure any more. Her heart twisted, and a deep ache set in. She didn't want to leave them like that. They deserved to know everything, but not now, not yet. Valhalla hadn't killed before, but Aegir was already dead. Could it even be considered killing? He would go on to do terrible things, but despite that, he had still shown love and care for his sons. Something of the man was still in there, so yes, she decided that it was still killing. His sons and Alistair would likely see it that way, too.

Shaking away the thoughts, Valhalla made up her mind. She would spare the Princes the deed. They would hate her for it, and she could live with that. Valhalla would deal with Aegir and Tamanna herself, no matter what.

54

Tamanna

Let's Just . . . Dispose of Them

Tamanna sat on the far side of the long council table, tapping an index finger on the sturdy, mahogany surface. Aegir sat opposite him. A single candle beside him cast its eerie violet light over everything in the room, its magic aiding him in controlling any caught in its light. The doors of the King's chamber were closed and fastened. A thick layer of dust covered much of the furniture, and grew all the worse further inside the long-unused bedchamber.

It had been some time now since he had poisoned the King. Concealing the runemark beneath the man's crown proved quite rewarding. It left a direct path to Aegir's mind, making controlling him more manageable, and as far as hiding places go, none would dare ask a King to remove his crown. To do so was to insult the King, which was a swift way to find oneself without a head. Aegir had been kept isolated and dressed himself each morning. Things had been exciting at first, but now, he was feeling bored with this place. Bored of Aegir's regrets and guilt for killing his wife. The King fought his control at first, but his fight seemed to die with his Queen.

He had thought long and hard about why Kiara sent him to Svartr; however, he made little progress in discerning her motives. The books on the histories of the massive, mythical sea serpent who aided the Oceanans in discovering and relocating to these lands were fascinating, but he had read them twice over. There was nothing else of note in this place. There was very little on draugrs or other undead creatures, which could strengthen his power in this region. It was infuriating. So much time wasted. The only promising thing to come of the venture was the practice he'd gained with the dark seidr sphere Kiara had provided him. The dead were easy enough to procure through his control of the King.

"What . . . What reason would Alistair have to betray me . . . like this?" Aegir said, his words coming with clear struggle. The King glared his disbelief at Tamanna.

That's right, he snapped out of his thoughts. He had been trying to convince Aegir that Emera, Valhalla apparently, was a spy working for the High Prince, plotting to dethrone him. Aegir had some history with Alistair, which complicated the process, but this was the fastest way for Tamanna to be rid of this place. The High Prince was a necessary stepping stone.

He reached inside his coat, sliding his fingers into the pocket that held the dark seidr sphere, and took it in hand. He was tired of the conversation and wanted nothing more than to expedite things. "So he can install a puppet on the throne." He replied, trying not to sound bored. "Someone he can control. He wants Svartr's resources for himself. I wouldn't be surprised if the High Prince has already convinced your sons to move against you. Your wife already planted the seeds of rebellion in Daemyn, after all. With the two of them united, Albrecht would be easy to sway."

Aegir's lips pulled back into a snarl. He balled a hand into a fist and slammed it down against the table. Finally, Tamanna thought, feeling the King succumbing to his influence.

"I will not stand for such treachery, not again!" The King barked with wide, wild eyes.

Tamanna's lips tugged into a smirk. There it was. Success was moments away. "Your Majesty, why not dispose of Hilliard's High Prince and that whore of his?"

Aegir rolled his eyes, sending a surge of annoyance through the Steward. "If

I openly oppose Alistair, war will break out. Regardless of the reason, *everyone* would side with Castle Gold. The High Prince is loved by the people." He then grumbled. "It would be easier were we talking about his sister, but someone already took care of her. Anyway, we simply don't have the army, nor the means, to face the might of Hilliard."

"Huh." Was Tamanna's only response. He hadn't considered that when coming up with this plan. Truth be told, he hadn't really put much thought into the plan, but how the High Prince dies was less important than the outcome. Tapping his finger on the table again, he rolled the dark sphere about his palm, making sure Aegir remained submissive.

After some time, a thought popped into his head. What if his death was an accident? Yes, that could work. "Your Majesty. What if, *instead*, we told the High Queen an accident befell her precious son? The young man went swimming and then a current just . . . swept him out to sea, or perhaps an accident while sparring." He sat back in his seat. "We put on a display of our sincere remorse, and you console the High Queen as she grieves. You recently suffered a loss as well, after all. Why shouldn't you two help each other through this tragedy? Then, when the time is right, make an offer of marriage. She will accept, and we place your oldest son, Albrecht, on Hilliard's throne. Daemyn then would become your heir to Svartr." Smirking now, he squeezed the sphere and imposed his will on the man. "But we must act quickly, before he turns your sons against you. The *whole* Queendom, or should I say *Kingdom*, will be yours, your Grace."

Aegir's expression flattened, giving Tamanna a moment of pause, his brow twitching. The King then stood and nodded like a good, soulless puppet should. His heart fluttered in triumph. He was going to finally be free of this place, and joy bloomed in the pit of his chest.

"Then by all means," the King answered, "let us be rid of these traitors."

55

Valhalla

A False Illusion

Valhalla stood before a pot in the castle's kitchen and conjured a fire beneath it. She stirred the stew of broth, vegetables, spices, beef, and chopped potatoes to loosen its thickening contents. It seemed the meal was nearly fully cooked, and yet someone had let the fire burn out; the stew growing cold. How odd, she thought.

She wasn't a great cook, not even a decent one, but as most of the work had already been completed, she thought it would be suitable enough for the Princes once it came to a boil. Now she just needed to find some bowls.

Scouring the cabinets along the right wall, a strange chill crept through the air. A shiver ran up her spine. Why was there no one else in the castle's kitchen? She was completely alone. Rubbing her hands together, she blew into her palms and summoned the fire within to raise her body temperature. The absence of any sound, save for her own, prickled the hairs on the back of her neck.

"Where is everyone?" She mumbled to herself, and she opened the last cabinet on this side of the kitchen. Still no bowls. "Maybe the other side?" Making her way around one of the islands, she tripped over something but just managed to catch herself.

"What did I—" Her breath caught in her throat. She had tripped over a woman's ankle. It belonged to one of the servant maidens, Amelia, if her memory was true.

Valhalla rushed to her side and shook her by the shoulders. Fortunately, the woman appeared to be breathing but wouldn't stir. "Amelia? Please, wake up!" She pleaded, but no luck.

Turning Amelia onto her back, her eyes were gently closed, and her breath came softly. It was as if she had simply grown tired and decided the floor was a perfectly suitable place for a nap.

Valhalla's heart began to race. "What's going on?" Glancing passed Amelia, she found the body of one of the cooks, and he too was asleep.

Something wasn't right here, and either these people had been poisoned or seidr magic was at play.

A scream pierced the silence, making her jolt. It came from somewhere in the halls just past the kitchen doors. She stood erect. Looking from Amelia, to the cook, and then the entryway she thought the scream had come from, she knew she had to make a choice. "Tsk! I'll have to come back to them; at least they're safe."

Running into the hall, Valhalla looked about for any sign of disturbance, but in the lights of the hanging lanterns, she saw no one. Before her, she spotted an open doorway which led into the throne room. It was as good a place to start as any, so she ran inside, expecting to find someone under attack.

There was no one. The great hall was well lit and completely empty. So, where did the scream come from?

"Hello?" Valhalla called out, her voice echoing off the walls. "Is anyone there?"

No reply. Someone was definitely in danger, and she began to get the feeling that it might be her.

Valhalla began making her way through the throne room, walking backwards and scanning the room for hidden dangers. She made her way to the large, closed gates that led out to the courtyard. That piercing scream had to have come from somewhere. The few staff she spotted since leaving the kitchen had been in the same state as the maid and cook. To say she was unsettled would've been an understatement. Her stomach churned. Whatever was going on, Valhalla sensed it was going to end badly.

Her heel bumped into the steps of the dais. She turned, but all there was at the top of the stairs was a black throne, leviathan ornamentation shining in the firelight. Valhalla's pulse raced, and another scream echoed through the great hall. It sounded as though it was coming from right behind her.

She spun around, but again, no one. Then, the flames of the candles began to snuff out. Chandelier by chandelier, darkness engulfed the throne room, spreading like untimely death. Her mind suddenly thrust her back into the storage space all those years ago.

"NO!" She roared and, with a twirl, summoned a ring of fire to hold the darkness at bay. Her arms extended outward to spread the light as far as she could, but whatever was powering the malicious seidr was too powerful. Everything beyond the border of her flames was consumed.

Valhalla scanned the void for any sign of the throne or a glimmer of reflected light on one of the handles of the doors. Whatever was going on, if she could only spot the way out, maybe she could warn the Princes, but there was nothing to guide her way.

Her heart pounded, and she fought to control her panicked breathing. Chancing a few cautious steps forward in an attempt to find her bearings, she froze, hearing something shuffle behind her. She spun around, ready for whatever she might find there, and whatever it was, kept to the darkness.

"Seriously, what the fuck?"

A sudden gust of wind crashed into her from behind. She nearly fell to the ground, but as she caught and righted herself, her heart sank. Her momentary loss of concentration had cost her the protective ring of fire. She watched helplessly as the last remnants of the flames extinguished. It was everything she could do to simply stay on her feet against the gale. The winds grew in strength and she shut her eyes. Her blood ran cold. She despised the darkness, and nothing good ever came out of it.

She wrapped her arms around her torso and hugged her sides, calling to the well of fire within her being. Valhalla would let it run dry if only to chase back the dark once more. All of a sudden, the wind ceased. Her eyes shot wide, expecting to see her assailant and readied to unleash her fire, only for a bright white light to shine behind her.

Turning her head to glance back, assuming the source to be the High Prince using his light seidr to brighten her way, but she was wrong. Who she actually saw standing there . . . someone that shouldn't have been. Couldn't have been.

"M-Mother?"

The woman was exactly as Valhalla remembered. Ebony hair tied back in a half ponytail, Aruvian pink eyes vibrant and beautiful, hangerok billowing lightly in the white light. Her smile was serene, and Valhalla stared at her, breathless and dumbfounded. Her mother, Saya Önníka, was supposed to be dead. Wasn't she?

"How . . . are you here?" Valhalla asked, afraid that her eyes were lying.

The woman, her mother, stretched out a hand, not saying a word.

Valhalla stood completely still, at first, but soon found she was raising a trembling hand in response. A thought gnawed at the back of her mind. There was something Hel told her, a warning, something to watch out for while in Svartr. What was it?

As their hands were about to touch, her mother's face suddenly turned from warmth to pure terror. Her eyes opened impossibly wide, and her lips parted as if she might speak. The moment only lasted a heartbeat, and then, she was gone. She was pulled violently back into the darkness, her light fading with her.

Valhalla felt herself being pulled with her mother, though she had not moved from where she stood. She jolted as the darkness engulfed her and yelled out, "Mother!" Valhalla ran after her mother, pushing her muscles to carry her swiftly forward. She hadn't gone more than twenty or so paces and slammed hard into something firm and wooden. The castle gates, her mind said.

Sliding her hands across the surface, she frantically searched for the crease to pry it open and give her a way out. Finally, she found it and pushed with all her strength. With a loud thunk and gentle creak, the gates started to move.

Leaning forward with all her might, she pushed until the opening was just wide enough for her to slip through, and so she did. Stumbling forward, she exhaled a deep sigh of relief. Her arms trembled from the strain. She glanced up toward the castle courtyard and startled, finding both King Aegir and Tamanna looking back at her. They were surrounded by thirteen bright, violet-glowing orbs that criss-crossed over one another in a constant circular motion.

Valhalla cursed at herself. Of course, the apparition hadn't been her mother. It was a damned illusion. As infuriated as she was by the deception, she was more upset that she fell for it. Her mother had been dead for thirteen years and had long since been taken through the gates of Valhalla. Of course, she wouldn't be here.

A lump formed in her throat as she balled her hands into fists, her nails feeling as though they might puncture her skin. "I suppose you've decided to deal with me sooner rather than later." She said, her expression hardening with anger.

"You and . . . Alistair . . ."

Noticing Aegir's demeanor had changed from when she last saw him, his expression was so flat and blank. He moved like a puppet, kept up right, and was not allowed to govern his own body.

"Will not have the chance to . . . turn my sons against me. I'll keep them safe from all threats . . . even if it means disposing of their childhood friend."

Her brows twitched. Aegir seemed as if he was stripped of every semblance of who he was. What had Tamanna done to him when they disappeared into the King's chamber?

"Turn them against you? Is that what Tamanna told you?" Valhalla questioned, her eyes narrowing at Tamanna. "Did you make false threats against his sons so you could fully take him over? And what of the vision just now, was that just cruelty for the sake of it?"

"A simple illusion to draw you to us," Tamanna answered with a mock smirk. "The spell brings out your deepest-held desire to see someone lost to death." He shrugged, hands deep in his pockets. "Must've been someone important to have you come rushing out like you did."

Ignoring his condescension, Valhalla took a deep breath. She wasn't going to allow herself to give in to his taunts and jibes. She needed to concentrate on how to deal with him, and . . . the King.

Glancing around the darkened courtyard, she hated how quiet it was. Not even the wind was making a sound. Just then, she glimpsed something at the edge of the violet lights. Squinting her eyes, she hoped her vision would adjust to the darkness, but it didn't. One of the violet spheres expanded, sending its light to where she stared at and Valhalla gasped. More bodies littered the courtyard, unmoving and asleep.

"What did you do to the people of the city?" Valhalla exclaimed.

"Not a thing," Aegir responded flatly. "They're . . . asleep. No one will get in our way."

She sighed, feeling a tinge of relief. If the city as a whole was asleep, then perhaps the Princes were safe in their chambers, but then so was Vardan, which meant she was completely alone in this fight. To her surprise, Valhalla was fine with it.

Squaring her shoulders, she walked down the stairs before her to join them standing before a fountain. "Hopefully, this will ease your burden, Your Majesty. His Grace has nothing to do with my being here. The High Prince came to see his two friends, nothing more. You *know* in your heart he would never do anything to bring them harm, nor you."

"Is-Is that . . . so?" Aegir slammed a hand to the side of his head, his face contorting as if fighting an unseen force in his mind.

Tamanna's brow twitched, and for the first time since she spotted them, he turned to the King. A glare came upon his face, and moments later, Aegir straightened, his expression falling flat once more.

"Is that so? We will see after I deal with you . . . and interrogate him," Aegir answered.

Valhalla twitched, the memory of the Queen's corpse and others still fresh in her mind. "You mean like your wife?"

Aegir's face twisted for a moment, then he lowered his head, casting his face in shadow. With hands trembling at his sides, Valhalla thought that perhaps she had found a way to get through to him after all, but as she stepped into the courtyard, all hope of that faded. He raised the back of his hand to her. It glowed a deep violet, and there, on his pale tawny skin, she spotted a faded skull surrounded in chains. At the center of the skull's forehead was a stack of runes, the same she'd seen in Tamanna's journal, which were meant to be under the King's crown.

Decrepit, grayed hands suddenly punched through the cobblestone ground all around her. They lunged at her with the speed of striking snakes. She cursed out a scream as they tore at her ankles and dress, ripping the black fabric and digging into the leather of her boots. She kicked and stomped at the dead hands, but they showed no end in their assault.

Finding an opening, she leaped back onto the steps. When the hands found only air in their path, they stopped waving and instead slammed their bony claws onto the ground, pressing down and pulling their undead masses onto the surface.

Each wore old armor, rusted to the point of indecipherability and dented beyond belief. They were covered in dirt and grime. Torn fabric and chainmail hung limply from their remains. They were haggard, and what was left of their skin was wrinkled, dry, and barely clinging to bone and muscle. Scraggy strands of hair draped down their faces and beneath broken helmets. Where eyes should've been were empty sockets. Valhalla's skin prickled as she remembered the draugr during her visit to Helheim. These may not have been the same creatures she had faced there, but she had never expected to deal with a foe like this, all the same. Aptrgǫngu-madrs, or undead puppets, could be just as deadly.

She sneered, ignoring the queasiness building in her stomach due to the stench of rotting flesh. "Oh please, I've seen and dealt with *much* worse!" Raising her hands before her, Valhalla summoned a whirl of flame which formed a long line and became her longsword.

Taking the hilt, she twirled the fiery blade about, quenching the flames, and took a defensive stance. She readied herself to face the ten aptrgǫngu-madrs and their broken swords. By the look of their gear, these poor souls must've predated the forming of Svartr, before the people turned to burning their dead on pyres.

Just as Valhalla was about to lunge, she heard the rush of footsteps exiting the castle behind her.

"Valhalla?" A familiar voice exclaimed, startling her into looking back, and her eyes widened with disbelief. The three Princes stood at the top of the stairs, to her surprise, awake and understandably shaken by what they were seeing.

"A-Are those draugrs?" Albrecht asked, all bravado gone and a slight tremble in his tone.

"No," Daemyn answered, a sullen look on his face. He held his purple and silver cane tightly in one hand. "These look very different from the ones I faced."

"How are you three—" Valhalla started to ask, but shook the thought away; this wasn't the time for conversation. "Never mind, just stay back!" Then, without waiting for their response, she roared and rushed at the undead, slicing, cutting, ducking, and dodging. She cleaved bone and body with ease, her dragon's blade sword reaping a devastating harvest; however, the dead wouldn't stay down. Many pulled themselves back together and stood again. Those whose bones were shattered beyond repair crawled after her. The dead moaned a constant, sorrowful dirge.

"Tsk! Forgot, I must remove their heads." Swirling her blade about, she slashed at two aptrgǫngu-madrs crawling toward her, and letting the momentum of the swing flow into her next attack, she decapitated the nearest foe as it raised its rusted sword over its head. All three fell limp and faded to dust.

With an exhale of relief, Valhalla renewed her defensive stance at the base of the stairs. She wasn't going to let a single member of the dead past her. They wouldn't be allowed to threaten the Princes. "So, which of you is next?"

"Tamanna," Aegir said, his eyes directed at Alistair and his expression difficult to read, "dispose of . . . Alistair."

"Aegir?" Alistair called to the man, confusion lacing his voice. Valhalla swiftly hurled an aptrgǫngu-madr over her shoulder, her heart twisting at the order as she spun to face where Tamanna stood.

"NO!" She screamed and watched helplessly as Tamanna raised his hand in the air and summoned a volley of black magical spheres around him. Then, with a flick of his wrist, they flew toward Alistair.

Valhalla rushed up the steps, knowing full well she wasn't fast enough to close the distance. She managed to climb one, two, three steps, eyes fixed on Alistair. He was going to die. The thought was like molten iron in her gut. Then, there was a flash of movement. Albrecht kicked Daemyn away from the castle gates, sending him stumbling to the ground, and in the same motion, grabbed hold of Alistair by the arm and back of the neck, pulling him the opposite direction. They all fell behind a half wall stone railing as the dark spheres sailed past where they had just been standing and bombarded the area, sending explosions of violet electricity and black smoke in all directions.

The stone grip around Valhalla's heart relaxed. "Thank the Norns."

"You would do well to not harm my sons!" Aegir growled at Tamanna.

Valhalla whipped her head around to Aegir and Tamanna, the Steward's brow twitching under the King's gaze. "My apologies, Your Majesty."

With jaw clenched, Valhalla readied to make for Tamanna, until the terrible stench hit her. Rotting flesh and dirt invaded her senses as bony hands grabbed her from behind. She lost her balance. Skeletal fingers clamped down on her forearm, trapping her longsword down at her side. A decrepit arm wrapped around her neck and squeezed.

"Shit, get off me!" She demanded as she raised her free arm high and threw her elbow back. Her elbow crashed into something incredibly solid, and a wave of pain spread down her arm. She had expected her assailant to be wearing leather, but it appeared that this thrall was buried in metal armor.

Valhalla's vision was starting to darken at the edges, and her feet lost purchase on the ground. For a moment, she thought it was simply her imagination, her mind slipping as consciousness waned; however, she realized it was the aptrgǫngu-maðr lifting her off the ground. Glancing down to the corpse's leg, she found torn trousers and bone. "Fuck this!" Sliding a foot back, she wrapped her leg around the exposed bone and kicked forward, separating tibia from femur. The aptrgǫngu-maðr toppled to the ground with a gravely moan and its arm around her throat loosened, allowing her a gasp of breath.

Landing on her feet, she glared down at the aptrgǫngu-maðr. Without hesitation, she cut off its head and returned the body to lifelessness. Struggling to catch her breath, Valhalla looked around and found even more of the creatures were coming into the violet light. Her fingers tightened their hold on her sword hilt, a torrent of aggravation and fear building within her. Tamanna was battering the half stone wall where Alistair and Albrecht hid with endless dark seidr spheres, and the undead were slowly surrounding her. Should things continue as they were, everything would be lost. If only she could reach Tamanna—

An aptrgǫngu-maðr rushed wildly toward her, its limbs flailing like a ragdoll. It swung its crooked sword at Valhalla, and she met the blow with her dragon's blade, cutting it in half and continuing her arc through the bone just beneath the base of its skull. As the corpse fell, she ran at the undead horde behind it, swinging away in a violent, tiring flurry. When she came to a stop, the brief gap in the enemy numbers allowed her to find Tamanna. He was now only several feet away. She was so close, but the undead suddenly surged to close the gap. Twirling, cutting down an aptrgongu-madr, Valhalla was caught off guard as another rushed out of the darkness. There was too little time to block its swing, so instead, she leaped away and bumped into someone far too solid to be a member of the undead.

Valhalla glanced back, raising her longsword defensively, and was taken aback by the flaxen-haired and vibrant sky-blue-eyed face she found there. They strained under the weight of an aptrgongu-madr's rusted sword, and she blinked at him in disbelief. "Your Highness?"

"I know, right!" Daemyn yelled through gritted teeth and pushed forward, unbalancing the corpse. With a swift, decisive stab of his silver rapier, the thin point of his blade pierced exposed vertebrae, and with a quick slash, his opponent's head fell free. "Here I am, shit filled pants, and I'm fighting against the fallen warriors of the past. What's the realm coming to?" He laughed with horror-struck delirium.

She quickly inspected him from head to toe, his stance defensive though distinct from her own, and saw through the shield of humor to his body quaking. Her heart pounded hard against her chest, and she understood all too well the fear he was holding back. They were fighting the dead, the actual dead of story and myth. Valhalla had at least already experienced those of Helheim, but even then, was terrified all the same. How much worse must this have been for Daemyn, or Alistair, or Albrecht?

Twirling her sword and bending her knees, she stood at the ready as more of the aptrgongu-madrs approached. "I don't know, but let's figure this out together."

Chuckling nervously, she heard a hint of confidence enter his voice as he answered, "Alright, I'll do my best."

The two met their attackers, slashing and striking as the aptrgongu-madrs came. As they fought, it became apparent that the aptrgongu-madrs were singularly focused. They were completely ignoring Daemyn, as if he were simply an obstacle to flow around. The young Prince did his best to cut them down as they passed him by, but their numbers were too great. Even through their combined effort, Valhalla was going to be overwhelmed. Her arms ached, and her lungs burned. Ebony strands of hair stuck to her neck and forehead, which were covered in sweat.

She caught sight of Alistair and Albrecht, still taking cover from Tamanna's volley. The stone protecting them was crumbling away, and every blast sent debris and dust down upon them. They, too, were running out of time.

She growled with annoyance as another aptrgongu-madr attacked. Tamanna was right there, a stone's throw away, and yet for all her fighting, might as well have been leagues from where she stood. "Dammit," her breath came heavy, "they just keep coming!"

"What about your fi—AGH!" Daemyn screamed out.

Spinning around, Valhalla found him on the ground, his rapier pointing at a aptrgǫngu-madr which was very, very different from any other among the horde. The figure was draped in a lavender, blood-stained nightgown.

Valhalla's eyes widened with recollection at the tall, frail body whose once pale blue skin was now haggard and as gray as stone. Her flaxen hair was chopped so short, the strands just barely brushed the bottom of her ears. Those milky white eyes no longer held the vibrancy with which Ayunli Nealfire Svartr, the Queen of Svartr and mother to Daemyn and Albrecht, had been known for. Her head had been sewn back onto the neck with black thread.

"Mo-Mother?" Daemyn choked.

56

Valhalla

To Kill, Or Not

Ayunli's fingers twitched and popped. She loomed before Daemyn for three long heartbeats, then lunged at him. Her bony hands clamped around her son's neck. He fell back, landing hard on the ground, eyes so wide they could've popped out of his head. His rapier clattered limply to the floor. He scratched frantically at her arms, trying to free himself to no avail.

"Dae—" Valhalla started, but her voice was cut short. Many aptrgongu-madrs slammed into her from behind, forcing her to her knees and bending her forward, her hair brushing the stones beneath her. A grunt escaped her lips as she turned her head to count her attackers. There were five aptrgongu-madrs in all. Movement in the corner of her eye caught her attention. Another of the creatures was fast approaching, a rusted sword dragging and scraping against the floor, no doubt intent on separating her head from her body.

Heart racing, she glanced to check on Daemyn, hoping he had managed to free himself, but no such luck. His eyes slowly rolled to the back of his head. He couldn't breathe. Valhalla knew she had to do something, but what? There were too many of the skeletal monstrosities to free herself through strength alone, and at this rate, Daemyn was going to die. She turned her attention to Aegir, wondering why it was that he was allowing this to happen. He stood as still as stone, staring ahead and seemingly not at all bothered about what was unfolding before him.

"King Aegir, you must stop! You're killing your own son!" She exclaimed, pleadingly and hoping that somewhere deep within the King was fighting for control. But he didn't answer. A cold, dismissive chuckle sounded from far behind her. The seidr bombardment suddenly stopped.

"Oh, don't you worry, girl, I'm not going to kill the young Prince, not yet, anyway," Tamanna answered instead of Aegir. "He still has his uses."

The man's words stuck in her mind, and a realization came to her. She thought on what she knew of seidr and what she had managed to glean from Tamanna's book. Turning her eyes back on the King, she then glanced to the aptrgǫngu-madrs all around. "That's how you're doing it. The King, you're using him as a link to the dead of these lands. He's what allows you to control them."

"And I will do the very same to the High Prince," Tamanna answered, confident that he had already won. "The magic, or seidr, whichever you prefer, is complex and beyond intriguing. There's a connection unseen by the naked eye, one I demand to understand. You and Alistair will be my links to the rest of this country. So, while it's true that I need you, you don't have to be alive to serve my purpose."

"VALHALLA!"

Hearing the desperation in the voice as it ripped through the courtyard, Valhalla whipped her gaze back toward the castle, to the origin of the cry. She peered beyond the aptrgǫngu-madrs holding her down, and after several agonizing moments, she found Albrecht's desperate, sky blue eyes on her.

"Tamanna's killing Alistair!"

Alistair was already down, his back flat against the floor at the top of the stairs. The High Prince convulsed and clawed at the strange, violet glowing rope about his neck. Valhalla's heart leapt into her throat, and dread ached in her chest.

A shadow fell over her, startling her, and she remembered the aptrgǫngu-madr who was coming for her. It raised its sword high above its head. She was out of time. Up until now, she had avoided using her fire, afraid that if she let loose, one of her friends might be caught in the chaos. That, or the fire might spread and someone else could get hurt, but now she was all out of options. If she did nothing, she and Alistair were surely dead. Daemyn and Albrecht would likely follow soon after. Tamanna had his sights on the realm and would spread like a disease if not stopped here and now. Closing her eyes, Valhalla looked inward and summoned every bit of fire she could muster, pushing beyond her simple völva powers, past her fjökyngi powers, all the way to the highest heights of her fródleikr powers, the strongest form of seidr known to the nine realms.

Her blood burned, and heat rose all around her. Runes bloomed on her skin, and energy swelled in her eyes, making her vision brighter, crisp, and more in focus. The flames raged through her veins, muscles, bones, and skin. The air about her superheated and churned into a cyclone. With fists clenched, her eyes shot open, and she bellowed, "ÓDR VILLI-ELDR[1]!"

Fire exploded out of Valhalla, pushing the aptrgǫngu-madr with its raised sword back. Those holding her down faltered, flames licking their decrepit hands and causing their hold on her to ease. Spinning on her knees, all the aptrgǫngu-madrs fell. As she twirled, her fingers touched against their bony arms, and her fire spread, burning them to charred ash.

Hopping onto her feet, her body enveloped by flame, she scanned her immediate surroundings and found the aptrgǫngu-madr who had meant to end her life. Its backward, bent body raised off the ground, blade scraping across the cobblestones, and as its torso snapped up, she grabbed the creature by its skeletal face and commanded her fire to rage forward. It fell in a heap of ash.

Hearing a clang behind her, she spun around, remembering Daemyn. His rapier lay beside him, and his body was terribly still beneath his mother. Alistair was still at the top of the stairs, Albrecht not far from him. Grabbing the hilt of her longsword in both hands, her fire engulfed the blade. Valhalla pointed the tip of her blade down and stabbed her sword through the ground, turning stone and soil to lava.

She was aware of her fire draining away inside of her, but it didn't matter; she needed to save her friends. Dragging the blade through the charred earth, Valhalla swung her blade forward in an upward arc, sending a wall of fire and lava erupting in a straight line, heading straight for Tamanna. With a yelp, he fell backwards, just narrowly dodging the attack. Flames lapped at his coat, but he managed to snuff them out before they caused any noticeable harm.

The High Prince let out a gasp and coughed as Albrecht helped him sit, rubbing circles on his back. While Valhalla was relieved Tamanna's concentration

---

1   Ódr Villi-eldr is Celnor(Norse) for Raging Wildfire

had been broken, she couldn't help but feel disappointed not to have taken the man out of the fight. Still, at least Alistair was safe for the moment. Turning her attention back to Daemyn, his eyes fluttering closed, she swung her sword in a horizontal arc, creating an arching blade of fire hurtling toward Ayunli. It crashed into her side, and the fire erupted around her. She released the young Prince and bent her back with a shrieking wail so loud it caused Valhalla to wince in pain.

With a shake of her head, Valhalla ignored the ringing in her ears and rushed the Queen, launching a foot into the corpse's face, kicking her off and away from Daemyn. He rolled onto his side, coughing and holding his neck. Tears streamed down his flushed cheeks. As the Queen screamed her death knell, burning away and succumbing to the flames, the young Prince slid his hands over his ears, likely trying to shield himself from hearing the last sounds his mother would ever make.

Valhalla knelt down beside him, placing a still-flaming hand on his shoulder, careful not to send the fire over him. He wheezed, curling in on himself with a terrible tremble. Her heart swelled for the young man. The terror and shock of it all; his recovery was going to be long and difficult. Valhalla wished she could do more for him. With a deep breath, she sent a bit of warmth into him, hoping it might help ease some of his misery.

Moaning and wails echoed into the courtyard, pulling her attention away from Daemyn. Looking about, she found more aptrgǫngu-madrs emerging from the darkness, dragging their broken blades behind them.

Her brows knit in frustration. "I need to deal with these aptrgǫngu-madrs. Now!" Calling forth more fire, she turned to Aegir. The man still stood before the fountain. His expression was blank as he silently called for more warriors of the past to awaken. She knew she had to deal with him eventually, but he would have to wait.

Closing her eyes, Valhalla took a deep breath. Her next spell was going to exhaust her, she was sure of it, but if it could stop the aptrgǫngu-madrs, then she was happy to pay the price.

Heat swirled around her once more, and she bellowed out, "Thollr ór Eldr[2]!" As her eyes flashed open, a ring of fire formed around her and Daemyn. The flames rose higher and higher, a towering wall of fire between them and what lay beyond. Daemyn startled, but she hadn't the time to explain herself. Concentrating on targeting the aptrgǫngu-madrs, Valhalla raised her free arm up before her, and with the flick of her wrist, unleashed the inferno. The wall of fire obeyed, instantly expanding outward and engulfing the undead. Aegir toppled

2   Thollr ór Eldr is Celnor(Norse) for Pillar of Fire.

back against the fountain's wall.

The fire ravaged the skeletal warriors throughout the courtyard and didn't dissipate until it covered every inch of the space. Valhalla let out a loud gasp. It felt as if she had been held under water. The air in her head thinned, darkening her vision, and cost her her balance. Body trembling and fatigue setting in, she ground her teeth together, cursing. She knew the spell would exhaust her, but hadn't realized to what degree. It was as though she would slip into unconsciousness and not wake for days.

"Shit," she huffed, "too much—I've used too much!"

Glancing up at the King, he was already starting to recover from her fiery push, his face contorted with aggravation. This was her chance. Valhalla needed to stop Aegir before he summoned more of the creatures; however, when she attempted to stand, the world began to tilt.

Muffled voices called to her, but Valhalla couldn't discern who they were or what they were saying. She shook her head to try to clear away the dizziness, and as she opened her tired eyes, they stung and filled with tears. Her heartbeat thundered in her ears. "I have to . . . I have to bury my sword into him. He's . . . The King is—"

Memories of the man flooded her mind. He was stern, but in his own way, he cared for his sons. His stoicism often masked his feelings; however, his true emotions could be gleaned in his actions. King Aegir got Daemyn a whole new piano when the young prince cut a finger changing out the wires in the old one. Aegir had often carried him to bed on the occasions he found him asleep at his desk. When he discovered Daemyn was running himself ragged, taking on a multitude of duties, he relieved him of that pressure. However, there was what she and the others discovered under the castle, what she read in Tamanna's journal.

Queen Hel's words returned to her as if reminding her of what needed to be done. *Any living being struck down by the sword of a Valkyrie, whether in defense or in bringing the swift mercy of death, will be transported directly to me, or Valhalla, should their soul be worthy.*

Valhalla's grip tightened about the hilt of her longsword. She had to do this. She had to see past the man he had been in life, past the genuine love that still shone through what he had become.

"Va-Valhalla," Daemyn coughed violently, his throat no doubt reeling from being strangled, "don't. Please!"

Forcing the young Prince's pleas into the back of her mind, Valhalla took a deep breath and steeled her conviction. Her eyes slid up to Aegir's crown. His eyes were closed, and he looked to be concentrating or listening to something.

She envisioned the mark on his skin and reminded herself that he was no longer among the living.

Gripping her longsword with both hands, she lunged at Aegir, who now stood as still as a statue. The Prince's pleas were nothing but muffled noises behind her. Valhalla readied to strike at the King with what strength she still had. As she hefted her blade high, she wasn't sure if it was the fatigue and adrenaline taking their toll or perhaps the sudden wind swirling through the courtyard, but her vision went blurry.

Her thoughts and body went heavy. Arms threatened to drop her sword, and legs felt as though she were wading through water. She could no longer tell how close she was to Aegir, but she wasn't going to get another shot at this and so she swung all the same, then tripped over her own feet. Valhalla hit the ground hard and was out of breath. Her sword clanged down at her side, and then there was another sound, more metal clinking to a stop against stone.

Opening her eyes, Valhalla found the man's crown had fallen only a few feet away. Had she hit him?

A few dark spots appeared on the ground before her, startling her. As she turned her eyes up, she found Aegir bent over and holding his face. Unmoving.

After a few breaths, he slowly stood again and removed a blood-filled palm from his face. A dark line now ran diagonally across the bridge of his nose, traveling up from the right of his cheek to his left brow. He towered over Valhalla, face still so uncomfortably unreadable, until his eyes opened. Inside of his sockets was blackness. Not empty sockets, but eyes so fully and completely devoid of anything that might be considered alive, swallowed in what couldn't even be called darkness, so much as an overwhelming absence of light.

The sight sent a shiver down her spine. She couldn't help crawling away from the King. Valhalla briefly glanced to her right, expecting to see Tamanna there, but to her surprise, the Steward was gone.

"Wait, where's—"

A deafening roar interrupted her, and a hand gripped her throat, lifting her high in the air. Valhalla let out a startled cry and followed the arm down to the man, trapping her in his vice grip, the face of King Aegir snarling up at her. Dark roots spread from his eyes and wound. In the center of his forehead was the stack of runes Valhalla had seen in Tamanna's journal.

She gasped for breath as he squeezed. Spots danced in her vision. Valhalla clawed at his wrist and kicked at his legs, but was struggling to reach him. Her eyes fluttered, and her arms weakened. The King suddenly grabbed her stomach, causing a shriek to escape her collapsing throat, and then she was soaring away from him. Just as she realized he had thrown her, she crashed into something with a loud crack, and everything went dark.

57

Daemyn

This is Goodbye

Daemyn let out a trembling breath. His eyes were fixed on Valhalla's motionless body lying at the edge of the circling violet lights about the courtyard. Something dark was pooling at the side of her head.

Although his body was racked with fear, he attempted to reach out and said, "Va-Valhalla?"

His father's imposing figure stood, and those blackened eyes glared down at her. Daemyn wanted to call to him, to ask him to stop all of this, but the words refused to come.

"We-We have to do something!" Alistair yelled as he struggled to hold his footing, then fell back to his knees. He rubbed his pained neck with a flurry of coughs.

"What?" Albrecht demanded through gritted teeth. "What the fuck do you expect us to do against my father? Against all of this?"

"I don't know," Alistair growled in reply, "but we have to do something!"

As the two argued, Daemyn returned his attention to his father. Aegir glared at Valhalla and raised a hand, palm facing down and fingers outstretched. The strange skull rune reappeared on the back of his father's hand, glowing a deep violet.

Something punched out of the ground around Valhalla, making Daemyn startle. It, or they, seemed to be more decrepit dead hands, each raising a fist toward the darkened sky. Their fingers uncurled and slammed down on Valhalla, grabbing hold of limbs, shoulders, her sides, and her head. The ground then started to shift. For several long heartbeats, a rumbling sounded from underfoot and then the ground began to churn, dragging her down.

"NO!" Alistair screamed out, almost launching himself down the steps, but Albrecht grabbed him and held him in place.

"Wait!" Albrecht said. "I-I just need a moment to think."

"She doesn't have a moment. Albrecht, let go!" Alistair attempted to push Daemyn's brother off him, but Albrecht wouldn't budge, squeezing him tighter.

Stunned, Daemyn looked down at his bandaged hands. He was scared, no doubt about that, but this . . . this was all wrong. The things he thought were long past, or pure fantasy, were real. The living undead, magic, whatever his mother had become. Yes, Alistair and Valhalla knew magic, but until now, he had rarely ever seen Alistair use it. As for Valhalla, he wasn't sure he believed his own eyes.

Daemyn flattened his hands against the ashy ground and attempted to stand. He wasn't going to just sit there and watch Valhalla die, especially not after everything she had done for him. She had been there to support him as everything else in his life was falling apart.

"I . . . I can't let this happen." Daemyn whispered as he grabbed his silver rapier, Silversnow, from the cobblestones. "I can't lose her, too!"

He recalled how gently she had tended to his hands, how she'd reprimanded him for falling asleep at his desk on more than one occasion, and how she posed as his model when he still thought his mother was ill. He'd come to think of her as an older sister.

"I was supposed to look after Mother and Father, but I couldn't. Didn't!" His eyes stung, tears filling his vision and falling to the ground. "So this will be my responsibility. My weight to bear!" He cried out as he turned to Silversnow, blade trembling in his grip. It was the last thing his mother would ever give him.

Turning to Albrecht and Alistair, he found them staring at him in stunned silence. He forced an apologetic smile. "Albrecht," he started as he took a few steps back toward their father, "I'm so very sorry." Daemyn then spun and ran as fast as his feet could carry him, the distance between them impossibly far and terribly close. He raised his blade and aimed to plunge it into his father's back.

His older brother's pleas were strangely muffled behind him. The wild winds dried the tears from his eyes. This was his fault, all of this. He promised Albrecht that he would watch over things, keep the peace, help their parents and their people, make sure nothing ill would befall their beloved Svartr. Yet despite his best efforts, he had failed. His mother was murdered, his father made into a puppet, and his friends and the people were all terrified. The signs were there, weren't they? How could he have missed them?

Closer and closer they came, his father mere feet away. Daemyn pulled his rapier back, roaring out in a surge of pure grief, and lunged Silversnow forward, striking only air. He was beyond stunned, and for a heartbeat stood there, dumbfounded. The blade of Silversnow then jostled, held at its very center by his father.

Was he always this fast?

Body shivering, he glanced up at his father, who snarled down at him with disappointment in those inky black eyes. Daemyn let out a shaky breath. "Fa-Father?"

He stared in horror as a black tear flowed from his father's eyes. The much taller man immediately grabbed Daemyn's vest collar. Aegir released the blade and struck his son straight in Daemyn's gut. He grabbed a handful of fabric and lifted the young man high in the air, making him yelp with surprise. One moment, Daemyn felt his feet leave the ground, and then the next, he was arcing over his father. Pain bloomed in his back. He lay against the ground, the wind knocked out of him, and his entire body aching.

Daemyn couldn't breathe. He was about to slide his arms back to lift himself when a foot slammed down on his shoulder. A scream echoed the courtyard, and it was several moments before he realized it was coming from him. Black and white spots danced in his vision.

He grabbed for his father's ankle, trying to push or slide it away, but the man only pressed harder. The young man whimpered and groaned, tears flowing like rivers down his cheeks. His eyes then widened as he realized his father had bent down and watched him retrieve Silversnow from the ground.

Daemyn's heart was racing. His breathing went erratic as panic set in. He kicked and clawed to get away, but he was trapped. "Fa-Father, please," he sobbed, "can't you—see me anymore?"

Aegir's expression was unreadable as he pointed Silversnow's blade at

Daemyn's heart. Daemyn's breath hitched. This couldn't be. This wasn't his father. This man looked like him, but it just couldn't be him. His father was stern, stoic, and outright intimidating at times. Daemyn wholeheartedly admitted that. But his father, Aegir Svartr, loved his family in his own, silent ways. Didn't he?

Daemyn's wide, bright blue eyes remained fixed on his father, who went still save for a slight tremble of his hand. The young Prince waited with bated breath. He feared moving, worried that even flinching might bring the blade down. There was a slight spasm in Aegir's face, only a twitch of the eye, and as the moments ticked by, Daemyn began to wonder if his father was still in there somewhere, fighting whatever hold was over him.

When the answer came, Daemyn felt a hollowness well up in his chest. His father drew his arm up, Silversnow high in the air, and just as he started to thrust the blade downward, his torso arched forward, changing the trajectory of the blow just enough that the blade struck the cobblestone inches from Daemyn's ribs. A black blade protruded from Aegir's chest.

The man gave out a brief groan, staring down with an expression of utter shock. The black in his eyes faded, and shock turned into disbelief as he dropped Daemyn's rapier. "D-Daemyn?"

Aegir's foot slid off his son's shoulder. He shuffled back a step but stopped as something, or someone, held him in place. He turned his head to look behind him, and his features softened into something akin to warmth. "Al-Albrecht?"

Albrecht pulled his hand and a half-longsword, Roaringserpent, from his father's body. Daemyn jolted, ignoring his aching body as he turned over onto all fours. Albrecht's breath was heavy, albeit controlled, tears rolling over his cheeks. Roaringserpent's tip touched the ground, the elder Prince's arm hanging like all the strength in him had been drained.

Their father attempted to turn toward his oldest son, his hand rising as his knees buckled beneath him. Albrecht startled, immediately dropping Roaringserpent and catching their father, carefully lowering him to the ground. The elder Prince's gaze turned frantic.

"A-Albrecht, you're here . . . you're really here." Their father attempted a warm laugh but choked as blood pooled in his mouth. "Albrecht, I-I'm sorry. For . . . everything I've done—I'm s-so sorry—" Another bout of coughs cut him off. Albrecht shook his head, mouth open to speak, but no words formed.

Daemyn's heart twisted, and he struggled to breathe. What had they done?

Their father's breath grew weak. His eyes darted about, searching but never finding purchase. "Daemyn? Where's Daemyn?"

A pang of guilt wormed its way into Daemyn's gut. He crawled to his father, taking the man's hand. Tears flowed as a lump formed in his throat, unable to respond.

A serene smile spread across his father's face as his eyes finally found Daemyn. "Ah, there he is. My . . . headstrong over-achiever of a son." He chuckled with a rasp, the sound somehow bringing the ghost of a smile to both Prince's faces. Sliding his hand out of Daemyn's grasp, he cupped the young man's cheek, and Daemyn pressed into his father's touch. "I was . . . forced to watch you grow up through eyes that were no longer mine . . ."

His expression wilted but didn't completely vanish. There was joy there behind the sorrow. "I-I would say that I don't have much time, but this . . . mark," he removed his hand from Daemyn's face and pointed with his thumb to the rune marker on his forehead, "is keeping me here. Please . . . for all our sake, wipe it away."

Both brothers shook their heads in refusal. Adjusting the man in his arms, Albrecht turned their father's face to look up at him. "Father, please, we can fix this. We just have to find Tamanna and—"

"There's no fixing death, Abrecht." Their father interrupted, sadness filling his words.

"W-What?" Albrecht asked, mouth agape in disbelief.

"I'm . . . no longer of this realm. Haven't been for some time. Please . . . let me leave this realm in peace before I hurt anyone else . . . Allow me to return to the sea." Bending one arm back, he cupped Albrecht's neck and did the same for Daemyn, pulling them both close in an embrace. Daemyn sobbed into his father's chest above the wound, Albrecht trembling vigorously beside him.

They didn't want to do it. Neither wanted to lose their father, but he was in pain, and already beyond reach, already dead. Daemyn realized that must've been what Valhalla was withholding from them. A glance at his brother told him he had come to the same realization.

"Just promise me," their father continued with a croak, "you'll take care of each other . . . and this city. Trials will come your way, no doubt . . . I never meant to leave you with so much responsibility so soon . . . nor with everything in such a sorry state, Albrecht, but I'm afraid . . . it can't be helped . . ."

The man suddenly coughed violently again. The brothers startled, but pleaded for him to hold on just a bit longer. More blood flowed from the corners of his mouth. The violet lights about the courtyard began to fade. "Please—It hurts—It hurts so much!"

Daemyn released a trembling breath, the pain and sorrow in his heart insurmountable and yet likely paling to what his father was going through. With a gulp, he turned to face his older brother, Albrecht's bright blue eyes already staring back at him. Both were in tears and stared at one another for a long moment, then Albrecht took a deep breath and raised a hand to his younger brother. He cupped the back of Daemyn's neck and pulled him in, touching foreheads together.

Albrecht was steady, but Daemyn could feel his older brother's heartache was equal to his own. It wasn't in the way he moved, or spoke, or even breathed. It was an ethereal thing, an essence, the bond between them allowing their souls to communicate in a way they would never be able to articulate. Albrecht was scared. His older brother was very good at putting on a brave face, but when it was just the two of them, just family, the walls sometimes came down.

With another deep breath, his words came softly, "He's lived on land long enough . . . Now he readies for his last wave. With the strongest of winds at his sails," Albrecht released a shaky breath and sniffled, "we say farewell as the valkyrs come to guide him to Valhalla."

Withdrawing his hand, Albrecht wiped the tears from Daemyn's cheek and, with a single nod, turned to their father. Daemyn's body couldn't stop trembling. As much as he didn't want to say farewell, deep down, he knew this was how it had to be.

Their father raised a hand to Albrecht, cupping his wet cheek as he brushed his thumb across the flowing tears. "My Albrecht, your strength and courage . . . they are unmatched even by me, and those qualities serve you well. But . . . do not be rash in your judgment. I believe in you."

"And Albrecht—" He wheezed, "a bit of advice about taking care of your brother—he has a—bad habit of taking on too many burdens, and refusing to ask for help."

Albrecht chuckled weakly. "I-I've noticed, Father."

"I know, just—try to be patient with him, please. Daemyn means well. It's the thing I love greatest about him. He has so much heart."

Albrecht quickly nodded. "I will. I promise." He answered as he raised a hand to their father's forehead, thumb resting just beneath the stack of runes.

"One more thing." Their father said, his words going soft between shallow breaths. "Please know—that I love you both so much." Tears flowed from his eyes, the first time he had ever cried in front of his children. "Your mother and I love you . . . what I did to her, it wasn't me. Know that I loved her dearly. Please know that."

"We do, of course, we do," Albrecht replied, bringing a small smile to their father's face. Aegir then slid his hand to the back of Albrecht's neck and pulled him down, pressing his lips to Albrecht's forehead.

"Thank you, Son." Their father released Albrecht and lowered his hand to

Daemyn's, squeezing him for several long heartbeats.

Albrecht's breath hitched, and his hand trembled, but with a gulp, swiped his thumb across the rune mark, smudging it as if it were simply a splotch of paint. A long breath escaped their father's lungs. His body relaxed in Albrecht's arms, yet his grip on Daemyn's hand held, and held, and held, until it didn't. His eyes closed, and then the King of Svartr, beloved father and husband, was gone.

A sudden boom like thunder sounded high overhead. The brothers startled and both looked up into the dark, stormy clouds, which were now dispersing. Rays of sunlight broke through the gloom, revealing the warm hues of daybreak. A light rain pelted the cobblestones. The cold brought gooseflesh to their skin and sent shivers down their spines.

"How long has it been?" Daemyn asked, confused by the sight.

Albrecht shook his head. "I don't know, but that unnatural weather is no more."

They both returned their gaze to their father, his eyes closed as if he were only resting, a glad smile peaceful on his face, and his body motionless.

"Father?" Daemyn called, not wanting to believe he was gone, and touched the man's shoulder.

"He's gone, Daemyn," Albrecht answered, gently placing their father down on the ground, then removing his coat and draping the fabric over their father.

"What are you doing?"

"The people are stirring. They don't need to see Father like this." Pulling the coat over their father's face, he bent down and touched his forehead to his father's one last time, and whispered, "I will always love and honor you, Father."

Daemyn took in a trembling breath. His heart ached. Pain rang through his head, blurring his sight and dizzying his movements. Even exhausted and bereft of strength as he was, he wasn't ready to move from his father's side or that of his mother's.

Groans and whimpers echoed into the courtyard. The people were questioning what had happened. As they rose to their feet and gathered together, trying to make sense of the situation, it was Alistair who approached them. He rested an arm over his stomach and bowed his head in apology.

Daemyn startled as Albrecht touched his shoulder. His older brother's sadness was heavy on his face and building in his eyes. He was trying his best to appear stoic, as their father would've done. "Listen, Daemyn, despite what has happened, and the fact there is much we still don't know, things are going to move quickly. For now, I just want you to stay with Father. Can you do that for me?"

Daemyn was taken aback and still clung to his father's hand. "Of course, b-but what are you going to do?"

"Valhalla," Albrecht answered and stood, rushing away.

"Oh shit!" Alistair exclaimed, running to where she should've been, but there was no sign of her on the surface.

Daemyn's heart raced. Valhalla couldn't be dead. She just couldn't be. Both Albrecht and Alistair slid to their knees, looking over the upturned brick and soil. Alistair shook his head, unsure of what to do.

Albrecht then reached into the mass of stones. "Alistair, dig!" He commanded and began tossing away brick after brick. Alistair did the same, until there were no more bricks, and continued digging into the soft dirt.

Alistair sunk his arm up past his elbow into the soil. "Dammit, I still can't feel her!"

"Then keep digging, come on!"

They dug like dogs trying to find a bone. Mounds of dirt piled up beside them until eventually Alistair's eyes went wide and he lunged down into the hole. "I found her arm!"

"Thank the gods, free her head first," Albrecht yelled.

They both vanished into the hole, and all Daemyn could see was dirt flying up as he held his breath. He whispered a prayer and waited. It was all he could do. Alistair emerged first. He pulled Valhalla free of the hole, but she wasn't moving. Albrecht appeared a moment later.

Holding her gently in his muscular arms, he pressed an ear to her chest and sighed with relief. "She's alright," Alistair proclaimed and hugged her close, "she's going to be alright."

Relief swelled in Daemyn's chest. At least they had managed to save her, he thought. He repositioned himself, sure to keep his grip on his father's calloused hand, brushing his fingers over the man's knuckles. So much had happened, things he had never anticipated, and now that the nightmare was finally over, it culminated in the loss of his mother and father. Feeling his eyes welling again with tears, he leaned down and rested his head on his father's chest, away from the wound. "Father, I promise, I *will* be beside Albrecht through every trial. I'll stand by him no matter what. I'll keep watch." Daemyn sobbed. "I vow to all the gods in Asgard, I won't ever let anything happen to him. That, I promise to you, Father. Mother."

58

Vardan

Bruises and Magic

ARDAN RODE HARD TOWARD the Svartr castle, the sun slowly
rising into the brightening blue sky. His heart thundered to the rhythm
of the hooves of his Clydesdale, Ótta. With jaw clenched and brows
furrowed, his fisted hands tightened on the leather reins of his horse.

The horse's black mane brushed against his face. He cursed for leaving
Valhalla behind. She was his daughter. His responsibility. Vardan would never
forgive himself if anything happened to her, and he felt foolish for not staying.

"Dammit." He growled through gritted teeth. "Dammit! Dammit, what
the FUCK happened last night?" The last thing Vardan remembered, he had
arrived at his abandoned longhouse. The grounds had been well maintained in
his absence thanks to the agreement he'd made with Svartr's royal lineage, and
he was gladdened for it. As he stepped through the threshold of the back door,

a wave of exhaustion hit him like a blow from Thor himself. Tamanna's journal and the lantern in his right hand slipped as his vision went black. He didn't even remember hitting the floor. When he awoke, he thanked his hamingja, a guardian spirit of luck, for smiling on him, for the lantern's flame had gone out, whereas it could've just as easily engulfed him and his home in his sleep. Luck was often a fickle thing.

He had no knowledge of what happened after Valhalla, and he parted the previous night, and could only hope—desperately—that she was alright. She had to be.

A large shadow loomed over Vardan, and as he glanced up, he found he had already made it to the gateway of Leviathan's Cove, the entrance to castle black itself. Centuries had gone by since his exile, and yet it still looked nearly the same. The stained glass windows were more colorful now, and there were more towers than he remembered, adding to the castle's already intimidating form, but the black stones and sea serpent statues were just as they always were. So much of the city had changed, the buildings more compact and alleyways narrowed, but it was comforting to find things that were familiar after all his long years of life in Midgard.

Riding past the long fountain at the center of the courtyard, Vardan pulled Ótta's reins for her to stop, his stomach churning as he caught sight of the castle gates. The left side looked as if it had been blasted open with explosives. Stone workers toiled at clearing away the rubble and taking measurements of the holes and craters that would need to be filled. Charred markings were all over the cobblestones, along with an array of unusual holes that seemed to have been punched through from underground.

An uneasy feeling settled in the pit of his stomach.

"What in Njörd's name happened here?" Vardan asked no one in particular.

In an attempt to not disturb the workers, Vardan guided Ótta toward the Servants Entrance at the right side of the castle, hidden within a simple maze garden. Passing under an archway of hedge, he found more and more workers scurrying about, among them the castle staff, gardeners, smiths, and stone masons. The more he saw, the greater his dread became. He hoped to find Valhalla, Aegir, and his boys alive and well, but sensed a great tragedy had occurred in his absence.

It then occurred to him that it had been nearly three years since he last heard from Aegir, well after Albrecht left for the Gran Mar War. He first grew worried when Ayunli stopped writing to him, and when he learned why, the news Valhalla brought about her death, he was devastated. As great as his own pain was, Vardan couldn't imagine what the young Daemyn must've been going through. After today, whatever had come to pass, he vowed to be more involved with the Svartr family, to make sure the descendants of his late best friend, the first King of Svartr, Velores, were alright.

As he approached the Servants' Entrance, a familiar voice cut through the commotion. Her accent was clear and brisk, with the clipped tones of most Oceanans. With time it had deepened, grown sharper. Rounding a tall, spiraling bush, he found an old woman with dark brown, graying hair and light tawny skin. Wrinkles had started forming on her face, but he knew her all the same. His brow twitched as he spotted the dark circles under her deep brown eyes, her expression weary, but her commanding voice was strong as stone.

Gently, he kicked Ótta's sides, moving close enough that he could be heard while remaining out of the woman's way as she ordered her staff about. "Mistress Lilianna."

Lilianna partly turned and, as she saw him, sighed, the tension in her shoulders loosening. "Oh, Vardan." She said, her tone soft, which chilled his blood even more than the cold that had yet moved on from this realm.

"I saw what happened at the front of the castle," he started, trying to keep his expression stoic to hide his growing concern, "please tell me she's alright."

Lilianna planted her hands on her hips. She rolled her shoulders and stretched. "I was wondering when you would show. The morning has been hectic, to say the least." Rubbing the back of her hand across her forehead, she glanced down at Vardan's horse and then back up to him. "Well, get down and come on. We don't have all day, and there are many things to . . . prepare."

He couldn't help but notice she avoided the question, which sent his heart racing, but he did as she asked and hopped down to the ground. Lilianna was one of the very few who knew the secret of who he was. His identity had been passed down over the ages from ruler to heir, just as it had from Head Servant to their successor, so that he would always be welcome should he visit the castle.

Just as Vardan stopped at Lilianna's side, she turned her gaze on the remaining staff and pointed at one of the young men. "You, take this man's horse to the castle's stable and see that she is tended to, please. As for the rest of you, if I haven't yet assigned you a task, go ahead and grab some breakfast and be ready to work when I return. Gods know this day is going to be a long one."

The gathered staff bowed in thanks, and the young man Lilianna had pointed to approached, a small smile coming over his face as he bowed in greeting. Vardan returned the gesture and handed the young man Ótta's reign, then gave her a quick kiss on her snout and brushed his hand across the solitary white diamond spot on her otherwise black coat. "You behave yourself, alright? I'll be back soon."

As he stroked Ótta's chin, she bobbed her head and nickered. With a light chuckle, he left her in the servant's hands and followed Lilianna inside the castle, patting his satchel to make certain Tamanna's journal was still tucked safely inside.

"Lia, please, I can't stand all this suspense. Is Valla alright?" He asked, his worry getting the better of him.

The two came to a set of stairs by the kitchen and began to climb. "She's fine," Lilianna answered, glancing at him without losing pace. "She's being tended to by the royals. I assume her secret was found out."

It was more a statement than a question, and since there was no use denying it now, Vardan nodded. "It was. The High Prince saw through her disguise and convinced her to reveal herself to the Svartr Princes, so they might help her in discovering what was going on."

"Hmm." Was Lilianna's only response. The rest of their climb was carried out in silence, and they eventually reached the fifth floor, where they stopped.

Wasn't this the floor of the royal chambers? Why had she brought him here? None of this felt right to him.

"Wait. Lilianna, what happened last night?" He touched Lilianna's arm, having her stop and turn to him. "The craters? The overturned cobblestones?"

She touched his hand and gave him a look which stole the words right from his mouth. "Trust me, Vardan, you'll find out, but I think it best that *they* be the ones to tell you. They were there for it, after all."

Vardan sighed defeatedly, and once he gathered himself again, he nodded for her to continue.

"I'll remind you to show your respect. His Grace, High Prince Alistair, and his Highness, Prince Albrecht, are no doubt still with Valhalla. They are NOT like his Majesty." Lilianna glanced back at him with narrowing eyes. "You better behave yourself."

His lips tugged into a challenging smirk. "Oh, come now, when do I not?"

"Most of the time." She rolled her eyes and continued forward. "Your time out at sea has made you crass, my Lord."

He shrugged, seeing no point in arguing with her, and followed after her. As they drew close to one of the doors leading into a chamber, Vardan was taken aback by the number of guards present. Four of the silverguards and an equal number of the blackguards were positioned before it. Just past them, only a few doors down, he spotted another set of blackguards standing watch. Uneasiness returned to his gut.

Lilianna stopped at the door with the eight guards and bowed in greeting. "Please excuse me, are His Highness and His Grace still with the young woman?"

"They haven't left her side since the Castle Healer finished, ma'am." One of the silverguards answered.

"Alright then, may we enter?"

The guards eyed Vardan wearily, each one of them looking as though violence was a breath away. He raised his hands in the air, putting some distance between them and his weapons.

Lilianna winced, realizing the guards' growing agitation. "Oh, right. This is the young woman's uncle. He only wants to see that she's alright. I assure you, he is no threat to anyone in that room."

The guards turned to each other for a long moment as if confirming each other's approval, and after several beats of Varden's heart, one of them nodded, and the group parted. Lilianna grabbed the handles and gently pulled the doors open a crack, peeking inside. From what Varden could see, it was fairly dark inside, and all the curtains were drawn closed. Candles and a fireplace bathed the chamber in orange hues. Lilianna then straightened and waved Vardan in.

Without hesitation, he stepped through the threshold, and as a moth drawn to flame, his eyes found Valhalla in moments. His heart leapt into his throat. She lay still on the canopied bed. The violet curtains were tied back at each of their posts. Bruises were visible on her neck, and dark circles hung under her closed eyes. A white linen bandage was wrapped around her head. He could barely move even as Lilianna closed the doors.

"My goodness, they should've slept in their own beds."

As she walked past him, he startled out of his shock and noticed a man at the lower left corner of the bed. He was sitting on a stool, arms crossed and head tilted in sleep. His dark brown hair was long and braided over his shoulder, his breath sounding a bit hoarse. Lilianna softly walked past toward someone else.

Wedged in the left corner of the chamber was another man seated in an ornate, mahogany chair. He was the spitting image of a much younger King Aegir. His arms were crossed over his chest, and his legs stretched out atop a footstool. Albrecht's head rested against the wall as he slept. His brown hair was brushed back and fell loose, his clothes were unkempt.

Vardan's brow twitched. He didn't like the idea of two men in his daughter's chamber, but they all looked so exhausted. Had they stayed with Valhalla out of concern, perhaps?

While Lilianna approached Aegir's heir, Vardan made his way around to Valhalla's side, opposite the High Prince. His anger with himself only grew as he took in the various bruises about her porcelain white skin, and his eyes drifted to the purple-blue fingermarks spread across her neck, a pang of guilt made his chest ache. Her breathing was almost nonexistent.

He drew closer, cupping her cheek, and as he did, Albrecht startled awake, shooting up from his chair. "Who're—"

"I'm a friend of Valhalla's." Vardan interrupted, gently turning Valhalla's head to the side. "I'm sure she's told you about me, however, likely not by name."

A weak groan escaped her lips. Her skin was too cool to the touch, likely a sign of exhausting her fire seidr, though he couldn't be sure.

"Oh, um, my apologies." Albrecht tapped his knuckles, averting his eyes to where Alistair slept at the corner of Valhalla's bed.

"Would you like me to—"

"No, I got him, um, Lilianna, was it?" Albrecht asked, turning to her for confirmation, and she nodded with a small smile. He sighed, seemingly relieved, and went quietly to Alistair, jostling him awake. "Alistair, wake up."

"Hmm?" The High Prince stirred and rubbed his sleepy eyes. Vardan was taken aback as Alistair lifted his head, just then remembering Valhalla mentioning the second skin tone on the man's body. Large sections of his flesh were, in fact, gold. "Is she awake?" Alistair asked with a yawn.

"Not exactly," Albrecht answered, nodding toward Vardan and Alistair followed his friend's gaze.

The High Prince's eyes widened, and he quickly stood. Alistair flattened his clothes, as if trying to look presentable. "I uh,"

Varden startled lightly as he spotted the strange bruising on Alistair's neck, not too dissimilar from Valhalla's, but managed not to show it. "I know who you are." He interrupted, taking account of the myriad injuries on each of the Princes.

"Vardan!" Lilianna scolded.

"Lilianna." He ignored the old woman's scowling and returned to Valhalla, gently tracing the bandage around her head, her midnight black hair pushed back and to the right. Clearly, she had suffered the worst of the injuries, but how?

First things first, Vardan decided. He needed to check her inner fire reserves. Valhalla's seidr was directly linked to her life, and if the seidr was too weak, it meant she might never wake.

At his right, he found a tall candle holder on the nightstand and grabbed hold of the ringed handle, pulling the candle closer to the edge. Then, he removed his fingerless, leather gloves, placing them by the candle. Hovering a palm over the fire, he held it there, allowing the heat to lightly burn his skin. He lowered his other hand to the edge of her nightgown and pulled it low to reveal the center of her chest.

Alistair and Albrecht shifted by the corner of the bed, and Vardan held back a snort. Clearing his throat, he placed his left hand flat on Valhalla's chest. Just as he started to close his eye, Alistair stepped forward, watching and wringing his hands nervously. "What are you doing?"

"She has a powerful connection to fire," Vardan answered. "I think she's used too much. While I can't conjure seidr myself, Valla here taught me about it. I might be able to see how much she has left in reserve."

"Might?" Albrecht raised a brow at him.

Vardan shrugged. "It only works if the element is nearby. I have to touch it, and fire hurts." He lifted his palm from the fire, revealing the darkening circle on his tawny skin.

The Princes cleared their throats and bowed their heads apologetically, allowing Vardan to continue. With a nod, he returned his hand to the fire and closed his eye. He breathed in deeply, and his world went dark. A flicker of light burned in the distance. Scrunching his face with concentration, he brought himself closer to the light. It was a small flame, dancing in the blackness of space, no larger than his thumb.

Releasing the breath with a sigh, he shook the pain from his hand and then rubbed it over his lap. "She overdid it last night." He said softly.

Turning his head to the right, he remembered the curtains were all drawn closed and stood, making his way to the closest window and letting in the sun's light. "Lilianna, help me with these curtains, please."

"Of course." Lilianna started at the opposite side of the chamber, helping him open the remaining curtains and tying them each with a crimson rope.

"Tell me what happened," Vardan commanded.

"My—" Albrecht paused, squeezing a fisted hand. His Highness sighed. "My father and the former Steward confronted Valhalla last night. By the time we got there, she was already fighting. There were undead soldiers everywhere. Eventually, my brother aided her in fending them off."

Vardan threw open the last of the curtains. He turned to face them, brows knitting in anger. "And what were you two doing?"

Albrecht twitched. "What are you implying?" He asked, his voice meeting the challenge.

Vardan's lip twitched with a smirk. The pup had some shark in him, which was a good quality in a future King, but then Varden remembered what this boy had done to Valhalla the day before, and his anger doubled.

"Albrecht!" Alistair grabbed his friend's arm, pulling him back. "Tamanna, the former Steward, attacked us with black magical spheres. Albrecht shoved Daemyn away from the entrance and dragged me into cover. The two of us were bombarded by volleys of dark magic. Daemyn was free and ran to Valhalla. We were just," He sighed, glancing with sorrow at Valhalla. "Trapped."

Vardan stared at Alistair for a long moment, his expression softening, and he slid his gaze back to Albrecht. "I'm not implying anything. I've only just arrived and learned the woman I've cared for as a daughter was attacked and is lying unconscious. You'll have to excuse me if I'm a bit prickly."

He turned away and opened the balcony doors, the salty sea air cool against his rugged face. The sensation was as comforting as it was nostalgic. This was his home, and being here always brought back a myriad of emotions. With a deep breath, he went back in and took his place at Valhalla's side. He glanced at the two young men, noticing the High Prince shoot a disappointed glare at the Svartr heir, who turned away, a perturbed frown on his face. This Albrecht struck him as rather petulant, though for everything he had been through, Varden supposed it was hard to fault him for that. Time would tell what kind of man he would grow into.

He wondered if perhaps the Svartr heir felt guilty about something and might just be lashing out, but before Vardan could ask, the doors of the chamber swung open. A young man with flaxen, disheveled hair and pale tawny skin rushed inside. He was out of breath and holding a folded letter pressed against a cobalt blue book, which was all too familiar. The young man, whom Vardan realized was likely Prince Daemyn, froze at the sight of Varden. It seemed he had something of importance that needed saying, but was wise enough not to say it in the company of a stranger.

"Daemyn?" Albrecht called to his younger brother, a hand over his heart, and sighed with relief. "Dammit, you fucking startled us."

The younger Prince jolted at his brother's words, and the two shared a look, a question in Daemyn's eyes. "Albrecht, F-Father told me if anything ever happened to him to-to——" His voice cracked, bright blue eyes shining with the faintest suggestion of holding back tears.

Albrecht rushed to join his younger brother and gently placed his hands on Daemyn's shoulders. "Take a breath, it's alright. What did Father want you to find?"

Daemyn stifled a sniffle and rubbed his puffy eyes, then presented the book, which had silver runes about the cover. "He said if anything happened to him, to . . . open this book. A-And when I did, this letter fell out."

Vardan brushed a strand of midnight black hair off Valhalla's round cheeks, then went still. *If anything happened to him.* The words echoed in his mind. Something had happened to Aegir. To the King. To his friend. Ignoring the churning knot in his stomach, he turned to the young prince. "Well, that's a book I haven't seen in a while."

As Albrecht accepted the book and the letter from Daemyn, Alistair stepped over to the head of the bed, wringing his hands and eyes locked on Valhalla. "Will she be alright? She——" He cleared his throat, no doubt trying to dislodge the lump in his throat. "She hasn't so much as shifted a finger since her fight with Aegir."

The High Prince's brows hung heavily over his mixed colored eyes, one amber brown, the other the same save for a splotch of a deep sapphire on the bottom right corner of the iris. Vardan's lips parted, touched by the sincere concern the man held for Valhalla. He hadn't expected that. Vardan focused back to Valhalla, and he decided his worry for Aegir would have to be secondary for the time being.

Vardan took Valhalla's hand in his, brushing his thumb against her knuckles, feeling a glint of warmth returning to her. "Firstly, I need you to relax. Your concern is appreciated, but Valla will be fine, I promise you. She's been through worse and always pulls through. This will be no different. Secondly," he looked up and met Alistair's gaze, "being a seidr user yourself, or magic if you prefer, you should already know how exhausting it can be to use. Based on the state of her reserves, she must've used some powerful spells in that fight." As he turned his eyes back on Valhalla, something beneath the strange bruising on her neck caught his attention.

"Right," Alistair chuckled awkwardly with cheeks reddening. He rubbed the back of his neck, "but I don't understand why you needed to open the curtains and the balcony doors."

Slipping a finger under a chain around Valhalla's neck, he paused, then raised a brow at Alistair. "Are you really asking why?"

The High Prince blinked a few times, clearly confused by the question. "Is it really so strange to ask?"

"Well, yes. You're a magic user like her, light instead of fire, right?"

"Yes, but um, I'm not as well-versed in it as I thought I was. In fact," something in Alistair's face shifted as he stared at Valhalla, soft and serene, "I'm nowhere near as amazing as her."

Vardan couldn't help but be a little stunned at that, and perhaps . . . gladdened. He'd known many in Alistair's position who would've felt threatened by her prowess, yet here was the High Prince of the realm, smitten. He let out a light chuckle. "The Celnor tongue didn't come as easily to me as it did her, but in Enskr, she's called an Eternal Sage. Sorcerers with her ability are able to rejuvenate themselves by bathing, or rather, consuming their elements. In her case, she's a fire sage, or mage, and needs to consume sunlight, the prime source of fire. " Vardan slid a hand over her forearm, her warmth slowly but surely returning. "It would be quicker to just set her bed on fire, though I doubt I would be welcomed back to the castle after that."

They both shared a laugh, and Alistair added. "Hopefully, the sunlight will do well enough, but it's good to have a backup plan."

Vardan nodded in agreement and returned to the thin chain tucked beneath Valhalla's nightgown. With a tug, he felt something weighted snag against the fabric. Sinking a finger into the garment, he fished out two medallions and a thick iron ring at the end of the chain.

"Oh!" Alistair blurted with wide, surprised eyes. "I didn't know she was still wearing that for me."

Vardan nodded again, carefully lifting Valhalla's neck and sliding the necklace free, handing it to Alistair. The High Prince took it with a sigh. It seemed the item gave him a great sense of relief, which only deepened Vardan's curiosity. He watched as Alistair traced a finger around the ring in his palm.

"Alright then, I need answers," Vardan said as he gently laid Valhalla back to rest.

"Of course," Alistair replied, sliding the necklace back on and concealing it under his buttoned shirt. "The ring belonged to my father."

"You entrusted it to her for protection. You must think quite highly of her, then." Vardan stared at him, seeing how he might react.

"I do. I trust her with my life." The answer came swiftly. A look of surprise then came over Alistair's face. It seemed he was coming to that realization right in front of Vardan, and then his expression turned serious. "With my life." Saying more to himself than to Vardan.

"Good," Vardan said, finding himself liking the lad, but didn't want him to know that just yet. He narrowed his one good eye. "Now tell me where these bruises came from? I couldn't help but notice you have one around your neck, too."

"What?" Alistair exclaimed and rushed to inspect himself in the vanity mirror behind him. His eyes went wide with disbelief. Gently running his fingers across the skin of his neck, he carefully traced the dark mark. "I-It actually left a mark?"

"Your bruise doesn't look to have been caused by hands, like Valla's, thanks to what you did to her yesterday, your *Highness*." Vardan chided and glanced at Albrecht, allowing some scorn into his tone and features. The heir of Svartr flinched. He had been reading the letter Daemyn had found and turned away. Clearly, he was ashamed of what he had done. Good, Vardan decided.

Turning his attention back to Alistair, the High Prince met his gaze with his reflection before falling to the vanity surface. His hands trembled over his neck. "Some . . . *Many* things happened last night. All terrible." As he spun back around to face Vardan, Alistair shielded his neck with a hand, his eyes still downcast. "It's just that I was being strangled, but it was through the use of magic. I didn't know—I didn't think—"

"You can do extraordinary things with magic," Vardan interrupted, allowing a gentleness into his words and squeezing Valhalla's hand, "but you can do terrible things as well. You said she faced Aegir last night. Please, tell me what happened."

"I'll tell you."

Both Vardan and Alistair looked at Albrecht, his gaze still on the letter. His words lingered for several heartbeats before he spoke again. The Heir's grip on the letter tightened, crinkling the paper. He then held out the cobalt blue book to Daemyn, who took it, then Albrecht knitted his brow and turned to Vardan.

"But first, I have to know something. Your name, what was it again?"

The corner of Vardan's lips twitched. Albrecht wouldn't be asking, unless . . .

Placing Valhalla's hand back on the bed, he stood and crossed his arms over his chest. Albrecht looked so much like his father had when the King was that age, save for those sky-blue eyes. Those had clearly been Ayunli's. Her gaze had a way of raging like a freezing blizzard when the woman was crossed. Vardan always considered himself lucky to have never been on the receiving end of that stare.

Lilianna then touched his arm and whispered, "Are you sure you should answer that?"

Vardan nodded. "I promised to reveal myself if . . . if anything happened to Aegir, and since his Highness is asking," his throat went dry, "then something must have happened. Am I right?"

Her expression saddened at the question, her stoicism failing. That was it then.

Vardan raised his head to Albrecht. "Vardan. Vardan Loyalen, your Highness." He answered with a bow of respect, hand held over his heart. "I'm Duke of this great city, and an Admiral of your fleets."

Vardan

There from the Beginning

"And," Lilianna added while gesturing at Vardan, "he was there when our ancestors first landed on these shores. In fact, he still owns one of the great ships from that time. What was it called again?" She asked, touching a finger to her chin. "The Anwen, was it?"

Vardan's expression softened. It was named after his mother. She was murdered all those years ago, and after all his centuries of living, he had forgotten why. Over time, the importance of why the act happened faded into irrelevance, and only the pain of her absence remained. The only thing he had left to remember her by was a carved statue figurehead in her likeness fastened at the prow of his ship. At least he had a few trinkets that belonged to his late brothers and father.

The chamber went deathly quiet. Young Daemyn hugged the cobalt blue book close to his heart. Alistair stood still, stunned by the man's story. Albrecht, on the other hand, watched him wide-eyed with disbelief and clutched the letter from his father in one trembling hand.

"What proof do you have of this?" He asked, an unsaid accusation in his tone.

Vardan scratched the back of his neck, trying to remember what his old friend Velores, the very first King of Svartr, had counseled. "The proof is in whatever you wish to ask of me. Your ancestors have most commonly asked for my knowledge of the first royal family." He smirked, feeling confident in his answer, but Albrecht's gaze turned angry, which surprised him.

With a deep breath, the older Prince looked down at the letter in his hand, clearly reading over the words again, and when he reached the end, returned his gaze to Vardan. "The records state that the first King of Svartr had three children, but that information is false. He had two more with another woman, bastards, unfortunately."

Vardan then guessed the contents of the letter. It was likely Aegir's backup plan to tell Albrecht and Daemyn about him. It was a wise choice, though it didn't bode well for Aegir's wellbeing, and now he had to relive a memory best left in the past. His index finger twitched at his side, still feeling a twist of grief for Velores's two forgotten boys after all this time.

"They were kept off the official records because the first Queen of Svartr wanted them stricken from history." Albrecht's eyes softened as his gaze slid to the rugged floor as he listened. "The first King refused, memorializing them in his own way."

Albrecht eventually seemed to relax and returned his now sad expression to Vardan. "What were their names?"

A smile tugged at Vardan's lips. "Honestly, you've surprised me. This is the first time anyone has ever asked about them." Sliding his fingers through his charcoal black hair, he felt a surge of warmth in his heart. "Velores had two bastards, as you said. Sons, to be exact, and probably some of the brightest souls," a lump formed in his throat, and try as he might, he couldn't make it go away. "I have ever had the pleasure of knowing."

Vardan turned to Valhalla and placed a hand over his heart, remembering a young girl of only five grinning from ear to ear as she ran about with blue ribbons in her hair, telling everyone in earshot that she was a flower fairy. He happily sighed at the memory, but then his mind flashed back to Velores' sons, one holding a wooden dragon and the other a wooden ship, both with great dreams of traveling to every corner of Midgard and beyond. Unfortunately, those dreams weren't meant to be.

"The youngest enjoyed art, music, and sculpting. He was never really fond of sailing the sea, but loved to be near it. His name was Daemon Oceanwave, immortalized as a pale blue flower edged with purple. You can find them—"

"In Mother's rose garden." Daemyn finished, utter surprise on his face.

Vardan gently nodded. "That's right. The oldest, now that was a boy destined to be a great warrior and sailor. He loved the sea so much he wanted to command his own ship one day." His smile faded as the memory of their end crashed into his mind. "His name was Alben Oceanwave, immortalized as—"

"A figurehead statue on," Albrecht interrupted, raising a hand to his forehead, looking as if realization dawned on him. "The Leoric, my family ship? I had no idea."

The lump in Vardan's throat held tight, his eye blurring with tears. He turned away and wiped his face. Those boys, taken so young. He missed them dearly.

"What happened to them?" Albrecht asked, an apology in his expression. "If you don't mind me asking."

Vardan turned to Valhalla with furrowed brows, trying to hold back the sorrow he'd buried away in his past. With a deep breath, he cleared his throat and continued. "Ánør-indi. It's been centuries, but the name of that disease is one I will never forget. It swept through the common district like fire. Their mother was the first it took. Velores begged me to shepherd the boys out of the city before they caught it, but I was too late, young Daemon was already coughing up blood by the time we reached the gates."

A dull ache settled into Vardan's chest. He could still picture the boils and rash that consumed their skin, the blood tears they wept, and the sheer hopelessness in their eyes. Alben was only sixteen, and Daemon just turned ten. Both were far too young. "What the disease did to them, it—"

"Don't," Albrecht said, raising a hand, "you don't have to. I know what that disease did to those who caught it. It's an end I wouldn't wish on anyone."

Still looking at Valhalla, Vardan reached out to stroke her hair, which had bunched by her shoulder. It was then he realized some color was returning to her cheeks, her skin no longer so ghostly pale. He gently ran a finger along the curve of her jaw, a small smile tugging at his lips.

"It was for those boys that you two have your names." Vardan met each of their eyes, seeing the surprise in their faces. "Aegir asked for me often during Ayunli's final month of carrying you two. Both times when I'd finally arrived, you two were already born." He straightened and loosely crossed his arms over his chest. "I was barely through the chamber doors when Aegir handed you to me, Albrecht. You were such a fidgeter back then, I worried I might drop you."

Vardan laughed, bringing a blush to Albrecht's cheeks as he glanced away with clear embarrassment. "As for you, Daemyn, your father was stuck with a council meeting when you were born. So your mother passed you to me herself. I don't think I'd ever seen a baby so small, so quiet, before that day."

Daemyn's reaction was no better than his brothers, but a smile found its way onto his face.

"You know," he chuckled and brushed his hair out of his face, "neither of them could come to a decision about your names, so they asked me. Believe it or not, it wasn't the first time I chose a name for a royal babe, but it always struck me as odd when it happened. For instance, I gave your great-great-uncle the name Aeldirmuc. He was an unpleasant boy and took after his father. Somehow, nobody had given him a name by the time he turned three, and when I brought it up to his parents, they told me that if it were that important, then I could have the honor. So, given his parentage and the boy's temperament, I chose Dwarvish slang for pig's ass."

Daemyn and Alistair chuckled at the story, but Albrecht only looked at him with a coldness returning to his eyes. "So then . . ."

Vardan glanced at the young man, something clearly on his mind, and decided to wait for Albrecht to piece together his thoughts. Eventually, the heir of Svartr's jaw set, and with a deep breath, he raised a scowl in Vardan's direction. "If that's the case, you were that close with our parents, then why weren't *you* here keeping my family safe? Why didn't you fight beside me in the Gran Mar War?"

A sudden gasp sounded from the bed. Startled, everyone's eyes turned to Valhalla. She let out a long groan, attempting to raise a shaky hand to her forehead and let her arm fall over her eyes.

Vardan flew to her side, cupping her cheeks. "Valla, what's wrong? Talk to me."

"Va-Vardan?" She whimpered, her face contorting with pain. "My-My head, it hurts!"

"The tea!" Alistair exclaimed and rushed to the nightstand on his side of the bed. Vardan hadn't noticed the teapot sitting over a melted candle and watched as the High Prince poured its deep crimson liquid into a teacup and handed it to him. "She'll have to drink it cold. The Castle Healer said as soon as Valhalla woke up, she needed to drink this to help with the pain."

Vardan nodded in thanks and took the cup as Lilianna lit a small candle to replace the one beneath the teapot. Sliding a hand behind Valhalla's neck, he carefully lifted her forward and pressed the rim of the cup to her lips. She drank without hesitation and emptied the cup.

Resting her back onto her pillows, Varden handed the cup back to Alistair to place beside the teapot. Valhalla's body shook, and she fidgeted under the sheets as if unable to get comfortable. Vardan brushed away a few loose strands of hair from her forehead, but due to the linen bandage, he couldn't quite remove them from her face.

"Just breathe and count to twenty." He said tenderly, then glanced at Alistair and whispered, "What happened during her fight with Aegir?"

"Ah, um," Alistair shifted, "as you said earlier, she exhausted herself so much that she could barely fight back. Aegir overpowered her, strangling Valhalla in her weakened state, and just . . . chucked her across the courtyard. She landed on her head pretty hard. The healer said she would be bedridden for at least a week."

"Vardan, please?" Valhalla called weakly, sliding her hand over his.

He leaned close to her, her eyes still closed. "There's no way I'll be able to keep this from them. You know they'll be worried." Vardan answered, assuming she wanted him to keep this secret from everyone in Asgard.

"No! Not that." She shook her head. "Th-The Princes?" Her mention of them seemed to startle the boys. "Are they alright?"

Vardan sighed as a small smile found its way onto his face. Of course, she would be thinking of them even while she was bedridden with injury. "The Princes are just fine. They're all here beside you."

Valhalla struggled to force open her eyes. He could just barely make out the pink of her irises as she searched for him in the room, her sight likely blurry. Eventually, it seemed she found him, and then her eyes turned to the three Princes lining up at the edge of her bed. She slid her arms back and attempted in vain to sit up, instead falling back on the bed with a screeching groan.

Vardan placed his hands on her shoulders and stopped her from trying again. "Dammit, lay still. You suffered a terrible head injury."

After a few breaths, she stretched out her right hand and began searching for something, sliding her palm across the sheets. Alistair watched for a moment, then hesitantly reached out for it. As the tip of his fingers touched the back of her hand, he glanced at Vardan as if he might lose his nerve. Perhaps he expected her to swat him away, but Vardan had a feeling that wouldn't be the case, and as he anticipated, she lifted her hand, allowing him to hold her between his hands.

Alistair then took a seat beside her. He smiled as he inspected her. "We're fine, Valhalla, I promise. You don't have to worry about us."

Valhalla's body relaxed, her breathing gentle, and the first hint of a smile tugging at the corners of her mouth. Sleep then took her once more.

Vardan let out a tired sigh. Hunched over beside Valhalla, relief easing the tension in his chest and he rubbed the back of his hand across his forehead. She was fine, that was at least some good news, but he was worried about how those who care for her in Asgard might react when they hear she nearly died. But that was an issue for another time. For now, he needed to focus on the conversation with Albrecht.

With another long breath, he answered the older Prince. "I promised Velores to always watch over his descendants, to be there for them when called upon." He glanced up at Albrecht and Daemyn, their expressions full of genuine curiosity. "Velores feared I would become a tool and be over-relied upon by the wrong people for my longevity. So, he exiled me until such a time that the next ruler had need of me, for war, guidance, or both."

"So," Alistair gingerly returned Valhalla's hand to the bed and met Vardan's gaze, his face turning sorrowful, "a new ruler would be your only chance to return to your home?"

"That's," he sighed, letting his arm fall to his side, "actually correct. Whenever the ruler of Svartr is on their deathbed, I am called back to meet the next in line." Vardan returned to Albrecht with a gracious smile. "That is, until Aegir was crowned King."

"My father?" Albrecht raised a brow, making Vardan chuckle.

"Let me explain. Your father was the first and only ruler to pull back on my exile because, and I'll do my best to quote him here, I am not some relic to be used and then discarded like an old, forgotten tome. I'm a man, living as he or any other." Vardan paused for a moment and then continued. "It was a surprise relief to hear him say that."

"Don't forget the but," Lilianna added, looking apologetic, but Vardan just shrugged.

"Aye, I know. *But* while I was allowed to come and go at my leisure, Aegir warned me not to attract attention and to keep my stays brief. If others were to catch on to my secret, he made it clear his protection would only go so far."

"And the wars?" Albrecht asked, his demeanor softening a bit.

"Ah," Vardan clapped his hands on his knees and stood, walking over to the balcony to feel the sea air on his face, "unfortunately, during the War of Lions," he glanced back at Albrecht, "I was out of the country at the time. With her."

"Where did you go?" Alistair asked, a look of fascination in his features.

"Weida Long, visiting a friend. We weren't far from Veerence, just a few miles from the Jade Bridge." Vardan stared out at the waters. "When I received word of what was going on, I asked Aegir if he needed me by his side. He declined."

"He did? Why?" Albrecht exclaimed.

"Your father was confident that with Hilliard and Rjóðr at his side, he would win. As for Gran Mar," he turned and fell back to rest on the doorframe, rubbing a hand down his face. The weariness of the night was starting to get to him. "Again, Aegir was confident, but bade me to observe. I was to only take part if there were no other options."

Albrecht narrowed his eyes, staring at Varden for several heartbeats, then turned away, lost in thought. "It was you." He eventually said, his words only a whisper. Whipping back up to Vardan, his face turned serious, a hint of surprise beneath his almost accusatory tone. "You saved me."

"Well, I don't know about that." Vardan corrected with a warm chuckle. "I promised to help. Sending letters, provisions for you and your sailors,"

"No!" The older Prince interrupted. "That's not what I meant, and you know it."

Vardan's smile faded. He knew exactly what Albrecht was talking about.

"Albrecht," Daemyn asked, seeming uncomfortable, "did something happen while you were aiding Zarago?"

"Yes," Albrecht said bluntly. "It was storming. The enemy came at me during the cover of night. There were no firelights. No sound carried across the waves. Nothing. We didn't see those fuckers coming. I defensively positioned my ship to rain cannon fire down on them, the two ships barring my path, then they suddenly went up in flames." He then did something Varden hadn't expected. The tension fell from his shoulders, and an expression of relief, maybe, crossed his face. "I heard thunder from above. The silhouette of a ship, similar to mine, appeared within a flash of lightning. You saved me that day. Then, after that day, more and more of the enemy's ships suffered the same fate. Their numbers dwindled at a staggering rate. That was all you, wasn't it?"

Vardan didn't answer, at least, not right away. He brushed the hair away from his face and watched the shimmering waves roll across the sea. Aegir would've wanted him to save his oldest son. He was sure of that, but his actions thereafter had been overstepping. Albrecht hadn't been completely out of danger, of course. It was war after all. But he was safe back within the lines of his men. Still, Vardan feared a repeat attack, and so he took it upon himself to intervene. He still wasn't sure if it had been the right thing to do.

"Would you be upset if I said yes?"

Albrecht instantly closed the distance between them and grabbed Vardan's arm. The older Prince looked at him with bewilderment. "Why would I be upset?" He exclaimed, tears brimming on his eyelids. "If it wasn't for you, I . . . I wouldn't be here to save—"

Sadness immediately shrouded his face. Then, when he thought Albrecht couldn't surprise him even more, the older Prince pressed his forehead onto Vardan's shoulder and began to weep.

This close, Vardan could smell the faint scent of musk mixed with the sea about the Prince. Vardan didn't say a word. His heart ached for Albrecht. For the whole family. Glancing at Daemyn, the young man was trying his hardest to hold back tears of his own. Alistair walked over to the younger Prince and pulled him into his arms. The High Prince silently caressed Daemyn's hair as he, too, cried. The care and ability to comfort one another, these two showed, made Vardan glad. It was a strength too few men allowed themselves to have. Such a bond was a boon in these troubled times. His focus then returned to Albrecht.

Vardan gently leaned his head against Aegir's older sons and hesitantly placed it on the back of Albrecht's neck, his fingers sliding through the Prince's brown hair. It was now or never. He didn't want to ask of their father as he knew the answer would likely only bring more pain to the boys, but he needed confirmation.

"Albrecht, please, tell me, what happened to your father?"

The chamber went quiet. An occasional sniffle broke the silence, and a tension set in between Vardan's shoulders. Albrecht's body was tense against Vardan's, and eventually, he answered. "After Valhalla was thrown across the courtyard," his words came soft and ragged, "my father attempted to bury her. I-I froze. I was scared. I couldn't decide what to do, but Daemyn," taking a deep breath, he let out a long sigh. "Daemyn knew what to do. He ran to-to stop him. To kill him."

Vardan gasped and turned to Daemyn, but the young Prince only buried himself deeper into Alistair's arms. The High Prince somberly obliged, hugging his friend tighter.

"However," Albrecht continued, his voice cracking, "Father caught him, threw him to the ground. He even——" He shivered, several heartbeats passing before he finished. "He stomped on Daemyn's shoulder, pinning him to the ground. I saw him raise my brother's sword in the air so I-I——"

"You did what you had to." Vardan completed for him, not wanting Albrecht to have to say it.

"Did I?" He asked, Vardan hearing hurt, and the confusion in his words.

Vardan took the Prince's biceps in hand and gently pushed him away, Albrecht's eyes red and puffy from crying. "Yes, because——"

He paused, just then remembering Tamanna's journal. He reached inside his satchel and pulled out the tome. Brushing a hand over the flat, leather surface, Vardan opened the journal to the last entry. He knew Valhalla had found something in here, but with how fast things went after that, he hadn't had a chance to confront her about it. "Valhalla found something in here, but after being discovered by Tamanna, we frantically left his chamber. Here. Have a look."

He handed it to Albrecht. The older Prince seemed so confused, but determination came back into the set of his brow. Taking the journal in trembling hands, he turned it over to look inside. "Is this supposed to be—"

"Tamanna's journal, aye. She took it with her after rushing out of the man's chamber. I'm sure the answers you need are in here. Read through it and show it to—" Vardan paused. "Show it to your council."

Albrecht startled at that, staring dumbfoundedly at him. Vardan grasped the Prince's shoulder, gently giving it a squeeze for comfort. "Your father has passed. The crown and throne is now yours. I'm not telling you to just accept what has happened, but to acknowledge your new reality. I'll be here to help you. If you need me, that is."

Albrecht let out a shuddering breath, his tongue tying as he attempted a reply. "Th-Thank you, Vardan."

He nodded and gave Albrecht's shoulder another squeeze. Looking around the chamber, Vardan went to one of the plush chairs by the fireplace, removed his satchel and coat, sword and various daggers, and placed his things on the chair. "Now, why don't—"

"Wait, please." Said Daemyn, wiping his face of tears as he stared at the cobalt blue book in his hands. "What you said, um, about the first King's bastards, Alben and Daemon, something about them sounds familiar to me."

"How so?" Albrecht asked.

"I think Mother told us their story when we were little." Daemyn held up the book to Alistair, showing him the title. "You heard it too, Alistair, but you were still recovering from your father's death and might not have been listening."

"Huh, I can barely remember," Albrecht replied with a tilt of his head. "Did the story go as Vardan said?"

"No, not exactly," Daemyn answered, opening the book and flipping the pages idly with a hint of a smile. "For starters, Alben and Daemon went on many grand adventures, both by land and sea. They even had a talking black falcon named . . . Vardan." He then turned his gaze to Vardan. Lilianna snickered by the doors of the chamber.

Vardan gave her a knowing smirk and winked. The book Daemyn was holding was one he wrote long, long ago, to immortalize not only Velores' bastards, but his family and Aura. He raised a fisted hand, index finger pointing skyward to count. "There's a magical talking horse the boys meet, named Aldridge, after my middle brother, who was an amazing rider. He fought on his steed as if it were a natural extension of himself." He extended his middle finger. "Then there's the talking black humpback whale named Catran, after my oldest brother, a strict whaler and fisherman. He didn't go after the big creatures unless there was no other choice and was always fair in divvying up their take, never giving himself more than his crew." Raising his ring finger next, "Then there's also—Well, I can't tell you who *everyone* is, I'm afraid. We'd be here all night." He gave Daemyn a playful wink and was surprised when the young Prince blushed shyly in return.

"That ring," Albrecht gestured at Vardan's index finger, "the falcon is the insignia of the Loyalen house," then turned to his sword resting on the side of the chair, "*your* house, I mean."

Vardan laughed softly and inspected the ring on his finger. "Both the ring and the sword, Sundfoerr, were a gift from Velores, given to me just before he passed away. The black falcon became the new symbol of my house, given to me after we landed on these shores."

"Wait, your herald wasn't originally the falcon?" Alistair asked.

He shook his head. "No. My family perished in a fire. Velores wanted to give me a new one, something he felt represented me better. I'm also pretty sure my flying companion helped." Vardan laughed.

"What was the creature's name?" This time, the question came from Albrecht.

"His name was Gríma. He was a gift when I was your age." Vardan pointed at Daemyn. "Gríma aided me greatly, delivering messages between the great ships when we were sailing across the great seas to get here. Poor thing passed before the castle was fully built. I never could will myself to get a new companion after that. Felt like a betrayal of his memory. By the way, remind me how the book ended. It's been so long since I wrote the damn thing, and I haven't read it to Valla since she was only ten falls young."

Daemyn jumped and closed the book, then brushed his fingers over the runes carved into the cover. "The name here says, Gjalpar Skaer." His eyes drifted from the title up to Vardan with a tilt of his head, an unsaid question hanging in the air.

Vardan was quiet for several heartbeats. It had been a very long time since his herald changed, but hearing the words of the old tongue, he could still picture his father's banner. "It was a saying long ago for wolf, my family's original insignia." He answered and returned to Valhalla's side, taking a seat beside her and sliding his hand in hers.

Alistair softly tapped Daemyn's shoulder. "Daemyn, how did the story end?"

"Oh, um," he returned to the book, his expression softening, "thinking about it now, it's . . . sad. At the end of Alben and Daemon's story, Vardan tells them that there's nothing left to see and that it's time to leave."

Alistair's brows curved, puzzled. "Leave to where?"

Daemyn's throat bobbed up and down, and he hugged the book closer to his heart. "To the golden city in the sky."

"Ah, I remember now," Vardan said, garnering their attention once more. "I had the falcon fly into the sky and disappear in rainbow light, summoning forth a warrior maiden in white flying a golden longship." He waved a hand in the air with a shrug. "It's all a bit grandiose, I know, but from there she helps them into her ship and sails them to the golden city, ending their journey." A tear rolled down his cheek, and he quickly swiped it away. "Valhalla loved listening to their stories when she was younger."

"I," Alistair took a deep breath, "don't suppose Valhalla's a character in the book?"

Vardan laughed, having not expected the question. "No, these stories were written well before she was born."

"Alright, everyone," Lilianna clapped, "I think that's enough for now. The four of you need to rest, especially you, Your Highness. No doubt you'll have a long day ahead of you."

Albrecht sighed. "You're right, but I have one more thing to ask. Vardan?"

"Aye?" Vardan responded with a knowing smile.

"Could you—Would you—"

"I would be honored to help you with whatever you need, Your Highness."

60

Alistair

NOW OR NEVER

"**A**lbrecht, come on,**" Alistair complained, feeling more than a little uncomfortable as Albrecht helped button his black vest and met his eyes with a knowing smirk, "I can dress myself."

"I'm well aware of that. You'll just have to allow me this distraction from what's to come." Albrecht slipped the last silver button into place and brushed a hand across Alistair's shoulders to remove the wrinkles from the white shirt.

Alistair understood his friend's trepidation and knew him well enough to see the sadness behind Albrecht's smirk. A tightness had gripped his chest ever since the fight in the courtyard. It had been two days since then, since Aegir's death and Tamanna's disappearance. In all that time, instead of allowing the Svartr Princes to grieve their father's passing, Svartr's remaining council and much of the upper society had prodded them for answers. The people's confusion and anger demanded justice for the deaths that laid at both mens feet.

In an attempt to appear as equals and show respect for Svartr's nobility, Albrecht never once took his seat in what had been until recently his father's chair at the head of the council table. In fact, he had never sat at all, preferring to stand opposite that chair with Alistair and Daemyn beside him, Vardan always leaning against the the chamber door. The days were filled with yelling and accusations, even after each of them had heard the contents of Tamanna's journal, they didn't let up. They sought answers that only Tamanna had, and in his absence, took out their frustrations on the brothers. Eventually, their ire toward Albrecht subsided when they realized he couldn't possibly have been in league with Tamanna due to his absence during the Gran Mar War, and so their anger quickly doubled and focused solely on Daemyn, since he didn't have such an excuse and was there when Tamanna first appeared.

It was at that moment when Vardan made his presence known, slamming a hand down on the table in outrage. Daemyn had been cursed by Tamanna and suffered more at the hands of that madman than most who were levying accusations at him, and Vardan didn't stop shouting until each and every one of them understood that fact. Both Aegir and Daemyn had barely, if any, autonomy over their choices and actions, and all in attendance came to understand that if any justice was going to come, they needed to find Tamanna to judge him appropriately.

Still, even with Vardan's scolding, tempers were high, and the council then turned to Alistair for the final verdict, as he was the High Prince and so had the power of final say on what would be done. That was the first time Alistair had ever been placed in such a position. Sure not to chide the council for their petulance, he assured them that he understood their frustrations and also sought justice for the pain suffered by the people of Svartr. He calmly explained that casting blame on Albrecht or Daemyn, when they played an integral part in toppling Tamanna's plans, was misguided. Aegir also couldn't be blamed as he was under the villain's command, which echoed Vardan's sentiments, and so urged the counsil to think on the matter for a time before making their judgment. In his opinion, all should join with Albrecht and Daemyn to find the man responsible, and the first step in doing so was to agree on a peaceful transition of power from ruler to heir. He cautioned against coming to a decision in haste, as nothing had to be decided right away.

Eventually, the council agreed, allowing Albrecht and Daemyn to give their father a proper Svartr send off deserving of the King he had been in life, and so now everyone was preparing for Aegir's funeral march.

Something then lightly smacked against Alistair's cheek, making him startle and turn, confronted by Albrecht's teasing gaze. "Stop it, I can tell when you're brooding. We'll have none of that." He had finished looping Alistair's jabot around his neck and tucked the ends under the vest. "Save the tears for the beach. Please."

"I—" Alistair flinched, a tear rolling down his cheek, and he wiped it away. "Yes. Yes, of course. Sorry, I . . . I didn't realize—"

"Don't worry about it. Your expression went distant, so I brought you back." He laughed warmly, and Alistair chuckled alongside him. "There, you're about done. Just need that coat and cape now."

Albrecht stepped past Alistair and opened the closet, sliding a black coat and cape off their individual hangars, and as he held them up, Alistair caught sight of the silver raven designs on them. "I didn't realize I had funeral garments."

"Oh, don't worry," Albrecht answered, "none of us did. It seems Father . . . no doubt thought of Mother's funeral."

Alistair winced and turned away, letting Albrecht slide the black coat over his arms. He slid his fingers over the silver ravens exploding out from under the lapels and down the cuffs about the sleeves.

His gaze then turned to Albrecht's coat, which lay over one of the room's orange couches. There were gold sea serpents swimming about the edges of the black fabric, the inside of the garment a deep crimson. "The designs are beautiful."

Albrecht chuckled, placing Alistair's black cape over his shoulders and fastening the clips with silver chains. Silver tassels hung against his biceps. "Of course they are. These were made for us after all."

Alistair rolled his eyes at that, and Albrecht shrugged, walking over to his things. With his coat on and the cape with Alistair's help, the two of them were just about ready. Looking at his doors leading out into the hall, his mind couldn't help but wander to Daemyn and Valhalla.

"Hey, how's Daemyn?" Alistair asked as he grabbed his silver, raven-decorated circlet and white gloves from his vanity mirror. "I haven't seen him since breakfast."

"He basically dragged both Vardan and Valhalla into his chambers to change," Albrecht answered with a raised brow and his usual knowing smirk.

Alistair snorted, understanding full well what that meant. "Oh no, maybe we should rescue them then?"

"No way. I want to see what my guppy of a brother has done to them." Albrecht slid his golden, ruby-encrusted circlet atop his head and opened the doors. At that same moment, Daemyn's chamber opened.

"Oh, you're done?" Daemyn asked, clutching his violet and silver, snowflake-decorated cane to his chest. As Alistair looked his young friend up and down, he was surprised to find his outfit was practically the same as Albrecht's, though the red fabric of his garb was notably brighter. Upon his head was the same plain black circlet he'd worn when Alistair first arrived in Svartr. It again struck him as odd, just as it had back then. He had never known Daemyn to wear something *that* plain.

"Of course, why do you ask?" Albrecht gave his brother a curious look.

The young Prince's bright blue eyes slid to Alistair, and a hint of judgment slid into his features. "With that hair?"

"What's wrong with my hair?" Alistair exclaimed.

"It's windy tonight. Do you really want your hair slapping you in the face?" Daemyn leaned forward with a challenging smirk. Alistair had always been fairly inept when it came to fashion, which made it easy for Daemyn to unravel his confidence in his appearance.

"Is it really that bad?"

"Don't worry!" Daemyn reached into his pocket and pulled out a thin, bright purple ribbon. "Luckily, I came prepared. Here, hold this."

Without warning, Daemyn tossed his cane to Alistair, who caught it with only a small fumble. The young Prince rushed behind him and grabbed hold of his hair a little too energetically, causing Alistair to yelp. "Careful, will you!"

A bellowing fit of laughter then echoed into the hall, grabbing Alistair's attention. Vardan emerged from Daemyn's chamber, and Alistair found himself taken aback. He had never seen the man dressed like a noble, which seemed to suit him quite well. The outfit was similar to his own, minus the cape, and featured bright blue falcon stitchwork. The biggest difference was the vast amount of laces blooming from his sleeves and hanging over his chest.

"Don't worry, Your Grace. Daemyn said the same thing about my hair, except I was fast enough to swat him away." Vardan shrugged with a wink, making Alistair snort.

"You look good, Lord Vardan." Alistair managed.

"Due to what today's events entail, I will allow the use of titles, but I swear, the thing I DON'T miss about Svartr is how the fashion always seems to involve more ostentatiousness." He sneered and swatted the hanging laces over his chest, causing Alistair and Albrecht to snicker.

"Oh, come now, if it was really so bad, you shouldn't have accepted the shirt from his Highness." A familiar voice called out from Daemyn's chamber.

Alistair's breath hitched as Valhalla emerged to stand beside Vardan. While her black garb was simpler than theirs, she looked the perfect image of nobility. Her skirt was layered, the underpart shining like silk, and her short coat fastened closed with sapphire gemmed buttons. Lace cascaded over her chest and sprouted from her sleeves. Valhalla's hair was done up in a braid and was adorned with a blue ribbon. Her vibrant pink eyes shone in the firelight. Her deep red painted lips and the kohl around her eyes hid all signs of injury.

"You know, Daemyn could paint her for you so it's less awkward when you stare." Albrecht grinned deviously. Alistair flinched, and his cheeks burned with embarrassment.

"SHUT IT! I didn't—I wasn't—"

"Aww, Alistair, are you blushing?" Interrupted Albrecht, not at all helping the situation.

"I think he is," Vardan answered, his grin reminding him of a hungry grizzly bear.

He hadn't realized he'd taken a step back until he bumped into Daemyn, who was still braiding his hair. "Shit! Daemyn, I'm s—"

"It's fine." He answered softly, the hurt in his young friend's voice bringing on a pang of guilt. Of course, he would feel that way, even after everything that had happened. Daemyn still had feelings for him, and here he was, absentmindedly ogling someone right in front of him. "I'm all finished anyway."

He smiled up at Alistair, but it was far from genuine, and tossed the dark brown braid over his shoulder. Alistair lifted it in his hand, seeing the little purple bow holding his strands together. "Oh, um, thank you, Daemyn."

Daemyn only shrugged, taking his cane back and standing beside Albrecht, who was now eyeing him warily. "Well, I suppose with all of that out of the way, Valhalla, you should really be wearing gloves. It's very cold out."

Daemyn then chuckled, causing Albrecht to raise a brow at him, and his smile faded a little. "Wait, are you serious?"

"To be fair, you did the same thing only moments ago." Vardan snickered.

"Alright, I'm missing something," Albrecht said flatly.

Daemyn's eyes beamed with excitement. "Aye! Valhalla, do the thing, like you did with me?"

"Wait, what?" Albrecht turned, cocking a brow at Valhalla and causing her to let out a shrill giggle.

For reasons Alistair didn't quite understand, his heart was sent a flutter.

"Here, let me show you, your Highness." Valhalla walked up to Albrecht and raised her hands in front of him.

He blinked at her a few times, confused for a few seconds, before playfully grinning and holding his hand up, displaying his Ring of Svartr. Tilting his head back in mock arrogance, he smirked. "You may kiss it when ready."

She rolled her eyes, unable to hide a smile of her own, and grasped his hand.

His shoulders flinched with surprise. He gawked at her hands around his. "How . . . are you doing that?" Albrecht asked, his free hand touching her knuckles, amazed.

"As Vardan told you, my connection with fire lets me control the heat of my flames, including my own body heat." She smiled sweetly and shrugged. "I can even raise your body heat if I want, but I need to touch you for that to work. The only time I struggle is when a fever is involved, but I can manage it well enough when I'm awake." Valhalla then released Albrecht's hand.

"Valhalla, may I?" Alistair asked, stepping toward her and offering his hand. She took it, giving him the same sweet smile, and he felt heat rise in his cheeks.

The moment her hands wrapped around his, heat soared through his fingers and up his arm. A new warmth then spread from the center of his chest, making him gasp and then laugh. "Oh wow, that truly is amazing. I bet winter chills never bother you."

"Not anymore, they don't." She laughed alongside him. He raised his free hand and cupped hers, and as he did, her breath hitched.

"Alright, you four, the sun is getting low," Vardan said as he glanced out the window. Alistair and Valhalla jumped, startled, and released each other.

The heat left him as quickly as it had come, leaving behind a subtle ache from the loss. To distract himself from the odd sensation, Alistair returned his attention to his best friends. They were hesitant to proceed. The two brothers stared at each other for several long moments before Daemyn grasped his brother's wrist, looking up at him and nodding as if a conversation had taken place. Albrecht nodded in return and stepped over to Vardan with Daemyn in tow.

"Vardan, Daemyn, and I were wondering if you would lead the procession? You were there for his birth and crowning." Albrecht swallowed, no doubt trying to remove the lump in his throat. "It . . . feels only right that you be the one to send him off."

Vardan held the brothers' eyes, stunned, but eventually grinned. "It'll be my honor, truly, but are you really both fine with that?"

"I am," Albrecht said.

"As am I," Daemyn answered, his voice soft while clutching his cane close to his heart.

"Very well then, why don't I start by leading you all to the throne room," Vardan said and then proceeded to walk ahead to the stairway, then paused, waiting for them to follow.

Albrecht took a deep breath and closed his eyes. The moment was upon them now. Soon, they would say their final farewells to their mother and father.

Exhaling steadily, he turned to look at Valhalla. "I plan to have Daemyn and Alistair beside me for the march. After what I did and everything you've already done in spite of that for my family, I know I don't have the right to ask this of you, but would you mind watching the rear? As much as I would like to believe we will be left in peace during the procession to the beach, I . . . am firmly aware of the fear my father instilled in the citizens of this city. Better to be careful. Is that alright?"

"Yes, of course," Valhalla answered without hesitation, pressing her hands to her heart. "I've replenished my fire reserve. If anyone *does* try anything, I'll make sure they regret it."

"Thank you. You don't know how comforting that is to hear." Albrecht then turned to his brother, touching his arm. "Daemyn, are *you* ready?"

Daemyn didn't meet his eyes but took a deep breath, his grip on the cane tightening. "As ready as I'll ever be."

Albrecht gently squeezed his shoulder and then looked at Vardan with trepidation in his bright blue eyes. "Alright, we're as ready as we can be."

Vardan nodded and began down the stairs. Albrecht wrapped an arm around Daemyn's shoulders and followed.

Alistair hurried to walk beside them without hesitation, aware of Valhalla falling in behind him. The brothers had been there for him when his world crumbled in the aftermath of his father's death, then again for the War of Lions. It was now time for him to repay their kindness, to be there for them. After everything they'd been through, he owed them that much.

61

Alistair

The Black Roots

The halls of the Svartr castle were quiet. No servants shuffled about, busy in their duties. No knights patrolled, though a few were posted here and there. Alistair's heart thumped so loudly between his ears, he thought for sure the others would hear it. It was a silly thought. He knew that. But the day was somber, and he didn't want his friends to worry for him when it was their day for grieving.

They grew close to the final set of stairs, which would lead them to the ground floor. Something bumped lightly against his hand. Looking down, Albrecht's hand was trembling, but what was curious was that he pinched Alistair's cuff between his index finger and thumb. It had been so long since Albrecht had done this gesture, since his own father's death eleven years past. He had only ever done this when fear took hold of him, which was a rare thing. The first time

Alistair noticed him do this was when Aegir and Ayunli found them on the beach with not a guard in sight. It was foolish, and they were just old enough to have known better, a point the King had made several times in the following days. The last time was on a trip into the city just before Alistair was to return home. Albrecht had accidentally gotten them lost, turning into unknown alleyways where they found themselves cornered and nearly mugged, were it not for the city guards who heard Daemyn's cry and came running. Again, they had not brought guards of their own, but after that day, Albrecht swore to never leave the castle without guards again.

Alistair's chest tightened. Moving his hand back, he slipped his cuff out of Albrecht's grip and took his friend's hand in his. "It's going to be alright, Albrecht," Alistair whispered. "You can do this."

Albrecht didn't respond, his expression betraying nothing, but his grip tightened, and Alistair knew his friend appreciated the support. Alistair smiled warmly, and he gently patted his arm. Facing the corpse of your loved one was never an easy thing. Now Alistair's stomach was beginning to churn, memories of his father's and his sister's corpses resting there on a wooden slab.

He shook the thought away. Those days were terrible, and he wasn't going to break down on Albrecht and Daemyn, not until he was alone, in his own chamber, where he wouldn't worry them.

As they reached the ground floor, Alistair heard a sob from Daemyn. Both he and Albrecht turned to the younger Prince, breath becoming heavy and curling in on himself. He rested a hand on the mahogany wall, the other clutching his stomach.

"Daemyn!" Albrecht rubbed circles on his little brother's back. "It's . . . It's going to be alright, we're—"

Vardan strode over to them and, before either had a chance to react, the big man wrapped them both in an embrace. The Svartr brothers were utterly stunned, but Alistair appreciated his presence. While not exactly fatherly, there was a parental glint in the older man's eyes when he looked at the brothers, which made Alistair glad for them. While they had suffered a great loss, they still had some family left, even if not directly blood related.

"You both are doing so well. Just try to keep a brave face a little bit longer. Save your tears for when you're in front of your parents, they're only in the next hall." Vardan then slid away from them, a hand on each of their shoulders. "You can do this. I know you can. Now come on." He walked away from them, but kept his one yellow eye on them as he went, flashing a small, encouraging smirk on his rugged face.

Daemyn straightened, but with his body still noticeably shaking, he stole a glance at Albrecht's arm. His older brother chortled softly and understood, bending the arm to him. "Just take it, you guppy."

As a tear rolled down his light tawny cheek, Daemyn slid his cane into its strap on his belt and wrapped his fingers around his older brother's arm. "Alright," he whispered, "I'm ready."

Albrecht touched one of Daemyn's hands and leaned on him, holding each other close as if they might be blown apart by a sudden gust of ill wind. Alistair touched his father's ring hidden under his clothes and felt some comfort from it, wishing he were here.

Alistair flinched, feeling a hand touch his arm and back. He turned and found Valhalla looking at him, her pink eyes meeting his with sadness and understanding.

She had experienced far more loss than he. A home destroyed. Family and friends murdered when she was only a child. Alistair's heart twisted as he imagined what that must've been like. The loss of his father had drained all color from his world. Every waking moment, he suffered a deep, aching emptiness in his chest, and in his dreams, his father's final moments played out over and over again. Then there was his sister's death. It had been a different kind of loss. Bringing anger and an all-consuming need to lash out at the world. Surely there had to be a breaking point where one would become numb to loss, though in this moment, he was keenly aware he hadn't reached it. The loss of Aegir and Ayunli weighed heavily on his soul, leaving a weight in his gut and a coldness in his joints.

He wondered how Valhalla managed to carry the burdens of her past.

"Do you need a moment, your Grace?" Valhalla asked, pulling him from his thoughts.

"What?" He glanced at the brothers, then back at her. "Yes. I mean no! I'm—"

"Alistair, you cared for our father as much as we did," Albrecht said, resting a comforting hand on his arm. "I understand if you need a moment before saying your final farewell."

"No, it-it doesn't matter how I feel," Alistair answered, startling both brothers.

Albrecht's brow knitted, clearly confused by his answer. He wrapped him in an embrace and Alistair's breath hitched in his throat.

"I don't know why you would say that, Brother," he whispered, "your feelings always mattered to us. Don't for one damn moment think it doesn't. Aegir was just as much a father to you as he was to us. You don't have to shield us from your grief." Albrecht squeezed Alistair tightly and he felt himself pressing into his brother's arms.

Daemyn cleared his throat to get their attention. "You've also suffered a loss very recently, so if you need a moment, then please just take it."

Alistair chortled at that, feeling a little embarrassed. "Losing our fathers and your mother," he sighed and pulled away from Albrecht, " has been hard. Losing Lorna, though, has been something else. No harder, but it has certainly left me drained and conflicted."

Albrecht shrugged in agreement, and Alistair thought back to several days before, when they were still waiting while things were still being set up for Aegir's funeral march. Albrecht sat both Alistair and Daemyn down by his fireplace. The three of them ate s'mores and drank warm apple cider together. It was such a pleasant surprise, but when Alistair realized the occasion was to help soften his mood for the brothers to ask about Lorna, it sat heavily in his stomach. He found himself unable to hold back his feelings about Lorna. Everything just poured from him unstoppered. It was uncomfortable at first, but he found himself glad of the experience afterward.

Straightening his clothes, Alistair cleared his throat and tapped Albrecht on the chest. "Come on, I think we've delayed long enough."

The brothers nodded, and the group proceeded to follow Vardan to a door leading into the throne room. Just as he started to pull the doors open, Alistair glanced back at Valhalla and mouthed, *Thank you*.

She smiled warmly and nodded her head, then followed close behind.

To their surprise, they were not greeted by the quiet of the throne room, but instead by the sounds of Albrecht's Court Council in heated discussion.

Albrecht rushed through the threshold, his brows knitting. "What's going on here?" He demanded.

The small group startled and turned to him with bows and curtsies. "Your Highness, we must express our deepest apologies for how we all acted toward you and Prince Daemyn. We should've," The Lord suddenly grew silent, and a woman beside him spoke up.

"We never should've doubted, nor questioned either of you. Please, forgive us. Allow us to continue to serve as your Court Council upon your coronation."

Albrecht's mouth fell open, clearly dumbfounded by the council's change in tone. He glanced at Alistair and then to Daemyn, who both shrugged.

"Um," Albrecht started, "I was already counting on working with each of you after I'm crowned, but I wasn't going to ask for another fortnight. Where's all of this coming from?"

The counselors glanced nervously at each other, then each stood, looking at the Svartr Scald Raven, the highest member within the Ravens of Ódin who oversee the order for each region of Veerence. He was second, under the High Raven in Hilliard. The man bowed low in respect to Albrecht, his dark brown hair peppered with gray under his raven-feathered hood. A cloth face mask covered half of the man's face, and Alistair couldn't see much of his features, save for his bright brown eyes and deep tawny skin.

Albrecht eventually bowed in return. "Thank you so much for overseeing my father's funeral march, Scald Yorath. Is everything prepared on the beach?"

"Aye, your Highness," Scald Yorath replied as he stood, touching the tips of his fingers together under his black and gold robes, "however, there's something I *must* show you. It pertains to your father."

Alistair glanced at Albrecht, seeing his shoulders tense. "I-Is everything alright?"

"That depends on you, Your Highness." Scald Yorath answered as he turned and walked to a figure resting under a black veil atop a wooden pedestal. Alistair recognized it immediately. It was made by the Raven Monks, and there were few like it. They used them to rest the dead upon. It was covered in knotwork ravens flying this way and that, and hollow, to make for easy carrying. Both his father and Lorna had rested on this one for a time, until they were inevitably moved to be burned on a pyre.

As Scald Yorath placed his hands on the veil, he returned to Albrecht with a stoicism in his eyes that gave Alistair the impression he had seen far too many dead. "After the Raven Sisters received your father in the Stave Temple, they immediately took to cleaning and preparing him for his funeral march. Despite the politics that were likely to play out in the castle, they were confident he would still receive this honor. Once finished, they left him be until it was time to be brought here."

He slid the veil from the figure's face, revealing the late King, and Alistair's heart fell into his gut. The corpse before him was Aegir, his brown hair peppered with gray, beard trimmed, his features just as sharp and chiseled as they had been in life. There was no doubt it was him, but his once pale tawny skin was now a terribly familiar stone gray. His eyelids and lips were impossibly shadowed, and black roots stretched across his face.

Daemyn let out a sharp gasp and clamped his hands over his mouth. Albrecht's eyes went wide. Moments crept by, and as the shock softened, Alistair remembered that Aegir had been poisoned. At the time he hadn't put much thought into what poison had been used but now the realization sent ice through his veins. Tamanna had used the exact same poison that had been used to murder his own father.

62

Valhalla

Grief and Pain were One and the Same

Valhalla swallowed a nervous gulp as she looked down at the late King. His skin resembled that of a statue. Black roots spread around his bruised eyes and lips.

She glanced to her left, to Vardan. His one golden eye was wide with shock, a shudder running up his body, and his lips firmly pressed in a frown. Both Albrecht and Daemyn were equally startled, the older brother's mouth hanging open while the younger brother hid behind his hands. Alistair fared no better, color draining from his face like he'd seen a ghost.

Alistair didn't seem to be breathing, seemingly transfixed by the late King. His body trembled as he took a hesitant step back, raising his hands before him to shield himself.

Valhalla furrowed her brows. Cautious as she stepped toward him, she raised a hand and touched his back, feeling him flinch. "Your Grace?"

His eyes rolled up into his head, and suddenly Alistair was falling.

The High Prince stumbled and crouched low to the ground, a hand over his mouth, the other clutching his stomach. He twitched and gagged. Valhalla knelt beside him and very carefully touched his shoulders, though he didn't seem to register it. Vardan rushed before the council and raised his arms at his sides, stopping them from coming any closer.

"Don't!" Vardan demanded. "He needs space."

"Alistair!" Albrecht dropped opposite Valhalla, rubbing circles on his back. "Alistair, please, tell me what's wrong?"

"Oh, Alistair . . ." Daemyn said softly, voice barely a whisper.

"Daemyn?" Albrecht called to his younger brother. "Do you know what's wrong with him?"

Daemyn gently shook his head as he lowered his hands from his mouth, still looking at his father. He eventually turned to his brother, eyes slowly rising to meet him. "The High King, Alistair's father, it's exactly the same!"

Everyone was taken aback, staring at Daemyn as the meaning of his words set in. That would explain Alistair's reaction then, Valhalla thought, Aegir's appearance forcing him to relive the death of his own father. If her memory was correct of what Eilis told her of her husband's death, Alistair was only ten springs young when his father died. The late High King passed away in his own son's arms. Something like that would no doubt haunt a person for the rest of their life.

"Oh fuck," Albrecht let out a shaky breath, "Alistair, I'm—"

"Does that mean we're at war?" One of the council members whispered, garnering a glare from Albrecht.

"Of course, this means war!" Another counselor started, "Raseela must pay!"

"That's enough!" Albrecht yelled, making both Valhalla and Alistair jump. "We'll have no more of that." He stood up, his expression stern and imposing, just like his father. "Tamanna's journal made it clear that he was banished. It didn't say for what, but I can only assume it was for experiments like those he committed right here beneath this castle. I wouldn't be surprised if he were as much a menace in Raseela as he was here."

"Surely you aren't asking us to forget about the land that deceitful snake hailed from?" One of the Council members glowered. Albrecht pinched the bridge of his nose, no doubt calming himself to avoid things devolving to yelling.

"No, of course not. I—What I mean is—NGH!" Albrecht groaned with annoyance. "This is supposed to be my father's Funeral March!"

The council flinched and quickly bowed their heads in apology to their Prince. Albrecht's glaring, bright blue eyes fell on each and every one of them, his fists clenched at his sides. Soon, tempers calmed, and he continued. "If this truly bothers you, know that Daemyn and I already made plans to speak with the dancers from Raseela. They're being kept in one of the inns in Sailors Reef. Vardan here also volunteered to set sail for Raseela with the aid of Eenheide. Of course, all this will have to wait until *after* my coronation within a fort—"

"Tomorrow." One of the Council members said flatly, their steely gaze locked on Albrecht, which took him by surprise, and before he could respond, another of the councilors chimed in.

"A lot has happened, and . . . a lot still needs to be done. We need a ruler now more than ever." They each bowed respectfully. "Please, take up the crown and become the King Svartr needs. We vow to support you as much as possible with your grief and that of the city. Things are sure to be exacerbated with a hasty coronation, but if a terrible evil is upon us, if war is truly coming, then it is necessary. We must be ready with you at the helm, Your Majesty."

Albrecht stood dumbfounded before them. Valhalla wasn't sure what to make of all this either. She was far removed from the responsibility of a crown. Was something like this appropriate?

She jolted as a hand grasped her wrist. "Valhalla," Alistair whispered, still staring at the ground, "can you help me up?"

"A-Are you sure? Just moments ago, you were about to vomit."

Alistair took a deep breath and nodded. "Sorry, I've . . . I've calmed. Promise."

Valhalla looked him up and down, and although she was skeptical, she nodded and took his hand. Slowly and carefully, she helped Alistair stand. He struggled for a moment to get his bearings, and his breathing was hard, but Alistair forced himself to straighten. As he caught sight of Aegir once again, he immediately averted his gaze, turning instead to the council. "You're asking a lot from Albrecht so soon after his loss, which is especially surprising given your doubts expressed just barely two days ago."

"We know, your Grace." Another of the Council members answered, keeping their heads low. "It's because of how we acted that we feel obligated to do all we can to make sure things run smoothly, given all that transpired under the final days of King Aegir's . . . reign. Allow us to aid the people while Prince Albrecht looks into Raseela to confirm they truly aren't a threat." A few of the Council members then lifted their heads. "We wouldn't be desperate if this situation weren't so dire, your Grace. Please, crown our King. Let us move forward from this unpleasantness."

Alistair's fingers twitched at his side. He slowly closed his eyes, took another deep breath, and looked as though he had come to a decision. "So be it, but *only* if Albrecht agrees to this. I will also remain in this city to offer what aid I can and will do so until he deems the threat passed."

"Wait," Albrecht said as he grabbed Alistair's shoulder, turning him and meeting his eyes, "are you sure? You don't—"

"I know, it's alright." He answered, touching his fingers to his temples. "That was . . . a startling sight, to say the least. I'm sorry for . . ." Alistair sighed and shook his head, no doubt unsure how to finish his sentence.

"You have nothing to be sorry for. This has been quite difficult on all of us." Albrecht glanced back at his father on the pedestal, his expression sorrowful. "This wasn't at all the homecoming I anticipated. I've lost both parents, gone before I even arrived, should that monster's journal be believed." A sob escaped his throat, and a shudder ran through his shoulders.

Alistair embraced his friend. Albrecht leaned into him, crying deeply into his shoulder. Daemyn shuffled closer to his father, also now crying and bent over the man, holding fast to Aegir's hands under the black veil.

Valhalla's heart twisted. She wanted to console Daemyn but wasn't sure if it was appropriate for her to do so in public. A hand brushed her elbow, startling her. She gazed down and followed the hand back up to Alistair's teary-eyed face. He forced a smile and gently nudged her toward Daemyn. Valhalla nodded in understanding and rushed to the younger Prince. Carefully placing her hands on his trembling shoulders, she bent down and embraced him as he cried into his father's chest.

She glanced at Vardan, his hands tightly clasped together at his waist. His golden eye shone in the firelight, and a few tears rolled down his rugged face. As he caught her gaze, he shook his head and pursed his lips.

Her brow twitched at that. Did he really not wish to say farewell to his friend, or perhaps he already had done so from where he stood?

Valhalla instantly stood, feeling a hand rest on her back. It was Albrecht. Alistair had a hand on his shoulder, as if he had guided him to stand with his younger brother. She stepped away, allowing Albrecht to take her place by Daemyn so the two could grieve together.

Her chest was tight. The sensation was familiar, the pain of loss dulled with time, yet cold as it was the day she lost everything and never very far from thought.

She glanced back at the sound of coming footsteps to see that Vardan had decided to stand beside her, his hand sliding across her back. He was trying to hold back his own sorrow. He hated losing someone as much as she did, and had likely suffered more loss than anyone else in the room. She tried telling herself that it was simply a part of life. That they all began and came to an inevitable end. That it was what made life so precious, that each life was a thread in the great tapestry of the realms, but as poetic as that was, it brought no comfort. What comfort was that to the life cut short, or to the mother, daughter, sister, brother, or father left behind?

Valhalla found herself turning and wrapping her arms around Vardan's waist. His arms wrapped around her and squeezed. The two held onto each other as tightly as they could, and while the force of his grip was mighty, the press of his being constricting, she said nothing. She welcomed the sensation, the burning it caused in her lungs as she breathed, and the creaking of her bones as they shifted under the weight, because any feeling at all was better than that which sorrow brought.

63

Alistair

Sea is Eternal

A S DAEMYN AND ALBRECHT STOOD TOGETHER, grieving their father, Alistair chided himself for getting lost in the past. Aegir's appearance had sent him reeling at the memory of his own father's death, and while his friends had understood, it only served to make him feel worse. He felt ashamed for reacting the way he did, as if he had given the pair yet another burden to deal with when they should be focused on taking care of themselves today.

He had been just a boy, celebrating his tenth name day. It was still early in the evening. His mother had just given a toast, and as she raised her chalice to drink, his father slapped it out of her hand. He had already drunk from his own cup moments before, and as everyone stared in shock, he strained out the word. Poison. At the time, there was no way for them to know that only his father's drink had been tampered with, but without hesitation, his last living act had been protecting his family.

Alistair's father, for whom he was named, was shorter than his mother and broad in his shoulders. He barely fit in young Alistair's arms when he collapsed down the dais, convulsing and gagging for air. His bronzed skin went impossibly gray. Eyes and lips quickly blackened. Dark roots spread across his face. Black liquid poured from his mouth, nose, eyes, and ears. He wailed in pain, making such noises that even Alistair's time at war had not come close to replicating. Later, Alistair was told he, too, had been screaming, though he had no recollection of it. All he could remember was helplessly watching as everything that was the man who had been his father changed, becoming a nightmare seared onto his very soul.

To say the experience haunted him would've been an understatement. For the longest time afterward, that moment was as ever present as his own shadow. When he slept, ate, went about his tasks, even in moments that might've otherwise been joyous, the memory was there to remind him that the world had ended, or rather, that what he thought the world was, had been irrevocably turned into an aberration full of cruelty, pain, and injustice. Alistair shivered. He couldn't shake the memory away. Not then. Not now. Of course, it didn't help that Aegir lay there before him, a reminder of his greatest personal tragedy.

He focused his eyes on his grieving friends, Daemyn in particular. Although older than he was when his father died, Daemyn looked no different crying for his father, except he was apologizing to the man. Alistair had been told he was repeatedly calling, pleading for his father to wake up. His heart twisted in his chest. He had no idea what to say to his friends. There was nothing he could do now to ease the pain Daemyn was feeling. The best he could offer was just to be there for him, to keep him company and not bring up his own issues, as he had so far failed to do.

A voice cleared, and most eyes raised to Scald Yorath. "The Raven Sisters, who looked after him, guessed that an illusion of sorts had been placed over him to hide what he truly looked like. Unfortunately, it has been such a long time since the realm as a whole practiced any such art, but I thought it best you know how your father was killed."

"A-Aye," Albrecht replied with a tightness in his throat, "thank you. Truly."

The Scald bowed his head. "Of course, your Highness. Now, the evening is growing late. Are you all ready to proceed?"

"No!" Daemyn yelled, making everyone jump.

Albrecht leaned closer to Daemyn, gripping his shoulders. "Daemyn, it's alright, he's—"

"No, you don't understand!"

"Then tell me what's wrong."

Daemyn bit back a sob. "I-I don't want anyone to see him. Not like this!"

Albrecht flinched and glanced up at Scald Yorath as if he might know what to do. "Your Highness, that's why I placed the veil over him. I had a feeling neither of you would want His Majesty to be seen like this. So, when you're ready, I'll slide the veil over his face once more."

Daemyn stared at the man with trembling eyes, silent but unflinching. Eventually, his grip loosened on his father, and Albrecht carefully pulled his brother off their father. A quick glance from Albrecht, and Alistair could tell he wanted him to stand on the other side of Daemyn, which he rushed to do. As he reached for his young friend's forearm, Daemyn grabbed his hand, holding onto him tightly. It startled Alistair at first, but he sighed and was glad he could do this small thing for his friend. He hugged Daemyn close as they stepped away from Aegir.

Scald Yorath then closed his eyes and lowered his head, signaling for his fellow order members in the throne room to do the same. "For many, death is a terrifying concept." The man began as he placed his hands down on either side of Aegir. "Traveling to that cold, bitter place isn't a pleasant idea, I will admit, but we must remember that Helheim is *not* a place to be feared. It's just one more destination on each of our journeys leading to Ragnarök."

"Here in Svartr," Alistair heard Vardan whisper just behind him, "*every* soul goes to Helheim first, to be looked after before being picked up by a valkyrie, to be guided to a hall of the *gods* choosing."

Alistair glanced back to see Valhalla's surprised expression. "Really? I had no idea." She whispered back.

Vardan chortled. "I know, that's why I'm telling you."

Valhalla rolled her eyes and stifled a giggle. Alistair had forgotten about the Svartr belief. It differed significantly from what was said in Hilliard. There, Helheim was seen as a place for the undeserving, where souls went to be *punished* by the Queen of Helheim herself.

"Young Hel," Scald Yorath continued, "was forcibly thrown into Helheim. There she was challenged by Ódin himself to face the realm and tame the horrors within, and despite what was woven by the Sisters of Fate, she did. Promising to safeguard the souls of the dead, safeguarding them from the deadliest beings the realm of Helheim had to offer, she was crowned Queen of the dying lands and given the title, Goddess of Death, by the King of Asgard himself. It was his way of showing respect, despite what he had done to her."

Raising his head to all in attendance before looking first to Albrecht, then Daemyn, and finally Alistair, and grabbed hold of the veil. "Remember that Helheim is not a place of misery, but one where King Aegir will be welcomed with open arms, and there he will await the arrival of the valkyrie who will send him into Njörd's hall. There, he will wait for Ragnarök. The sea is life. The land is temporary."

Scald Yorath placed the veil over Aegir's face, concealing him under its thick black lace, and everyone repeated the words: The sea was life, the land was temporary. They were the words of Svartr. The man then stepped away, waving at the waiting Raven Monks to surround Aegir, grabbing hold of the eight outstretched wooden handles of the stretcher.

A Raven Sister approached the Scald with a brightly lit lantern, and the two stepped over to Albrecht. "Your Highness, the lantern is full of oil and brightly lit, as you can see. Will you light the way, or do you wish to ask another to do so in your stead?"

Albrecht released a long breath and took the lantern. "I know the perfect person to carry the lantern for me."

The Scald nodded. "Very well, then call upon the one you wish to light the way."

Albrecht turned his head and stepped before Vardan, carefully holding the lantern as though it were a precious thing. "Vardan, I-I call upon you to light the way for us. Would-Would you—"

"Of course I would." Vardan chuckled, bringing a small smirk to Albrecht's face. He then took the lantern and made his way into his position at the head of the procession, several feet before Aegir.

Albrecht took another deep breath and turned to Alistair and Daemyn. "You two ready?"

Before they answered, another Raven Sister stepped beside Scald Yorath. She was holding a violet urn decorated with white roses, painted around its base. "Before we head out," Daemyn's eyes widened as Albrecht turned to the man, wincing as he saw the urn, "we gathered what we could of Queen Ayunli. Do you still wish to carry her to the beach yourselves?"

"Aye, thank you," Albrecht answered, his words sounding choked, and took his mother's urn from the Scald. He cradled her carefully as one would a newborn babe close to his chest. With a bow, he whispered something Alistair couldn't make out, and gently kissed the porcelain surface. He then walked to his brother. "Daemyn, do you still want to do this? If it's too hard I—"

"I'm ready." Daemyn swallowed, tears falling freely down his tawny cheeks. There was only a moment of hesitation before he reached his trembling hands out and touched them to the urn. He pulled his mother close and bowed his head, just as Albrecht had done moments before. But instead of a final message, Daemyn gently kissed the porcelain surface and stood.

Now it was their turn to take their places behind Vardan. The gates of the courtyard were left wide open. Looking up, the sky was fading from orange to a deep violet. Stars slowly blinked in and out of existence. It was so clear that had Alistair not seen the storm which ravaged the city with his own eyes, he wouldn't believe it had happened at all.

His heart was beginning to race. It was time. As he looked past Vardan, through the opening into the courtyard, he was taken aback to see a sea of candlelights lighting the way. "Wait, are the people—"

"Thanks to Scald Yorath," Albrecht interrupted, also staring out into the courtyard, bright blue eyes shining with tears, "he was able to rest many of the fears over my father. I wasn't going to force anyone to march with us, nor did I want to force them to meet with us as we walked, but," he looked at Alistair with a small shrug, "I was told to expect a mass all the same."

"When the Lantern Bearer is ready, the march shall begin." The Scald called out from behind Aegir, wielding an iron orb, white incense smoke billowing out of it.

Alistair's heart drummed in his chest. The march to the black beach was upon them, but he didn't at all feel ready for it. Albrecht took a deep breath and slid a hand around Daemyn's arm, squeezing him tight, as if to keep him from slipping away. Glancing down at his own hands, Alistair realized he too was trembling. He then looked up at Albrecht, feeling a flutter in his chest as his friend smiled warmly back, nodding him over to do as he had done.

Alistair took a deep breath and approached Daemyn, carefully sliding his hand around Daemyn's other arm, feeling him squeeze into his touch. His heart warmed at that. He shifted his weight, unsure of what to do with his other hand. It startled him as a pair of hands slid around him. Looking to see who it was, Alistair was taken aback to find Valhalla stepping in beside him. An explosion of warmth flowed up his arm, and he let out a breath.

"Thank you." He whispered.

She nodded with an encouraging grin.

Swallowing, he struggled to turn his eyes away from her, and suddenly asked, "C-Could you—"

"If you'd like me to."

Somehow, she knew exactly what he was going to say, that in this moment he needed her company, just as lungs needed air, and her response lifted a weight from his shoulders. "I very much would."

Valhalla pressed in closer to him, wrapping her arm around his and lacing her fingers between his own, causing butterflies to flutter in his chest.

"Alright, Vardan," Albrecht said, looking at the man, "we're ready."

Vardan nodded, then proceeded out the gates of the castle. Daemyn was first to step forward, pulling Alistair and Albrecht along after Vardan. As they grew closer to the threshold of the castle, Scald Yorath began his chant. His voice was soothing, his elegant tones echoing out from the throne room, and soon joined by the other members of the order. The chant grew in volume as others in the gathering added their voices to the mass until it felt like the whole of Svartr was feeling the same despair that was nesting in Alistair's chest.

Now, outside, Alistair was taken aback by the sheer volume of people who had shown up for the procession. From the chant alone, he knew to expect many, but seeing them lining the sides of the cobblestone road, candles in hand to light the way, drove home just how well regarded Aegir had been. Children held a myriad of species of flowers, violet and black roses, little blavises, and bright dahlias, to name a few. As Vardan reached the first of them, the children tossed the flowers at his feet, a custom dating back all the way to the first of Aegir's line, a sign of the people's respect for the royal family.

It was a long walk to reach the edge of the city, but from there it would only be a short way further to the Stairs of Svartr, which led to the black beach below. Darkness had crept over the realm. Stars twinkled above so vividly that it looked as though the sky itself was weeping.

Alistair looked down at Daemyn, who was, to his surprise, smiling serenely at his mother's urn in his arms. Albrecht's gaze stayed locked forward, seemingly not focused on any one thing or person but to something only he could see. Perhaps it was a future that would now never come to pass, or a glimpse of memories from when his father and mother were still alive. Alistair chose to believe it was his father's spirit he was seeing, guiding him on the path forward. If that were true, then maybe Daemyn was smiling because his mother's soul was whispering to him that all would be okay and that she loved him dearly.

Alistair found himself squeezing Valhalla's hand and forced his grip to soften. He was thankful that she hadn't once pulled away, likely sensing his anxiety and taking it upon herself to help shoulder his burden, which seemed to be so natural a thing for her to do. Though their meeting had been under the worst of circumstances, she had shown her quality time and again, and it meant the world to him to have her at his side in this moment. Without her, he honestly wasn't sure if he would have had the strength to make this march. He had always hated this part of the funeral march. It was the anticipation that built during the long walk. Waiting to get to the destination. Waiting to place the dead on their pyre. Waiting for goodbyes. Waiting for the flames to take the dead.

Waiting. Waiting. And more waiting.

He would've much preferred to say farewell and set the deceased aflame before their home. This, he believed, would be easier for both the deceased and those left behind. To him, doing so would allow the living to gather together where the dearly departed had lived, to spend time mourning together and reminiscing, telling stories and celebrating all which the deceased had accomplished in life, good and bad. This would also, in his mind, give the departed a place to rest in comfort as their spirit awaited the Valkyries, where they could survey all the lives theirs had touched. The procession, on the other hand, felt painfully cold, and while many were in attendance, it always made Alistair feel more alone.

With that tiring thought, he snapped back to the present and found himself exiting the final gate leading out of Svartr.

The Scald and the rest of his order had moved on to a new chant. The farmers and sailors who lived outside the city had cleared a path to the stairs situated on the city's left side, which would take them to the beach. He could hear the waves crashing against the shores below.

They rounded a grassy dune, and an extravagant longship came into view, awaiting them half on land and half in the water. It was surrounded by more members of the Ravens of Ódin, each holding a long torch with its end embedded in the dark sand. Continuing down the black stone steps to the beach, Vardan stepped aside, allowing the Raven Monks carrying Aegir to go on ahead to the longship, and as they reached it, they became as statues awaiting the Scald to finish his chant.

Alistair released his hold on Daemyn and grasped his father's ring nestled safely under his clothes. It was almost time for Aegir's send-off, and while he had known this would be difficult, he hadn't realized the depths of pain that would resurface in going through this ceremony yet again. He wanted so badly to numb these feelings, to be the pillar of strength his friends would need, though he knew they would never ask nor expect that of him. Still, he wished he could do that for them, and as a trickle of guilt flowed into his chest, he recalled Albrecht's words, which washed over him like the cool waters lapping on the beach. Aegir was just as much a father to him as he was to them. A breathy sob escaped him, and he felt Valhalla's embrace tighten on his arm. He distantly wanted to look at her, to thank her, but Alistair couldn't tear his eyes away from Aegir's silhouette under the veil.

Scald Yorath finally finished his chant and turned to Daemyn. "We shall settle the Queen, before we settle her King."

Raven Monks then approached Daemyn. Alistair could feel him shiver as they drew closer and was sure it wasn't only due to the freezing, salty wind. Albrecht held his brother close and leaned down, whispering something in his ear. A shaky breath escaped the young Prince, and moments later, he handed their mother's urn to the monks. Tears spilled down his cheeks. "I'll miss you, Mother."

One of the monks accepted the urn and bowed low to Daemyn, softly offering him their condolences. Cradling Ayunli carefully in their arms, the monks walked to the longship and gently set her in the center of a circular gap. After which, the Scald waved those carrying Aegir over, and they too set him on the boat atop Ayunli.

Vardan stepped toward Albrecht and grasped his shoulder. "Do you want to loose the arrow?"

With a deep breath, his eyes not flinching from his father, he nodded. "Aye." His voice came with a croak.

A Raven Sister approached the pair, holding a black bow intricately decorated with a sea serpent, the symbol of the Svartr house, and an arrow with its head wrapped in an oily cloth. Albrecht took it, and both he and Vardan walked into the waters, their ankles getting soaked by the rolling waves, and the monks began pushing the longship from where it rested in the sand.

"The great sea serpent, Vidir, escorted us to these lands, giving us these safe grounds for generations." Scald Yorath exclaimed for all to hear. "Being part of Lord Njörd's domain, we ask Vidir to recognize these two great souls, so that after they travel to Helheim, the valkyries will carry them to his great hall overlooking the sea. The sea is life, the land is temporary."

Everyone on the beach repeated the saying, and as the water picked up the longship, it began carrying Aegir and Ayunli out to sea. Albrecht, without missing a beat, knocked the arrow, and Vardan opened his lantern, allowing him to touch the flame with the oil-soaked cloth, which immediately burst into flame.

Sucking in a deep breath, Albrecht aimed skywards and pulled the arrow back, holding the arrow but not releasing. As time slipped away, still he didn't release. Alistair looked to him and noticed his friend's shoulders were trembling, and he heard him curse with a grimace.

Vardan then carefully placed a hand on Albrecht's shoulder. "It's alright, just take another breath and whisper a final farewell into the arrow. It'll reach your parents, I promise."

Albrecht seemed to ease a bit with that and then did as Vardan suggested. With a gulp, he whispered something into the shaft of the arrow, lightly touching his tawny cheek, and after one more deep breath, he released. The fiery arrow shot into the dark night sky. Half a moon shone its light across the water's surface, brightening the way as the flame arched and fell, striking true.

The fires spread quickly and bloomed as brightly as the sun. All were quiet. The only sounds were those of the crackling ship and waters lapping against the black sands.

Daemyn bent over beside Alistair, holding his stomach, which gave him a fright. Albrecht reacted faster, spinning around and dropping the ceremonial bow to the sand. He ran several paces to his little brother, followed closely by Vardan. As they reached him, they stood Daemyn erect, the young man unable to hold back the stream of tears running down his face as he gasped between sobs. Albrecht wrapped his arms around his brother's shoulders, and Daemyn's hands latched onto his older brother's back.

Albrecht gently caressed Daemyn's flaxen hair as they knelt into the sand. "We can stay out here for as long as you want, until you're ready to go home."

Daemyn only responded with a silent nod, and the two watched their father's longship sail into the distance until it was nothing more than an orange dot on the dark horizon. Alistair sat close beside them. As he reached down to run his fingers through the sand, Daemyn surprised him by grabbing hold of his hand and holding it, their hands resting atop his lap. Alistair was taken aback for a moment, but smiled warmly at his friend, squeezing tightly in return. Vardan set his lantern on the sand and took a seat close to Albrecht, and Valhalla remained at Alistair's side.

As the five of them sat, silently watching the waves crash against the sands, Scald Yorath knelt behind Albrecht. "Your Highness,"

Albrecht glanced back at him, then returned to the water. "I'm sorry, everyone is free to return home."

The Scald bowed his head in appreciation and made his way back onto the grassy land, announcing that the procession had ended and all were free to return home. They left the torches lit, ends buried in the sands to anchor them in place. One of the Raven Sisters retrieved the bow and followed after the rest of her order. The sounds of the crowd faded from the beach as most took leave, leaving only the occasional clanking of metal from those of the silver Queensguard and the black Svartr Kingsguard who remained by the steps. After Aegir's death, it made sense that the guards wouldn't want to leave them alone on the dark beach.

Eventually, a new sound caught Alistair's ears, footsteps crunching the sand and approaching. Alistair glanced back to see a member of Albrecht's council approach and bow. "Your Highness,"

"You'll have my answer tomorrow morning," Albrecht interrupted, throat tight and not looking back, "for tonight, please leave my brother and I be."

"Of course, your Highness. For what it's worth, we are sorry to have to push this decision on you. May you have a good night."

Albrecht didn't respond and hugged his little brother closer. The Lord bowed his head low again and left them be. A whistle caught Alistair's attention, and he found Vardan looking at Valhalla, miming something with his hands, and she nodded, seemingly understanding. Alistair raised a questioning brow at them.

Adjusting herself into a kneeling position, Valhalla cupped her hands over her mouth and blew into them, causing a bright orange glow trapped within her palms. Tossing her hands forward, she conjured a fire just large enough to bathe them in its light and warmth.

Albrecht chuckled lightly and raised a gloved palm to the flames. "That feels wonderful, thank you."

Daemyn then blurted out, "Did I ever tell you about the time I almost burned down the castle's kitchen?"

"WHAT?" Both Alistair and Albrecht exclaimed.

The younger Prince straightened, seemingly comfortable in his place wedged between his brothers, and sighed. "It was while you were gone. I wanted to surprise Father with a special nameday breakfast."

"So, instead of asking one of the cooks to make something, you tried to cook it yourself? With absolutely NO experience?" Albrecht teased, a grin forming.

Daemyn dropped his face into his hands, trying to hide his shame. "I thought it would mean more coming from me, alright!"

Alistair shrugged. "I always ask the cooks to teach me when I find myself wandering into the kitchen. It's not difficult to learn. "

"Speak for yourself," Valhalla grumbled, looking away and cheeks turning a deep shade of red, her clear embarrassment making Alistair laugh.

"Still," Daemyn continued, "I accidentally left the fires unattended, and one thing led to another. I thought Father would be furious, but he only sighed. Mother laughed. Thankfully, no one got hurt, and the fire was dealt with before it got out of control. He just told me that next time I find myself inspired to try something new—"

"To ask someone who knows what they are doing?" Both Alistair and Albrecht said together, followed by more laughter.

Daemyn pouted and raised his nose. "Well, excuse me for not being so naturally gifted at cooking."

"Says the one who can paint as if gifted by Bragi himself." Albrecht teased, poking his little brother's puffed-out cheeks.

"Not to mention being so musically inclined," Alistair added.

"Vardan, can you please help me out here?" Daemyn pleaded with a roll of his eyes.

Raising his hands in the air, Vardan chortled. "Don't look at me, I was taught to cook before we fled from the old lands, but you're not alone." He pointed with a thumb at Valhalla, "This one here can't cook at all. If it came down to starving to death or surviving only on her concoctions, I'm sorry to say I'd choose death."

Valhalla let out a flustered gasp, making all three Princes burst out laughing. "Well, I NEVER! Excuse me for trying." Crossing her arms over her chest, she ignored Vardan's apology and looked away.

It continued like that for the rest of the night. One of them would share a memory of Aegir and Ayunli, usually something that ended with embarrassment for the one telling the tale and leaving the rest roaring with laughter. Vardan shared inspiring stories, adding some diversity to the evening and leaving them all a warm feeling in their hearts. As the night grew later, even long after Aegir's fire had disappeared under the horizon, not one of them showed signs they were ready to return to the castle, for if they did, it would bring them one step closer to tomorrow. One step closer to Alistair crowning his best friend the new King of Svartr, and none of them were ready for that next step.

64

Alistair

Take a Breath

Alistair paced in his bedchamber. Wringing his hands together, he tried to focus his breathing to calm the churning in his stomach. It didn't help. He was sure he'd vomit before the day was done.

Stopping, he looked himself over in a tall mirror that had been brought out for him to inspect his attire before the coronation. He was dressed in all white, the crowning ceremony outfit meant only for a member of the Hilliard high royal family, but made in the Svartr style to match their fashion. A long pointed coat reached his ankles. His long cape would have dragged behind him as he walked had he not been clutching it in his hands so as to not trip. Silken gloves covered his hands, and an eight-buttoned vest and buttoned shirt fit snugly to his torso. A cascaded jabot spilled over his chest. Silver accents adorned his attire in the form of buttons and raven stitch work on the coat, cape, and vest. Instead of his usual simple silver circlet, he now donned his mother's silver raven crown.

After sending word of Aegir's death by raven, in a few days, Alistair's mother surprised him with a parcel containing her crown, with a note of her own. Due to the suddenness of Aegir's death, she was certain the council would demand a coronation as soon as possible and so sent her crown by the fastest route in her stead. It arrived by boat at the city of Erevol, and then was shepherded here by horse. Alistair's crowning garments had been another surprise gift from Aegir. As with the funeral garments, the late King knew Alistair would be around in the event of his death to crown his son. It surprised Alistair and Albrecht both at just how prepared Aegir had been for this outcome. Perhaps a part of him had resisted Tamanna's control just long enough to put these safeguards in motion, or maybe this had been something he'd set in motion years before and had garments prepared annually. There was no way to know now that he was gone.

Anxiety thrummed through Alistair's veins. His chest tightened, and he began pacing once again. "Come on, you can do this. Just remember the words . . . Wait, what were the words again? Fuck!"

He rubbed his forehead beneath his mother's crown, its weight an ever-present reminder of the pressure he was feeling. "There are three questions, right? Or maybe there were four? NGH! Come on! The crown goes on Albrecht's head after-after—What is he supposed to say?"

Tripping over his feet, Alistair's hip crashed into the vanity, and he gritted his teeth with a groan. Slamming his back against the wall beside it, he rubbed the tender spot on his side. It was all so overwhelming. The responsibility of it all. At least he was crowning his best friend. It was the one silver lining in this mess.

The doors of his chamber swung open. Looking up, he couldn't quite make out who it was, his vision blurring from the stress.

"Alistair?" A voice called.

It was Daemyn. Alistair recognized his light voice instantly. Pushing himself off the wall, he reached out to the young Prince but found himself falling forward. Someone caught him with a groan but who it was, he didn't know. His mind floated, and the world spun.

"I-I don't think I can do this." Alistair managed to say, his body trembling as he shut his eyes.

"Don't you start too," Daemyn said with a chuckle.

"Too? Wait, don't tell me Al—" A hand slid over his back, and a chin rested on his shoulder.

"Take a deep breath, Alistair." A new voice said, Albrecht, his friend's calm breathing brushing against his ear. "You *can* do this."

Alistair stopped, feeling Daemyn's steady heartbeat under him and Albrecht's steady breath. His hands shook, but he managed to raise them up and grabbed hold of their shoulders, lifting himself upright. The room started to clear.

"S-Sorry, I—"

"Oh, shut it, you." Daemyn cut him off.

Rubbing his eyes, Alistair gazed down and found Daemyn's teasing smile beaming back up at him. He sighed with a soft chuckle. "Listen, my anxiety almost made me pass out."

"And I was here to catch you." Daemyn placed a hand on Alistair's chest, and his expression shifted, likely feeling Alistair's ring hidden beneath his clothes.

Albrecht then cleared his throat. Daemyn jumped and stepped away, his cheeks a bright shade of pink. He turned away, and Alistair caught the quickest glimpse of his friend's bright blue eyes turning sad, making him feel a pang of guilt.

"Anyway," Albrecht said before Alistair could speak, "how're you feeling?"

"I uh," Alistair fiddled with his thumbs, "honestly, I want to vomit."

"Well, that won't do. How about I open the balcony doors and windows while you finish getting ready?"

"What? Wait, what do you mean? I-I am ready?" Alistair exclaimed, eyes wide and spinning to look himself over in the mirror again. Two Gentlemen of the Bedchamber helped him get dressed. There was no way something could be wrong with what he was wearing.

Albrecht snickered and gingerly grabbed the long loose strands of Alistair's dark brown hair, which draped his shoulder. "You going to just leave your hair loose like this?"

Alistair's cheeks grew hot. He hadn't even considered his hair. Was there a proper way to wear it? "Oh fuck! Should I tie it up? Leave it down? What should I—"

"Alright, alright, relax. I'm sorry I teased you." Albrecht laughed, taking his shoulders and shaking Alistair a little.

"I just really don't want to mess today up for you. It's important."

"It is important, but it doesn't matter if you fumble a little over the words or don't quite look the part, not to me anyway." Albrecht shrugged with a smirk.

"I suppose." Alistair sighed.

"Alright, I'll open some windows and Daemyn will braid your hair." Albrecht patted his shoulders and set about opening the balcony doors while Daemyn pulled Alistair toward the vanity. He removed the silver crown from Alistair's head and allowed him to cross his arms over the furniture's surface, where he leaned and let his head fall forward.

"I can't imagine how you're feeling."

"Eh, better now. Daemyn had the foresight to open the windows in my room." He took in a deep breath of the salty sea air. "The ocean's always helped to calm me. I swear, once there's a lull in all this chaos, I'm taking the three of us sailing. No ifs and no buts. We're going. Is that clear?"

Alistair laughed and Daemyn grinned, still brushing Alistair's hair. "I'll be holding you to that promise," Daemyn muttered.

"Same." Alistair agreed.

"Hmm, you have a lot of hair. I think I'll just do a simple braid." Daemyn said as he placed the brush on the vanity and started his work.

"Aww," Alistair mocked lightheartedly, "don't stop now, it was sooooo relaxing," but Daemyn only shrugged, that usual warm smile of his not wavering in the slightest. Something about that stuck him as odd. His calm demeanor suddenly felt false. Was he just pretending to be fine for their sakes? That notion brought on an all-new nervousness in Alistair's gut. His young friend was simply too calm. "Daemyn, how're *you* doing? You better not be shouldering everything yourself again."

"Oh, trust me, he's shouldering pretty hard," Albrecht answered for him and walked over to join them, plucking a thin white ribbon off the vanity and handing it to Daemyn, who pursed his lips. "No matter what I say, I can't get the damn guppy to open up to me today."

Alistair sighed. "Daemyn, I—"

"Listen, after the two of you passed out on my bed last night, I . . . had a long while to gather my thoughts," Daemyn said as he carefully twisted Alistair's hair into braids. "You both took care of me yesterday, so today it's my turn. Let me return the favor."

"But—OW!" Alistair yelped.

Daemyn yanked Alistair's hair back, arching his neck and head back so their eyes could meet. "Be honest with me, you were pretending today wouldn't come, weren't you?"

Alistair blinked up at him. He searched for a response, but no words came to mind. Daemyn knew him all too well, even if they hadn't seen each other in over three years.

"Thought so. I thought long and hard about today, about every day after, and . . . I vowed to Vára, the Goddess of Oaths,"

"You didn't!"

Daemyn planted a hand over Alistair's mouth, his expression determined and serious.

"I vowed to be there for both of you, no matter what. There will be days the crown sits heavily, weighing you down. So, I will be there to carry that weight. Lend an ear when you need to vent. Or offer solutions to puzzles that seem impossible. Maybe even take on new responsibilities when you two need—"

Alistair yanked Daemyn's hand from his mouth, his brows knitting with anger. "You think you're being strong for us, but all you're succeeding in is hiding from your *own* troubles. What makes you think we'll be alright with that? I'm not THAT blind to miss—"

Daemyn slid his arms around Alistair's shoulders and buried his face into his neck. "Listen, I'm happy you're here, I really am, and even though these recent days have been hard, I'm beyond thankful for you and Valhalla. You helped us. Helped Father."

Alistair startled as he felt hot tears spill down his neck.

"I need to repay both of you for what you did, and this is the solution I came up with. So just . . . shut it and take my help, alright. I already had this argument with Albrecht and can't do it again!" A ripple of sadness ran through Albrecht's otherwise stoic expression as he leaned against the wall with arms crossed, silently listening to words he'd apparently already heard. "He lost so much time with Mother and Father because of the war, so godsdammit I'm going to do what I can! Yes, my heart hurts, and it'll hurt for some time. Just let me do this."

Alistair swallowed back the lump forming in his throat and raised a hand to one of Daemyn's wrists. He didn't know how to respond. What could he say? Everyone grieves differently, and who was he to deny his friend's wishes? If purpose and obligation of duty were what he needed . . . then so be it.

"Besides," Daemyn let out a soft chuckle, "you could always order me to take a break. You both outrank me, but only in social status."

"I—" Alistair's voice cracked as he met Daemyn's eyes in the reflection of the mirror. "I shouldn't have to."

"Yes, well, that doesn't change the fact that it's true." The young man answered, standing and wiping the tears from his cheeks. "You've heard it from Father and Valhalla both. I get so focused on my tasks that I forget to take care of myself. True, it's something I need to work on, but in the meantime, I'll have to rely on you. So," Daemyn raised a braid and gently placed it over Alistair's shoulder, a white thin ribbon tied at the base, "you both will just have to get used to the idea of me shadowing you for now."

"For now, but when my mind healer arrives, you'll admit all your burdens to him. That's the deal." Albrecht narrowed his eyes at his little brother.

"Aye aye, I promised I would. Now then," Daemyn waved and stepped past

Alistair to retrieve his mother's crown, then gently placed it on his head, tucking away a few loose strands of hair. "Are you ready?"

Alistair cursed, momentarily forgetting all about the ceremony. His heart quickened again. Dammit all, he hated feeling like this. He often asked why crowds bothered him so, but in truth, he knew the answer. He had been like this ever since his father's death, when he was surrounded by all those eyes staring at him as he held his lifeless father. He was just a child after all. The impact of those judgmental looks had stayed with him. He could power through his nerves as long as he was not the central focus, but when the masses' attention fell on him, all the emotions of that day sent his nerves soaring. Now, today, he would stand before so many people, to crown a friend—a King. Alistair was responsible for ascending a new ruler to the throne in front of the whole city.

Did people expect him to do this flawlessly? He hoped not.

Planting his hands on the vanity, he struggled but managed to stand, noticing in the corner of his eye as his friend's expressions turned to worry. He managed one entire step before doubling over, grabbing at his chest, searching for his father's ring.

"FUCK! No. No, I don't think I can—"

"Hey, hey hey hey hey hey! Alistair, look at me." Albrecht planted a hand on his shoulders, forcing him back to his feet. Albrecht held him upright, and Alistair latched onto his arms to keep himself steady, terrified that he might fall again were he to let go. His eyes welled with tears.

Breathe. He couldn't breathe.

"Alistair, look at me!" Albrecht exclaimed. "Take. A deep. Breath."

Alistair's body shook, and he felt small under Albrecht's bright blue stare, but he did as commanded and sucked in a small breath.

"Now hold it."

His eyes went wide with disbelief. Why? There wasn't much in his lungs to begin with. He needed—wanted to breathe, and he looked at his friend with confusion

"Just follow me, alright?" Albrecht answered and took one of Alistair's hands, holding it to his chest. He then placed his free hand over Alistair's chest, likely feeling his heart banging against his ribs. "Now, I'm going to count to ten. One."

Alistair's lips parted. Why was he so nervous? Albrecht continued to count. "Three. Four."

Alistair's vision went blurry.

"Seven. Eight. Nine. Ten. Exhale."

Alistair let out the small breath he had been holding and gasped. He felt like he'd been underwater, but then a sensation washed through him, faint but there. It was the beginning of relief. He could hear, feel Albrecht's steady breathing and rhythmic thumping of his heart. It was like a guide, and he felt his body easing into synchronicity.

The two stood there before one another, one breath in, count to ten, one breath out. They repeated the steps over and over. He didn't fully relax, not really, but as they continued the ritual, he regained some semblance of control. He shook his head. "I can't do this."

"Yes, you can. Don't rush this. Don't force it. We will take the ceremony as slowly as you want. One step at a time, isn't that what the common folk say?" He chuckled softly.

"But . . . I'm not you, Albrecht." Alistair whispered.

Albrecht smirked at that. "You're right, you're not."

Alistair was taken aback. Not because of what he admitted, but because he did so genuinely, with no mockery behind it. Albrecht slid his hand from Alistair's heart to the back of his neck, pulling him close and touching their foreheads together. "And that's alright. You're you, Alistair. Just you. And that's all anyone expects from you. I may be able to hold myself together when the need calls for it, but that doesn't mean I don't feel fear." He chuckled as a look of guilt crossed his face. "You nearly rushed headfirst after Valhalla when she was pulled into the earth by those aptr—whatever she called them, and what did I do? I just sat there holding you back, because . . . I was afraid I was going to lose you, too. You were brave when I wasn't."

Albrecht gazed at Alistair with a sigh, letting his head fall back as he stared up into the firelight of the crystal chandelier above. "Afterward, she told me to not worry about it, that she understands the hold fear can have, that fear can hold even the bravest among us."

He rubbed his face, his expression turning amused.

"I told her that I wished fear hadn't held me down, that if it weren't for that, she wouldn't have been buried. She then told me, in her no-nonsense sort of wisdom, that we're only human. She understood my fears and asked how often I found myself faced off against the undead and dark magic." He laughed and brushed his fingers through his loosely tied hair, fastened in a deep blue ribbon.

"Fighting against the living beings who can feel fear and pain is vastly different than fighting something like that." Alistair shrugged.

"I know, I'm straying off topic, what I was trying to say is this," Albrecht cupped Alistair's hands in his, "it's normal to feel scared. It's normal to be nervous. I certainly am, but so long as you and Daemyn are with me, I can get through this. All you need to do is put a crown on my head. If we can survive fighting against the undead, we sure as fuck can survive a crowning." The three of them shared a laugh, and Albrecht clapped Alistair on the shoulder. "Feel better?"

He exhaled but grinned. "Barely. I don't know if I'll ever get over crowds, but I suppose you're right about one thing,"

"And what's that?"

"I can face this, so long as the two of you are with me."

Albrecht grinned. "That's the spirit. Although this day came much sooner than any of us had expected, it is still a day Father and I had been looking forward to, a day he made sure I was *ready* for, no matter the situation. So, let's go make Father proud."

65

Alistair

The Crowning of a King

Alistair stood before the doors of the throne room, hearing the murmur of the crowd on the other side. A bead of sweat slid down his brow. Tapping the tips of his thumbs against his fingers one by one, he took a deep breath, holding it to a count of ten, and then released it.

Albrecht placed a hand on his shoulder. "You ready?"

He took another deep breath before answering, his nerves not as frayed as they had been, yet still somewhere between panic and calm. "As ready as I'll ever be."

"I know," Albrecht said and glanced at Daemyn. "Do you mind standing by us on the dais? Even after I kneel?"

He was noticeably taken aback. "O-Of course! Honestly, I wasn't even sure where I was supposed to stand in all this."

Albrecht snickered. "Somehow, I *had* a feeling. Alright," he patted Alistair's back, practically pushing him forward, "lead the way, your Grace."

Alistair rolled his eyes. He couldn't find any joy in his friend's teasing at the moment; instead, far too concentrated in holding himself together.

Looking at their guards before the doors, they snapped to attention and awaited his cue. With another deep breath, he ordered, "Go ahead."

They nodded and opened the doors. The metal hinges creaked loudly. The entire hall instantly fell quiet as all eyes set upon him. With a gulp, trying to keep his expression as stoic as possible, he took a step, then another, and another. He couldn't stop his heart from racing, but knowing both Albrecht and Daemyn were close behind helped.

As they climbed the dais, he kept his eyes off the throne. He didn't want yet another reminder of Aegir. He then noticed a familiar Scald standing to the left side of the Svartr throne, accompanied by a young boy of about eight, with deep tawny skin, holding an iron crown. It looked to have been crafted after Svartr's leviathan, with sparkling sapphire eyes, resting upon a deep blue pillow.

Before greeting Scald Yorath, Alistair planted his hands on his knees and grinned. "Hello, and who might you be?"

"The name's Thorin, um,"

"Your Grace." Scald Yorath whispered down to the boy.

"Your Grace! I'm Lilianna's grandson." The boy, Thorin, flashed Alistair a grin with some crooked teeth.

Alistair appreciated the child's excitement. "It's a pleasure to meet you, Thorin. Did she ask you to take care of Albrecht's crown?"

"Aye! In fact, my papa was the one who made it for the late King."

Alistair was taken aback at that. "R-Really? Is everyone in your family close to the Svartr's?"

"Young Waylonsson here has family that dates back to the very, *very*, beginning, your Grace." Scald Yorath answered, and despite the half mask over his face, Alistair was sure the man was smiling underneath.

"That's amazing! You promise you've been taking good care of my friend's crown?" Alistair shot him a raised brow, and Thorin just nodded enthusiastically.

"Uh huh! Grandmama told me it was reeeeeal important. So I made sure not to drop it."

Alistair snorted, amused alongside Albrecht and Daemyn. "That's good to hear. Well, ready to take your place beside me then?"

"Aye!" Thorin rushed to Alistair's side.

He and Albrecht then faced one another, his friend and soon-to-be King winking as their eyes met and he bent a knee. Taking another deep breath,

Alistair raised his gaze to the crowd and was surprised to find Valhalla at the very back of the hall, leaning against the large gate out of the castle, Vardan beside her. Her bright azure cloak was a stark contrast to everyone else's dark attire.

She noticed his stare, giving him an encouraging smile and a small wave.

Unable to pull his eyes away from her, he felt his posture relaxing and in that moment decided that she would be his focus while addressing the crowd, pretending it was just the two of them alone in a chamber as he had in Hilliard.

"Many things have happened these past several months that are . . . hard to explain." He started, his throat tightening at what Daemyn had told him about Aegir. "The late King was brainwashed by a man whom he thought to be a friend. This sorcerer poisoned King Aegir and used him to orchestrate the unfortunate events which have been felt by each and every one of us."

The people bowed their heads low, some looking somber while others were unreadable.

"However, despite those dark months, let's not forget the good memories we all share of the late King. He loved and cared for his sons, as well as his people." Recalling all his memories of Aegir, those days when Aegir would pull Alistair and Albrecht aside to show them blueprints given to him by inventors, architects, and alchemists. Alistair realized too late the importance of those plans. "From looking for innovative ways to keep this castle city safe and well fed, to sending those he trusted to check on his son in a war leagues away."

Although Vardan leaned against the wall with arms crossed over his chest and eye closed, projecting what was likely a practiced show of indifference, Alistair caught sight of a small smirk on the man's rugged face. Even Albrecht grinned at that, touching the Ring of Svartr on his finger, which had been one of the last gifts given to him by his father when he still lived.

"King Aegir will be missed. Land is temporary, sea is eternal." Alistair finished, and the crowd repeated the Svartr saying.

It was now or never. Looking at Thorin, the boy's smile stretched from ear to ear, and Alistair forced a smile of his own. The boy raised the crown high to Alistair, and with a deep breath, Alistair carefully accepted it, pressing his cupped hands around the swirling base and presenting it aloft for all in the throne room to see.

"Do you, Albrecht Svartr, promise to care for these lands for the rest of your days, until death takes you?" Alistair enunciated as loudly and clearly as he could.

"I do," Albrecht replied, courage burning in his bright blue eyes.

"Do you, Albrecht Svartr, promise to keep the peace not only within your lands, but with the lands touched by others both far and near?"

"I do."

"Do you, Albrecht Svartr, also promise to cast aside all selfish ambitions, to rule this land with a kind heart and a strong mind?"

"I do," Albrecht answered every question without hesitation, his usual stoicism worn with practiced perfection, and after the final question he smirked with a wink.

Alistair's heart warmed at the sigh. He knew Albrecht would do all that he could to keep his castle city, his region, and the people who lived there safe and prosperous. Albrecht wouldn't roll over for anyone, least of all him, but if Alistair were to ask for aid, he knew Albrecht would do everything he could to help.

With a small nod, Alistair placed the crown on his friend's head and announced to all in the throne room, "Then rise, King Albrecht Svartr, first of his name. May Ódin's light bless your path and Njörd's seas remain forever calm."

Now it was Albrecht's turn to take a deep breath, and as he stood, he did so as though no weight pressed against his shoulders. His posture was strong and confident, and with a nod to Alistair, he spun to face the crowd. He pushed his deep blue cape back and stared them down, waiting to see how they would react. First were his black kingsguards, pounding their fists against their chests with a loud clang in salute to their new King. Then a wave of claps echoed in the halls, growing to thunderous applause, the people cheering, "Land is Temporary, Sea is Eternal. Take the helm, King Albrecht!"

Daemyn was the first of the three to sigh with relief, making Alistair chuckle. He then grabbed Alistair's arm, pulling him to stand on the other side of his brother. Before he had a chance to let the tension drain from his shoulders, his older friend, now King, grabbed his hand and raised it high before the crowd, symbolizing continued support and friendship with the Hillard royal family. It took his breath away as the cheering drowned out his beating heart.

Looking out over the crowd, he gave the people a bashful smile and attempted to hold himself as confidently as Albrecht, but his gaze kept drifting to the very back of the hall. Valhalla clapped and grinned at the pair, but Vardan didn't. His posture was just as it had been the last time he looked at him, but now an encouraging smirk rested on his face. The moment, though, was short-lived as just as Alistair had looked at him, the man hopped off the wall and exited the castle gates. Valhalla, seeming taken aback and confused by her friend's actions, followed after him.

66

Valhalla

There's More to this Life

"Vardan," Valhalla called out, "are you sure you don't want to stay? At least until the festivities have wrapped up?"

He stopped before the stairs that led down into the courtyard. Pulling out a black and gold ornate pipe and rectangular tin filled with tobacco leaves and matches, he tapped the metal surface and sighed. "I'd like to. I really would. To be able to walk these streets with the Svartr royal family, it sounds wonderful." Vardan then looked at her with a crooked smile. "I do so miss this place, but these boys' safety must come first. We have to know if Tamanna's home country seeks war, or if, as I suspect, they too were an unfortunate victim of that man's experimentations."

"Then why not wait and hear from these dancers staying in Sailors Reef?"

Vardan just shrugged, popping open his tin and stuffing several of the dried tobacco leaves into the bowl of his pipe. "Prince Daemyn will speak with them for me while I ready my ship in Flotnar. It'll be at least a week before I can leave. Making preparations and gathering a crew for the journey will take time. So, any information he garners from them can be sent to me by raven in Svartr's sister city."

"I suppose." Valhalla wove her fingers together over her stomach and gazed at the ground. There was a strange aching sensation in her chest, like an invisible hand was squeezing her insides.

"By the way," Vardan said, then took a long drag from his pipe, an orange glow brightening in the bowl, "did you give the journal back? If you don't find any more information there, you should leave it for Albrecht and his council for further inspection."

Valhalla's shoulders slumped. "I scoured through that book front and back. There was only one entry on Kiara, and even then, there was barely anything there except that she came to him with her dark crystals. I just need to figure out *why*."

Vardan grunted and leaned against the stone railings of the stairway. "*You* don't need to do anything. Lady Vitalia told you to stop inquiring about her daughter. Just tell her and Aura what you found, and let them take care of the rest."

Valhalla rolled her eyes and crossed her arms in defiance. Intellectually, she knew if it came down to another fight between her and Kiara, she was completely outmatched by the ex-Valkyrie, but she couldn't shake the urge to continue digging.

Vardan narrowed his one eye at her and, with sternness in his tone, called out, "Valhalla."

She scoffed. "Fine! I'll tell them what I know, but this is so damn—"

As she turned to pace, she bumped into someone and startled, recognition blooming in her face. "Your Grace?" She exclaimed. "I'm sorry, I wasn't paying attention."

Alistair laughed warmly and gently caught her by the shoulders, steadying her. "No, I'm sorry. I didn't mean to startle you from your conversation like that."

"But you did mean to startle me?" She regained her composure and raised a brow, flashing him a smirk so he would know it was a jest.

"No, you're right. Anyway, I saw you two leaving without so much as a farewell and wanted to check on you. Is everything alright?"

"Oh, um," she turned to Vardan, hoping he might have an answer, but he was now completely lost in smoking his pipe. So it was just her, it seemed.

"Well, firstly, I learned what I could from Tamanna's journal and left it on Albrecht's desk this morning."

"Thank you. Albrecht wanted to check for any hideouts the man may have written about. Now that the council has calmed down, we should be able to read through the passages more carefully, catch anything we missed the first time. If we're lucky, there may be clues as to where he's heading next. By the way, were you able to find what you needed?"

Valhalla dismissed his concerns. "Trust me, you don't need to worry about my issues, Your Grace. However, if you do find Tamanna, can you ask him more about this Kiara woman he briefly mentioned in his journal?"

"Of course, anything specific?"

Valhalla's mind began to swirl with possibilities, but there was one thing she wanted to know more than anything else. "Just, does he know what her goals are?"

"That's all?" He asked with a tilt of his head. Her chest fluttered at his curious expression, and as much as she would've liked to tell him everything, that certainly would lead him into danger. If she revealed her entire history with Kiara and that the woman had nearly killed her when she was fourteen falls young, Alistair would surely take on her burdens. But he had enough on his plate already and would be safer left out of Kiara's sight.

"Yes. That's all."

"Alright then, I'll let Albrecht know."

"Let me know what?" The voice of the newly appointed King rang out.

Both Valhalla and Alistair jumped. Albrecht apparently was just as stealthy as Alistair.

Alistair laughed and patted his chest. "Are you sure you should be out here right now?"

"I could be asking you the same thing." He shot Alistair a playful look and stopped beside him. "Besides, I gave them the same half truth you did; just needed some fresh air." Albrecht shrugged, then nudged him with an elbow, causing Alistair to purse his lips.

"Now, what did you want to tell me?" He turned to Valhalla.

"She just wanted to know if Tamanna knew what this Kiara is up to," Alistair answered. "I think I remembered seeing her name pop up in the journal at least once."

"Same. I'll do what I can after we find the murderer, but there's little to go on. I'd squash any expectations you harbour that he knows anything more."

"I know." Valhalla exhaled. "I'll take anything by this point, and I appreciate you looking into this for me."

"Of course, after what you did for us, it's the least we can do." Albrecht grinned. "Whatever we get out of Tamanna, I'll send word to Vardan. It's a town called Alf, right?"

Vardan puffed out several gray rings of smoke and nodded.

"Alright, now what else? You look like you have more to tell us."

Valhalla startled. Was she that easy to read? Scanning the ground between them, she thought about what she found concerning Daemyn in Tamanna's journal. Albrecht now had the book, but by the time they found what she knew, it might be too late.

"It has to do with his Highness, Prince Daemyn." She finally said, garnering new concern from Alistair and Albrecht.

"What about me?" Another voice joined the conversation.

It was Daemyn's voice. Of course it was, she thought. How was it that all three of them were so good at sneaking up on her?

Albrecht cleared his throat. "And here I thought you were distracting the sharks for me."

"Don't change the subject. I heard my name, so what's wrong?" Daemyn's expression was so uncharacteristically serious that it startled each of them.

Alistair and Albrecht both turned to Valhalla, Daemyn's gaze following just after. A flicker of fear showed through the young Prince's eyes, as though he already knew the topic, and before she could answer, he asked, "What did he do to me?"

That answered that, then. She knew she'd likely have to be the one to tell them, Daemyn especially, and there was no knowing how long it would take to find Tamanna. With a deep breath, she answered, "While looking through the journal, it seemed Tamanna had many methods of control he inflicted on his victims, one that especially caught my eye involved the use of nightmares and inducing fears into the victim's mind."

Daemyn clutched his hands to his chest and stared at her with wide eyes. "Am I-Am I cursed?"

"I—" She sighed, hating that this was only causing him more worry. "I believe so. I'm not adept in curses, especially those pertaining to dark magic, but from what I *can* remember, you need to place yourself in a stress-free environment and over time, the magic should fade."

"That means, should any nightmares plague you after today, you *better* not keep them to yourself," Vardan added with a narrowing stare, but Daemyn glanced away.

"But what if they get worse?" He asked, voice soft.

"That's why I'm saying you need to tell me if that happens. I know someone who can help."

"Then why not call that person here now?" Albrecht asked, desperation clinging to his voice.

Vardan shook his head. "She's not that easy to reach. Besides, she always comes to me."

"Do you want me to ask for her?" Valhalla said softly, but he shook his head again.

"I'm going to be gone from these lands for some time, and you know how *you know who* keeps his warrior maidens busy. No, just tell her I could use her aid when she becomes available. As for you two," he turned to Alistair and Albrecht, "make sure the guppy here doesn't overwork himself, alright?"

"I'll do my best, Lord Vardan." Albrecht teased with a smirk and a bow of his head.

Vardan sneered, which seemed a weak attempt to hide his smile. "I'm outta here." He said and started down the stairs, waving farewell, and he headed to his black Clydedale, Ótta, already waiting for him with Lilianna. "I'll be back as soon as I can."

Valhalla and the others snickered. "He truly does care about this place," Daemyn said, smiling as he turned to her, "doesn't he?"

She nodded. "He does. I promise you, there's no one more loyal than Vardan to have on your side. Please, don't misuse him."

"That's a promise I'll be honored to keep." Albrecht raised a hand outstretched, and she took it, cupping her hand with his other. "Also, thank you once more for helping us. If you ever find yourself in Oceana, Svartr especially, please say hello." He then leaned close and whispered so only she could hear. "Also, don't tell Vardan, but with Lilianna's help, I'll be sprucing up his estate, whether he likes it or not." He winked, making her giggle shrilly.

"Thank you, that would be greatly appreciated. From what I was told, it was a beautiful longhouse back when it was originally built. I'm sure it'd warm his heart to see it so again." She smiled warmly at them while sliding her grip out of Albrecht's. "Take care, the three of you."

Valhalla then followed after Vardan, and about halfway down the steps, a memory of the three of them exiting the castle came to mind, of when she was attacked by aptrgongu-madrs and facing off against Tamanna and Aegir. Everyone in the castle city had been put to sleep, or they should've been. Vardan even explained what happened to him after reaching his longhouse. So, how did it not affect the three Princes?

"Valhalla?" Alistair called her name, making her jump in place.

"Sorry, um, something about the night I faced Tamanna and Aegir has me curious. Tamanna said he placed a sleeping spell over all of Svartr, so how was it that you three were awake?"

Alistair let out a sharp breath as Albrecht's and Daemyn's eyes fell upon him. Raising a hand to the back of his neck, his brows knitted. "It's . . . hard to explain." He eventually answered.

"Alistair was pacing in my chamber while waiting for you to get back. He claimed he had a terrible feeling all that day that something bad was going to happen, to you or just in general." Albrecht glanced at Alistair, then at the ground with an irked frown. "Safe to say he was right. After the spell was likely cast, Alistair here said he heard a voice?"

Alistair nodded. "It was like hundreds of whispers flooding my mind all at once. These two didn't hear a thing."

"A black mist nearly consumed Albrecht and I," Daemyn continued. "Alistair was the first to notice it, and he—"

"In my panic, I-I somehow summoned a dome of light which shielded us from the mist." Placing a hand on his hip, the other wiping his forehead, confusion and worry crossed his features. "I don't even know how. I didn't even say the command spell!"

Valhalla's brows furrowed. "Somehow?"

"The magic came from me, that much is certain. I just, I don't—"

Valhalla rushed back up the steps, heart fluttering, and took Alistair's hands in hers, surprised by the warmth that came from his touch despite wearing gloves. "Your Grace, your magic isn't something to fear. Light is a repellent to darkness, and vice versa. You told me you were relearning your light magic, correct?" Alistair nodded wordlessly. "But didn't you already know some protective spells?"

"I—Well, yes, but—"

"Your magic," she placed a hand on his chest, feeling what was likely his father's ring under his clothes, "i-is as sentient as you and I. Depending on your emotions, the magic within you can react on its own. That happens to many novices in training. When I started out, I literally burst into flames whenever I got angry."

The boys all chuckled at that. As she withdrew her hands, Daemyn waved at her. "Alright, spiking emotions aside, should he still be acting that way? He's been practicing it since he was young."

"Well, that depends, how easy does it come to you?" She smirked at Alistair with a raised brow. He turned away, cheeks turning a bright shade of pink. "Just keep practicing until the most basic of spells come as easily as breathing."

"Do you . . . think I can?" Alistair hesitantly asked.

She took his hand gently and grinned. "I know you can. The power is clearly within you, trust me, I can feel it. You just need to tap into it, call on your light, and make a connection. Once you establish a link," she tapped the center of his chest with a finger, "you'll be able to better protect yourself and those closest to you."

Smiling softly and trying to ignore her racing heart, Valhalla took several steps back and shot a twirling hand up in the air. Flames spun overhead and formed into a dome-shaped shield around them. Their eyes widened in surprise and amazement.

Albrecht raised an arm to block the heat. "You're such a show off!" He laughed, and she quickly dismissed it, pulling the fire back into her chest.

"I'm just showing His Grace what he can do, with enough practice." Valhalla shrugged with a teasing smirk and took her leave down the stairs.

Reaching her friend who now sat in his saddle, she took Vardan's hand, ready to climb up, when Alistair called from up the stairs. "Valhalla, wait!" She stopped and glanced up at him. "The next time we meet, I hope it's under a more joyous occasion." His grin beamed down at her, and she couldn't help but do the same.

"I look forward to it, Your Grace."

Vardan then pulled her up. She lifted a leg over the saddle and situated herself behind him. With a snap of the reins, Ótta was off, racing through the gate out of the courtyard. Watching Alistair become a blurry haze behind her, she fell into Vardan's back and tightened her hold on his waist.

Had she grown feelings for the High Prince? Why now, after all this time? Did he feel the same? There had been those who admitted feelings toward her in the past, but she never reciprocated. She had been even less inclined to do so after him, when he attempted to force himself on her. But *he* was long ago before ever meeting the High Prince.

What made Alistair different?

"Valhalla," Vardan called back, "what you're feeling, it *is* normal. Some go half a lifetime before finding someone, and others never do at all. There's nothing wrong with you, I promise."

Valhalla knew she should listen to Vardan. He had already spent centuries seeing much and meeting many, and too many of them were no longer among the living. But she couldn't shake the discomfort.

"That may be true, but . . . do I even *want* these feelings?"

67

Tamanna

Only a Pawn

UGGING the hood to hide his face, Tamanna hugged the shadows of the alley walls as he made his way through Svartr. Looking up, he could barely see the sky beyond the overhanging shingled rooftops and sneered. It had been several days now of trying and failing to find his way to Sailors Reef, where he could finally make his escape from the castle city. Now, with the clarity of hindsight, he lamented his overconfidence. The thought of losing control of the city hadn't even crossed his mind. Because of that, he'd not been concerned with studying the map of Svartr, and due to that incredible lapse of judgment, he'd gotten lost on more than one occasion. It was either a miracle or sheer luck that he had managed to avoid the city guard this long.

Not even the dancers he'd hired would be of any help. Guards were seen scouting the inn they were staying in, and so any allies he might've found there were out of reach. He was sure he was close to the city's exit; he had to be. Tamanna just had to remember which way would lead him out of the alley he currently found himself stuck in.

"Dammit all, I never expected that woman's magic to be *so* powerful. I mean," he paused, placing a hand on the cold stone brick beside him, "her eyes glowed a bright crimson. How? Why would they do that? Dammit, there's so much I still don't know!" Tamanna snuck a hand into his coat pocket, squeezing the dark sphere Kiara had given him in what felt like ages ago.

Pulling the sphere from his pocket, he slowly spun it around in the air above his palm, admiring the deep violet glow emanating from it. "No matter. Clearly, Hilliard is where I need to go to understand this land's magic. It's so bountiful. So powerful! And yet, how does it all work? There's an energy flowing through this world that I still don't understand. Now," he thumbed his chin, "if I can get myself a horse and some supplies, and a map of Veerence, I should be able to make my way there. I just need to avoid the High Prince until I have control of his mother. Well," he smirked, "it'll no doubt be some time before he leaves this place. That should leave me plenty of time to sink my teeth into her, and then he will no longer be an issue. I'll find the answers to this magic once and for all."

Sliding the sphere back into his pocket, Tamanna rounded a corner and startled as someone emerged from the shadows. He recognized her in moments. She was clad in unmistakable raven-decorated armor, and the sight of her silhouetted by the sinking sun made his heart skip.

A shiver shot up his spine. "O-Oh, Lady Kiara, it's you." He chuckled nervously, Kiara's expression completely unreadable under her visor. "You really shouldn't sneak up on people."

Silent as the grave, she reached out an armored claw, palm up, and just stood there. He stared at her for a long moment, unsure of what it was she wanted. When she did finally speak, his blood turned cold, and fear bloomed in his chest. "Sphere."

"Alright, h-here." He slid a trembling hand back into his coat and withdrew the sphere again. Just as he handed it over, the violet light brightened, and he caught a glimpse of her face. Her features darkened beneath her visor, and he realized then his next words would be crucial.

"I—" Tamanna swallowed the lump in his throat, his nerves on a razor's edge. "I encountered a minor inconvenience, but I'm sure I can learn much more in Hilliard. If you don't mind hel—"

A sudden wrongness plunged into his gut. A moment of pressure that his body registered before his might caught up, and then came the pain.

Kiara's eyes were on the dark sphere held between her clawed fingers. A thin, warm liquid spilled out of his mouth, which now tasted of metal. Tamanna gazed down at his stomach and found Kiara's free arm slowly disappearing deeper inside of him. Those clawed fingers working their way into his chest brought on a new wave of pain that, while he understood it his death was imminent, he couldn't help but feel like he was watching it all happen to someone else. His body coughed, and he felt the air slip from his blood filling lungs.

"Why?" He croaked, but she ignored him.

The sphere continued to brighten, hurting his eyes as he tried to stare directly into it. Kiara's skin also seemed to glow. She twirled her hand that held the sphere, letting the object drop into her gloved palm. The shadows around them began to writhe. Bright, violet markings appeared across her body, like the runes he'd studied in Svartr's old tomes, scrolls, and paintings of the country's past.

The glowing crystal then absorbed into Kiara's hand. She gasped, closing her eyes, and the runes flared, but then, just as quickly, faded. "You misunderstand the reason for which you were given my crystal. Thanks to you, I'm closer to achieving what needs to be done, but as a parting gift for your contribution," she leaned down close to his face and smirked menacingly, "I'll leave you with this."

Summoning a black, one-handed sword into the hand that had held the sphere, Kiara slipped her other claw free of Tamanna's gut, which made him stumble forward. Blood spilled in buckets down his clothes. His knees quaked, ready to buckle.

Clutching the large wound in his stomach, mouth open and eyes incredibly wide, he watched as if time had slowed for him to soak in every last moment. Kiara thrust and stabbed her blade into his chest and out of his back. Tamanna gave out a tight gasp, and as she twisted the blade, there was a terrible crack. His body was weirdly cold. It wasn't like that of a chill in the air. It was something coming from inside him. More blood filled his throat.

She instantly pulled her sword out, and with a twirl, sent the blood flying off the blade, then turned away and started back into the darkness of the surrounding buildings. Tamanna thought of reaching out to her; however, many alabaster-white, decrepit hands suddenly sprang out from his own shadow and pulled him down.

A scream came from his lips. Tamanna clawed for purchase on the cobblestone ground before him, the skin on the tips of his fingers ripping and nails breaking free as he was dragged deeper into his freezing shadow. "NO! You promised me knowledge, you promised! Why are you doing this?" He cried out, but Kiara said nothing.

Darkness filled his vision. He caught sight of Kiara glancing back, only once, but even then, she still gave no response. The last thing he registered as the blackness swallowed him whole was the disinterest in her deep blue, monolid eyes, and then nothing.

Glossary of Terms

This is a general guide for readers who are unfamiliar with the terms used in this story, however, many of these terms have nuance and history that can't be expressed in a blurb. I encourage you to go search out your own information, either using the internet or with the reference page I've added.

Æsir: One of the tribes of Gods that live across the nine realms, but who call Asgard home.

Aptrgøngu-maðr: One who walks after death/undead/zombies.

Asgard: One of the nine realms, home to the Gods. Also called the Golden Realm.

Bifrost: The rainbow bridge that connects Asgard to the other eight realms. The dome gateway is looked after and protected by Heimdall the Keeper of the Bifrost, Guardian of Asgard, and the God of Protection.

Draugr: Undead warriors that haunt and seek vengeance on those who killed them dishonorably, basically zombies.

Fensalir: Frigg's personal home in Asgard.

Einherjar: Óðin's army/warriors that reside either within the Halls of Valhalla or by Óðin's palace in Asgard.

Einmánuður: The last winter month, it coincides with the end of March to the middle of April.

Endispretta: A festival to celebrate the end of spring.

Gungnir: Óðin's famous spear that never misses its mark.

Gullhrafn: Heimdall's sword.

Hávi: Another name for Ódin the King of the Gods of Asgard, also means High One.

Helheim: One of the nine realms, home to the damned and Queen Hel the Goddess of Death. Also called the Dead Realm. Sources do say that this realm may not be one of the nine realms, but like Svartalfheim, it depends on interpretation by this point. I also took liberties with this realm, as sources say the residents of Helheim aren't damned, but souls who did not die in battle and/or did not die honorable deaths, but to be fair, dying of old age was also considered not honorable, so take that as you will.

Himinbjorg: Heimdall's personal home in Asgard.

Járngreipr: Thor's gauntlet that allows him more strength, actually this magical item helps him wield his own hammer, Mjölnir.

Jórsalafarar: Crusaders.

Jotunn: One of the tribes of Gods that live across the nine realms, but who call Jotunheim home.

Jotunheim: One of the nine realms, home to the Jotunns, also called Giants depending on interpretation. Also called the Rainbow Realm.

Meginjörð: Thor's belt that doubles his strength when worn.

Miðgarð: One of the nine realms, home to the humans, aka not Earth. Also called the Mortal Realm.

Miðsummarblot: A traditional celebration of the sun. Midsummer refers to the middle of summer, and in modern times usually indicates the summer solstice. The word blot can be simplified as "sacrifice", but more literally it's a request towards the Gods, or a trade. Celebrations included enormous campfires, song, dance, drink, and offerings made to the Gods. It is still celebrated in Scandinavian countries and by pagan/heathenistic/wiccan religions.

Mjölnir: Thor the God of Thunder and Battles most powerful and famous of weapons.

NiflheiM: One of the nine realms, once home to the dragons. Also formerly called the Dragon Realm, now the Grár Realm. Depending on sources, Niflheim is another realm, unsure by historians and scholars, if it really is of the nine. It could be Helheim, or vice versa. This is another, depends on interpretation.
The Norns: The Sisters of Fate in Norse Mythology. There is Urd of the Past, Verdandi of the Present, and Skuld of the Future. They were always sought after when needing to know your future or fate, especially by Ódin.

OstaRa: A traditional celebration of spring. It is still celebrated by pagan/heathenistic/wiccan religions.

ThoRRablot: A traditional midwinter festival/celebration. It is named after the month Thorri and the word sacrifice, meant to also honor the Thunder God, Thor.

RaGNaRÖK: In Norse Mythology, Ragnarök is an event, the final battle of gods and monsters, and the coming of the end. In my story, Ragnarök is a deity made born, but he still signifies the end of life if he is ever awakened from his slumbering prison.

SeiÐR: Viking age magic.

Vala: Seers/Fortune tellers.

Valhalla: Hall of the Slain and one of Ódin's most famous. Depending on sources, Asgard and Valhalla could be one in the same, but that also could be because of the Christianization of the mythology. Here is where Ódin's Einherjar would be kept.

ValKyRie: Powerful warrior maidens that serve Ódin, their goal is to fly to earth, either on swan wings or flying horses, depending on sources, gather souls that were slain in battle, and take them to Valhalla, where there they would wait for the coming of Ragnarök.

VaNiR: One of the tribes of Gods that live across the nine realms, but who call

Vanaheim home.

Völva/Völur/Völvx: Practitioners of seidr. Sources say that this was mostly a female dominated position as it was seen as an unmanly profession, but one of many they could do was see a person's fate, contact the dead, and speak to the gods.

Yggdrasil: The Great Ash Tree that connects the nine realms together, also known as the World Tree.

Acknowledgement

Well, after ten plus years(I actually lost count a couple of years ago) working on this story, *Valhalla the Valkyries Fire* is FINALLY out in the world. Valhalla herself was born after watching the *Claymore* anime while Alistair was born after playing *Dragon Age: Origins*, but the story itself didn't start coming to fruition until my Mythology class in college and I fell down a Norse mythology rabbit hole, in fact, I'm not sure I got myself out of it lol. Since then VTVF has been written, rewritten, reworked, expanded, moved around, the works. Why? Because I was stubborn and I love these characters so much, which is funny because even they have been redone several times since their inception too. I didn't want to let this story go, but now I have to, so you guys can finally have it in your hands and hopefully enjoy it.

I definitely want to thank my husband for suffering through with me until this story worked, it's the biggest I've done, so thank you for also sticking with her for all this time. I also want to thank my beta readers for going through this, especially Marta, your input helped fix some things I didn't think about. Also also I want to thank my writing group in *Bookwyrm Den*(Discord) for helping me figure out affordable resources for this monstrous manuscript. Seriously, I think I would've been pushing *VTVF* off even longer if I didn't have ideas on how to handle some of those steps. Can't forget my awesome cover artist Nicole Deal for bringing Valhalla and Alistair to life, and I'm so so sorry for mostly crying during the whole process, I was just so happy to finally see them on a cover. And of course, I want to give a huge thank you to Cat Rector, author of *The Unwritten Runes* duology, for helping me realize what I CAN do with the world of Valhalla. This whole time I thought I had to stick with what was known about Norse mythology, when really I should just have fun and repurpose it to fit the fantastical world I created. There are a lot of theories and facts about what is known about these pantheons of gods, monsters, and magic, but *Valhalla* is also an epic fantasy, so I reworked my mind and reminded myself that the knowledge out there is my guide to figure out what to do, while also reminding myself, this pantheon is just so weird lol. If you asked me if you should look at least a little into Norse mythology, my answer would be yeah, it's fascinating and interesting and really defies logic that sometimes I found myself laughing, while also learning the impact this pantheon had/has on Europe. Just remember to open your mind and expand, and to take breaks because these are not small infos.

Lastly, I want to thank you, the reader, for giving *Valhalla The Valkyries Fire* a chance. A lot of blood, sweat, and tears went into this story and there's more to come, so please don't forget to leave a review, it lets me know that people do in fact want to read more.

Thank you again so so much <3

~A.J. Torres

About the Author

Adlin(A.J.) Kennedy Torres is a writer who likes to dabble as an anime artist for fun. She enjoys Fantasy and Science Fiction stories. Adlin particularly loves to write Fantasy and easily gets immersed in books like *The Goddess of Nothing at All* and *Daylight's Curse*. She's loved Fantasy stories ever since she was a kid picking up *The Lord of the Rings* and *Eragon* for the first time.

Nowadays, you can find her in the hot and horribly humid sunshine state of Florida, hanging out, playing video games with her husband, and chasing her son around the house with a needy dog and a very chill cat.

Instagram/Thread and Twitter: @A_J_Torreso
TikTok: @A.J.Torreso
BlueSky: @ajtorresauthor.bsky.social

www.ingramcontent.com/pod-product-compliance
Lightning Source LLC
Chambersburg PA
CBHW031020030726
47497CB00004B/939